The WILD WEST Brides

★ ★ ★

3-Book Series from a Bestselling Author

LORI COPELAND

Print ISBN 978-1-63409-037-7

eBook Editions:
Adobe Digital Edition (.epub) 978-1-63409-385-9
Kindle and MobiPocket Edition (.prc) 978-1-63409-386-6

All scripture quotations are taken from the King James Version of the Bible.

This book is a work of fiction. Names, characters, places, and incidents are either products of the author's imagination or used fictitiously. Any similarity to actual people, organizations, and/or events is purely coincidental.

Published by Shiloh Run Press, an imprint of Barbour Publishing, Inc., P.O. Box 719, Uhrichsville, Ohio 44683, www.shilohrunpress.com.

Our mission is to publish and distribute inspirational products offering exceptional value and biblical encouragement to the masses.

ecpa Member of the Evangelical Christian Publishers Association

Printed in the United States of America.

The Peacemaker
Book 1

Prologue

Cole Claxton reined up and sat for a moment looking out over the soggy landscape. New Orleans lay before him, the place where he and the other riders planned to split up, each man going his own way. The men had fought for their own states, but the weeks following the war had thrown them together and forged an indelible bond.

The war was over. Cole had begun to think this day would never come. Since he'd left his home in the Ozarks four years earlier, the days had merged into weeks, and then into years, blurring into an endless repetition of fighting and regrouping, killing and dying.

Trey McAllister—tall, handsome, with curly red hair—voiced the thoughts of all the men. "Well, boys, it's finally over and we came out alive."

The dark half-breed, Dallas Ewing, said little, but his friends knew he was a man of few words. Dallas would be heading home to Oklahoma.

Bill Trotter, short, blond, and a lot thinner than he had been when he joined up, spat a stream of tobacco juice. "I'm heading back to Ohio. Gonna put my boots 'neath the welcome table."

The others laughed, throwing friendly gibes in jovial Bill's direction.

"Me?" Elmer Cox put in. "I'm heading straight for Fort Knox, Kentucky, brothers. Gonna get me a kiss and a batch of fried chicken—in that order."

"Amen, brother. Me, too." This came from Elmer's brother, George.

"Home sounds mighty good," Cole agreed, looking at his brother, Beau. He'd miss these men. But it was time to go home. He held out his hand. "Fellows?"

One by one the men shook hands and turned their horses in the various directions they called home.

As Cole and Beau moved away from the others, Bill Trotter called over his shoulder. "If you ever need anything. . ." He didn't need to finish the thought. *If any one man ever needed anything. . .*

Cole reined up to watch the men ride off, disappearing into the mist and fog. Then, with a word to his horse, he hurried on to where his brother waited. Together they would make the final leg of the journey home. *Home.*

Chapter 1

July 1865

Wynne Elliot coughed and daintily lifted a handkerchief to her nose as clouds of choking dust swept through the open stagecoach window. She flashed a weak smile for what seemed like the hundredth time at the gentlemen who sat across from her, and fervently wished the tiresome trip were over. She'd never dreamed it would take so long to travel from Georgia to Missouri.

Turning back to the scenery, she compared the harsh countryside to her own beloved Georgia. July, a time when flowers were blooming, when breezes were moist and balmy and moss draped through the trees like a bride's spidery veil.

Here the ground was hard, the grass dry from lack of moisture. While there was little evidence of the death and destruction her dear South had endured, there were still visible scars. Burned homesteads. Barren fields. The war had taken its toll here, too, but not with the terrible devastation she had witnessed farther south.

The farther the coach traveled, the more rugged the contour of the land. Ozark mountain country, she'd been told, was a place where people either survived or didn't, and given the landscape, she could well imagine why.

Low mountains with virtually untouched forests dotted the landscape, and the road they traveled twisted and snaked through gaps and valleys with endless walls of shale and limestone. On at least two occasions the coach had stopped and the driver and guard had removed fallen rocks from the way. Wynne had taken to watching the hillsides looking for rolling boulders, although if she saw any moving in their direction, it would already be too late to avoid impact.

She feared that at any turn in the road a band of outlaws would gallop from behind those massive boulders to waylay the coach. During the last rest stop, she'd heard mention of Alf Bolin and his men, an unsavory faction that waylaid unsuspecting travelers. And there was talk about Ozark vigilantes meting out their own bloody brand of justice. The men's casual conversation had given Wynne the willies.

It wasn't the first time she'd heard such shocking tales. Stage hands at the way stations delighted in relating such stories to shock and distress lady passengers.

But she had to admit that nothing she had been told had prepared her for Missouri's rugged beauty. And the land was beautiful. Great oaks and maples. By the size of the trees alone she guessed them to be hundreds of years old. Colonies of ferns spread a lacy carpet across the forest floor. Branches as big around as her waist reached out to form a canopy over the trail. Sturdy tree trunks sank deep roots into soil that was alternately black loam and rich red clay, but so stony that no plant could hope to survive. Still, natives of the area appeared to eke out an adequate living, and apparently in Springfield—a regular metropolis, she'd heard—businesses were thriving. Just yesterday she'd overheard that the railroad and more stores and hotels would locate there soon. If this was true, then Missouri would come out of the Great Conflict in better shape than her own beloved Georgia.

She sighed as the stagecoach tossed its passengers about. How much farther to River Run? Traveling by coach had not been easy—the jostling about, the dust, and the insufferable heat. How she longed for a bath—a long, hot bath with scented soap and shampoo. She sighed longingly. Revenge could indeed be tedious at times.

Absently, she rubbed the smooth, odd-colored stone she'd carried for over a year. He had given the token to her. Strange that she hadn't rid herself of this last painful reminder of him. She didn't need anything to remind her of Cass Claxton. His image was burned into her mind.

That man.

The worthless trinket worn smooth by the continual wash of river water had become her worry stone. Her thumb fit perfectly in the tiny hollow, which looked as though it could have been formed for such a purpose—but then, Wynne knew worrying was not of God. Nor was revenge, for that matter. She couldn't expect the Almighty to look with approval on the purpose of her journey, but her blood ran too hot, her anger too deep, to forgive and forget.

Her fingers endlessly smoothed the rock in silent litany:

I'll get him. . . . I'll get him if it's the last thing I do. . . . I'll get that man.

The journey to Missouri had been long and tiresome, and it wasn't over yet. She tried to bolster her wilting spirits by reminding herself that it wouldn't be much longer. As soon as she caught that deceiver. . .she would go home. Home to baths and warm food, a comfortable bed and people who loved her. Home to Moss Oak, the plantation where she had been born and raised. The only home she'd ever known.

Wynne wiped ineffectually at the small trickle of perspiration that escaped from beneath her hairline, and then adjusted her hat. It was hard to stay presentable, but she wanted to look her best. When she finally ran Cass to the ground, she wanted him to see what he had walked away from.

Her attention settled on the flamboyant young woman dressed in red sitting next to her. Now here was a fascinating example of womanhood. One that she had never expected to find in her circle of acquaintances.

Miss Penelope Pettibone was on her way to a new job at Hattie's Place. According to Penelope, Hattie's Place was a drinking establishment where a man could go for a hand of cards and "other gentlemanly pursuits." At the mention of "other gentlemanly pursuits," Wynne's eyes had widened knowingly, and she had felt her cheeks burn. She had never met one of "those" women before, and she found she had a certain adverse fascination with Miss Pettibone. Penelope smiled and winked at the man sitting opposite her, and Wynne fanned herself quickly and turned back to the Missouri countryside. A lady never winked, or if she did, she should have something in her eye.

Only that scoundrel, that disgraceful, deplorable, unforgivable Cass Claxton, occupied her thoughts now. The mere thought of that rogue left her breathless with anger. Not only had he left her standing at the altar in complete disgrace, but he'd also managed to walk away with every penny she had except the small pittance she kept in a tin box under her mattress for extreme emergencies.

True, she'd been foolish to fall in love with a man she knew so little about, and even more imprudent to offer financial assistance to a business venture he was about to embark upon, but she had always been one to put her whole heart into everything—especially in matters of love. Of course, she'd not had all that much experience with matters of love, but after studying at Miss

Marelda Fielding's Finishing School for Young Ladies, she considered herself a sophisticated woman of the world. That's why it hurt so much that she had let Cass Claxton take advantage of her.

If it hadn't been for the war and her suspicion that Cass had enlisted the day they were meant to marry, she would have tracked him down like a rabid skunk and put a hunk of lead straight through his thieving heart for sullying her trust—not to mention her character. But surely it would have been considered treason to shoot a Confederate soldier, a defender of the homeland, no matter how much he had it coming. However, the fighting had ended, and now she felt free to wreak her vengeance on the lout who had taken advantage of her in such a shameful way.

Her temper still boiled when she thought how gullible she'd been. Well, she was no longer gullible. Quite by chance she'd been told by a close acquaintance of Cass that he had indeed enlisted, survived, and had been seen in Kansas City a few weeks ago. The friend had said Cass was en route to his home in River Run and should arrive any day now. She intended to be there to meet him.

Wynne clenched her fan in her hand; her eyes narrowed pensively. It had been a long time coming, but Mr. Cass Claxton would soon pay for his sins. She smiled in satisfaction. Very soon Cass would rue the day he'd ever heard of Wynne Elliot.

She'd learned a valuable lesson: no man could be trusted. She wasn't necessarily permanently soured on men—Papa had been a man of sterling reputation, but Papa had been an exception. She would never allow herself to be fooled by a man again. Not even one as good-looking as Cass Claxton.

The coach lurched along. Wynne studied the two male passengers dozing in the seat across from her. Undoubtedly they were scoundrels, she speculated. After all, they were *men*. She could rest her case. Argument closed.

She had to admit she liked to watch the way stuffy Mr. Rutcliff's fat little jowls jiggled every time the stage hit a rut in the road, but when it came to females, she'd bet he was just as fickle as all men, even if he was nearly seventy years old. She guessed age didn't make much difference where men were concerned.

Covering her mouth with her handkerchief, she'd managed to keep from laughing out loud a couple of times when a bump had nearly unseated the small man. He'd snorted himself awake and angrily glanced around as if to ask *who* the culprit had been that had dared interrupt his napping. After a moment his eyes had closed, and soon he could be heard snoring again. Fat little jowls ajiggle.

Henry McPherson, the second gentleman traveler, was younger than Mr. Rutcliff and boringly polite. He constantly tipped his hat and said, "Yes, ma'am" and "No, ma'am" in response to any comment either she or Penelope ventured.

Wynne had the impression the two men had been scared to death of Penelope since they'd overheard her discussing her destination with Wynne. She doubted they'd be dropping into Hattie's Place for any "gentlemanly pursuits." But then, who could tell? They were, after all, men, and therefore could not be trusted. Miss Marelda had definitely been correct on that score.

Miss Marelda had never married, claiming the natural cupidity of men as the reason, but Wynne wondered if maybe the biggest reason was that she'd never been asked. Wynne's conscience smote her. She needed to ask God to forgive her for such unkind thoughts, although to tell the truth, since she'd set out to bring Cass Claxton to justice, she hadn't been on comfortable terms with God. How could she ask Him to bless her plans when she knew He would want no part of them?

The coach picked up speed, and Wynne glanced out the

window at the scenery now rushing by. "Does it seem to you we're going faster?" she asked of no one in particular. A frown creased her forehead. Surely such excessive speed on this rough road couldn't be safe.

"We can't go fast enough for me," Penelope said with an exasperated sigh. "I can't wait for this trip to be over." She made a useless effort to knock the layer of dust off her dress and grimaced in distaste when it only settled back on the light material. "I really expected the journey to be more genteel." She flashed a glance from under her eyelids at Mr. McPherson, who blushed and looked away.

Puzzled by the increasing momentum of the coach, Wynne peered out the window. Her mouth dropped open, and she immediately jerked her head back in. "My stars! I think we're about to be robbed!" she blurted in disbelief.

Both men's eyes flew open. Mr. Rutcliff craned his neck out the window to verify her statement. "Oh my! I do believe you're right!"

Penelope sent up an instant wail, fluttering her fan and looking like she was about to break out in tears. "I knew it! I knew it! We'll all be killed!"

Wynne shot the young woman an impatient glance. Over the past few days she'd noticed that optimism did not seem to be the girl's strong point. "Penelope, really! I'm sure we are well protected." The guard, the driver, and two male passengers: there was no cause for immediate alarm. The team could probably outrun the outlaws without the slightest problem. At least she hoped her assessment of the situation was accurate.

A few minutes later her optimism sagged. Her heart beat wildly as gunshots filled the air. Another glance out the window showed the riders drawing steadily closer.

Wynne cast a worried glance at the gentlemen seated across

from her, noticing that neither man looked overly confident. She doubted either one would be much help in case of a holdup. They didn't even appear to be armed.

"Shouldn't we do something?" she asked, clutching the worry stone in her fist. The two men peered out the coach window apprehensively. Neither one seemed to be inclined to action. Penelope looked like she might faint at any moment. Wynne dismissed them all as useless in the present situation.

"There's nothing to do but pray," Mr. Rutcliff murmured in a barely audible voice.

Pray? Wynne blinked back hot tears. When was the last time she'd prayed—asked God for anything other than bodily harm toward Cass? What was the use of continuing to try to fool herself? She couldn't ask God for anything except forgiveness for what she had planned, and in order to do that, she'd have to change those plans. She wasn't ready to consider doing that. But she sure hoped God would be patient enough with her to spare them injury or worse at the hands of these outlaws. She'd heard Missouri was filled with violent men who weren't afraid to break the law. Apparently those rumors were correct. She dropped to the floor when the masked riders slowly but surely gained ground on the wildly swaying coach.

Wynne tried to pray, but the words stuck in her throat. She couldn't even think clearly. It looked like she was on her own this time.

The noonday sun bore down on the two dusty riders like a flatiron on a hot stove. Cole and Beau Claxton rested their horses on a small rise overlooking a field of withered corn. A faint, teasing wisp of a breeze grazed the horses' manes. The heat was so intense it was hard to catch a deep breath. July in the Ozarks. You could stand still and sweat.

"Look at it, Beau. Home." Cole, the older of the two brothers, spoke first, his deep baritone husky with emotion. He'd dreamed about this view: thought of it at night around the campfires and on waking in the morning. Nothing he'd seen in the time he'd been gone could rival the Ozarks for pure natural beauty. It was God's country, and he was so glad to be back he could shout for the pure pleasure of hearing the surrounding hills throw back an echo.

He sat leaning forward, resting his elbow on the saddle horn and looking out over the rolling hills of their southwest Missouri home, just savoring the moment, which had been a long time coming. "Looks good, doesn't it?" Cole asked.

"It sure does," Beau answered.

Cole let his reins go slack as he slumped wearily in the saddle, his eyes hungrily drinking in the familiar sight spread before him. There had been times he hadn't expected to see it again. A lot of good men wouldn't be coming home from the war. He had much to be thankful for.

The gently sloping terrain was no longer the lush, fertile green that would have met their eyes if it had been spring. The blazing summer sun had taken its toll on the land and crops, burning them to dry cinder. But it was still a long-awaited, welcome sight to one who had seen nothing but death and destruction for the last few years.

Four years. Four years of not knowing if he would ever see home again. Four years of watching men die by the thousands and wondering if he would be next, living with the unspeakable horrors of war day after day after day. Through it all, he'd grown closer to God. War had that effect on a man. Every day you didn't die was like a personal gift. He didn't know why he and Beau had been spared when so many others hadn't. Seemed like God might have had a purpose for letting them live, but he didn't know what it could be—unless it was Ma's and Willa's prayers. Whatever the reason, he was grateful. Mighty grateful.

Home. The word held a new and more sacred meaning. He breathed silent thanks to his Maker for bringing him intact through the carnage and destruction.

"There were times when I thought I'd never see this again," Beau confessed.

"I had those times, too."

Beau echoed his thoughts. "We were lucky, you know. There are so many who won't come home—"

"Hope Ma and Willa have some of that chicken 'n' dumplings waiting for us," Cole interrupted. He'd had enough dying and sorrow to last him a lifetime. He wanted to forget the past four years, not relive them. Wanted to shuck them off like worn dirty clothes, like this uniform, and get back to being a civilian with nothing more to worry about except getting in a crop and looking into that marshal's job.

He thought about his ma and their Indian housekeeper's cooking. Willa had been with the family since he was a baby and had been as much of a mother to the three Claxton boys as their own ma had been. When the family had moved from Georgia to Missouri back in the late forties, they'd established a homestead and built a new life. Samuel Claxton died five years into the adventure, leaving behind a wife with three young sons to rear. No one could argue that Willa had been nothing short of a godsend to Lilly Claxton.

"I can eat six pans of corn bread and three dozen fried-apple pies before I even hit the front door," Beau said. "Makes my mouth fairly water to think of it."

"If I were you, I'd eat that pie and corn bread even before I went over to see Betsy." Cole teased him with a knowing wink.

"You're right," Beau said solemnly. "Only sensible thing to do."

The brothers broke out in laughter. Cole knew the first place Beau would head would be Old Man Collins's place. Beau and Betsy had been about to be married when the war intervened. Now the wedding would take place as soon as possible.

"Who wants ol' Betsy when they can have Willa's cooking?" Beau grinned mischievously, his eyes twinkling. "You know, now that the war's over, you ought to think about settling down, too, Cole."

Cole chuckled softly, letting his gaze return to the valley below them. "Betsy's the prettiest girl in the county, and you're claiming her. Who would I marry?"

"Aw, come on," Beau chided. "You know you wouldn't marry Betsy if you could. I'm beginning to worry about you, Cole!"

Cole laughed. "Well, don't. When the right woman comes along, I might give marrying some serious thought."

"It'll never happen," Beau said. "You're never going to find a woman who'll suit you because you're too everlasting picky."

"I'll run across her someday. Happen to favor a woman with a little spirit." Cole's gaze drank in the familiar surroundings. This was a familiar argument, one his whole family had utilized. Cole's mother and Willa were fond of questioning when he, the eldest, was going to marry and produce offspring.

"Spirit, huh? What about Priscilla, Betsy's sister? There's a fine figure of a woman if I ever saw one." Beau grinned. "Strong as a bull moose, healthy as a horse, and sturdy as an oak fence post. Why, I've seen her and her father cut a rick of wood in a couple of hours and never raise a sweat. She'd make some man a fine wife. Got a *lot* of spirit, too," he added. "Saw her hand-wrestle an Indian brave once, and she didn't do badly."

Cole's mouth curved with an indulgent smile. "She didn't win, did she?"

"She didn't win, but she didn't do all that bad," Beau insisted.

Cole chuckled at the younger man's sincerity. "Somehow, little brother, the thought of a woman hand-wrestling a brave, cutting a rick of wood in a couple of hours, and never raising a sweat doesn't appeal to me."

"Well, what *does*? I've seen you go through more women than I can count, and not one of them suits you. You're just too picky!"

Cole shifted in his saddle. His bones ached, and he was dead tired. "Don't start with me, Beau." Little brother could nag as long and hard as any granny when he set his mind to it, and Cole was in no mood for a lecture on women. "When I find a woman who can wrestle the Indian brave and *win,* then turn around and be soft as cotton and smell as pretty as a lilac bush in May, that's the day you'll see me heading for the altar."

Beau shook his head. "I've never known a woman to wrestle an Indian brave and then smell like a lilac bush in May," he complained.

Cole took off his hat and wiped away rolling sweat. His eyes scanned the valley below then narrowed and lingered on the cloud of dust being kicked up in the far distance.

"Stage coming in," he noted.

Beau leaned forward in his saddle, his eyes centered on the road below. "Driver's sure got the horses whipped up—will you look at that!"

Leather creaked as Cole's horse shifted restlessly beneath his weight. His eyes followed the path of the coach barreling along the dusty road. The driver whipped the horses to greater speed. The coach careened crazily as the team tried to outrun the small band of riders galloping after it.

Beau whistled under his breath. "Looks like trouble."

Cole set his hat back on his head and took up his reins, his eyes focused on the frantic race. "Better see what we can do to help."

The brothers spurred their mounts, and the powerful steeds sprang forward, covering the ground with lightning speed, steadily gaining on the swaying coach.

Six masked riders had brought the stage to a halt, and the passengers were filing out with their hands held high above their heads. Penelope sobbed quietly, while Wynne tried to master her fear. She wasn't about to let these ruffians see her true emotions.

The leader of the grizzly pack vaulted out of his saddle. While he held a gun on the driver and guard, others began pulling luggage off the top of the coach.

"Don't anybody make a move and you won't get hurt," the second rider warned in a gravelly voice. "Driver! You and Shotgun throw down your guns and the gold box."

The driver and guard looked at each other. *Don't do it*, Wynne thought, and wondered if she had spoken the words out loud. The driver reached for his pistol as the guard lifted his rifle. Before they could bring them into firing position, two shots rang out. The driver and the man who rode shotgun sagged against the seat, weapons falling from their limp hands. Penelope screamed and covered her eyes as the bodies tumbled from their high perch. Even as inexperienced as she was, Wynne realized that the men were dead by the time they hit the ground. She closed her eyes, feeling sick to her stomach. Those men never had a chance. They had been gunned down in cold blood.

Three of the bandits returned to dragging valises off the top of the coach, ripping through the contents in search of valuables.

The passengers stood by in dismay, watching as their personal items were strewn about in the frenzied search. Wynne stood in shock. Her undergarments were being handled by rough, dirty hands, the lace pieces thrown into the dust with no regard to the fragility of the material.

In a vain attempt to stop the robbery, Penelope edged forward and batted her eyes coyly at the leader. Wynne watched, fascinated. So this was the way a woman like that charmed the men. "Really, sir, we have nothing of any value," Penelope said. "Won't you please let us pass—?"

The man angrily pushed her aside. "Out of my way, woman." His hand caught the large emerald brooch pinned to the front of her dress and ripped it free of the fabric. Penelope stumbled and almost fell.

Wynne gasped at the outlaw's audacity. For a moment she forgot her own paralyzing fear and marched to stand protectively in front of the sobbing girl. "Why don't you pick on someone your own size, you inconsiderate brute!"

Her heart beat like a tom-tom when the robber's eyes narrowed in rage. He reached out with a huge hand and caught the front of her dress. Her heart nearly stopped beating altogether when the bandit jerked her up close to him and made a thorough search of her body with his beady eyes. He held her that way for a moment before releasing her. She pressed her lips together, staring back at him. He grabbed her fist and quickly relieved her of the pearl ring on her left hand, scraping her knuckle painfully in the process. Before she could stop him, he jerked her purse from her arm and rummaged around in it, removing all the cash. He focused his attention on her. "This all you got, lady?"

Her eyes met his in what she hoped was a cold stare. "I am not a fool. Of course, you have it all. . .and please get out of my face." She tilted her head to avoid his offensive odor. Thank goodness he had a mask over his face to dull the stench of his odious breath.

"Ah, am I offending Her Majesty?" He chuckled and jerked her closer, lifting his mask above his mouth. The sight of yellow, tobacco-stained teeth made her stomach lurch.

Slowly his greedy gaze lowered to the décolletage of her emerald-colored dress, lingering there. "What's the matter, honey? Ain't I pleasing 'nough for you?" He laughed when she continued to avert her nose from his rancid smell. "Yore a pretty little filly." He breathed against her ear. "How's about giving ol' Jake a little kiss?"

"See here! Rob us if you will, but I must insist on your treating the ladies with respect!" Henry McPherson stepped forward in Wynne's defense. One of the masked men lifted a gun butt and promptly knocked the young man unconscious.

His body slumped to the ground, and the assailant waved his pistol in a menacing manner. "Don't anyone else try anything foolish if you don't want to get hurt."

"Come on, Jake! Quit fooling around and get on with it!" Another bandit shot an apprehensive glance at two riders fast approaching from the west. "We got company coming."

Jake laughed once more and shoved Wynne aside. "Sorry, honey. We'll have to take this up another time."

"In a pig's eye we will." Wynne retained enough sense about her to speak under her breath.

The bandit paused, and his evil eyes narrowed angrily. "What'd you say?"

She grinned weakly. "I said, yes. . .some other time. . .surely."

"Come on, Jake! Would you quit socializing and come on?"

After another degrading sweep of her body with cold, dark

eyes, Jake brutally ripped the fragile gold chain from around Wynne's neck.

"You give that back!" she screeched, snatching for the keepsake. He stuffed the necklace into the bag he was carrying.

"Sorry, Red, but I just got a sudden hankering for little gold chains." He chuckled again and strode in a rolling gait to his waiting horse.

"That necklace isn't worth anything," she protested angrily, "except for sentimental value to me! My father gave that to me minutes before he died—"

Her words fell on deaf ears. The man tipped his hat in a mocking salute. Then the six riders spun their mounts and galloped off.

"Well, all right then! Take the necklace, but I won't forget this!" Wynne shouted into the cloud of dust their horses kicked up. She grabbed her tilting hat and stared at the robbers' retreating backs. Seconds later the other two riders neared and quickly took off in hot pursuit of the culprits.

The dazed passengers just stood around looking stunned. Wynne rushed to kneel beside the injured Henry, who was beginning to come around. He moaned and opened his eyes to look about in bewilderment. "What happened?"

"Lie still, Mr. McPherson." Wynne reached for one of the pieces of scattered clothing to place under his head. "You were knocked out by one of the ruffians, but they're gone now." Glancing around, she saw the others hadn't moved.

Mr. Rutcliff snapped out of his stupor and immediately knelt between the driver and shotgun rider. Shaking his head, he glanced back to meet Wynne's questioning gaze. "Dead as a doornail. Shot 'em both clean through the heart."

Penelope collapsed in tears.

Wynne got to her feet and absently reached over and patted

the young woman's shoulder. "It's all right. They're gone now. Why don't you go sit under that tree until you get yourself under control?"

"But we all could have been *killed*," Penelope wailed. "I tried to stop them, but you saw what happened—"

"But we weren't killed," Wynne said, asking the good Lord to give her patience. "Mr. Rutcliff, are you all right?"

The elderly man looked pale and mopped at the perspiration trickling down inside his collar. "Why, yes, I believe so. Quite a disturbing chain of events, wouldn't you say?"

"Yes, I would say that." Wynne blew a wisp of hair out of her face. "Quite disturbing." He called that right enough. If only she'd had sense enough to carry a gun. After all, she was out on a mission of vengeance. She should have had enough forethought to provide herself with a weapon.

Cole and Beau pushed their horses to the limit, but the gang of robbers was already disappearing into the distance. As Cole watched the outlaws fade from view, he realized they were long gone. About all he and Beau were accomplishing was eating their dust. He'd suspected from the beginning they couldn't do anything about the robbery, but a man couldn't stand by and watch when others were in a bind. He pulled his mount to a halt.

"What do you think?" Beau shouted as he reined up beside Cole, his shirt flapping in the stiff breeze.

"They're too far gone. We'll only wind the horses more."

Beau's eyes followed the cloud of dust. "You're right—but I'd like to have caught them. Let's go see what we can do to help the passengers."

Cole shook his head. Beau never gave up. That good-hearted streak of his was going to get them both in trouble one of these days. It evidently didn't bother him that they had been outnumbered six to two and this wasn't their fight.

He pulled his mare around and followed his brother back to the stage.

When the two riders came into view, Wynne paused in picking up her scattered clothing. She watched warily as they approached. One of the guns was still lying on the ground, and she lunged for it, leveling the muzzle at the approaching pair. One robbery a day was all she was going to put up with, thank you. If these two ruffians had come for the same purpose, she would take care of this personally.

Penelope, huddled under a nearby tree, crying and fanning herself, was useless in a situation like this. Mr. Rutcliff was trying in vain to comfort the injured Henry McPherson. That left only Wynne to defend what was left of their meager possessions. She shot a disgusted glance in their direction. A lot of help they were. Leaving a woman to protect them.

The two men cautiously reined in their horses, wearing incredulous expressions as they looked down the barrels of the twelve-gauge shotgun Wynne pointed at them.

"Throw your guns down, gentlemen," she commanded in a firm voice.

"Now, ma'am," the younger one said, "we don't make a habit of parting with our guns—"

"Now!" She hefted the shotgun an inch higher on her shoulder. As if she cared about their habits. She had a few more important things to worry about.

Both men slowly unbuckled their gun belts and let them drop to the ground.

"Now your rifles."

"Ma'am. . ." the young one protested. "I'm not about to let my Springfield be taken away by anyone." He looked like he wanted to laugh.

Wynne knew she probably didn't look very frightening with her torn collar and dust smudges on her face. And this hat! Whatever had possessed her to purchase the wide-brimmed straw hat topped by a bird in a nest? The silly thing kept tipping forward, so she had to keep nudging it back, causing the gun to sway in a most disconcerting manner.

The young man smiled. "Judging from your charming Southern drawl, I'd guess you're from Georgia. I've heard that speech pattern before."

I'll just bet you have, she thought. *Yankees.* They'd overrun her beloved state. She'd heard their *nasal twang* before, too. Way too many times.

"Never you mind where I'm from. I said throw down your rifles." She waved the gun in their general direction.

Moving slowly, the man carefully slid his rifle to the ground. Only then did she lower her weapon a fraction. "Now, if you don't have anything more to say, I think you two best be moving on."

The young man swung his hat off and flashed what he evidently hoped was a winning smile. She'd seen better.

"The name's Beau, and me and my brother, Cole, was wondering if everyone was all right here. We thought we might be of service. Looks like you had a run-in with a gang of thieves."

In Wynne's opinion, this newest set of strangers didn't look a whole lot better than the last one. The men were rumpled and dirty, both in need of a shave and a haircut and wearing the wrong kind of uniform. The only difference she could discern between these two and the band of unsavory hoodlums who had fled was that they didn't smell as bad—at least not from this distance.

She studied the two carefully. Both men were large in stature and impressively muscular, if one liked that sort of man. But they were the exact opposites in coloring. Beau, the one who had been doing all the talking, had hair streaked whitish blond by the sun and dancing blue eyes. He sat in his saddle with a rakish air. Cole, the second one, was older, his skin toasted to a deep nut-brown, his hair jet-black with a trace of unruly curls softening his rugged features.

They were wearing the ragged blue uniforms of the North. She prayed that on top of everything else this rotten day had brought her she hadn't had the misfortune to meet up with a pair of renegade Union men. She'd heard what their sort was capable of.

Wynne swallowed hard and steadied her hold on the shotgun. My stars, the thing was unbelievably heavy! "Don't come any closer," she warned as the men's horses shifted.

"Ma'am, why don't you put the gun down?" Beau coaxed. "Someone might get hurt."

Wynne took a firm step forward to show them she was not in the least intimidated by their presence. She focused the length of the gun barrel on Beau, figuring he was trying to wheedle her into relaxing her guard. "It's quite possible someone might—namely, you. I'm warning you, mister, you'd better not rile me. You'd best state your business and move on, or I'll have to use this."

"I don't think that'll be necessary." Beau turned slightly in his saddle to face the other man. Wynne let her eyes follow his. She had a hunch he would be the most dangerous. Right now he was keeping a fixed eye on her trigger finger.

Beau shifted. "I'd better state our business, Cole."

He started to dismount and stopped short as Wynne's voice rang out. "Stop right there!" she demanded.

Deciding she'd better let them know in no uncertain terms who had the upper hand, she marched forward, determined to settle this once and for all. Unfortunately, she stumbled over a discarded valise in her path, giving her shin a painful crack and pitching her forward. Still clutching the gun, she twisted to the side, falling to one knee.

Cole and Beau ducked as the gun went off, spraying buckshot over their heads. Confusion reigned. Wynne fought to regain control of the gun and her destroyed composure. She grabbed her hat when it tilted over her face, blocking her view. Beau and Cole rolled out of their saddles onto their knees, still hanging on to their horses, which were prancing and shying away.

Wynne staggered to her feet, kicking the valise aside, the gun firmly back on her targets. "Gentlemen, don't be misled," she cautioned. "I assure you, I *do* know how to use this gun and shall not hesitate to do so if the need arises. I suggest you move on. My fellow passengers and I have nothing left but the clothes scattered in the road, so you're wasting your time if you've come to rob us."

Wynne glanced uneasily at the dark-complexioned rider slowly getting to his feet. His face was grim, and his eyes narrowed. She didn't like the set of his mouth. In fact, she didn't like anything about him. Probably a ruthless desperado preying on innocent victims.

She knew she looked like an utter fool, but then she had the gun and he didn't.

Cole's electrifying blue eyes centered directly on her. He studied the scene before he remounted his horse. His face looked like it had been carved from a slab of oak, hard and unyielding. The glance he shot her was contemptuous enough to shrivel a weaker woman. Wynne tilted her chin. Who did he think he was, looking at her like that? She was merely defending what was hers along with protecting her fellow passengers.

"Ma'am," Beau protested with a weak grin, "I think you've got the wrong idea. We're here to help, not rob you."

"Oh, really?" Wynne's eyebrows lifted with skeptism. He did

have a point, though. They had chased the gang off, but it could have very well been for their own evil purposes. After all, she had decided not to trust *any* men, and these two were quite definitely men. Rather attractive ones, too, under all of that travel dust.

"Honest," Beau declared. "We're sorry we weren't in time to prevent this unfortunate mishap." He swept his hat off and bowed gallantly. She was once more the recipient of a most charming smile.

"That may be so, but you're still a *Yankee*!" She spit the words out as if they left a vile taste in her mouth. "And I wouldn't believe a thing a *Yankee* said!"

"Ma'am, the war's over. Can't we let bygones be bygones?"

She took aim at his heart. "Easy for you to say. *You* won. Now you listen to me. I'm in no mood for argument. I'm sweating like a mule, I'm hungry, and this has been the worst day of my life."

Sweating like a mule. Miss Marelda would frown on that choice of words, but truth was truth.

Beau shrugged. "I had help with the war."

Wynne shot him a dirty look. He wasn't taking the situation seriously.

He slowly eased his way over to her. "Why don't you calm down and let me and my brother take you and the other passengers into town?"

Wynne glanced at the lifeless bodies of the driver and guard and realized she was at this man's mercy even though she was holding the gun. It was obvious that neither she nor Penelope could drive the stage, and the two male passengers were in no condition to attempt such a feat.

"Well. . .maybe that would be a good idea, but bear in mind, I'll have this gun pointed at you all the way in case you try something underhanded." She shot the other brother a warning look. "And that goes double for you."

Cole kept silent. Wynne tilted her chin and stared back at him. His expression seemed to say that if it had been up to *him*, he'd have taken the gun away from her ten minutes ago and turned her across his knee. She'd like to see him try.

"What's the matter with him? Can't the pompous fool talk?" Wynne whispered crossly, motioning to Cole. All the man had done since he arrived was stare at her as if she were a raving maniac!

Beau glanced over his shoulder. "Who, Cole? Sure he talks, when he wants to." His gaze switched back to her, studying the hat, which was tilting again. "You don't have to be afraid of us. Do we look like the type of men who would take advantage of a lady?"

Wynne studied him for a moment before her gaze drifted involuntarily to Cole. His posture remained aloof as she looked up and met his direct gaze.

Beau didn't seem the type to take advantage of a woman, but his brother certainly looked questionable. Wynne gave a fleeting thought to what it would be like to have a man like him take advantage. . . She pulled her wandering thoughts back into line. What had come over her? Miss Marelda Fielding would be horrified to think of one of her students being so. . .so unseemly. Wynne had best be attending to business.

"Nevertheless, you've been warned," she stated then turned toward the stage. Somehow she got her feet tangled in one of Penelope's stray petticoats lying on the ground. In the scuffle to retain her balance, her own skirt wrapped itself around her legs, pitching her forward. She threw out her hands to keep from falling, and the gun spun out of her grip to land in the dirt at Beau's feet. Dust puffed up around her, filling her nostrils as she hit the ground. She sneezed and barely halted the automatic move to wipe her nose. How had she ended up flat on her back staring up at the sky? She looked up directly into the brilliant blue eyes of silent brother Cole, who was watching her as if she were the main attraction in a sideshow. She flushed with embarrassment, realizing she wasn't coming off too well in this encounter.

Beau reached down a hand and helped Wynne to her feet. She dusted off her seat, twitching her skirt into more orderly folds. He handed the gun back to her with a courtly bow and a polite smile. "Allow me, ma'am."

"Thank you. . .sir." She felt her cheeks flame. She snatched the gun back and reached up to straighten her hat, which as usual had gone askew in the turmoil. "I'll get the passengers in the stage," she announced.

"That would be fine, ma'am." Beau grinned.

He made his way to where Cole sat on his horse watching the fiasco. Wynne strained to hear the men's brief exchange while trying to look as if she wasn't paying attention. But she heard—oh, she heard, all right.

"What do you think you're doing?" Cole asked calmly.

"Getting ready to escort the stage back to town," Beau answered.

"Why did you give that gun back to her?"

"Oh, that." He adjusted his hat. "She's not going to shoot anyone. She's just scared."

"I *know* she's not going to shoot anyone intentionally," Cole said, "but I think we're in serious danger of getting our heads blown off by her stupidity."

Wynne fumed. She'd like to show Mr. High-and-Mighty how well she could handle a gun. She'd teach him a lesson that would wipe that smirk right off his face. Call her stupid, would he?

"Come on, Cole. Look at them. They're as helpless as a turtle on its back." Beau's gaze shifted to the shaken passengers filing slowly back into the coach. "Let her think she's running the show. It's not going to hurt anything."

Wynne stiffened. Let her *think*? Of all the arrogant. . . If she didn't need them so badly she'd send them packing. Just who had the gun here? She *was* running this show, and he'd better not forget it.

Cole looked in her direction. "In my opinion, everything is under control, and one of the men can take the stage on into town."

She waited, holding her breath.

Beau shook his head. "They need help, Cole."

"You're a born sucker when it comes to a pretty face."

Beau reached for his reins. "Might be, but it's our duty to get them into town safely."

Cole sighed. "We made it all the way through a war without an injury, and I'll be blamed if I'm about to have some snip of a woman ruin my perfect record less than ten miles from home. There's no reason for us to get mixed up in this. We can send Tal out to help them when we ride through town."

"I don't want to do that," Beau argued. "We can't just ride off and leave the ladies out here unprotected. It won't take fifteen minutes to escort them to town, and then we'll be on our way."

Cole's unshaven jaw firmed. "I say we stay out of it."

"If you don't want to help, then I'll do it myself."

"You've got a cross-eyed mule beat when it comes to stubborn. All right, all right, I'll help. But I'm warning you, she's going to be trouble."

"Don't have to like her," Beau grumbled. "All you got to do is help. Wouldn't be right leaving them alone." The last passenger clambered aboard the coach. "You drive the stage; I'll load the driver and guard onto our horses and be right behind you."

Cole, still grumbling, dismounted and strode over to the coach, leaving Beau to take care of the dead bodies.

Wynne breathed easier. They may look like outlaws, but apparently they were going to escort the stage back to town. She had no illusions as to what a mess they'd be in if left to their own devices. An injured man and one who might as well be hurt, no more help than he'd been so far, and a flighty woman who wasn't any better. They'd be sitting pigeons for the next band of outlaws who might happen along.

Cole had planted his foot on the wheel of the stage and started to climb aboard when Wynne tapped the barrel of the gun on his shoulder. He slowly turned around to meet her calculating eyes.

"Don't forget. I'll be watching you, mister."

He bit out his words impatiently. "Ma'am, I'm quivering in my boots." His drawl was a mixture of Georgia softness and Missouri twang.

Wynne narrowed her eyes. There was something vaguely familiar about this man, though she was certain she had never met him before. Something about his eyes. . .

In spite of herself, she found herself admiring Cole's very even and white teeth, and though he had obviously been riding for some time, he was not nearly as dirty and offensive as the bandits had been. The humidity had curled his dark hair around his tanned face, and his eyes—well, she'd seen blue eyes in her time, but she'd never seen that particular shade before.

For a brief moment she tried to imagine what he would look like with a shave, a haircut, and clean clothes. The image was disturbing. She shook the thought away. There wasn't the chance of a snowball in July she'd ever see him again, yet as she turned away, she couldn't shake the feeling that he reminded her of someone.

Wynne primly tucked herself and the gun into the coach and slammed the door. "Like I said, I'm watching you. Drive directly into town. No detours, no unnecessary stops."

Beau rode up, and Wynne saw Cole shoot his brother a dirty look. "I don't know why I let you talk me into these things!" he snapped.

Beau was still grinning when Cole, with an impatient whistle, slapped the reins. The team bolted, and with the barrel of a shotgun pointed straight at his head, Cole headed for town.

Chapter 2

The stage rolled into River Run, Missouri, to the sound of jangling harnesses and a cloud of boiling dust. The townspeople came running, clearly surprised to see Cole sitting in the driver's seat. Cole could have told them he was a bit surprised himself. If Beau hadn't been such a stubborn, mule-headed so-and-so they could have been home by now instead of playing Good Samaritans.

"Cole, boy!" Tal Franklin, county sheriff, climbed aboard the coach and slapped him soundly on the back. "Good to see you, son!"

Cole could have sworn Tal's eyes misted before he dragged out a large handkerchief and hurriedly wiped his nose. The crowd pressed closer, and Cole grinned. Looked like the whole town had turned out to meet them, and it was a heartwarming sight.

"Good to see you, Tal." Cole grinned, clasping the sheriff's calloused hand. Mere words were inadequate for the emotions that blocked his throat when he looked at the face he'd known for most of his thirty years. It was good to be home!

"Looks like you come through the war without a scratch." Tal beamed; then his smile faded. "Have you seen either of your brothers?" The sheriff looked like he hated to even ask the question, probably dreading the answer he'd heard too often in the past few months. Cole understood. A lot of boys who went away wouldn't be coming back, and too many of the ones who did make it home were destroyed by their experiences. And like him, they were bone-weary and disillusioned.

"One of them is right behind me." Cole set the brake. "I ran into Beau a couple hundred miles back, and we rode home together."

"Aw, your ma's going to be beside herself! Two of her boys home the same day!" Tal slapped him on the back again. "What in the world are you doing driving the stage?"

Beau rounded the corner by the saloon, leading Cole's horse with the bodies of the stage driver and shotgun guard draped across the saddle. The town gave him a wide berth. Sheriff Franklin turned to look over his shoulder. "What's going on here?"

"Stage was robbed about five miles back." Cole waved at several friendly voices that called out to him, and his heart felt like it was about to burst with gladness. Home. He was finally home.

There was old Nathan at the blacksmith shop, grinning at him with his gold tooth shining in the afternoon sunlight. Nute Brower leaning on his broom on the front porch of his general store, watching all the commotion taking place. The way everyone was acting, it was almost like a holiday celebration.

Mary Beth Parker, town spinster, sat in the post office window and waved her hankie at him. He remembered Miss Parker's smile from when he was a small boy and his ma would send him into town to pick up the mail each month. Mary Beth had been the postmistress of River Run over fifty years, and it wouldn't seem right to come home and see anyone else sitting in her place.

Cole threw the reins to Jim Parker and climbed down off the high seat. The townspeople made room for him as he walked back to the coach and opened the door. Finis Rutcliff barreled out.

Penelope Pettibone was next, stepping lightly into Cole's waiting arms. He swung her small frame down easily and then quickly doffed his hat. "Ma'am, I hope the ride wasn't too uncomfortable for you."

Penelope's sultry gaze slid over his shoulders and chest as she removed her arms ever so slowly from around his neck. She batted her long black eyelashes at him. "Why, thank you, sir. I surely do appreciate your being such a gentleman. I'm feeling much better now, thank you." Her soft Southern accent drifted as lightly as jasmine on the hot, sultry air.

Cole felt his smile widening to a silly grin, and he mentally caught his emotion. How long had it been since he'd seen such a sweet-smelling, pretty-looking woman? Too long.

His grin spread over his face as he reluctantly set Penelope aside and turned to the next passenger. Instead of warm flesh, his hand came in contact with cold metal. His grin died a sudden death. He'd forgotten that fool woman and her gun. It was a wonder she hadn't blown his head off yet. It looked like his guardian angel was still on the job.

Wynne Elliot forced the burdensome shotgun ahead of her and tried to work her billowing skirts and the hatbox she was carrying out the narrow doorway. The brim of her hat scraped the door frame, tilting over her eyes.

Cole didn't make any move to help her. He knew he'd probably overdone the courteous treatment with Miss Pettibone, and he felt guilty about not helping Miss Elliot in the same considerate manner, but if he offered his hand, she'd probably take a shot at him. Most cantankerous woman he'd ever met.

Miss Elliot didn't seem to notice as she stubbornly worked her purse, the hatbox, and the gun out the narrow door. A dog barked somewhere close by. She jerked as though the sound startled her, and her foot slid off the bottom step. The hatbox was crushed against the door frame, and the gun barrel reared upward as she slid feetfirst out the door.

Cole ducked quickly to one side and automatically flinched against the anticipated blast. The gun didn't go off. He straightened in time to see Miss Elliot sit down in the dust, flat on her backside, the gun and hatbox beside her. That silly hat was tilted down covering her eyes, and the bird looked like it was giving serious thought to flying south. Her feet stuck straight out in front of her, revealing trim ankles. She shoved the hat back and shot a frustrated look in his direction. Her face flamed a bright red when she saw the smirk he couldn't conceal.

Cole bit his lip to control the laugh he knew was ready to explode. The tough, gun-toting Southern belle couldn't keep from tripping over her own feet. They were just lucky she hadn't shot anyone by accident. She sat there looking like she didn't know what to do next. The humiliation in her eyes got to him.

Drawing a resigned breath, he picked up his hat, dusted it off on his uniform, and jammed it back on his head. Against his better judgment, he walked over to Miss Elliot and leaned down until his face was level with hers. With an expression as serious as gallstones, he spoke in as polite a manner as he could manage without bursting into a guffaw. "Miss, allow me to assist you with your hatbox."

Something akin to a growl escaped her tightly compressed lips. She struggled to her feet, steadfastly refusing to look at the gawking crowd. The smothered chuckles from the bystanders brought blood rushing to her face again. He had a hunch she felt like this was the last straw. Poor kid. She'd had a tough day, but she hadn't lost her spunk.

She glared up at him, green eyes blazing. "Thank you. . .*sir*, but

I believe I can manage by myself."

He felt a twinge of remorse. She had a right to be angry with him, but he wasn't going to say so. He'd helped Miss Porcelain out of the stage like a high-priced doll and then let *her* fall out on her backside. Ma would have been ashamed of him.

Miss Elliot shook the dust from her skirt and reached for the hatbox. Cole's hand snaked out to snatch the gun away. When she would have protested, he said—with a smile—"Please, I insist on being of service. At least let me carry your weapon."

With an obvious effort, she gathered the shredded remnants of her composure, squared her shoulders, and lifted her small chin. "Yes. . .well, thank you. That would be most helpful." Her nose tilted a fraction higher. She lifted the hem of her skirt and brushed past him.

He followed, grinning. The townsfolks' welcome made him feel so good he couldn't be angry at this little Southern spitfire. Even if she was a royal pain in the neck.

Tal Franklin was talking to Beau, discussing the details of the robbery as Wynne approached. "I'm certainly glad to see you, Sheriff." She dropped the hatbox onto the ground beside him, ignoring Cole, who had followed her, still carrying the gun. "You will find the culprits today?" She peered up at Tal while adjusting her hat and tucking up stray strands of hair, which now dangled like wet noodles around her dirty, perspiration-dampened face.

Cole watched as Tal regained his composure. He had witnessed Wynne's unseemly stage exit, and you could bet those shrewd eyes of his had noticed the obvious animosity between the two of them. Tal noticed everything. That was why he was the best sheriff west of the Mississippi. Right now he had a stunned expression on his face as he eyed Wynne's hat. Eastern fashions were slow to get to the Midwest, and generally the ladies were interested in seeing the new styles, but Cole would bet his last dollar not a woman in town would be caught dead wearing that thing.

"I'll sure try my best, ma'am," Tal said, "but the gang got a pretty good head start on me. One of my men's rounding up a posse right now, and we'll be on our way soon as they get here."

Wynne's shoulders slumped. "I'd hoped you'd know who they were."

"From the description Rutcliff gave me, sounds like it's the Beasons. They've been giving us a peck of trouble lately. If it's them, they'll head straight for the hills, and it'll be nigh onto impossible to find them." Tal's tone of voice didn't offer much encouragement.

Wynne kicked dust. "But you will find them? They stole every cent I have plus the locket Papa gave me. I haven't anything left except my clothes!"

"Sure sorry, ma'am. We'll do everything we can. You'll excuse me now? I've got things to see about." Tal tipped his hat to her and hurried over to help one of the men lift the lifeless body of the guard off Cole's horse. The driver already lay stretched out on the ground.

Cole trailed after him, pausing to talk to his brother.

"What about the women?" Beau asked.

"Penelope told me she's here to work at Hattie's," Cole said. "She didn't say, but I assume that's where the crazy one's headed, too. So you can stop playing mother hen."

Beau's gaze studied Wynne's small, wilted form, and he looked disappointed as Cole's words registered. "Oh? I wouldn't have thought she'd be one of. . .those kinds of women."

"Well, apparently she is, so let's just play it smart and move on." Cole resettled his hat and turned toward his horse. "If you want to spend time socializing with the lovely Miss Pettibone in the future, you can always ride back to town."

"Like thunder I can," Beau said, but Cole thought he sounded tempted. Cole knew, like him, it had been a long time since Beau had enjoyed a female's company, and Penelope was a very pretty young woman. "Betsy would wring my neck like a Sunday chicken."

Wynne sank down to sit on her hatbox as she tried to think what to do next. The sun hammered through her hat, making her feel faint, and the air was thick with dust. Her cotton dress stuck to her moist skin. She fanned her heat-flushed face with her handkerchief. How could Missouri be so hot?

She sighed, plucking absently at the drawstrings of her purse. She was indeed in a pickle and needed advice. Sound advice. She was penniless without the slightest idea of what to do next. She'd been carrying every last cent she had left, but at best she would only have had enough to see her through a few months.

By then she'd planned to have her revenge on Cass Claxton and be on her way back to Georgia to try to sell the only asset she had left in this world: the land her family home had been built on. Now she was stranded in a strange town, impoverished, and without a vague notion of where to turn. Since Papa's death the only family she could claim was a distant aunt in Arizona, whom she didn't think would even remember her name, let alone wire money.

She could get a job, but she wasn't trained for anything other than being a lady. Five years at Miss Marelda Fielding's Finishing School for Young Ladies in Philadelphia had given her genteel manners and behavior befitting a proper lady, but Miss Marelda had hardly prepared her students to be sitting in the middle of the street on their hatboxes, alone and flat broke.

Wynne fanned herself harder and forced back a hysterical giggle. Miss Prim-and-Proper Marelda Fielding would positively *swoon* if she could see the fine muddle Wynne'd gotten herself into this time.

Cole and Beau talked in low undertones. She watched them, thinking they seemed to be arguing. The younger one, Beau, was all right, but that Cole was the most arrogant, irritating male she had ever met. She caught them casting an occasional glance in her direction. Somehow she had the feeling they were discussing her situation, and it unnerved her.

The sheriff motioned to Cole, and Beau strolled back to where Wynne sat and knelt down beside her. "I think we're through here. Sheriff Franklin will notify the families. Are you going to be all right?"

"To be honest, Mr. . . ." She paused, searching for a name. She'd given her name earlier, as well as the other passengers', but the two strangers had not reciprocated.

Beau swept off his hat. "Beau, ma'am."

"Yes, Beau." Didn't the man have a last name? "And you may call me Wynne."

"Wynne. That's a right pretty name."

"Thank you. . .Beau. . .but as I was saying, I'm afraid this robbery has left me in quite a quandary." She drew a deep breath, shooting him a timid smile.

"Oh?" Beau frowned. "Well, I know you must have been real scared, but you're safe now."

"I'm not concerned for my safety," Wynne confessed. "It's. . .well, they took all my money, and now I'm not quite sure what I'm going to do." She fought the tears hovering precariously close to the surface. She couldn't sit here in the street forever, but she had no idea where to go or what to do.

Beau dropped his gaze from hers, looking decidedly embarrassed. "Why, I don't imagine you'll have to worry about your keep," he said weakly. "I've heard—though I have no firsthand knowledge—that Hattie takes right good care of her. . .girls."

Wynne stared back at him vacantly. "Hattie?"

"Yeah. . .you know, Hattie Mason. . .she runs the local saloon and. . .well, you know, the lady who owns Hattie's Place—"

Wynne felt the blood drain from her face. "Hattie's Place!" She sprang to her feet, and Beau's head snapped back.

He rose more slowly. "Well, yeah. . . Cole said he thought you and Miss Pettibone were headed for the same. . ." His voice trailed off as she drew herself up as far as her small stature allowed.

"Oh, he did, did he?" She shot a scathing glance in the direction of the gossipy, ill-mannered lout. "Well, you can tell *him* he'd better get his facts straight before he starts maligning my good character!"

"Now, ma'am," Beau soothed, "my brother doesn't mean any harm. He just sort of assumed since you and Miss Pettibone were traveling together. . .you know, you two being such pretty women and all—"

Wynne stamped her foot and glared up at him. "Well, he assumed wrong!"

"Yes, ma'am. I'll tell him," Beau agreed.

Wynne snorted and shot visual daggers at Cole, who was still immersed in deep conversation with the sheriff. "Hattie's Place. How dare he!"

Cole glanced in Wynne's direction at the sound of her upraised voice, and she sent him a scathing glare that could rightly singe pinfeathers.

Beau changed the subject. "Now, don't you be fretting yourself any. Cole and I will be happy to take you to your folks, and hopefully, in a few days, the sheriff will arrest the Beasons and return your money."

Wynne barely heard his optimistic predictions. Her angry gaze bore into the tall, dark-haired man who had finished his conversation with the sheriff and was now making idle conversation with Penelope in front of the saloon. She seriously doubted Cole would be thrilled about Beau's generosity.

Her temper simmered when she noted the respectful way Cole treated Penelope. She couldn't help comparing his chivalrous manner toward the petite blond with his egotistical behavior toward her a few moments earlier. His gentility had taken wing when he had let her fall out of the coach and make a complete fool of herself for the second time today!

"You don't understand." She interrupted Beau's attempt to soothe her ruffled feathers. "I don't have any family."

Surprise flickered briefly in his eyes. "None?"

"None," she confirmed.

"You're not from around here?"

"Savannah is my home. . .or was until Papa died last winter."

"Georgia." Beau seemed surprised. "What's a young lady like you doing traveling to Missouri alone?"

Her eyes narrowed to viperous slits as she reminded herself why she was here. That no-account Cass Claxton! It was his fault she was in this mess. Another score she had to settle with him. "I'm looking for someone."

Relief crossed Beau's features. "Good, at least there's someone. A lady friend?"

Wynne shrugged lamely. "A man. I heard his home was in River Run. Even though I know he's been off fighting the war, I understand he's coming back now that the fighting's over."

"A man." A devilish gleam lit Beau's eyes. "A beau, huh? Well, take heart, Miss Elliot. Me and Cole have lived in these parts all our lives, so we know about everyone in the area. If your friend lives around here, we can help you find him."

Wynne's face lit with expectation, her concerns suddenly lighter. It would save a lot of time if they could direct her to where Cass lived. Wouldn't the varmint be surprised when she showed up? She'd teach him a lesson he wouldn't forget. She smiled up at Beau. "You'd do that for me?"

"I certainly would!" Beau affirmed. "And about your lost money. . .don't worry about that. We'll take you home with us. Ma always has room for one more, and she'd be ashamed of us if she found out you was in trouble and we hadn't done our Christian duty."

"Oh no. Really, I couldn't impose on you like that," Wynne protested.

"Impose!" Beau appeared to warm to the idea. "We'd be right proud to have you come along with us. Soon as me and Cole get settled in, we'll start looking for your man." His face creased in a disarming grin as he offered Wynne his arm. "No more arguments. You're coming home with us."

She placed her hand in the crook of his elbow, and he picked up the hatbox and escorted her to his horse, assuring her all the while that everything would work out. "You ride with me," he said. "I'll get Cole to take your bags."

Wynne wasn't sure she was doing the right thing; she knew going home with two perfect strangers was highly improper, but she suddenly found herself being lifted up and set firmly on the back of Beau's horse.

She leaned over to catch his arm. "Don't you think you should check with your brother before you invite me to your home?" She could imagine what *his* reaction was going to be to this latest piece of news.

Beau swung his large frame up behind her and grinned. "Not

to worry, Miss Elliot. He won't care. He's been gone four years; all he wants to do is get home. He doesn't care who goes with him."

She cast a dubious glance toward the man in question. "I still don't think he'll be too happy about all this."

"He won't care," Beau insisted.

Beau nudged the horse's flanks gently and set the animal into motion. Seconds later they ambled up beside Cole and Penelope. Cole glanced up, and Wynne bit back a smirk when surprise flickered across his face. Seeing her mounted in front of Beau had to unnerve him. In spite of Beau's assurances to the contrary, she realized Cole would definitely mind her going home with them.

"You about ready to leave?" Beau inquired pleasantly. "Wynne's coming home with us."

Wynne bit her lip hard when Mr. Smarty-Pants's jaw dropped like a rock, but he recovered quickly. "I thought she was headed for Hattie's."

"It so happens you thought wrong," Wynne said. She proceeded to bestow on him one of her loveliest—albeit snootiest—smiles, one Miss Marelda Fielding would have been proud to witness. "Your brother has kindly offered the hospitality of your home until I can regain my financial losses." Her voice dripped honey. "Beau said you wouldn't mind one little bit carrying my valises." She crossed her hands over her chest in mock admiration. "My, your chivalry simply leaves me without words!"

Cole glanced sharply at Beau then back at Wynne. He had a grim set to his mouth. "My mind cannot comprehend someone as fair as you without words, Miss Elliot." He bent his head respectfully. "Ladies—Miss Elliot, if you would excuse us for a moment I'd like to have a word with my brother."

Beau slid down off the horse and handed the reins to Wynne

with a knowing wink. "I shall return."

Wynne stiffened. The cad. She'd caught that thinly disguised salutation. *Ladies,* meaning Penelope.

"Pompous idiot." She hadn't meant to speak out loud, but a quick check satisfied her that no one except Penelope was close enough to hear her caustic observation. Not that she would mind all that much if that ill-mannered lout had heard her. Someone needed to take him down a peg.

The two brothers disappeared around the corner of the building while Wynne said her good-byes to Penelope.

The minute they were out of sight of the women, Cole grabbed Beau's arm and demanded, "What are you doing this time?"

"Hey, calm down." Beau glanced back over his shoulder. "I knew you wouldn't be too happy about the arrangement, but the poor girl's up a creek, Cole."

"I fail to see where she's our responsibility." Cole's jaw set in a grim line. "She's Hattie's problem."

"She told you. She wasn't coming to work for Hattie. Penelope is the only one planning to work there," Beau explained.

Beau sounded so reasonable, Cole wanted to box some sense into him. Crazy kid. Hadn't he learned anything from being in the war? You didn't just pick up strange females and take them home with you. "Then what is Miss Elliot doing tramping all over the country in that silly hat and falling out of stagecoaches? Crazy fool woman." Just his luck to run into her. Look how they'd already been delayed by her shenanigans. If Beau hadn't insisted on getting them involved in this mess, he would have been sitting down to supper right now.

"She's looking for a man."

Cole snorted. "I bet she is—let's hope, for his sake, she doesn't find him."

Beau sighed. "What have you got against her? She hasn't said ten words to you and you act like she's done something wrong. Besides, you're the one who is always carping about wanting a woman to have a little spirit. Well, she's spirited enough."

"I don't want a spirited, addlebrained female." Any man who took her on could count on a short, frustrated life. If she didn't shoot him by accident, she would drive him to shoot himself.

"So she doesn't know how to handle a gun. Is that what you've got against her? Lots of women don't. Betsy and Priscilla don't—"

"I don't want to hear any more about Priscilla! Okay?" Cole felt he had just about reached his limit. He didn't want a woman. All he wanted was to get home, see Ma, eat some home cooking, and start getting his life back to the way it used to be before the war had changed everything.

"Okay, okay. But you can't hold not being able to handle a gun against Wynne," Beau pointed out. "For the life of me, I can't understand why you're so dead-set against helping her. You're usually a little more gentlemanly when it comes to women. Ma would be ashamed of you."

Cole took a step back and crossed his arms. He raised his eyebrows. "Now it's 'Wynne'?"

"She said I could call her by her first name."

"You're asking for trouble," Cole said. "I say we turn her over to Tal and be on our way."

"I can't do that."

"You can't *do* that," Cole repeated in exasperation. "Why *can't* you do that? She means nothing to us one way or the other. We stumbled on a robbery! We didn't take her to raise!" And he sure didn't want to take her home with him. He didn't want strangers spoiling his homecoming.

"I know, but somehow I sort of feel responsible for her, Cole. Look at her. Does she look like she can take care of herself? Don't ask me why, but I think the Lord's put her right here with us, and I'm going to take her home to Ma for now, and then I'm going to help her find the man she's looking for." Beau crossed his arms. "All I'm asking you to do is carry her valises. Is that asking too much?"

"You're a fool." Cole pulled off his hat and swiped a forearm sleeve across his forehead. He'd helped raise this boy; why hadn't he taught him some plain common sense?

Beau's lips firmed. "So be it, but that's the way I'm going to do it. Now, are you going to carry her bags, or am I going to have to make another trip back into town to get them?"

Cole raked his fingers through his dark hair. "I don't know why I let you talk me into these things," he muttered. "She's only going to be trouble for us. Remember that when she turns into more headache than she's worth."

"I'll remember—as long as you're carrying her bags." Beau grinned and slapped him good-naturedly on the back as they walked around the corner. "I'll tell Tal she'll be out at our place if he needs her. I'll only be a minute."

Cole grunted and went over to pick up the two bags sitting on the ground in front of the stage. After hefting them up onto his shoulders, he walked back to his horse and started tying them on.

He watched as Wynne fanned herself energetically, swatting at the flies buzzing around her head. Aggravating female. Seemed like if there was any way she could be a problem she would find it. He yanked hard on the leather strap he used to bind the bags behind his saddle. And Beau was just as bad. Couldn't do a thing with either one of them.

Now she slid off the horse and walked toward him. Should have known she couldn't sit still and stay out of the way. Maybe if he ignored her she would leave, but he knew he couldn't be that lucky.

She stopped some three feet away and cleared her throat. "Excuse me."

Cole glanced up. Even with a dirty face and her hair straggling in her eyes she was still pretty. Too bad she didn't have a lick of common logic to go along with her looks. He went back to fastening her bags on his horse. His horse. This poor animal was as tired as he was, and now thanks to his scatterbrained brother, it was being used as a packhorse, too. Sometimes he wondered about Beau. Well, he might have to take Miss Elliot home with him, but he didn't have to like it.

"Sir?"

This time he stared at her, and she smiled back timidly.

"Are you speaking to me?" he asked.

Her smile faded. "Well, of course I'm talking to you. Who do you think I'm talking to? The horse?"

"Wouldn't surprise me." He went about his work, dismissing the strained conversation. There wasn't anything that said he had to talk to her, either. He should have known it wouldn't be that easy. She wasn't the kind to give up.

She cleared her throat again. "Since we'll be in each other's company for the next few days, we should properly introduce ourselves."

He grunted.

"I'm Wynne Elliot." She extended her hand.

"And I'm Pompous Idiot," he replied evenly, cinching the rope around her bags. He ignored her hand.

A flush rose up the column of her neck as her gaze slid away in embarrassment. "Oh dear. You heard that."

"I'm pompous. Not deaf."

"Well, I must apologize—is it Cole?"

He shot her another prickly look and continued his task. Why didn't she do something about that hat?

"I suppose this whole ordeal has unnerved me, and I have completely forgotten my manners." Once again she extended her hand in a friendly gesture. "My name is Wynne Elliot, but you may call me *Miss* Elliot." Apparently she was willing to give only so much in the name of peace. That was all right with him. He didn't feel much like going the extra mile himself. Turning the other cheek was all very well, unless the person slapping you down just kept on slapping. He'd about had enough of *Miss* Wynne Elliot.

Cole stared at her hand, dirty from her recent fall. He hesitated, not wanting to accept it, but Ma's teaching ran too deep to be ignored. He took the grubby little paw in his own. "*Miss* Elliot"—he bowed mockingly—"I wish I could say it was an honor to make your acquaintance."

Her lips tightened, but she made an obvious effort to ignore his deliberate attempt to rile her. "I'm sorry I called you a pompous idiot."

"And I'm sorry I called you what I did."

She frowned. "What did you call me?"

"Addlebrained. Careless. That's two that come to mind right off," he confessed. He grinned, knowing he was irritating her all the more.

Her frown deepened. "Addlebrained? You called me addlebrained?" She jerked her hand free. "I suppose you think I'm addlebrained because I dropped the gun and tripped over it?"

"That was part of it, and then you fell out of the stage," he confessed. "That's where the *careless* came in."

The corners of his eyes crinkled with amusement when she shook her head in anger and the hat slipped over her nose. She shoved it back on her head, and the bird rocked in its nest. He grinned, thinking if there were eggs in that nest they must be scrambled by now.

"Well, I can assure you I am *not* careless or addlebrained," Wynne said. "You happened to catch me at a bad moment."

"You can think that if it pleases you, Miss Elliot." Cole picked up the reins of his horse and swung into the saddle. "Seems to me you're just being yourself."

Beau came out of the sheriff's office and approached them, looking ready to go.

"I'll follow you," Cole said. "Let's try to make it home for supper." He hoped they didn't come across any more stagecoaches being held up or any more damsels in distress. One addlebrained female was one more than any sane man could be expected to put up with.

"Sounds good to me!" Beau agreed as he helped Wynne up onto the horse and then mounted behind her. He gathered up the reins and gave a loud rebel yell as he kicked his horse into action. Wynne shot a cross look in Cole's direction as they rode out of town in a cloud of dust.

He grinned when he heard her mutter, "Addlebrained indeed!"

Chapter 3

This was the hour Cole had relived for the past four years. In his mind he'd walked the old paths, climbed the hills, slept in his own bed. Nothing he'd seen in the East or South could compare with the sights, the smells around him now.

July was too late to see the wild roses in bloom, but the golden flowers of the black-eyed Susan lined the roadway. The blue stars of chicory mingled with the white of Queen Anne's lace. Ma would probably have a big bouquet of wildflowers in the old ironstone pitcher sitting on the library table in the front room.

Life felt pretty good. Cole had been afraid of what he would find here. Even though he'd been a long way from home, he'd heard about the fierce border war between Missouri and Kansas. Guerrilla bands had fought back and forth, the Missouri men called Bushwhackers and the Kansas ones called Jayhawkers or Redlegs. He supposed it didn't matter what you called a man; there wasn't much difference in war.

Quantrill's band of Bushwhackers had fought here, and from what he'd heard, Frank and Jesse James had ridden with him. The James boys, like a lot of young men, had been forced into this war to protect what they saw as theirs. And what they believed. Frank and Jesse had been Southern sympathizers. Cole had fought for the Union.

The war had turned neighbor against neighbor, brother against brother. As for him, he'd never felt like he had a choice. He'd never been able to think that anyone Almighty God had created should be held in slavery because they looked different or belonged to a different race. Didn't seem right somehow.

He focused on Wynne Elliot, riding in front of Beau. One hundred pounds of trouble on the hoof. Ma would probably take her in all right. She'd take in a stray dog, had lots of times, but they'd be lucky if this stray didn't shoot someone or set fire to the house. Miss Wynne Elliot was an accident waiting to happen.

Life was unpredictable. Wynne clung to the saddle horn and thought how odd it was that she was here, in Missouri, trusting her very life to strangers. Not all that long ago the only thing she'd had to worry about was the color of her next ball gown.

Life had been grand back home in Georgia—before both Mama and Papa passed away. She'd been an only child, raised in an affluent home by doting parents. Moss Oak had been one of the biggest cotton plantations in the South before the fighting broke out.

Then the war had come, and Papa had sent her away to the East to learn the fine art of being a lady, which he thought she sorely needed. Real ladies weren't supposed to know the basics of farming. She wondered what he would say if he could see her now, riding astride a horse in front of a man she had met for the first time today. Papa definitely wouldn't have approved.

Beau was taking her to see his mother. Well, she'd had a mother, too, before she'd been taken ill with a strange sickness. Papa had brought Wynne home from school to be of comfort, but nothing had been the same since.

She clung tighter when Beau urged his horse to a canter, remembering the feeling of helplessness as she and her father stood by and watched Rose Elliot struggle to overcome the sickness that ravaged her. There was nothing doctors could to do to still the nausea and the swift weight loss that beset her frail body. Then came the terrible pain. Wynne was still tormented sometimes by the memory of her mother's soft sobbing in the night and her father's agonized voice trying to ease her torment and contain his own. Weeks had seemed like years back then.

Tears stung her eyes. Why was she thinking of that now? Was it because Beau and Cole seemed so anxious to get home and see their mother again? Well, she could identify with that. She'd spent hours praying that the good Lord would relieve the suffering and take away the agony they all were experiencing.

She guessed God had His own way of looking at things. He hadn't saved her mother, and He had done nothing to stop the war. All that killing and dying, and for what? Nothing she could see. Surely the problem of slavery could have been solved another way.

At least she could be grateful her mother hadn't lived to see the destruction of the plantation she loved so dearly. When the end came, Rose Elliot simply went to sleep and never woke up.

Wynne watched the unfamiliar scenery rushing by. She was used to cleared fields and stately houses. The trees here grew so close together it was like riding through a green tunnel. The few houses they passed looked neglected, like no one cared about them. Papa had taken good care of their home. Or he had before her mother's death had ripped the heart out of him.

Her mother's sickness had been heartbreaking enough, but the pain was nothing compared to her father's grieving his life away after her mother's death. He'd roamed the halls at night in search of something that Wynne had never quite understood. Once she'd passed his study late in the evening and heard the tortured weeping of a man who had suffered an unspeakable loss, one with which he could not cope.

The horse stumbled, and Wynne caught her breath. If this fool horse fell, he'd kill them both the way Beau kept urging the animal to a faster gallop. She knew he was in a hurry to get home, but as long as they'd been away, surely a few minutes couldn't matter. Not enough to take a chance on having a fatal accident. She turned slightly, observing Cole. Now there was a man who'd take a lot of taming—far more than she could fathom.

She turned back, tightening her lips, suddenly flushed with anger. Men. It was just after Mama's death that Cass had come into her life. He'd been a gentle, loving man who had helped her through the agony of loss with his sunny disposition, quick wit, and remarkable charm.

She'd met him through a mutual friend at a Christmas ball. When she questioned why he hadn't enlisted in the Southern cause, he'd explained that he had family obligations, and he had paid someone to take his place. The idea that any man could pay his way out of service to his country bothered her. For five hundred dollars, another man would fight on his behalf. She even knew it was customary practice for men of means to do so, but the thought still disturbed her.

Undoubtedly Cass came from an affluent and prosperous family, which should make it easier to find him. From what she'd seen of River Run there couldn't be too many families around here that met the criteria. You had only to look at Cass to know he came from good stock. He had been in Savannah visiting kin—

prominent, wealthy pillars of the community. She had been so totally captivated by Cass's impeccable manners and his chivalrous ways that all else seemed secondary in her mind.

She supposed there was some excuse for the way she fell for him. After all, it had been such a rare treat for the belles of Georgia to have a fascinating, eligible young man in their midst. She had simply forgotten about the war and let her heart be won by those pretty words that had dripped off his tongue like rich, warm honey—lying, deceitful words that she still hated to admit she had actually been gullible enough to believe!

He'd caught her at a vulnerable time, of course.

A scant six weeks after her mother's death, she'd heard a shot ring out in the night. Papa had chosen to leave his daughter behind. By his own hand he had gone on to be with the woman he had loved so much he no longer wanted to live without her. For months she had heard the reverberation over and over again.

She'd been left alone and more frightened than she had ever been in her life. And then the Yankees came through and burned Moss Oak and the surrounding buildings. Mercifully they had left the main house standing, but they had ransacked and carried off the furnishings while she and the servants stood by and watched the pillaging in stunned silence.

"Are you comfortable?" Beau's voice broke into her painful thoughts and drew her quickly back to the present.

Immersed in her sad memories, Wynne had forgotten her uncomfortable perch in a saddle too large for her and the closeness of the man riding behind her. She plucked at the material of her dress, attempting to allow some air to circulate against her skin. The sun was a ball of fire in the sky, making her nearly limp with heat. She was anything but comfortable, but considering how kind Beau had been, she decided it would be ungrateful to complain.

"I'm fine, thank you." She shifted slightly, increasingly aware of the pressure of Beau's arms around her as he held the reins. Surely it couldn't be much farther. "Are we almost there?"

"Another three miles or so. We can stop and let you rest a spell if you'd like."

"That won't be necessary. I'll be fine."

She was most appreciative of what he was doing for her. Not all men would have taken her under their wing the way Beau had.

She turned her head slightly, her eyes fastening on the rider trailing a safe distance behind them. *He* certainly would have left her for the buzzards to pick clean.

For a reason she couldn't understand, that train of thought made her think of Cass, handsome rogue that he was, which set her to seething all over again.

The only good thing Cass Claxton had done was to be there for her to lean on during the most tragic time of her life. And in all honesty, he had never failed her once during those dark days. He'd helped her face reality, always there when she swore she couldn't bear the sorrow, wiping away her tears and confidently assuring her that through God she could bear all things. For a young man of twenty-two, he readily admitted he didn't have all of life's answers, but together they would find them.

Then one day he'd been offered an opportunity to go into business with one of his cousins. They wanted to buy a plant that manufactured gunpowder. Wynne had been ecstatic. The business venture meant Cass would be staying in Savannah. She suspected now that she had been happier about the business prospect than he was. Had she pushed him into accepting the offer? She'd wanted to keep him close. Even began dropping marriage hints, viewing Cass as a most pleasant avenue to salvage her broken life.

As further enticement she'd offered the money from her

inheritance for the business prospect. It wasn't long before she persuaded Cass to accept her generosity. Now that she'd had time to think about it, seemed like she'd done an awful lot of persuading, and maybe she'd brought some pressure to bear on the marrying part, too. The night before they were to be married, she handed over all her money—with the exception of the meager amount she kept in that small tin box under her mattress—assuming his business endeavor would be concluded early the following morning.

Looking back, she wondered if Cass ever really loved her or if he had asked for her hand in marriage simply to appease a heartbroken girl for whom nothing in life had gone well lately. Certainly his family could have lent him the money to go into business, but instead, Cass had asked her to marry him. So surely he'd cared about her, but if so, why had he left her literally standing in front of the church?

Her cheeks felt hot when she recalled her "wedding day." The morning had dawned cold and gray with the promise of rain in the air. Tilly, her mammy since childhood, had lovingly dressed her for the ceremony, fretting over her like a mother hen.

Even now, she could remember smiling and gazing at herself in the large looking glass in her parents' bedroom, the soft, delicate folds of her mother's ivory wedding gown billowing out around her and sweeping to the floor. She had stared back at the reflection that could have been Rose nineteen years earlier, her eyes misty with grief.

"Do you think Mama and Papa would approve of what I'm doing, Tilly?" she'd asked softly.

Tilly had heaved a big sigh and patted her shoulder reassuringly. "A body's got to do what they think best, sweet baby." The large, rawboned servant gently tucked a lock of red hair behind Wynne's ear. "I'm sure your man will be real good to you."

Wynne shrugged. She supposed Tilly had been right. Cass would have been good to her—had he made it to the wedding.

The pain and humiliation she'd felt standing in front of the church, anxiously awaiting her bridegroom's arrival, still hurt. She and the guests had waited at the church for Cass to arrive that afternoon. And waited and waited and waited. . . . She could never forgive Cass Claxton for that. She could almost overlook the money, though that was bad enough, but nothing could ever make her forget the way she had felt, standing there in the growing twilight, witnessing the pity in the eyes of friends and neighbors she had known all her life.

That was why Mr. Cass Claxton was going to pay for what he had done.

Wynne ignored the tremor of discomfort—as if God might be reminding her about forgiveness. And she'd forgive Cass. Indeed she would, the moment she'd made him sorry he'd ever been such a lying, thieving, two-timing polecat.

Why else would she be here, enduring heat and holdups and Cole—a man whom she'd bet could best Cass in the ornery-man department.

She'd left the morning after the unfinished wedding to return to Marelda Fielding's Finishing School, a feeble effort on her part to put her life back together.

The death of her parents, the war, and Cass's humiliating rejection—all had taken their toll. It had seemed to her she just had to take some sort of revenge.

Slowly a plan—a very simple plan to avenge her pride and uphold the Elliot name—began to take root. She would find Cass Claxton and kill him for what he had done to her. Put a lead slug right through his double-dealing heart. Not only had he stolen her blind, but he had made her the laughingstock of Savannah in the process! Surely such action could not go unpunished.

Cass Claxton had not seen the last of her. She would find him if it was the last thing she did, and before she killed him, she would demand an explanation for his despicable behavior. She shut her mind to the nagging voice that kept whispering, "*Vengeance is mine. . .saith the Lord.*"

This time the Lord was going to have a little help. Surely He wouldn't begrudge her this one slightly irregular take on the eye-for-an-eye suggestion.

Squinting against the glaring sun, she turned to look over her shoulder. The man riding behind seemed intent on his destination, his dusty features hidden beneath a thick dark beard. It was either her vivid imagination, or else *he* even *looked* like Cass. No, that couldn't be. She turned to look straight ahead. The two men only looked alike because she had been thinking about her former fiancé. Other than being uncommonly handsome, they bore no similarities.

But her imagination wasn't playing tricks on her. It suddenly dawned on her why she thought she'd met Cole before. Cass had the same brash but completely charming way of addressing a female. Of course, Cole hadn't been all that charming to her, but he'd oozed with appeal when he was talking to Penelope. She leaned back in the saddle, peering more closely at the brother trailing behind. Even the remembered set of Cass's chin suggested the same stubborn streak she now suspected might be in Cole's, hidden beneath that thick beard. It wasn't so much that they looked alike, but the personality similarities were unmistakable. Both were self-assured, arrogant, not to be trusted. Her eyes skimmed the rider's tanned features and paused at the opening of his shirt. A mat of thick dark hair shadowed the neckline.

Wynne's pulse quickened.

Powerful and ruggedly virile, Cole sat in his saddle with the same aura of authority that Cass possessed, and for a moment Wynne found her heart thumping at the remembrance of being held tightly against the broad expanse of a chest.

She wasn't certain why her gaze lifted suddenly, but it did, and she found herself staring into a set of mocking blue eyes that held ill-concealed amusement at her disgraceful observation of him. She felt color flood her face, and she hurriedly looked away, but she could feel his arrogant eyes boring into the back of her head. She refused to give him the satisfaction of looking back.

She was sure her face was bright as a sunrise!

"Did you say something?" Beau called above the clatter of horses' hooves.

"Nothing!" At least she hoped she hadn't voiced her thoughts out loud. For the remainder of the ride she carefully kept her eyes fixed on the scenery and her mind blank. When the two riders finally turned into a winding lane and let their horses have their head, Wynne breathed a sigh of relief.

The horses thundered down the road. Cole and Beau grinned mischievously at each other and apparently reverted to their childhood, each trying to outrace the other home. Wynne held tightly to the saddle horn, fearing both men had taken leave of their senses.

Flanking the mare's side, Cole shot around Beau and galloped the remaining half mile to the farmyard. With a whoop of joy, he sprang from his saddle before the horse stopped, and enfolded in his arms the woman who had burst out the door, waving her apron. Lifting her high above his head, he swung Lilly Claxton around and around, his face a wreath of smiles. "I'm home, Ma!"

"Cole!" Tears filled Lilly's eyes, and her laughter joined his. "Oh Cole, you're home. Thank God."

His mother's eyes searched his face, and Cole saw the worry

wrinkles that hadn't been there when he left. He knew she'd have spent hours on her knees interceding for the sons who were so far away and in danger. He watched her blink away her tears, and he waited while her searching fingertips examined every contour of his face, looking for signs of the boy who had ridden off to war. He knew those signs weren't there. He'd seen too much, heard too much, fought too many battles. You didn't have much innocence left after four years of hell.

"Beau? Have you heard from Beau?" she questioned.

Before he could answer, Beau and Wynne rode into the barnyard.

A second round of joyous praise and laughter erupted. Beau tumbled off the horse and caught his mother up in his arms. He laughed as he tossed her up into the air and caught her safely back in his arms. He gently set her back on her feet, smiling down at her.

"Beau and Cole! Back home on the same day. Praise the Lord!" Tears spilled over and she reached to clasp her arms around both men's necks, hugging them tightly, as if she would never let them go.

"It's good to be home, Ma," Cole said.

"And your brother. . . Have you seen or heard from him?" Her eyes mutely pleaded for the right answer.

Cole met her question with surprise. "Isn't he here with you?"

"No—no, I got a letter a few months ago. Said he had joined up—"

"I thought he was staying here to help out." Beau took off his hat.

Lilly wiped the corners of her eyes with her faded apron as she tried to defend her youngest son. "I know, but. . .well. . .he always had a wandering streak in him. . .just like your pa."

"Don't worry, Ma. Now that the war's over, he'll be riding in any day." Cole tried to console her, but his heart was heavy. Why in tarnation couldn't that boy have stayed home and taken care of Ma the way he was supposed to? That's why they'd paid five hundred dollars to keep him out of the war in the first place—so she wouldn't be here alone.

Lilly flung her arms back around her boys' shoulders, hugging them simultaneously. "Well, I thank the Lord you're here. I can't believe you're both home at the same time! When we heard the war was over, we started looking for you to come, but since we hadn't heard anything from either one of you in so long, we didn't know what to expect."

"I would have written, Ma," Beau apologized, "but I figured I'd probably get here before the letter did."

"And what's your excuse?" Lilly put her hands on her hips and turned on Cole with accusing eyes that only a mother could manage. He'd never realized how *much* he'd missed her until he got back home. Now he grinned and let his shoulders rise in a lame shrug.

"Ah, Ma. . .you know me. I never was good at writing letters."

For the first time since all the excitement had broken out, Lilly glanced up at Wynne and smiled. "Land sakes! All this ruckus and we plumb forgot our manners! Who have you brought home with you?"

"Ma, this is Wynne Elliot." Beau walked over and lifted Wynne off his horse and set her down on the ground. "She was on the stage to River Run when it was robbed. The Beason gang stole all her money, and since she don't have any kin around here, we brought her home to stay with us for a few days."

"Robbed! Why, that must have been real frightening." Lilly reached out and pumped Wynne's hand warmly. "I'm glad Beau brought you home. You're welcome to stay as long as you like."

Cole looked on cynically. Like he figured, Ma would take her in and feed her. To tell the truth, he'd forgotten about her in the excitement of being home. Well, they'd gotten her here, and he could wash his hands of her. What she did now didn't concern him, and he was going to make sure it stayed that way.

"Thank you," Wynne murmured gratefully. "I should be able to move on in a few days. The sheriff is looking for the bandits right now."

Cole leaned against the porch and watched Miss Elliot try to talk her way into Ma's good graces. What was a woman like her doing out here by herself? Looking for some man, Beau said. Well, if that man was smart, he'd keep running while he had the chance. He narrowed his eyes thoughtfully. Something about Miss Wynne Elliot didn't quite ring true. He'd survived the last four years by recognizing a lie when he heard it, and while he wouldn't go so far as to say that Miss Elliot had lied, he wasn't so sure she had told them the whole truth.

"Well, don't you fret, honey. Tal will find those thieves if anyone can. He's a good man. Now, come along." Lilly wrapped her arms around her sons' waists and gave them another motherly squeeze. "It just so happens Willa and I have a big pot of those chicken and dumplings you're so fond of simmering on the stove. 'Course, you're not either one going to sit at my table till you shave and wash some of that road grime off you." She tugged affectionately at Cole's beard.

Beau's face lit with expectancy. "No kidding, Ma? You really have chicken and dumplings? I was just telling Cole this morning how I hoped you would. Now that's real luck."

"Luck!" Lilly scoffed. "We've had a pot of them chicken and dumplings on the stove since we heard the war was over. Almost wiped out the flock, and I've eaten so many dumplings I'm sick of the sight of them. We've been praying and waiting for you two to come home and eat them for months!"

As suddenly as it appeared, the laughter drained out of her voice and her eyes misted. "I guess I'm going to have to stay down on my knees an extra long time tonight and thank the good Lord He seen fit to send you back to me." She reached up and pinched Cole's cheek. "It's good to have you back, son."

Cole grinned. "Thanks, Ma. It's good to be home."

Chapter 4

Man alive, it was hot! Bertram G. Mallory mopped his forehead with a lank handkerchief and studied the scene before him. A merciless, blazing afternoon sun beat down, sending a shimmer of heat haze across the landscape.

There it was: Springfield, Missouri. He was close now.

He reached up and took another swipe at the sweat rolling from his hatband and looked up for some sign of relief, but the endless blue of a summer sky met his gaze. His weary horse plodded along, its hooves raising little of the dust from the dry road. It had been more than three months since it had rained in these parts, he'd heard. Too long. Brown, scorched grass—dry streambeds. Hotter than an oven on baking day. His patience was wearing thin. Not only with the weather, but also with Wynne Elliot.

Every time he got near that stubborn filly she somehow managed to slip through his fingers. But she wouldn't do it again. He ran a long, lean hand over his prickly beard. No sir, he'd make sure he had her this time.

He reined in the horse and with a low, painful groan slid out of the saddle. His hand automatically went to shield his still-tender left side. The result of the untimely accident he'd encountered a few weeks ago was sensitive to the touch, not to mention the thought. His eyes narrowed when he recalled the harrowing incident that had left him with three busted ribs and a splitting headache for days.

When he'd heard that Miss Elliot was reportedly attending a finishing school for ladies back East, he'd set out to capture the little spitfire. But when he'd arrived in Philadelphia at Miss Marelda Fielding's Finishing School for Young Ladies, Miss Fielding had told him that Wynne wasn't there. Apparently the Elliot woman had decided to pay a visit to Missouri. River Run, Miss Fielding had said. Well, he knew right then that meant a peck of trouble unless he could get to her before she got there.

At the time, it had seemed like a good idea to hop the train. River Run, by stage, was a good several weeks' travel from Philadelphia. Since he had very little time to catch up with her, he'd decided to catch the first train going west and hope it would take him to within a reasonable riding distance of River Run.

It was a good plan and ought to have worked.

He'd sold his horse and pocketed the money, figuring that when he arrived in Missouri by train several days ahead of Miss Elliot, relaxed and completely rested, he would buy another horse. No need to waste his money on a ticket. He'd wait until the train passed under a big bluff and then jump on top of the car and stay there until the conductor collected the fares. Then he would casually blend himself in with the other passengers and enjoy the ride.

He flinched when a sharp, excruciating pain rippled through his side. The plan would have worked, too, if his timing hadn't been a fraction off, and if the train had run as far as Missouri.

He'd jumped off the bluff as planned and hit the top of the railcar with the speed of a bullet. His calculation had been a mite off. The train had been traveling faster than he'd figured—not much, but enough to throw off his rapid descent.

He landed wide-eyed in spread-eagle position flat against the top of the fast-moving boxcar. He'd frantically grasped for something to hold on to while the train shot around a bend in the track. Even now he could remember the terror he had felt when his fingers began to slip and he'd realized he and the train would soon be parting company.

He'd tried to dig his toes in for support, but there wasn't anything to get a toehold on, so to speak. He'd lost his grip on the deepest bend. The train's speed catapulted him off the side of the car, and his life had flashed before his eyes when he hurtled through the air. His body had been flung like a rag doll to the ground, where he rolled for what must have been fifteen minutes down a deep, briar-blanketed ravine. When he came to it was night and he was certain every bone in his body had been shattered. An old prospector was bending over him.

Probably hadn't helped much to be ridden into town slung over the back of the old man's donkey. The prospector had left him with the doctor and, after refusing payment, which had been right neighborly of him, had waved off Bertram's gratitude and disappeared out the front door.

Bertram straightened and caught the small of his back. He was still amazed that he was alive. The harrowing brush with death had left him with three cracked ribs, a bad back, and a busted skull. The accident had been enough to lay him up at the local hotel for several weeks.

Then he'd found out that all the pain and inconvenience had been for nothing. The track had ended twenty miles down the road.

How was he to know that?

Merchants throughout the country had a hard time getting goods delivered overland by wagon, not to mention the toll it took on animals. Terrible road conditions in most states brought about railroad fever. Tracks were springing up all over the country, and the people were crying for rail service. He'd been certain he could get to Missouri with no problem.

When he healed, he'd worked long enough to buy another horse, and then once more he set off in pursuit of the elusive Miss Elliot.

Bertram shook his head. He was just too reliable, that's what. Too loyal. Any other man would have given up by now, but not him. He'd been forced to go back to Miss Marelda Fielding's Finishing School for Young Ladies, hoping that by now Wynne might have returned. He could still remember the sinking knot in the pit of his stomach when Miss Fielding told him she assumed Wynne was still visiting in Missouri.

But he had given his word. Bertram G. Mallory was a man to whom a promise meant something. A man's word was his honor. He would go to great lengths to fulfill an obligation, and his responsibility was to find Wynne Elliot, no matter how long it took.

Now his mission was finally nearing an end. And none too soon. He winced, bringing his hand up to shield his ribs. River Run was just a half day's ride from Springfield. By late tomorrow afternoon, he hoped to meet Miss Elliot face-to-face.

Tonight he'd rest a spell. He longed for a clean bed, a bath, a shave, and a hot meal, but he knew that was foolish thinking. He didn't have funds for that sort of luxury. Instead, he'd settle for a campfire and a bedroll on the outskirts of this fair metropolis.

His eyes skimmed the town ahead. He was surprised to see so much activity on the streets at this hour. Pulling a watch fob from a side pocket, he noted it was nearing six. He'd figured most folks would be home taking supper about now. He rewound the timepiece before carefully placing it back in his pocket and refocusing on Springfield. Big towns had a faster way of life, he decided.

Even from this distance, he spotted a group of bedraggled-looking women standing next to the livery. It wasn't unusual to encounter hundreds of female Confederate refugees swarming about the towns, looking for food and shelter. That worried Bertram. The females were a destitute, heart-wrenching sight, and he didn't like to think about a woman being alone. Women should be taken care of, pampered, and held gently. It always saddened him to see those women. After what he'd experienced during the war, he'd have thought he would have become accustomed to the poverty and degradation the conflict had brought upon the people, but he hadn't and he guessed he never would. He had fought for only a few days when he suffered a wound that had sent him back to Savannah. But he'd seen all the killing he cared to.

Picking up the reins of his horse, he rode the short distance into town and threaded his way along the fringes of the crowd milling about, conversing in low tones. They all seemed to be waiting for something. He wondered if one of those medicine shows might be coming to town.

Suddenly the hushed murmurs stilled. Everyone stood quietly waiting. Bertram's puzzled gaze studied the small crowds gathered in the doorways and alleys surrounding the square, and his brow furrowed with curiosity.

As far as he could tell, there was nothing unusual happening, yet the crowd seemed apprehensive and watchful. He threw the reins over the nearest hitching post and stepped onto the porch of the general store, where he spoke to one of the old-timers leaning back in a chair, whittling on a piece of wood.

"Howdy."

The man's knife paused, and he glanced up at the newcomer, giving him a friendly grin. A battered hat sat on his head, and his snow-white beard was spotted with tobacco juice. The man didn't have a single tooth left in his head.

"Howdy," the old-timer said, leaning over the rail to spit a long stream of brown liquid into the dust.

Bertram stepped out of the line of fire then pushed his hat back on his head before he hunched down beside the man's chair. "Hot, isn't it?"

"Shorely is."

"Could use some rain."

"Yep." The old-timer leaned over the rail and spat. "It'll rain soon, though. Saw a black snake in a tree this morning." He spat again and wiped at his mouth with the cuff of his sleeve. "Hit's a sure sign rain's on the way."

"Yeah. So I've heard." A black snake in a tree was about as accurate a prediction of rain as Bertram could think of, with the exception of birds flying low or walking on the ground. They always meant rain, and he was grateful for any small sign the drought would soon be over.

"You're a stranger to these parts, ain't you, boy?"

"Just passing through."

"Humph." The old man leaned over and spat on the porch.

Bertram surveyed the milling crowd. "What's going on?"

"Gonna be a shooting," the old man said. His gnarled hands gently rubbed the carving he was working on.

Bertram wasn't sure he'd heard right. "A shooting?"

"Yep."

Bertram's wary gaze sought the restless crowd. "Who's going to be doing it?"

The old-timer looked up, and a toothless grin spread across his weather-beaten face. "You ever heard of Wild Bill Hickok?"

Bertram blinked in surprise. "Hasn't everyone?" It was a

well-known fact that Wild Bill's reputation and skill with a gun had made him the constable of Monticello, Kansas, when he was still a teenager. Rumor had it that young Bill had worked as a Union sharpshooter and scout during the past few years. Bertram had even heard speculation that Wild Bill had been a spy for the Union, posing as a Confederate throughout southern Missouri and Arkansas.

"Well, Wild Bill's gonna get his watch back today," the old-timer announced, chuckling.

Bertram frowned. "Someone took his watch?" He whistled under his breath. That sounded mighty daring to him. Most men gave Wild Bill a wide berth. He couldn't imagine anyone being foolish enough to steal the man's watch.

"Guess you could say that. Him and Tutt ain't exactly the bosom buddies, if you know what I mean. They've had some real hard feelings over Susannah Moore, a woman they both had a hankering for, but that's not what they're fighting about."

"Oh?"

"Nope, they ain't fighting over her this time. They were playing cards the other day, and after Hickok had won most of Dave's money, Dave reminded him of the thirty-five dollars Bill still owed him from another time they had played. Well, Wild Bill said he owed him only twenty-five dollars, and he laid it on the table in front of Tutt."

The old man appeared to warm to the subject, his fingers fondling the carving as he ran the sharp knife blade over the soft wood. "Tutt took his money all right, but he also took Wild Bill's gold watch that was a-laying there, saying he figured that would about make up for the other ten Bill owed him."

Bertram would have sworn that Tutt would have been a dead man before he could have gotten the watch in his pocket. "Wild

Bill let him have the watch?"

"Oh, wouldn't say that exactly. Bill jumped up and told Tutt to put the watch back down on the table. But Dave ignored him and left with the watch anyway. The air's been real thick betwixt the two ever since."

"And that's what the shooting's about?"

"Yep. Wild Bill warned Tutt not to wear the watch in public, but he paid Bill no heed. Went right ahead and wore it anyway. We knowed something was bound to happen, and sure enough, it has."

A stream of tobacco flew across the porch and raised dust beside the walk. "Some of Tutt's men sent word to Bill that Dave would be crossing the square around six o'clock tonight if he wanted to try and get his watch back. Hickok sent word back that Dave wouldn't be carrying his watch across the square unless dead men had started walking." The old man cackled.

Bertram fumbled in his pocket and hastily withdrew his watch, noting with dismay that the appointed hour was upon them. "It's six o'clock now. Dave Tutt's a fool for taunting Hickok like that. Hickok will kill him for sure."

The old man leaned closer. "Maybe, maybe not. Dave Tutt ain't exactly shabby with a gun himself. But there's one thing for certain. Trouble like you ain't never seen is gonna break loose in a minute."

If there was one thing Bertram had no desire for, it was to become remotely entangled in a shoot-out on a public street with two known gunslingers. Even watching the spectacle held no interest for him. "Well, I think I'll just mosey on—" He turned when a breathless hush fell over the crowd.

Up the street to one side a bearded man stepped into view. About the same time another man with shoulder-length dark hair and a long brush of a mustache appeared on the opposite side of the square. The flat-crowned hat, black coat, and tucked shirt identified the second man as Wild Bill Hickok.

"You'd better stay on that side of the square if you want to live, Tutt," Hickok warned. His words echoed down the now-deserted town square.

Spellbound, Bertram watched the exchange.

Tutt made no effort to reply. But neither did he dally. He merely stepped out into the street, drawing his gun as he walked.

In a flash, Hickok drew, and both men fired at the same time. The bullet from Hickok's gun went straight through Tutt's heart, and he fell dead in a crumpled heap in the dusty street.

Hickok quickly whirled and pointed his gun in the direction of Tutt's friends, who by now had drawn their own weapons. "Holster those guns or there'll be more than one man dead here today."

Bertram had seen enough. He spun and started for cover. But as luck would have it, his foot caught on a loose board. It was like a hand had come out of the sidewalk and grabbed his ankle, jerking him to a sudden stop. He reeled off the porch onto the street, landing with a thud beneath the watering trough. His ankle throbbed with excruciating pain.

The old-timer jumped up from his chair and peered over the trough. On the square, Tutt's men slowly holstered their weapons and melted into the crowd.

With one final glance around him, Wild Bill calmly walked over to Tutt's body and recovered his gold Waltham watch and chain then turned and sauntered to the courthouse to surrender his pistols to the sheriff.

"Here, boy. Let me help ya. Are you bad hurt?" The old man rolled Bertram over onto his back.

Bertram groaned and held on tightly to his rapidly swelling ankle. If he didn't get the boot off soon, he knew he'd have to cut it off, and he couldn't afford another pair.

"I think I busted my ankle." He gritted the words out. The pain was white-hot and searing. He was having trouble breathing, let alone talking.

The old man squatted beside him and gingerly rotated the injured foot.

"Aaagh!" Bertram screamed.

"Yore right," the old-timer said. He motioned for some of his cronies still sitting on the porch whittling to lend a helping hand. "We'll have to get you over to Doc Pierson's and let him have a look-see."

A busted ankle! If his foot didn't hurt so bad Bertram would have kicked something. That was all he needed now to lay him up again for another who knew how many weeks!

He groaned when four elderly men hovered above him. They seemed hardly strong enough to support their own weight, let alone carry him, but each man dutifully scooped up an arm or a leg. Bertram bit down, clenching his teeth, when they unceremoniously hauled him across the street to the doctor's office, like a wilted sack of flour, and folded him onto the doc's operating table.

"Take care of my horse," Bertram shouted as the old men melted back out the doorway.

"Shore will. He'll be at the livery," the old-timer assured him.

Bertram groaned. Now a livery bill! What else?

The doctor leaned over him. "All right, son, let's see what's happened here."

A firm hand clasped Bertram's boot, and he clamped his eyes shut when pain shot through his leg. He prayed to pass out.

Chapter 5

"The war's over, but there's still men out there in the bushes who don't know that yet." Cole glanced up and smiled at his mother, who had just cut him another thick slice of gooseberry pie. "Careful there, Ma; you're going to have me so big I can't get back on my horse," he complained, but Wynne noticed he had no trouble polishing off the second serving of dessert.

Now that Cole was freshly bathed and cleanly shaved, she had to admit he was even more handsome. Only his despicable disposition spoiled everything.

"You're skinny as a shitepoke," Lilly said, quickly slipping another piece of pie on Wynne's plate before she could stop her.

"Thank you, Lilly, but I really couldn't eat another bite," she protested. For two days she had sat at the dinner table and nearly burst. Willa's meals were large and plentiful. She was surprised at such an abundance of food on the table each day, especially when every other homestead she had passed while riding the stage seemed to be in a depressing state of shortage of even the barest essentials.

She had been surprised by the house, too. True, whitewash and repairs were needed, but the home reflected an affluent lifestyle she'd not expected to find. The house was quite large, with the parlor and family rooms on the main floor. The five upstairs bedrooms, each furnished with a double bed, a clothespress, a nightstand, and a full-length mirror, were much like her room back home at Moss Oak.

There was also almost a Southern flavor to their lifestyle. Meals were at set times, and manners were observed religiously. The best china, glass, and silver had been used on the night of Cole and Beau's return, and in this house they thanked God for their food before every meal. All of this was comforting to Wynne, although it brought a faint sadness along with memories of the home she used to have that was now gone forever. The house was still there, of course, but what good was a house without the presence of the people who had made it a home?

Lilly's voice broke through her thoughts. "It wouldn't hurt for you to have a little more meat on your bones," she told Wynne as she busied herself refilling their cups with the dark chicory coffee that Wynne had come to despise. The brew was tangy and bitter, and she would just as soon do without than have to drink it.

"Praise the Lord the garden's doing well," Lilly murmured, almost as if she had read Wynne's mind. "And Elmo Ferguson's been seeing that we have fresh meat on the table at least twice a week."

"I'll have to stop by and thank Elmo for looking out for you," Cole said with a roguish twinkle in his eye. "I'll bet he's been invited in for a piece of sweet-potato pie every now and again."

"Oh, occasionally I've had one cooling on the windowsill," Lilly said. "So, you're a captain now. I'm real proud of you, son. Now you can settle down and see to the farm."

Wynne noted she had quickly changed the subject. She suspected Lilly didn't like to be teased about Elmo, and Cole knew it. It would be just like him to latch on to something a person didn't want to talk about and drag it into the conversation. He had to be one of the most contrary men ever to draw breath.

"Thanks, Ma—I'll help around here, but I'm going to look into that U.S. marshal job."

She frowned. "Oh Cole, I wish you'd reconsider. Seems you love to put yourself in harm's way—a true man of the saddle."

He leaned over and pinched her cheek. "That's me, Ma, and law's my life. When the good Lord says it's my time to go, then I'll be leaving this old earth whether I'm hunting down a wanted man or sitting here eating fried chicken. Of course, I'd prefer the latter, but I'm not afraid of the former."

Wynne felt his eyes on her as she quietly pushed the second piece of pie aside. She didn't want to offend Lilly, who had immediately taken her in and treated her as part of the family, but she was stuffed as tight as a tick. "If you don't mind, I think I'll save this for a little later on," she murmured as she looked up and saw Cole watching her.

A set of cool, distant blue eyes locked obstinately with hers for a moment before he looked back down at his plate. "A lot of people would be glad to get that pie, Miss Elliot," he said curtly.

Wynne resented his attitude. For two long days Cole had purposely gone out of his way to ignore her, speaking to her only when forced to and, in general, treating her as if she were something he had picked up on his boot in the barnyard instead of as a houseguest. She had tried to overcome the impression she had made at the stagecoach, but evidently Cole wasn't one to forgive and forget. Too bad *he* couldn't have spent some time at Miss Marelda Fielding's Finishing School. Miss Marelda would have taught him some manners.

Because Cole was beginning to fascinate her, she had taken the opportunity to observe him and his relationship with his mother. With Lilly, he was kind and thoughtful, even nice. Cole and Beau treated their mother with the utmost respect. There was genuine, honest warmth among them, evidenced daily by the continual bantering that volleyed back and forth in the household.

After being around Lilly for a couple of days, it wasn't hard to see where Beau had gotten his soft heart and sense of humor. Wynne only wished some of that goodwill had rubbed off on Cole. The tension between the two of them seemed to grow with each passing day, even though Wynne had gone out of her way to be pleasant to him. Well, if not out of her way, then she had at least made a conscious effort to be polite to him, far more than he had done for her.

"I'm aware there are people going to bed hungry tonight," she replied, daring him to look her in the eye, but when he complied, his eyes were so stern her hand reached feebly back for her fork. "Well. . .maybe a few more bites."

Cole polished off his pie and drank the chicory substitute for coffee. Now that he'd had time to observe Wynne Elliot, he realized she was pretty, about as pretty a woman as he'd ever seen, but she had the disposition of a bad-tempered sitting hen. Get too close to her private space and she could turn and flog a man until he ran for cover.

She was eating her pie now, and he felt a sneaky satisfaction that her capitulation had something to do with him. It was good to win one, even if it was over a piece of pie. He'd not won too many battles with Miss Elliot, which brought up an interesting question: What was she hiding? He didn't really care, but after spending four years fighting to survive he had developed certain instincts, and they were all on alert where this woman was concerned.

"That's all right, dear. I'll put the pie in the warming oven, and it will be there when you get hungry again." Lilly took her place at the end of the table and reached for her cup. "I wish Beau and Betsy would hurry and get back."

"They'll be here soon enough," Cole said. "You can't expect them to hurry. They'll have a lot to talk about. Four years is a long time."

"Too long." Lilly sighed. "I don't know how those two have endured the separation. They're so crazy about each other."

The sadness in his mother's voice made Cole realize those four years had taken a toll on the women left behind. Take Betsy for instance. There wasn't a school close to town anymore, so she had accepted a teaching job in a small community about twelve miles from River Run. She was there today, cleaning her schoolroom for the fall session. Beau had gone to help her and visit with her family for a few days. Seeing Beau and Betsy together again was good. The war had disrupted and destroyed too many lives. He was glad to see some sort of normalcy returning to his family. Beau and Betsy had a wedding to plan, and he intended to be there to kiss the bride.

This war had affected everybody. A state of martial law had existed in many areas during the past several years. Schools had closed, and churches had been disbanded. But the small community of Red Springs, where Betsy taught, had not been directly affected by the fighting. Although the community could barely afford to provide a roof over the new teacher's head and three meals a day, the board wanted its children's education to go on uninterrupted, and Betsy had answered the call.

She was a woman to be proud of, and Beau was a lucky man. For a minute Cole wished he could find a woman who would suit him as well. He cast a sour glance at the female sitting across from him. If he ever found one, she'd be as different from Wynne Elliot as possible.

He pushed away from the table. "That was some meal, Ma. I wish you and Willa had gone along to cook for us. Army cooks have a lot to learn."

No, he didn't really wish that. He never wanted the women in his family to see what he had seen. He wasn't sorry he'd gone to war, but he sure hoped he never had to fight in another one. Seemed like war brought out the worst in a man.

Outside, the sound of hoofbeats interrupted the early twilight. Several riders rode up to the house and reined to a halt.

"Now, who could that be?" Lilly frowned. "It's nigh onto dark, and I can't think of a neighbor who would come calling at this hour."

She hurried over to pull the curtain aside to peek out, and Cole reached for his gun belt hanging on a peg next to the back door.

"Why, it's the sheriff," Lilly announced, her face breaking into a friendly smile. She pulled the door open and hurried outside onto the porch, leaving Cole and Wynne to follow.

No one could argue that at fifty-two the sheriff of Laxton County wasn't still a fine figure of a man. His six-foot-three frame sat in the saddle with an air of undisputed authority. The hint of gray in his sideburns was the only concession to getting older; his dark hazel eyes were as clear and sharp as they had been thirty years ago. His body was honed as hard as steel, and the elements had tanned his skin to a deep bronze. Cole wondered if the ladies of River Run still blushed when he turned his smile in their direction.

"Evening, Lilly." Tal tipped his hat politely, his eyes warm and his smile extra friendly. Lilly smiled and blushed, fussing with her hair as Tal slid out of his saddle and handed the reins to one of his deputies.

Cole half-turned as Wynne came up to stand beside him. He

was suddenly conscious of her in a way he didn't like. She smelled pretty—and she looked. . .complete. Sort of put together in a way that didn't have much to do with her physical build. She fit somehow. He sniffed. What was that scent? Lemon? Ma must have loaned her some of her special shampoo. That meant his mother liked the Elliot woman, which might prove to be a problem if he found out what she was really up to. When his mother gave her approval to someone, she pretty well stuck with it.

Wynne's voice broke into his thoughts. "Are the sheriff and your mother. . .attracted to each other?" she whispered.

Cole glared at her. What did she mean by that? No better woman ever lived than Ma, and she wasn't the kind to be "attracted" to men. She was a decent, God-fearing woman who had raised her children right and had never looked for any man to replace Pa.

He stared at her coldly. "I wouldn't know."

"Oh, they both are," she said. "Can't you see the way they're looking at each other?"

The outrageous notion took Cole by surprise. He'd never considered his mother looking at another man that way—at least no one other than Elmo. Elmo was harmless.

"No, they're not," he said curtly.

Lilly's and Tal's heads snapped up at the sound of his annoyed tone. "Did you say something, dear?" Lilly called.

"No." Cole lowered his voice. "You have an overactive imagination, Miss Elliot. And remember, that's my mother you're talking about."

Wynne glanced at him, looking surprised. "I know she's your mother. I wasn't casting any aspersions on her. *You* obviously don't have a romantic bone in your entire body. I was making a simple observation."

"Well, stop making observations. Ma's got a full life here."

What else could he expect from some soft Southern lady? Wynne Elliot probably never did a day's work in her life. She wouldn't have any ideas about real life. Probably couldn't imagine a woman being capable of handling her business without a man's help. He couldn't imagine her raising three small children on a hill-land farm with only Willa to help, the way Ma had done. It took grit and common sense to do that. While he had to admit Wynne Elliot had plenty of grit, such as it was, she was definitely lacking in the common sense department. Still, her remarks bothered him.

He turned back to stare at his mother and Tal. *Ma and the sheriff?* The two were about the same age, and now that he thought about it, they were both reasonably good-looking people. He studied his mother in a new light. She still had a youthful, trim figure, laughing blue eyes, and pretty dark blond hair with only a few threads of gray running through it. He realized she was beautiful. From the look on Tal's face, he was of the same opinion. But Cole knew his mother. She wasn't looking for another man. Last thing on her mind.

He growled in Wynne's ear, "Pa died in a hunting accident after my youngest brother was born, and Ma has never looked at another man except old Elmo, and that's purely in a friendly fashion—nothing more."

Wynne smiled at him sweetly. "It isn't my fault you can't see what's right under your nose."

He snorted. "That bird on your hat must have pecked a hole in your head."

She made a face at him and he itched to walk off, but she'd probably follow him, and besides, Ma would be upset if he acted rude in front of Tal.

"Won't you and your men come in and have some supper with

us?" Lilly asked as the sheriff reached for a small leather pouch tied to his saddle horn.

"Can't, Lilly. The men want to get on home before dark. I stopped by to bring Miss Elliot something." He held the bag in his right hand, but Cole noticed Tal's attention was still centered solely on his mother. He wished the Elliot woman had kept quiet about her suspicions. He didn't need her putting foolish thoughts in his head. And he sure wasn't going to mention it to Ma. No use getting her to start thinking about things she had no business thinking about. She had enough on her plate without taking on a man.

Wynne approached the posse. "You have something for me, Sheriff?"

Tal colored slightly and diverted his attention from Lilly, obviously trying to get his mind back on the business at hand. Cole glowered at him. If the subject ever came up so it was convenient, he'd let Tal know there was no need to be getting notional about Ma. She wouldn't welcome the attention.

"Uh, yes, Miss Elliot, ma'am." Tal held the small pouch out to her. "We brought your ring back."

Wynne smiled and hurried down the porch steps to accept the bag. Cole watched as she loosened the drawstring and dumped the pearl ring out into the palm of her hand. The iridescent pearl centered on the gold band gleamed softly in the dim light. "Oh, this is marvelous! Where did you find it?"

"Down the road apiece from where the stage was held up. Must have dropped out of the bag when the Beasons was trying to make their getaway."

Cole had stepped off the porch to come stand beside Wynne, thinking it was time he got Ma off the hook. The way she blushed, she was probably embarrassed at Tal's attention—or if she wasn't she should have been.

The sheriff nodded at him. "Evening, Cole."

"Evening, Tal." Cole glanced at the ring in Wynne's hand. It didn't look like much to him, but he knew womenfolk, and the little circlet of gold and pearl probably had sentimental value to her. "This all you were able to find?"

"Afraid so," the sheriff admitted. "The gang seems to have gotten clean away this time, but as soon as me and my men rest up we're going out again."

Tal didn't have to say he had his doubts about his manhunt turning out to be anything but useless. Cole knew these hills, and he knew how easy it would be for a few men to disappear into some lonely hollow and never be seen again. He'd heard the Beasons had a cave hideout somewhere. Could be anywhere. These hills were riddled with underground caverns known to only a few people.

Wynne's shoulders drooped, and for a moment Cole felt sorry for her. "Do you think you can recover the rest of my belongings?"

The sheriff shook his head. "It's been two days since the robbery. Those men are no doubt long gone by now. Like I said, we'll try, but I can't make any promises."

"Thank you anyway, Sheriff." Wynne sighed. "I'm thankful that you were able to recover my ring."

"We'll try to pick up the Beasons' trail in the morning," he promised her.

"You sure you won't come in and at least have a cup of coffee with us?" Lilly invited again, but the sheriff swung into his saddle.

Wynne looked over at Cole and grinned smugly. He shot her a censuring look. If she said one word to make it look like Ma was inviting the sheriff in for any reason except in a purely neighborly fashion, he'd straighten her out in a hurry. It was bad enough he had to have the Elliot woman in his home without her going out of her way to stir up trouble.

The sheriff shook his head. "I'd love to, Lilly, but we need to be getting along. Some other time, I promise."

"Thanks for your trouble, Tal." Cole reached out and shook the older man's hand. Tal hadn't needed to come by tonight to bring that piddling little pearl ring. It had been nice of him to do so, but Cole would be foolish to let an addlebrained Southern belle get him all het up over a so-called attraction between his mother and the sheriff. Trust Wynne to get all stirred up over some imagined romantic nonsense.

"No trouble," Tal said. "Just wish I could have gotten the rest of the little lady's things back for her." He tipped his hat politely at Wynne and Lilly. "Evening, ladies."

Cole nodded as the posse rode away. Just as he thought. A friendly gesture on the sheriff's part. No call to think otherwise.

Wynne watched with a heavy heart as the small group of riders left the yard in a cloud of dust.

Cole and Lilly had already started back to the house when her gaze dropped to her tightly clasped hand. She opened it slowly, feeling a mist of tears rise unexpectedly in her eyes as she stared at the ring cradled in her palm. One pearl ring. Not much to show for her life, but that was all she had left of the personal possessions she had brought with her. All her money was gone, her other jewelry, which would have been worth much more than the ring, lost. Of course, there was still Moss Oak, but that was of no value at all right now. Home was merely an empty house and a piece of land with charred fields and no owner to oversee its use. Even sadder was the thought that she didn't have anyone to care, much less to help her with her plight.

Lord, I never expected things to get this bad. It's just been one blow after another. These people have been good to me, taking me in like this, but I can't stay here forever. With both Papa and Mama gone, I don't have anyone except You to hold on to.

A memory of her plans popped into her head. Was her current run of bad luck because God wasn't happy with her plans for revenge?

She sighed. Well, right or wrong, here she was, and it looked like she had burned about every bridge behind her.

Chapter 6

Late Saturday afternoon, Beau returned from Red Springs with Betsy. Wynne watched while he lifted his fiancée down from the buckboard as carefully as if his hands held a precious jewel. He stole a brief but thorough kiss before he set her lightly on her feet.

The young woman turned a pretty pink, but her eyes shone with a radiant love. She primly straightened her hat and tried to pretend displeasure with Beau's rowdy ways, but it was plain to see she enjoyed his teasing.

Wynne felt a stab of jealousy. If Cass Claxton hadn't been such a mule-headed deceiver, she would be a married woman with a husband to love and protect her instead of being alone on this wild frontier. Of course, if she had Cass here right now she'd shoot him, which wouldn't help her situation a whole lot.

Beau grinned at Wynne. "I see you're still here."

"I'll be leaving soon. The sheriff came by and said he hadn't been able to recover my money—but he did find my ring." Wynne held out her hand to show him the recovered pearl ring.

He leaned closer, clearly impressed. "Well, that's more than I thought he would find." He introduced her to Betsy, and Wynne liked the young woman at first glance. Betsy had an air of innocence about her that was refreshing. Judging from his air of pride, you could bet Beau wouldn't leave her waiting at the altar.

"Beau told me all about the robbery," Betsy said. "I know it must have been terrible for you. What about your family? Will they be worried?"

"I don't have anyone," Wynne confessed. Seeing Beau and Betsy together had brought home to her how alone she really was. She did have Tilly, the black servant who had taken care of her most of her life, but that was all. She wasn't even sure Tilly was still there. Wynne hadn't told her old friend where she was going when she left. What would she do after she found Cass and meted out the punishment he had coming? She could go home to Savannah, and probably would someday, but not right now. At the moment she had unfinished business in River Run.

"You find that man you were looking for?" Beau asked.

"Are you looking for someone?" Lilly asked, looking interested. "Who might that be?"

Wynne blushed. "Just an acquaintance."

"Friend?"

She smiled. "Acquaintance."

"Well, that's good news," Lilly said. "When you find your gentleman you'll have someone to take care of you. A woman doesn't have any business traveling alone these days. It's too dangerous."

Wynne kept quiet, feeling anything she had to say about her so-called acquaintance would fail to ease Lilly's fears. She wished Beau hadn't brought it up. She couldn't tell Lilly what she had in mind. Lilly was a lady. Well, so was she. A graduate of Miss Fielding's school. But she had a mission, and while Lilly might sympathize with her, she couldn't expect anyone else to understand the anger and humiliation that drove her to follow a man across several states with the intention of killing him. She wasn't sure she understood it herself.

Beau left to see about the horses, and the three women were alone. Lilly made a big fuss over Betsy, telling her how much she had missed seeing her in church on Sunday mornings, while Betsy smiled and nodded. Wynne felt left out. Lilly looped her arm through her future daughter-in-law's and walked her around to the side of the house to show her how well her flower bed was doing this year.

Wynne trailed behind, listening to the two women chatter about flowers and remembering the lovely gardens that had surrounded her home in Savannah. Her mother had loved flowers, too, but the gardens had gone to ruin long ago. Trampled under soldiers' feet. The Yankees hadn't cared what they were doing to people's lives or property. They had come to destroy. Beau and Cole had worn those blue uniforms, too, but somehow she couldn't imagine them taking part in the wanton destruction of the sort that had taken place at Moss Oak.

"I have to water every evening," Lilly confessed. "If it doesn't rain soon, I'll have to stop. I can't have the well going dry, and the vegetable garden's going to need watering more than these flowers do."

She leaned down to touch a delicate lavender petal. "They sure are pretty, though. The world's seen too little beauty since the war began. Too little beauty, too little happiness, too many tears. But thank God it's over now."

"They're truly lovely," Betsy said.

Wynne bent down to smell a big pink zinnia. Yes, the war was over, but putting her life back together would take a long time. A lot of people had lost everything, though. She at least had a house, and Lilly's home had been spared. They had a lot to be thankful for.

Beau rejoined them. "I've taken care of the horse and buckboard, and my stomach is reminding me I haven't eaten since early this morning. I hope we haven't missed supper."

Lilly laughed. "No, Willa's frying chicken, and I was just getting ready to put the biscuits in the oven."

Beau sniffed the air appreciatively. The aroma of meat sizzling in hot fat filled the late afternoon. "I hope she's fixed plenty."

"There'll be enough, son." Lilly had a sad expression as she patted his arm. Wynne knew she was remembering that this child of hers had gone with bare rations and little or no meat while he was fighting. Maybe that accounted for the large quantity of food Willa put on the table every day. Trying to make up for all the hardships Lilly's sons had endured. War was hard on everyone—the ones who went and fought and the ones who were left behind.

They started for the house, catching up on the news as they walked. "Cole rode into town this morning to see what kind of supplies he could buy," Lilly said. "He should be back any time now."

"It will be so good to see him again." Betsy smiled. "Beau says he's fine."

"He looks real good." Lilly beamed. "Thin, like this one here, but I'll have them both filled out in no time at all."

Wynne had liked Betsy from the start. They became friends almost immediately. She missed her friends back home and at the school. Betsy was the first person her own age she felt at ease with since coming to Missouri. There was Penelope, of course, but she had an entirely different way of looking at life. No, she didn't have much in common with Penelope. Betsy was different.

Lilly went to the kitchen to help Willa, and Wynne followed Betsy upstairs and waited while she washed and changed her travel-stained dress before supper. She sat on the side of the bed and listened attentively as Betsy chattered on about how she had known all of Beau's family since she was born, and how she had been in love with Beau for as long as she could remember.

Wynne sighed. Would she ever have someone she could love, who would love her in return the way Betsy and Beau loved each other? She tried not to be jealous, but she couldn't help remembering her own disastrous venture into romance.

Cole rode into the courtyard as they were starting back down the stairway.

"Now, that's another man who's going to make some lucky woman a fine husband one of these days," Betsy confided in hushed secrecy. "Isn't he about the most handsome thing you've ever seen? I mean, next to my Beau, of course."

Wynne hesitated to dash Betsy's high opinion of Cole by admitting that she wasn't impressed with Beau's older brother in the least. Oh, he looked well enough if you didn't mind his arrogant, overbearing manner. But *lucky* wasn't the word she'd apply to the woman unfortunate enough to hitch up with brother Cole.

"I suppose he would appeal to some women," Wynne replied evasively.

"Some women? Are you serious?" Betsy laughed, a delightful tinkling sound, like the wind chimes that had hung in the garden back home. "My older sister, Priscilla June? Why, she would absolutely swoon if Cole would ask her the time of day."

"Really?" Wynne forced her tone to remain agreeable. "What's the matter? Can't Cole tell time?"

Betsy looked blank for a moment then broke out in a fit of giggles. "Oh Wynne, you're so funny!" Her cornflower-blue eyes widened expectantly. "Listen, are you spoken for? Or is the gentleman you're looking for your fiancé?"

"No." Wynne smiled. "The man I'm looking for is not my fiancé." *Or a gentleman*, she longed to add but didn't. Maybe when she got to know Betsy a little better, she would confide in her about Cass. It would be nice to have someone to talk to, and somehow she sensed Betsy would understand and sympathize if she just knew the facts. But that had to wait until they knew each other better.

"Then you're not spoken for?" Betsy's grin widened. Her expression had matchmaker written all over it.

"I don't care to be," Wynne added quickly. "I've decided to be a spinster." She had even given serious thought to entering a convent as soon as she found Cass and took her revenge. By then she would have a whole list of grievances to be considered. The thought gave her sudden pause. Maybe she wouldn't be good enough to join a convent. They must have requirements. Killing a man probably wasn't one of them.

Betsy's face wilted with disappointment. "Oh my, what a shame. . . ."

"Yes, isn't it," Wynne agreed serenely. "Some women just aren't meant for marriage, and I fear I'm one of them." She led the way down the last few steps, hoping her expression would convince Betsy the subject was closed.

Willa was setting heaping platters of fried chicken on the table when they entered the dining room and sat down at the long, well-appointed table.

Beau smiled at Betsy when she picked up her napkin and placed it in her lap. Cole started to pass a bowl of potatoes and completely ignored Wynne as she took the chair opposite him. She twitched impatiently. The man had the manners of a goat. How could a son raised by a lady like Lilly behave in such an obnoxious manner?

"We'll have prayer first," Lilly admonished, and Cole promptly set the potatoes down as they all bowed their heads.

"Lord, we thank You for the bounty we are about to receive, and for giving us another beautiful day of life," Lilly said softly.

"We thank You that You've seen fit to put a stop to this terrible war, and I want to tell You again how much I appreciate You looking over Cole and Beau, and sending them home to me, safe and sound. I'm mighty beholden to You, Lord.

"If it wouldn't be too much bother, I'd ask that You send my baby home real soon, because I'm worrying about him something powerful, too. But I know You have a lot of things on Your mind right now, and I want You to know I'm not demanding anything, just wanted to remind You about my baby in case You might have forgotten. If You have time, Lord, we could sure use some rain. Garden's getting awful dry, and the well's threatening to do the same.

"Well, guess I'll close now. Supper's getting cold. Wanted You to know we love You, and ask that You'll forgive us for anything we might have done today that You wouldn't be right proud of. We didn't mean You any harm, Lord. You've been mighty good to us, and we won't be forgetting that. Amen."

"Amen," Cole and Beau echoed.

"Now"—Lilly looked up and smiled—"you may pass the potatoes, Cole."

"You know, Wynne, I've been doing some thinking about that robbery," Beau said while he spooned a mound of pole beans onto his plate. "You think you could recognize those men if you ever saw them again?"

Wynne glanced up, surprised at the question. "I don't know; they wore masks, but one of them did pull his off momentarily. I might recognize him." She suppressed a shudder at the memory of the outlaw's yellowed teeth and rancid breath.

"Well, I was wondering. . ." Beau hesitated. "Cole, you don't think that Frank and Jesse had anything to do with it, do you?"

"Frank and Jesse?" Lilly answered before Cole could. "Why,

those James boys wouldn't do anything like that!"

Cole spared his mother an indulgent look. "Ma, Frank and Jesse have been riding with Quantrill's Raiders, and they certainly haven't been holding Sunday school picnics."

"And since when have I gone addlebrained? Their pa was a preacher, if you recall. And those boys were good boys; at least they were until the Jayhawkers took it in their heads to persecute them."

Wynne's mind was not solely on the conversation but rather on how she was going to get through another meal without popping the buttons on her dress. Now she looked up, caught by the unfamiliar word. "What is a Jayhawker?"

"Missouri is mostly Southern sympathizers," Beau explained. "Some of the men would up and march right over the border and kill all the Kansans they could find. Of course, the Kansans didn't take right friendly to that sort of thing, so they up and marched right back and knocked a few Missourians' heads together. Missouri men were called Bushwhackers; the Kansans were called Jayhawkers or sometimes Redlegs."

Cole glanced up, a steaming biscuit in his hand. "Or sometimes something not all that complimentary."

"Who are Frank and Jesse?" Wynne asked, passing the bowl of potatoes to the left.

"Frank and Jesse James." Beau repeated the names as if they should mean something to her.

"You sound as if you know them personally," Wynne said.

Cole shrugged. "Our paths have crossed a few times."

"Frank and Jesse floated in and out of Missouri during the war," Beau told her. "There's not a better place to hide than in these hills and hollers. We've got some of the roughest country you'll ever see. A man could get lost a hundred feet from his cabin in a few of those valleys, and down around the White River country is about the best place to start. There's where you'll find Frank and Jesse, if you're looking for them."

"Well, I'm not," Wynne said. "And I hope I never have the occasion to meet them." She had her own particular men problems. So Missouri was mostly Southern, but Beau and Cole had worn blue. She met Cole's eyes, and apparently he saw and recognized the question in hers.

His chin firmed. "I never felt comfortable with owning another human being, Miss Elliot. You got a problem with that?"

Wynne shook her head. "Certainly not." She wasn't about to refight the War Between the States sitting at Lilly's dining-room table. That would be right unmannerly. Not that it would bother Cole in the least. He didn't have any manners to speak of anyway.

Lilly shook her head. "Next thing you know, those boys will be robbing banks."

Beau gave Betsy another moonstruck grin and picked up the bowl of poke greens and handed it to her. She shook her head, and he smiled with the most besotted expression Wynne had ever witnessed. Betsy didn't know how blessed she was.

"Have you and Betsy thought about a date for your wedding?" Lilly inquired.

"Thinking about maybe the last Sunday in October." Beau grinned. "It'll be cooling off by then."

Betsy's face flamed scarlet. She hurriedly groped for her water glass to avoid choking on the bite of chicken she had in her mouth.

"I mean. . .well, what I meant is. . .I thought. . .," Beau stammered, his face turning as red as his fiancée's.

"I think we know what you meant, Beau," Cole said dryly.

"Well. . .no. . .you see, what I meant was—"

"What he meant was he and Betsy want to wait until early fall to get married so that Cass will be back home," Lilly intervened mercifully. "There'll be no marriage in the Claxton family unless the whole clan's present to wish Beau and Betsy well."

Wynne's fork clattered off the side of her plate, and four pairs of eyes switched in her direction all at once.

Cass Claxton.

Had she heard wrong? She fervently prayed she had.

"Are you all right, dear?" Lilly's fork paused in midair, and she peered anxiously at her guest.

Wynne realized that her face had suddenly gone white. She had actually felt the blood drain all the way to her toes. "No. . .I. . ." Her mind churned with confusion. Had she actually heard Lilly say Cass Claxton was her son? No—it wasn't possible, yet Lilly had clearly said Cass would be home and the *Claxton* family would be together. Well, wouldn't this rock your boat? She'd been dropped right into the viper's own nest this time! *Well, Lord, what do I do now?* If there was a way out of this mess she couldn't see it. How could she kill Cass in front of his mother? Particularly since Lilly and Beau had been so kind to her.

"Wynne?" Betsy's concerned voice slowly seeped through her paralyzed stupor. "Are you ill?"

Even Cole had stopped eating. She could feel his eyes on her when she removed her napkin from her lap and rose carefully on shaky limbs. She had to get out of this room before she fainted. "If you'll excuse me," she blurted, "I think I need a bit of fresh air."

She turned and bolted out of the room, knowing the others at the table were staring at one another in bewilderment. How could she ever explain her behavior?

Cole pursed his lips, thinking about Wynne's hurried escape from the table. What had set her off like that? He had been suspicious of her from the start, and he had a feeling he was close to finding out what the woman was up to. She looked like she'd had a sudden jolt.

"My word, what do you suppose happened?" Lilly asked.

"I can't imagine!" Betsy exclaimed.

"Maybe all that talk of war and Frank and Jesse upset her," Beau said.

Betsy rose from her chair. "I'd better go see about her—"

"Let her be, Betsy." Cole let his voice slice through the air.

Betsy whirled and faced him. "But, Cole, she might be ill. . . ."

"Finish your supper," he snapped. "If she was sick, she would have said so." If anyone checked on Miss Wynne Elliot it would be him. He had some questions to ask her, and it was time he got some answers.

Betsy glanced expectantly at Lilly.

"He's right, dear. Maybe the past few days have finally caught up with her and she needs time alone," Lilly said. "Why don't we give her a few minutes to herself, and then one of us will go check on her?"

Betsy obediently sank back in her chair. "Well. . .maybe just a few minutes, but then I'm going to see about her."

They finished the meal in strained silence. Betsy looked upset, and Lilly didn't have her usual composure, but with Cole's eyes on them, they stayed at the table. When Willa brought coffee and dessert, Cole stood up and excused himself and left the room.

He looked over his shoulder and noticed more than a few relieved looks being exchanged.

Chapter 7

Wynne stood on the front porch, arms gripping her waist so tightly she could hardly draw breath. *Where do I go from here? Oh, why, Lord?* Why did it have to be Cass's brothers who had befriended her? Hadn't she been hurt enough by the Claxton men?

She swiped angrily at the tears that suddenly threatened her composure. The Claxton family was probably wondering why she had left the room so quickly. How could she face them again? Right now she couldn't think of a convincing explanation for her behavior.

She stepped off the porch and looked up at the sun, sinking in a big, fiery orange ball behind the grove of cherry trees on the west side of the house. She headed in that direction. The hot air, so still and heavy, made breathing difficult. A furnace-blast wind burned her flushed cheeks, and she wondered when, if ever, she'd felt so betrayed, so emotionally wronged.

Where are You, God? Why don't You do something to help with all of these problems that keep coming, one after another, until I'm so overwhelmed I don't know what to do next?

When she was a small child, she'd healed disappointments and cried out her frustrations in the arms of a gnarled tree at Moss Oak. Somehow she'd drawn strength and security from that old tree. The cherry grove here seemed to beckon as though the trees would offer refuge for her inward turmoil, a haven for the chaos that had again come so unexpectedly.

Once she'd reached the shelter of the grove, she sank down in a thick carpet of grass. Above her, fruit was sparsely scattered about the branches. The aroma of sunbaked earth, sweet cherries, and the sultry end of a summer day teased her senses. Overcome with sadness and defeat, she dropped her face into her hands and let the tears flow.

After a few minutes she managed to regain control of her emotions. Betsy might come looking for her, and she didn't dare be caught crying. She had enough to explain as it was. She rubbed the backs of both hands across her cheeks and sniffed like an injured child.

The leaves on the cherry trees rustled in the evening breeze like gossipy women. The grass beneath her was soft and already turning brown. High, puffy clouds that held no promise of moisture burned in the afterglow of the sun's rays. Lilly was right, she thought dismally. If it didn't rain soon, everything was going to dry up and blow away. She hiccupped. Maybe, if she were lucky, the wind would take her right along with it.

She tilted her head, staring up at the sky through the tree branches. *Fool! Fool! You've done it again! Made a complete fool of yourself by stumbling right into the arms of Cass's family.* She buried her face in her hands again, wanting to hide from the world. The irony of the situation struck her, and she chuckled mirthlessly. Lowering her hands to her lap, she stared at a distant line of trees. What was she supposed to do now?

Her restless fingers found a loose thread hanging from the waist of her dress. Yielding to irritation, she twitched the fine string off and tossed it away. *Literally thousands of people between here and Savannah, but who did Almighty God send to rescue me?* She laughed out loud, a bitter sound in the evening quiet of the orchard. *Cass Claxton's brothers! That's who.* Even sent his dear saint of a mother to feed and shelter her. If it hadn't been so ironically funny, she would have bawled. She angrily brushed away ready tears.

Lord, I don't understand. Why, out of all the people in this world, would You let me stumble into this nest of vipers?

That wasn't fair, of course. Lilly and Beau were nice. So was Willa, and Betsy was a darling. Only Cole and Cass were snakes.

She leaned back against a tree, resting her head against its thick trunk. A hopeless sigh escaped her as she pondered the disturbing similarities in Cass and his family. Not his whole family, of course, but that rotten Cole was just like his brother—cold, calculating, and totally heartless. He'd never done anything spontaneous in his life, she'd bet. And he thought her the most foolish thing in the world—and he just might be right.

She was always reacting without thinking, but she'd thought out well what she'd do to Cass Claxton. She had a plan and she was going to work that plan, and nothing would stop her.

It didn't matter that his family had taken her in when she had no place else to go. Nothing could change the enormity of what Cass had done to her. He couldn't toy with her feelings and steal her money without paying for it! And now that she was in the confines of his family she could no longer delay putting her plan into effect.

For days she'd lingered, praying that Sheriff Franklin would be able to recover her money, but now that she knew she was staying with Cass's family, she would have to move on. Oh, granted, she could just sit right here and wait for the rat to return to his nest.

That would be the easiest way to handle the situation. Lilly had no idea who she was or her intentions—nor for that matter did Cole or Beau. Cass would undoubtedly return home one day soon, and she could shoot him and then be on her way.

Her hand absently toyed with her worry stone. But she had to face facts. If she stayed around until Cass returned, it was possible she would let slip what she was about to do, and then Cole would thwart her plan. She shot a dirty look toward the house. He'd love to get the best of her.

Her conscience nagged her. She sighed. Well, all right. Staying here wouldn't be ethical. Not if she planned to shoot Cass on sight. She couldn't very well kill him in front of his mother. She owed Lilly that much. No, she would have to make other arrangements.

The pearl ring the sheriff had returned would be her ticket to freedom. She would walk into town first thing tomorrow morning and see if the bank would accept the jewelry as collateral on a loan.

Wynne felt better now that she had a plan. The bank would lend her a small sum. She'd only need enough to live on for a few weeks while she continued her search for Cass. It wouldn't take a great deal. Only enough for food and lodging, and she would assure the banker that she ate very little and required a minimum amount of sleep. She was aware it was a rather slim hope that she might encounter Cass while he was on the trail, but at this point she really had little other choice.

And who knew? Maybe she would be lucky and find him right away. Wynne sat up straight. She might get even luckier and he would still have a portion of her money on him. After all, she was overdue for a stroke of luck. She glanced back at the Claxton farmhouse. Long overdue.

Her stomach felt slightly queasy at the prospect of removing personal belongings off a dead man, for that's exactly what Mr. Claxton would be two minutes after she found him. She'd come this far, so she supposed she could do anything she had to do. At least if Cass was dead, she could search his pockets without fear of his objecting.

Once her mission was accomplished, she could return to Savannah and try to rebuild her life. She'd have to make some recompense to God for carrying out her plans for revenge. Wynne had an uneasy feeling that simply admitting she was sorry wouldn't be quite enough for the Almighty.

Her mind went back to her Sunday school lessons and the Ten Commandments. "Thou shalt not kill." That was rather plain speaking on God's part. But it wasn't as if she really *wanted* to kill Cass. Killing a man, even if he did deserve to die for what he'd done, did not please her. But death was the only suitable punishment for a man like Cass. Left to live, he'd do the same thing to yet another unsuspecting woman with stars in her eyes. Surely God wouldn't want that to happen.

Looking at it another way, God probably knew Cass needed killing, and Wynne was the weapon He chose to use. In that sense, she had a *responsibility* to shoot the sorry excuse of a man on sight.

Why had she not realized immediately that Cole was Cass's brother? Why had she thought the similarities were only coincidental? The brothers looked so much alike it was almost scary, but she had been so preoccupied with all her other problems she never dreamed fate would throw another Claxton in her path! What were the chances of something like that happening? Wynne fixed her eyes on the first star of the night. She had delayed long enough. Tomorrow she would take up her search for Cass Claxton again, and with God's help, she would find him.

Cole strode toward the orchard, his eyes on Wynne as she sat staring at the branches of the cherry tree overhead. She appeared to have calmed down, but something had upset her. He waited to see if she would bolt and run when he approached.

The muggy air had a hint of reprieve. The sky was clear, the evening stars barely visible. It was his favorite time of the day. He decided he'd wasted enough time watching a sharp-tongued female who barely had a passing acquaintance with the truth. She may have Ma and the others fooled, but she wasn't getting anything by him. He could smell a liar at twenty paces. Wynne Elliot was up to something, and he meant to find out what.

"You didn't finish your supper."

She started at the unexpected intrusion, then stiffened, her body language indicating the last thing she wanted was to put up with his company. "I suddenly lost my appetite."

"So I noticed." He leaned against a tree opposite her, his gaze narrowed on her averted face. "I hope it wasn't anything we said that caused your sudden. . .indisposition."

Defiance gleamed in the eyes she lifted to meet his. "Certainly not. What would make you think that?" Her chin tilted at an angle that said she didn't care what he thought, and the sharpness of her voice indicated that it was none of his business.

He shrugged. "No reason—just thought it a shame to leave so much food on your plate when others are going to bed hungry." He tipped his hat back and crossed his arms over his chest.

She shifted beneath his penetrating gaze, staring down at her hands, which now rested primly in her lap. Finally she raised her eyes to meet his scrutiny. "Do I have food on my face?"

"No."

"Then why are you staring at me?"

Cole's shoulders lifted. "I was just wondering how you could keep such a straight face and lie the way you do."

Her gaze dropped back to her hands. "I have no idea what you're talking about."

He made a clucking sound with his tongue and shook his head. "Didn't that fancy school you went to back East teach you that a lady never tells stories? At least not the big whopping ones you've been telling lately."

Anger flared in her eyes before she looked away. "Mr. Claxton, did you want anything in particular, or are you here merely to heckle me?"

"Heckle you? My time is more valuable than that. A prissy little old thing like you bothers too easy." He watched her face redden under the impact of his words and wondered if she would flare up in a temper fit. He hoped so. Sometimes people said more if they were angry than they ever would when they were calm.

"I'm not prissy." She absently picked at a loose string around her waist. He watched as she jerked at the thread, unraveling it a bit further.

Cole studied her as she sat under that tree, picking at a string on her dress. Soft hands, pale skin—never did a day's work in her life. All fluff and ruffles with a bird on her hat. She wasn't wearing the hat now, of course, but any female who would pick out something like that and no doubt pay good money for it. . . He pitied the poor soul who hitched up with her, and the words were on the tip of his tongue to say so, but he wasn't inclined to start another argument. He had more important issues to discuss with Miss Elliot.

He pushed away from the tree and edged closer to where she

sat absently wrapping the loose thread around her finger. "Mind if I sit a spell?" he asked.

She shrugged. "Never known a polecat to ask for permission to do anything."

Well, now, he was going to ignore that remark. They sat in silence, gazing at the hovering clouds brushed with rose and pearl gray by the fiery blaze of the departed sun. "Going to be a nice night," he observed pleasantly.

She shrugged again.

"Willa can sure fry chicken, can't she?"

Wynne slid a sideways glance at him as if she wondered why he was being so cordial all of a sudden. She jerked another string off her dress. "Yes."

He removed his hat and laid it on the grass beside him. It had been a long day, and he was tired. He leaned back against the tree trunk, gazing off into the western sky ablaze with purples and oranges and golds where the sun had disappeared from view. "It's good to be home."

"Were you away long?"

"Four years. Seemed like a lifetime."

"And Beau was gone that long, too?"

"We left about the same time." Cole studied her from beneath lowered lashes, watching to see how she reacted. "My youngest brother, Cass, hasn't returned yet."

Wynne's back stiffened perceptibly. Her voice sounded remote, as if she was totally detached from the subject. "How sad. Where is he?"

"Fighting—like Beau and I. Last I heard he was in South Carolina."

Her mouth dropped open, and she shot him a surprised look that didn't quite come off. "He's been away fighting?"

Cole hunched down more comfortably. "When I left, Cass was supposed to stay around and help Ma with the farm. We even paid to have a man fight in his place, but it seems he took off a while back to visit family in Savannah, and then all of a sudden he decided to join up." He glanced at her, watching her expression. "You sounded a little surprised, Miss Elliot. Any particular reason?"

"No, I–I'm just surprised. I thought he was just away—maybe on business. . .somewhere."

"No, he's been in the war," Cole repeated. "He didn't join until late in the conflict. Ma's pretty worried about him. You heard her at the supper table. She's hoping he'll ride in any day now."

Wynne pulled at another string on her dress. "She hasn't heard anything from him lately?"

"No, but he'll not keep her worrying for long." Cole observed with interest the rising flush of color staining her cheeks.

"How gallant of him!"

Cole's eyes snapped up to meet hers. *Sarcasm?* "Gallant?"

She shot a look at him that he didn't have any trouble reading. She knew Cass; she just didn't plan to admit it.

"I mean, that will be very considerate of him," she amended. "I hope he's fared as well as you and Beau."

Cole momentarily turned his attention back to the fading sunset. "Yeah, that's what we're all hoping. How old are you, Miss Elliot? Seventeen, eighteen?"

"Nineteen," she said curtly.

"Nineteen? I didn't think you were that old. That's about Cass's age. He's twenty-two."

"I suppose he followed your leadership and became one of those Yankees." She turned an accusing gaze on him, and Cole remembered the blue uniform he had been wearing the first day he met her. She probably had reason to hate the uniform. Georgia had borne the brunt of the Union offensive. He wondered absently if her home had been destroyed in the fighting. Truth be told, both sides had done plenty to dishonor the colors they wore.

"Yankee?" He shook his head. "As a matter of fact, Cass chose to fight for the South. If you'll recall, Missouri was divided in its opinion of the war, and so were the Claxton men."

Wynne nodded. "Cass was the only one of you who knew right from wrong. He worried about the war all the time, even though he'd paid someone to fight in his place. He fretted over how it was going, about getting back to take care of your mother."

Her voice trailed off lamely, as if she suddenly realized what she'd said.

"Really." Cole's brow lifted thoughtfully. "Do you know my brother?"

"Oh, heavens, no," she said, a shade too quickly to be believable. "I was. . .just guessing." Her laugh sounded nervous.

"Amazing." His lips pursed thoughtfully as he studied her. "For a moment there you sounded exactly like you might have met him—even been friends. You did say you were from Savannah, didn't you?"

"Yes."

"Cass was in Savannah for a while," he mused.

"Really, Cole." Her laugh sounded more confident this time. "Savannah is a large city. I couldn't possibly know everyone who goes there."

He watched as her fingers flew over a stone she held in her hands.

In the blink of an eye he grabbed her shoulders, pinning her back against the tree. She looked up at him, eyes wide, lips parted as if to scream. His eyes locked with hers, and even he was startled at how deadly he sounded. "Then explain what you're doing with his worry stone."

"His..." She dropped the stone like hot lava.

Cole's voice was menacingly low when he spoke again. His face so close to hers he could feel the warmth of her breath, see the gold-tipped lashes framing her eyes. Her shoulders were warm and soft beneath his hands. He jerked his thoughts back to the business at hand. "Come on, Miss Elliot. I'm dying to know how you happen to have my brother's worry stone, yet you say you've never met him." He kept his eyes pinned on hers, his fingers relentlessly pressed into her shoulders.

"You're *hurting me*," she gritted between clenched teeth. She struggled, attempting to break his hold, but her puny efforts were useless. He wasn't about to let her go until she told him the truth.

They glared at each other defiantly. Her breath was soft and sweet against his face, and she smelled fresh, like soap and water. Good clean smells, the way a woman ought to smell, and like a scent of heaven to a man who had lived too long with the stench and decay of the battlefield.

He threatened her again in a stern tone. "I can stay here as long as you can, lady." He didn't want to hurt her, but if she knew anything about his brother, she wasn't leaving here until she told him, no matter how appealing she happened to be.

She lurched toward him, her curved fingers clawing at his face. Caught by surprise, he stepped back out of her reach then caught her wrists, holding them tight as she struggled to get away.

"Let me go, you brute!"

He laughed in her face.

Suddenly her body went limp. For a moment he thought she had fainted, but she batted her big green eyes at him prettily. "Is all this brute force necessary, Cole?"

Her voice was soft and her drawl as sugarcoated as those special cookies Ma used to make. It made him sick to hear it. Warning bells were sounding in his head. All this sweetness and light wasn't like her. She was acting like that Penelope who had come to work at Hattie's.

"I do declare, you're crushin' the little ol' life right out of me." She blinked coyly. "Surely a big, strong man like you doesn't have to threaten a poor innocent girl just to ask her a simple question."

He blinked back at her mockingly. "Coming on a bit too strong, aren't you? You tell me where you got Cass's worry stone, and I'll let the 'poor innocent girl' go about her business—but not until she learns to tell the truth," he snapped. "If she doesn't tell the truth, she just might get her pretty little ol' behind whipped right here and now."

"Why, you big lout! Let me go!" Feminine wiles flew right out the window. Because he was momentarily surprised by the way she lurched away from him, he lost his grip on her wrists. Wynne doubled up her fists and hit him squarely in the rib cage.

Deciding retreat was the best maneuver at this point, Cole covered his head with both arms, but when her blows continued to rain, he lost all patience with this contrary female. With one swipe of his arm he moved her aside, out of hitting reach. Before he could grab her shoulders and pin her down, she twisted away from him and landed on her knees. She tried to struggle to her feet, but he caught her around the waist and pitched to one side, pulling her with him.

Wynne broke his hold, but this time she lost her balance and rolled over the edge of a slight incline. Cole's arm snaked out and pulled her back. His hands pressed against her shoulders, pinning her to the ground.

"I am out of patience with you!"

She glared up at him, all fire and fury. "You get your hands off me!"

"I will," he said pleasantly, "as soon as you answer my question. Where did you get Cass's worry stone?"

"What makes you think that silly stone belongs to your brother?" she grated.

"Because I *gave* it to him, and Beau and I have one to match. I found all three stones in a riverbed not too far from here when I was just a kid. Cass would never willingly part with it, so save yourself another lie."

"He gave it to me!" she shouted in a most unladylike display of temper.

Cole relaxed his grip in brief surprise at her outburst. He blinked at her. "He *gave* it to you?"

"That's right. He gave it to me. Now leave me alone."

He studied her hot, flushed face. So she *did* know him. "Not yet. When did he give it to you?"

"In Savannah. Two days before we were to be married."

He felt his mouth go slack. His hold loosened. Wynne quickly seized the opportunity to escape. She pulled away from him, and Cole let her go. He stared at her in disbelief.

"Cass was going to *marry* you?"

"That's right." She drew a deep breath and reached up, trying to straighten her hair, which by now had tumbled around her shoulders in a fiery mass. "But don't worry, Cole. He didn't marry me. Your precious little brother *left me* standing in front of the church. But not before he made off with almost every cent I had in the world."

By now Cole had managed to regain his composure. If she thought he was going to believe this tale, she was off the mark. No brother of his would do anything like that. He'd helped raise Beau and Cass, and he knew them to be fine, decent men, not the type to take advantage of a woman.

He tried to keep his voice under control. "Now I know you're lying. Cass wouldn't steal anyone's money, let alone a woman's."

"Well, that just goes to show how much you know. He *did* take my money, and when I find him, I'm going to shoot him first, ask questions later."

Cole's eyes narrowed in sudden realization of what was going on here. "Then Cass is the man you're looking for?"

"That's right." Her defiant gaze met his, and he wanted to shake her.

"And you're going to shoot him when you find him?"

"That's right."

"So. . .that's what you're doing out here," Cole mused. "Looking for my little brother so you can kill him."

"So I can blow his thieving head off," she said.

"I doubt that."

"Don't. I'll do it. I promise."

"Not if I can help it, you won't."

"You won't be able to do a thing about it." She looked as smug as a cream-stealing cat. "First thing tomorrow morning I'm going to take my ring to the bank and get a small loan. Then I'll buy another stage ticket and be on my way. Unless you want to trail me all over the countryside, there's not one blessed thing you can do to stop me."

"Just where do you think you're going to find Cass?" he asked. "None of us know where he is."

Wynne pushed to her feet, not looking quite so assured. "I—I know that, but I inquired about his whereabouts everywhere the stage stopped, and I know he was seen in Kansas City a few weeks ago, and he was supposed to be on his way home. That's why I came to River Run. Obviously he hasn't made it yet, so now I'll just head west toward Kansas City and hope to find him somewhere along the way."

Cole sagged with relief. "Then he's alive?"

She glanced at him, looking guilty. "For now."

Cole shook his head and thrust his long fingers through thick hair. "Ma will be relieved to hear that." She could have told them sooner, knowing how worried they all had been. But he guessed if she had passed out that information she would have had to say how she knew and what she was doing here. Evidently she hadn't realized they were his family.

"Are you"—Wynne straightened her spine defensively—"are you going to tell Lilly about me? She's been awfully good, and so has Beau. I wouldn't want to cause them any more worry, although Cass has handed me more than my share of trouble."

Cole studied her for a moment and then chose his words carefully. "I don't know what happened between you and Cass, but I do know my brother is an honorable man. Whatever he's done, he had good cause to do it. That's why I'm not going to say anything to Ma about any of this, but not because of you. Number one, I don't want her to worry any more than she already is. Number two, I think my brother can take care of himself." He let his eyes skim over her, showing his contempt. "Especially when it comes to little Eastern finishing-school girls."

She pointed her finger at him. "You'd better fear for his life."

"Like I said, Cass can take care of himself." Cole rolled to his feet. "And number three, you haven't a prayer of finding him in the first place. In case you haven't noticed, lady, there's a lot of territory between here and Kansas City, and a woman traveling alone is asking for trouble."

"I'm nineteen years old, and I am perfectly capable of taking care of *myself*. I made it out here alone, didn't I?" Wynne pushed at that fiery mop of hair that kept falling in her face.

"You did—barely. But I'd have to argue with you about being able to take care of yourself."

"Why?" Her mouth firmed, and her chin rose automatically to challenge his statement.

"For one thing, you're standing there in nothing but those frilly little breeches you women wear—"

"Frilly breeches! What are you talking about?"

He grinned as Wynne's gaze dropped to her waist, and her mouth gaped open with astonishment. The skirt of her dress had slipped to the ground and lay in a puddle around her feet. Apparently the loose strings she had been jerking away at had been there for a purpose, and in all the scuffling the material around the waistband had given way, leaving her standing in nothing but her linens!

"Ooooooh! How dare you!" Her face flamed as crimson as her hair. She swooped down to pick up her skirt and step back into it, shooting him a glare that would have felled a lesser man. "I hope you were enjoying yourself!"

A smile played about his lips as Cole observed her growing frustration. "No, as a matter of fact, I wasn't. You're not my type. And if you call getting robbed and being stranded in a strange town without a penny to your name taking care of yourself, then I guess you have," he said, going right back to the conversation as if nothing unusual had happened. "But the next time you might not be so lucky. Next time you might run into highwaymen who are looking for a little more than money, or you might meet up with Bushwhackers who haven't seen a woman in a few months, or there're still splinter groups of Quantrill's Raiders riding in these parts. One of them might take a fancy to a pretty face."

The more he talked, the more uneasy Wynne looked. "You're—you're just trying to scare me."

"You think so?" Cole kept his expression as solemn as a preacher's. "There're a lot of men riding these roads nowadays. Most of them have been away from home for a long time, and they wouldn't be too particular how they treat a woman."

A rosy blush painted her cheeks. "You can talk all you want, but I'm leaving tomorrow morning."

"Fine." He shrugged indifferently and reached down to pick up his discarded hat. "If you want to be bullheaded about it, then it's your skin you're risking, not mine. Have it your way." He turned and started to walk away, then had second thoughts. "Oh yeah. Tell Cass, when you see him, that Willa's keeping his supper warm."

"I'm not about to give that no-good man any message," Wynne snarled. She gathered the waist of her skirt in one hand, the hem in the other, and marched to the house.

Cole followed, feeling like Missouri's biggest villain, but she had it coming. Maybe he'd been a little rough on her, but Cass was his brother. She had no call to lie about him. Miss Wynne Elliot needed to be taught a lesson, and he was in a mood to teach.

Chapter 8

The sun was grazing the horizon when Wynne stole silently out of the Claxton house the next morning. She tripped lightly over the rutted path, carrying two brown valises, her mood brighter than it had been in days.

It was going to be another scorcher, but she comforted herself with the thought that it couldn't be a very long walk into town, and she would enjoy the peace and solitude.

She choked back a laugh when she thought about the way Cole had accused her of being incompetent—incapable of coming in out of the rain. She'd show him she could take care of herself. He looked so much like Cass it was easy for her to muster up true revulsion. And it wasn't just the way he looked. Cole Claxton was the meanest. . .the most aggravating man she had ever met. But as much as she detested him, she despised his brother more.

Wynne sighed and shifted her grip on her valises. She wished she could catch up with Cass and get this entire episode behind her. This urge for revenge surely did tire a soul out.

Her thoughts turned to the man she was leaving behind at the farm. If Mr. Cole Claxton could see her now, he'd strangle on his own smugness. She was properly dressed in a pale blue sprigged dress with tatted lace trim, the waist nipped in to emphasize its narrowness. Her hair was upswept with miniature curls nested at the crown, *and* she was on her way into town to take care of her own affairs.

She was a lady well versed in running a plantation—Papa had made sure of that—so dabbling in the business world wasn't new to her. She knew Cole thought she was a pampered Southern belle, but she'd had her share of work. Oh, maybe not cooking and cleaning like Lilly and Willa did, but she knew the workings of a plantation and how to manage servants. He'd see just how helpless she was.

Granted, the superintendent at Moss Oak had been experienced and conscientious, considering that many overseers had up and deserted the plantations during the war, leaving their employers helpless in the care of the few servants left behind and the crops in the field. Many landowners had sat and watched their heritages disintegrate before their eyes.

But Moss Oak had survived, not without a great many problems, but the land was still there and in the Elliot name. The fields were parched, no crops in the ground other than the small truck garden, which fed the servants who remained. Her childhood home would eventually be coaxed back to fertile land; she'd see to that. And she sincerely hoped that whoever bought the plantation would love it as much as Wesley Elliot had.

She sniffed disdainfully. Though she had been stripped of her personal belongings and set afoot in a Missouri town, she was still an Elliot of Savannah, Georgia. The Elliot name counted for something back home.

Dust puffed up with every step she took. An irritating gnat hovered around her sweat-slicked face. She used her handkerchief for a fan. Mercy, it was hot! Wynne glanced at the sun, beating pitilessly down on her and it barely seven in the morning. Already the lace collar chafed her skin. Her black, high-top, buttoned shoes were fashionable, but the footwear was not intended for long-distance walking. She had progressed only a short way when the fact became achingly evident. If Cole Claxton had cretin manners he'd have offered to drive her into town. Considering he'd be rid of her that much faster, she would have thought the idea would have appealed to him.

Even the perky bird sitting serenely on top of her hat looked slightly more wilted than when her journey first began. And the humidity! Her hair straggled down her neck in limp strings.

The sun was a blazing ball of fire now. Wynne used her handkerchief to mop ineffectually at the perspiration pooled on her brow. She thought of the cool veranda at Moss Oak and how she used to sit there, rocking gently, sipping fresh lemonade. Right now her mouth was as dry as a cotton ball. Why hadn't she thought to bring water? Fresh water, drawn from the cool depths of the Claxton well. She stiffened her back and marched on.

She had only a meager amount of clothing in her valises, but they seemed to weigh ten pounds more than they had when she started out. Her arms ached from carrying the cases, and these shoes were ruining her feet. She hadn't realized exactly how far it was to River Run from the Claxton farm.

Another mile down the road and a large blister started forming on her right toe.

Another two miles found her angrily sorting through the valises and stuffing only the essentials into one then discarding the other in the middle of the road.

By the time the town of River Run came into view, her disposition could best be described as something less than sunny. It was a good thing she didn't meet up with Cass in this mood; the way she felt, she would have shot him on sight even before she told him what a rotten hound he was to have treated her so shamefully.

The sound of approaching hoofbeats reached her. The animal wasn't moving very fast, just a smooth, ground-covering lope. Curious, Wynne turned to see who it might be. Perhaps whoever it was would give her a lift.

Oh no! She groaned. Him! She'd recognize Cole Claxton's arrogant bearing anywhere. What was he doing here? Coming to drag her back, no doubt. Well, he had another think coming. She turned around, eyes on the road, and stepped out at a good clip, unwilling to let him see how tired and hot she really was.

The horse drew nearer. Her chin lifted a notch higher and she mentally prepared a scathing rebuttal for when he demanded she return to the Claxton homestead.

When his mare was abreast of her, her mouth shot open to refuse his offer, but he rode right past her! Didn't even look her way.

Before she realized it, she had been standing in the road for a full five minutes watching him disappear from sight. Her cheeks bloomed scarlet. That wretched man was playing with fire! Didn't even wave, passed her like she was a fence post. She harbored a furious thought about taking care of her business with Cass and then making Cole pay for the way he had ignored her.

She shot an apologetic glance heavenward. *Sorry, Lord. I don't know what I was thinking. I know vengeance is Yours, and I shouldn't be having such thoughts about Cole, but he is certainly the most arrogant. . .ignorant. . .well, words fail me when I try to describe him. I won't shoot him, honest I won't. Just Cass. And You know he's got it coming.*

She trucked on down the road, more determined than ever to accomplish her purpose. The farther she got from River Run and the Claxton family, the better for her. She'd meet up with Cass between here and Kansas City. There weren't that many roads, and he'd have to be traveling on one of them. A no-account man would be no competition to a determined woman. And she was getting more determined by the minute.

Cole stood in the window of the general store drinking a cold sarsaparilla when Wynne trudged into town an hour later. He probably should have stopped and offered her a ride, but she would have refused. Besides, she was out to kill his baby brother. Not that he thought she could shoot straight enough to achieve her purpose, but so far her luck had been so bad she was overdue for a victory. It was a wonder she hadn't shot someone the day the stage had been robbed, waving that gun around like a drunkard. He took another low swallow of the ice-cold drink.

"Three pounds pinto beans, sugar, and flour." Nute Brower laid the items out on the counter. "Anything else I can help you with today?"

"That should do it, Nute. I'm killing time until Tal gets here." He didn't really have any business with the sheriff, but one excuse was as good as another, he supposed. As a matter of fact, he needed to be home working, but he'd gotten to worrying about the Elliot female so he'd ridden behind her—to see if she made it to town all right. But seeing she was safe didn't mean he had to coddle her. She'd chosen to walk to town—so let her walk.

"Tal's not in town," Nute said. "He rode out with a posse before dawn to look for the Beason gang. Thinks they might be the ones who killed the stage driver and the guy riding shotgun."

Cole finished off the last of his drink. "I doubt that he'll have any luck."

Nute shook his head. "Something's got to be done about that

bunch. They're getting real dangerous."

Cole set the bottle back on the counter. "Might not be the Beasons. The witnesses weren't too clear on who'd done the robbing. Could be the James gang. Heard they were operating in this neck of the woods."

"Last I heard the James boys had moved their operations farther west. Seems they're getting their kicks robbing banks these days. Some say the boys are heroes, robbing from the rich and giving to the poor, but I've got money in that bank across the street, and I'd hate to see it wind up in the James boys' pockets."

"I'd have to agree with you." Cole watched Wynne limp up the steps to the bank's front door and wondered if Elias would be fool enough to loan her money on a ring. Once she had cash in her hand, she'd be out of town faster than a scared rabbit, and he'd bet his last dime that she wouldn't be back to pay her bills. A woman who would deliberately set out to kill a man wouldn't be too concerned about her credit rating.

He glanced at the bag sitting on the mercantile floor; he'd picked up the valise she had abandoned. What was he going to do with it?

&

Wynne staggered through the bank door, dragging her dust-covered valise. She blew a strand of hair out of her eyes as she caught a glimpse of herself in the mirror hanging on the back wall. No doubt the mirror was installed so the banker could keep a close eye on employees and customers, but her reflection didn't do much to boost her flagging self-esteem. Her face was as flushed as one of the stripes on Old Glory flapping in a lackluster wind atop the courthouse. Her hat was cocked crazily to one side, and the bird she had thought was so fashionable when she had purchased the thing now looked as if it had been shot at and hit. Her dress was soaked with perspiration, her hair hung in limp strands around her face, and her eyes were so ringed with dust she looked like a rabid raccoon. Not a spectacle guaranteed to inspire confidence in a banker. She wasn't much of an endorsement for Miss Marelda's school, either. No one looking at her would take her for a finished young lady. In fact, she looked decidedly unfinished.

She dabbed her cheeks and neck and sagged weakly against the polished pine railing, letting the cooler air of the bank's overhead fan wash over her. If it hadn't been for making a spectacle of herself, she would sit right down on the floor under the revolving blades and stay there until her temperature dropped.

Elias Holbrook, bank owner, approached, speaking pleasantly. "Howdy, ma'am. It's going to be a warm one."

She smiled lamely. Yes, you could certainly say that. She forced herself to respond politely. "Quite warm. It isn't nine o'clock in the morning, and the heat is suffocating."

Elias poured a glass of water from a pitcher sitting on his desk and handed it to her. Wynne accepted it gratefully. The tepid water felt cool to her parched tongue. She emptied the glass in one long swallow then drew a deep breath and returned it to the corner of Elias's desk. Air from the fan and the drink of water had restored some of her sense of well-being. She breathed the way Miss Marelda had taught her. In, out, in, out—guaranteed to calm nerves. And she was about as stretched out as she could handle.

Her foot throbbed like a sore tooth. There was a chair right next to the oak desk, and without thinking, she sat down and peeled off her right shoe, exposing a throbbing blister the size of a silver dollar covering her big toe. She sighed in relief as she wiggled the smarting appendage. Land sakes, the last mile had been so painful she had been afraid she would be reduced to crawling the rest of the way. She tucked the skirt of her dress around her legs and then brought the injured foot up to her lap. Blind to her surroundings, she cradled her foot, poking gingerly at the puffy spot.

Elias leaned forward, peering at the proceedings with growing interest. "My, my. That looks terrible." He clucked sympathetically.

"It hurts like the blue blazes," she said. Immediately she realized her unbecoming posture. Her jaw dropped. What must he think of her?

She slid her foot slowly off her lap and, as circumspectly as possible, tucked her bare foot and her shod one beneath the dusty hem of her skirt. A lady would never enter a bank and take her shoe off in front of a man. She could just hear what Miss Marelda would have to say about that! Papa would have had a fit, and Miss Marelda would probably have collapsed in such a swoon it would have taken a bucket of smelling salts to bring her around. Wynne never would have imagined this quest for revenge would mean such a lowering of her standards.

She cleared her throat and crossed her hands in her lap, trying to restore a shred of her lost dignity. Elias waited, looking patient, as she drew a deep breath and pasted on what she hoped was an utterly charming smile. She figured she needed to change his first impression of her as quickly as possible. She kept her voice sweet and genteel, the mark of a true lady. "Would you perhaps be the man I would talk to about obtaining a small loan?"

Elias straightened his vest. His face brightened. "Why, yes, my dear! I certainly am." He extended a cordial hand. "Elias Holbrook, at your service."

"Mr. Holbrook." Wynne accepted his hand with a graceful nod. "Charmed to make your acquaintance, sir. My name is Wynne Elliot." When she shook his hand, her hat tilted dangerously to one side. Probably made her look like a scatterbrained female. Cole's favorite word rose to her mind. *Addlebrained.* She hurriedly reached up and adjusted the offending headgear.

Elias beamed. "Wynne. What a lovely name, my dear. You're staying at the Claxton place, aren't you?"

"Yes. . .I don't know if you heard about my misfortune."

Of course he had; nothing in a town this small went unnoticed and most certainly not a stage robbery that took the lives of two men.

"Yes, yes, I did." He frowned. "I'm terribly sorry."

For a moment her smile dimmed. If he knew about the robbery, then he was also aware of the spectacle she'd created when she fell out of the stage with the rifle. Her cheeks burned with embarrassment. If Cole Claxton had been gentleman enough to assist her—the way he had Penelope—she wouldn't have fallen on her. . .well, fallen in the middle of the street.

"Yes. . .well, about the loan. Your establishment comes highly recommended," she said, hoping he wouldn't suspect how desperate she was. Actually, the suggestion about someone recommending his bank was not entirely true. Not a single soul had suggested she try the bank, but she thought she might sound more businesslike if she took a professional approach.

"Oh my. Why, that's wonderful," Elias exclaimed. He scurried around his desk and sat down, reaching for a pen and paper. "Now, what amount did you have in mind, Miss Elliot?"

"Well. . ." Wynne twisted her handkerchief in her lap. "I think perhaps ten dollars would be sufficient." She hoped that amount would be enough. Papa had always taken care of purchasing what she had needed, so she had very little idea of what it would cost to travel by stage to Kansas City. There would be food and other travel expenses. The amount didn't seem to shock the banker, so she relaxed a little, enjoying the thought of soon having her financial problems under control.

"Hmm. . .ten dollars. . .yes. . ." Elias scribbled as they talked. "And other than the Claxtons cosigning the note, what sort of collateral would you personally be able to offer?"

The Claxtons cosigning the note? Wynne stared at him as if he had suddenly started spouting a foreign language. He had most certainly misunderstood her. As if she would accept help from the Claxtons! Well, any more help than they had already given, that is.

She cleared her throat and smiled sweetly at him. "I have this lovely pearl ring my father gave me on my sixteenth birthday." She hurriedly slipped the circle off her finger and handed it to him. "Isn't it nice?"

Elias stared at the tiny loop resting in the palm of his hand then glanced back at her. He didn't look as impressed as she'd hoped. "This is the collateral you have?"

She mustered up her most engaging smile. "That's all I have with me right now, but it is truly a lovely ring, don't you think?" She scooted to the end of her chair. "See? The natural pearl is large, and the gold setting is stunning. Wouldn't you agree? Are you aware that a pearl signifies love, happiness, affection, and generosity? I'm sure the ring would bring half as much again as Papa paid for it."

She could see the seed of doubt begin to sprout in his eyes, and her heart sank.

He bent and closely examined the token. "It is lovely, but I would need more than the ring to make such a loan," he said, handing the ring back to her. "Have you nothing else of value?"

"I have a whole plantation back in Savannah," Wynne said. Surely mention of Moss Oak would reassure him that she was a woman of means.

"A plantation, you say?" Elias seemed more interested. "Well, that's more like it. May I see the deed, please?"

"Deed?" She stared at him, her heart sinking for the second time.

"Proof of ownership. You do own the land free and clear?"

"Yes, but I don't have the deed with me." Did anyone carry a deed to their land?

Doubt clouded Elias's face. "No deed."

"But I *do* own the land, and I could send for the proper papers—"

"That might take months," he pointed out gently. "Perhaps the Claxtons' signatures would suffice—"

She interrupted. "The Claxtons will not sign a promissory note for me." When they found out what she intended to do with the money, they'd burn in hades before they'd help.

Elias carefully placed the ink pen back on his desk.

"But the ring is collateral. . . ." Her voice trailed off when he began to shake his head negatively, and she realized with a sinking heart he wasn't going to give her the loan.

For over ten minutes she argued everything she could think of to make him change his mind, but he remained firm. The bank could not issue the loan in a woman's name.

"But that's not fair," she spluttered. "I own land—a fine plantation. The fact that I'm a woman shouldn't come into it at all."

"Miss Elliot, may I make a suggestion?" he said gently. "Why don't you talk this over with Cole Claxton and then you and he come back tomorrow morning? Perhaps something can be worked out—"

Wynne flew to her feet. "Cole Claxton! Never!"

"Now, my dear—" Elias stopped and started over. "It pains me greatly to refuse you a loan, but you must realize the bank is not in the habit of making loans to women—"

"It pains me, too," Wynne snapped. She stuck her foot in her shoe and sucked in a painful breath when the leather grazed the blister. "Thank you for your time, sir."

"Miss Elliot. . .perhaps a private investor? Nute Brower, owner of the mercantile, sometimes makes small loans. . . ."

She limped across the bank lobby, snatched up her valise, and slammed out the front door.

The temperature felt as if it had shot up ten more degrees when she stepped out of the bank. Wynne slipped the ring back on her finger where it would be safe and surveyed the crowded street, people going about their business, and no one paying the slightest attention to her. No one cared about her dilemma. Oh, it was a cruel, cold world when a banker wouldn't do business with a fine, upstanding customer just because she was a woman. Someone needed to do something to correct such an injustice.

Oh yes, Banker Holbrook had thought the ring was lovely, but completely insufficient collateral for a ten-dollar loan. And he wouldn't give her a loan because she was a woman! But it wasn't until he suggested that Cole come talk to him, that perhaps *he* would be willing to cosign the note, that she'd known her goose was cooked. She could well imagine the arrogant Claxton sneer he'd flash if she even suggested such a thing.

No matter how she'd argued—presented her case, she amended for Miss Marelda's sake—Banker Holbrook had not been persuaded.

Well, she wasn't whipped yet. She shifted the valise to her other hand, stepped off the sidewalk, and limped toward the mercantile.

Mr. Holbrook had suggested that she find a private investor. He'd said Nute Brower sometimes made small loans in exchange for personal property. But Mr. Brower didn't need a pearl ring.

Neither did Tom Clayborne or Jed McThais or even Avery Miller, for that matter. Not one person in River Run had use for a lovely pearl ring or any money to lend, either.

Wynne slumped down on a bench in front of Hattie's Place and glumly surveyed the pearl on her right hand. Hot tears sprang to her eyes. She thought it was the prettiest ring in the world, and she'd been so sure it would be an easy task to exchange the priceless trinket for the cash needed for the journey.

The saloon was extremely quiet this morning. She supposed Penelope would still be sleeping. Wynne toyed with the idea of marching right in there and rousing Hattie out of bed and asking for a job. She was completely alone, broke, in a strange town, and didn't know where her next meal was coming from.

Time had come for desperate measures.

She stood up and edged to the saloon door, hoping she wouldn't see anyone she knew. How could she bear it if Cole Claxton should see her peering into Hattie's? He'd mistaken her for one of the madam's girls before. Her anger kindled at the memory.

She raised herself on tiptoe and peeked inside at the dark interior. She couldn't ever recall seeing such an establishment before. Papa would never have permitted it, and it was quite possible he was turning over in his grave right now because of her shamelessness. Ladies of her acquaintance back in Savannah would have swept past a place like this, pretending it didn't exist. But then those ladies hadn't been alone and broke with no place to go.

She could barely make out a lone man sweeping the floor. Chairs were stacked neatly on top of tables, and a low ceiling fan was trying its best to move stagnant air. The stout odor of stale smoke and brackish beer stung her nostrils. She wrinkled her nose, thinking what it would be like to work here. She was desperate all right, but not that desperate.

If you're going to kill a man, Wynne, then you certainly should be able to go inside a saloon, she reasoned.

For a moment she felt an insipid stirring of apprehension. The thought of actually murdering a man turned her stomach. What would it be like to walk up and point a gun at Cass's big, broad chest then deliberately, coldly, cruelly pull the trigger? Revulsion snaked through her. Actually she'd been so consumed with bitterness that she'd never really stopped to think about the act itself.

She stood there, holding on to the saloon door and thinking of what it would be like to shoot someone. When it happened, would Cass look at her with amusement or with scorn or maybe even with a hint of remorse? Or would he throw his dark head back and laugh at her, his even white teeth glistening in the sunlight, having his own revenge, even as he stood at death's door?

Could she really take another's life?

Tilly had taught her the Ten Commandments, and she could recite the scripture by heart. One of those commandments was a stern warning: "Thou shalt not kill."

Her resolve wavered. Would God punish her the way she planned to punish Cass? She'd tried to reason away her doubts as to God's acceptance of her behavior, but she had an uneasy feeling He might not agree with her assessment of the situation. And what about Cass? What would he do when she showed up breathing fire and accusations? She knew he was enough like Cole that he might be hard to kill, but she'd cross that bridge when she reached it.

She stepped away from the door and sat back down on the bench. She wouldn't know Cass's reaction until she found him, and she couldn't find him until she had a mode of transportation, and she couldn't get that transportation unless she sold her ring.

Across the street a small crowd had gathered at the general store. A sign advertised a wagon train leaving the following morning. Mr. Brower had suggested she try to sign on, but when she'd inquired about the prospect, she'd been told she would have to have a husband or a guardian, preferably a family member. It was a man's world all right. A woman like her didn't have a chance.

She heaved a deep sigh. Obviously, she didn't have a spare "uncle" around, and her chances of finding a husband by daybreak tomorrow were about as slim as selling the pearl ring.

Her gaze fell on the livery stable, and it occurred to her that she hadn't tried there yet. Now here was a possibility she hadn't thought of before. Of course, how stupid of her! She probably wouldn't be able to sell the ring there, but perhaps the owner would have a horse he would trade for it.

Riding a horse wouldn't be the most comfortable way to travel to Kansas City, but she supposed she could do it if she had to. She'd ridden nearly every day before she'd gone away to school. And other women braved their way across the rugged frontier, didn't they? She'd gotten this far on her own, hadn't she? She lifted her chin. Women were a lot smarter than men gave them credit for; she wasn't whipped yet.

Feeling slightly easier about the whole situation, Wynne picked up her valise and hobbled across the street.

The blacksmith was busy shoeing a horse as she approached. He was a huge, burly sort of fella with a big gold front tooth. He towered above her small frame.

Combined with the heat of the day, the inside of the stable felt insufferable. The forge gave off a hot blast. Not a thread of the smith's clothing was dry. Rivulets of sweat poured off his forehead and ran in streams down his neck; his muscles bunched and relaxed as his hammer beat a steady rhythm to shape a red-hot horseshoe. He threw her a brief glance then refocused on his work.

Wynne cleared her throat and smiled. "Good morning, sir."

He answered with a grunt.

"It's extremely warm," she said and then realized how absurd she sounded. It was hot as a summer skunk in here. How on earth did the man stand it? She had thought it was hot outside. It made her think of Pastor Burke back home. He had a habit of preaching on hell so convincingly, Mattie Pearson said you'd have thought the man was born and raised there. Well, he'd probably gotten his inspiration for his sermons in a blacksmith shop.

The smithy grunted again and moved aside to pick up more shoeing nails, cradling them in his large, soiled apron.

"Could you tell me how far it is to Kansas City?" Wynne asked.

"Over two hundred miles."

Wynne squinted. "That far?"

He nodded and drove another nail.

She glanced around the stable. There was a solid-looking horse standing in one of the stalls. The animal was large *and* sturdy-looking, and had a glistening coat of the most beautiful rust-colored shade. The mare looked as if she would have a gentle gait—and Wynne desperately wanted a soft ride if she had to travel two hundred miles!

Wynne cleared her throat again. "Sir, I was wondering. . .would that horse over there happen to be for sale?"

The blacksmith's gaze followed her finger. "It is." He returned to the job of shaping another horseshoe.

Wynne set down her valise and walked over to the stall. The horse stuck its head over the gate and whuffed at her. She smiled and rubbed its velvet-soft nose. "Pretty girl," she whispered. *Oh yes, this one will do nicely.*

She quickly stiffened her resolve and turned back to the smithy. "Well." She spoke again, more loudly.

He didn't even look up.

"I'm sure you've heard about the stage robbery. I was on that stage and the thieves stole my money, and now I have no way to get to Kansas City," she explained in a rush of breath. "But I do have this lovely pearl ring; I'm sure you'd like it. I would trade the ring in even exchange for this horse—"

The blacksmith's eyes promptly narrowed; his mouth firmed.

Wynne's mouth went suddenly dry. "I didn't mean that *you* might be interested in the ring," she hurriedly added. "I thought maybe you might know someone you could give the pearl to—like a wife? Daughter. . .?" She trailed off hopefully when she saw the man's attention unwillingly drop to the ring on her right hand. Quickly she thrust the jewel toward him. "See? It's very appealing."

His dark eyes took in the fragile object with little sign of interest. She waited, and he leaned toward her a fraction more, studying the piece of jewelry more closely. Wynne held her breath. Her heart beat so strongly she was sure he must see it beneath the cotton fabric of her bodice. If he wouldn't trade the horse for the ring, she'd have no choice but to go to Hattie's and ask for a job.

The blacksmith straightened and scowled. "What would I do with a little play pretty like that?"

"You could give it to your wife—"

"Don't have a woman," he interrupted.

"Well, then, you could give it to—to a lady friend," she suggested. She flashed the ring, waiting for him to deny he had a lady friend. That probably was a bad suggestion. It would be a miracle if he even had a female acquaintance.

But apparently he didn't find the suggestion preposterous, because his gaze had switched back to the ring, lingering there. For a second he seemed to be seriously considering the offer.

A stream of tobacco juice whizzed by her ear. The spittle had come so close to her face she was positive that a remnant of the repulsive spray hit her left cheek.

"I don't know. . ." he said.

Wynne tried to keep from gagging (because Miss Fielding had repeatedly warned that a lady does not gag in public). She fumbled hastily in her pocket for her handkerchief and wiped her face. She had to have that horse!

"Any lady would adore the ring," she encouraged, turning her hand from one side to the other to catch the light.

Fifteen minutes later she rode out of the stable on the back of a glorious white mule, grinning ear to ear. She'd made a deal and she'd done it all on her own.

The blacksmith wouldn't trade the horse for the ring, but he would trade the old mule. It seemed the animal had wandered into town a couple of weeks ago, and it was widely speculated that it had once belonged to a prospector. Perhaps he'd died somewhere out on the trail, and the mule had wandered wild for a while. The animal was of no value to the smithy, just one more mouth to feed, and the ring didn't eat anything.

The trade had come complete with the prospector's pack equipment. Two filthy blankets, various mismatched eating utensils, a pick and a shovel, three pie-shaped pans for gold panning—should she happen to run across a gold mine, here in Missouri—and an old rusty pistol. The unexpected weapon would be a godsend if she were to complete her mission successfully, for she had wondered where she would get a gun. She was sure she couldn't run Cass down and club him to death, although if it came to that alternative, she'd do it.

Once again, she pushed thoughts about God aside. Seemed like her anger at Cass overrode everything else. She didn't use to be like this. Back at Moss Oak, she had sat in church and thought pure thoughts. Now all she thought about was how badly Cass had treated her and what she intended to do about it.

She was proud of her mule and all the equipment, though. There was a lot of other paraphernalia that she couldn't readily identify, but she was sure everything would come in handy once she was on the trail. All in all, she thought with a satisfied smile, she'd driven a very shrewd bargain.

The only problem was that she'd always ridden sidesaddle. Because, she suspected, he had felt sorry for her, the blacksmith had thrown in a worn saddle with the deal, and she had to ride astride. Adapting was going to be a little tricky, and the animal had a peculiar gait, more of a lurching from side to side than the smooth horse stride that she was accustomed to at Moss Oak.

The blacksmith had helped her mount. At first she thought about insisting upon riding properly like a lady, hooking her knee around the saddle horn, but the smithy had warned her that would be a poor choice.

"You'd best set like a man," he'd said, "or the ornery thing will pitch you headfirst in the middle of the road."

Of course she didn't want the "ornery thing" to do that, so she'd primly tucked her skirt around her legs and shinnied up on the back of the mule as gracefully as shinnying allowed.

"Excuse me. Exactly what direction is Kansas City?" she'd asked moments before she started out on the long journey.

The blacksmith had absently scratched his head and then sent another brown stream of juice flying by the mule's head. "You sure you ought to be doing this, lady? If you don't know what direction Kansas City is in, I don't think you should be setting out for it by yourself."

She adjusted the bird hat. "Thank you for your concern, but if you would kindly point the way?"

He shook his head then pointed due north. "Keep bearing north, little lady. Just keep bearing north."

Cole leaned against the porch railing of the general store and watched Wynne ride out of town on the back of a mule. It would be hard to miss her departure. Pots and pans clanging, skillets and gold pans banging. The procession made as much racket as a marching band. The pack was fastened firmly behind the saddle, but the utensils were tied on loosely and clattered noisily when the mule and its rider ambled slowly down the street.

Elias Holbrook had refused to loan money on that ring. You had to get up early to catch an old fox like Elias. Banks weren't in the habit of loaning money to women, particularly to strange women with birds on their hats and no apparent roots. The here-today-and-gone-tomorrow type didn't inspire a banker's heart.

Cole guessed she'd traded the ring for the worn-out mule and that pile of junk she had tied on it. One thing for sure: Cass didn't have to worry about her taking him by surprise. Little brother would hear her coming a mile away. He sighed.

He didn't actually think she had the skill to kill his brother, even on the remote possibility that she could find him. But there was always the chance she could accidentally kill him if she came upon him unexpectedly. Cass probably wouldn't know he was in danger until it was too late.

Cole pushed away from the post. He'd have to follow her and see that she didn't achieve her purpose.

The last he saw of Wynne Elliot, she was bouncing in the saddle like a proud prairie hen, heading for Kansas City.

She had about as much chance as a snowball in August of getting there.

Oh, what a *glorious* feeling it was to ride down the center of town knowing she was once again in charge of her own destiny. The only thing that spoiled her newfound paradise was the fact that *he* was there outside the general store taking note of her departure with an irritatingly cool detachment. He didn't even wave as she rode past him.

Wynne didn't care how blue his eyes were against the dark tan of his face. It didn't matter that his white muslin shirt was open at the neck to reveal the shadow of a patch of thick dark hair across his chest. Or even that his sleeves were rolled up to reveal corded forearms. His hat was tilted rakishly to the back of his head, and a fringe of hair that was a bit too long framed his strong face.

The cad was so handsome it nearly took her breath away.

Cole Claxton was ill-tempered, arrogant, and a complete egotistical old goat. But there was something about him that commanded her respect. Maybe it was his posture—or his attitude—or even the impenetrable stance he'd shown toward her. She liked a man who knew his own mind.

Feelings ran deep in the Claxton household; that was evident. The family came from a background of wealth and gentility. Their home reflected pride, and Lilly's ingrained Southern mannerisms left no doubt of her heritage.

But then, Wynne came from a similar background. Only trouble was, she was alone. She didn't have family to love her, support her, or defend her from men like Cole and Cass Claxton. The thought hurt but was nonetheless true. If there was any defending to do, she'd have to do it. She firmed her lips. Well, she was up to the challenge. Wynne Elliot was capable of taking care of herself.

With a decisive lift of her nose, she kneed the old mule to a faster gait and loped out of town, aware that a smirking Cole Claxton stood on the mercantile porch, arms crossed, silently laughing at her. *Good riddance,* he was undoubtedly thinking.

The same to you, sir.

She was glad to be rid of the troublemaker.

Chapter 9

"Guess we could always cross the street and wet our whistles." The old-timer shot a wad of tobacco juice off the porch then wiped the brown stain outlining his mouth on his left shirt shoulder.

It never ceased to amaze Bertram G. Mallory that a man could be so disheveled. It wasn't that he dressed all that upscale himself. He was no dude, but a man could keep himself clean.

"Better not. We were over there earlier." Bertram winced and shifted his broken ankle to a more agreeable position. The heavy splint encasing his foot was cumbersome, and his leg itched like crazy. And the insufferable heat wasn't making conditions any better.

"We could go wet a line, if you were of a mind to."

For some reason the old-timer thought Bertram was his responsibility. From the moment he'd taken a headlong plunge off that porch, Jake had befriended him—stuck closer than wool underwear on a hot day. The old codger insisted Bertram stay with him until the break healed. Since Bertram was once more at the mercy of fate—and low finances—he had little choice but to accept the offer.

Jake lived alone in nothing more than a shack on the outskirts of town. The accommodations weren't great, but Bertram had stayed in worse, and Jake was friendly and wouldn't take any money for his help. His wife had died back in '51, and his only son had been killed in a gunfight the year after. In short, Jake was a man starved for company, and he welcomed the young stranger's companionship. And it hadn't been all that bad, except Jake talked a lot and got on Bertram's nerves something awful. Still, the old man was the salt of the earth. Bertram couldn't complain.

"I could put you on the back of old Millhouse and walk you down to the river," Jake offered.

Every morning Jake unceremoniously hefted Bertram atop the old mule's back and led him into town. Bertram was fond of good horseflesh, and it hurt his pride to jolt along on a jenny, of all things. The animal's rough gait wasn't comfortable, but Jake insisted, and the ride was better than lying in bed all day. For the rest of the day, the two men sat on the plank porch in front of the café. Sitting and talking with Jake, chewing and spitting, got a mite old real quick. Bertram counted the hours until he could leave Springfield and resume his mission—one he wished he'd never accepted.

"Not in the mood for fishing," Bertram said. "Just want to sit here and finish this cow I started." He held up a piece of pine, poorly fashioned to bear a mild resemblance to a four-legged bovine. Jake could turn out a pretty good piece of whittling. You could almost always tell what it was. Bertram eyed his cow. Could be a horse, or an ox. Could be anything you wanted to call it, but it took a lot of imagination for anyone to see a cow in his work.

He appreciated the way the old-timer tried to keep him busy, but he was getting mighty bored. He needed to find the Elliot woman and get this business over with once and for all. Once he was through—and only then—would he be able to resume a normal life.

"Why, that's right nice, boy." Jake studied the carving Bertram was holding.

Well, it wasn't, and Bertram knew it. The miniature carving didn't look anything like a cow. More like an old notched-out piece of wood, but Jake had worked hard to teach him to whittle. Bertram didn't have the heart not to at least try. He appreciated the encouragement though. Seemed like there wasn't enough of that commodity to go around these days.

This afternoon the porch was full of Jake's counterparts, all whittling and spitting in unison. Bertram hadn't taken up tobacco chewing yet, but he suspected that would be next if he didn't get out of Springfield soon. Sometimes he had nightmares of himself sitting here for the rest of his life, stuck in this one-horse town like one of the old-timers. Woke up in a cold sweat a time or two. This wasn't any life for a young man.

An annoying jingling, jangling racket woke everyone up. Bertram blinked in amazement at the apparition headed their way. All eyes centered on the woman atop a white mule who seemed to have appeared out of nowhere. The animal lumbered through town, with the pans and other artifacts tied to it rattling and tinkling to beat the band. The young, pretty redheaded girl wearing a silly hat with a bird on top didn't look too comfortable, and she couldn't control that mule worth spit. It would be a miracle if she didn't get dumped on her. . .well, dumped in the middle of Main Street.

Bertram pushed slowly to his feet, wincing when he heard the woman shout a blistering command. The mule stopped dead still in the middle of the road, pitching the girl forward. She grabbed its mane to keep from falling.

"You *filthy*, stubborn piece of *dogmeat*! I ought to—" She glanced toward the porch full of gawking men and stopped mid-shout, as if she had suddenly become aware of the exhibition she was making of herself. She reached up to push a lock of hair out of her heat-flushed face and flashed an enchanting smile. "Afternoon, gentlemen," she trilled.

One by one the men left their chairs—all except Bertram; he couldn't leave that easily. A couple tipped their hats and offered toothless grins.

The girl sat astride the mule, holding court. The men gathered close, engaging in friendly introductions. *Act like they've never seen a female before*, Bertram thought.

He leaned back in his chair and grinned at her obvious dilemma. "May we be of assistance, ma'am?"

She shot him a lame smile, but about that time the mule decided to move on. Without warning the contrary animal lurched ahead. The girl grabbed for the reins and yelled, "Whoa!" but the mule ignored her. By the time they hit the end of the street, the mule had worked up a full gallop.

The last Bertram saw of the girl was a white streak bounding out of town in the midst of the banging pots and pans. The old-timers stared after her, looking dumbfounded.

Jake climbed the porch steps and sat down in his usual chair. "You see that?" he demanded.

"Yep. I saw her." Bertram shook his head in amusement. He picked up the wooden cow once more. "Sure was an unusual method of transportation for a lady, wouldn't you say?"

Jake grinned. "Didn't seem like she had much to say in the decision to go or stay, did it?"

Bertram laughed. "No, I'd say the mule was driving."

A few minutes later Jake said, "Here comes Fancy Biggers."

Heads pivoted to watch the young woman crossing the street. Fancy worked at the saloon, and Bertram had observed, in the two weeks he had been in town, how the other women picked up the hems of their skirts and made sure they didn't touch any part of Fancy's gown when they passed.

Bertram was concerned for Miss Biggers's soul. Clearly, she wasn't living by the Good Book, but other women had no cause to treat her like a bad smell.

Miss Biggers couldn't be much older than eighteen, maybe nineteen, he guessed—hard to tell with all that war paint on her face: heavily rouged cheeks, black kohl lining baby-blue eyes. She was pretty; he was certain of that. Her hair shone like a shiny new copper penny in the afternoon sunlight.

She was thinner than most. Looked to him as if she could stand a few square meals under her belt. The emerald gown she was wearing was indecent by any standards; couldn't argue that. The shiny satin made her waist look tiny—why, his hands could span her waistline and still have room left over. And the neckline—well, the material dipped way too far to be modest. 'Course, he didn't mind the dress all that much, but he could see where the other womenfolk might get a little upset with Fancy's style. This morning she was carrying a matching green umbrella, twirling it absently between her hands as she walked.

Fancy stepped onto the porch, and the men's chairs came back down on all four legs with loud thuds. "Afternoon, gentlemen," she drawled.

Bertram witnessed a second outbreak of toothless grins and nervous twittering at the men's appropriate responses. Yep, he needed to be moving on in case that sort of behavior was catching.

Fancy focused her smiling attention on Bertram. "Afternoon, Mr. Mallory."

"Afternoon, Miss Biggers." Bertram managed to struggle respectfully to his feet when she approached. His stomach fluttered. He didn't know why.

"Lovely day," she remarked, meeting his direct gaze.

"A mite hot."

"Yes. Surely could use a good rain."

"That we could. Looks kinda threatening to the south. Maybe we'll get a shower before the day's over." Jake grinned at her as he butted into the conversation.

"I wouldn't mind rain at all, but it's such a lovely day for a drive, wouldn't you think?" Fancy's eyes refused to leave Bertram's, and he felt his face grow hot when he heard the other men's knowing chuckles behind him.

"I guess it is. Real nice." Was she inviting him for a ride?

"I know you're not exactly up to driving a team at the moment, but the saloon has a buckboard I could borrow. I was wondering if you might like to go for a ride with me."

Well, you could fell him with a two-by-four. Would he like to go for a ride with her? Was the earth round?

"Why, yes. . .a ride would be real nice," Bertram said, wishing the other men would stop their dad-blasted giggling. They were worse than a bunch of old women.

"Oh, that's lovely." She smiled, showing her pleasure. "I'll get the buckboard and be back for you in a few minutes."

Bertram endured the usual male ribbing before Fancy finally reappeared, driving a horse and buckboard. He gazed up at her, sitting there behind the horses looking so pretty and so friendly, and decided the affable jesting was worth it. The old-timers hoisted him aboard, and shortly he and Fancy were leaving the town behind.

Those old geezers could laugh all they wanted to, Bertram thought when he sent an admiring glance in Fancy's direction. A warm summer ride in the countryside with Fancy Biggers was a whole lot better than carving another one of those blasted cows. And Fancy was prettier and better company than he'd been accustomed to lately. He settled back against the seat. Yes sir, things were looking up.

&

Wynne shoved her hat out of her face and stared up at the sun. Sakes alive. She was burning up! The mule had turned stubborn again, and she rued the day she'd traded the pearl ring for a misbegotten, ill-tempered piece of meat and hide that was going to be the death of her.

She'd gotten the short end of the deal.

That mule had been nothing but trouble from the moment she left River Run. It didn't want to walk, and it didn't want to sit down. It wanted to exist—nothing more.

Two miles out of Springfield she'd had to slide off and drag the contrary beast several hundred feet before Wynne made up her mind that they were going to have to get a few things straight, one being that she was the boss, and the mule was not.

The sun was hotter than a two-dollar stove burning pitch pine bark. Another hour and she would be baked to a crisp, basted with her own perspiration. She knew from Miss Marelda's teaching that a lady didn't sweat. Men sweat. Ladies glowed. Well, if she glowed any more, they could use her for a lamppost. She angrily jerked off her hat and fanned herself, trying to catch a breath of air.

The blister was paining her something awful, so she hobbled to a grassy patch and took off both shoes, wiggling her toes. After a few moments of blessed relief, she hobbled back and stuffed her shoes into her valise, which she had tied on the mule's back along with all of her other newly acquired possessions.

After a sip of tepid water out of the canteen, she turned her attention back to the mule, her current problem. She'd heard animals were smarter than they looked. Well, when they looked as ignorant as the mule did right now, you still might not have all that much to work with. Maybe if she tried to explain her predicament, this poor excuse for a beast of burden would be more cooperative. At least it was worth a try. The horses at home had liked to have her talk to them.

"Now, mule, you and I have got to have an understanding," she began in her most cajoling voice. "I've got a job to do, and you're here to help me do it."

The mule didn't look overly interested.

"I know you had a nice stall in that stable, and I've brought you out here in the hot sunshine, which you probably resent, but we're going on an adventure." That was it. Lie to it. Perhaps. . .oh, fie! It didn't really matter what she said. This worthless animal didn't understand a word she was saying! And it couldn't care less.

Besides, who was she trying to fool, herself? Adventure, ha! She was out to kill a man, and she was beginning to wonder if she was really equipped to handle the job.

Wynne sat down again, holding one rein while the mule stood facing her with a simple, placid look on its face. Whatever smarts were floating around out there in the mule kingdom had evidently bypassed this animal. She was glad no one had seen her trying to hold a conversation with this misbegotten reject from the equine race.

Cold reality was beginning to appear on her horizon, and some of her earlier enthusiasm for the task she'd set herself to was beginning to seep away. "If the truth be known, mule, I think I may have bitten off more than I can chew," she confided.

Miss Marelda was very strict about things like serving tea

properly and carrying on a charming conversation, but her course of education had been lacking somewhat on the subject of the proper way to kill a man. Even one you hate with all your being, which should add enough incentive to help Wynne develop her own method—preferably something quite painful. She'd done a lot of thinking about how painful it should be. She was sure even *Godey's Lady's Book* had absolutely nothing to say about the way to handle that task. In fact, it probably said quite the opposite. A proper young woman did not attempt revenge. She was supposed to be above that.

"Such trifling with a lady's heart should be avenged by the men in her family," Wynne assured the mule. A deep sigh escaped her. There were no men in the Elliot family now. They all were gone. A tear rolled down her cheek.

A long rumble of thunder—like dominos falling over—rolled across the horizon. "Oh flitter, mule. If it rains, I don't know what I'll do." She stood up and tugged on the reins. "Come on. Please, please cooperate," Wynne begged, but the mule didn't budge.

She searched for shelter. Other than the ominous-looking dark clouds on the horizon there was nothing but trees and scrub brush and hundreds of grasshoppers, surrounding her like a miniature spitting army. The lack of rain had made the pesky creatures abundant this year. They clung to her skirt and hopped around her feet and made a squishy sound when she accidentally stepped on them.

A grove of hickory trees off to the right looked promising. Her eyes narrowed when they focused on what seemed to be some sort of primitive dwelling hidden among the trees. Dense foliage almost obscured the sight, but on closer inspection Wynne decided that it must be an old log cabin.

If she were fortunate, the owners would allow her to take

refuge when the storm broke, but the first thing she had to do was get the mule to move.

She turned her attention back to the animal, tugging on the rope halter as she tried to force the beast back to its feet. The beast, of course, enjoyed his sit. "Ohhh!" Wynne jerked the halter, and the mule brayed louder than Gabriel's last trumpet.

"My word!" She dropped the reins to cover her ears. She'd never heard a mule with such lungs. So far that bray had been the only part of this animal that had consistently worked.

Cole slowed his horse to a walk as he zeroed in on the scene below him. He rested his arms on the saddle horn and watched the spectacle with budding amusement.

Wynne had the mule in front of her. The contrary thing had planted itself squarely in the middle of the road. The two of them hadn't made it much past a couple miles out of Springfield, but somehow that didn't surprise him.

What did surprise him was that she was standing there shaking her finger in the animal's face and, from the look of it, preaching a sermon.

Fool woman, he thought irritably. Why was he wasting precious time following her, time that could well be spent on a hundred other things? While he was away, the farm had gone steadily downhill. Ma had done her best, and he'd hoped Cass would stay there to help out, but he'd gone off and left the farm to go to ruin. Fences to be mended, ground to be tilled, crops to be planted, and what was Cole doing? Chasing a crazy female, that's what.

He'd blamed himself all afternoon for giving her a second thought. He'd told himself that whatever happened to her was just due, but as the day wore on, her pitiful plight kept coming back to him. She was a city woman, unaccustomed to the Ozarks terrain.

The thought had nagged at him all day, and by late afternoon he'd decided to follow her another few miles. So, instead of mending fences, he was trailing Wynne and an ornery mule. And it was getting ready to pour. He glanced up, studying the churning clouds.

Stubborn female. She'd been nothing but trouble from the day he and Beau had come across her, and now he was going to be following her across half the state. He was not her protector, and she wasn't his responsibility.

He found it hard to believe that Cass had actually left Wynne standing in front of the church, but if he had, the boy would answer to Cole. Cass was the baby; Cole had always been overly protective of him since he'd never known their pa, but neither of his brothers would get away with breaking his word. If a Claxton man gave his word, then he'd honor it. Although he'd hate like blazes to see Cass, or any other man for that matter, bound to the Elliot woman. No man deserved a fate like that.

He sighed and shook his head when Wynne's frustrated screeches filled the air. Seems like there was no end to the trouble she could cause. Now he was going to have to lie to Ma. Wire her some far-fetched story about unexpected business that would take him to KC for a few weeks. His conscience hurt him. He didn't make a habit of lying. It surely wasn't the Christian thing to do, and to lie to his mother seemed to double the guilt. And it was all because of that fickle female. Now, was that fair?

The little twit sat in the road, her feet firmly planted as she pulled on the mule's halter. The animal lurched up, knocking her flat on the ground, and then stood over her, braying.

Cole grinned when Wynne screeched with indignation. She

was living up to redheads' reputation for bad tempers. He kneed the mare forward and walked it down the slope, pulling up a scant five feet from her. His eyes skimmed her pitiful condition: rumpled dress, filthy hands and face. She raised her eyes and sent him a disparaging look.

Cole eyed her bare feet. Surely not Southern ladies' proper attire. He casually leaned forward and peered down at her. "The mule a little disobliging, Miss Elliot?"

"What are you doing here?" she snapped.

He let an ornery smile trace the corners of his mouth. "Why, Miss Elliot, you act as if you're not happy to see me."

"How astute of you. I'm not." She got to her feet, brushing the dust and grasshoppers off her skirt.

Cole watched while she fussed with her appearance, trying to conceal her bare toes beneath the hem of her dress. Her hair had come loose from its pins, and limp curls hung down her back.

"I thought you were going to take the stage to Kansas City," he said.

"I decided it would be better to travel by. . .mule. If I'd gone by stage, I might have missed Cass on his way home."

"Well, here I was thinking maybe you couldn't get a loan at the bank, so you went all over town trying to sell your pearl ring, and that didn't work, either, so you finally had to go to the stable and swap the pretty little thing off for this old mule and backpack."

"Well, you thought wrong," she said, squinting. "Now, how did you know all that? There are obviously a bunch of busybodies in River Run."

Cole shifted in his saddle, grinning at her growing frustration. "Where's your little bird hat?"

Wynne strode to the side of the mule and jerked the hat out of her valise. She flung it at him. "Right here!"

He ducked when the bird sailed past his head, but he was still grinning when he straightened and clicked his tongue. "Did anyone ever mention you have a nasty temper, Miss Elliot?"

"Mr. Claxton, I'm sure you have not ridden all the way out here to discuss my personality traits," she replied icily. "What do you want?"

"Oh, I don't know. Maybe I missed you, and I decided to ride out and see how you were doing."

"Very amusing." She wasn't buying that in the least.

"Maybe I wanted to make sure you had a rain slicker." His grin widened when he saw her getting madder by the minute. His gaze shifted to the south. "Looks like it's going to pour, and maybe I got to worrying about that little bird on your hat. I sure wouldn't want a little sparrow to get wet, so maybe I rode out here to—"

He ducked when a black shoe flew past his head.

Cole straightened in the saddle once more and clucked as if amazed at her behavior. "There you go getting all riled again. And I'm trying to be nice to you."

"Ha! That's a laugh! You have never been nice to me. Will you kindly move on, Mr. Claxton, and leave me alone?" She grabbed the mule's reins.

"No." The saddle creaked when he shifted. Suddenly the situation didn't seem so funny. "I can't do that, Miss Elliot."

"And why can't you do that, Mr. Claxton?"

"Because now that I know you're out to kill my brother, I have to stop you."

"Well, you can't stop me."

"Protect him from your. . .oh, shall we say, ineptitude? You're not a professional gunslinger, are you? Haven't made a name for yourself?"

Her face turned hard and impassive. Her eyes skimmed the

area. "I'll have you know I can shoot a—a grasshopper's eye out at a hundred feet!" she boasted.

He whistled in mock admiration. "A grasshopper's eye at a hundred feet, huh? Well, I have to admit, that's pretty fancy shooting."

"That's right. It certainly is." Their gazes locked, and her lower lip jutted out until she looked as stubborn as the white mule.

"But you'll have to do better than that, because I can shoot a grasshopper's eye out at a hundred and fifty feet." He seriously doubted if he could *spot* a grasshopper that far away, and he didn't bother to point out the fact that there would be nothing left of the grasshopper to support this boasting should they actually engage in such a childish duel.

Wynne bulled up like a thundercloud and stared back at him. "I do not want your despicable company a moment longer. I don't care if you can shoot a hummingbird's eye out a mile away."

"I don't want yours, either," he said. "But we're stuck with each other. Don't make the mistake of thinking I'm here for you. I'm here for Cass. So don't come running to me when you get yourself in a peck of trouble you can't get out of. I'll be right behind you all the way, Miss Elliot. I want you to be aware of that. And if you do happen to run into my brother, I'll be there looking over your shoulder." All trace of teasing had disappeared from his voice. "I'm giving you fair warning; I will not stand by and watch my brother killed, even if it means one of us gets hurt in the process."

Wynne paused in rearranging the pack on her mule, and he was relieved to see she looked apprehensive. He was doing his best—using a stern tone of voice—to convince her he was not making idle threats. He would stop her from shooting Cass any way he had to.

He knew she was itching for a way to call his bluff, but he didn't plan to give her a chance. His eyes locked with hers. "One final piece of advice, Miss Elliot." He turned his horse and prepared to ride off. "It would be smart to quit while you're ahead."

Still, half a mile up the road he paused and dropped his canteen in the middle of the road. He had extra; she wouldn't think of refilling her canteen until she drank the last swallow.

If she walked right past the water, he couldn't help it.

Chapter 10

In the two days Cole had trailed Wynne Elliot, she'd been caught in a brief but drenching rain, fallen in the river twice, and shouted at the mule in a most unladylike manner. But even that had only been a prelude to the hissy fit she'd pitched when she discovered she couldn't start a campfire because she had insisted on swimming the mule through the deepest part of the streams during river crossings and invariably got everything wet, including her matches, her clothing, and her bedding.

The old adage held true: God made the rain to fall on the just and the unjust.

And on fools.

She must have slept in a wet blanket every night since she left River Run. The fool jenny wouldn't walk half the time, its obstinacy matched only by the pea-brained stubbornness of a Savannah tidewater belle toting a grudge a mile long.

Cole rested in the saddle and observed Wynne on the trail ahead of him. As far as he knew, she had eaten very little since her trip began. She had found the water he'd left—he'd doubled back and made sure of that—but he'd bet she was getting mighty hungry.

She was a mess by now, clothes limp and permanently wet, her hair hastily piled up on top of her head. But he was not going to help her. Helping her wasn't part of his plan. He wanted her to get discouraged enough to quit this crazy vendetta of hers and go home—back to that Georgia plantation where she belonged.

During the day, he had trailed her at a safe distance. At night they had made camp not two hundred yards from each other. Every night he had a fire going in minutes, coffee bubbling over the coals, and bacon and beans sizzling in the pan. The aroma of the simple but filling food drifted on the humid air.

Wynne had steadfastly ignored his presence. And he had ignored hers.

Tonight was different; tonight, he noted with disgust, she had chosen the most exposed location she could find. Anyone with a lick of sense would have known better, but he guessed they hadn't taught survival skills at that fancy women's school she had attended. She'd picked an open space, too far from water and without protection should an enemy approach. If she did happen to get a fire started, anyone could spot the smoke a mile away.

Why didn't she give up and admit that she was beaten? Why was she so all-fired intent on killing a man anyway? He wouldn't have expected her to be the type to let revenge eat her alive. She wasn't the first or the last woman to be wronged by a man. If a woman had left him at the church, he'd have said good riddance and thanked the Lord for saving him a lot of heartache.

Cole picked a campsite deeper into the brush. Wynne had already pulled her pack off the mule and spread her blankets. From the looks of them when she tried to shake them out, they were sopping wet. He studied her unraveling hem, and the sight reminded him of the night in the cherry orchard when she'd accidentally unstitched her skirt from her bodice. There she'd stood in her bodice and white cotton bloomers, the crimson cloud of hair making her look even younger than her nineteen years.

He'd never seen a woman look more vulnerable—or more attractive.

Waiting for his supper to cook, he clasped his hands behind his head, leaned back against his saddle, and closed his eyes. The campfire's gentle hiss soothed his weary bones. His muscles slowly began to relax. During the war he'd ridden as much as two days without closing an eye, but sometimes he thought he was getting older, and his body wouldn't take the strain anymore. Sleeping on the hard ground wasn't as easy as it used to be. If it wasn't for Miss Pain-in-the-Neck Elliot, he could be home, sleeping between sun-dried sheets, eating Willa's biscuits and gravy every morning. . . .

The stars twinkled overhead like diamonds, but toward the west, occasional flashes of heat lightning marked the sky. The smells of rabbit roasting over the fire and coffee boiling in the pot softly infiltrated the twilight.

For some reason he felt guilty that she was sitting in the dark beside an unlit pile of sticks, hungry and scared. But after all, it wasn't his fault. All she had to do was give up this insane idea of killing Cass and ask for help. The town would have been glad to take up a collection to send her home—come to think of it, he'd have been one of the major contributors. But she wouldn't accept help—oh no, not her. Pride. The woman had more pride than a lizard with two tails.

He shifted on the hard ground, ignoring his conscience. He'd warned her about making this trip, but she'd refused to listen. The chances that she would find Cass were close to nil, and every day he expected her to give up her crazy jaunt and go back to Savannah where she belonged. Maybe after she'd spent another night on the hard ground, hungry, listening to the coyote's howl while she sat alone in the dark, she would reconsider what she was bent on doing.

He didn't have to be told that Ma wouldn't approve of the way he was behaving. She had brought her boys up to respect women, and to live by the Good Book. Ma firmly believed the man should be the head of the house in spiritual matters, but when she had been left with three small boys to raise, she had done her best by them physically and spiritually. Cole couldn't remember a time he ever went to bed hungry, or a time when his mother hadn't thanked God for her blessings. She'd made sure he learned about Jesus and salvation at an early age, too, and she'd wept tears of joy the day he was baptized. He wondered if Wynne Elliot was a Christian. Likely not, or she wouldn't be so blamed determined to kill a man.

He let his thoughts drift aimlessly, ignoring the waif who sat next to a cold pile of logs while he basked by the dancing flames of his own campfire. He couldn't imagine what had gotten into his younger brother. If anything, Cass was like Beau, generous to a fault. He wouldn't think of stealing a woman's money. The Claxton men were gentlemen, with Cass being the gentlest of the three.

Beau had his soft side. He was always the one to take in injured animals and defend the smallest child in school. Then again, like Cole, he could be angered when provoked. Cole had to admit that Cass was the ladies' man of the three. Being the youngest, Ma had spent more time with Cass—taught him more of the Southern way than he and Beau had absorbed. That was one reason Cass had gone to Savannah to visit relatives Cole and Beau had never met, and the reason Cass had joined the Southern sympathizers when he'd enlisted.

Cole sat up and tested the rabbit on the spit, now tender and dripping with fat. He settled back against his saddle, pondering what he was going to do about Wynne Elliot. How long would it take for her to give up and give in to the fact that she wasn't going to achieve her purpose? And what would he do then? She wasn't his responsibility, but he knew he couldn't walk away from her. It wasn't in him to abandon a woman without money or any means of support. After he'd gotten to know her, he had been convinced she wasn't the type to work at a place like Hattie's. That meant someone was going to have to help her get back to Georgia, and it looked like he was elected—unless she managed to kill his brother. Then all bets were off.

He sat up again and gingerly tipped the cross stick loose and off the forked stands of the spit. He couldn't get Wynne's purpose out of his mind. Someone other than Cass had jilted the woman. Maybe someone was using his name. Whoever had taken advantage of Wynne had not been a Claxton. Cole knew that better than he knew his own name. No Claxton would do anything so despicable. That was the only logical answer. But if that was the case, where was his brother now?

Cole pulled a leg free from the rabbit and tasted the succulent meat. His conscience bothered him so much he couldn't enjoy the tasty fare. Wynne had to be hungry. And while the days were blistering, without a fire the night air could seep uncomfortably into the bones. Maybe he should give her a few of his matches.

One match couldn't hurt anything. The simple gesture wouldn't be contributing to his brother's imminent death.

Wynne was miserably hungry—wretchedly, pathetically starved.

The aroma of roasting rabbit saturated the air. She sat huddled next to the unlit pile of sticks and envied the flickering glow of Cole's campfire. It looked so warm, so comforting. She shivered as a cool breeze rippled through the underbrush. If only she could dry her blankets so she could at least get warm. She was apt to catch her death out here with no shelter. And hungry—so hungry.

Her stomach growled, and she drew the blanket more tightly around her shoulders. Her skin felt clammy and dirty. Her head itched, her face was gritty with trail dust, and her dress was destroyed—and all because of that horrible mule.

She glared at the animal, standing not ten feet away, looking placid and docile. "Why can't you act like that in the mornings when I'm ready to ride instead of being so blamed stubborn? Wretched mule." She had traded her pearl ring for this? And thought she had gotten a bargain. That blacksmith had taken advantage of her. He had her lovely ring, and she had this white, long-eared, misbegotten son of Beelzebub.

Her stomach rumbled. That rabbit smelled heavenly, and the coffee's rich, full aroma drove her crazy. *He's torturing you, Wynne,* she argued with herself. *It probably isn't even coffee, just some old stuff he's made with chicory.*

But she wouldn't have minded having a cup if it were made with weeds. Something warm in her stomach would be heavenly. And rabbit? Real food? Just thinking about it made her dizzy. For the past two days she'd lived on nothing but the tough jerky she'd found in the miner's backpack. At first she had been too squeamish to think about eating it, but as the hours had worn on she'd decided that eating the leathery stuff was better than starving to death.

She rested her head against her knees and fought back bitter tears. She wasn't one of those crying ninnies. It took a lot to make Wynne Elliot cry, and it sure wouldn't be over the smell of Cole Claxton's coffee.

Wetness trickled down the sides of her cheeks as she sniffed and swiped at the unwanted tears. She pulled the blanket up tighter. Why was he following her anyway? Did he really think he could keep her from killing his worthless brother? If so, then he'd never dealt with an Elliot before.

Tomorrow she would practice shooting. The blacksmith had been kind enough to include bullets in the trade, so she didn't have to worry about running out of ammunition. And she couldn't argue that she needed the practice. She had to make certain that when she found Cass, she could outshoot him and his contrary brother.

Her gaze returned to his firelight, and she absently licked the salty wetness trickling into the corners of her mouth. By tomorrow night she would be a good enough shot to kill her own supper, and then she'd just see whose mouth was watering!

She would get a fire started, even if she had to resort to rubbing two sticks together. She'd already tried that numerous times in the past two days, and the method hadn't worked for her, but tomorrow night she'd keep at it until she had a nice roaring fire. Mr. High-and-Mighty Cole Claxton wasn't about to get the best of her. She jerked at the blanket and winced when she felt water ooze down her neck.

She tried to pray, but she didn't have any sense that anyone was listening. Maybe God was through with her. When she was feeling discouraged, like now, she could admit this manhunt was wrong. The commandment about not killing haunted her waking moments. But then she would think of Cass spending her money in Kansas City, or see Cole sitting by his warm campfire, eating his rabbit and drinking his coffee, and she got mad all over again. And she guessed you couldn't be mad and repentant at the same time. God's forgiveness didn't seem to work that way.

But then, God's mercy didn't seem to work for her, either. She'd lost everything and gotten nothing in return. Had the beliefs she'd learned in church been a lie? No, she didn't really think so. Her mother's faith had been strong even when she endured the horrible pain of dying. Wynne admitted the problem was probably with her and not with God. She just didn't know how to make things right again.

She eyed the fire then sniffed the air, hoping to absorb the smell. Rabbit. Delicious, hot rabbit.

Oh, he thought he was torturing her, but he wasn't. She could take anything Mr. Smarty-Pants dished out. He'd see.

At daybreak the next morning, Cole was awakened by the sounds of a gunshot and a bullet loudly ricocheting off his coffeepot.

He was on his feet in a flash, gun in hand. As his heartbeat slowed to normal, he realized he made a wonderful target standing upright like that. He took two steps backward and dropped behind the large log he'd drawn up beside his fire. Cole stared over the wooden barrier, still half dazed and trying to figure out who was doing the shooting—and why were they shooting at him? He hadn't done anything to anyone. At least nothing bad enough to be jerked out of a sound sleep by someone banging away at his coffeepot.

He peered cautiously over the log toward the fire. Black liquid trickled out of the gaping hole in the coffeepot and into the faintly glowing embers. Steam and the scent of scorched coffee drifted on the morning air.

A movement to the side of his range of vision caught his attention. His gaze swiveled upward in that direction to find Wynne towering above him. Her red hair tumbled wildly about her head, her green eyes sparkled angrily, and her mouth was set with determination. "Hand over what's left of that *rabbit*!" she demanded.

"What—" Cole, wide awake now, stared blankly up at her. Every muscle in his body was taut and ready for a fight, but instead of a Bushwhacker standing over him, he saw a five-foot piece of fluff gripping a pistol. And she was pointing it straight at his head.

"Don't argue with me!" She took a menacing step forward, the metal of her gun barrel glinting wickedly in the early-morning sun. "I said, hand me that *rabbit*!"

Cole cautiously got to his feet.

"Don't come any closer," she warned. "I'll shoot—I mean it."

She looked hungry enough and mad enough to hand-wrestle a bear.

"Easy." Cole leaned down and picked up what was left of the meat. "Here's the rabbit. Now put that gun down before you hurt someone."

She waved the barrel toward the coffeepot. "Pour me a cup of coffee before it all seeps out," she ordered.

He put his hands on his hips. "How do you expect me to pour you a cup of coffee when you just blew a hole the size of Texas through the middle of the pot! What am I supposed to do for coffee now?"

"You'll do just what I've been doing," she said without the slightest trace of pity. "Without. Now, pour that coffee before it all runs out on the ground."

If it hadn't been for the fact that she had the gun, he would have put a stop to this nonsense once and for all. But he valued his life more than he did the coffee, so he grudgingly obliged her request.

"Set the cup down on that stump."

He had hoped he could get close enough to take the gun away from her, but he decided he'd better do what she said. He wasn't fool enough to mess with a woman in this mood.

He placed the cup where she indicated.

Wynne nodded. "Now, you stand over there out of my way."

He did as she ordered, silently gritting his teeth at his awkward situation. Wynne picked up the cup and started slowly backing away from his camp.

Cole stood with his hands on his hips, watching her. Robbed by a woman. It was too much.

"Oh"—she paused in flight—"give me some matches, too."

"What?"

"You heard me!" She steadied the gun, holding the meat and tin cup with her other hand. "Give me some matches!"

And he had been about to give her matches the night before. "You steal my rabbit, shoot up my coffeepot, and now you want my matches? Lots of luck, lady."

She leveled the gun barrel directly at his chest and repeated in a low, ominous growl, "I said I want some matches. *Now.*" Her finger hovered near the trigger.

He wasn't certain how tight that trigger was set. Let her grip it too hard, and he could be dead where he stood before the fool woman realized what she'd done.

He bent and flipped open his saddle pack then tossed a small packet of wrapped matches toward her.

When they landed in the dust, Wynne waved the gun. "Pick them up and put them where I can reach them. Do it nicely."

Moments later she had her matches and was backing her way out of camp. When she was in safe running distance, she whirled and fled.

Cole stood watching her, his jaw open in disbelief. She'd done it *again*! How many times was he going to let her get the best of him? The woman was a menace to society!

Wynne dropped down on a nearby rock and began stuffing the

meat in her mouth, keeping one eye on the enemy camp. She had to admit that what she'd done wasn't very nice, but right now she really didn't care. It was only after she had eaten her fill and drunk the barely warm, bitter coffee that remorse began to set in.

Her life of crime was increasing every day. She sighed, licking remnants of the tasty rabbit off her fingers. Just how was she supposed to explain this moral lapse to God? Another commandment broken: "Thou shalt not steal." Well, really, she hadn't broken the one about killing because she hadn't exactly killed anyone yet. But she certainly had plotted in her heart to kill, and Pastor Burke had insisted that holding the thought was the same as committing the deed. That didn't really make sense to her, but she was willing to admit he might be a bit more versed on the Good Book than she was. Still, it did seem that until she actually pulled the trigger, she hadn't broken the mandate.

Would she really have shot Cole back there in his camp? She didn't know. He had looked so. . .well, attractive. . .and vulnerable, waking up all surprised like that. Still, she had been terribly hungry, and he had that rabbit. Hunger did odd things to folks. If Cole Claxton had even the smallest scrap of manners he would have offered her some of his food. She rested the gun on her lap and stared off into space, wondering how she had come this far from the way she had been raised.

The whole mess had started with her simple—and completely understandable—determination to avenge herself and get her money back. Then she had decided to kill the man in the process, and now she had resorted to robbery.

Miss Marelda Fielding would swoon.

More to the point, Wynne had a feeling God was taking a dim view of her present behavior. Surely He would take into account that during the present atrocity she had been extremely hungry, if not actually starving, and irrational behavior had won out. And it should count for something that Cole Claxton had food aplenty but hadn't offered to share. Wasn't that a biblical command: to share with those who were in need? Well, she had been in need, and he hadn't shared. In that light, you could say that she had just taught him a lesson in Christian behavior. God was probably looking approvingly on the way she had handled the situation.

She sighed. No matter how hard she tried to justify her actions, she knew she had done wrong. There was no justification for stealing and shooting up a man's belongings.

If she felt this bad about shooting a coffeepot, what would she feel like after she shot Cass?

That woman was asking for trouble! Having Wynne Elliot best him didn't sit well with Cole. The very thought that a pint-sized woman weighing a hundred pounds less than him could waltz into his camp and demand he hand over his food at gunpoint was nothing short of humiliating.

If she had been a man, she would have lived just long enough to hear the sound of his gun explode. Cole squirmed uncomfortably in his saddle. He was hungry. Last night he had purposely eaten only half that rabbit so he could have the remainder for breakfast. But Miss Elliot had taken care of that.

Well, she wouldn't take him by surprise again. And the next time, the fact that she was a woman—and a pretty one to boot—would make no difference.

By evening he was too beat to ride another mile. The heat sapped his spirit and his energy, and when he noticed Wynne making camp earlier than usual, he did the same.

At least this time she'd chosen a decent camping space. She had stopped in a pine grove beside a clear stream. The peaceful setting looked cool and inviting. Much more so than the bare expanse of rocky ground he would have to bed down on if he was to keep her in his sights. But again, why should he be uncomfortable because she was in the lead?

Having made his decision, he rode to within fifty feet of where Wynne was bent over trying to start a fire. She glanced his way then quickly turned her attention back to the sullen spark she was striving to coax into life.

He made camp and had a good fire going long before she had fanned the tiny flame to life. Remounting his horse, he tipped his hat to her in a mocking gesture and rode out. Game was plentiful here, and it took only two shots to bag a couple of plump rabbits. He was going to cook both of them and eat in front of her tonight. See how she liked that. He'd heard her trying to kill her own supper all day—it would have been hard to miss all the rounds of ammunition she had wasted. Made him nervous, too. As unhandy as she was with a gun, he half-expected to hear a shot come over his head any time. And if it had, he wasn't at all sure it would have been accidental. She had a redhead's temper all right. It was a shame that someone that pretty had such a cantankerous disposition.

Wynne straightened, placing her hand in the small of her aching back, and watched as Cole took two rabbits down to the edge of the stream and began to clean them. She didn't watch the process, knowing it would only upset her stomach and ruin any success she might have in killing her own dinner. She pushed aside any thoughts of having to clean anything she was lucky enough to shoot.

But the stream was inviting. She was tired and grungy. Her hair had been whipped and matted by the dry wind, and her skin felt about to crack from the heat. She had never in her life been this dirty.

She decided that since she would be going to bed hungry again tonight, she could at least be tidy. The old prospector's gear didn't offer much in the way of luxuries, but she gathered the scrap of soap she had packed in the valise and the last of her clean clothing and walked downstream in search of privacy.

Around a small bend in the stream there was an inviting pool deep enough to meet her needs.

The setting sun bathed the tranquil waters in a fiery orange glow. Wynne left her clothes in a pile lying on the bank and stepped into the creek, wearing only her chemise. The lowering sun gilded her dampened skin as she cupped water in her hands and let it flow over her shoulders and arms. It felt so good to wash away the trail dust. She'd sleep better tonight for bathing, even if she went to bed hungry.

When Wynne didn't return, Cole reluctantly went looking for her. He followed the bend in the stream and saw her standing in water to her waist with her damp red locks flowing around her like molten copper. She was lathering soap in her hair, working the rich creaminess through the crimson mass.

The sun had turned her fair skin to warm honey. It occurred to him that when he had seen her this morning up close, over a steel gun barrel, her nose had been sunburned and her cheeks sprinkled with freckles.

The deep water and the chemise she wore protected her modesty, and the fall of her hair reached to her waist, like a scarlet cape. She was the most beautiful woman he had ever seen. He wished, for a moment, they weren't enemies, then swiftly pushed the thought away. This wasn't a battle he had sought. Wynne Elliot might be a beautiful woman, but she had only one thought in her mind, and that was to kill his brother.

He moved cautiously back through the underbrush, hoping she hadn't seen him spying on her. When Ma had brought him up to respect women, she hadn't divided them into categories. His mother was as cordial to Hattie and her girls as she was to the women in church. When she said *women*, she meant all women. He guessed that included Wynne Elliot. Ma had taught her boys their Bible, too. He had a strong belief in God, and he knew what had happened to David when he had seen Bathsheba taking a bath. A man couldn't be too careful in these matters.

In a few moments he was back at his fire and spitting the rabbits, wishing he were anywhere but here. This was no place for a God-fearing man. If he wasn't careful, Miss Elliot could become even more trouble than he wanted.

He made certain the meat was roasting properly then gathered his own clean clothing and went to bathe farther downstream.

That night Wynne lay in her bedroll and forced herself to ignore the smell of Cole's supper lingering in the air. His campfire had been banked, and she presumed he was fast asleep by now.

They had not exchanged one word since they'd made camp, but that wasn't unusual. They rarely spoke to each other unless it was to argue.

In a way she wished that weren't so. She was lonely, and maybe just a little bit afraid, if she would let herself admit it.

This miserable journey was the first time she'd ever been so alone, and she hated it. She glanced at the other campsite and wondered if Cole had ever felt so lonely. Since he had served in the war, he would be used to being out in the dark night, beside a campfire with only the sounds of crackling bushes and wild animals.

Did he ever wonder what those strange noises were, or whether they were dangerous? Probably not. He was a man of experience; she could tell that. A man who'd experienced war and killing and death every day. She stared up at the stars, wondering how many times he had lain out on the battlefield wondering if he would see another day. It was difficult to imagine Cole Claxton being a man with natural fears, but surely he experienced his own devils. The only reason he was following her now was his concern for his brother.

She could understand why Cole felt resentful toward her, why he must hate her. She would have felt the same way if someone were trying to kill one of her kin; yet it would seem that since they were traveling in the same direction, alone, maybe it wouldn't hurt for them to talk a little once in a while. They could discuss the weather, or he could tell her where he had fought in the war, or maybe they could just talk about nothing in particular.

The ache in her stomach reminded her of her hunger. And the thought that Cole still had one whole rabbit left—for his breakfast the next morning—didn't help any.

She knew she didn't dare try to take it from him again. He had let her get away with robbery once, but she probably wouldn't be so lucky the next time, especially since he had witnessed her deplorable inaccuracy with a gun today. He'd no doubt laughed all day at her bumbling antics. How embarrassing. Her cheeks burned in the darkness. How utterly stupid he must think her.

She propped herself up on one elbow, squinting toward his campfire as she tried to locate the leftover rabbit. There it was lying next to the fire—all brown and juicy-looking.

Get your mind off that rabbit! She dropped back onto the lumpy bedroll. *He would break your arm if you tried to steal it from him again. Surely tomorrow you'll be able to kill your own supper.*

Her gaze switched involuntarily back to Cole's camp, and she sighed. She was so hungry. He had at least enough rabbit left for two people, and if he was any sort of gentleman at all, he would have offered to share his food with her.

She bit her lower lip, thinking. Maybe she could just sort of sneak over there and take a bit of the meat while he was sleeping. He would never miss it. She would take a piece so tiny he would never know it was gone.

Wynne slipped out of her bedroll and tiptoed on bare feet across the short space between her camp and Cole's. She crept closer to where he lay peacefully sleeping, holding her breath lest the slightest sound wake him. A soft snore quivered on the breeze and helped still her growing apprehension of what she was about to do. It appeared Pastor Burke was right: once you committed a sin, the next one was easier. Right now it didn't bother her a bit to take part of Cole's rabbit. She was only afraid he'd wake up and catch her.

Her steps faltered. She'd best make sure he was actually asleep. He could be trying to trick her. She certainly wouldn't put it past him. She leaned over and studied his expression. His eyes were closed, the dark lashes a smudge against his tanned skin. Dark curls tumbled over his forehead, and her fingers moved involuntarily to brush them back, but she caught the gesture just in time. His lips were parted, lightly snoring. She leaned closer, listening to the even pattern of his breath. No, he wasn't trying to trick her. He was asleep.

The plump rabbit beckoned. Wynne tiptoed closer to the fire. One teensy little piece. Smarty-Britches would never know the difference, but the food would mean that she wouldn't have to lie awake all night with an empty stomach.

Cole opened his eyes and watched when Wynne approached the rabbit he had left out as bait. She had to be starving, and his conscience wouldn't let him be. He'd never let anything go hungry. Every stray dog or cat, every traveling saddle tramp knew they could find food at the Claxton farm. He'd tried, but he couldn't go back on his raising. Still, she had to be taught a lesson.

He carefully got to his feet as she reached out to snare a plump, succulent morsel.

Her fingertips were actually touching the rabbit when he yelled at her. "Oh no, you don't, Miss Elliot!"

She whirled, staring at him, her mouth open, one hand clasped to her throat. He wanted to grin at her stupefied expression. He'd probably looked as thunderstruck this morning when she woke him by taking a shot at his coffeepot. Well, turnabout was fair play, and it served her right.

"You were trying to steal my rabbit again, weren't you?"

"I most certainly was not!" she said indignantly.

"Oh yes, you were, and this time you're not going to get away with it." He grabbed her shoulders and gently shook her. He was going to scare the wits out of her this time.

She stared up at him, sobbing, tears rolling down her cheeks. Cole released her, feeling like a whipped dog. He fought the urge to take her in his arms and dry her tears. What was wrong with him? This woman could turn him inside out just by looking at him.

Now he'd made her cry. She was a thief—and planned to be a killer—and he felt sorry for her. Was he losing his mind?

He reached in his back pocket and took out his handkerchief.

"From now on, if you want anything that's mine, you come and ask me—nicely." He wiped the tears from her cheeks.

"You're. . .a. . .big. . .bully," she said, sniffling.

"I'm not a bully. I know that's what you think, but I'm only trying to help you. You can't go through life stealing from others. You're going to get yourself killed."

"But I was hungry, and you wouldn't let—"

"I know, and I'm sorry I wouldn't help you shoot your meat." He put the handkerchief back in his pocket and reached out to lightly place his hands on her shoulders. His eyes met hers, and he tried to look stern. "From now on I'll see that you have enough to eat."

She sniffed, nodding. "And a fire. Please."

This time he couldn't hold back the grin. "And a fire." His gaze lingered on the soft curve of her mouth. She sure looked kissable.

He slowly bent his head forward until his mouth touched hers.

She sighed—a soft, kittenish sound—and her arms automatically wound around his neck. He pulled her closer, and his mouth closed over hers in a kiss that left him feeling shaken.

Cole dropped his arms and stepped away. He cleared his throat. "Please, forgive me, Miss Elliot." He had no idea why he had done that! Well, yes, he did, but he didn't plan on doing it again.

Wynne backed away from him, her eyes wide. "It's—it's quite all right, Mr. Claxton."

"Listen"—he moved over to the fire to retrieve the extra rabbit—"you take this and go on back to bed."

"I couldn't," she said politely. "It's your breakfast."

He glanced at her in disbelief. *Females!* Five minutes ago she was ready to steal it from him. "I insist." He generously extended the meat to her. "But this doesn't change our situation. I will do everything in my power to prevent you from finding Cass."

She shrugged. "A man's got to do what he's got to do. That's what my father always said."

He blinked, surprised at the platitude dripping from her honeyed lips. Somehow he could never second-guess her.

Her hand flew out to accept the gift before he could have second thoughts. "If you're sure. . ."

"Yeah," he said dryly. "I insist."

He watched as she sprinted back across the grass with an air of triumph and a sneaky smile on her face.

She probably thought she had brought him to heel with her tears. He grinned, feeling smug. He'd figured she'd come sneaking around tonight if she got hungry enough.

Little did she know that he had killed that rabbit for her in the first place.

Chapter 11

Wynne awoke minutes before the sky began to slowly shed its heavy mantle of darkness. She lay in her bedroll, watching the spreading light with a strange sense of detachment from the beauty unfolding before her. The sun sent out exploratory rays, brushing the few clouds with gold.

Her mind was still on Cole's kiss. The kiss he had taken would be the appropriate description. For she would never willingly have allowed that man such liberties with her! But she had to admit, Cass had never kissed her like that.

If she was truthful, she had to confess, though it made her uncomfortable to do so, that she'd done very little to stop the unexpected embrace; in fact, she might have actually encouraged him in the matter. However, she much preferred to think of herself as the victim who had once again been made to suffer at the hands of a Claxton.

The longer she lay and thought about what had happened, the easier it was to convince herself that she'd had nothing to do with the kiss and that Cole had had everything to do with contributing to her damaged pride.

Oh, she would grudgingly admit the kiss had been nice, but

certainly not pleasant by any means; a bit stimulating, perhaps, but only mildly so. Nothing to make her lose sleep. She had only tossed and turned because the ground was hard as a stone. Her restlessness had nothing to do with Cole *Claxton.* She thought of the way he had looked while he had been feigning sleep. For a moment she had felt guilty about taking advantage of him while he had been vulnerable, but he had only been pretending. Acting a lie.

No, of course she hadn't wanted him to kiss her. In fact, a gentleman would not kiss a woman the way Cole Claxton had kissed her.

The man should be ashamed of himself!

Still, it had been. . .interesting. Being a proper young lady, she'd never been kissed all that much. In fact, her experience with Cass, limited though it might be, had been her only experience with the art of kissing. She felt unfaithful to the fiancé who had jilted her to have enjoyed Cole's kiss so much. Well, no, now that seemed a bit complicated and not at all what she meant. Perhaps she wasn't sure what she meant, but one thing she knew: the only reason the kiss had stimulated her in the least was that Cole resembled Cass so strongly. That was the only reason why her mouth still tingled and she grew slightly breathless when she thought about last night. She knew she was being a fool. Cole Claxton had probably kissed a hundred women.

Wynne rolled onto her side and glared in the direction of his camp. She couldn't see him, couldn't see that devilishly handsome face. But in her mind she could see those penetrating blue eyes, that thick curly hair that a woman would long to push her fingers through.

Oh yes, Cole Claxton was steal-your-breath handsome—Wynne groaned aloud with frustration—but he was also cruel, unrefined, uncivilized, and a big bully with little regard for a woman's gentle nature.

Yet considering her own eagerness to be captured by his younger brother, and considering the way the two men resembled each other, it was little wonder that she was only one of a number of women intrigued by Cole.

Still, she wasn't about to make the same mistake twice. She wanted Cole Claxton out of her life. She was good and tired of his following her day after day, taunting her, laughing at her lack of experience in the wild. And she intended to do something about it, starting right now.

She crawled out of her bedroll, talking to herself as she folded the blankets and tried to smooth some of the wrinkles out of her dress. She was going to lose that scoundrel if it was the last thing she did. She was more than capable of taking care of herself, regardless of what he thought.

Once she had her mind made up, it took very little time to wash her face and hands, change into a fresh dress, and break camp. In a few minutes Wynne was urging the mule out of the grove of trees as the sun rose over the Missouri hilltops.

"Giddyap, you ornery critter!" she commanded in a hushed tone, giving the animal a smart kick in the ribs. For once the mule complied with her wishes and set off in the bone-jarring trot that rattled her teeth and jerked her neck about painfully. She smiled, thinking how surprised Cole Claxton would be when he woke up this morning. That would teach him to grab a decent woman and kiss her. He wouldn't be so impulsive the next time.

Cole leaned against a spreading oak, whose base was shielded by a thick undergrowth of wild grapevines, and watched the mule lope away with its ungainly rider. He shook his head.

Now what was she up to?

She'd carefully smoothed her hair and perched that silly hat back on top of her head. Why she insisted upon wearing that hat and her Sunday dress he'd never understand.

He pushed away from the tree trunk and strode toward his own camp. What he ought to do was turn around and go home. He was tired of sleeping on the ground and having to hunt for every meal. He'd lived like that for the past four years, and he was sick of it. He'd looked forward to getting home after a four-year absence, and here he was riding around the countryside keeping an eye on an addlebrained female who was probably going to get them both killed.

Going home was such a persuasive thought that it almost brought him pain, but then another equally disturbing idea worked its way back into his mind. For a brief moment Cole let himself think about how good it felt kissing Wynne last night. Even having been on the trail for days, she still smelled feminine—nice, like the lilac bushes that grew wild across the countryside. And her hair. The copper strands had felt like that piece of material he'd bought Ma for Christmas one year. The tinker had had a bolt of it in the back of his wagon. Silk, he'd called it, and it was real pretty. Wynne's hair had lain across his bare arm like rich, elegant silk, and it made a man long to run his fingers through it.

Cole irritably cinched his bedroll onto the back of his horse and stared in the direction she had taken. He was tired—tired of responsibility, tired of duty. Just once he wished there was a simple answer to a problem. But he'd looked after Beau and Cass since the day Pa died, and he guessed he wouldn't be stopping now.

Not when Wynne Elliot was running around the countryside, threatening to blow his brother's brains out.

It was truly a glorious morning. Songbirds chattered in the trees, and the sound of an occasional woodpecker held Wynne's attention as the mule trotted along.

She turned her face up to the sky and took a deep breath, smiling happily. It felt marvelous to be free of the specter of Cole Claxton following her within hailing distance.

She urged the mule in a more northerly direction, concentrating on making her trail harder to follow. By the time Mr. Know-It-All woke up, she'd be only a memory.

Wynne prayed she could keep her sense of direction and not become hopelessly lost. The blacksmith had said to steer north, and that's what she had been doing.

She had to laugh when she thought about how incensed Cole would be when he realized how easily she had ridden out of his life. *It only serves him right,* she thought smugly. It was high time he was made aware he wasn't dealing with a complete imbecile. Mr. Cole Claxton was dealing with Wynne Elliot, a courageous woman who had survived the deaths of her parents, who had held a plantation together—if only for a little while—and who could take care of herself on the trail and do just fine without a man's help.

Her delighted laughter rang out over the hillsides. He might not believe she was capable of anything other than making a fool of herself, but Mr. Claxton would know differently soon enough. Oh, would he ever!

By midafternoon the sun was a blistering red ball, the heat so oppressive that Wynne could hardly breathe. The mule had slowed until it barely ambled along, picking its way over a narrow trail of overgrown prickly briars and thicket. Vines trailed across the path, brushing her face and catching her hair. She had abandoned the main road hours ago to guarantee her getaway but was still careful to travel northward.

Wynne periodically reached up to swipe halfheartedly at the moisture beading her flushed features. She would give anything she still owned for a drink of cool water, but in her haste to break camp, she had forgotten to fill the canteens.

Ordinarily water shouldn't have been that hard to come by, but with the recent lack of rain, most of the streams and gullies she had crossed had been bone-dry.

She really should stop and throw this blasted corset away before she fainted from the heat. She wasn't sure what was causing the most agony: the pantaloons, the corset, the layers of petticoats, or the lack of water, but she wasn't about to part with any of the three items of apparel. A lady should maintain propriety even in the wilderness. At least she remembered that much of Miss Marelda's teaching. She dabbed daintily at her cheeks and throat.

If and when she ran into Cass, she wanted to look her best, although she had to admit her dress was sadly lacking in style. Of course, she had two other dresses packed away in the valise, but they were not nearly as nice as the one she was wearing. It was foolish to dress so nicely every day on the remote chance she might actually encounter Cass, but her pride prevented her from traveling in comfort.

Her hand absently reached up to readjust her hat, and a thin layer of dust trickled off the brim and caused her to sneeze. When he saw how beautiful she looked, Cass would be absolutely sick that he had walked out on her. She wanted him to hold that thought, just before he became absolutely dead.

A few hours of daylight remained when Wynne finally had to admit she couldn't go another mile. She halted the mule on a hill overlooking a deep valley. A growing sense of despair threatened to sap what little fortitude remained. She was tired, hot, sticky, and convinced by now that she had no idea where she was or if she was even going in the right direction.

Gnats flew around her face and stuck to her bare skin. The sun had burned her face and cheeks in spite of the hat, and the tops of her hands were blistered. The tip of her nose itched and was peeling, and she didn't want to guess what it looked like. It was impossible to go on, yet she didn't know what else to do.

The combination of heat and lack of food and water made her head swim. It was all she could do to hold herself upright in the saddle, and she still had to make camp and try to find something to eat before darkness fell.

For a moment she almost wished the pompous idiot were still following her. She turned in the saddle and peered almost longingly behind her. He wasn't there, of course. She had been too thorough in her escape. By now he was probably on his way back to River Run, where he would have a wonderfully clean bed to sleep in and a huge plateful of Willa's chicken and dumplings to gorge on. The thought of all those rich dumplings swimming in golden gravy with plump pieces of tender chicken made Wynne feel faint.

She straightened her shoulders and forced herself to think. This was no time to start feeling sorry for herself. She had a goal, and she was going to reach it no matter what.

She had two matches and plenty of bullets left. Surely to good ness she would be able to kill one small rabbit for her supper. She was getting better at hitting the targets she chose.

Wynne nudged the recalcitrant mule with her heels, holding on tightly as she urged it down a steep incline. Rocks tumbled over the mountainside and hit the walls of the shale canyon, but she refused to look down. She was dizzy enough. It was all she could do to hold on because the dumb mule kept trying to brush her off on the scrub brush that grew close to the narrow path. Vines and limbs reached out and snatched at her clothes and hair. At one point the mule nearly succeeded in knocking her off against a jutting oak covered with strange-looking vines. Right after she shot Cass, if she had a bullet left, she was going to use it on this mule. Anything this cantankerous and contrary didn't deserve to live.

Wynne decided to plan her next steps as a means of keeping her wits about her. She would camp at the bottom of the valley tonight. With luck there would be water available. She closed her eyes and prayed that would be the case. Then she would try to find something to eat, a rabbit or a squirrel, but most likely just berries again. Her mouth watered at the thought of fresh meat roasting over a fire. Maybe she'd catch a fish with her hands—though she hadn't spotted any in the shallow streams.

It seemed to take forever for the mule to make its slow descent, but the path finally widened and leveled off.

The air was a bit cooler down here. The tall limestone bluffs gave partial shelter from the sun's burning rays. She pushed at the thick mass of hair on her neck and vowed to find something to tie it away from her face before she started out again in the morning, even if it meant ripping a piece of cloth from her petticoat. She brushed at the leaves that had settled and caught in the material of her dress.

By now she had removed the hat—her one concession to ease her agony—and tied it on the saddle horn. She could always put it back on should she run into Cass unexpectedly, and it was sheer heaven to let the faint breeze blow freely through the thick mass of her hair.

Suddenly a new aroma filled the air. Her nose lifted slightly at the unmistakable smell of fatback sizzling over an open fire.

Cole! Had he followed her? But jubilation quickly turned to smoldering resentment. How *dare* the man continue to follow her when she had made it perfectly clear she didn't want his company?

Still, the aroma of his dinner tempered her anger somewhat as she urged the mule into a faster gait. Perhaps he would be kind enough to share his meal with her tonight, although that might be pushing optimism to the very limit.

In her eagerness for food she let the mule break through the clearing with the grace of a runaway stage. She quickly yanked the animal to a halt as six revolvers came out of their holsters and centered directly on her.

Wynne's eyes widened, and she stared openmouthed at the tattered, dirty men standing around the open fire. Realization slowly dawned. She had not smelled Cole's fatback cooking. Somehow she had blundered into a camp filled with frightening-looking men. She didn't think they were the outlaws from the stage robbery, but they looked like they were cut from the same bolt of cloth.

"Oh dear." She yanked the mule's head around and kicked his flanks. While she knew escape was futile, she had to at least try and correct this newest blunder.

The mule hadn't taken three strides before she was hauled off the animal's back and roughly flung to the ground. In another part of her mind, Wynne was aware that the sleeve of her dress was ripped from the bodice. She kicked and screamed, trying to scratch the eyes of the man holding her down, but to no avail. Recognizing defeat, she went limp, staring up at the bearded face of her captor.

"Well, well, boys, look what we got here," her assailant crowed. His thin mouth twisted into a smile as a lusty gleam lit his eyes.

A thread of real fear raced down Wynne's spine. She remembered the way Cole had warned her of renegades who prowled these hills. By sheer bad luck, she had just ridden into their camp like a ninny. *Addlebrained.* That was the proper word for her.

The bully hauled her over his shoulder and carried her, kicking and twisting, to where the others stood around the campfire, drinking coffee. He dropped her unceremoniously at their feet, and she hit the ground with a thump. The odor of his unwashed body was so strong it made her stomach roil, and she had to swallow hard to fight the growing nausea that threatened to overtake her.

For the first time in her life, Wynne lost her voice as a cold, paralyzing fear froze her vocal cords. The men surrounding her were a terrifying sight to a lone woman. Besides the one standing over her, three others stood around the fire, and another sat on a large rock. He caught her attention momentarily. It looked as if he was reading a book! He didn't appear to be the slightest bit interested in what was happening, and his apathy chilled her.

A sixth man stood a little way from the group, almost hidden in the shadows at the edge of the small clearing. Apparently he was on watch while the others ate their supper.

Wynne swallowed hard and sat up a little straighter, determined to look death straight in the eye. Even while she willed her pounding heart to quiet, her mind automatically formed impressions. None of the men looked to be more than twenty-five. They were filthy and unkempt, with long hair and untrimmed beards, their clothes worn and dirty. They stared at her with callous observation that made her feel like a thing rather than a woman. She was afraid to guess what they might be thinking.

One of the men called out, "Right pretty-looking girl, Sonny. Invite her to supper!" He stepped over to examine Wynne more closely. Her breath caught when he reached a grimy hand out and touched her head. He grasped a lock of her hair, absently sliding the shiny mass through his fingers, all the while staring into her terrified eyes.

"Real pretty," he repeated. Something in his voice compelled Wynne to study him more closely. He looked young, terribly young.

"Please," she finally managed, "let me go—"

"Ah, Jesse, you think they're all pretty." One of the men chortled, and the others broke out into a new round of laughter. But the young man holding a lock of Wynne's hair seemed unruffled by their friendly kidding.

"That may be rightly so, but this one's *real* pretty." He seemed to be speaking more to her than to the men, and his voice was soft and soothing.

"Now look, Jesse, I got her first," Sonny said.

"Maybe so, but I'm not sure I'm going to let you keep her," Jesse returned, his attention centered on Wynne. "Where you going in such a hurry, honey?"

"Nowhere—to Kansas City," she corrected hurriedly when his eyes narrowed.

"Kansas City? That's a mighty long way for a woman to travel alone."

"I'm not exactly alone," Wynne lied. "I—I have this man with me. He'll—he'll be riding in any moment. . . ."

The men laughed at her attempted bravado.

"I'm supposed to be making camp while he hunts our supper." She continued her bluff. "He'll be quite upset if he finds out you have detained me, gentlemen. He's big and short-tempered, and he doesn't put up with a lot of nonsense." She began to edge slowly back toward the mule.

"Ohhh me, oh my! *He* probably will be real upset if we detain her, gentlemen," one of the men mocked in a feminine voice. The men roared again, and goose bumps brushed Wynne's arms.

The man reading the book glanced up and frowned as if the racket bothered him. He carefully placed the book on the rock, stood up, and stretched. Wynne's eyes widened in disbelief when she noted the title of the book: *Venus and Adonis* by William Shakespeare.

Jesse turned and grinned at him. "Where you off to, Frank?"

Frank and Jesse. The men's names rang a bell in Wynne's muddled mind, yet she couldn't think where she had heard them before.

"Thought I'd check the horses," Frank announced.

"Ah. Did we bother you?"

"No," he said. "Just thought I'd stretch my legs."

"Do you mind if I go with you?" Wynne piped up in a shaky voice. She had no idea if this man was as bad as—or possibly worse than—the rest of them, but anyone who read Shakespeare didn't seem so frightening.

"No, you can't go with him," Sonny exclaimed. He jerked Wynne back toward him. "You're staying right here, sugar face."

Wynne sent him a sour look. She'd sugar his face with a round of buckshot. First chance she got.

Sonny seemed amused by her dour expression. He dragged her close to the fire and shoved her down onto an old blanket. "How about some supper, honey pie? We was jest about to 'dine' when you dropped in."

"No, thanks." As badly as she needed nourishment, she refused to take anything from this bunch of brigands.

"Aw, have we spoiled your appetite?" Sonny grinned. "Better eat a bite while you got the chance."

Jesse's gaze lingered on her.

Fear had eliminated her hunger, and she shook her head at Sonny's urgings to eat. She stared into the fire, trying to bite back her fear. If only she had been content to leave well enough alone.

She'd brought this on herself. Cole was stubborn, but she knew she could trust him. Now she was in deep trouble with no way out that she could see.

"Better eat, woman," Sonny urged. "Chow's hot."

Wynne shivered and looked away. Sonny shrugged and filled his plate. She turned her back to the men and plucked ineffectually at the torn threads of her sleeve. What was going to happen to her now? She blinked away the tears that hovered very near the surface. These men would probably take crying as a sign of weakness. She knew almost instinctively that if she let them see her fear, it would only bring out the worst in them.

Her gun was in the saddlebags on the mule, and the one they had called Frank had led the animal away a few minutes earlier. There was no way they would allow her to go hunt for it.

It hurt her pride even more when Cole's numerous warnings about the likelihood of such an occurrence bounced loudly in her head. Why hadn't she listened to him? Why had she undertaken such a ridiculous venture in the first place? This time she couldn't hold back the tears.

It was getting dark when the men had finally eaten their fill. Some stretched out on the ground to let their meal settle, while others sat and drank coffee. They had eaten like swine, belching and smacking, eating with their fingers since there were no utensils.

Wynne found herself comparing the motley group before her with the way Cole and Beau had looked the first time she met them. Actually there was no comparison. The Claxton brothers had been dirty, but not bone-deep nasty like these men.

Cole's image kept running through her mind, and she suddenly, desperately wished she hadn't been so foolish. Even if he did annoy her, and she got on his nerves something powerful, and she had to take food from him at gunpoint, she knew he would have protected her from this, no matter how much he disliked her.

A rumble of thunder broke into her thoughts. She glanced up and saw dark storm clouds rolling overhead. The thought of rain held no elation for her now. A flood of raindrops would never be able to wash away the pain and degradation she was about to experience.

The realization of what was going to happen made her bury her face in her hands and weep in silent despair.

Chapter 12

Well, now the fat was in the fire. Cole kept a tight grip on his horse's reins as he crept closer to the camp. If Wynne Elliot didn't get them both murdered, he'd be a monkey's uncle. And it was going to rain like pouring water on a flat rock in about three seconds. That fool woman could come up with more ways to cause trouble. Of all the ruffians out here she had to pick the James gang to fall in with.

The summer storm rolled in, heralded by a cannon roll of thunder and flares of intermittent lightning. Wind picked up, lashing the treetops. Showers of red sparks spiraled from the campfire and skipped across the parched earth.

Cole hoped the storm would distract the outlaws. He recognized a few faces—Frank and Jesse James, Sonny Morgan—desperados, every last one of them, most happy when they were causing trouble. Frank and Jesse might have had reasons during the war for their rebellion, but the war was over and they had no call to prey on unsuspecting females.

"Looks like it's a bad'un," one of the men shouted above the roar of wind.

Cole watched as Jesse scanned the ever-darkening sky.

Greenish-looking clouds boiled and churned and puffed out periodic gusts of wind that stripped leaves and sent tufts of dried grass rolling over the hollow. Cyclone weather. He wouldn't have been surprised to see a funnel dip down at any time. No wonder Jesse was nervous.

Cole kept his head down, hoping the approaching weather would distract the outlaws. He crept closer, moving as silently as possible. The roar of the wind helped mask the sound of his movements. Now all he had to do was wait for the ideal moment to make his presence known—not that he was looking forward to the encounter, but one thing he knew for certain: someone would walk away with Wynne Elliot, and he planned to be the one.

Wynne's hair whipped wildly in the fury of the wind. Cole watched as she struggled to bat fire off the hem of her dress. Men shouted and raced about, trying to quiet the animals spooked by thunder and lightning.

Chaos reigned, and the wind blew gale force. Suddenly Wynne bolted for freedom, running straight at him. His jaw dropped. Did she know he was here?

Sonny lunged after her, long arms flailing. He caught her around the waist.

Wynne screamed and fought like a wild thing, scratching and kicking as Sonny dragged her back to the camp. His laughter rose above the screeching wind.

Cole tightened his grip on his rifle. He didn't want to kill Sonny, but it looked like he might have to.

The outlaw dropped Wynne on the ground and stood over her. "No need to run, sweetie. Ol' Sonny'll take care of you!" Laughter rang out from the others, and Sonny lifted his face to the sky. "Whooeee! Got us a fighter here, boys!"

A woman with spirit, Cole thought. Just what he'd thought he wanted. Beau would have a field day with this one.

Sonny reached down and yanked Wynne to her feet.

"You slime!" She sank her teeth into the outlaw's meaty forearm, but he only laughed harder, shaking her until her head whipped back and forth like a broken doll.

Cole tensed; his anger burned brighter. He shot a glance in the direction of the others and decided he'd have to make his move.

Wynne spat in Sonny's face, and he slapped her, hard.

Cole took a deep breath and stepped into the clearing holding the barrel of his Springfield rifle leveled squarely at Sonny's chest. "Let go of her, Morgan."

Cole's arrival was met with a startled silence. Sonny stood slack-jawed with surprise. Cole's eyes swept the men, making certain the six he'd seen from where he had been hiding were well within the range of his rifle. Wynne couldn't have picked a worse group to annoy. Frank and Jesse James and some of the others had ridden with a splinter group of Quantrill's Raiders during the war. Sonny Morgan was plain mean, with a reputation as long as your arm. Lawmen everywhere were looking for this bunch, and Wynne had found them without trying; think what she could do if she put her mind to it. He silently shook his head. The thought was enough to make a grown man weep.

Wynne sank her teeth into Morgan's hand. Pain crossed his rugged features, but he held tight. "Claxton? What are you doing here? This ain't none of your business."

The men had begun to move in closer but then stopped when Cole motioned for them to throw down their guns. They reluctantly unbuckled their belts and let them drop to the ground.

Cole spared a glance in Wynne's direction, sending a clear message that she had foolishly gotten them into this sticky situation, and she was going to hear about it if they made it out alive.

"Are you all right?" he asked curtly.

She nodded. "They—I didn't know they were here."

"Obviously."

She flushed, and he figured she'd gotten his message that this was all her fault and it would be a miracle if they got out of this mess in one piece.

He turned his attention back to Sonny. "Okay, Morgan. Let her go, and we'll ride out without any trouble."

"Ah, Claxton, what's it to you?" Sonny argued, pulling Wynne possessively to his chest. "I found the little spitfire, so I figure that makes her mine."

Cole's gaze never wavered. He raised the barrel a fraction higher. "Sorry. This one's mine."

Sonny was slow, but he got the point. His smile wilted. "How come? Never knowed you to argue 'bout a woman."

"Perhaps this little lady is different." Jesse made the observation in a casual tone. He tipped his head in a mock salute to the man holding the gun on him.

Cole waited. He'd met up with Jesse during the war, and they had taken each other's measure. Neither one of them would want to go up against the other.

Jesse's grin didn't reach his eyes, but he echoed Cole's thoughts. "You don't want to go up against Captain Cole, Sonny. He's fair when it comes to a fight, but he doesn't make empty threats. I believe it might be best to hand over the woman, particularly when he's got a rifle and we don't."

Sonny sent Cole a resentful look. "She your woman?"

That was a tricky question, one Cole didn't care to answer. He shrugged noncommittally. "Let's just say I'm looking after her interests at the moment." His finger rested on the trigger. "Hand her over real gentle-like, Morgan, and we'll be on our way."

Sonny glanced expectantly at Jesse, who nodded his silent agreement. After weighing the situation for a few moments longer, Sonny shoved Wynne roughly away from him. "Take her. She weren't nothing but a peck of trouble anyways."

"You noticed that?" Cole drawled.

Wynne shot him a look that should have struck him dead in his tracks, but she edged closer to him, like she was afraid he'd go off without her. He guessed she'd rather be with him than against him in this situation.

He slipped his arm around her waist and started backing slowly out of the camp. "Good to see you again, Jesse," he said pleasantly. "You and Frank still reading Shakespeare?"

"Nice to see you, Claxton." Jesse still wore a slight grin, but there was that air of danger about him that spoke louder than the smile. "Still reading Shakespeare."

"Frank doing all right?"

"I'm fine, Cole," the man standing on the right side answered quietly. "Good to see you again."

Cole nodded briefly and continued to retreat in measured steps. He could feel Wynne trembling against his thin shirt, and he squeezed her waist in quiet assurance.

"Looks like we're going to get a good rain," Cole continued conversationally. The tension in the air was so thick you could have cut it with a bowie knife, but he kept his voice moderate, as if they were enjoying a Saturday-night social.

"Sure could use it," Jesse agreed.

Rain peppered down. Cole reached behind him for the mare and then helped Wynne into the saddle. He swung up behind her, still keeping the gun leveled at the men who watched his every movement.

"Take care now," he said politely.

Jesse nodded. "You do the same."

The storm struck with hurricane force. Cole reined the mare in a half circle and set home the spurs. Thunder rocked the hollow. A blinding glare of lightning was followed by a deafening cannonlike blast. The scent of sulfur cut the air. A huge oak to the right of the camp split down the middle. Cole clutched Wynne against him, thanking God for the cover of the storm as they rode straight into the heart of the deluge.

"My mule!" Wynne shouted above the pounding rain.

"What about it?" Cole yelled as he urged the horse over the uneven trail. He doubted the men would follow, not in this downpour, but he wanted to make sure there was plenty of distance covered in the shortest possible time.

"We forgot it!"

Well, that did it. Like he hadn't been busy enough trying to save her neck; she expected him to cart along her mule, too? Let Sonny have the mule! Come to think of it, you could say it was an even trade. Sonny got an old white mule and Cole got Wynne Elliot. He figured maybe Sonny got the better deal.

"You want to go get it?" he asked.

"No! But now I won't have anything to ride or wear. And my gun! What about my gun?" she yelled. "And I'm about to drown. Can't you slow down a little?"

"Pipe down!" he yelled back. "I'm a little out of sorts with you, lady!"

"Me?"

"You! That was a crazy trick you pulled this morning, and you're lucky I stuck around to save your hide!"

"Why, of all the nerve! I didn't need your *help* in the least!"

"No? It sure looked to me like you did!"

"I didn't!" She twisted around, trying to look at him.

Cole tried to ignore her. He'd risked his neck to save her, and she didn't appreciate a thing he'd done. For two cents he'd take her back and make Sonny Morgan a gift of her. No. He couldn't do that. A conscience was a terrible handicap. Being a decent, God-fearing man had its disadvantages sometimes.

"I was about to make a run for it when you showed up!"

"I saw how well you made the break," he snapped.

"How long were you standing there, Cole Claxton?"

He'd been there almost from the first moment she'd wandered into the James camp, but he'd decided to teach her a lesson. As long as she wasn't in immediate danger he thought he'd let her sweat. From now on she'd listen to what he had to say. "Long enough to see you were in over your head." His arm tightened around her waist.

"Stop!" she screeched, nearly busting his eardrums.

He hauled back on the reins, and the horse slowed. "What's the matter now?"

"You're going back the same way we came," she said.

"Oh, for—just be quiet, will you!" Cole nudged the mare in the flanks. He wanted to get out of this jungle and back on solid ground. Little rivulets of water had begun to flow down the hillsides. The trail was slick with wet leaves and mud. Wind-driven rain lashed the ground and struck his unprotected shoulders with needlelike force. And this addlebrained woman wanted to argue. How much was one man supposed to put up with without taking matters into his own hands?

"We've already covered this ground," Wynne yelled. "Now we'll have to double back, and that will take more time!"

Really, Cole thought. *Well, how about that?* He didn't care how much time it took her. If he could delay her by an hour, he'd jump at the chance.

The horse lumbered up the hump of the slope and out into a clearing. A flash of lightning exposed the road, and Cole breathed a sigh of relief. He'd been afraid the mare would lose her footing on the steep trail.

The horse raced through the stormy night into the teeth of the worsening storm. Deafening claps of thunder shook the earth, and lightning cut ragged paths across the sky. They'd be lucky if a fire bolt didn't strike them. It was beginning to dawn on Cole that the person who was in the biggest danger of getting killed could be him.

The rain slacked enough to improve visibility. Cole figured they had lost any pursuers who might have tried to follow. He had a hunch Jesse and his boys would have had their hands full taking care of their own affairs in this downpour. He reined the mare to a trot. Storm clouds rolled in the distance. Sullen rumbles of thunder still rattled the silence, but the rain had slowed to a fine mist.

He squinted, trying to see through the gathering darkness. Had to find shelter. Both were soaked to the skin. The full load of his grievances hit him again. Aggravating woman. He could have been killed back there, and did she care? Not a bit. What he should do was set her down in the middle of the road and let her walk to Kansas City. That's what he should do. She'd been nothing but a thorn in his side from the moment he'd met her. Wouldn't listen to a word he said—constantly goading him, not to mention her unmitigated gall.

He wasn't going to forget that she took his rabbit at gunpoint, either. Nor would he forget the reason for this ill-conceived trip across Missouri.

Even if she did smell like lilacs.

They rode in silence now. Wynne slumped against him, exhausted. For the first time since he'd met her she'd been quiet for at least ten minutes. A record, he believed. His anger cooled, and he remembered how helpless she had been back in camp. He knew exactly what would have happened to her at the hands of that bunch of outlaws. He was thankful he'd managed to get there before things got out of hand.

I hope she's learned something valuable from this experience, Lord. I might not be around the next time. . . .

Things had changed since the war, and roads weren't safe anymore. Given time, he guessed things would settle down, but feelings still ran deep. A woman traveling alone sent the wrong message to the wrong men. He tightened his hold on the reins, aware that he liked the way she felt nestled against him. They fit right—like two pieces of a puzzle. He mentally groaned. How was he going to ride all the way to Kansas City with her on the same horse and keep his distance? He had to keep reminding himself of her intentions to shoot Cass. Blood ran deeper than—what? This feeling he suddenly had for her?

Now that he thought of it, she might shoot Cass. Baby brother's luck was bound to run out sometime. Be a pity if he survived the war only to be shot by a vengeful woman.

Cole looked down at the curve of her cheek, felt the softness of her hair brushing his face. He sighed.

He should have gone back and gotten the mule.

Wynne realized he was watching her. She leaned back against him, relishing the strength of the arms that held her. There was something solid and comforting about Cole Claxton. She thought of the men at the campsite. Rough, dirty, violent. She knew in her bones Cole would never mistreat a woman. Look at the way he had followed her to make sure she was safe after she'd tried to run away from him.

Why was she so hateful to this man? He'd risked his life to save her. And instead of being grateful she'd vowed that she didn't need him, which wasn't true at all. She'd been awfully glad to see him standing there, six feet tall, all brawn and muscle, with that Springfield rifle leveled at Sonny's chest. Wynne shivered as she remembered the glint in those icy-blue eyes as he had challenged the men. She couldn't remember when she had ever been so glad to see anyone.

The outlaws hadn't argued with him, either. She was beginning to suspect there was more to Cole Claxton than she had realized. He didn't like her. Had told her so to her face. Didn't want to be anywhere near her, but still he had come to her rescue. She'd fought him and resented him, but in spite of it all, she knew he was a good man. Funny, because of Cass she had vowed never to trust another man. Now Cass's brother, because of his actions today, had taught her to trust again.

The horse plodded on, and weariness overtook Wynne. She sagged against Cole, grateful for his chest to cushion her back. Odd how utterly safe she felt when he was there. From the moment he had showed up on her trail, she had felt more at ease, less alone. Oh, she had fought with him, even stolen his food and tried to hate him for not helping her, but even when he camped some distance from her, she felt comforted just to know he was close by. There was something reliable about Cole Claxton—and wonderful and exciting and breathtaking.

She could feel the strength of him at her back, the warmth of his breath against her cheek. Strong arms held her close against him. Unbidden, the memory of his kiss, of his mouth touching hers, pushed its way to the forefront of her mind.

Her cheeks heated when she realized where her thoughts had

led her. This was risky territory. True, Cole had helped her today, but he had no interest in her. That kiss was just something that happened. It didn't mean anything to him. It didn't mean anything to her, either. It was only because he reminded her so much of Cass that she let herself even think about such things. He was only following her to keep her from hurting his brother.

Cole's mannerisms reminded her of Cass quite often, but the brothers were as different in nature as corn and sweet rolls, she found herself thinking a few moments later. Cole had a certain maturity about him that Cass had yet to acquire. She thought Cole was the more dependable of the two. Certainly Lilly depended on him.

And she had also come to the conclusion that their looks weren't *all* that much alike. Now that she had been around Cole more, she saw that he was the handsomer of the two brothers. His hair was thicker, curlier, and coarser than Cass's. And their eyes—both were blue, but Cole's had a deeper, more vibrant hue. Cole was taller and heavier, while Cass had the body of a young man yet to fully mature.

It suddenly occurred to her that if she had met Cole first, she might never have given Cass a second thought.

Now her mule was gone. So were her clothes and her gun. She was completely at Cole Claxton's mercy; she should be frantic, but strangely, she wasn't.

If Cole had been decent enough to save her from a fate worse than death with those horrible men, then he would surely see that she was taken care of, at least for tonight. Tomorrow she could start worrying again.

Having a man around might not be all that bad, she thought as she grew drowsier. If a woman was lucky enough to find the right man. She was beginning to suspect that she had made an error in judgment with Cass. Surely all men weren't liars and deceivers.

Wynne sighed. Perhaps she would reconsider going into a convent when this was all over. It was entirely possible she would find a man someday who would love her and respect her the way Beau did Betsy.

For the first time she noticed that her resentment of Cass was actually beginning to be more trouble than it was worth. Try as she might, she couldn't seem to summon that terrible, gut-wrenching agony she had experienced toward him only a few days ago. Not even a hint of the bitterness she'd clung to so desperately the past few months. What had happened to change her?

She thought of something else. No matter what happened it seemed to work out for the best. The stage had been robbed, but Beau and Cole had shown up to help. She'd found Cass's family and discovered that they were nice people. She'd run away, but Cole had followed her. She'd been hungry, and he fed her. Now he had risked his life to save her.

It was almost as if God had sent him. She examined that idea more closely. It was hard to imagine Cole Claxton as a God-sent protector, but perhaps she hadn't been abandoned after all. Could it be that God wasn't angry with her?

"In my Word I've said, 'Thou shalt not kill.' "

The words echoed to the beat of the horse's hooves. Words she didn't want to acknowledge. A chilly rivulet from her wet hair trickled down her nose. She surely had a lot to think about.

Wynne stirred and sat up straighter then almost immediately sagged back into Cole's arms. Such a nice place to be. . .

"You've gone without eating again today, haven't you?" His stern voice broke into her thoughts.

"How did you know?"

"I've followed you all day."

The admission should have upset her, but it didn't. "I'm glad you did."

"Glad? You were chewing me out a few minutes ago."

"That was a few minutes ago. I'm thanking you now—so don't make me mad again." They rode in silence for a while before Wynne spoke again. "Why did you follow me? You could easily have ridden away and been rid of me."

"I wanted you to learn a lesson."

"You would." She sighed. "But I'll admit I probably have learned a lesson. From now on I'll listen more closely to what you say."

"I'll have to see that to believe it. Want a drink of water?"

She'd been without that precious commodity all day. The rain had come too fast, too hard to do more than get her wet. All that water and nothing to drink. She swallowed against the dryness of her throat. "Please."

Cole leaned sideways to unsnap his canteen and handed it to her. "Don't drink too fast," he warned.

She drank long and greedily until he pulled the container away from her. "That's enough for now. You'll make yourself sick."

She submitted to his authority, leaning back against his chest as she gazed up into the sky. Low clouds raced across the horizon, and in the distance traces of lightning could still be seen, but the storm in all its fury had moved on.

"Who were those horrible men?" she asked when Cole replaced the lid on the canteen.

"Frank and Jesse James, plus a few men they ride with."

She shuddered. "Are those the men Lilly and Beau and Betsy were talking about at dinner the other night?"

"They're the ones."

"They're disgusting—except the one called Frank. He seemed

more. . .civil than the others." She remembered the book he had been reading. Sonny Morgan probably never read a book in his life.

"They'd just as soon shoot you as look at you—Frank included."

Wynne turned to look at him. "How do you know those men?"

"The James boys have been around for a while. They're Missouri born. As for the others, you meet all kinds in a war. A woman is looking for trouble if she's running around the countryside without a man's protection."

She could have argued, but the past few hours had made her realize that he was right. This was the second time he had saved her. He and Beau had arrived just in time at the stagecoach. God and Cole Claxton had kept her safe both times.

Wynne settled more comfortably in his arms. He smelled nice. Like rain and soap and pine needles. And he believed in God. Lilly Claxton had raised her sons right. "Where are we going to camp tonight?"

"We passed what looked like a deserted cabin earlier this afternoon. I thought we might hole up there for the night." His eyes scanned the sky briefly. "My guess is it'll rain again before morning."

"I don't recall seeing any such lodging." She hoped he was wrong and the storm had blown itself out. A handful of stars twinkled overhead, but this was Missouri. One of the men on the stage had talked about the way the weather here could change in hours.

Cole shifted in the saddle. "Couple of miles more. We'll be there soon."

The horse plodded down the rain-soaked trail. The air was cool now and smelled of damp earth and moist vegetation. Wynne dozed, roused, and nodded off again. She was so tired she couldn't think straight any longer.

Finally they rode into a clearing. Cole suggested she stay on the horse while he checked to see if the dwelling was occupied. In a few moments he was back with good news: it was empty.

When he lifted her off the horse, it occurred to her that a temporary truce now held between them. *Thank You, God. Please give me the wisdom to amend my earlier behavior.* She was indebted to Cole now. Owed him her very life.

Guilt beset her. Would God forgive her if she carried out her mission? He loved His children, and she was His child. . .and she was acting like a child. Peeved. Spoiled. Self-centered. Besides, if Cole knew God, it was entirely possible Cass did, too—which made Cass God's child. And God probably loved Cass as much as He loved her. Wynne sighed. Life had gotten awfully complicated since last night.

Cole carried the saddle into the small lean-to. "Let's see what we have here."

Wynne followed him inside and looked around at what would be their home for the night. The cabin was barely adequate shelter. There were a few stray pieces of furniture strewn about the dirty room. Dust and cobwebs conquered corners and rafters, and the sound of rats scurrying for cover when they'd entered was a bit disconcerting.

Yet the cabin looked like a castle to Wynne. At least it would be a roof over her head tonight, and that was more than she had been used to the past several days.

Cole knelt in front of the hearth and began to build a fire to dry them out and cook their supper. Some other weary traveler must have used the cabin before them because the wood box was filled with dry wood. Wynne huddled close to the fireplace, her teeth chattering, wondering if she would ever be warm again. Her rain-wet dress clung to her. Her hair was soaked and stringing around her face. Her shoes, which were coming apart, pinched her toes where the leather had begun to dry.

A flame shot from the kindling, licking at the dry wood. Cole straightened. "I've got the valise you left in the road on the way to River Run. I'll step outside while you change out of those wet clothes."

The rainstorm had cooled the air until it was almost chilly. She glanced about and located an old blanket lying on a bed in the corner of the room. It wasn't clean, but it was better than catching her death of cold from wearing wet clothing. Her nose was already tickling with a sneeze.

A few minutes later she had peeled off her wet dress, keeping her pantaloons and chemise on for modesty's sake. She draped the blanket around her shoulders, covering herself from head to toe, suddenly glad Cole Claxton was a God-fearing man. She'd never been in a situation like this before, and she felt extremely vulnerable.

By now the fire was going and the room was cozy. She busied herself hanging her dress over the back of a chair so it would dry.

Cole returned with her bag and left again while Wynne quickly dressed. Imagine him carrying it all the way from River Run. If she hadn't been so contrary with him, he'd probably have given it to her much sooner. On second thought, it was a good thing he hadn't, or this one would be back in the campsite with her mule.

Cole brought in his saddlebags, and within minutes she smelled salt bacon frying and coffee boiling.

"Well, looks like we'll eat tonight," she said, smiling.

Rain had started to fall again. Wynne could hear it on the roof as they settled around the fire. Looked like another front had moved in.

The day had been long and arduous, and Wynne realized she was exhausted. Had it only been this morning she had tried to run away from Cole? Why had she done anything so foolish? It wasn't the first time her impulsive nature had gotten her into trouble, and probably wouldn't be the last. She thought about the way she had bolted from Moss Oak, determined to find Cass and wreak her vengeance on him. Had that been another leap-before-she-looked moment? Seemed like time and the recent events had sort of changed her outlook.

They ate their supper in silence, wrapped in blankets before the roaring fire. Wynne glanced in Cole's direction, but he seemed deep in thought, so she let him be. Nothing she had learned from Miss Marelda Fielding had equipped her for this awkward moment.

She cleared her throat. "Penny for your thoughts."

Cole stared glumly into the fire. What a mess he was in, all because he had to play the hero and go riding to the rescue. Now he was obligated to this woman; now he was responsible for her safety. How could he find himself in such a trap? If he followed his inclination, he would ride off for home in the morning, and she could come along or stay. But he knew that he wouldn't, because men like him didn't leave a woman alone in the wilderness, helpless, prey to every no-account renegade that came along. He could never live with himself if he did that.

He glanced at Wynne out of the corner of his eye, aware she was waiting for an answer. Penny for his thoughts. She wouldn't like them. The light of the flames painted her skin with a rosy glow. Her eyes were shadowed, but he knew them the way one knew a favorite, well-read book. Knew when they laughed, when they sparked with anger, or when they were thoughtful and pensive, like now.

He had never met a woman who could annoy him so quickly yet make him forget all about anger when she leveled those strange-colored green eyes on him. She was feisty, unreasonable, bullheaded, and had the fortitude of six women. Yet she was one of the most beautiful creations he had ever met.

He'd read somewhere that the eyes held the essence of the heart. If that was so, he had looked deep into the heart of Wynne Elliot.

And he didn't like her! Why did he keep forgetting that?

She reached up to brush a damp lock from her face, and his eyes traced the line of her throat.

Lord, I need help here. I never asked for this situation, but it's been handed to me. Don't let me face any kind of temptation You and me together can't handle.

He got to his feet, reaching for the coffeepot. "I believe the rain's stopped. Think I'll go check the mare."

He shut the door behind him, relieved to be out of there. The thought crossed his mind that right now would be a good time for Sonny Morgan to get even if he happened to be passing by. He'd left his guns inside, hanging over the back of a chair. That's what happened when a man let a woman invade his thoughts—made him crazy. Good way to get them both shot.

He sucked in a breath of fresh air, waiting for his racing pulse to slow. When he felt he'd given himself enough time to clear his thoughts, he went back inside. She turned to face him with a hesitant smile. He figured their being here like this was hard on her, too. Not as bad as it was for him, though.

Women didn't have the same impulses as men had.

Wynne lowered her eyes. Her hands smoothed her skirt. "Still raining?"

He sat down in front of the fire. "It's about over." He picked up the poker and stirred the fire. "You'll want to go to bed."

She looked startled, and he backed up. "You're tired—right?"

"Oh. . .yes, I am."

He shifted uncomfortably. Now, wasn't that just like her? Most of the time she chattered like she'd been vaccinated with a phonograph needle, but she hadn't said a dozen words since they'd got here. This wasn't easy for him, either. She could help him out here.

"You take the bed," he said. "I'll bunk on the front porch."

Relief flooded her eyes. An emotion he had never associated with Wynne Elliot. He reached out to touch her hand, and her expression stilled. "It's all right. You're safe. Nothing's going to bother you now."

Her eyes met his, and he saw a new expression in their depths. Something he'd never expected to see. . .trust.

They got to their feet at the same time, standing close. She lifted her face to meet his eyes. And then it happened. Like a moth irresistibly drawn to flame, he slowly lowered his head, not intending to but unable to help himself. His lips hovered a breath away from hers; his arms went around her, pulling her close. Blood pounded in his temples when she reached up to lock her hands behind his neck.

Her eyes closed; her lips parted softly. It was the hardest thing he had ever done, but he reached up and pulled her arms down, holding her hands lightly in his. He'd asked the good Lord to help him, so it seemed only right that he do his part.

He touched her cheek with one finger. "Sleep well."

She gazed up at him, serious, eyes searching his as if looking for answers. Then she nodded and, without a word, stepped away from him.

Later, he lay on the porch, reliving the moment. He could have kissed her so easily. It would have been effortless to lose control, which would have put him pretty much on the same level with Jesse and Sonny. Something he never wanted to happen. Even during the war, he had never mistreated a woman.

Besides, a man like him didn't kiss a woman like Wynne Elliot unless he had marrying on his mind, and he sure didn't. He wasn't the marrying kind, and even if he was, Wynne Elliot wasn't his kind of woman.

The words rang a little hollow, even to Cole.

Chapter 13

Wynne opened her eyes and blinked at the unfamiliar surroundings. The cabin looked even worse in daylight. Cobwebs hung in every corner. The floor was filthy, the furniture shabby and broken. But last night it had been a haven.

A watery sun streamed through the broken windows, signaling that the storm had moved on. She sat up and swung her legs over the edge of the bed, wondering if Cole was still asleep. Her bare feet touched the rough, splintery floorboards. She stood up and tiptoed to the front door, opening it as quietly as possible. Her brave rescuer was snoring louder than the last trump.

He looked different in sleep. The tired lines around his eyes and mouth had softened, making him appear much younger. It was hard to believe this was the same man who could make her so angry without even trying. She had to admit he was the handsomest thing she'd ever seen. Nothing back home could compare with Cole Claxton. True, he was as cantankerous as a bear with a sore paw, but she had a feeling the right woman could tame him. Not that she was looking for the job. She had better things to do.

The kiss two days ago had been so soft, gentle. Cass had kissed her a few times, but he hadn't stirred her the way Cole did. She absently scratched her arm. That blanket must have been slept on by a mangy goat, or something even worse. Even after the thorough soaking she had received from the storm, she needed a good scrubbing. In fact, this entire cabin needed a good cleaning, but she didn't plan to be here long enough to play housekeeper.

Wynne sighed. One had to be honest, and to be perfectly honest she wished Cole Claxton would kiss her again. And she was humiliated to even think such a thing. Her gaze traveled back to the sleeping form rolled so tightly in a bedroll.

It was even more painful when she thought about the fact that he was a Claxton. Maybe if Cass had not broken her heart and trampled on her pride she would have felt differently. She might even, in time, have fallen in love again.

That new and disturbing thought brought her meanderings to an abrupt halt. No, that was ridiculous. She couldn't be falling in love with Cass's brother. Until last night she hadn't even liked the man. You would think, after the misery she'd been through the past few months, she'd have learned her lesson about men. Yet, strangely, it seemed she hadn't.

She scratched her arm harder, and it felt heavenly. A large, irritated area spread long pinkish fingers almost up to her elbow. Wynne frowned as she studied the tiny, watery blisters with growing concern. What in the blue blazes was that? Fleas? Flea bites?

Whatever it was, it was annoying and painful. She thoroughly scratched the area, but her clawing fingers brought little relief. It felt good when she scratched, but as soon as she stopped it was like fire burning her skin. She'd never experienced anything like it before.

Cole stirred as she watched him, scratching his chest beneath the blanket. He mumbled something unintelligible. Wynne bent over to peer at him and saw the same watery blisters erupting in patches on his arms. Whatever she had, it must be contagious.

She switched her attention from his arm and chest to his face, and encountered a pair of arresting blue eyes now open and staring up at her. "What are you doing?"

"Looking at your arms." She bit her lip in vexation, wishing she could take back the words and give a more proper answer.

He grinned, a completely male reaction.

She shook her head impatiently. This was no time for humor. Whatever was wrong, he had it, too.

Cole drew back, squinting at the arm she suddenly shoved in his face. "What is it?" she demanded.

"I don't know. . . . Flea bites?"

"Maybe—but you have them all over your arms, too."

Cole glanced at his own arms, and his eyes widened in disbelief. He reached out and grasped her arm, peering at it more closely. "I don't *believe* this."

"What? What is it?" she asked, looking half-afraid.

"It can't be!" He sat straight up in the bedroll. He'd had all kinds of luck since meeting this woman, all of it bad, and this was the worst of the lot. He exhaled in disgust. "It looks like poison ivy!"

"Oh, is that all?" She released a sigh that sounded like pure relief. "The way you acted I was afraid you were going to tell me it was some horrible plague."

Cole was busily inspecting his chest for further signs of the outbreak. "What do you mean, is that all? I'm sensitive to this stuff."

"Then you should have stayed clear of it."

"I do stay clear of it! I have since I had a particularly bad case of it when I was a kid. I must have got it chasing after you."

"Me! Why does it always have to be me who causes the

trouble?" Wynne jumped to her feet and glared down at him. "Just what makes you so sure I led you through poison ivy, and who asked you to come chasing after me anyway?"

"Because I'll ride five miles out of my way to avoid getting the stuff on me," Cole snapped. "Can you say you've been as careful, Miss Elliot?"

"How would I know? I don't know what poison ivy looks like."

"Obviously not." With bleak resignation he indicated her arms, which were puffing up by the moment. "You must have rolled in it somewhere!" And there'd been enough juice on her clothes to infect him. He'd ridden through the rain with her clutched against his chest, and in return she gave him what looked like a rousing case of poison ivy. That's what he got for trying to be a gentleman. If he had it to do over, he'd have let her walk.

Wynne's temper flared. "There is no reason to be so snippy. I suppose you could be right. I *did* wade through a lot of thickets and briars, and I *did* fall off the mule a few times. There were some strange-looking vines on that old oak tree the mule brushed against. I guess if you were following me, you probably went through some of the same vegetation, but I'm so tired of always doing the wrong thing."

Suddenly, to Cole's horror, she burst into tears.

He rolled hastily to his feet. He'd rather face the James gang any day than to have to deal with a squalling woman. "Don't cry. It's not the end of the world."

"But I'm—I'm for-e-ev-er doin-g su-ch stu-pi-d th-in-gs," she sobbed. "Now I've caused you to get poison ivy."

"Come on now, stop getting yourself all upset." He fumbled in his back pocket for his handkerchief, intending to hand it to her if he could get her to stop bawling long enough to take it. There were very few things that could bring him to heel, but a woman's tears were one of them. He'd do anything, short of grabbing her by the shoulders and shaking some sense into her head, to make her stop. But he was afraid in her agitated state he might make her even madder. Not that he was afraid of her—but she could be unpredictable. At least she didn't have a gun in her hand this time.

He shifted uneasily. All the blubbering and sniveling was making him uncomfortable.

She snatched the cloth out of his hand and buried her face in it, sobbing harder.

He let her cry it out, casting uneasy glances in her direction. All that squawking and bellowing was going to make her sick, but he didn't know how to put a stop to it without bringing on more of the same.

When the squall finally abated, Wynne lifted red-rimmed eyes to meet his.

Cole sagged with visible relief. "Feel better?"

"N–o," she said, and hiccupped.

"You'd better hurry and get it all out of your system," he said, trying to be nice so she wouldn't turn on the tears again. "We have work to do."

She viewed him with open skepticism as she blew her nose. "What work?"

"We have to find a whole lot of jewelweed. As fast as possible."

"Jewelweed?" She peered up at him as if he had lost his mind. Well, the same thing had occurred to him several times in the past few days. "What for? I wouldn't know a jewelweed plant if it came up and spit in my face!"

"We make poultices out of the weeds and hope they'll keep the poison ivy from spreading." He paused, not wanting to set her off again. It wasn't easy to smile like an idiot. "Mind you, I said *hope* that it won't spread any further."

"But it could?"

He shrugged, absently scratching. "With my luck? It'll spread like wildfire. By night we'll both be miserable. You don't know the meaning of trouble until this stuff spreads."

The woman was a menace—no longer any doubt about it. He'd come through the war without a single bandage. He'd led his men into battle day after day, watching them fall around him in droves, yet he'd managed to escape unharmed. But now, after becoming a one-man rescue mission for the most infuriating female that had ever been born, he was faced with a threat he feared even more than death. *Poison ivy.* The words struck dread in his heart.

When he was a kid, he had been flat on his back in bed with the dreaded ailment for more than a week. After that, his mother made sure he was dosed heavily each spring with sulfur, molasses, and a pinch of saltpeter. He wasn't sure it had helped, but as bad as it had tasted, it surely had cured something. At any rate it hadn't killed him.

He'd come to recognize the little three-leaved vine from a mile away and to avoid it. Wynne wouldn't have noticed the plant, and since the juice had probably been all over her clothing, she might have a worse case than he did.

Too late to worry about it now. If he hadn't been so intent on keeping up with her, he'd have paid more attention to where he was going. *Let there be a mess of jewelweed growing somewhere nearby, Lord.* The plant was usually found in the vicinity of poison ivy, as if God wanted to provide an antidote.

His gaze drifted back to Wynne, who was trying to pin up her mass of hair. How could someone so aggravating be so beautiful? Women were a mystery to him. In his opinion, God never intended for them to be understood. They were put on the earth to irritate men. Look at what Eve had done to Adam in the Garden of Eden. Adam had been enjoying life, going about his business, naming the animals. Then God had created woman, and the trouble started. And she had been causing trouble ever since.

Cole figured he could rest his case.

Take Wynne, with her hair straggling down like that, dress dirty, shoes coming apart. She was still easily the loveliest woman he'd ever seen. Even someone as pretty as Betsy couldn't hold a light to Wynne. It seemed odd to him that God would make such a soft, pretty woman and give her a disposition that would sour milk. A man wouldn't have a day's peace with a woman like that sharing his home.

A woman of spirit... He dismissed the thought, instead recalling how soft her lips had felt beneath his. Warm, inviting. Inexperienced. Not that he was an expert, but he could tell she hadn't been kissed many times. Probably Cass had— He stopped right there. It made him uncomfortable to think of Cass holding Wynne in his arms, or anyone else holding her for that matter. He had been ready to shoot Sonny last night, and the world would be a better place if he had. Sonny Morgan was a menace to society, including himself.

He sighed, relieved Wynne had quit crying, but the pensive look on her face bothered him. What was she thinking up this time?

Cole gathered up his bedroll. "You start breakfast. I'll be back shortly."

"There now. Are you feeling any better, Bertie?"

"It's getting bearable." Bertram G. Mallory rolled to his side as Fancy gently tried to help him into a more comfortable position. "Agghhh..." A low groan escaped him. "The ache runs straight up my spine."

"Doc said if you needed any more laudanum, he would send you over some."

"Have I taken the whole bottle already?"

"Almost." Fancy picked up the brown glass container sitting on the table among all the wooden animals he had carved these past few weeks. A regular Noah's Ark. His carving was getting better; he could almost tell the last one he'd worked on was a horse. He wondered if Fancy would want to keep them to remember him by when he left.

Fancy plumped his pillows, fussing over him in a most pleasing way. Bertram G. Mallory hadn't had many women fuss over him. It was a real nice experience.

"I brought dinner, Bertie. Hope you're good and hungry tonight."

He sniffed the air, eyeing the tray covered with a red-checkered cloth she had set on the table. "What'd you bring me?"

"Stew and corn bread."

Bertram grinned. "Stew's my favorite, and you know it. Wouldn't happen to be a piece of blueberry pie on that tray, would there?"

Fancy grinned back. "There just might be."

"You're going to spoil me, Fancy."

"I want to, Bertie."

Bertram humbly knew that he was about the best thing that had ever happened to her. In the time he'd been delayed in Springfield, the "soiled dove" had fallen deeply in love with him. She'd said that he was the kindest, gentlest man she had ever met and that she wanted to cry when she thought about how empty her life would be when he left town. He thought he might shed a few private tears, too.

Fancy was about the sweetest woman he'd ever met. He'd take

her with him if he wasn't on this mission that seemed doomed from the start. But he'd come back for her. Just see if he didn't.

He knew the fact that he was looking for a woman worried Fancy. At times when he'd talked about it he'd sounded desperate, and at other times he'd been frustrated when he talked about his leg healing so he could go on with his trip. He couldn't stop until he found Miss Wynne Elliot and did what he had to do. He wished he *could* talk it over with Fancy and ease her fears, but ethics demanded he keep quiet.

Fancy had told him she couldn't imagine him being on a spiteful mission. He was too kind to be an evil man, and he appreciated her vote of confidence. Yet every time she tried to question him on why he was looking for this Wynne Elliot, he'd had to clam up. His mission was of a personal nature; he had to find the woman. Period.

He knew he spoke in riddles. Fancy didn't know what he meant, but she said she was sure it was important for Bertie to complete his mission. Bertie. That's what she called him. He liked the name, and it made him feel good the way she was willing to trust him.

His mission would be over and done with if he hadn't stopped to help Elmo Wilson fix a wheel that had come off his buggy Sunday morning.

He'd been leaving for River Run when he'd come across Elmo and his wife, Sadie, sitting in the middle of the road, hot and sweating in their Sunday best. He could tell Sadie was about to expire, so he got off his horse and offered to help. Elmo had instructed Bertram to lift the left side of the buggy up easy-like so he could slip the wheel back in place. Wouldn't take a minute and they all could be on their way.

Well, what was a man to do? Bertram had agreed the task was

simple enough for a strong man like himself, so he had proceeded to heft the left side of the carriage, when all of a sudden his back went out. He got so mad words poured out of his mouth he didn't even know he knew. Didn't even care if Sadie was listening, because his back hurt so bad he thought he was going to be sick right there in the middle of the road. And throwing his back out was going to delay him. Again.

Sadie had almost jumped right out of her skin because his salty language scared her so badly, but the pain grabbed him around his middle something fierce. Even worse than the time he fell off the train and more ghastly than when he broke his ankle. He simply couldn't help letting off a little steam.

And what with his leg being fresh out of the splint just that morning, the jolt had set the fracture aching like all get-out. Seemed like this assignment had brought him nothing but pain and frustration.

He looked at the pretty face bending over him, concern in her beautiful eyes. Well, there was some good in everything, he guessed. If he hadn't been trying to find Wynne Elliot, he would never have met Fancy.

Elmo and Sadie had brought him back to Springfield and taken him to the doctor's office. Then they'd thoughtfully sent someone to inform Fancy about the accident, since the two of them had gotten awfully close lately. He guessed the whole town knew and gossiped about his friendship with Fancy, but they'd better not say anything to him. He'd not stand still for anyone bad-mouthing a sweet little thing like her.

Fancy smoothed his pillow and sat down on the bed beside him. "Poor Bertie. You're having a terrible run of problems lately."

Bertram thought that was an understatement if he'd ever heard one.

Fancy went on talking in soft tones; her voice sounded as sweet as a spring breeze. "However, Bertie, sweetheart, I'm just elated to have you around for a while longer."

Bertram caught her hand in the middle of all her fussing and brought it to his lips. "You're mighty good to me."

"Aw, I'm not, Bertie. You deserve so much more than somebody like me caring for you." Fancy dropped her eyes, looking shy when his grip tightened on her hand. He knew she'd known a lot of men in her time, but somehow this quiet, almost naïve woman could make him feel like a schoolboy again. He had a notion that Fancy wanted out of the kind of life she lived. People didn't always get a choice in this world. If things had been better, he didn't believe she'd have ever gone into saloon work. There wasn't much else for a woman to do to support herself if she didn't have menfolk to take care of her. Fancy was as much a prisoner of her world as he was of his. Soon as he could find the Elliot woman and do what he had to do, he was going to come get Fancy, and they'd go somewhere else and make a world all their own.

"I don't ever want to hear you say such a thing," he said. "Why, you're the best-hearted woman I've ever known, Fancy."

Bertram meant it. Other people might judge her harshly, but he didn't. He saw beyond the saloon-girl paint and glitter. He saw the lonely, sometimes frightened woman she really was. The woman who wanted a different life than the one in which she was trapped. Bertram understood, and he loved her.

"Thank you, Bertie. It's not true about me being nice—you know what I do. But I surely do appreciate you thinking so." She tenderly smoothed thinning hair away from his forehead.

"You *are* nice," he whispered, "and as soon as I finish what I'm sworn to do, I'm going to come back and get you, Fancy. Then I'm going to marry you and take you home with me."

He knew Fancy thought that when he left she would never see him again. No one had ever cared enough about Fancy Biggers to come back for her, but Bertram would be back. He loved sitting beside her talking, or holding her in his arms while they lay on an old blanket and looked up at the sky. He'd make up silly stories about people who would travel out there among the stars someday, and she would laugh and declare that he was getting addlebrained.

No, she never would let herself believe that she would someday marry Bertram G. Mallory, but she was in for a surprise. God willing, he'd complete his duty and he'd be back for her. They'd get married, have three or four children, and the two of them would grow old together.

Bertram kissed the palm of her hand and winked at her. "Now don't start doubting me. You wait and see. One of these days you're going to be Mrs. Bertram Mallory or I'll eat my hat."

She wanted to believe—he could see hope reflected in her eyes. He wanted to say, *Believe, Fancy!* "We're going to live in a big house sitting on top of a hill—"

"With a big white fence around it," she said, playing the game.

He smiled. "And lots of flowers and a big vegetable garden—"

"And kids"—she grasped his hand tighter—"at least six kids, Bertie. . .maybe more."

Bertram laughed. "However many you want, Fancy. A dozen—maybe more."

"Oh Bertie." Fancy couldn't hold back tears. "I love you with all my heart."

He gently patted her hand. "As soon as I get my business taken care of, we'll start our new life. I'm even going to change professions when this is all over. The one I have now is too harrowing. My body can't take all these injuries."

"Oh Bertie."

"I'll take care of you, Fancy. From this moment on, you don't have to worry about another thing." He meant it, too. She was the best thing to happen to him in a long while.

She rested her head on his pillow and sighed. Tears slipped silently from the corners of her eyes, and he used his fingertip to blot them. "About you going to River Run. . ."

"Yes?"

"I know you're looking for someone, but maybe that person won't be there anymore. After all, you've been here so long. You said this Wynne Elliot was supposed to be visiting there."

Bertram frowned. "I've thought about that."

"What if this woman's left by now?"

Bertram sighed, a long, weary sound. His hand absently stroked the top of her head. "Then I'll have to keep searching until I find her."

"I wish you'd tell me why it's so all-fired important for you to find her."

"Because Bertram G. Mallory is a man of his word," he stated.

And that was that. He would not stop nor say another thing until he stood face-to-face with Wynne Elliot.

Chapter 14

One month. It was hard to believe they had been gone for almost a month and still weren't more than twenty miles out of River Run. For the past two and a half weeks they had been holed up here, and Cole had cabin fever.

He lay on the old bed in the cabin and stared at a wasp circling the ceiling. His face was still a mass of puffy red welts, he itched all over, and his body was covered with crusted, oozing sores. The places that were healing had formed new skin, but he still had a lot of rash that was just starting to blister. He knew not to scratch, but sometimes he couldn't help it.

He could hear Wynne humming happily as she worked around the cabin. *Oh*, she *could hum*, he thought resentfully and gritted his teeth to keep from clawing at places already raw from his fingernails. Her case of poison ivy had turned out to be mild, while his had raged out of control.

And if that wasn't enough, the horse had pulled up lame. He figured riding that steep trail in the dark had contributed to the injury. At any rate they had to wait until the animal's leg healed. Good thing, because while he could have traveled, it wouldn't have been pleasant. He thought he'd had trouble with poison ivy before, but this outbreak was the worst he'd ever had.

He was puzzled by Wynne's behavior. He'd thought she surely would have stolen his horse and gone in search of Cass, but surprisingly she had stuck around to care for him. She wouldn't have gotten far on a lame horse, but as impulsive as she was, he figured she'd have tried. Instead, she'd slept on a pallet she had fixed on the porch, without complaining. Every day she fed him, brought water for him to bathe, and made new poultices to apply to his swollen body.

In the long night hours, while she slept undisturbed, Cole tossed and turned, plotting ways to get even with his little brother for putting him through this nightmare. Cass had a lot of explaining to do.

Wynne noticed Cole was awake and crossed the room to check on him. "Good morning. How are you feeling?"

"Rotten."

"Oh, you always say that. Surely you're feeling somewhat better today." She was getting so used to his complaints they no longer bothered her. She tried to examine the progress of his rash, but he brushed her hand away.

"I'm all right."

"Fine. I was only trying to help." She went back to arranging wild daisies in the empty glass jar she'd found in the refuse dump behind the cabin.

While Cole slept during the heat of the day, she'd taken to searching the area, looking for edible wild roots and berries for their supper. Until now she'd been successful, but all she had come across today had been the lovely flowers. She'd brought them back to the cabin in the hopes of cheering up Grumpy, but it looked as if her efforts had been wasted.

She knew their forced delay had been hard on Cole, so she didn't begrudge his being a bit touchy. If she'd been as sick as he was she would have acted the same way—well, maybe not exactly the same way, but close. The unexpected turn of events hadn't upset her in the least.

Cole was worried about the horse, too. That injured leg didn't seem to be healing as fast as it should. The mare needed the enforced stay. Wynne led her around the open space in front of the cabin every day, but her left hock was still swollen and sore.

Actually Wynne welcomed the short reprieve. It was wonderful to sleep with a roof over her head every night and be able to walk down to the pond and bathe every morning. At times she even found herself forgetting why she was here in the first place. There were hours when she no longer cared whether she ever found Cass. It was hard to hold on to the blazing anger and humiliation she had felt when he'd left her standing at the church waiting for a bridegroom who never arrived.

The bitterness and anger were slowly leaving her, and suddenly she found herself. . .well, almost happy once again. Even thinking about Cass failed to dampen her spirits like it once had. She was drawing closer to God again, too. She'd taken to praying while walking in the woods or lying on her front-porch bed. Seemed like the more she thought about God, the less she hated Cass. And the less she hated Cass, the more she wondered what she'd ever been thinking to have been so determined to kill him.

"What would you like for dinner tonight?" she asked.

"Since when is there a choice?"

"There isn't, actually. I tried to catch a fish out of the pond this morning, but I'm not fast enough with my hands."

He grunted and closed his eyes.

She searched her mind for some topic of conversation to keep him interested. As long as they were cooped up here together, they might as well try to get along. He was probably extremely uncomfortable, so obviously it was her duty to keep him entertained.

"When I was a small girl, Papa used to take me fishing. We had this large pond that was close to the house, and it was stocked with all sorts of interesting-looking fish." She continued to arrange the flowers as she chatted. "You know, fish are really fascinating. Have you ever noticed that?"

Cole grunted but didn't open his eyes.

"Some of them are truly magnificent, with nice, plump bodies and charming characteristics. And then there are those poor things that have nasty dispositions and are just plain ugly—big, bloaty-looking eyes and horrendously fat lips."

She glanced at him and thought he looked a little strange, sort of green. "It's a shame folks don't eat the mean ones and leave the cute ones alone." She glanced back to check on him. "Don't you agree?"

One blue eye opened, showing pained tolerance. "With what?"

"That the ugly fish should be eaten first."

"I've never given it a moment's thought."

It suddenly occurred to her he might be trying to rest. "Am I bothering you?"

"No."

"Well, as I was saying—"

"What about supper?" he interrupted.

"Oh." Her thoughts returned to the earlier discussion. "Well, I could always make stew again."

He sighed. "Anything but berries."

"Cole! You really should be grateful for what the Lord has provided. At least we haven't gone hungry."

"I am grateful. I'd just like a change in the menu."

"Well, I couldn't find any berries today, so you're in luck." She hoped God wouldn't be hard on him for his complaining. Surely the Almighty could see he was a sick man. Although to be honest, he didn't sound much better when he wasn't sick.

Some people just didn't have a gift for being grateful.

❧

She called that luck? He called it God being merciful. He was sick of berries. She couldn't hit the broad side of a barn with a gun, so they would have to eat that unappetizing root stew until he could get back on his feet and kill fresh meat.

It didn't matter. He'd had very little appetite lately, and it hadn't been helped by the nauseating messes she came up with. He wondered what she put in that stew. Dig the wrong kind of root and you could have just bought yourself a one-way ticket to the pearly gates. Was she smart enough to know poisonous plants from the good ones?

Wynne stuck a daisy into the jar, cocking her head to examine the effect. "If you would lend me your gun, I could go and kill a rabbit for our dinner."

He wanted to laugh, knowing she was irritated because he had hidden his gun from her and she couldn't find it. He rolled to his side, and a new round of itching hit him. "I'm not letting you have my gun."

She turned to face him, holding a flower in her hand. "That's not *fair*. You're sick, and I'm the only one able to provide our food."

"If I give you the gun, either you'll run away and leave me stuck here without a horse or a way to protect myself, or you'll shoot yourself and I'll have to get up and bury you. I don't feel well enough to tackle that yet."

She rested her hands on her hips. "I'm hungry, Cole. Now give me the gun. I won't run away. If I had wanted to do that, I would have left days ago."

"I said no."

She shrugged. "Then I'll just have to think of another way to kill our supper, because I'm not going to bed hungry again tonight."

"Good luck."

A slamming door signaled that the slaughter was about to begin. He figured any game in their immediate vicinity could probably plan on living to a ripe old age.

Cole stared at the ceiling. He should get up and move around more. Spending so much time lying around was getting to him. He'd be so stiff that he couldn't move if he didn't get more exercise. He watched dust motes drift aimlessly in a vagrant ray of sunshine. This enforced time of doing nothing had given him time to think.

He'd never really thanked God enough for keeping him safe during the war—not only him, but Beau, too, and hopefully Cass. He credited Ma's prayers for that. Oh, he'd prayed, too, every day, but praying in an emergency was different from spending time with God in a slow, leisurely way, not much on your mind but just talking and listening to Him. Cole had learned to enjoy the listening. Seemed like he'd never had time before. The war had taken a lot from him, but he knew nothing would ever take away the joy of his salvation.

For the next couple of hours he dozed off and on. The cabin became an oven, and he woke up once drenched in sweat and itching all over again.

It was late afternoon when he heard a terrible ruckus erupt in the front yard. The sound of feathered wings flailing in the air and terrified squawks, mixed with Wynne's screams, shattered the stillness.

Cole shook his head to clear his mind. The fracas got louder and more intense. He eased off the bed and fumbled for the gun he had hidden under a loose floorboard. The fight outside raged unchecked as he rose to his knees. There was no telling what the woman had gotten into this time, but it sounded as if the Battle of Vicksburg were being fought again on the doorstep.

About the time he reached the door, Wynne burst through, a triumphant grin on her flushed face. Her soiled dress was hanging in tatters, and her hair was matted with twigs and chicken feathers. She held the proof of her earlier words dangling limply from her hands. "Look what I have, Mr. Claxton!"

Cole stared blankly at what looked like a chicken, minus its head, dripping blood on the cabin floor. "Where did you get that?"

"I ran it down," she exclaimed. "And then I swung it around and around until its head popped off! I've watched the servants at Moss Oak do that. Getting the head off wasn't as easy as it looked, but I managed."

His lips twitched. "I see you did. It must have been quite a battle. Sorry I missed it."

Her cheeks pinkened. "It was wandering around in the woods, and I ran until I finally caught it, and then I brought it back here. Isn't that marvelous?"

"Well, yes, I'd call it that." And miraculous—and a gift from God. He didn't have to eat either roots *or* berries tonight.

"I don't need your gun anymore, sir," she informed him, then grinned impishly as she swirled the chicken in a wide circle like a drawstring purse. "I think I've finally got the hang of it!"

Cole groaned and sank weakly into a chair. *What will this woman do next, Lord?* Now he'd have to hunt down the farmer who owned the chicken and pay the man. Chicken thieves weren't taken lightly in these parts, and if she had been thinking, she'd have realized it was stealing. But she acted then thought.

Seven more days passed before the horse's leg showed real signs of improvement. During their extended stay, Wynne had settled into the cabin as if it were to be their permanent house. The room looked a lot different now than it had when they came.

Cole looked around, noticing the changes. It looked. . .homey. Wynne had ripped off the lower half of her petticoat and made several cleaning cloths. The cabin was spotless now, the old floor scrubbed clean, and fresh flowers sitting on the table every day.

She'd managed to stretch the chicken over an entire week and then miraculously went out and ran down another one. She'd even discovered an old root cellar in the back of the house and found a leftover bushel of apples and two jars of honey. Somehow she managed to turn the fruit and sweetening into a tasty dessert.

Cole watched her move about the cabin and noticed that not all of Miss Fielding's teachings had gone astray. There was a certain beauty and elegance about Wynne that he had failed to notice earlier. She went about her work with the grace and refinement of the most regal Southern woman, even when she was down on her hands and knees, scrubbing the rough wooden floor with a scrap of petticoat.

Instead of the clumsy, addlebrained girl he'd first encountered, Wynne was proving every day that she was indeed the genteel lady her papa had raised her to be.

At night they lay in the dark—he in the bed she had insisted on his taking and she on the front porch—and talked through the open window, surrounded by hoot owls and cicadas. Wynne told stories of growing up on a large cotton plantation, while Cole regaled her with tales about the war. They had grown so comfortable with each other that one night she even told him about Cass and how they had met and fallen in love.

When she started weeping, Cole had lain in the darkness, hurting as her bitterness and grief spilled over. After the tempest had passed, they talked long into the night. Cole now believed that his brother was partly responsible for her unhappiness, although he couldn't understand how it could be. The boy hadn't been raised to act like that.

He told her all about Cass and how he had been as a child. With each word he could sense more of the rancor slowly draining away from her. Cole told her he was the strong one, Beau the optimist, and Cass the dreamer of the Claxton family. Three men with the same parents and background, but each one different.

Then one morning he took Wynne outside the cabin and gave her a lesson in shooting.

"Why are you doing this now?" she asked, her eyes questioning his motives.

He couldn't blame her, considering the way he'd refused to let her touch his gun. "If anything unforeseen happens, you'll be able to take care of yourself."

Alarm filled her eyes. "But nothing's going to happen to you," she protested.

"Nothing's going to happen to me," he assured her. "But you need to know how to take care of yourself." He couldn't shake the image of Sonny manhandling her. If he could help it, no one would ever touch her that way again.

They were sitting in the yard, and she asked the question he had been dreading. "Aren't you afraid that I'll use this new knowledge to harm Cass?"

He didn't allow his gaze to waver. "I know you'll do what you have to do, Wynne." It was the closest he could come to saying he understood why she was doing what she was, but he hoped it was enough.

"Thank you. I appreciate your faith in me."

He nodded briefly and returned his attention to the lesson.

Wynne proved to be a fast learner. After only a few tries she hit the target, a scrap of paper he had nailed to the trunk of a large oak. He'd found some old bottles at the refuse dump behind the cabin and considered using them for targets, but decided against leaving a mess of shattered glass for someone else to clean up.

He watched as Wynne took careful aim, grinning as she frowned in concentration. She tackled everything with total abandon. The first time she had pulled the trigger she hadn't held the gun butt close against her shoulder. The resulting kick had made her yelp, but she hadn't quit. He was beginning to suspect that word wasn't in her vocabulary.

He found himself enjoying the way she stood, head slightly bent to sight down the rifle barrel. The wind teased loose strands of that bonfire-bright hair into unruly tendrils that curled and clung in a very enticing way. Standing at the side like this he had a good view of her womanly shape, too. Small and slight, she would be a mighty sweet armful.

She pulled the trigger, and a tiny piece of paper fell from the target. "I hit it," she crowed, swinging around to face him. "Did you see that?"

He ducked, throwing up an arm for protection, although he couldn't say what protection he thought it would be against a bullet. "Point that thing somewhere else!" Why in the name of good common sense had he put a gun in the hands of this harebrained female?

"Oh, sorry." She moved the gun barrel a scant four inches from his head. "Did you see me hit it?"

"I saw it," he gritted from between clenched teeth. "Watch where you point the barrel, and never point it at anything you don't plan to shoot. Can't you remember anything I told you about gun safety?"

"Of course I remember," she sputtered. "Why do you always talk to me like I'm lacking somewhat?"

"You're lacking a whole lot." And he was about to list a few of the ways. They should have had her fighting on their side in the war. She'd have wiped out a whole battalion of Johnny Rebs without batting an eye.

"I happen to be a woman—" she began.

"Yeah, I noticed. You're not lacking in that area."

"Oh." She flushed. "Oh, well. . ."

He grinned, enjoying her discomfiture. It wasn't often he bested her. Victory was sweet.

She flounced around, pointed the gun at the tree, and without taking time to aim, fired. The recoil knocked her flat. He couldn't help it. He laughed. She glared at him, temper blazing in her eyes.

Too late he remembered she had the gun. "Sorry about that. Are you hurt?"

She got to her feet, brushing off the back of her skirt, the barrel of the gun swinging in erratic circles. "Much you'd care if I was. You are the most despicable, infuriating man I have ever met."

"Yes, ma'am. I apologize; I surely do, but that thing has a hair trigger, and I'd be a lot more comfortable if you would point it in a different direction—preferably one that I don't happen to be occupying."

She glanced at the gun in her hands. "Oh, yes? You think I'd shoot you after you saved my life? Is that the sort of poor, disloyal creature you think I am?"

"No, ma'am, not on purpose, but you do seem sort of accident prone."

Wynne bit her lip, tears beading her eyelashes. She hurled the rifle on the ground and Cole winced. That was *his* gun.

"Hey, where are you going?" he demanded when she took off down the trail, arms swinging, stepping out smartly as if she knew exactly where she was heading.

When she didn't answer, he ran after her, puffing to catch up. He was out of shape, which came as no surprise. Time spent lying in bed recovering from a roaring case of poison ivy and living on roots and berries hadn't done much to develop his muscle tone.

He grabbed her arm, swinging her around to face him. "Hey. What's wrong? Don't run off like this. It isn't safe. You know that."

She turned her face away, but not before he saw tears streaming down her cheeks. He pulled her into his arms and smoothed her hair back from her flushed forehead. The silken strands clung to his fingers, as if binding him to her. Her eyes, blurred with tears, blinked up at him.

"Honey, I'm sorry. I didn't mean to upset you. It's just that I don't think too well with a gun pointed at me, and while you probably didn't intend to shoot me, you sure looked mad enough to try. You can't blame me for being a little shook."

"You laughed at me."

"I did, and I certainly won't do it again."

He tried to keep his mind off the way she felt in his arms. Almighty God had created something wonderful when He made a woman so soft and so cuddly and who smelled so good. He caught a glimpse of the fire still burning in her eyes. Almighty God had a sense of humor, too. His greatest creation had a temper that could ignite a forest fire.

"Ah, come on, honey. Don't be mad. What would you have

done if that old gun had knocked me flat? Wouldn't you have laughed just a little?"

She started to grin then clamped her lips shut in a hard line.

"Just knocked me backward, bruising my dignity something fierce. You know you'd have thought that was funny," he said.

A twinkle started in the depths of her eyes, and then a chuckle erupted, followed by a full-blown laugh. They clung to each other, laughing like idiots, tears rolling down their cheeks.

His knees felt weak. The scent of lilacs filled his nostrils. Their eyes locked, and he could see the wonder in hers. He lowered his head as her lips parted to receive his kiss. She met him halfway, standing on tiptoe to clasp her hands around his neck. His senses reeled. If he didn't get a grip on his emotions, this situation could get out of hand in a hurry.

He lifted his head and looked down at her lashes, lying like shadows on her cheeks. The days spent out-of-doors had tanned her complexion to a soft gold. Her lips were as sweet and as red as wild strawberries. He wanted to push her away, get on his horse, and ride off, but even as the thought crossed his mind, he knew it was a lie. What he really wanted was to stand here like this, warmed by the glow in her eyes.

Cole knew he was playing with fire and that the mistake would follow him the rest of his life. He didn't want her in his heart—but she was already there. Somewhere between here and River Run he'd fallen in love with this woman, and he no longer had the will to ignore it. Yet he had no idea how he would deal with the knowledge, either. How could he have fallen in love with a woman who had vowed to kill his brother?

He sighed, letting his arms drop. *I didn't want this, Lord. What am I going to do? Why did You let me fall in love with the one woman I can't have? Why couldn't I have found her first?*

Wynne stared up at him, a question in her eyes.

"We'd better get back to the cabin. It's not smart running around here unarmed." Which it wasn't, and he should have known better. He was glad to see the clearing in front of the cabin was empty, the rifle still lying where she had flung it. All that target practice would have been audible for miles around. They'd be lucky if every gang and wannabe bad guy in the county didn't pay them a visit.

That night he lay in bed, listening to the sounds of tree frogs and katydids in the grass and trees outside the cabin. A stray shaft of moonlight tied him to Wynne, who slept on her porch pallet. Tomorrow he was taking her back home with him. The horse had been walking better, barely limping. They could have left a couple of days ago if he'd been willing to walk, but he hadn't wanted this time to end. He didn't think Wynne was as determined to catch up with Cass as she had been. Maybe a few days spent with Ma and Betsy would bring her to her senses. He didn't know what he would do if she refused to go.

The moon was going down behind the cabin when he finally fell asleep.

The following morning Cole was sitting at the table when Wynne finally awoke.

"Hello." She smiled, waltzing into the cabin as pretty as a sunrise.

"Hello."

"Why didn't you wake me?"

He shrugged noncommittally. "There was no need."

Wynne stretched lazily. "Did you sleep well?"

"Yes."

She grinned. "I did, too. Your rash looks almost gone this morning."

He shoved back from the table and began pulling on his boots.

"Where are you going?" she asked.

"Home."

"Home? River Run?" She turned to stare at him.

"That's right." The boots were on, and he straightened to face her.

"But what about me?"

"I think you would be wise to come with me," he said.

"But why?"

He felt his expression lose some of its earlier harshness, but he dreaded the coming fight. "Give it up, Wynne. Come back to River Run with me. There's no telling where Cass is—he may even be back home by now. It would be crazy for you to keep looking for him. You don't have a horse or a gun."

"You could stay with me," she pleaded. "When I find Cass, you can be there to warn him about me." She was talking desperately, he knew, any feeble excuse to keep him with her, but he couldn't stay. Not now.

"I can't do that." He turned away from the pleading in her eyes for fear he would give in; he couldn't do that, either.

"Why?" Her fingers grasped the sleeve of his shirt and turned him back around to face her. "Why *not*, Cole? Hasn't our time here—together—meant anything to you?"

Meant anything to him? It had changed his life. "I'm leaving in thirty minutes. If you want to go with me, then I promise to see that you get back to Savannah safely. If you don't want to come"—he looked away from her—"then I guess you're on your own."

He knew the words were cut-and-dried, unemotional, and final. Sometimes life wasn't easy, but if he gave in now that would make them both fools.

Tears gathered in her eyes and her hand came up to cover her mouth. He could see the hurt in her eyes from the lie he'd perpetuated: that the past few weeks had meant nothing to him.

"Well?" Cole ignored her tears and got up and reached for his hat.

"All right," she said lifelessly. She kept her face averted.

"You'll come back with me?"

"Yes. I don't guess I have much choice."

He nodded and walked to the door. "I'll saddle the horse."

Chapter 15

So they started home. Cole knew he was doing the right thing, but he already missed the companionship he'd shared with Wynne at the cabin. Granted, he'd been sick most of the time, but the time they'd spent together would be an experience he would always remember. He guessed marriage wouldn't be so bad after all.

With the right woman.

Wynne rode sheltered in his arms, but they spoke only when necessary. She seemed weary, and most of the fire had gone out of her. He didn't feel like talking much himself.

An hour before dusk, they stopped to camp. Wynne prepared the meal while he brought wood and water and took care of the horse. They worked well together, sharing the tasks in silence. There was a barrier between them. A barrier he had erected and couldn't tear down. At least not yet. If ever.

At night they lay across the campfire from each other, not speaking. The silence was deeper than anything he had ever imagined. He watched the flames playing over her bedroll, and it was as if a great gulf lay between them. As much as he wanted to deny it, she'd had some sort of relationship with his brother. Until he learned the truth from Cass, he wasn't free to express his love to

Wynne. He was alone in his own private world without the right to ask her to share it with him.

Whatever had been between Wynne and his brother was over for her—he was certain of that—but he hadn't heard Cass's side of the story or how he felt. He'd been like a father to both of his brothers. He couldn't take Wynne from Cass any more than he would try to take Betsy from Beau.

Cass was a charmer, no doubt about it. What if, when they met again, he used that charm on Wynne? Could he stand aside and let his brother have the woman he loved? Cole sighed. Life didn't use to be this complicated. He always figured once you fell in love you spent your time having a lot of romantic thoughts. Well, he had the thoughts all right, but he couldn't act upon them. If the good Lord had ever created a more exasperating woman, Cole had yet to meet her.

Morning dawned after another sleepless night. He carefully avoided the hurt in Wynne's eyes. It was hard speaking of things that weren't important and pretending the past few weeks had never happened. He knew she didn't understand the change in him, and he didn't have the words to explain. All he could do was take care of her and keep his distance. There were matters they needed to talk about, but he was waiting for the right time.

He talked to God often, asking for guidance. Trouble was, God wasn't doing much talking back. The past few days Cole had felt like he was stumbling through the fog, trying to find his way. Maybe that was what the preachers meant when they talked about living by faith. He'd always thought if you trusted in God the path would be clear—lit by constant sunlight. At the cabin, when he talked to God, Cole had felt like he was walking in that sunlight, but out here on the trail it was different. Colder even in the hot sun. Maybe it was supposed to be that way. Sometimes you walked in the light and sometimes you walked in deep shade, but either way God was there. If you could see where you were walking all the time, he guessed you wouldn't need faith. And right now faith was all he had to hold on to.

He rode behind Wynne, repeatedly challenging his sanity at the way he had let himself fall in love with this woman. Even if she were to give up the foolish idea of killing his brother, she would always bear a deep resentment toward Cass.

The family would be divided, something he found intolerable. How could he choose between the woman he loved and his family? His prayers were disjointed dialogues with God, alternating between raging disappointment and abject apology on his part. So far God wasn't contributing much to the discussion.

The Claxton family had stood together through thick and thin. It was inconceivable that an outsider, wearing a crazy little bird hat, could waltz into his life and come between him and family, yet the thought of putting Wynne on the stagecoach back to Savannah tore him apart. Right now he couldn't imagine what his life would be like without her.

Toward evening of the second day they stopped to water the horse. Wynne knelt beside the stream and splashed a handful of cool liquid against her grimy face. Trail dust was thick and ground into her dress. Her hair straggled from the few remaining hairpins, and weariness etched her features. He thought she had never looked more beautiful.

Cole watched as she closed her eyes and trickled water over her neck. She had been no trouble at all lately, doing her share of the work and never complaining. She'd been submissive and unusually quiet, not at all like the fireball he'd found standing in the middle of the road one day, waving a gun at him. The change only served to deepen his anguish.

Wynne shaded her eyes and watched a rider approach. The stranger paused across the stream, dismounted, then led his horse to the water. Maneuvering down on his knees with stiff, careful movements, he bent to cup his hands and drink. It appeared he was wearing some sort of brace on his back. He had no waist motion, and bending seemed an effort. She watched as he quenched his thirst.

"Someone you know?" Cole asked.

She frowned. "I think I've seen him before."

Cole's brow lifted sourly. "Oh?"

She watched awhile longer, her face pensive.

"Let's move on." Cole waded the horse out of the stream and waited while Wynne took another long drink then rose and joined him.

Their eyes met as she waited for him to help her up. He reached out as if he meant to touch her face then let his hand drop back to his side.

She gazed up at him expectantly. "What's the matter?"

"You have water on your nose."

"Oh." She reached up and wiped away the droplet then smiled at him. "There. Is that better?"

Cole nodded, keeping his eyes averted, and quickly lifted her into the saddle.

She was incredibly close, near enough for him to see into the depths of her green eyes. "I wish you wouldn't look at me that way," he said.

"And I wish you didn't look the way you do." Both tones were tempered with something close to affection. She watched him closely.

He gathered up the reins and turned away.

"Aren't you going to ride?" she asked when he walked the horse down the rutted lane.

"No, ma'am. I'm walking."

She stared at the stubborn set of his shoulders. Something was bothering him. Well, good. She was bothered, too. Their time together at the cabin had opened her eyes. She had never loved Cass. Not with the strong, sweet emotion she felt for Cole. She wanted to tell him how she felt, but she knew he wouldn't want to hear.

The time spent at the cabin had taught her something: she could never have killed Cass. That had been hurt and anger talking. She didn't believe God would have let her pull the trigger. She had sinned: lied, stolen, and determined in her heart to commit murder. God wouldn't let those sins go unpunished, and she feared her punishment would be more than she could bear. She'd learned what it was to love, but Cole could never be hers because the man she had planned to kill was his brother.

They made camp early. Wynne appreciated the thoughtful gesture. Both knew this would be their last night on the trail. Cole shot a rabbit, and she roasted the meat on a spit.

She glanced up to see him watching her, a look of sadness and regret in his expression. "What?"

"Nothing."

"There must be something. You've been watching me like that since we left the cabin."

"I was just thinking how pretty you are."

She stared at him before erupting into a laugh. "You can't be serious. Look at me. I've worn this dress for weeks, my hair is hanging half down my back, and I'm covered in trail grime. I know how I look. Try again."

He shook his head. "You beat anything, you know that? Try to give you a compliment and you throw it back. Is that any way to attract a man?"

Wynne jumped up, hands on hips, eyes flaming. "What makes you think I want to 'attract a man,' as you put it? Have I made any effort to *attract* you?"

"No, ma'am, you sure haven't," he said. He'd had women set their cap for him, and he knew the tricks. This one had mostly tried to kill him or get him killed. Maybe that was why he *was* attracted to her. The change of pace had thrown him. A man sort of expected a woman to be all wide-eyed and admiring. Cute and cuddly. This one looked at him like he was out of his mind. And probably he was. What else could explain the way he felt? His pulse raced like a sixteen-year-old's in the throes of puppy love, and this old dog had better rein in his imagination before he found himself walking down an aisle.

Wynne was peeved. Did that man *really* think she was attracted to him? Well, she was, but that didn't mean she had to put up with his behavior. From the moment they had left the cabin he had been acting funny. Like when they had seen that other rider at the stream. He'd seemed disturbed that she might know the man, and at first she had thought he was jealous, but then he froze her out until she felt like an outsider again.

"I didn't ask you to follow me," she said.

"Don't start that again." He pointed a finger at her. "You know why I followed you. I had family obligations."

"Well, you carried them out. I'm not after your brother anymore." She knew she was picking a fight with him, but she didn't care. At least if he was angry at her he was talking, and he'd done precious little of that since leaving the cabin.

Cole stared into the campfire, eyebrows knitted tightly together. "If Jeff Davis had given you a gun and put you on the front lines, the war would have been over in a week. The troops would have been so whipped down no one would have had enough gumption to fight."

She glared at him, unable to trust her ears. "I can't believe you said that. What have I done that makes you think I'm such a hooligan?"

She thought he was going to choke. "What *haven't* you done would be more like it. Think back a little. I believe you stole my rabbit."

Her jaw dropped in amazement. "That was weeks ago. I can't believe you're still upset about that. Are you the type to carry a grudge?"

He glared at her. "Who's the man back at the stream? The one you were so interested in."

She laughed. "You're jealous."

"I am not. I am, however, responsible for getting you back safely. So I'm asking you again, who is he?"

He was jealous. She was delighted! "I don't know who he is, but I've seen him somewhere—maybe on the first part of my journey—except then he had a splint on his leg. This time he seemed to have something wrong with his back." She grinned. "Very handsome man, don't you think?"

She laughed at the expression on his face, as if he had just bitten into a sour pickle. Cole might act like he was indifferent, but she had a feeling he was more aware of her than he let on.

Let me have him, Lord, and I'll never ask for anything else again.

"If you ask me, he looked kind of puny," Cole said.

"I didn't ask you." She resisted the urge to stick her tongue out at him. She flipped the stick away from the fire and removed the rabbit. "Supper's ready."

The following morning, Cole released an audible sigh of relief when the Claxton farm came into view. Wynne's close proximity the past two days had his nerves humming like telegraph lines. She had gone from saying nothing to picking on him. He could hear the teasing in her voice, and she seemed to be laughing at him most of the time. He couldn't turn her over to Ma and Betsy to see if they could do anything with her fast enough. In his opinion, which she hadn't asked for, no one could do anything with Wynne Elliot when she made up her mind to oppose him, which seemed to be about 100 percent of the time.

The courtyard was busy when he lifted Wynne off the mare. Tables and chairs had been set up in the cherry grove, and there was a general air of festivity.

"What's going on?" he wondered out loud.

"Looks like your mother's having a party."

Willa waved from the clothesline, her large body dipping up and down rhythmically as she retrieved the wet pieces one by one and pinned them into place.

Cole waved back, taking in all the commotion, then watched as Wynne started toward the house, her steps gradually slowing. Considering how she had sneaked out after Ma and Betsy had been so good to her, he figured she was having a case of guilt.

His heart contracted. She looked so shabby. He wanted to pick her up, dust her off, and protect her from curious eyes. But he couldn't do that. Wynne, like everyone else, would have to take the consequences of her behavior, and Ma and Betsy had a right to an explanation. He hoped Wynne didn't reveal her real reason for leaving. Ma probably wouldn't take kindly to hearing the woman she'd taken under her roof planned to shoot her baby boy.

Betsy came out of the house, her face lighting when she spotted the newcomers. She grabbed Wynne and hugged her exuberantly. "I do declare, you're a sight for sore eyes. Where in the *world* did you disappear to?"

"I had to leave suddenly." Wynne glanced at Cole, her face as red as the blossom on the rambler growing over the fence at the side of the house.

Cole watched, fascinated by the way women acted. Men would have shaken hands, and that would have been the end of it. Women, now, they hugged, cried, got embarrassed, talked, and made noise. A lot of noise.

Lilly poked her head out the door then flew across the porch, her feet barely touching the steps. "Wynne, darling, how good to see you back! And Cole! I do declare, this is a happy day!"

After a tight hug Lilly held Wynne's thin shoulders and surveyed her disreputable condition. "Oh dear, I suppose this means your trip has been unsuccessful. You didn't find your friend?"

Wynne looked down. "No, I wasn't able to find him."

"I'm so sorry."

"It's all right. I've changed my mind about trying to locate him." She lifted her eyes to meet Lilly's. "I'll be going back to Savannah instead."

"Well. . ." Lilly heaved a sigh and glanced in Cole's direction. "I suppose that would be for the best, but I was hoping you would stay for a while."

Cole approached the group of chattering females, figuring it was time to make his presence known.

"Land sakes alive! Finish your business in Kansas City at last?" Lilly hugged her oldest son, peering hopefully around him. "I don't guess you ran into your brother anywhere along the way?"

"No, Ma, but I heard Cass made it through the war."

"You did!" Lilly clapped her hands together. "Well, praise the Lord! I just knew he would. Surely he'll be riding in any day now."

Cole grinned and shrugged. "I suppose anything's possible."

"Why, of course it's possible," she said. "He'll be home anytime—you wait and see." She turned back to Wynne. "How did you get here, dear? I only heard one rider."

Cole slipped an arm around Wynne's waist. "I ran into Miss Elliot a ways back on the road. Her, uh, animal bolted and ran away, so I gave her a ride."

"Your horse ran away?" Lilly's face instantly filled with concern. Her eyes ran over the bedraggled young woman standing forlornly beside Betsy. "Why, I thought you left on the stage."

"No—no, I decided to buy other means of transportation."

Cole grinned at Wynne, and she kept her eyes on Lilly. He noticed she didn't mention the mule. She couldn't without telling the rest of the story. He didn't think she would want Ma and Betsy to hear the extent of her adventures.

"Great day! I'm glad I didn't know that." Lilly sighed. "I'd have worried myself to death. I hope you weren't hurt when the horse threw you, dear."

Wynne smiled. "Not a scratch." She brushed grime from her dirty dress, looking embarrassed. "But of course all my clothes went with it. Now I don't have a thing to wear."

Betsy rushed to allay her worries. "Don't you worry a bit. We'll get you into a hot tub of water, and after you're bathed, you can borrow some of my things. I'm a little larger, but I have a yellow calico that will look wonderful on you!"

"Thank you, Betsy. I would appreciate it." She glanced at Cole then looked away. Betsy draped a protective arm around her shoulders and led her toward the porch. His future sister-in-law was still chattering like a blue jay as the two women disappeared into the house.

Lilly followed at a slower pace, her arm wrapped around her son's waist. "You think she's really all right, dear?"

Cole's eyes pursued Wynne until he could no longer see her. "She's okay, Ma."

"She's sure a lucky little thing. Imagine, you coming along at the right moment to save her." Lilly glanced up, meeting his eyes. Cole felt a slow burn creep up his collar. Ma was smart; she'd give him the benefit of the doubt, but she knew coincidences were rare. He recognized that gleam in her eyes. She was matchmaking. She wanted her boys married to good, decent, God-fearing women. Well, she didn't know it, but he'd marry Wynne Elliot in a heartbeat if Cass hadn't proposed first.

"I suppose," he said. "Where's Beau?"

"Mending fences. He'll be along after a while to eat his dinner. How'd your business go in Kansas City?"

"Fine." His eyes took in the cherry orchard once more. "What's going on?"

"Oh, Beau and Betsy were getting all astir to announce their engagement. We decided we'd have an informal party—let friends and neighbors know that the wedding was still on."

"You were going to have an engagement party without me and Cass?" Cole said with mock astonishment. He knew Lilly would never consider such an event without having her entire family present.

"Why no, dear, the party isn't an official engagement announcement—more like a Saturday-night shindig. Beau and Betsy's actual wedding announcement won't be until later in the fall."

Cole squeezed his mother's shoulder. "I'm just teasing you, Ma. I know you wouldn't do that."

She reached up and tugged the wiry growth that lay dark and thick across his face. "I look at you and I see your daddy. My firstborn, and you're Sam Claxton all over again. It makes me want to shout for joy that the good Lord has left a small part of him on this earth to give me such comfort."

Cole grinned down at her. "Don't go all sentimental on me."

She playfully slapped his shoulder. "You think I don't know you and your tomfoolery by now? You get on into the house and tell Willa to fetch you some bathwater. There's going to be a party tonight." Her eyes sparkled with anticipation. "There's going to be singing and dancing the likes of which you haven't seen or heard for four long years!"

Chapter 16

Around four o'clock, buggies started arriving. Buckboards and surreys filled the Claxton courtyard. After four long years of war, folks were ready to celebrate. The melodious tones of fiddles and guitars filled the air, and the sound of laughter floated over the hillsides as the party got into full swing.

Wynne listened to the sounds of merriment floating through the open window while she finished dressing. She studied her reflection in the mirror and wondered if she'd ever feel the same. She had changed so much since leaving home. She looked the same on the outside, until she looked herself in the eyes. An older, wiser woman looked back at her. She had arranged her newly washed and dried hair in a mass of curls on top of her head and dusted a smidgeon of Betsy's face powder to conceal the freckles. Long days in the sun had damaged her skin. Tilly would be upset, and Miss Marelda would say she should have been more careful.

Wynne didn't care about her skin; it was her heart that had irreparable damage.

Tonight was intended for celebration; she didn't begrudge the silly shenanigans going on below, but her smile slowly faded when reality closed in on her. She only wished that she and Cole could be a part of the lightheartedness.

What a wondrous delight it would be if they could overcome the differences that lay between them. She wished he would swing her up in his arms and haul her off to the barn to steal a kiss. But Cole would never do that. He never teased her or showed his feelings, except for the brief moments when he let his guard down. And he would most assuredly never haul her off to the barn in front of everyone. Lilly would never stand for that sort of tomfoolery.

And she shouldn't be thinking of such things. Miss Marelda Fielding would be disappointed in her. According to her, ladies never thought about what she called "baser traits" until after marriage. Well, you could be fairly certain that Miss Marelda had never spent weeks alone with a man in an isolated cabin—all perfectly innocent. Cole had been nothing but a gentleman.

Her own thinking had been altered, though. She'd spent a lot of thought on the way she felt when Cole held her—particularly on the way she felt when he kissed her. She could tell Miss Marelda a thing or two about kissing and thinking that would make her eyes pop.

Wynne smoothed the skirt of the yellow calico. She would miss Betsy when she left. Good friends were hard to come by, and Betsy was a good friend. God had granted Beau someone special, and by the look in his eyes when he held his fiancée, he recognized the gift. The two would have a good life together. She was happy for them, but she couldn't shake the envy.

The two women had talked long into the afternoon. Betsy had encouraged her to stay in River Run, but Wynne would not be convinced. She planned to leave on tomorrow's stage, and her decision was final. There was absolutely no reason for her to remain where she was not welcome.

Cole's aloof behavior during the ride home proved to her that he would make no effort to change her mind. She had teased and goaded him, trying to get a rise, but he had remained steadfastly detached. If he cared about her, he would have said something—anything—to keep her from leaving, and he hadn't. On the contrary, he'd offered to pay for the stagecoach ticket.

She rested her case.

When she'd informed him of her decision an hour ago, he'd met her announcement with the same indifference he had shown when they first met. He'd merely asked that she be ready by first light, and he'd take her into town and *buy* a ticket, if that was what she wanted.

So tomorrow morning she would be on her way back to Savannah with a broken heart, but at least it would be a fresh break. She would do her best to revive Moss Oak and turn it into a paying plantation again, but her heart and thoughts would always be back here in Missouri.

It would have been better if she had never set off on this wild chase for revenge, but God had taught her a lesson, one she should have known all along. Sin brings shame to the name of Christ, and her heart had been full of sin when she met Cole. Sin robbed her of God's blessings, and most of all, sin only complicated life, not enhanced it.

She leaned her arms on the windowsill, watching the people below. *I knew all along it was wrong to want to kill anyone, Lord. And I know that thinking those thoughts was a sin. I know I couldn't have gone through with it, and I'm glad I was never put to the test. Wherever Cass is, give him a safe trip back home to Lilly. She's so worried. And please, God, when I leave tomorrow, don't let me cry until I get out of town.*

Betsy's knock on the door interrupted her prayer. "You ready to go down now?"

"As ready as I'll ever be."

They walked down the stairway together and were greeted by whistles of male admiration. Beau waited at the foot of the stairs to claim his Betsy, while Wynne was surrounded by friendly, smiling men anxious to catch her attention. But there was only one man's reaction she wanted, and he was nowhere to be seen.

It was late evening before Cole joined the festivities in the cherry orchard. Wynne's heart threatened to stop when she saw him pause to speak to Betsy's sister, Priscilla June. He looked utterly striking: clean shaven, wearing a jacket and dress pants. Wynne was certain that her love for him was written so clearly on her face that everyone would know her secret.

She wasn't the only one who had spotted his entrance. A crowd of women had gathered, vying for his attention, but Priscilla had already staked her claim. She cooed and fussed over Cole until Wynne wanted to march over and snatch her bald-headed.

Cole glanced up from saying something to Priscilla, and their eyes met; suddenly for Wynne, every other person at the party disappeared.

She struggled to hide her emotions but knew she failed miserably. She could only stare back at him with her heart in her eyes and pray he wouldn't look away.

The blue of his eyes darkened as they gently ran the length of the yellow calico. She knew the dress fit her nicely—and was her color. Betsy had given her a locket, and the gold sparkled at her neckline. Her hair was arranged in the latest style. Funny how knowing you looked good gave a person more confidence. She lifted her chin, smiling slightly.

Waiting.

For a moment they stood transcended in time. It was as if the world held no one else but them. And then he smiled at her, a slow, easy smile that told her he had not forgotten what they had shared.

She smiled back, enough to let him know that she understood and shared his remembrances. They would be all she had to cling to after tomorrow. No matter what the future held for her, the days spent with Cole at the cabin would be a golden treasure to be kept forever.

The magic was broken when Priscilla took his arm. Wynne moved through the crowd, biting back welling tears. Cole would marry Priscilla June. Or he would if Miss Pris got her way. No matter. She wouldn't be here to see it. Let him do whatever he wanted. She didn't care.

The night blurred. She danced and laughed and tried to forget that after tomorrow she would never see Cole Claxton again.

Around midnight she gave up all pretenses and slipped quietly around the corner of the house to go to her room.

Cole's voice stopped her when she reached Lilly's flower garden. "Turning in so early?"

Her footsteps faltered. Closing her eyes, she took a deep breath. She didn't have the strength to stand another encounter with him tonight. "I'm a little tired."

"I can imagine. It was a long trip, and you have another one facing you tomorrow."

"That's right." Wynne could only see a darker shape where he blended into the shadows of the shrubbery, but his cologne drifted to her. Soft. Musky. "If you'll excuse me?" She gathered her light shawl around her shoulders and started to walk on.

"What's your hurry, Miss Elliot?" he asked in an easy tone.

Her steps faltered again. *Walk on. Walk on!* "I told you. I'm very tired."

He stepped out of the shadows and joined her. Her breath caught and held as she gazed up at him. The rays of the silvery moonlight played across his face, and she longed to have him take her in his arms and tell her that he loved her, that it didn't matter what she had been about to do to his brother. The only thing that really mattered was that she was in love with him now, and it would be sheer insanity to throw away that rare, wondrous miracle simply because of her past foolhardiness.

He could do worse in a bride, Wynne told herself. She could make him proud. She would use all the skills Miss Marelda had taught her until one day he would look at her as a lady, not some bumbling nincompoop!

But how did she tell him without making a complete fool of herself? He'd made it clear that he didn't return her feelings. He would only laugh and tell her she obviously didn't know what man she loved. First Cass, now him.

She could never bear that.

She turned and started on, but his hand reached out and blocked her. "Don't go in yet." His earlier arrogance was gone. Instead, his tone held a soft, almost urgent plea. Her breath caught when he swung her roughly around and into his arms.

She melted like snow on a warm day. The world stood still. This was what she'd wanted, what she'd longed for all evening. His mouth lowered to kiss her.

She could only guess where the embrace would have ended if Beau hadn't interrupted. "Wynne? Are you out there?"

Cole caught her back possessively. "Don't answer." His mouth captured hers again with fierceness that shook her to the core.

Beau's voice persisted. He came closer to where they stood sheltered in the shadows of a lilac bush. "Wynne?"

"I have to answer," she whispered between broken kisses. "In a few minutes he'll see us, Cole."

He must have realized the truth of her words, because he slowly released her. A moment later she stepped quietly out of the shadows. "Yes, Beau?"

"Oh, there you are." He came forward with a large grin on his face. "There's someone here looking for you."

"Me?" Wynne asked with surprise.

Beau shrugged. "Yeah. Some fella came riding in a while ago. Said he would have been here earlier, but his horse threw a shoe. Oh, hey, Cole. Didn't see you standing back there." His grin widened.

"Who's looking for her?"

"Don't know. Some man who says it's real important that he talk to Wynne."

"She's not talking to any man tonight," Cole said flatly. "Tell him to come back tomorrow morning and call on her proper."

"Good heavens, Cole. He's not *calling on* me," Wynne protested, thrilled to hear jealousy seeping into his voice. She couldn't imagine who her visitor could be. She didn't know anyone in River Run. "Where is the man, Beau?"

"He's waiting in the parlor. Ma made him sit down and drink something cool. He looked a mite peaked when he got here."

Wynne glanced at Cole. "It wouldn't hurt for me to see what he wants, would it?" She couldn't bear the curiosity until morning.

Cole shrugged, looking cross. "I don't like it, but go ahead. Talk to the man."

She smiled and turned to leave when Beau spoke up again. "Aren't you going to go with her?"

"I don't tell her who she can talk to," Cole said curtly, but Wynne was pleased to see that he followed at a distance. After all, she didn't know who was waiting out there. It might even be

Sonny Morgan coming to press his claim to her. She felt better to know Cole would be close by.

When Wynne entered the parlor, the young man waiting for her smiled in spite of his obvious discomfort. She could see the back brace he wore was hot and bothering him something fierce. He looked frazzled, as if it was the end of a long and particularly tedious day.

When Wynne approached, his face immediately went slack with astonishment. For a moment the two stared at each other. Then she broke into a smile and moved across the room to take his hand. "Well, hello again." He was the same young man she had seen twice before. Once sitting on a porch, whittling, when she had ridden through Springfield, and again when she and Cole had stopped to water their horse.

"*You're* Wynne Elliot!" His voice cracked, sounding as though he were in the throes of puberty.

She smiled expectantly. "Yes."

A protruding Adam's apple bobbed up and down as he tried to regain his composure. "Miss Elliot. . .I had no idea that was you. . . ." His voice trailed off.

Wynne continued to smile at the pale young man, wondering what in heaven's name he wanted with her. If Cole thought she was addlebrained, he should meet this man. He seemed to have trouble putting his thoughts together.

He wiped his hand nervously on the side of his trousers then politely extended it to her. "Bertram G. Mallory, ma'am."

"Mr. Mallory." Wynne tipped her head and accepted his hand, the way Miss Marelda had taught her. Perhaps this was another one of the lawyers from her father's estate, though he certainly didn't look like a lawyer. Matter of fact, he looked like a saddle tramp, but you couldn't always tell.

"Oh ma'am, you don't know how nice it is to finally meet you!"

"Why, thank you." She smiled again. "I believe you wanted to speak to me?"

"Oh yes, ma'am. I still can't realize you're standing in front of me. I'm with Pinkerton's National Detective Agency—you've heard of us, haven't you?"

Wynne nodded. She had read about Allan Pinkerton from Glasgow, Scotland, in a paper one time. He now lived in Chicago and had made a name for himself by recovering a large sum of money for the Adams Express Company. The paper had said he was also credited with foiling a plot to murder President Abraham Lincoln.

"Well, ma'am, I was hired by Mr. Claxton to return this to you." He began to search through his pockets, extracting his billfold, a comb, a pocketknife, and his gun, all of which he promptly handed to her. "Excuse me, ma'am, could you hold these for a moment?"

"Yes, certainly." Wynne took the items, and he continued his search. "You said Mr. Claxton sent you?"

"Yeah. . .yeah. . .now, wait. . . . I know it's here somewhere." His face suddenly brightened. "Yes! Here it is!" He quickly slapped a leather pouch into her hand and immediately smiled as if a ton of weight had just been lifted off his shoulders.

"Cass. . .Claxton?" she asked. Her smile faded.

"Yes, ma'am. It's the money you lent him."

Wynne's hand clasped the pouch and the wallet and the comb and the gun. Her eyes narrowed in anger. If this was someone's idea of a joke, it wasn't funny. "The money I *lent* him? What are you talking about?"

"It's all there, ma'am. Every cent of it—with interest. Cass gave it to me to give back to you the day you two were supposed to be married." Bertram peered back at her from eyes that were bloodshot and ringed with road grime, but they were good, honest eyes. "I've tried real hard to find you, ma'am. I surely have. I had been in bed with a bad case of the miseries the day Mr. Claxton came to my door, so I couldn't bring the money over then. I got up early the next morning and went to your house, but you were already gone back to Miss Fielding's school, so I went looking for you there, but I missed you again."

He sighed hopelessly. "From then on every time I got close to you, either you disappeared again or I had another one of those. . .accidents."

Wynne smiled sympathetically. "I noticed you had been injured."

Bertram sighed. "Just thinking about my ordeals makes my ribs, my legs, and my back start to pain all over again. I've not had an easy time, ma'am, and I'd appreciate it if you told Mr. Claxton so—on account of me being so late in finding you."

He drew a cleansing breath. "Then I heard you were on your way to River Run, so I figured I'd try to catch you before you got to Mr. Claxton's folks. He told me he came from River Run originally, and he'd been visiting kinfolk in Savannah. I was afraid you'd arrive ahead of me and be under the impression Mr. Claxton swindled you out of your money, which would be a tragic misunderstanding, because Mr. Claxton has the highest ethics. I'm afraid it was I who dropped the ball." Bertram hung his head sheepishly. "Sure sorry I didn't make it in time. I know you must be thinking all sorts of bad things about Mr. Claxton—and, ma'am? About his intentions to marry you? I am to inform you that he loved you, but he developed a case of what is known as cold feet. I believe he decided it would be unfair to you to continue with the nuptials—and he didn't have the heart to tell you. He told me he knew he was making the mistake of his life, but his conscience prevented him from marrying."

While Bertram rattled on, Wynne battled through a range of emotions: disbelief, jubilation, incredulity, exultation. If what Mr. Mallory was saying was true, then these horrendous past few months had been for nothing! She had been running around vowing revenge on a man who was guilty of nothing more serious than marriage aversion. Cass hadn't wanted to *hurt* her even more by going through with an ill-advised wedding, which actually made a lot of sense.

Wynne's knees turned to water, and she stared at Bertram's gun, still in her hand. What if she had been able to find Cass? She would never have actually killed him—she couldn't. No, never. In a way Cass's rejection had been a blessing. She knew now that what she had felt for him was not love, not when she compared her feelings for Cole. Her smile faded. And what was *he* going to say, other than "I told you so," when he learned that his brother had made provisions to return the money all along? She had been too busy seeking revenge to stop long enough for Mr. Mallory to find her.

She breathed a long, deep sigh. It was all very confusing.

"Ma'am?" Bertram looked like he wasn't quite sure how she was taking the news.

She glanced up. "Yes?"

"Are you. . .all right?"

"Oh yes. Better than all right, Mr. Mallory." Or at least she would be as soon as she was able to digest the shocking news. "I can't thank you enough for finally locating me. You've made me a happy woman."

"Oh, that's all right, ma'am." Bertram gathered up his wallet and comb from her safekeeping. "Mr. Claxton paid me handsomely; I'm only doing my job."

"Nevertheless, I am grateful. You have a great dedication to duty, Mr. Mallory."

"Thank you, ma'am; I try."

She thought he looked rather sad. Perhaps his back was hurting him.

Outside someone let out a loud war whoop as the sound of approaching hoofbeats thundered into the yard. A crescendo of voices rang out. "Cass! Cass is coming!"

Bertram stepped to the window and lifted the curtain. "Oh my, looks like Mr. Claxton could have delivered the money a whole lot easier. Uh, maybe there's a back door? If so, I'll excuse myself and be on my way. I have my own wedding to attend in Springfield."

Wynne suddenly came back to life, the shock of the past few moments finally wearing off. "Good heavens! Cass is home!"

An hour ago those words would have meant very little, but now all she could feel was extreme joy. Cole and Beau would have their brother back, and Lilly's youngest son would have returned home safely.

Letting out a squeal that would have shocked Miss Marelda right down to her prissy old corset, Wynne bolted toward the front door. She wanted to be one of the first to greet him. Cass was home, and he wasn't the scoundrel she had thought him to be at all! She had to tell him she forgave him and make peace. Then maybe she and Cole. . .

She skidded to a stop halfway across the parlor and whirled around to rush back and give Bertram a large, energetic hug. "Oooooh, thank you, Mr. Mallory; thank you ever so much!" She spun around and raced out the wide parlor door at full speed.

"Ma'am, my gun—"

Wynne heard him, but his words barely registered. Cass was home.

Cole was on his way to check on Wynne when she buzzed by him like an angry hornet, flailing a gun in the air, nearly bowling him over in her hasty exit.

"Hey, where's the fire?"

He reached out to slow her passage, but she shrugged his hand away and yelled over her shoulder, "Can't stop now! Cass is home!"

A man Cole vaguely remembered seeing before ran past him, calling in a panicked voice, "Ma'am, my gun!"

The smile on Cole's face drained when the meaning of Wynne's words sank in. And she had been waving a gun. He tore off after her.

"Wynne, wait!" he shouted.

Wynne burst through the crowd on the porch and down the steps, racing toward the rider who had just entered the courtyard.

Bertram was making progress in his dash to intercept her when Cole rushed by like a streak of lightning. Mallory slowed and grabbed a nearby table for support.

"Sorry, fella." Cole hurriedly steadied the swaying form. Bertram straightened up and readjusted his hat, and Cole started running again. "Wynne!" he shouted. "Don't do it!"

He had the impression that everyone had stopped what they were doing and frozen in position, like a child's game where no one could move except on command. He knew he and Wynne were making a spectacle of themselves and that he was going to have to come up with a full explanation to Ma for acting like this when guests were present, but he had to stop Wynne before she made the biggest mistake of her life.

"Wynne! No! I won't let you do it!"

A dog ran between his feet, slowing him. He took a flying leap and tackled her as Cass reined his horse to a skidding halt.

Cole knew Cass was sitting openmouthed on his horse, watching his older brother knock Wynne Elliot off her feet. He had to be wondering what was going on. Well, join the party. So was half the county. Cole had always been conscious of his position as the head of the family, but now he had just driven a woman to the ground in front of practically everyone he knew. His reputation was shot.

Over to the side, the stranger had managed to get one foot in the stirrup, but his horse was antsy with all the racket going on. The man couldn't mount, nor could he get his foot loose.

Cole knew someone should go to the stranger's rescue, but he had his hands full right now. Evidently his landing on her had not only surprised Wynne, it made her mad. Extremely mad.

"Get *off* me!" she screeched, kicking and elbowing him. "What in the world is the matter with you?"

"Don't do it!" Cole tried to still her flailing limbs, fighting to gain control of the gun. His heavy body pinned her to the ground. He grasped her wrists tightly and pinned them above her head. "Don't. . .Wynne."

"Don't *what*? What are you babbling about?"

"Don't shoot him—please."

"Shoot him? What are you talking about?"

Cole's eyes locked with hers, and he pried the gun from her hand. He saw realization dawn in her eyes. She looked down at the handgun he now held out of her reach.

"Oh darling! I wasn't going to shoot him!" she exclaimed. "I was going to thank him for being so honest and nice. . ." Her words trailed off when his eyes narrowed with disbelief.

Cole felt anger swell his chest to the bursting point. He knew from the expression on Wynne's face that he was scaring her.

"*Thank* him!" he exploded.

He had nearly killed himself these past few weeks trying to prevent his brother from being ambushed by her, and now she was going to *thank* Cass for being so nice! What was wrong with this woman? Was it asking too much for her to act sane? He never knew where he was with her, and that was a real handicap to a man who was used to being in charge.

"Well, yes. . ." Wynne slowly got to her feet, dusting off the yellow calico. "You see, that man who wanted to see me in the parlor. . ."

Cole listened with amazement to her explanation until the sound of running horses caught their attention.

With a boil of dust and a loud "Ho! Ho, there!" a buckboard driven by a rather flamboyant young woman swung crazily into the yard. She bounded down in a flash of red satin and rushed to the stranger's rescue.

"Fancy!" the man blurted, dancing on one foot to keep up with the horse.

"Oh Bertie, darling, let me help you." She grabbed the reins of the horse and managed to still the animal while Bertram jerked his bound foot free from the stirrup.

"What are you doing here?" he asked.

Cole watched as the woman reached out and reverently touched the man's cheek. "I thought you might need me, Bertie, and I wasn't taking any chances. You, Bertram G. Mallory, are a rare man, and you are *mine*."

"Aw, Fancy, I do need you." Bertram grinned humbly. "For the rest of my life."

Cole shook his head, thunderstruck. Now that was a woman who knew how to treat a man. He hoped Wynne was paying attention. She could stand a lesson in men versus women—and come to think of it, he probably could stand one, too. He was glad to be home and glad Cass was all right, but he had some business of his own to take care of.

By now Cass had leaped off the horse, and Lilly had him in a tearful embrace. Cole wasn't going to worry about him anymore. He gave his full attention to Wynne Elliot and her continuing explanation, most of which he had missed in all of the commotion.

"—and so you see, darling, I don't *hate* Cass anymore," Wynne was saying. "He didn't steal my money or my heart. I just thought he did."

"You. . .*thought* you were in love with him."

She nodded. "But I'm not."

He heaved a relieved sigh. "Then you've finally got all this avenging nonsense out of your head?"

Wynne nodded, gazing up at him.

Cole cocked his head and looked back at her. "Any idea of what man you might love?"

She nodded.

"Well?"

"I'm not saying until you say what you're supposed to say."

"What if I say it and you don't agree?"

"That's what we'll have to find out, isn't it?"

She had him beat. He was in love with her, and she knew it. Clearing his throat, he said softly, "I don't know how good I'll be at saying it." Cole had never told any woman he loved her.

"Just say it," she begged, her hands framing his face.

"I love you," he admitted. "I think I loved you the day I met you. I know you might have reason to doubt those words coming from a Claxton, but I mean them, Wynne." He pulled her closer, his mouth only inches away from hers. "You *know* I mean them."

She gazed up at him with those beautiful eyes, looking lovelier and more kissable than any woman ought to look. "You really do?"

Cole suddenly felt playful. "Are you strong as a bull moose, healthy as a horse? Can you wrestle an Indian brave, cut a rick of wood without raising a sweat, and still be soft and fresh as lilacs?" He already knew the answer; he'd known it for weeks.

She smiled at him sweetly. "I can be anything you want me to be."

He pulled her closer. "I really love you, lady." They kissed, oblivious to the stares.

She drew back only momentarily. "Well, there is Moss Oak. . . . I don't know. . ." The teasing light in her eyes said she was joining in the fun.

"We'll live at Moss Oak, or we'll live in Missouri, but wherever we are, we'll be together. I believe God has brought us together, Wynne, and I want you beside me every day of my life."

She turned serious. "You honestly believe that?"

"I do, and I think we've fought Him long enough, don't you? Do you want a double wedding or one of our own?"

She didn't hesitate for a moment. "Which will be the quickest?"

He grinned. She blushed.

"Our own, then. Next Sunday. I'm an impatient man, lady. What's so funny?" he asked when her grin widened.

"I thought you didn't know the meaning of romance, but I'm learning you're a romantic at heart."

Cole bent to kiss her a second time. "Well now, you've got a lot to learn about me, lady."

"Ummm," Wynne whispered, "I can hardly wait." He had a feeling life with this woman would never be dull.

He smiled. *God, let me be up to the challenge.*

THE DRIFTER
BOOK 2

Prologue

Missouri, September 1867

The day started out like any other. The pungent aroma of earth mingled pleasantly with the tangy smell of sweat rolling in rivulets down the back of the tall, powerfully built man gently urging the team of oxen to pull the heavy plow. Overhead, the bright sun hammered down on man and animals as they steadfastly went about furrowing the ground for fall planting.

Nature's elements rarely bothered Beau Claxton. Truth be told, nothing much bothered him because he was an inordinately happy man. The good Lord provided a roof over his head, food on his table, close family ties—and he had the prettiest, sweetest woman in all of Missouri for his wife.

As far as Beau was concerned, he had everything a man could ever want.

Oh, he had to admit that times were hard. The country was trying to put itself back together since the War Between the States, and many people still went to bed hungry every night, but he knew the Claxtons had fared better than most. God had been good to him, and life couldn't be better.

Beau's mother, Lilly, still lived on the old homestead a couple of miles down the road. His father, Samuel Claxton, had moved his wife and their two sons from Georgia to Missouri when Beau and his older brother, Cole, had been tykes. Cass, his youngest brother, had been born shortly before Samuel died. Cole and his wife, Wynne, now lived two miles on the other side of Beau's land. Fifteen months ago they'd produced a baby boy named Jeremy, who was growing like a weed and cute as a bug's ear.

Beau had to grin when he thought about how downright silly Cole was about his wife. They both acted like love-struck youngsters whenever they were together. He would've bet his spring crop that no woman could have worked Cole Claxton into such a lather, but two years ago the feisty little woman from Savannah had waltzed in and stolen Cole's heart, and the man hadn't been the same since.

But Beau understood how Cole felt. He gave a sharp whistle for Sally to pull right, and his grin broadened. Hadn't Betsy Collins done the same thing to him? He recalled how they'd no sooner decided to marry than war had broken out. He'd left to join the fight, and when he returned, Betsy was waiting for him. Though they'd married two years ago, she could still make his insides go soft when she smiled up at him with those big eyes the color of a January sky.

The thought of holding her in his arms made his heart skip a beat. He thanked the good Lord every day for giving her to him. Any day now, they'd be having their own child—a son, he hoped, though a little girl wouldn't upset him any. It had taken forever for Betsy to get in the family way, but the doc had said she was healthy as a new pup and should be able to have all the babies they wanted. Beau wanted a large family.

"Easy, girls, easy." Beau turned the oxen and leaned over to wipe his dusty face on the sleeve of his sweat-dampened shirt. The days were still hot, even though they were nearing the end of September. He'd be glad to welcome the cooler days and crisp October nights. There was still a lot of work to be done before winter. He had to butcher the old sow, lay in a good supply of firewood, and stock the root cellar. . . .

The sound of Betsy's voice caused him to glance up and slow the team's pace. He grinned at her and waved. Must be close to noon, and she was bringing his dinner. His mouth watered at the thought of the fatback and corn bread she'd have in his dinner pail. She'd been making fried-apple pies when he'd left the house. No doubt she'd packed a couple of those, too.

He heard her call again, and he whistled for Kate and Sally to stop. Strange, he thought, Betsy wasn't running toward him like she usually did. He enjoyed watching her move, smooth and graceful as the prairie grasses rippling in the wind. After their meal, they'd often lie under the old cottonwood tree talking and kissing. Like as not, it'd be well past his allotted rest hour when he'd finally go back to work.

Betsy called his name a third time, and Beau's smile began to fade. He dropped the reins and shaded his eyes against the hot sun to see her more clearly.

Her slender frame, swollen with child, was silhouetted against a broad expanse of blue sky. For a moment he hesitated, expecting Betsy to start toward him again. But she lifted her hand feebly in the air and then dropped to her knees.

Cold fear shot through him. Something was wrong. The baby. *Yes, that's it,* he reasoned. He started running. The baby was coming, and Betsy was scared. How many times had he told her not to be afraid; he'd be there with her when their child was born? He'd be there to share her pain, to hold her hand, to tell her how proud he was that she was the mother of his child. Together they'd share an incredible joy when their son or daughter came into the world.

He was running fast now, sucking long, deep breaths as he watched Betsy slump to the ground. His feet covered the hard-packed dirt with lightning speed. "I'm coming, Bets!" he called to her. *God, don't let her be afraid.*

She lifted her head once as if she was trying to answer him, but with growing horror, Beau saw her fall back limply to the ground.

"God. . .oh God. . .please." Beau's lungs felt as though they'd explode. He ran harder. Something deep inside told him that this was more than labor pains, but he refused to listen. On he went, over rough tufts of ground, his boots gouging the dry, crusty earth, his eyes never once leaving the silent form crumpled close to the woodpile.

It couldn't be anything serious. She was teasing him. . . . No, Betsy never tried to scare him. . . . It had to be the baby. . . . Maybe she was going to have a harder time than most. The pains were sharp, and she'd dropped to the ground to wait for him. That must be it.

Gut-wrenching fear gripped his windpipe. Beau pushed himself faster. Betsy wasn't moving. She lay on the ground in deathlike stillness.

When he finally reached her, he fell to his knees and gathered her in his arms. His heart pounded, his breath coming in painful gasps as he cradled her head and called her name.

At the sound of his voice, her eyes slowly opened and she smiled at him. She reached up with trembling fingers to touch his cheek, and he saw his tears drop gently on her hand.

"What is it, sweetheart? The baby. . .is it the baby?" he prompted.

"My baby. . ." she whispered softly, so softly that he could scarcely make out her words. "Dear God, Beau. . .our baby. . ."

"Bets, what's wrong? Tell me, sweetheart. Should I get Ma or Wynne?"

She lifted her hand to cover his lips. "Snake. . .over by the woodpile. . .rattler. . .don't worry. . .dead now. . ."

Rattler! The word hit him with the force of a bullet, and suddenly he felt his heart drop to his stomach.

He whirled, his distraught gaze searching the woodpile by the house until he saw the horrifying evidence. A timber rattlesnake, almost seven feet in length, was stretched out on the ground. Its head, severed by a hoe, lay in the dust some distance away. The small pile of wood Betsy had been gathering was scattered about the area, mute testimony of what had happened. Betsy had encountered the snake unexpectedly while gathering wood for the stove.

Frantically, Beau began searching for the fang marks. If she'd been bitten by a rattler, there wasn't much time.

"Where's the bite?" Beau's voice trembled, but he fought to remain calm. He didn't want to scare her more. She moaned softly, and he remembered that she should be still. The more she moved, the quicker the poison would spread through her body. "Don't move, sweetheart, I'll find it, I'll find it!" His eyes and hands searched her body. It didn't take long to locate the two small puncture marks on her right arm. He bit back a curse when he saw the angry swelling. The rattler's fangs had hit the vein dead-on.

Beau swallowed the tight knot in his throat. He knew without being told that the poison would go straight to her heart; there was nothing, nothing he could do to save her.

Swiftly, he pulled his knife from his pocket and cut two small slits across the vein. He brought her arm to his mouth and sucked the venom then spat it on the ground while he stemmed the tears brimming in his eyes.

When he'd done all he knew to do, he talked to her in soft, reassuring tones. "I love you, Bets. More than I can ever say. We've had a good life together, and we're going to have a lot more good days, you and me and our baby."

She didn't answer, and he held her closer. "Don't be afraid, darlin'. I won't let anything hurt you."

Her eyelids fluttered open, and he brushed a lock of hair back from her forehead. "I'm sorry I was so neglectful. I'll keep that wood box filled every day from now on, I promise."

He should have done that anyway, he agonized, though Betsy had insisted on carrying the wood herself.

"Don't leave me, Bets," he pleaded when he heard her moans growing weaker. "I have to go for help," he murmured. "I have to get the doc out here—"

"No. . .no. . .stay with me, Beau." Her hands anxiously clasped him, and he rested his head on the swollen mound of her stomach. They both started to sob.

Beau lifted his face to the sky. Tears streamed down his face. "Dear God. . . Oh, please, God, don't let her die. I know I've not been all I could be, but don't make Betsy pay for my sins. Lord, I love her so much. If You'll spare her, I promise I'll do better. I'll live my life for You every day."

Betsy's lashes fluttered, and he could see a change—but not the one he wanted to see. Anger filled him, anger at his Maker. "You're supposed to be a God who cares, a God who watches over us!" Just last Sunday the pastor had spoken of a benevolent God who wanted to do good things for His people. Surely such a God wouldn't take Beau's wife and child from him in such a cruel, senseless act.

"What kind of God are You?" he raged. "How can I trust You when You let this happen to Betsy? She trusted You!" He could see her slipping away from him, and his heart turned to stone.

Paralyzed with fear, Beau clutched Betsy and crooned to her, rocking her gently back and forth, back and forth, until the sun dipped low on the western horizon. The golden rays spread across the parched earth, enveloping the young couple in an ethereal light. Still Beau wouldn't let go.

He didn't know the exact moment she left him. His arms had grown numb from holding her, yet he would not release her. If he put her down, she'd be gone from him forever. He couldn't accept that.

His brother Cole found them.

Cole's tall frame swung out of the saddle as he dismounted and hurried to where Beau sat cradling Betsy in his arms.

"Beau? What's wrong?"

Beau cried openly—deep, heartrending sobs that shook his entire frame. He clasped his young wife tightly to him, murmuring her name over and over. He saw Cole's concern, but he couldn't find the words to answer. He moved his head, indicating the snake.

Cole's eyes focused on the lifeless body of the rattler on the ground beside the woodpile.

The horror of his expression told that he realized the full extent of what had happened. "Oh Beau. I'm sorry."

Cole gently reached to lift Betsy from his brother's arms.

"No. . .no. . .don't take her, Cole." Beau spoke for the first time, his voice steady.

"I have to take her."

Beau tightened his grip around his wife's body. He shook his head.

"Give her to me," Cole commanded softly.

Since the day Sam Claxton had died of a heart attack, Cole had been father and brother to Beau and Cass. He'd been there for them through the good and bad times, and they still looked upon him as head of the household. Beau couldn't go against years of strict obedience. He reluctantly relinquished his hold.

"Don't hurt her," he whispered hoarsely.

"I'll take good care of her."

Carefully lifting her in his arms, Cole stood and carried Betsy into the house. Beau stumbled after him. He'd built that house for Betsy, and they had lived and loved here, planned for their family. He'd thought they would grow old together here. Now the house they'd loved was an empty shell. Betsy was gone.

The Claxtons were a prominent family in River Run. Just about everyone turned out for Betsy's funeral. "Such a lovely young thing," the townspeople whispered among themselves. Why had tragedy struck such a fine couple when they'd only begun to live? What would poor Beau do now? She was so young. . .and the innocent baby she was carrying. . .why, it would have been born soon. . .horrible. . .just terrible. . .simply unthinkable. . .

Beau hadn't shed a tear since the afternoon Cole had found him holding Betsy. Standing straight and tall between his two brothers, he kept his face an empty mask as the preacher droned on.

At the graveside, he watched as his mother, Lilly Claxton, wrapped her arms around Betsy's mother and suffered with her. He knew as far as Lilly was concerned, Betsy had been more than a daughter-in-law; she had been one of her own.

Beau showed no emotion until the first spade of dirt fell atop the simple pine coffin. When the sound reached his ears, he flinched as if he'd been burned, but he kept his eyes dry and his face stoic. Betsy, his Betsy, was in that pine box, lost to him forever, and he had nothing left to live for. After the burial he turned and walked away without a backward glance.

Wynne Claxton, flanked on either side by Cole and Cass, approached Beau. Wynne handed baby Jeremy to his father and enfolded her brother-in-law in her arms, hugging him tightly. "We share your pain, Beau, and we love you very much," she whispered.

"I don't know how I can go on. . . ." Beau's brave facade shattered, and his voice filled with raw emotion. Even God had forsaken him.

"But you will. You will, Beau."

For a fraction of an instant Beau tightened his arm around Wynne; then he dropped it back to his side and walked on.

Cole matched stride with his brother as Beau marched to his horse.

"Why don't you come over and spend a few days with Wynne and me?" he invited. "You don't have to go back home until you're ready."

"Thanks, but I'll be leaving for a while." Beau paused and turned to face his brothers.

"Leaving? Where are you going?" Cass demanded.

Beau's gaze rested upon the small mound of newly turned dirt. "I don't know. Away somewhere."

"Aw, Beau, I can understand you feeling that way, but don't you think this is a bad time to be running off?" Cass protested. "Tell him, Cole. He shouldn't be wandering around by himself. . .not right now."

Cole shook his head. "I think he should do what he feels he has to, Cass."

Beau looked into Cole's clear blue gaze and saw a silent understanding. He nodded. "Thanks. Bets. . .well, she'd have appreciated all you've done. . . ."

Cole clasped Beau's shoulder. "Let us know when you're ready to come home."

"I will. I want you to take Kate and Sally and the rest of my stock."

"I'll see to them for you."

Beau reached out and touched Jeremy's nose, drawing a happy gurgle from the baby. "Take good care of this little fella." Bright tears stood in Beau's eyes. He thought about his own baby and what might have been.

"You take care of yourself," Cole said.

Beau nodded. "Tell Ma not to worry." Slowly, he mounted his horse and pulled his hat low on his forehead.

"She'll worry anyway—you know Ma," said Cass. Beau realized his younger brother still wasn't sold on the idea of his leaving. "A man needs his family at a time like this. Let us know where you are, you hear?"

Beau's eyes returned to Betsy's grave and lingered there. "I hear."

Trouble was, he didn't care.

Chapter 1

Kansas, November 1868

"Shoo! Shooeee! Get out of here you—you. Shoo! Shooee! Get out of here! You—you miserable. . .ungrateful. . .ham hock!"

Charity Burk was determined to show no pity as she swatted the old sow across her fat rump and herded her back out the front door. It was a sad day when a woman couldn't step outside to hang the wash without being invaded by pigs!

She slammed the heavy wooden door and leaned against it to catch her breath. She had to do something about getting the fence back up.

Her husband, Ferrand, had died in the war four years ago, and since his death Charity had been on her own. Not that she wanted to be—far from it. She wasn't equipped to homestead in this desolate land, nor had she ever entertained the least desire to do so, but shortly after they'd married, her husband had decided to take advantage of the federal government's Homestead Act, signed into law in May of '62.

She could still remember how excited he had been the day he'd come home, swung her into his arms, and announced they were moving to Kansas. "A hundred and sixty acres, Charity. Think of it! They'll give us a hundred and sixty acres of whatever land we stake out."

Kansas? For a girl who'd spent all her life in Virginia, Kansas sounded like the end of the earth. Charity had paced the parlor of her ancestral home, wondering aloud why Ferrand would want to run off to some foreign land when they had a perfectly good home right here with her parents.

Her husband had been patient, reminding her that Kansas wasn't a foreign land. But to a woman accustomed to nannies and servants who attended to her every whim without a moment's hesitation, the idea had seemed foreign enough. Certainly Kansas was not a place she wanted to live.

Ferrand Burk came from an old, aristocratic line in Virginia. His father could have well afforded to buy any amount of land his son desired. Why, even her own pa had offered to purchase Ferrand a plantation on their wedding day. They didn't need to travel hundreds of miles to acquire a mere hundred and sixty acres.

But Ferrand wanted land of his own, not something her father or his had provided. The Homestead Act was the answer, as far as he was concerned. All a person had to do was begin improvements on the land within six months of the time he filed for application and then stay there for five years, and the land became his, free and clear.

Charity filled a bucket with the wash water and carried it outside, emptying it away from the path. The cold November sky threatened rain or snow. Folks in town were predicting an early winter. The wooly worms were completely black this year, which meant bad weather and lots of it. She'd cut open a persimmon seed back in October and found a spoon. A sure sign of a lot of snow, according to Laughing Waters and Little Fawn, two Kaw Indians who had chosen her for a friend.

The Kaws were a friendly tribe and had often dropped by

the homestead, before they broke camp and moved away, leaving Laughing Waters and Little Fawn behind. The two women came and went whenever they chose. They'd never been known to knock, and sometimes they drove her to distraction, but they had taught her about herbs and native plants, and she had learned to accept their unexpected visits.

Charity leaned against the tumbledown fence and thought about the way Ferrand had held her close and kissed her, promising an adventure. Well, he had surely delivered on that. She'd had about all the adventure she could stand.

Sometimes she hadn't understood her husband.

She had loved him, and her papa always said a man was the undisputed head of his household, but still. . .given her choice, she would have stayed in Virginia. Charity carried the bucket back to the wash kettle, remembering how Ferrand had also promised her life wouldn't change much. There would be plenty of people looking for jobs in Kansas, and she could hire all the help she'd need to do the work. Turned out there had been virtually no one looking for a job. Everyone had enough to do trying to survive life on the frontier.

She straightened and rubbed her aching back. She'd had to learn to cook and clean, do all the things someone else had done for her. At first she had missed Mama and Papa and Jenny and Sue, her sisters. Ferrand had promised her family could come visit when they'd got settled on their homestead, but that hadn't worked out either. To tell the truth, she was sort of relieved Papa had never seen how she lived. Kansas was different from Virginia in more ways than one.

She'd worried about the war, too, afraid her husband might have to leave any day. Her husband had laughed and said they'd worry about that when the time came. Well, the time had come a lot sooner than Charity had planned.

They hadn't lived on their new settlement for more than a few months when Ferrand decided it was his duty to join the fight for the Confederacy. She'd been left to face the bewildered looks of her neighbors when they found out he'd decided his loyalties still belonged to the South.

She emptied the last of the rinse water and propped the washtub against the side of the house to drain. Kansas was hundreds of miles away from Virginia, and her family hadn't been able to make the long trip to visit. After they'd learned of Ferrand's death, they had written, urging her to come home. When she had informed them she was staying on to claim the land, Mama had begged her to reconsider.

Charity brushed her hair out of her eyes and stared out over the unrelenting landscape. She was a stubborn woman; too stubborn for her own good, she suspected. She was determined to stay in Kansas, though at times she hated every waking hour in this wild, uncivilized land, where the winds were fierce and the winters long and unbearably cold. The heat could be suffocating and the droughts endless. There were tornadoes and grasshoppers and Indians. And wolves. She hated the wolves, too. They prowled around her log cabin at night, snapping at her dogs, Gabriel and Job, while she huddled in a corner grasping Ferrand's old rifle and praying they wouldn't break through the door.

Still, she couldn't bring herself to relinquish her right to the homestead. In a strange, inexplicable way, she felt a certain pride to think she owned the land—or would, if she could hold on one more year.

Then maybe she'd go home. The thought was mighty tempting. There hadn't been any servants or nannies out here to take care of her. In truth, she'd barely been able to manage.

She felt herself smiling, something she rarely did anymore, when she thought of how poor Ferrand had struggled to mold her into a pioneer woman. He'd been good to her. He'd seen her through her crying spells and days of loneliness. Sometimes weeks would pass before they'd see another human being, and at times she thought she couldn't bear the solitude.

But she'd survived. When the news of her husband's death had reached her, she'd had a good long cry, but by then she'd begun to adjust to the harsh realities of the world. Oh, she'd been furious at him for getting himself killed in that foolish war and leaving her all alone to care for a miserable chunk of worthless land. But the feeling had passed, and she'd started remembering what a really good man her husband had been, and then Kansas didn't seem all that bad. It was home now, her home, so she guessed she'd best make do and quit feeling sorry for herself.

A hawk hovered against the overcast sky before dropping like the weight on a plumb line, straight down. The hawk would devour some helpless rodent. Life was hard out here and not likely to get easier. She sighed and turned back to look at her home. Not fancy compared to what she'd left in Virginia, but what she and Ferrand had shared had been special. Despite all her domestic failings, she knew she had to do this one last thing for him. He had worked too hard in the brief time they'd been granted together for her to be fainthearted now. She'd see this thing through. Though she had to admit, she couldn't understand how she was going to do it.

From a purely practical standpoint, she needed a man. She'd have to make improvements on the land to keep her claim, but she simply didn't have the knowledge, the strength, or the necessary skill.

Thanks to Grandmother Pendergrass's personal tutelage, Charity knew how to piece a pretty quilt and bake a tasty blackberry pie, but she didn't know how to build a barn or plow a field. Oh, she'd tried. Her hands, once lily-white and soft as rose petals, were now calloused and beet red.

When it had come to setting posts and planting wheat, she'd done an embarrassing job. Ashamed for anyone to see the way her fence posts leaned westward when they were supposed to stand straight, she had ripped them out and cried herself to sleep that night.

A man was her only answer.

But a man was a rare commodity around these parts. It was unlikely that anyone would walk up and knock on her door and say, "Well, hello! I hear you're looking for a husband, Mrs. Burk. Take me." She laughed out loud at the notion.

Though the town of Cherry Grove wasn't far from her land, she rarely socialized. Once a month she made the trek into town to purchase staples and yard goods from Miller's Mercantile, but suitable marriage prospects weren't plentiful. Oh, there were the usual cattle drovers who came through town, bringing their longhorns up from Texas to ship them out by railroads. Of course, the travel-worn herders were always looking for female companionship, but Charity despised their slovenly ways and drunken antics. They carried on like the devil himself. Their cattle brought them a good price back East, but she wanted nothing to do with such men. They were rovers and drifters, and she needed a man who'd stick around for a spell.

She sighed in despair and turned her face heavenward, as she increasingly did these days. "Well, it's up to You, Lord. I'm at the end of my row."

Beau Claxton slowed his horse beside the stream and paused to let the animal drink his fill. Unkempt and dirty with a heavy beard covering the lower half of his face, he felt older than his twenty-eight years. He slumped in the saddle, body aching with fatigue. A light drizzle had been falling for the last half hour, and his beard was caked in ice.

He'd been on the trail long enough for the sun to cook his skin and the wind and weather to lash him into a blank acceptance of a life that no longer held purpose.

He knew he looked bad, but he couldn't seem to care.

He didn't eat the way he should. He was at least forty pounds lighter than he had been a year ago. During that time, he'd rambled down one winding road after another, going wherever the next one took him. He'd tried to get through one day and then the next and then the next. Sometimes he'd noticed when he crossed a state line, but if anyone had asked him where he was, he wouldn't have known or cared. Life was one long day after the other.

Betsy had been gone a year now, or close to it. Beau didn't know what month it was, but summer and fall had come and gone so he'd guess it was November now.

The memory of his wife brought a smile. Their baby would've been over a year old by now. Boy or girl? Suddenly, he realized he'd never let himself ask that question. Well, he guessed it didn't matter. Nothing mattered anymore.

He slid from his horse and knelt on the bank to break the ice then reached into the stream, cupping his hands for a drink of freezing-cold water. When he finished, he splashed a handful of icy wetness down his neck to wash away the stench.

He had straightened and prepared to mount when his horse shied nervously. "Whoa, girl, easy." Beau gripped the reins and pulled himself into the saddle as the mare whinnied and side-stepped. "Easy. . .easy. . ." He glanced toward the surrounding woods, wary now.

"What's the matter, girl?" His eyes scanned the area and his stomach tightened. Standing not twenty feet away, partially hidden in the undergrowth, was one of the biggest timber wolves he'd ever seen.

The horse trumpeted and pranced in alarm. The wolf's lips curled back above its fangs. It growled a low, ominous warning. Its eyes had a bright, feverish sparkle to them; its back paw dangled limply.

Beau could see fresh blood dripping from the wound onto the frozen ground. Probably been caught in a trap. Slowly, he backed his horse out of the stream, taking pains not to make any sudden moves. The animal would be in no mood for socializing, and neither was Beau. He could shoot it, but his draw would have to be lightning quick, and he didn't want to chance it.

Before he could choose his next move, the decision was out of his hands.

With a lunge the wolf sprang from its hiding place. The horse reared, pawing the air.

Beau reached for his gun at the same time the wolf charged. The air was alive with the screams of the crazed horse and snarls of the wild animal locked in a life-or-death struggle. Beau managed to pull his gun from his holster, but the wolf fell, regained its footing, and sprang again, clamping its teeth on his leg. Beau tumbled out of the saddle and landed in the water, trying to shield himself from the animal's sharp teeth.

He fought to get away. The wolf repeatedly slashed at his unprotected body.

Charity stopped kneading bread and cocked her ear toward the open window. The dogs were setting up a howl on the front step, and in the distance she could hear what sounded like animals in some sort of fight.

She wiped flour from her hands. Pesky coyotes, she thought irritably, reaching for the rifle. They'd probably attacked a stray dog or calf. The noise increased as she stepped out of the cabin and started toward the stream.

She'd be forever grateful to Ferrand for choosing this particular piece of land. In this part of Kansas, a shortage of rain, coupled with high winds and low humidity, sometimes left a pioneer at a serious disadvantage. But the Burk home was built near an underground spring that provided a stream of cool, clear water year-round.

A shrill squeal rent the air, and her footsteps quickened. Good heavens! Something had attacked a horse! Her feet faltered as she entered the clearing, her eyes taking in the appalling sight. A large timber wolf was ripping a man apart as his horse danced about him in terror.

Charity hefted the rifle to her shoulder and took careful aim. A loud *crack* sliced the air, and the wolf toppled off the man. The gunfire spooked the horse, and the animal bolted into the thicket. Charity waded into the stream, flinching when she edged past the fallen wolf. The gaping bullet hole in the center of its chest assured her that her aim had been true. Her husband had taught her how to be a deadly, accurate shot. She'd learned her lesson well.

She knelt beside the wounded man and cautiously rolled him on his side in the shallow water, cringing when he moaned in agony. He was so bloody she could barely make out the severity of his wounds, but she knew he was near death.

"Shhhh. . .lie still. I'm going to help you," she soothed, though she was afraid he could neither see nor hear her.

His eyes were swollen shut from the lacerations on his face. As she watched, he slumped into unconsciousness.

She hesitated, not sure whether to hitch Myrtle and Nell to drag him out of the water. He was a tall man, but pitifully thin. Though she was small and slight, she was a lot stronger than when she'd first come to Kansas. She decided she wouldn't need the oxen to move him.

It took several tries to get him out of the water. He wasn't as light as he looked. She tugged and heaved inch by inch, pausing periodically to murmur soothing words of encouragement when he groaned. Though she handled him carefully, his injuries were so great she was sure he suffered unspeakable pain.

Once she had hauled him onto the bank, she hurriedly tore off a small portion of her petticoat and set to work cleaning his wounds. He fought when her hands touched torn flesh.

"Please, you must let me help you!" she urged.

She was accustomed to patching wounds on her stock, but she grew faint looking at this man's injuries. But she shook off her queasiness and looked after his needs.

As her hands worked, she studied him, recoiling not only at his injuries but at his general condition. He was so unkempt, so dirty, so. . .slovenly. She wasn't used to that. Ferrand had always kept himself clean and neat. No doubt this man was a drifter, or perhaps one of those drovers. He certainly hadn't had a bath in months—maybe even years—and he was in need of a shave and haircut.

She peeled away the torn shirt and washed the blood from his broad chest. She could count his ribs. Obviously, he hadn't had a square meal in months. With more meat on his bones he'd be a very large man. . .powerful. . .strong. . .

Strong enough to build a barn and set fence and work behind

a team of oxen all day. Her hands momentarily stilled.

A man. Here was a man—barely alive perhaps, but a man all the same. He could be the answer to her problems. Her hands flew feverishly about their work. She had to save him! Not that she wouldn't have tried her best anyway, but now, no matter what it took, she'd see to it that this man survived!

As far as men went, he wasn't much. . .disgusting, actually, but she reminded herself she wasn't in a position to be picky. She'd nurse him back to health, and once she got him on his feet, she'd trick him into marrying her. No, she amended, she wouldn't trick him. . .she'd ask him first, and if that didn't work, then she'd trick him.

But what if he has a wife? an inner voice asked.

Don't bother me with technicalities, she thought. *I'll cross that bridge when I get to it.*

Her hands worked faster, a new sense of confidence filling her now. He would live. She knew he would. The good Lord wouldn't send such a gift and then snatch it back. Would He?

The man moaned, and Charity lifted his head and placed it possessively in her lap.

He was a gift from God.

She was certain of that now. Who else would so unselfishly drop this complete stranger at her door?

Charity gazed down at her unexpected gift and smiled, lifting her face heavenward.

She would be able to claim her land.

In her most reverent tone, she humbly asked for the Lord's help in making this man strong and healthy again, at least strong enough to drive a good, sturdy fence post.

She closed her petition with heartfelt sincerity. "He's a little. . .well, rough looking, Father, but I'm not complaining." She bit her lower lip and studied the ragged, dirty, bloody man lying in her lap. With a little soap and water, he'd be tolerable. She shrugged, and a grin spread across her face. "I suppose if this is the best You have to offer, Lord, then I am surely beholden to You."

Chapter 2

Charity dragged the stranger up the ravine and then the quarter mile to the house. By the time she managed to pull him onto her bed, she was gasping for air.

She sighed and surveyed his pitiful state. The nearest doctor was over an hour's ride away. The stranger would die before she could make it to Cherry Grove and back.

No, if his life was to be spared, she'd have to use whatever skills she possessed, and she had to admit they were deplorably few.

It would take a lot of nursing, and the mercy of God, to see him through this, she realized.

Though he remained in a state of unconsciousness, the man's face was swollen and contorted with pain. The angry six-inch gash across his chest oozed blood. She knew he would bleed to death if she didn't stem the wound.

She rolled up her sleeves and moved to the hearth. After filling a wash pan with scalding water from the teakettle, she tore an old petticoat into soft bandages. She'd stitched up livestock, she reminded herself. Her hands automatically went about her task. When Nell had gotten tangled in Ansel Latimer's fence last year, she'd been the one who'd cleaned the torn flesh and stitched it back together. She took scissors and a needle from her sewing basket. Of course, Nell's wound had been nothing like this poor man's, but the ox had healed beautifully.

And she'd assisted with a few births, but helping a woman deliver a baby was easier than sewing a man back together. She selected a spool of black thread and absently closed the lid on the basket. Doctoring wasn't her favorite thing, but then she had no choice if she wanted the man to survive. God would ultimately decide his fate, but she'd do all she could. . .and not for purely selfish reasons. She had an obligation to her fellow man.

It took a half hour to cut away his clothes. She choked back nausea as she bathed his wounds in cool water. Drawing deep breaths of fresh air to quell the urge to empty her stomach, Charity turned back to the injured man.

She wasn't sure she could go on. Most likely the man would die in spite of her efforts. No one could survive such injuries, she reasoned. But she thought of her own miserable plight and resolved anew to save his life.

The laceration across the middle of his back was the deepest. She carefully rolled him onto his stomach, cringing as she poured a small amount of carbolic acid into the wound. The man stiffened, screaming in anguish. He tried to twist away, but Charity held firm, throwing her slight weight against his large frame, pinning him down until he drifted back into unconsciousness.

She found herself biting her lower lip till she could taste her own blood. Her hands worked feverishly to stitch the open gash. When she finished with his back, she rolled him over and continued to stitch the other lacerations. At any moment he could wake up and overpower her, and then what would she do?

The darning needle, which she'd held in the fire, slid in and out, in and out. . .until she thought she'd faint. The room was stifling.

She dipped a cloth into the bucket of clean water and pressed it to her flushed features. Once the lightheadedness passed, she continued.

The afternoon shadows lengthened, and Charity's back felt as if it would break, but she worked on. She heard Bossy standing near the front door, bawling to be milked.

"Not now, Bossy," she called out softly, praying the old cow would wander off.

It was nearing dark when she finished. Tears welled in her eyes when she listened to the sounds of his suffering. She dropped weakly into the rocker and stared unseeingly at the cooling stove, numb with fatigue. She'd felt every agonizing prick the needle had made in his bruised flesh as surely as if she'd been the one injured.

Her body, as well as his, was sticky with sweat and blood, and she knew she must bathe the both of them before she could rest.

The man mumbled and thrashed about on the bed. Charity feared he'd reopen his wounds. If he did, she wasn't sure she'd have the strength to sew them again.

There was nothing to ease the stranger's agony except the bottle of brandy Ferrand had kept for medicinal purposes. If this wasn't a medicinal purpose, she didn't recognize one. She hurriedly pulled the bottle from the cupboard and carried it to the bed. He moaned when she scooped his head up from the pillow and cradled it in the crook of her arm. She tipped the bottle to his lips, letting the strong brown liquid trickle down his throat.

When he choked, she set the bottle aside and patted his shoulder, trying to soothe him. He screamed in torment when the wound across his chest threatened to escape the bounds of the slender thread.

When he regained his breath, she tipped the bottle again, and the nerve-racking choking started all over again. It took several minutes to get enough of the liquid down him to dull his senses.

He'd fought her with a strength that was surprising for a man so gravely injured. Twice he'd nearly knocked the bottle out of her hand, but she was as determined as he. The spirits took full effect, and he lay so still that she leaned forward to be sure he was still breathing.

Assured that he was she released a long sigh. *He's going to make it. He has to.* If she could clean and stitch his wounds without fainting, then he could live! She eyed the unconscious male lying in the middle of her bed.

He was a pitiful sight. His chin was covered with stubble; his ribs poked through his sides like those of some half-starved animal. But it didn't matter, she told herself, trying to bolster her sagging morale. He was a man, and good Lord willing, she was going to see that he lived. He obviously needed someone to take care of him, and she needed a man. Surely a satisfactory arrangement could be worked out, once he regained his health.

He was still breathing, and she took small comfort in that. By morning he'd be awake, and she'd find out who he was and where he'd come from. Mustering up enough strength to walk to the fuel box, she tossed a few buffalo chips on the fire then stumbled back to the rocker and dropped into an exhausted sleep.

Wind howling down the chimney penetrated Charity's dulled senses. Her eyes opened to slits then closed again. For three nights, she'd hovered over the stranger, alternately bathing him in cool water and changing the bandages.

His wounds didn't look good. The long, angry lesions were beginning to fester, and her heart pounded with fear when she looked at them.

The man was hot and feverish—delirious at times, calling out for "Betsy." If she had known Betsy, she'd have gladly fetched her. She'd try anything to ease his torment, but nothing helped.

Only once had he shown a sign of consciousness. Last night, when she'd been sponging his burning forehead, his eyes had opened to stare at her with a blank plea in the deep, tormented pools of indigo.

Charity had smiled and spoken to him in soft, reassuring tones, running the damp cloth gently across his reddened skin. "There, now, you're going to be fine." Her heart had skipped a beat when his eyes had grown incredibly tender and he'd returned her smile.

It had been so long since a man had looked at her that way. Then she realized that it wasn't Charity Burk he'd been seeing but his Betsy. His feverish mind continued to play tricks on him.

The stranger had grasped her hand and brought it to cradle lovingly against the rough stubble coating his jaw. His eyes had slid shut, and she'd heard him whisper faintly, "Bets, I knew you'd come back, darling." Charity watched with an aching heart when tears rolled from the corners of his eyes to dampen the pillow.

Slowly his eyes had opened again, and she'd caught her breath when he pulled her head down to meet his. She had been transfixed when their lips touched and lingered. Because he was so ill, the kiss had lacked substance, but nothing could have disguised the love he'd transferred to her. His kiss had taken her breath, and she'd felt herself growing weak.

When their lips parted, Charity had seen a look in the stranger's eyes that she'd seen before in Ferrand's. It had been such a look of love, so strong that Charity felt warmed by the adoration shimmering in the tormented depths. Then he smiled at her again and said softly, "Bets, I love you."

Charity had never encountered such striking eyes: clear, vibrant blue. . .the color of morning glories that grew on the trellis beside the porch when the first rays of summer daylight nudged them gently awake. Somehow she knew those eyes, now bright with fever, could sparkle with merriment during better times. Despite his pitiful condition, the stranger was still the handsomest man she had seen in a long while.

And he loved a woman named Betsy.

The wind was rising. Charity noticed a chill in the air, and she rose to throw more chips on the fire. She stoked the glowing embers and thought of the stranger. A frown played across her features. Maybe he wouldn't be able to help her. Then what would she do? She'd lose the homestead, that's what.

She thought of Ferrand and how hard they'd worked together to build the cabin. It hadn't been easy traveling to the Great American Desert, as Kansas was sometimes called.

They had taken a steamboat part of the way. My, what a glorious time that had been, churning up the wide Missouri on a big old paddle wheeler. By then, Ferrand had convinced her that an exciting new life awaited them; all they had to do was reach out and take it.

Charity walked back to the rocker and sat. It was still early; the sun wasn't up yet, so she could dawdle for a spell before she milked Bossy. Rocking back and forth, she let her thoughts remain in the past.

How she had loved Ferrand Burk.

When they'd arrived in Kansas, they'd immediately found a piece of land, staked their plot on good level ground, and stripped the spot of grass. They'd worked from daylight to dusk, clearing the land of rocks and debris.

From sunup to sundown, they'd cut logs to build the one-room house. A tough job for a pampered Southern woman raised a lady.

No sitting on a cushion sewing a fine seam here. She'd worked like a man, like one of the slaves on her father's plantation. *You never know what you can do until you have to do it,* she thought.

After the logs had been hewn, she'd helped load the heavy timber into the spring wagon. Working together, they had built their house, and more important, they had created a home. Tears sprang to her eyes when she remembered how happy they'd been. She dabbed at the wetness with a corner of her apron and tried to push memories aside.

What good did memories do her anyway? Ferrand was gone, and crying wouldn't bring him back. She wouldn't cry again. She was just feeling tired; that was all. Sitting up with the stranger for three nights straight had taken its toll.

She returned to the bed and touched the stranger's forehead. Still hot. She didn't know how much longer the fever could rage before it either broke or killed him. It would do one or the other soon.

She settled back in the chair and sighed. Ferrand seemed to hug the fringes of her mind this morning. Perhaps because he'd always loved this time of day. Charity let herself dwell on her husband's quiet strength, and somehow that eased her mind.

She leaned her head against the smooth wood of her chair and thought about how he'd made the rocker and given it to her on their first Christmas together. She tried to remember his eyes. . .blue, like the stranger's. . .no, they were hazel, weren't they?

The slow creak of the rocker ceased. Blue. . .no, hazel. She frowned. Blue or hazel? Which one was it? Strange, she couldn't recall. Setting the chair in motion she thought about how tall and handsome Ferrand Burk had been. She could remember clearly what an attractive man he was. Oh, he might not have had a broad-shouldered frame like the stranger, but Ferrand had had a firmness about him that she'd found most attractive.

And he'd held his own when it had come to working the land. He might've been raised in a home where servants had done all the backbreaking chores, but he hadn't been afraid of hard work. Neither was she.

Her eyes wandered lovingly around the room. The cabin was all she had left of Ferrand, and if she lost it, she feared she'd lose what remained of his memory. Oh, she knew this house they'd built wasn't fancy like her ancestral mansion in Virginia. But it was home.

Charity's gaze surveyed the meager furnishings. Not much—a buffalo-hide carpet on the floor, a wooden bed with a straw-filled mattress, some goods boxes fashioned into tables, and a few barrels Ferrand had hewn into chairs. She'd managed to save enough egg money to buy material to make pretty gingham curtains. The two richly patterned patchwork quilts that had once belonged to her grandmother brightened the room.

All things considered, Charity loved this home. That's why she had to keep the stranger alive. He might be pitiful, but if she could enlist his strength once she nursed him back to health, he could save her homestead.

She didn't know how she'd make him stay once he recovered—provided he did recover. This Betsy would be an obstacle, but perhaps the stranger could be persuaded to help out while he was mending. It would take a good long while for him to regain his full strength.

Suddenly she slapped the arm of the chair, and her frustration erupted. Oh, it cut her to the core to have to depend on someone else! Her life should have been so different. She hated the miserable, senseless act of war that had snatched Ferrand away from her!

Wind whistling down the chimney added to her fury. While

she was mad at everything, she thought angrily, she might as well include the Kansas grasshoppers, tornadoes, and blizzards, along with the incessant wind that had withered what little crops she'd planted.

Wearily she rose from the chair and blew out the tallow candle on the kitchen table. The sun was up now—a new day. Maybe this one would shine more favorably on her and the stranger.

She poured water into the kitchen basin and washed her face and hands then pulled the pins from her hair. The soft black cloud fell like a shawl around her shoulders. She picked up a brush and pulled it through the tangled locks, pausing to stare at her reflection in the mirror. Frontier life had been hard, and she feared her beauty—what there was left of it—was fading.

Her hand absently fingered the faint crow's-feet around her eyes. Come next month, she'd be twenty-three years old. Twenty-three years old! An old widow.

Most women her age were busy raising families and tending husbands, but she had neither. Instead she had a dead husband, an unclaimed piece of land, a few chickens, a few old sows, two dogs, a cow, two oxen, and a gravely ill stranger about to meet his Maker.

The sound of a buckboard rumbling into the yard caught her attention. Charity hurriedly repinned her hair, wondering who could be calling at this hour. She took a final glance in the mirror then quickly smoothed the wrinkles on her dress and answered the knock.

She was surprised to find her neighbor, Ansel Latimer, standing on her doorstep, his face pale, his mouth set in a grim line.

"Good morning, Ansel." Charity peered on tiptoe around his large frame. "Is Letty—?"

"Letty sent me to fetch you," Ansel interrupted curtly. "She's—she's feeling right poorly this morning, and I don't know what to do for her."

"Is it the baby?"

"I don't know. It ain't time for the young'un to be born, but Letty—she's been hurting all night."

Ansel and Letty Latimer had been Charity's closest neighbors until a few months ago when the Swensons and several other families staked their claims. The Latimers lived a good five miles away, but Letty and Charity visited back and forth once a month, excitedly planning for Letty's new baby, due in late November.

The women were about the same age, and they had developed a close friendship while the Latimers and Burks homesteaded their properties. Ansel and Letty were the closest thing to family Charity had, now that Ferrand was gone.

Charity was reaching for her shawl when she remembered. "Of course I'll come, Ansel, but will you step in for a moment?"

Ansel removed his hat and walked into the warmth of the cabin. "We'd best hurry, Charity. I hate to leave Letty alone any longer than need be."

"Of course. I'll only take a moment." Charity motioned for him to follow her to the bed. "I want you to see something."

He strode across the room, a tall man, still handsome at forty-three, with brown eyes and dark hair streaked with gray. He was twenty years older than Charity, and she valued his intelligence and common sense. Many times since Ferrand's death she'd gone to him with her problems. If anyone would know what to do about the stranger, Ansel would.

Slowly his puzzled gaze focused on the bed. A frown crossed his rugged features. "Who is he?"

"I don't know. Three days ago I found him in the stream. A wolf attacked him. I shot the animal and managed to drag the stranger to the house."

Ansel bent over and lifted one of the bandages. Charity watched his frown deepen. "Infection's set in."

"I know. I've tried to keep the wounds clean, but they look worse every day."

Ansel lifted the other bandages and shook his head as he viewed the angry lesions. "He needs a doctor, but even then, I don't believe he'll make it."

"I know. Oh Ansel, what should I do?" Charity heard the quiver in her voice. "He's going to die!"

Ansel patted her shoulder reassuringly. "Looks to me like you've done about all you can. I've never seen a better job of stitching. But the man's wounds are too serious. It'd be more merciful to let him go to his reward in peace."

Her eyes filled with tears. She stared down at the stranger's flushed features. His face was pathetically swollen and hot with fever. She felt such a closeness to the man, yet she couldn't explain why. She'd fought so hard to save his life that it seemed unthinkable to let him go.

Still, she knew Ansel had spoken the truth. Wouldn't it be kinder to let him pass away? In three days she'd managed to get only a few drops of water and a couple spoonfuls of broth down his parched throat.

The man was so weak Charity could barely hear him call for Betsy. She wondered how much longer she could bear to watch his suffering.

Ansel gently touched her arm. "Let him go, Charity. You've done all you can. He's in the Lord's hands now."

She nodded, tears of resignation trickling down her cheeks. Ansel was right. She had to let the stranger go. There was no mercy in letting him suffer this way.

"Come with me. We'll tend to Letty; then I'll bring you back this evening and help you bury him," Ansel said.

She nodded again and reached to tuck the sheet tenderly over the man's chest, realizing Ansel expected him to be dead by sunset. "I know it's best, but it. . .it seems awful just letting him pass away alone." Her voice caught. Tears ran in swift rivulets.

"Nothing more you can do." Ansel put his arm around her shoulders and led her away from the sight.

She knew he was right. Ansel was always right, but it seemed wrong, leaving a man to die alone. Charity wanted to be with him when it happened. . . .

"Letty needs you," Ansel reminded gently.

"Oh. . .yes, Letty. . .of course." Charity had almost forgotten her friend. Letty should be her first concern, but her eyes raced back to the still figure lying on her bed. Ansel helped her with her shawl.

"Bundle up real good. Chilly out this morning."

"Put plenty of chips on the fire. I—I don't want him to be cold."

Ansel did as she asked then opened the door and quietly commanded, "Charity, Letty needs our help, girl."

"Yes. . .yes, of course." She glanced one final time at the bed before she turned and walked through the door.

"May the mercy of the Lord be with you," she whispered, wishing desperately that his Betsy could be here to see him safely home.

Chapter 3

The old buckboard rumbled along the rutted trail, bouncing Charity back and forth on the wooden seat, but she barely noticed. Her thoughts were on the stranger. She wondered how long it would be before he. . . He could be dead at this instant, she realized, and the thought made her shiver. Another time a ride across the prairie would have been a source of pleasure, but not today.

The roadbed ran along Fire Creek. She, Ferrand, Letty, and Ansel had enjoyed picnics here on lazy Sunday afternoons. Willow trees lined the bank along with grapevines and hazel bush. In warm weather, Charity and Letty had spent hours gathering the wildflowers that grew in colorful profusion along the roadbed while the men discussed their crops.

A killdeer sang his tuneless note. A meadowlark called. The old buckboard lumbered across the shallow stream and rattled up the steep incline toward the Latimer homestead.

Charity noticed Ansel had said little during the ride, commenting only occasionally on the weather. His face remained pensive; worry lines were grooved deep at the corners of his eyes.

She knew how much he loved Letty, and she sympathized

with his concern for his young wife. He and Letty looked forward to their first child like youngsters waiting for Christmas. Charity sighed deeply, wishing Ferrand had left her with a child. It would have been a part of him to love and to hold when the nights were long and the wind wailed around the cabin. A child to carry on Ferrand's name. Her heart ached with the loss. Best not to think about such things. What was done couldn't be undone.

She couldn't imagine what was ailing Letty this morning. She'd seemed fine at church on Sunday. After the service the two women had lingered outside, discussing the new dress they'd make for Letty after her baby came. They'd use the fine blue-and-yellow sprigged calico they had dawdled over the last time Charity had ridden to Cherry Grove with the Latimers for supplies.

Charity suspected Letty's weakness for dried-apple pie was the source of her discomfort, but she didn't think Ansel had any notion to hear her opinion.

The buckboard clattered along the prairie, and soon Charity could see the chimney pipe of the Latimer dugout poking out of the ground. Whenever she visited Letty, she always came away thankful that Ferrand had built a cabin instead of a dugout.

Letty was forever complaining that her home was dark and damp year-round, and she said it was practically impossible to keep things clean, what with dirt from the roof and walls sifting down on everything. Whenever it rained, water poured in through the roof and under the door. Letty had to wade in mud until the floor could dry out.

Bull snakes got into the roof made of willows and grass. Letty said sometimes one would lose its hold at night and fall down on the bed. Ansel would jump up, take a hoe, and drag the snake outside.

Charity shuddered at the thought. There were no snakes in her cabin. In summer it was cool as a cavern; in winter, a snug, warm refuge from the howling Kansas blizzards.

"Looks like Letty's allowed the fire to burn down," Ansel remarked. He drove the buckboard alongside the dugout and drew the horses to a halt. Only a faint wisp of smoke curled from the stovepipe.

He set the brake, jumped down, and lifted Charity from the wooden seat.

"I bet she'll have dinner waiting," Charity predicted, trying to ease the worry lines on his face.

When they stepped inside the dugout, her optimism faded. It took a moment for her eyes to adjust to the small room. A ray of sunshine filtered through the one window, and Charity squinted to locate Letty, who lay on the bed, her hands crossed over her swollen stomach, her lips silently moving.

Charity hurried across the room and knelt beside the straw-filled mattress, reaching out to smooth back the damp tendrils of carrot-red hair. "Letty, it's me. I'm here."

For a moment she thought Letty hadn't heard. Then Letty's lips moved, and Charity leaned close to understand her words. "Ansel. . .make him go outside. . . ."

Charity's heart started to hammer. Something was terribly wrong. This was far more serious than a case of eating too many dried apples. She touched her friend's delicate hand and discovered it was unusually cold. "Ansel's here, Letty, and so am I. Can you tell us what's the matter?"

"Ansel. . ." Letty's voice was stronger. "Make Ansel. . .go outside," she repeated.

"Letty. . .why?"

Letty's tears fell across cheeks sprinkled generously with girlish freckles. "Just make him go, Charity. Make him leave. . . ."

Charity turned in bewilderment to face Ansel, who was standing quietly in the shadows. "She wants you to leave."

"I heard." Without questioning his wife's unusual request, he turned and walked out.

Charity turned to Letty and began smoothing the rumpled bedding. "Now, let's get you comfortable." She paused, frowning when she felt a warm, sticky substance on the sheets. Shock moved through her. She stared at the blood on her hand.

Gently, she shifted Letty's body. The girl was pitifully thin except where she was swollen with child. Charity pressed her hands to the bottom sheet and discovered it was saturated with Letty's blood. Her gaze flew back to her friend's pale features, and the young woman on the bed whispered softly, "It's the baby. It's coming. . .and there's something wrong."

Letty cried out then bit her lower lip, muffling an agonized scream. She reached to grasp Charity's hand, holding on tightly until the spasm passed.

As soon as she could turn loose of Letty's hand, Charity snatched up a clean sheet and used it as padding to stem the flow of blood, but already she could see the crimson fluid soaking through the wadded-up cloth. How could anyone bleed like that and live?

Charity grabbed a rag from the basin on the floor beside the bed and gently sponged Letty's flushed face. She spoke in low, soothing tones. "There now, everything will be fine. The baby might be a few weeks early, but I'm sure it'll be strong and healthy. Perhaps Ansel should go for the doctor?"

Letty reached up and halted the movement of the wet cloth, her dark eyes fearful. "There isn't time, Charity. Something's wrong."

Charity tried to speak with assurance even though she was afraid. "It's going to be all right. I'll help you, and God is with us."

Now was the time to pray if there ever had been one. She wanted to help her friend so badly, but she didn't know what to do.

A violent seizure racked Letty's slender frame. Sweat stood out across the girl's brow. She buried her face in Charity's shoulder to muffle her scream. "Don't. . .want. . .Ansel. . .to. . .hear," she panted.

"Don't worry about Ansel," Charity soothed. When the pain abated, she ran the wet cloth across Letty's pale features. "How long have you been in labor?"

Letty shook her head and stiffened with the onset of another contraction. This time the seizure was so violent, so savage, that Letty screamed and clung to Charity's hand so tightly that Charity bit her lip to keep from crying out. The baby was very close to being born. She needed to tell Ansel to stoke the fire, to bring the kettle to a boil.

Letty's amber eyes grew wide with fear, her body shook with convulsions. She called Charity's name. The horrible shaking subsided. Still trembling, Letty began the Lord's Prayer with whispered fervor, "Our Father, which art in heaven. . . Hallowed be Thy name."

She screamed and clutched the sides of the bed then continued, ". . .Thy kingdom come. . . . Thy will be. . .done. . ."

Charity couldn't think straight. She knew it shouldn't be happening this way. She'd assisted at other births, and they hadn't gone like this.

"Give us this day. . .our daily. . ." Letty whispered. Another contraction seized her. "Ansel!" she pleaded in a high-pitched wail.

The dugout door flew open and Ansel rushed into the room, his eyes wild with fear. "Letty. . . Oh, dear God!" His words sounded like a prayer.

"Leave!" Charity tried to shield him from the pitiful sight. Letty thrashed wildly on the bed, screaming Ansel's name over and over.

"Charity—do something for her!" Ansel watched his wife in stunned horror. Letty's body was consumed with spasms as the child pushed from the confines of its mother's womb.

"And lead us. . .not. . .into. . .temptation. . ." Letty murmured, stopping to pant, her eyes squeezed tight in torment. "Ohhhh. . .Ansel, help me!"

Throwing her full weight against his frame, Charity tried to shove Ansel toward the doorway, hoping to spare him further agony. "Go outside," she pleaded, raising her voice above the sound of Letty's terrified pleas. "I'll tend to her. She'll be fine."

But Ansel wouldn't leave. He leaned against the heavy wooden door, mumbling to himself. "God, help her, she's dying. Letty's dying."

He sagged against the door frame and then slid down in a crumpled heap on the dirt floor, pressing his hands over his ears to block out her screams, tears of helpless frustration rolling down his cheeks.

Charity reached to support the baby coming out bottom first.

Letty's screams ran together. She clawed the sheets, her eyes bright with terror. "I'm goin' to die, Charity. Take care of. . .my. . . baby. . . . Take care of my baby. . . ."

"No!" Charity protested, her voice rising in hysteria. She couldn't permit Letty to die! "You have to hold on, Letty—you have to fight!" The baby was nearly out now. Charity grasped the small mound of flesh and pulled, blinking back tears.

"Tell Ansel. . .I. . .love. . .him. . .take care. . .of. . .baby!"

Before Letty could finish she convulsed violently one final time. The baby slid free of her body into Charity's waiting hands.

Charity stared at the scrap of humanity. "It's a girl, Letty! You have a daughter! Look! She's beautiful!" Charity held the squalling, red-faced bundle up for Letty to see, her words slowly fading in her throat.

She blinked back tears when she realized Letty would never know she had a fine, beautiful daughter. She lay peacefully in the folds of the soiled linen, her screams silent now. Deathly silent.

Ansel glanced up when Charity held out the bundle in her arms, tears running down her face.

"Ansel?" she spoke softly, knowing how much he must be hurting.

He gazed back at her, eyes blank.

"You have a lovely baby daughter." She carefully pulled back the folds of the blanket and held the baby so that her father could inspect her.

He stared awkwardly at the tiny wrinkled face. "A little girl?"

"Yes. She looks real healthy."

His eyes slowly lifted to search Charity's. "Letty?"

Charity shook her head. For a moment the anguish in Ansel's eyes was more than she could bear.

Tears streamed. He looked at Charity. "She's. . .gone?"

She nodded, her own tears blinding her.

His gaze dropped to the baby. "A little girl. We was hoping for a boy," he said. All trace of emotion was gone from his voice.

"Would you like to hold your new daughter?"

"Oh. . .no. . .not now. . ." He turned and stumbled from the room. "Think I'll take a walk right now," he murmured.

"Ansel, don't go." Charity's heart was breaking. She wanted to go to him and lend him comfort, but she couldn't. He needed time to grieve.

"I'll be all right. You'll—you'll see to my wife's needs, won't you?"

"Of course." Charity would bathe Letty and dress her in her Sunday best for viewing.

"Good, good." Ansel stopped and drew a deep breath then looked up into the sky. "It's a fine day, isn't it? Couldn't ask for any finer. Letty would have found it real enjoyable."

"Ansel." Charity watched numbly as he ambled off alone. She glanced down at the tiny bundle in her arms and recognized Letty's pug nose and thatch of bright red hair. *Letty will live on in this child*, she thought with sad jubilation. Letty would live on, but what would happen to poor Ansel?

She lifted her face to the sky—and as if Letty could hear her, Charity finished Letty's last thought in a heartfelt whisper.

"For Thine is the kingdom, and the power, and the glory. . .for ever. Amen."

Beau drifted in and out of consciousness, neither awake nor completely under. He had no idea where he was, nor did he care. The pain was unbearable. Voices drifted around him. Were they speaking Kaw, or was he dreaming?

"White Sister asleep."

The words meant nothing to him. From a long way off another voice answered, "This no White Sister."

Something touched his chest, and he wanted to scream with the sudden jolt of pain.

"Gold Hair lives, but sick."

A clucking sound. "Ohhhh, big sick. Heap big sick."

Beau clutched the tattered edge of sleep around him and drifted off on a sea of dark water. He knew he was dying and he welcomed the release, but something drew him back to the light.

Rough hands stroked his fevered forehead. "This good man. Good."

Good?

He didn't know about that. He wasn't wicked, but he wasn't a saint. He'd done his share of bad things, but those days were behind him. Truth be told, he'd been a better man after marrying Betsy. Now Bets was gone, and there wasn't any reason to live.

"No, Little Fawn, man White Sister's," the stern voice admonished someone. Didn't make sense, though. He didn't know anyone named White Sister.

"You wrong, Laughing Waters. White Sister gone. She leave Gold Hair to meet Wa-kun-dah alone. I take care. Make Gold Hair strong again."

A ripple of interest skipped through Beau's mind. Laughing Waters? Little Fawn? Where was he? Gold Hair? If this was a dream it was a strange one. No pictures, just voices talking babble.

"He fine strong buck." The voice came again. "When he well, Little Fawn call him Swift Buck with Tall Antlers. He be fine father to many papooses."

"I think he fine man, too. I make him well, call him Brave Horse with Many Wounds."

Beau struggled to open his eyes, but it was too much for him. He must be dying. Maybe he was hearing angels, but he'd never heard of angels speaking Kaw. . . . But who was he to question Almighty God? The voices had stopped, and he drifted off again.

Hours—maybe days passed. He stirred uncomfortably on the bed. Hot! It was hot.

He wanted to force his eyes open, but the effort was too much. Every inch of his body ached, and his mouth was so dry he could spit cotton.

Where was he? He willed his legs to move, but he found them so heavy they refused to budge. A trickle of sweat ran down the sides of his head; when he tried to wipe it away, he realized his hands wouldn't move.

Paralyzed. He was paralyzed! The wolf's image with its great slobbering jaws rushed back, and he realized with a sinking sensation what had happened.

He was dead. The wolf had killed him.

The thought was strangely disappointing. He had to admit that he hadn't wanted to live since Betsy died, but he hadn't necessarily wanted to die either.

That must be what had happened. The wolf got him.

So this was what dead felt like? Somehow he had expected something different, like harp music and angels singing. He'd never counted on hurting and feeling heavy and hot. So hot!

He drew a shaky breath and found the air stifling, like a furnace. A new, even more disturbing thought surfaced. If he was dead. . .and it was this hot. . .

He groaned and willed his eyes to open. If he was where he thought he was, he might as well face it. Slowly, his lids fluttered open, and his eyes roamed the darkness. He was lying in some sort of bed. . .in a room. Did they have private rooms here? He'd never heard of that, but then he'd never known anyone who'd actually come back and said anything about the facilities. His heart hammered, and sweat rolled in rivulets off his forehead and dripped into his eyes.

The rosy glow of red-hot flames danced wickedly across the wall in front of him, and he groaned and clamped his eyes tightly shut. "Oh God, help me," he prayed, limp now with fear. He really was here. Hell.

Well, it wasn't fair, he thought, resenting the fact that he hadn't had a chance to explain the bad things he'd done in life—not that there'd been all that many.

You'd think God would have cut him a little slack. He'd lived a good life after marrying and settling down. Been a good husband.

Loved the Lord with all his heart. . .until Bets died. That ought to count for something, but his luck must be running true to form. This last year had been one thing after another. And now this. What would Ma say?

He did have a few things on his conscience, like that hundred-dollar debt he owed the general store, which he meant to pay once he got back to Missouri. But it would have been nice to be allowed to tell his side of the story, even if God did have his transgressions written down in some big book.

No, it wasn't fair. Ma had taught him to obey the Ten Commandments, and with a few minor exceptions, he'd done it.

Cole had been worse.

His younger brother, Cass, even worse than Cole.

He wondered if he could talk to someone and get this mess straightened out. He hadn't seen anyone when he'd opened his eyes. Maybe he was in some kind of holding pen.

He carefully opened one eye and moved it slowly around the room, surprised to discover hell looked much like the inside of a log cabin. He'd never stopped to think what hell would look like, since he'd never had any intention of going there.

But it sure was hot down here. Preacher Adams had got that right.

He tried to wipe the sweat off his forehead only to discover he was wrapped tight as a tick in some sort of blanket. He shifted, trying to free his hands. Suddenly he glanced up, and his heart jumped into his throat.

Standing over him was the biggest squaw he'd ever seen. On closer examination he saw she was young and she was smiling a wide, toothless grin.

"Gold Hair wake. Good."

Gold Hair? Where had he heard that name before?

He wondered if he was expected to say something back, though he preferred not to. He might be in hell, but he didn't have to socialize this soon. From all he'd heard, the people who came here weren't the kind he'd choose to associate with.

A second woman suddenly loomed above him, her massive bulk blocking the flickering flames on the walls. She began to unwrap the tight blanket.

Beau groaned and jerked away. "No! Don't!" he pleaded. Pain shot through his side. "Listen, there's been a mistake."

"No talk, Gold Hair," the second woman grunted. "Save strength."

His eyes widened when the first woman reached out and touched a lock of his hair, smiling as she fingered the silken locks. "Pretty, like rocks in water."

"Listen, who's in charge?" Beau asked. What was going on here? A stench filled his nostrils. The second woman hurriedly stripped off the blanket.

"No hurt, Gold Hair. We make well," the first woman promised.

He tried to fight them off, but he didn't have the strength of a stray kitten, and who was this Gold Hair they kept nattering about? There'd been a mistake. He was in the wrong place; why couldn't they see that? Someone had gotten the records mixed up and "Gold Hair" was up there with the streets of gold, where Beau was supposed to be, and he was down here being roasted like a spit pig.

The women ignored his protests. They dipped their large hands into a pail beside the bed and slapped moist, vile-smelling mud all over his body.

He gagged and winced when a series of sharp, excruciating pains shot through him like stray bullets. He realized that this must be part of his eternal punishment, though he'd never imagined it would be administered by a pair of loud-talking squaws.

Preacher Adams had never mentioned a word of this. What Bible verses said that he had to put up with this sort of treatment? Some of those minor prophets, he'd bet. That was his last rational thought before he mercifully slipped back into sweet oblivion.

Chapter 4

LETICIA MARGARET LATIMER
BELOVED WIFE
MAY SHE BRING AS MUCH JOY IN HEAVEN AS SHE BROUGHT HERE ON EARTH

Charity's heart nearly broke as she watched Ansel lovingly carve the inscription onto a wooden cross for Letty's grave.

She had dressed Letty in her wedding gown, made of the finest ivory silk. When she'd unpacked the dress, she'd found a pair of satin shoes tucked beneath the folds. She had slipped the shoes on the young girl's feet, thinking of her well-to-do family back East, who'd married their daughter to Ansel Latimer in grand style, only to have her die in a dugout on a Kansas prairie. They'd have to be notified of her death, but that was Ansel's job.

She brushed Letty's hair until it was the color of a fiery sunset and fastened a cameo brooch at her neckline. Ansel had given the cameo to Letty on their first Christmas together. It had been her most cherished possession.

Charity gazed down at her friend, and her eyes filled with tears. Letty looked so small, so young. . .so helpless.

She draped the kitchen table with Letty's grandmother's lace tablecloth then called Ansel in from the lean-to, where he'd been building the small pine box.

When he stepped hesitantly into the room, she slipped past him to leave, allowing him time alone with his wife. Her thoughts returned to Ferrand. She hadn't been there when he died—no chance to say good-bye. Maybe that had been for the best. She'd been spared the memory of seeing him suffer. Ansel would never forget the horror of Letty's death.

She remembered the stranger lying on her bed back home. By now he was dead. Maybe in heaven with Letty. Maybe not. She didn't know his faith or if he had any.

Was there a special place up there for newcomers, one where they could get acquainted? Were Letty and the stranger looking down right this minute, watching them today? If they were, would the man she had tried so hard to save forgive her for leaving him to die alone? Could she have done anything to help Letty? Not the way the lifeblood had poured out of her.

Charity leaned against the rough bark of a sycamore tree and cried for Letty, for Ansel, for the stranger, for Ferrand, and for herself. Most of all she cried for that poor motherless baby girl who would never know the wonderful woman who had given her life.

When she went back into the dugout, she and Ansel hoisted the simple pine box onto the middle of the kitchen table then gently placed Letty in it. Charity lit a single candle that would burn until they buried Letty in the morning.

She stood for a few moments looking down at her friend, fondly recalling how they'd sat around that same table, laughing and giggling like two schoolgirls. For hours on end they'd made plans for the new baby, stitching tiny gowns and lace bonnets and knitting booties. So many dreams had come to an end with Letty's death; so many hopes would be buried with her.

The funeral was small. Only a handful of neighbors stood in a circle around the open grave, singing "Amazing grace, how sweet the sound, that saved a wretch like me."

Letty had known that grace. She was at rest now, gone home.

Pastor Olson held his worn Bible, looking over the small group of neighbors with compassionate eyes. "We are gathered here to say good-bye to Letty. This young wife and mother loved God. She lived in obedience to His commandments. And our lives are richer for having known her.

"She was a good friend, a good wife, and she would have made a good mother—but unforeseen circumstances took her from us. God did not cause Letty to die, and we must not place the blame at His doorstep. But we can be sure He received her with open arms, and He had a place prepared for her.

"Although she left this life, leaving behind a husband and daughter, she did not go alone. A loving heavenly Father sent His angels to carry Lazarus home, and those same angels cradled our friend in their arms and carried her to that place where there are no more tears, no more sorrow, no pain.

"We grieve today for Letty. We will miss her, but she is in a far better place, and someday we will be reunited with her. Until then we will remember her with love, and we thank God for the privilege of having had her with us for a precious while. Letty is not gone—she lives in our hearts and minds, and she will live on in her precious baby daughter. We will not forget her. Let us pray."

The baby cried, and Charity gently patted the tiny back until she quieted. Neighbors paused to shake hands and murmur words of condolence, leaving one by one until only Charity and Ansel were left.

She waited, letting him take the lead, but he only stood staring at the raw earth heaped over the casket. The baby whimpered, and he cast one blank look in their direction and turned away. Charity walked alone back to the dugout, carrying Letty's daughter. Ansel didn't come in to eat until long after she had fed the baby and rocked her to sleep.

Friday dawned dark and dreary. A cold, gray mist fell from a leaden sky and encompassed the buckboard as Ansel and Charity rode without speaking.

Occasionally she crooned to the tiny infant carefully wrapped against the weather and cradled closely in her arms. Ansel drove the team of horses with methodical movements, seemingly unaware of either her or the child.

Had it been only two days since she'd traveled this same road? To Charity it seemed an eternity had passed since Wednesday, the day Ansel had come to fetch her for Letty.

Dear, sweet Letty. It was still hard to comprehend that the fresh mound of dirt behind the Latimer dugout was all that remained of her friend.

Death had come so swiftly she hardly had time to get it all straight in her mind. Letty was in heaven, leaving her precious baby motherless, and poor Ansel, all his hopes and dreams dashed. No wife and a newborn babe to look after. Her heart went out to him.

The baby started fussing and Charity looked up. "She's hungry again." Without the benefit of her mother's milk the infant seemed insatiable.

It bothered Charity that the baby hadn't been named yet. When she'd mentioned the subject at breakfast, Ansel looked at her vacantly. Instead of answering, he'd responded vaguely about his crop for next spring.

Letty had wanted to name the baby Mary Kathleen, if she should have a girl, but Charity wanted Ansel's blessing on the name. He glanced down at the infant, and she wondered if he was aware it was his child. At times, she didn't think he knew. He'd barely acknowledged that the child had been born, leaving the baby's sole care to her.

She was sure Ansel was acting strangely because his grief was so profound. He didn't cry or express his sorrow overtly. Charity knew if he'd just hold his new daughter, somehow a small part of Letty would return to him.

The babe looked so much like her mother. Letty's laughing, amber-colored eyes stared back at her. Letty would live on in this tiny morsel of humanity. She had to make Ansel realize that.

"We'll be at your place soon," he said quietly, his tone unchanged by the sucking noises the baby made on her fist. "The child can eat then."

Charity lifted the infant to her shoulder and gently bounced her up and down. The soothing motion stilled her fretfulness for the moment. She worried how Ansel would care for the baby alone, once he returned home. Perhaps, she sighed, it would be good for father and daughter to be on their own. She'd promised to help find a woman to care for the baby, but she knew that could take time. Most everyone in these parts had their own young'uns to see after. In some ways, though, she felt that might be for the best. Ansel could become acquainted with his daughter, and Mary Kathleen could help fill the void in his life.

The baby whimpered as the buckboard topped a rise and Charity's cabin came into view. Her thoughts turned to another, even more perplexing problem: the stranger in her house. He would have to be buried immediately.

She'd been gone much longer than she'd expected, and his remains would have to be disposed of quickly.

She glanced at Ansel and prayed he'd spare her the unpleasant task. Her heart still ached from having left the man to die alone.

The buckboard rumbled into the yard, and Ansel brought the horses to a halt. Charity noticed a heavy plume of smoke roaring from the chimney.

Ansel jumped down from the wagon and lifted Charity and the baby to the ground.

"Someone has built a fire," she remarked, puzzled. She stared at the rising smoke. Was it possible the stranger was alive? A thrill of expectation shot through her, though she quickly suppressed the unlikely hope. There had to be another explanation for the smoke.

She glanced around the yard, looking for a clue. The stack of buffalo chips next to the house was the exact height it had been when she'd left two days ago. The oxen grazed stoically. Old Bossy, her bag heavy with two days' milk, bawled from the small pen beside the lean-to. A few hens roamed outside, scratching in the dirt.

Gabriel and Job lay in front of the door, lazily wagging their tails, apparently waiting for Charity to come and scratch behind their ears.

Everything looked exactly like she'd left it, except for the strong smell of smoke in the air. She turned to ask Ansel how he'd explain the strange occurrence, but he was already climbing back onto the seat of the buckboard.

"Ansel, why don't you rest for a spell before you leave?" She knew he'd need the wagon to carry the stranger's remains to the gravesite.

"Thank you, but I'd best be getting along." He picked up the reins and released the brake.

Charity's jaw dropped. "Ansel," she protested lamely, "you can't be leaving!"

"You take care now, you hear?" He whistled and slapped the

reins across the horses' broad rumps. The buckboard rolled noisily out of the yard amid the jangle of harness and creaking leather.

Charity watched the wagon roll off in the direction it had just come. She glanced from the bundle in her arms to the disappearing buckboard. Great balls of fire! He was leaving.

"Wait!" she shouted, running after the wagon. "You forgot your baby!" But in moments she was out of breath. Her footsteps faltered.

She released an exasperated sigh and stared down at the infant in her arms. If this wasn't a fine kettle of fish! How dare Ansel ride off and leave the child in her care!

The baby started to cry, thrashing her fists angrily in the air, demanding her dinner. Charity trudged toward the house, wondering what had gotten into Ansel. Surely he'd have the good sense to remember he'd forgotten his daughter and come back. Meanwhile she was left to care for the infant, and face the unpleasant task of burying the stranger, by herself.

If her thoughts weren't disconcerting enough, the baby was screaming at the top of her lungs when she finally reached the cabin. She pushed the door open and sucked in her breath when a blast of suffocating air nearly knocked her to her knees.

"What in...?" Charity pushed the door wider and stepped into the room, trying to adjust her eyes to the dim light. When her vision cleared she couldn't believe her eyes.

Two squaws sat before the fireplace in rocking chairs they had pulled up to the hearth. They had built a roaring fire, and the flames were licking wildly up the chimney.

Charity wrinkled her nose, her attention momentarily diverted when she noticed the several large pans of herbs and roots bubbling on the stove, filling the room with a vile odor.

The stranger lay on the bed, swathed tightly from head to toe in a bedsheet. He reminded Charity of a picture of an Egyptian mummy she had once seen in a book.

The room was so stifling hot she couldn't breathe, and the smell rolling from the stove made her stomach lurch. She stood speechless at the door, clutching the baby against her bosom.

Little Fawn caught sight of Charity and gave her a wide grin. "White Sister return?" Her smile wilted. She scrambled to her feet, dragging Laughing Waters with her. "We take care of Gold Hair."

"Little Fawn? Laughing Waters?" Charity stared at the two disheveled women with growing bewilderment. The heat in the room had flushed their faces with perspiration. Buckskin dresses clung to their massive forms. Sweat rolled from beneath their dark hairlines and dripped off their chins.

"What is going on here?" Charity glanced to the bed, where the stranger lay. Her heart leaped when she heard him moan weakly, trying to break free of the bindings.

Little Fawn crossed her arms over her ample bosom, and a combative glint came into her eyes. "We make Gold Hair better."

Charity couldn't believe he was still alive. It was nothing short of a miracle, but the man had survived. "He's better. . . . He really is? Oh, thank You, God!"

Laughing Waters grunted. "Little Fawn and Laughing Waters make Gold Hair better," she said curtly.

Charity hurried to the bed. Yes, he was alive. His eyes were open and staring. His nose was visible through an opening in the sheet.

"Why is he wrapped so tightly?" she asked in a whisper. Was he aware? Fully conscious? She didn't know.

"Make medicine work," Little Fawn explained. She scurried to the bed and edged Charity out of the way with a large hip. Her fingers picked up a stray lock of his hair, and the man's eyes widened fearfully. She smiled and stroked the golden strand. "Pretty, like rocks in water. I keep."

The man groaned and clamped his eyes shut.

"I think he's trying to say something." Charity reached to unwrap the bandage wound so tightly under his chin that it prevented him from speaking. Little Fawn's hand shot out and stopped her. The squaw sent her a stern look. "We help Gold Hair!"

Charity glanced up, surprised to hear the possessive note in her voice. For months, Laughing Waters and Little Fawn had made a habit of visiting the cabin, making themselves at home. Whenever they came, they examined every nook and cranny, satisfying their natural curiosity.

She never scolded them, even when they peeked in the cooking utensils or pried open the storage bins. If she wasn't busy, she would let them watch her work the spinning wheel. Sometimes she would snip a piece of yarn or a colorful ribbon and give it to them. They always left delighted with their new treasures.

Apparently they'd happened by to visit two days ago and discovered the wounded man, and now they had laid claim to him.

"Thank you very much for tending. . .Gold Hair. . .while I was away," she said carefully. She would have to convince them that the man was hers, not theirs.

"Gold Hair heap good man," Little Fawn proclaimed. She grinned.

"Oh yes. . .yes, I can see that. He's very. . .nice. He's. . .mine."

Little Fawn's face dropped.

Laughing Waters's eyes narrowed. "Why you leave Gold Hair? Heap big sick."

"I know he is." Charity wasn't sure how much they understood, but she sensed they were waiting for an explanation. Remembering the baby, she smiled and unwrapped the blanket, proudly revealing a grumpy Mary Kathleen. "See? I've been away helping my friend have her baby. That's why I had to leave Gold Hair."

The women lowered their heads in unison and stared at the child. "Papoose." Little Fawn tickled under the baby's chin.

Charity noticed Laughing Waters wasn't impressed. "Gold Hair heap big sick. We fix; we keep," she announced.

Since the Indians had never seemed threatening, Charity wasn't alarmed. Apparently the two women had been able to do for the stranger what she hadn't, and she was grateful. But not grateful enough to let them have him.

"You see, my friend, Letty, was very ill. She was about to have her baby, and she needed my help," Charity explained. "Since Gold Hair was asleep, I thought it would be all right to leave." That wasn't exactly true, but Charity knew the women would have no way of knowing otherwise. Broken English was their only means of communication. Actually they understood very little short of their native tongue.

Laughing Waters was clearly skeptical. "Where mother of papoose?"

"She. . .died," Charity admitted.

Laughing Waters still wasn't convinced. "Where papoose's father?"

"He's. . .not here right now. . .but he'll be back soon. Because my friend died, I was gone longer than I intended. I'm thankful to see you and Little Fawn have taken such good care of Gold Hair."

Little Fawn and Laughing Waters exchanged noncommittal looks. "If you'll show me what to do, I'll take over now." Charity prayed they'd buy her story. "He was attacked by a wolf, and I haven't been quite sure how to care for him. I see you have him on the mend."

Laughing Waters grunted. It seemed unlikely the two would

relinquish their rights to the white man. They went off into a corner and gestured animatedly, whispering to each other.

Charity held her breath. She glanced at the bed and found the man eyeing all three of them warily. His eyes were as blue as she remembered, and she tried to reassure him with a discreet nod.

Laughing Waters returned and grudgingly handed Charity a large cup of vile-smelling liquid. "Make Gold Hair drink."

Charity nodded and released a pent-up sigh of relief. She set the cup on the bedside table. "Thank you. I will."

"We be back Big Father's Day," Little Fawn stated firmly.

The baby began to fuss, and Charity absently rocked her back and forth in her arms. She thought she'd faint from the heat. "Sunday? Yes, Sunday will be fine." They were not going to give him up easily.

"Keep fire burning. Heap big sweat. Make Gold Hair better."

"Yes. . .yes, of course," Charity promised, wondering why she hadn't thought to try and sweat the poison out of him herself.

"Put medicine on hurts."

Charity stared at the bucket of herbs and roots sitting next to the bed. "I will."

Little Fawn walked back to the bed and touched a strand of golden hair. She gave the man a flirtatious wink and displayed the wide gap of missing front teeth. He shut his eyes.

"We go now," Laughing Waters announced.

"I'll take good care of Gold Hair," Charity promised.

Laughing Waters started past her and paused to look at the baby again. "Gold Hair make stronger papoose," she grunted.

Charity watched Little Fawn and Laughing Waters open the door.

"We be back Big Father's Day," Laughing Waters repeated.

"We'll be here."

The door slammed, and Charity sank weakly onto a chair. The baby began to scream. *What a disagreeable day,* she thought numbly.

Most disagreeable.

❧

Beau lay wrapped in his cocoon, relieved the two squaws had left. He didn't know what the women had in mind for him, but he had a hunch it wasn't anything he'd enjoy. The woman who'd gotten rid of them tried to soothe the infant.

She kept casting worried glances toward the bed as she rushed around the room, trying to calm the baby's wails, which were getting more frantic by the minute.

Even the warm milk squeezed through a clean cloth didn't help. The baby screamed at the top of her lungs, her tiny face turning red as a raspberry. The woman paced the floor, jiggling her up and down in her arms.

The more she jiggled, the louder the baby cried. Obviously she hadn't had much experience with babies.

Still trussed up like a Christmas goose, Beau lay on the bed watching the growing ruckus. When the infant erupted into a full-blown tantrum, holding her breath until her tiny features turned a strange, bluish white, the woman panicked and broke into tears. Both woman and child were sobbing noisily when Beau cleared his throat, hoping to get her attention.

He'd felt relief when he'd finally realized he wasn't in hell—at least he wasn't in the fiery pit described in the Good Book. But exactly where was he?

Wherever it was, it was strange. Two Indian squaws fussing over him, slapping foul-smelling something on his wounds. Now he was faced with a baby howling like a banshee and a woman who obviously didn't know the first thing about motherhood.

He cleared his throat and squirmed about, but the woman and baby were too busy crying to notice. Glancing around, he focused on a tin cup filled with tea sitting on the stand beside the bed. He inched his way across the straw-filled mattress and nudged the cup with his shoulder, knocking it off the table.

The contents splattered on the bed, leaving a dark stain on the white linens, but the cup had the desired effect of hitting the floor with a resounding clatter.

Both woman and baby ceased their wailing at the same instant. She looked his way, and he tried to motion with his eyes for her to remove the tight bandage confining his chin.

The baby resumed screaming while the woman continued to stare at him.

"Were you speaking to me?"

"Ohmmhgtynm."

"You want me to untie the bandage?"

"Ohmmmhgtynm!"

"Yes, of course."

She used one hand to try to loosen the knot in the bandage, attempting to converse over the baby's screams. "I'm sorry, I know we're disturbing you, and I'm trying to get her to hush, but she won't!"

The knot came undone, and Beau felt like he'd been released from a bear trap. He worked his jaws back and forth, wincing at the painful stiffness yet grateful for the overdue freedom.

"I don't know what's gotten into her," the woman apologized. "Nothing I do seems to help."

"Get the scissors and cut me out of this sheet," Beau whispered hoarsely.

"Oh, I don't think I should. Little Fawn and Laughing Waters said—"

"I know what they said!"

Startled by the snap in his voice, the infant screamed louder.

"Just get me out of this!"

"You're scaring the baby." The woman turned mulish. She patted the baby on the back, which only made her cry harder. "If I remove the sheet, it'll disturb your wounds. I don't want to do anything to hinder your recovery. You've been very ill."

Beau interrupted, making a conscious effort to lower his voice and speak calmly. "Just get me out of this. I'll help with the baby."

Evidently those were the magic words. He'd figured she'd do anything to stop the baby's crying, and he'd been right. She grabbed the scissors and started snipping away at the sheet. The baby lay on the bed beside Beau, kicking and bellowing at the top of her lungs.

"Your bandages need changing." Beau sucked in his breath when she lifted the fabric Little Fawn and Laughing Waters had carefully lain over the tender wounds.

"Ow! That hurts. Take it easy!"

"I can't help it; I'm trying to be gentle." She gingerly peeled away another layer. "You don't have to be so cranky."

"You let a wolf gnaw on you for supper and see how full of brotherly love you are. Ouch! Look out; that hurts!"

There was a time when he would apologize for yelling at a female, but much had happened to change him in the past year. He gritted his teeth in renewed agony when cold air hit his wounds.

"There, now...one more..." She removed the last bandage, and he sagged with relief.

Raising himself up, he sucked in his breath at the pain and closed his eyes until the room stopped spinning. He didn't know a man could hurt like this. Foul-smelling mud encased his body; the odor made him sick.

The woman sat down in a nearby chair and rocked the baby.

"You remember the wolf?" She stared at him as if she was afraid he'd keel over.

"I try not to." He winced when the baby's howls continued. "Hand her to me."

She glanced at him in surprise. "You feel like holding her?"

"I can hold her better than I can stand to listen to her."

She hurriedly gathered the baby in her arms and carefully handed her to him. Beau caught his breath when one tiny flailing fist hit one of his wounds.

"I'm so sorry!" She started to take the infant, but Beau shrugged her away and eased the tiny bundle into the crook of his arm. He laid his head back on the pillow, feeling as limp as a piece of worn-out rope. A fine sheen of sweat stood on his forehead. To his relief, the baby promptly ceased crying and snuggled deep into his side.

The room became quite peaceful. Beau gazed down at the infant in his arms. "You know, little one, you're picking up some bad habits," he said softly. "Some man's going to have to take that fire out of you someday if you don't control that nasty temper."

The baby hiccupped then stuck her fist in her mouth and sucked loudly.

"She's hungry," he said.

"I know she is, but she refuses to take her milk."

"Give me the cloth."

The woman fetched the cloth and gave it to him. In moments the baby was sucking contentedly.

"How did you do that?" She seemed awed by the way he handled the child.

The tiny baby girl settled snugly next to his large frame, her big amber eyes drooping with exhaustion.

"I've always been good with kids. I have a nephew I used to visit every day. We got along real well."

Beau refused to think about the child he'd lost.

He held the baby until she slowly dropped into a peaceful slumber. She nestled trustfully against him, and somehow the pain in his heart began to ease. The image of Betsy, heavy with child, drifted into his thoughts. *Oh God, not now, please.* He didn't want to think about Betsy. . .didn't want to remember it could have been his child tucked against his side. He could feel the aching sadness creep back to overwhelm him.

"Would you like me to move her?" the woman asked.

Beau tucked the baby's blanket snugly around her. "She'll be fine right here."

"I need to put clean bandages on your wounds."

"In a while." He lay back, exhausted. As soon as he got his strength he was getting out of this madhouse. Toothless women torturing him, a squalling baby, and this woman who watched him like a hawk. Did she think he was going somewhere? In his condition? From what he could tell, she was still young. Small and slender with hair the color of a raven's wing, nice green eyes, and a wide, generous mouth—certainly nothing about her appearance to turn a man away. He realized he hadn't noticed a woman in a very long time, and he didn't plan to start now. There would never be another Betsy in his life. Not ever.

Charity tried not to stare, but her eyes wandered back to the bare expanse of masculine chest. She remembered how protected, how wonderful she'd felt when he'd held her, even if he had thought she was his Betsy.

She suddenly realized that she missed having her own man, missed being held and kissed and loved.

She didn't think of Ferrand as often, but then she hadn't thought of him any less. Having this man in her house was improper, but surely God would condone compassion. Human compassion of which the apostle Paul spoke so eloquently.

After her husband's death she'd sworn she'd never love another man, never again risk the hurt he'd caused her by going off and getting himself killed in that senseless war.

It occurred to Charity that she'd been angry at Ferrand for a long time. Now she could feel that anger subsiding. For the first time since his death she found herself thinking that maybe it would be possible to love again. To feel again.

She longed to have her own child. Mary Kathleen was precious, but she wasn't hers. Taking care of Letty's baby only reminded her of the emptiness in her heart, the void. If only she'd had Ferrand's child the last few years she wouldn't have been so lonely. Her gaze drifted wistfully back to the stranger, and she wondered anew why she found him so attractive. His hair was shaggy, he hadn't shaved in weeks, and his large frame was whipcord thin. The two large wounds across his middle were covered with a thick, sticky poultice. His ribs were poking through his skin. Still, she found him extremely. . .interesting.

Charity found the admission disturbing. Would her growing feelings for this stranger only serve to bring her new heartbreak?

"I guess we should introduce ourselves." She willed herself to take one step at a time. She drew her palm across her dress to dry the moisture from it and extended her hand. "I'm Charity Burk. I shot the wolf. This is my cabin."

The man glanced at her extended hand but made no effort to take it. "You shouldn't have bothered."

"Oh. . .no bother." Charity faltered. She thought he'd be immensely grateful that she'd saved his life. She paused, waiting for a thank-you, but when "God bless you" didn't come, she dropped her hand to her side. "What did you say your name was?" He hadn't said, but she thought it only decent he supply some sort of information about himself.

"Claxton."

Charity smiled. "Just. . .Claxton?"

"Beau. Beau Claxton."

"That's nice. I'll bet your mother chose that name." Charity noticed he was losing interest in the conversation. "Well, Beau, I must admit, there were times when I thought I'd never know who you were." She watched his eyes droop with fatigue. "Are you from around here?"

"No." His voice sounded weaker than before.

"I'm sorry I had to leave, but Letty—the baby's mother—she needed my help. I'm so thankful Laughing Waters and Little Fawn happened along when they did."

"I'm not sure I'm all that thankful, but I'm too tired to think about it. How long have I been like this?"

"Nearly a week, but you're getting better." It was a relief to see his wounds starting to improve. He still had many weeks before he was healed.

He was silent for a moment. "You said the child's mother died?"

"Yes, I'm afraid she did."

"That's too bad. A baby should have its mother."

"Would you like some broth? I see that Laughing Waters and Little Fawn left some on the stove for you."

"I'm not hungry. Just tired. Bone tired."

"Rest a spell. We can talk later." Charity leaned to tuck the sheet around him and the sleeping infant. The two made a fetching sight. His eyes drifted shut. She stood and gazed fondly from the baby to him. In moments they were sound asleep, his large arm wrapped protectively around Mary Kathleen's tiny shoulders.

I hope there's no Betsy waiting for you to come home. Charity found herself appalled by her thoughts. Startled by her wistful thinking, she realized how selfish she sounded.

If he was married, she would write and inform his wife of her husband's injuries straightaway. And yet. . . She reached to brush a lock of golden hair from his forehead and sighed.

Maybe. . .just maybe, Betsy was his sister. But no, he wouldn't kiss a sister the way he'd kissed her. Could Betsy be an acquaintance? The possibility sent a pang of jealousy through her. Jealousy? Now, where had that come from? Beau Claxton was a stranger. But she couldn't forget the way he looked, lying there helpless, and she couldn't forget those blue eyes. Anyone could tell from the way he acted he'd been brought up a gentleman.

Well, no matter who Betsy was, Beau Claxton was a fine man. If there wasn't a legal Mrs. Claxton, there'd be one soon—if she had anything to say about it.

Chapter 5

The smell of corn bread baking in the oven woke Beau next. He had no concept of time. The tempting aroma filled the cabin, and his empty stomach knotted with hunger. How long had it been since he'd last eaten?

He glanced down at the small bundle snuggled against his side, and a smile touched the corners of his mouth. The baby was sleeping peacefully.

Without disturbing the infant, he shifted to ease his stiff joints. The movement hurt, but not as much as before.

Settled more comfortably, he let his gaze drift toward the window, where he noticed the last rays of sunshine glistening on the pane. *It must be late afternoon,* he thought, realizing this was the first time he'd been able to distinguish the hour of day. His head felt clearer, more alert. How long had he been drifting in and out of darkness that had threatened to sweep him away forever?

His gaze moved on, roaming aimlessly around the room. The bright gingham curtain hanging at the window looked freshly washed and ironed. A buffalo rug covered the floor. Everything was tidy.

The room had a woman's touch. The colorful red-and-blue

patchwork quilt draped across the foot of the bed reflected long hours spent on the intricate rows of tiny stitches. He didn't know much about such womanly pursuits, but he'd watched his mother sit beside the lamp in her parlor, working late into the night on a coverlet much like the one he saw now. Bets had brightened their home with pretty things. His chest tightened when he remembered the home he had built with such high hopes. He'd planned to grow old there, raise a fine family of Claxton men and women. When Betsy died, taking their child with her, he'd lost everything: his home, his will to live—even his trust in God. He felt ashamed at the way he had acted. Just walked away from the people who loved him, away from the values he'd been taught; he sure hadn't been living the way a Claxton had been taught to live.

He'd been drifting for a long time, bitter, angry, and not caring if he lived or died, but now it seemed God had decided that he'd live. He guessed one couldn't run far enough or long enough to get away from God. Beau knew it wouldn't be easy, but he was going to have to make a life for himself again. Life went on, whether a man wanted it to or not, and the time had come for him to bury Betsy and let her go. He had to get up and go home, back to Missouri. Maybe he'd talk Ma and their housekeeper, Willa, into coming to live with him. The women could tend the house while he worked the fields. It wouldn't be the rich, full life he'd had with Betsy, but it would be livable.

The sound of a voice humming "Dixie" distracted him. His head slowly pivoted on the pillow, seeking the source of the clear, sweet tones.

He saw a young woman standing at the stove, stirring a large pot with a wooden spoon. Instead of the foul-smelling brew the pot had formerly sent off, a delicious aroma of meat and vegetables rose from the steam.

Who was this girl? Beau searched his memory for her name. Charita? Cherry? He couldn't remember.

"Well, hello. You're finally awake." Charity's voice interrupted his thoughts. She set the spoon aside and wiped her hands on her apron. "Dinner will be ready soon. I hope you feel up to eating a bite."

His gaze drifted back to the pot on the stove. The smell of stew simmering piqued his interest. "I believe I could eat."

"Well, good!" Charity brought her hands together enthusiastically. "That's the most encouraging sign of recovery so far." She ladled the thick stew onto a plate, adding a piping hot wedge of corn bread and slab of freshly churned butter, then arranged everything on a tray along with a large glass of milk.

The baby was beginning to stir when she approached, so she set the tray on the small table beside the bed and gently scooped Mary Kathleen into her arms. "Best you eat slow," she cautioned. "It's been a long time since you've had solid food. Too much taken too fast might upset your stomach."

"Aren't you going to eat?" His eyes were on the corn bread, thick and crusty—just the way Ma used to make it.

"I'll feed the baby first." Charity returned to the stove and removed the bottle of milk she'd warmed, pouring some in the dish she'd used earlier. She tied a knot in the end of a square of cheesecloth and dipped it in the milk. "You and Mary Kathleen had a nice long nap."

Beau picked up the piece of corn bread and took a cautious bite. The exquisite flavor burst in his mouth. It'd been a long time since he'd tasted anything so good.

"Looks like snow to the west." Charity sat down in the rocker and held the baby, who was eagerly sucking from the cloth. "Sure could use a good soaking. It's been real dry."

Beau took another bite of the corn bread and chewed it slowly. "What time of the year is this?"

"Late November." Charity cocked her head to one side. "Why?"

November? He'd been wandering for over a year? The thought astounded him, and he felt a pang of remorse. His family must be sick with worry. "Exactly where am I?"

"Kansas, why?"

"No reason." Beau picked up the spoon and brought a bite of stew to his mouth.

"This is my home. . .mine and my husband's until he died."

"I'm in Kansas? I'm not in Missouri?"

Charity laughed warmly. "You're in Kansas. Not far from a town called Cherry Grove."

"Kansas?"

"Kansas," she repeated. "What part of Missouri are you from?"

Kansas? How had he ended up so far from home? Ma must be nearly out of her mind with worry. Lilly Claxton was a mother hen, never happy until all of her sons were safe beneath her wings.

"I. . .River Run. . .I think."

Charity thought his answer was odd. Had the sickness affected his memory? In a way, it would be to her advantage if he couldn't remember his past. If he couldn't remember who he was, then he might be more easily persuaded to stay and help her. She decided to face her biggest obstacle first.

"Who's Betsy?"

He met her inquiring gaze, and a defensive light came into his eyes. "Who?"

"Betsy. You kept calling for her while you were unconscious." Charity bit her lower lip, praying Betsy would be anyone but his wife.

Beau pushed his plate away, though he'd barely touched it.

"You're finished already?" Her tone rang with disappointment.

"I've had enough."

"But you barely touched your food."

"I lost my appetite."

Charity hated to hear that. If he didn't eat properly, she knew he'd be slow to regain his strength. "I'll put your plate in the warming oven; you'll feel like eating more later."

He seemed to ignore the suggestion. He settled back on the pillow and closed his eyes.

Charity felt like crying. They had been getting along so well until she mentioned Betsy. She hated to ask him again, but she had to know. If he had a wife, then she'd nurse him to recovery and then send him on his way. She sighed. Maybe she should give up and go back home. Her family would welcome her.

No. She had to stay and fight. Ferrand had worked too hard for her to turn her back on this land and walk away.

When Mary Kathleen finished the milk, Charity lifted her up to her shoulder and patted her back gently, savoring the sweet fragrance of the baby's skin. Once more her thoughts turned to the baby's father and where he could be. All afternoon she had been expecting him to return for his daughter, but it was getting dark and she feared he wasn't coming.

If he didn't come tomorrow, she wasn't sure what she'd do. Send someone to fetch him? She didn't know who it could be. And it would be impossible to leave Beau and the baby alone. You'd think Ansel would be hungry for the sight of this precious child. Mary Kathleen was all he had left of Letty, and she needed her father. Maybe he was making arrangements for someone to help him care for his child.

Grief had rendered Ansel temporarily forgetful, she reasoned. It was the only explanation she could come up with to explain his puzzling behavior. Surely tomorrow he would come for his daughter. She needed milk bottles not cheesecloth to drink from.

Returning to the present, Charity remembered that Beau hadn't answered her question about Betsy. Was it an oversight, or had he deliberately avoided the subject? There was only one way to find out. She could be what Ferrand had always called downright nosy. She decided to chance it.

"You never answered me about Betsy."

This time, she was sure he was deliberately avoiding her question. He lay on the bed, eyes closed, hands folded peacefully across his chest. Ignoring her.

The baby burped loudly, filling the silence that had suddenly crowded the room. Beau remained silent.

"Well?" Charity prompted. She wasn't going to give up until he answered her.

Finally he drew a deep breath and opened his eyes. He met her gaze across the room, his face twisted into a pained expression. "Betsy is my wife."

Disappointment ricocheted like heat lightning through Charity's heart. She'd known it was a possibility that he was married, hadn't she? Hadn't she warned herself not to get her hopes up? But nothing could dull the dismal feeling of frustration closing in on her.

"Oh. . .I—I thought maybe that's who she might be." Her voice sounded high and hollow even to her own ears.

Well, Charity, you've no one to blame but yourself for getting the foolish idea in your head that he was sent to you as a personal gift. It was plain he wouldn't be any use to her now. He had a wife, Betsy, waiting for him when he recovered. She recalled the love in his eyes when he had been so terribly sick and had mistaken her for Betsy. He wouldn't stay. She couldn't expect him to.

She sighed and squared her shoulders. "First thing tomorrow morning, I'll write your wife a letter informing her about what's happened and where you are."

Beau stared at the ceiling for a moment with expressionless blue eyes. Charity thought she detected a veiled sadness creeping into them. "Yeah, you can do that, but I don't see how you're going to have it delivered," he said softly.

"Shouldn't be too hard. It's about time to go into town for the mail. I'll send the letter then. It will take a few weeks to reach your wife, but—"

Beau interrupted. "You can't do that. Bets is dead."

Charity's gaze lifted to his, witnessing the grief in his eyes. She ached for his loss, but she couldn't smother the faint glimmer of hope for what this might mean to her.

"I'm so sorry."

Dead. Betsy was dead! Relief filled her, and she was instantly ashamed for being so heartless and selfish. It was plain to see that his wife's death had nearly destroyed him.

"Yeah." He took a deep, ragged breath. "So am I."

"How long ago?"

"Over a year. She was carrying our baby, and a rattler. . .bit her."

Charity knew this couldn't be easy for him. Memories of Ferrand's death flooded back. She listened to Beau speak about his wife's accident in quiet, almost reverent tones. She had a feeling he didn't talk much about Betsy. The way he said her name, the flickering pain in his eyes, told her this was something too private to share with many people. She felt honored he was opening up with her.

"It didn't take long. . . ." His voice broke momentarily, and then he cleared his throat. Charity was surprised to see him reach for his plate again. He calmly picked up the spoon and ladled a bite of vegetables into his mouth. He chewed for a moment, absently, like he didn't taste the stew. When he glanced back at her it was almost as if he'd forgotten she was there. "I loved my wife very much."

"I'm sure you did," Charity said softly, feeling his pain as deeply as she'd felt her husband's loss. "It's hard to get over something like that. I lost my husband four years ago."

"Oh?" He looked surprised, and she realized he hadn't given a thought to why she was living here alone in the middle of Kansas. He'd been too wrapped up in his memories to care about anyone else. She could understand that. Been there herself.

"The war?" he asked.

She nodded. "Ferrand was riding with Sterling Price's Confederate raiders in the fall of sixty-four. When the Confederacy made its last offensive west of the Mississippi, Curtis Steward, with the help of Alfred Pleasonton's cavalry, whipped the Confederates and drove them back into Arkansas. Ferrand was killed near Westport, Missouri."

"The Confederacy?" Beau glanced up. "Your husband fought for the South?"

"His decision was very difficult—especially for me. But I understood his reasons. There was a lot of talk. You must remember, in the Civil War Kansas sent a larger number of Union soldiers to the field, in proportion to its population, than any other state. But my husband and I came from Virginia, and your upbringing is hard to forget. Our families still live there. Ferrand was torn at first, but when it came right down to it, he felt he had to fight for what he believed in. Of course, all he did was go and get himself killed."

"It must have been hard on you."

"Still is," she confessed. "We had barely started homesteading this piece of land when Ferrand decided to join up. For a long time after his death I didn't know what I should do. My family wanted me to move back to Richmond, and that would probably have been wise. But my husband said I was as stubborn as a stuck door when it came to holding on to what's important to me. After all the hard work we'd put into this cabin, I couldn't just walk away and leave it for someone else."

"You have been trying to work the land by yourself?" It was a question, but she could see the knowledge in his eyes. And behind the knowledge lay understanding. The war had left a lot of widows. Women forced to do work they'd never had to do before and for which they were ill suited. She was just one of many.

He shook his head. "I'm having trouble seeing someone your size driving a team of oxen and building fences."

"I've been doing a miserable job of it," Charity admitted. She wasn't too proud to confess. "The fences are mostly down, I haven't had a decent crop in two years, and I haven't begun to make the improvements the state requires to grant me a title." She looked down at the baby. "I must admit, I was near my wits' end when you happened along."

Beau finished the stew and corn bread and drained the glass of milk. She took the tray from him. "I hope the food's setting easy in your stomach. You need to eat if you're going to get your strength back." He couldn't drive posts while he was weak as a newborn calf.

His eyes narrowed. "Why haven't you remarried?"

She shrugged. "We have a real shortage of men out here, Mr. Claxton. Besides, other than my husband, I've never met one I'd want." She looked at his blue eyes, the gold of his hair, the way he was built and knew she had just told a bald-faced lie. She'd met one all right. She couldn't believe she was feeling this way about a man who was more stranger than friend. She suddenly felt bashful. "Never met one I'd want to have underfoot all the time," she corrected.

He smiled, a nice, soft gesture. "I know the feeling. Since Bets died, I haven't been interested in a woman. Doesn't matter, I guess, because I'm never going to marry again."

Charity arched her brow slightly. "Oh?"

"I loved Bets. No one could come close to taking her place."

She overlooked his pessimism. "Do you have family in Missouri? I can write and tell them about your accident."

"I have family, but you don't need to bother getting in touch with them. I've been wandering around ever since Bets died." He paused for a moment before continuing. "I'll write them and let them know where I am, soon as I'm up and around."

"You've been drifting all this time?" She wondered what that would be like. Shut the door on everything she owned and ride away. Some days she'd been in a mood to do just that, but she guessed it was different with women. Some women, like her, needed a home, a permanent place. . .roots.

"Yeah, just drifting."

"Didn't you ever think about home?"

"I don't believe I thought about much of anything. Just trying to outrun the memories."

"You can't run far enough to leave the memories behind," she confided.

"I couldn't. Tried, but I couldn't." He glanced at Mary Kathleen asleep on Charity's shoulder and changed the subject. "Where's the baby's father?"

"I'm not sure. Ansel brought me home yesterday then up and disappeared."

"Disappeared?"

"I don't know what to make of his strange behavior. Ansel's wife, Letty, died giving birth to the baby a few days ago. Now he seems so lost—not like himself at all. When he brought me home yesterday, I thought naturally he'd take the baby with him, but he didn't. He climbed back in the buckboard and drove off." Charity shook her head, still puzzled by Ansel's peculiar behavior. "I figure once he comes to terms with his grief, he'll be back."

She rose and walked over to lay Mary Kathleen at the foot of his bed, her mind going back to what he had said about no other woman ever replacing his wife. She didn't know why that bothered her. It was only natural for him to feel that way. She wouldn't be asking for his love. All she needed was his strength and stamina for the next few months. To clear land and set fences.

It was just as likely that no other man would ever replace Ferrand in her heart. What she felt for Beau Claxton was an attraction, due to the fact she hadn't seen a good-looking, unattached male since she became a widow. This marriage—should she convince him to stay—would be strictly a business proposition. If he'd agree to marry her, they'd be starting out even. And she supposed she shouldn't be beating around the bush about her intentions, either. Now was as good a time as any to tell him about the plan.

"Mr. Claxton," she began in a formal tone.

"Call me Beau." He'd closed his eyes again now, looking relaxed and comfortable. Well, she was getting ready to wake him up.

"I understand how you feel about the loss of your wife, and I can sympathize with your feelings about not wanting to marry again. I loved Ferrand with all my heart, but I've discovered that sometimes you have to put personal feelings aside and go on with life. . . ." Her voice trailed off.

"That's what they say."

Trying to gather enough courage to proceed with the conversation wasn't easy. Like pulling hen's teeth. She wasn't an aggressive woman. Asking this man to marry her was going to be one of the most brazen things she'd ever undertaken, but she'd never before faced losing everything either.

Necessity overrode her fear in this instance. She knew she had him at a certain disadvantage. He was still too weak to walk out on her if he didn't take to the idea right away. If he did balk—and she was fully braced for that possibility—she would at least have a few days to make him change his mind.

"You're wondering about what?" he asked.

She took a deep breath and shut her eyes. There was no easy way to do it. She'd simply have to be blunt and forthright before her courage failed her again.

"I was wondering. . .would you marry me?" Her voice suddenly sounded downright meek. And brazen. Definitely brazen.

For a moment it appeared her words had failed to register. His eyes remained shut, his head nestled deep within the pillow.

"Ordinarily I'd never be so blunt," she rushed on, determined that he wouldn't think her a sinful, immoral woman. "But I'm afraid I'm in a terrible quandary." Her voice picked up tempo when she interpreted his continued silence to be a hopeful sign. "You see, if I don't make the required land improvements within a year, I can't claim title to my homestead. To be candid, Mr. Claxton, I need a man. That's why I think it was God's care—you know, the way I found you in my stream. I dragged you back to the cabin and worked day and night to save your life—though I suppose most of the credit should go to God, then to Little Fawn and Laughing Waters. Regardless, I worked just as hard, and if it hadn't been for Letty desperately needing my help, I would never have dreamed of leaving you here. . .to die. . .alone." She paused. "But, of course, you didn't die, and I'm tremendously grateful that you didn't. Now"—she paused again for air, preparing to make her next recitation in one long breath—"you'll find I work hard, cook decently, bathe regularly, and make a good companion." She hurried to the side of the bed and sat down, enthusiasm growing as she explained the plan. "I figure if you'd be so kind as to marry me, then at the end of the year, I can claim my land and you can be on your way."

Beau's eyes remained closed. She prayed he hadn't fallen asleep during the discussion. "Of course, I realize I'm asking you to spend the whole winter here, but I think it will take many months for you to fully regain your strength. In the meantime we can make the needed improvements on my land, weather permitting. Naturally, I'm prepared to pay you well for your time and effort," she promised. "I'm not a rich woman, but I do have a small nest egg, and I can assure you I'll see that your generosity is handsomely rewarded." She paused, bending closer to see if he was listening. She couldn't tell. "It wouldn't take very long, and I'd be most grateful for your assistance."

Beau's left eye slowly opened.

Charity held her breath. If he refused, she wasn't sure what she'd do next.

Both eyes opened wide, staring at her in disbelief. "Marry you?"

Her smile wilted. She might have been a bit hasty in revealing her plan. Maybe she should have waited a few days, let him get to know her better. . . .

"I realize this may have come as a bit of a shock, but you see, Beau—"

"Mr. Claxton," he interrupted curtly.

Her chin tilted stubbornly, and she ignored his frosty attitude. She understood this might be disconcerting for him. She was a stranger. "Mr. Claxton, I'm afraid my unfortunate circumstances have forced me to come directly to the point, though to be honest, I don't know any other way to be. I've been truthful by telling you why I'd make such an unusual suggestion, and while I can't fault you for being shocked, I don't think you have a right to act like I've escaped from an asylum for the insane. I'm. . .desperate." Her tone switched from meek to pleading.

Beau stared at her, looking like he found the sudden turn of conversation incredible. "Let me understand. . .you're seriously asking me—a man you know nothing about—to marry you? For all you know, I could be a worthless drifter, a debaucher, a hired killer, and there you sit offering to be my wife—and pay me for the privilege?"

"I am indeed," Charity stated firmly. "I need a man."

He shook his head, frowning "Lady, this is—"

"I need a man's strength. Someone to help me work the land, meet the requirements so I can keep what Ferrand and I have invested our lives in." She felt her face color. This was so embarrassing. What would her husband think if he could see her now? The heat intensified at the thought.

"Why in the world would you ask a stranger to marry you? Are you addlebrained?" His tone was less than charming. "A woman should never ask a man to marry her, regardless of the circumstances."

"I'm not addlebrained, and I told you why,'" she said. "I don't want to lose my land, and I'm going to unless I come up with a man soon."

"So you propose marriage to the first man you meet?"

"You're not the first man I've met. You're just the first available man I've met," she corrected.

The baby started to fret. Charity rose to pick her up. "Besides, you're not a stranger—not really. In fact, I feel rather close to you." Caring for him had brought an intimacy much like she'd known with Ferrand. He didn't know it, but he'd kissed her, even if he'd thought she was someone else. "I know your name is Beau Claxton; I know that once you've recovered from your accident, you'll be a strong, healthy man—healthy enough to clear land, set fence posts, and drive a team of oxen. I know you come from Missouri, you're widowed, and because of your injuries, you're going to be laid up here for a good long while." Charity turned and smiled at him. "That's all I need to know, Mr. Claxton."

"You must be addlebrained," Beau muttered. "You don't know a thing about me, and I told you, I don't plan on ever marrying again."

"Are you refusing my offer?" She had the sinking feeling that he was.

He glared at her again, disbelief reflected in his blue eyes. "Of course I am."

"You won't at least think about it?"

He shut his eyes again, and it appeared he was praying for patience. "I feel obligated to you for saving my life, but not enough to marry you."

Silence fell between them for a moment. Charity tried to digest his words. He wasn't going to marry her; that was plain as the nose on her face. Well, she hadn't wanted to take advantage of the situation, but he was leaving her little choice. The silence had grown thick and dark.

He glanced over at the rocker, and from the expression on his face, his temper was starting to simmer. He took a deep breath. "If you're so desperate for a husband, what about Mary Kathleen's father? Seems to me he could use a wife right about now, and the two of you know each other."

"Ansel?" Charity looked up in surprise. She had never considered him. He'd be the logical choice she supposed, but it would be months before he could think of taking another wife. She quickly discarded the idea. Ansel was out of the question. She needed a man right now if she hoped to save the land.

"Ansel isn't my answer." Charity hated to resort to underhanded tactics, but it seemed clear she'd have to force Beau's hand, however unpleasant.

"Then I'm afraid you're up a creek without a paddle," Beau said.

"Maybe, but you're in the same boat."

He glared at her. "How do you figure that?"

She shrugged. "If you won't at least consider my idea, I'll have little choice but to turn you over to Little Fawn and Laughing Waters."

Beau's eyes widened. "Those two squaws—"

"The lovely women who took care of you in my absence." She felt almost shameful for being so mean. But not quite. "They're very enamored of you, you know. I had a terrible time convincing them that you're my man. They feel they have a certain claim to you since they played a large part in saving your life."

Beau's chin jutted stubbornly. "No one has a claim on me." But his tone of voice said he wasn't all that sure. She didn't blame him; Little Fawn and Laughing Waters were rather formidable.

"I know it's disconcerting." Her tone turned soothing, but she could be as heartless as he if he wouldn't cooperate. "I'm afraid if you don't marry me, then I'll have no alternative but to give you to them. They're coming back Sunday. I'll tell them you're not my man after all. They'll take you to their camp, nurse you back to full health, and then"—Charity's eyes narrowed, and her tone turned venomous—"you'll be on your own, Mr. Claxton, because they both want you." All traces of pleasantness were gone. She straightened, smiling. "Of course, if you'd prefer Laughing Waters and Little Fawn over staying here and helping me save my land, then I suppose there's no point in our talking."

"You know what? I'm getting out of here. Missouri is looking better to me all the time. If those two women come back. . ." Beau struggled to the side of the bed and sat up, grabbing the edge of the table. He groaned and lay back on the pillow.

Charity watched, feeling vindicated. He was too weak to outrun Little Fawn and Laughing Waters, even though they were too big and clumsy to run very fast themselves. She had no intention of turning him over to the squaws, but he had no way of knowing that. She felt a little bit sorry for him, realizing how hard it must be for him to be cornered by a woman half his size.

"I could still die," he threatened.

"I don't think so. You've already missed your chance. Besides, I can't understand why you find marrying me so offensive. You obviously don't have anything else to do; you said so yourself."

"This is blackmail." The pillow muffled his voice. "You're crazy if you think I'm going to let you get away with it!"

"Suit yourself." Charity walked to the rocker and sat down, gently rocking the baby back and forth, humming "Dixie."

She knew she had him. He was sensible enough to know when he was bested. When he'd had time to think about it, he'd choose marriage to her over facing an uncertain fate with Laughing Waters and Little Fawn. Who wouldn't? The room was warm and comfortable compared to the tent they lived in. And she hoped she wasn't completely unappealing to him.

"I mean it." Beau eyed her sternly. He was sitting up now, his head bobbing weakly back and forth. "I'm not marrying anyone, least of all two crazy squaws or an addlebrained girl."

"We'll see. Do you know what day it is, Mr. Claxton?"

"No."

"Saturday." Charity sent him a smug look. She should be ashamed of herself; he was still very sick and could do little about the circumstances facing him. But she was desperate, and desperation turned nice people into monsters.

"So?" he sneered.

"Big Father's Day is tomorrow." She hummed softly.

"Big Father's Day?" Beau slumped back on the pillow, and Charity knew her words had just sunk in. He would remember the two women saying they'd be back on "Big Father's Day."

He looked back at her with dawning horror in his eyes. "Tomorrow is Sunday?"

She nodded, smiling.

He glared at her. "You can threaten all you want, but you can't make me marry you. You're bluffing. Just bluffing, and I'm not about to fall for it."

Charity kept rocking. And humming.

She felt sorry for him.

Chapter 6

The sun rose earlier than Beau would have liked. He'd been awake most of the night, trying to figure a way out of his entrapment. Sleep would have been impossible anyway: the baby had screamed the entire night. He lay on his side of the curtain Charity had rigged across the room to provide privacy and thought about where he had ended up and how he had gotten there. Kansas was a long way from home. For the first time in a long time he had a yearning to go back.

Beau had to admit he felt sorry for Charity. He'd heard her pacing the floor, trying everything she could think of to quiet the baby. Nothing had worked. The infant had only stiffened in anger and cried all the harder, throwing a real temper fit.

The sun was coming up when Mary Kathleen finally dropped into an exhausted slumber. Charity had placed the infant in the small crib she'd fashioned from a drawer and tiptoed to the rocker, dropped into it, and fallen into a sound sleep.

Beau lay quietly thinking about Charity and her demand. Marriage? Over his dead body. He was grateful to her for saving his life, and he wouldn't mind fixing a little fence if it would help her out. There wasn't any denying he was beholden to her, and a

Claxton always paid his debts; Cole had drummed that into him early on.

He knew he'd left some unpaid bills back in Missouri when he'd walked out, and he fully intended to make them right if Cole and Cass hadn't already done so. But what he owed Charity couldn't be paid with money. It was a debt of honor.

That didn't mean he had to marry her, though.

He didn't plan on getting married again, but if he ever did, he'd do the asking. Still, he couldn't say he didn't feel sympathy for her predicament. There were a lot of women facing the same situation—husband a casualty of war.

This woman was stranded on the Kansas frontier with a seriously injured man and a baby who wasn't hers. Didn't seem rightly fair. With her tending his needs, and the baby's, she'd barely had time for chores. No wonder she looked like she was worn to a frazzle. She was too small, too delicate to have to work like this. If she had any sense she would pack up and go back home to her family in Richmond. She wasn't cut out to be a pioneer wife. Ferrand should have taken better care of her. Beau felt downright indignant at the thought. Running off to the war when he had a wife to see about.

Not only did he sympathize with her, he was starting to feel guilty because he'd let her sleep in the rocker the past two nights, allowing him the luxury of the soft, straw-filled mattress. Truth be told, neither of them had gotten any rest, what with the baby crying. It was amazing how one little infant could make so much noise.

He heard Charity awaken and begin to move around in the small quarters. It was unjust that so much misery could fall on one woman, but he wasn't about to let compassion overrule common sense. Marriage was out of the question.

He could see where it would benefit her, but what could he gain from it? Saddled with a woman he barely knew. While it was easy enough for her to say he could ride away at the end of the arrangement, he knew he wasn't the kind to take vows and then walk out. Once he gave his name, he was duty-bound to make good on it.

He shook his head. While he could pity her plight, he wouldn't let himself become part of it. As far as her threatening him with Indian squaws was concerned, she was downright crazy if she believed she could scare him into marrying her. He didn't scare easy, but if he had been the kind to scare, those squaws would do it. Little Fawn had a gleam in her eyes he fully distrusted.

Charity might be flighty, but she wouldn't actually make good on her threat, and he knew it. No one would be that callous. He was a sick man, helpless to defend himself. She wouldn't do that to him. Or would she? No telling what a woman, particularly this woman, might do. He needed to concentrate on getting well. Then he would be in a better position to defend himself. A man too sick to get out of bed was helpless.

He shook his head, thinking of all that had happened to him since that day at the stream when the wolf had attacked him. Two Indian women determined to cart him off. Charity talking marriage when she didn't know a thing about him. As soon as he was able, he was going to leave here and head for Missouri. At least the women back there were sane.

Charity pushed the curtain aside and brought his breakfast. They both carefully avoided the subject of marriage. Still, he kept one ear tuned to the door, listening for signs of Laughing Waters and Little Fawn. When they hadn't come by midmorning, he relaxed, figuring Charity was running a bluff. They couldn't kidnap him in broad daylight. He agreed to keep an eye on the baby while she went to the stream for fresh water.

She returned with the full buckets and set out to gather chunks of dried dung left by grazing cattle and buffalo, along with dry twigs, tufts of grass, hay twists, woody sunflower stalks, and anything else she could find to burn.

Later, while Mary Kathleen napped, Charity built a fire outside the cabin and set a large black kettle filled with water from the spring over it. Beau watched out the window as she used a bar of lye soap and a washboard, scrubbing the baby's diapers and hanging them to dry. The weather had turned unseasonably warm.

When she came in the house he asked, "What day is this?"

"Sunday."

Actually, he'd known the day. "That's what I thought. Most of the women I know don't wash on Sunday."

It wasn't right. Sunday was supposed to be a day of rest.

Her face reddened, but when she spoke she sounded civil enough. "Normally I don't wash on Sunday, but I have very few diapers for Mary Kathleen, and the baby's needs come first. God will understand."

"Well, yes." Beau allowed that she did have a point.

"Remember that verse about getting the ox out of the ditch?"

He did.

"This isn't my ox and I didn't drive it in the ditch, but the baby needs diapers and I'm the only one who can wash them." This time her words carried a bite.

Beau figured it would be a good time to take a nap. He didn't want to rile her any more than he had. He was still dependent on her for basic needs. He shut his eyes and pretended to doze.

By the time Charity had finished the wash, the baby was awake and demanding to be fed again.

"I'll do that," Beau offered. Charity warmed the milk, carrying the baby in one arm to still her hungry cries.

She glanced at him. Her hair hung in limp strands around her face. "Are you sure you feel up to it?"

"I'll manage."

He figured it was the least he could do. He didn't suppose she felt much better than he did after the morning she'd put in.

When Charity placed the baby in his arms, Mary Kathleen quieted down immediately. She handed him the cheesecloth and warm milk and tucked the baby's blankets snugly around her. "She seems to like you."

"You're going to squeeze the life out of her," Beau said. "Give her room to breathe." He loosened the blanket, and Mary Kathleen made a funny little sound, like she was heaving a sigh of relief.

"I don't want her to catch a chill."

"She won't. Babies don't need so much mollycoddling." When Beau put the cloth in Mary Kathleen's mouth, she began nursing hungrily. "Soon as I can I'll rig up a bottle. She'll get more milk."

"She's real cute, don't you think?" Charity bent over his shoulder and peered at the baby, looking flushed with maternal pride. And the baby wasn't even hers. He could imagine how she would be with her own child. He closed his eyes.

She smelled fresh and lemony. It had been a long time since he'd noticed how a woman smelled. When he opened his eyes he studied Mary Kathleen's wrinkled, reddish face and decided it reminded him of a scarlet prune. He answered the question. "Not really. . .but she might be, given a few more weeks."

"Oh, what would you know about babies?" Charity moved to

the stove and slid the skillet on the fire.

"My brother Cole and his wife, Wynne, have a baby. Jeremy must be getting nigh on to three years old now." He felt an unexpected tenderness when he talked about his family. He'd never realized how much he missed them until he woke up in this little cabin in Kansas. He needed to let them know he was all right.

"Do they live in Missouri?"

"They have a piece of land not far from my place."

"Is your brother taking care of your farm while you're gone?"

"He said he would." He gazed thoughtfully down at Mary Kathleen. "Don't you think someone should see about getting this baby's daddy to assume his responsibility?"

Beau didn't think it was fair for Mary Kathleen's father to have waltzed off and left the baby with Charity, even if he was grieving over his wife. If his and Betsy's baby had lived, he was certain he'd have seen to its care. Couldn't imagine leaving a cute little bug like Mary Kathleen for someone else to take care of.

"I thought Ansel would be here by now." She sank down wearily in a chair by the kitchen table and began peeling potatoes. "I'll ride over to his place this afternoon while the baby's napping—"

There was a sudden knock at the door, and both Charity and Beau looked up.

"That's him now." Charity hurried to the door, and Beau held his breath, praying it wouldn't be Laughing Waters and Little Fawn. He didn't want a run-in with those two anytime soon.

When Charity found Ansel on her doorstep, hat in hand, a pleasant smile on his face, she gave a cry of relief. "Where in the world have you been?" Her voice sounded more critical than she'd intended, but she was bone tired and he'd been downright irresponsible.

"Miss Charity. I hope I'm not disturbing you?"

"You're not disturbing me," Charity said curtly. "I've been worried sick about you. Where have you been?"

"Worried about me?" He stared vacantly at her. "Why?"

"Why? Because you rode off and left Mary Kathleen with me."

"Who?"

"Mary Kath—oh, never mind. Come in." Charity ushered the baby's father into the house and closed the door.

He stopped in his tracks when he saw Beau lying in the bed and glanced back at Charity with a puzzled look. "Didn't know you had company."

"Company?" Charity looked at him, bewildered. "I don't have company."

His gaze switched to Beau. "Who is he?"

Charity glanced at Beau then back to Ansel. "The man I found in the stream." She was more confused than ever by her neighbor's odd behavior. What was wrong with the man? It was as if he'd forgotten all about the stranger. "You know—the one the wolf attacked?" *And the one you left ME to bury,* she wanted to add but didn't.

Ansel walked to the table and sat down, seeming to dismiss Beau for the moment. "It's right pleasant out this morning."

Charity was surprised by the almost immediate change of subject. "Ansel, are you all right?" She moved to the table and knelt beside his chair. "I've been so worried. Where have you been?" she asked for the third time.

"Been? Why, I've been at home. Why?"

"Home. . .well, I've wondered. . . Are you sure you're all right?" He didn't act all right. If she didn't know him so well, she'd think he'd been drinking. But Ansel and Letty had never allowed alcohol in their home. Ferrand hadn't held with serious drinking, either, but he did keep a bottle on hand for medicinal purposes. Ansel had refused even that.

He looked up and smiled. "Yes, Letty, I'm just fine. How are you today?"

"I'm good." Charity frowned. He had called her Letty. Was that a slip of the tongue? "And the baby's fine. Would you like to hold your daughter?"

Ansel's face brightened. "Why, yes, I think that would be nice."

Now that was encouraging. This was the first time the man had shown any sign of wanting to hold his little girl or even remembering that he had a daughter. She hurried to the bed to retrieve Mary Kathleen from Beau's arms. Of course he'd want to hold her. Why else would he be here except to claim his precious daughter?

Charity introduced Ansel to Beau, who'd been watching the exchange. "I know you'll be glad to hear Mr. Claxton is doing fine now. When I got back, I discovered he was being nursed by Little Fawn and Laughing Waters—I think I've mentioned them to you before. The two women stopped by to visit and found Mr. Claxton and knew exactly what to do."

Ansel didn't look much like he cared one way or the other. Charity glanced at Beau and shrugged her shoulders, dismayed by her neighbor's apparent bad manners. Ansel did have a lot on his mind. A body had to make allowances.

Charity settled Mary Kathleen in his arms. "There now, isn't she beautiful?"

He gazed down at the tiny bundle, his face growing tender with emotion. "Oh, she's real pretty."

"She truly is."

Mary Kathleen opened her eyes and stared angelically at her father. He returned her smile and hesitantly reached to trace his forefinger around each rosy cheek. "She looks like you, Letty. Just like you," he whispered softly.

Charity wasn't sure if he was speaking to her or his deceased wife. Would he talk to Letty out loud like that? It didn't seem right. Still, she knew enough about grief to allow him some leeway. He was still lost.

"She does look exactly like Letty. She has the same eyes, the same color of hair. She would be proud," Charity acknowledged softly.

"Yes, yes, she would." Then, as quickly as he'd accepted the baby, Ansel handed Mary Kathleen back to Charity and stood up. "Well, I mustn't overstay my welcome. My chores need tending."

Charity blinked at his sudden change of attitude. But she guessed he'd be wanting to get the baby settled. Still, his departure did seem a trifle abrupt. She began gathering the baby's belongings, keeping up a running line of chatter. "You're always welcome, Ansel, but I understand your wanting to get back home. Mary Kathleen's a sweet baby to care for. She's a bit fussy at night, but I think you'll get along fine. I don't have a bottle and nipple; I've been giving her milk through cheesecloth. She's been eating about every two—"

The sound of the front door closing made her whirl in disbelief. The room was empty, except for Beau and herself—and Mary Kathleen. Charity faced Beau. "Where'd he go?"

He shrugged. "Said he was going home."

Charity raced to the door and yanked it open in time to see Ansel's buckboard rattling out of the yard. "What in tarnation is wrong with that man?" She slammed the door shut. The baby jumped with fright, puckered up like a thundercloud, and started squalling. Wonderful! Just what she needed. As if her nerves weren't stretched to the limit.

Beau tried to quiet the baby while Charity stormed around the cabin, mumbling under her breath about the injustices of life. She slammed the iron skillet on the stove and angrily spooned lard from a can and flung it into the pan.

"I can't imagine who he thinks he is to leave me with his baby! I can't take care of a baby and fix fences and drive oxen and— Letty was my friend, but there's a point where friendship ends. I can't take on any more responsibility!" Charity irritably questioned Ansel's sanity—and her own—as she chopped potatoes and onions and dropped them into the sizzling fat. She had her limit, and Ansel Latimer had just gone past it.

Beau managed to calm Mary Kathleen but left Charity alone. He figured only a fool would try to talk to her now. And he hadn't been raised to be a fool. He had no idea what was going on, but it was plain to him that Ansel wasn't in full control of his faculties. The realization did little to calm him. Maybe because he'd been in a similar situation and he hadn't been all that much in control, either. He could still remember the fog that had blanketed his mind. Couldn't think, couldn't do much of anything except ride away. A man wasn't responsible for his actions at a time like that. Still, Ansel had a child; he needed to pull himself together for Mary Kathleen's sake.

If Ansel Latimer had gone off the deep end because of his wife's death, Beau was going to be left as the only candidate to help Charity save her land, and that grim prospect made him even more uneasy. He felt like he was in a deep canyon and the walls were closing in on him.

He wasn't a man who liked change. He and Bets had been building a good life together, and in one short afternoon, it was all gone. He'd stood beside his wife's grave, knowing his plans and dreams for the future had died with her. Beau Claxton was an empty shell of a man with nothing left to give. He'd always heard Almighty God could bring good out of bad, but he couldn't imagine any good coming out of losing Betsy. Now here was Charity wanting to marry him so she could hang on to her homestead, and he had a feeling she wasn't the kind to take no for an answer.

As if she understood his turmoil, Mary Kathleen burst into tears.

Charity slammed a bowl on the table and began mixing a batch of corn bread, still mumbling heatedly under her breath.

"I know how you feel," he confided to the baby. "It's a mess, isn't it?"

Monday morning Beau drained the last of his coffee. The front door burst open, and he mutely stared at the dark outline of the two squaws silhouetted starkly against a noonday sun. They were back.

Both women's arms were piled high with stove fuel. Stories of people being burned at the stake flashed through his mind. They didn't still do that, did they?

The memory of Charity's earlier threat closed in on him: *"If you won't marry me, I'll have no other choice but to hand you over to Laughing Waters and Little Fawn. . . They both want you for their husband."*

Husband? To both of them? Was that legal? How could he explain that to God? Let alone try to explain it to Bets if he ever did make it to heaven, which was looking more doubtful every day. Bigamy, that's what it was, and he didn't plan to partake.

"Laughing Waters! Little Fawn! How nice to see you." Charity stood at the table washing dishes. She cast a pointed look at Beau and then wiped her sudsy hands on her apron. She stepped forward to greet the two visitors.

"We come see Gold Hair." Little Fawn stated their purpose, and Laughing Waters's stern, austere expression reinforced it. Well, Gold Hair didn't want to see them. How could he get out of this? There was only one answer: Charity had to help him, but she was looking far too happy to suit him.

"Well, how nice. Please come in. I know he's been anxious to see you." Charity smiled pleasantly at Beau and reached for her shawl hanging on the hook beside the door.

Beau shot her a warning look, but she ignored it. Was she out of her mind? Did he look phased?

"I'll feed the chickens and gather the wash while you three visit."

"Charity!" he snapped.

"Yes?" Charity turned to face him with a look of wide-eyed innocence that was as crooked as a barrel of fish hooks. He'd get even with her for this. She'd rue the day she tried to threaten him.

"You have company. It's not proper for you to leave." Though he kept his voice firm, he knew she could hear desperation. "Besides, the baby will be waking up any time now."

"Little Fawn and Laughing Waters aren't here to see me." She paused to tie the string on her bonnet. "They've come to visit you, Gold Hair. Don't worry; I'll listen for the baby. You go right ahead and enjoy your visit." She sent a gracious smile at the two women. "Make yourselves at home, ladies."

Charity reached for the egg basket. Little Fawn and Laughing Waters set their bundles of chips by the doorstep and silently walked into the cabin.

"The fuel is a nice gift," Charity said. "I'll see that Gold Hair is warmed by it."

Beau couldn't believe she would be callous enough to desert him! "Charity. . .now, hold on a minute!"

"Papoose asleep?" Laughing Waters asked.

"She's sleeping soundly. Would you like to see her?" Charity invited. She sent another pointed look his way.

The squaws edged toward the table where Charity had placed the baby's drawer crib. The women's dark eyes intently surveyed the infant until their curiosity was satisfied. They slipped back to stand quietly at the doorway.

"Well, I'd best get to my chores," Charity announced.

How could she walk away like this? Did she save him from the wolf to abandon him to an even worse fate?

Laughing Waters nodded, and Charity hung the egg basket over her arm and slipped out the door. Little Fawn stretched her mouth in a wide grin and began creeping toward the bed.

Beau froze. Charity Burk had thrown him back to the wolves.

"Gold Hair heap better," Little Fawn said. "No longer pale. Look healthier now, and handsomer and stronger than any other warrior." Her dark eyes moved to Beau's hair. He noticed her fingers wiggling like she was itching to get hold of him. Scalps? Did the Kaw do scalping? He had no idea. He looked around the bed searching for a weapon, anything to defend himself, but the only thing his groping fingers found was the edge of his pillow. Somehow a pillow fight seemed lame.

They were fixated on his hair. He'd been around enough Indians to know that while the men of other tribes let their hair grow long, Kaw men shaved their heads, leaving only a well-curved tuft on the crown where they wore warriors' eagle feathers.

Only when grieving a death would a Kaw allow his hair to

grow, proof of his inconsolable sorrow.

Little Fawn's eyes glittered. "My heart beat faster just looking at you. Soon, Swift Buck with Tall Antlers will be mine, and I give thanks to Wa-kun-dah, the All Powerful, for sending me such a fine, strong brave."

Beau recognized the possessive light in her eyes and drew back defensively into his pillow. He didn't know who this Swift Buck with Tall Antlers was, but he was welcome to Little Fawn. If she already had her eyes on a man, why was she looking at him? He'd seen a cat eye a baby rabbit like this once. The rabbit didn't have a chance. This woman with her wide, toothless grin made him uneasy.

"Now, don't you go messing with my hair," he warned in a voice that he hoped sounded like it brooked no nonsense.

"Gold Hair speak! See! Gold Hair speak!" Laughing Waters quickly joined Little Fawn at Beau's bedside, and the two smiled down at him. Where was Charity?!

"Ohhhh, Gold Hair heap better," Laughing Waters said. "I take Brave Horse with Many Wounds back to camp," she exclaimed. "White Sister claim Gold Hair, but we have more right. We save his life."

Little Fawn frowned. "Swift Buck with Tall Antlers go with me."

Laughing Waters waved a dismissing hand. "We settle this later. No time now."

After a minute Little Fawn nodded. "White Sister come back soon. We must hurry."

Beau shifted restlessly. They were planning to take him with them. "I'm not going anywhere. You two ladies forget all this nonsense." He had a good, solid name; he didn't plan on being called some outlandish name like Swift Buck. . .or Wounded Horse?

Laughing Waters shook her head. "You come. We been alone

too long. Speckled Eye, Little Fawn's husband, die of smallpox last winter. My husband, Handsome Bird, rode off on buffalo hunt three years ago." She held up three fingers. "No come back."

Beau shook his head. Considering Laughing Waters's lack of charm, he would have kept going, too. A man could ride a fair piece in three years, and if he ever got free from Charity Burk, he was going to do the same.

Little Fawn frowned. "You belong to us. We save life. Not let White Sister keep you. We have a plan."

Laughing Waters giggled. "Very good plan. Almost work once before. Will work this time. Can't fail."

Beau sighed. A new stubborn look, one he didn't like, had entered Little Fawn's expression.

"The plan won't work," he said. "I'm not going with you or any other woman. Do you understand that?"

Laughing Waters shook her head. "We not speak English. Not good. Not understand."

"We bring you gift," Little Fawn announced.

Beau knew he had to put a stop to this conversation and fast, or he could find himself running around half naked, hunting buffalo for the rest of his life. "I don't want to hurt your feelings, but—"

Laughing Waters slyly withdrew a bottle from beneath her red blanket and handed it to him. "We bring *pi-ge-ne*. Make you heap better!"

Beau cautiously took the bottle of amber liquid and examined it closely. "What's this?"

Little Fawn proudly displayed another toothless grin. "*Pi-ge-ne*—firewater!"

"Whiskey?"

Laughing Waters and Little Fawn's heads bobbed enthusiastically.

"Where'd you get this?"

"Trade pony and two buffalo robes," replied Little Fawn.

He couldn't take their whiskey. He'd sworn off whiskey when he became a Christian, and Betsy had been dead set against alcohol of any kind. He quickly handed the bottle back to Little Fawn. "I appreciate the thought, but I can't drink this."

Their faces fell. "You no like *pi-ge-ne*?" Little Fawn asked.

Beau shook his head. "I can't accept your gift."

"White Sister no like *pi-ge-ne*?" Laughing Waters prodded.

"That's it. White Sister no like *pi-ge-ne*." Pin the blame on Charity, he decided. If it hadn't been for her, he wouldn't be in this mess. She wasn't around to hear, so what could it hurt? He figured if he let the squaws think he belonged to "White Sister," they'd be on their way and out of his hair, literally.

Little Fawn turned to Laughing Waters, her eyes openly puzzled. "Gold Hair no want *pi-ge-ne*."

The squaws were noticeably upset by his lack of gratitude. Despite their infatuation with him, he had to admit that if it hadn't been for their dedicated care, he'd probably be dead right now. They'd been good enough to stay with him in Charity's absence, applying the healing poultices to his wounds, stoking the fire, and here he was, treating them unsociably.

"I appreciate all you've done for me, but we might as well get it straight. I'm not going to marry either one of you."

The women exchanged frank looks. Little Fawn whispered sharply to Laughing Waters.

Dark eyes suddenly riveted on Beau. Laughing Waters immediately turned sullen. "Gold Hair no be husband to Little Fawn and Laughing Waters?"

"No," Beau said. "I'm beholden to both of you for saving my life, but as soon as I'm able, I'll be moving on. I'm not going to marry anyone."

"No be husband to White Sister?" Little Fawn asked.

"No, no be husband to White Sister," Beau confirmed, noticing the squaws' faces swiftly light with renewed expectation. "No be husband to anyone," he stated. "I'm not the marrying kind."

They looked puzzled. "No like gift?"

"Nice gift," he agreed. "But I don't drink whiskey."

"We trade pony and two buffalo robes," Laughing Waters said. "You belong to us!"

"No, I belong to no woman. You get that through your head." Talking to these two was like spitting in the wind. Useless.

"Okay, no marry," Little Fawn said.

Laughing Waters nodded. "Gold Hair has spoken."

Beau relaxed. That was more like it. About time they started showing some sense. He glanced out the window and saw Charity throwing corn to the chickens.

He felt smug when he thought how shocked she was going to be when she discovered how easily he'd outfoxed her and the two squaws. She thought she'd backed him to the wall with her threats of "marry me or else." He smirked. Once more, he'd proved you couldn't tangle with Beau Claxton. At least, not a puny little woman like Charity Burk.

Little Fawn reached out a tentative finger, grinning at him. "Swift Buck with Tall Antlers have pretty hair."

Beau drew back. He thought they had that settled. How many times did he have to say it? He tried to be diplomatic. "Don't touch my hair, ladies. We'll get along better if you leave my hair alone."

Laughing Waters grinned. "Never see warrior with hair like yours. We be envy of tribe. Brave Horse with Many Wounds handsome warrior. Make strong papooses."

Beau's grin felt a bit uneven. "Brave Horse do no such thing."

She could get that thought right out of her head. Well, all right, maybe he hadn't gotten through to them as well as he'd thought. He'd try again. "Look, ladies, I do appreciate all you've done for me, and when I can, I'll reimburse you for the pony and buffalo robes, but I'm not going with you. Subject closed."

Little Fawn looked cross. "No go with us?"

Beau shook his head. "No go anywhere with anyone. That's final."

Laughing Waters bit her underlip. She nudged her sister. "We have powwow."

Beau felt his temper rising. "There is nothing to talk over. I've said my piece. Now, you go on along about your business and leave me alone." He stared out the window. Charity was taking her sweet time feeding the stock.

Lord, You've got to help me out here. They're not taking no for an answer.

The two women stepped to a corner of the cabin and engaged in a furious Kaw exchange. Little Fawn kept shaking her head no. Beau watched the argument, wondering what they had in mind now. They eventually reached an agreement because they approached the bed, marching in quickstep. He instinctively drew back against the pillows, wishing Charity would get in here.

Laughing Waters grinned. "We give up Gold Hair. Let White Sister have you."

Beau didn't like the sound of that. They wouldn't give up this easily. They'd hatched another plot. "I don't think so, ladies."

"We want to help."

Or trick him; he wasn't a fool.

Little Fawn reached out to touch his hair, and he jerked back. "None of that now. I don't want you messing with my hair."

Little Fawn grinned. "We glad Gold Hair feeling better."

Laughing Waters nodded. "You need to get strength back now."

"That would be nice." It couldn't happen fast enough for Beau. He wished God would speed up the healing process. The minute he was strong enough, he wouldn't let his shirttail hit his back until he was on his horse and headed back to Missouri, where the people were normal.

Laughing Waters said, "You want to get strong fast?"

Beau sighed. "That would make me very happy."

She nodded. "I fix tea."

"Now, hold on here," he said. "What kind of tea?"

"Good tea. Make you very strong," Little Fawn said. "We fix."

"I don't know," Beau said. "Charity might not want you in her kitchen."

"White Sister no care," Laughing Waters assured him. "She say to make ourselves at home."

She had said that, Beau reflected. So let them make the tea and leave. He didn't have to drink it.

Laughing Waters was at the stove pouring hot water over something. He watched her with a jaundiced eye. She approached, holding out a cup. "Gold Hair drink. Make strong."

He took the cup, sniffing the contents. "What is it?"

"Tea, made from plant. Good plant. Not know name, but just what Gold Hair need to get well." She grinned. "Trust me."

Trust her? Beau wanted to laugh. Still, they had saved his life. They had used herbs then. Evil-smelling things that had sucked the poison out of his body and made him breathe whether he wanted to or not. Maybe the tea would work.

He sipped the hot liquid and found it not all that unpleasant. Sweetened with honey, mild tasting. He drank again, and Laughing Waters beamed at him. "That right. Drink it all. Make much better."

He finished the tea and leaned back against his pillow. The

two women stood at his bedside, waiting. A white fog crept slowly through his mind, swirling peacefully, lightly. The two sisters suddenly blurred. He fought to keep his eyes open, but his eyelids were too heavy. He felt giddy. Someone giggled, and to his horror, he realized it was him.

Tricked. He'd been tricked and fallen for it. Someone was running their fingers through his hair. He tried to tell them to stop it, but all he could do was laugh. What in the Sam Hill had they given him? Whatever it was, it had made him as helpless as a newborn calf.

Chapter 7

Guilt was starting to set in. Charity felt bad about leaving Beau alone with the squaws. She was desperate for a man's help, but her conscience told her it hadn't been right to leave him to the mercy of Little Fawn and Laughing Waters. They'd scare him half to death. They were so big, bigger than a lot of men, and determined, too. He was still weak as a kitten.

Her hand dipped into the corn bucket, and she scattered kernels on the hardened ground for the flock of chattering hens. She'd been heartless to threaten to turn him over to Laughing Waters and Little Fawn if he didn't marry her. It hadn't done a bit of good and more than likely had made him more stubborn. She'd never been able to bluff Ferrand, not once.

He would have been ashamed of such underhanded tactics. He'd always said a person was only as good as he was honest. Charity had to face it: she'd seriously jeopardized her integrity lately. She didn't see another choice, though. She couldn't lose the land and all the work that had gone into the place.

Something else troubled her. She'd lied and tried to trick a man into marrying her. Lying and dishonest dealing were sins. Her Bible said so, plain and simple. There wasn't any way to justify what she'd done, and now that she'd had time to think about it her conscience hurt her something fierce. She stopped scattering corn and stood looking up at the sky, talking to God in her heart.

Lord, I'm sorry. I knew better; it's just that I'm so tired of trying to do it all by myself. I don't have the know-how or the strength to improve this place, and now there's a sick man and a baby to take care of and I'm worn-out. She didn't know if God would accept her excuses, but it was the Gospel truth, and He'd know that. Life had sort of caved in on her right now.

She'd do her best to make things right, apologize to Beau for behaving so badly, and furthermore, she'd assure him that she wouldn't hinder his return to Missouri once he'd recovered. It would be hard to keep that promise, but she'd do it. Come hell or high water.

She would consider asking Ansel Latimer to marry her. She knew him to be strong and kind. After he weathered the initial shock of losing Letty, he'd need someone to help him raise Mary Kathleen, and Charity would love the child as dearly as if she were her own. She already did.

But in truth, she knew marriage to Ansel would be disappointing. He'd never make her stomach flutter the way Ferrand had. No one would ever give her that delicious, giddy feeling again, and she might as well accept it. He could smile a certain way, and her pulse would race with heady anticipation.

There wouldn't be any surprises with Ansel. What you saw was what you got—quiet, dependable, but he was also a trifle boring. He had been right for Letty, but he wouldn't be right for her. On the other hand, Ansel would never mistreat her, and she knew Letty would be proud to know Charity was raising her daughter.

She heard the door open, breaking into her thoughts. Her jaw dropped when she saw Laughing Waters and Little Fawn haul

Beau out of the cabin, spread-eagled between them. His backside dragged the ground, and he had a silly, stupefied grin on his face. What did they think they were doing, and what was the matter with Beau Claxton? Why would he let them manhandle him like a sack of grain?

She dropped the corn pail, spilling the contents, and sprinted toward the cabin, trying to catch up. The two women weren't wasting any time. Their legs pumped and their flat feet thundered over the crusty ground.

"Hold it!" Charity shouted. "You bring him right back here. Now!"

At the sound of her voice both women glanced her way but made no effort to slow their rapid departure up the hillside.

Beau grinned and waved. " 'Lo, Mrs. Burk!"

"Hey! I said wait a minute!" Charity broke into a run when she realized the two women had no intention of stopping. She couldn't imagine what was going on. Did they really think they could just carry him off like that? She'd been fully aware that Little Fawn and Laughing Waters were smitten with Beau, but she'd had no idea they'd take their whimsy to this appalling extent!

And Beau! He not only appeared indifferent to his abduction, but it looked to Charity as if he were a willing participant. It hadn't been half an hour ago when he was begging her not to leave him alone with them. What had happened while her back was turned? She should have known she couldn't trust that man.

Well, she had found him first. Beau Claxton belonged to her, and she wasn't in the mood to share.

"We go, White Sister," Little Fawn puffed over her shoulder when Charity gained on them. "One sleep, come back."

Beau looked like he had passed out; he was oblivious to the flight. The women carried him swiftly along with his backside bumping the ground every third step.

Charity finally got close enough to grab Laughing Waters's shoulder, jerking her to a sudden halt. She paused for a minute to catch her breath before taking them to task. "Now see here! You can't just come into my house and tote this man away like a sack of flour!"

"Gold Hair no care." Laughing Waters stubbornly planted her solid frame in front of Charity, keeping a firm hold on Beau's bare feet. Charity was relieved to see that the women at least had the forethought to put trousers on him.

"Well, we'll ask Gold Hair if he minds or not." She leaned over Beau's limp body. He opened an eye and grinned up at her.

"Hallo there, Mizzz Burk. Didja feed all them chickens?"

"What is wrong with you?" He looked and acted like he was drunk. She bent over him, sniffing for whiskey, but she couldn't smell anything. "What have you been drinking?"

"Had a little tea party with these two fine women. You know Laugh. . .Little. . ." He frowned, waving his hand in a dismissing manner. "Whatever. . . Fine ladies."

"What kind of tea?"

He shook his head. "Jus' tea. Had a little cuppa tea. Feel better already."

"I can't believe this!" Charity confronted the two squaws, her anger flaring. "You carry him back to the house—immediately!"

She could see Laughing Waters and Little Fawn had no intention of obliging, and their stoic expressions proved it. So now what did she do?

"Gold Hair come with us," Laughing Waters announced, lifting Beau's feet—a signal to Little Fawn to move on.

"Hold on." Charity stepped around to block their path. "He can't go with you. I thought I made it clear: Gold Hair is mine."

Little Fawn looked to Laughing Waters for direction.

"Gold Hair say he no marry White Sister," Laughing Waters argued.

"But he no marry Laughing Waters or Little Fawn, either."

"Ladieees, ladieees, don't fight. I no marry any of you," Beau informed them.

Charity gritted her teeth. If he couldn't help the situation, she wished he would keep quiet. This was serious business. These two women had their hearts set on having Beau, and she knew he was in no condition to save himself. If he was to be delivered from this, it would be solely up to her. She frantically searched her memory for a bartering tool. She had so little left.

The brooch. Ferrand's grandmother's emerald brooch. It had been his gift to Charity on their wedding day. Little Fawn and Laughing Waters had admired it extensively since the first day they had discovered it in the tin box she kept under the bed. The brooch was her greatest treasure, but she couldn't stand by idly and let Beau be abducted.

She held up one hand, trying to gain their attention. "Let's hold on a minute. Surely we can reach a satisfactory solution."

Laughing Waters and Little Fawn held their ground, watching her with suspicious eyes.

"What White Sister mean?" Little Fawn finally offered.

"I agree you helped save Gold Hair's life, and I suppose you could argue that he is partly yours." She didn't want to go too far down that road. After all, possession was nine-tenths of the law, and they definitely were in possession.

Laughing Waters eyed Beau. She wasn't following the logic. "We save Gold Hair. We like. We take."

"I saved Gold Hair, too."

"You leave Gold Hair to meet Wa-kun-dah, alone."

"I had a good reason. I was called away to help the papoose's mother, remember? She was very ill, too."

From their stoic expressions she could see they remembered, but it was also clear they didn't care.

"Gold Hair heap good man. We want," Laughing Waters repeated sullenly.

"True; that's why I'm prepared to make you a trade."

Little Fawn hurriedly shook her head. "Gold Hair make good papooses. We keep."

Charity glanced at Beau, who had fallen back to sleep. "I'm sure he would. . .but I'm prepared to offer you my brooch. The one in the tin box. Remember how much you liked those pretty green stones? You said they sparkled like morning dew on the grass."

Laughing Waters exchanged a dubious look with Little Fawn but then curtly nodded.

Charity felt faint with relief. Ferrand had given her the brooch, thinking the heirloom would remain in his family. She pressed her lips together tightly, ready to do whatever was necessary to save Beau Claxton once again. "I will trade you my emerald brooch for Gold Hair."

Laughing Waters's eyes immediately lit up. "Green Rocks for Gold Hair?"

Charity knew the woman was completely taken when it came to bright, shiny things. Laughing Waters had wanted the emerald brooch from the first time she had seen it. Surely she would accept the trade. Little Fawn might be harder to convince.

Drawing a deep breath, Charity closed her eyes and repeated before she lost her nerve, "The brooch for Gold Hair."

The squaws looked at each other.

"We talk. White Sister stay," Laughing Waters said.

They dropped Beau's limp body in the dust, where he landed with a resounding thud, bringing him wide awake.

He sat up, looking dazed. "What's going on?"

"Serves you right," Charity snapped. "Because of your foolishness, I have to give up Ferrand's grandmother's brooch."

"Whose what?" He sounded befuddled. "My head's spinning like a wheel."

"Ferrand's grandmother's. . .oh, never mind." Charity knew he couldn't possibly understand anything in his sorry state. "You'd better hope they accept the trade or you're in serious trouble, Beau Claxton!"

Beau looked around him in a daze. "What? I wish somebody would make some sense. What am I doing sitting in the middle of the road? It's hot, and. . .I'm sick."

His bid for sympathy, if that's what he meant it to be, was wasted on Charity. She had too much on her mind to stand here and chat. He didn't look all that alert, either, even though he talked more sensible and he wasn't slurring his words as much.

"I'm not interested in how you feel," she said curtly.

Beau looked hurt and eased back down.

Charity dismissed him, watching Laughing Waters and Little Fawn still conferring in hushed tones. Their prolonged conversation worried her. She had thought they would be happy to exchange a sick man for an emerald brooch that sparkled like sunlight on water. Occasionally, one would raise her voice, and the other would shake her head and angrily wag her finger. Clearly the discussion was getting a bit heated.

Charity decided to go over their heads. *Lord, I need help here. I can't let them take him; that wouldn't be right. I'm sorry I threatened to let them have him. I wouldn't have done that; You know I wouldn't. Please convince them to take the brooch. I don't have anything else to offer.*

She watched the two women, wondering what she would do if

they refused to give up their claim on Beau. She was outnumbered and they could run faster. She was winded after the short chase, and Mary Kathleen was alone in the cabin and probably squalling her head off. Beau Claxton, that miserable lout, had gone back to sleep in the middle of the road. She had a good notion to boot him.

Charity slanted a look heavenward. "Sorry again, Lord. It's just that he makes me so mad."

The tense conversation went on for a full ten minutes. Charity was beginning to despair. If they refused the brooch, she didn't know how she'd prevent them from taking Beau away. She took another look at him and wondered why she cared.

He lay curled up in the road, sound asleep and blissfully ignorant of what was taking place. Charity wondered if he was really worth a brooch. Seemed like she was always having to rescue him, and as far as she could see, she wasn't getting anything out of the effort but extra trouble.

Finally, Little Fawn raised her arms, shook her hands in the air in exasperation, and stalked off. With a satisfied smile, Laughing Waters scurried back to Charity. "We trade Gold Hair for roach."

"Brooch."

Laughing Waters grinned. "Yes. Roach."

Charity heaved a sigh of relief. "Good. And Little Fawn? Does she agree?"

"She no care."

Charity seriously doubted that. "Now, when we make our trade," she warned, "it's final. You must leave Gold Hair alone, for he will be mine."

"Laughing Waters no see Gold Hair again?"

"That's right. Little Fawn must agree to relinquish her claim as well."

Laughing Waters thought for a moment and then shrugged

agreeably. "Me tell Little Fawn. Gold Hair White Sister's. We no take."

"Very well."

They reached down in unison, and Charity picked up Beau's feet and Laughing Waters carried his hands.

"We make good trade," Laughing Waters said proudly as they carried Beau's limp body back to the cabin.

Charity nodded glumly but truthfully. She had just grabbed the short end of the stick. She had given away her prized brooch, and she wasn't one inch nearer to saving her land.

But at least her integrity was intact, and for that she was grateful.

The old rooster stretched, flapped his wings, and loudly crowed in a new day. Rays of dappled winter sunlight spilled through the cabin windows, spreading a golden path across the wooden floor.

Charity groaned and stirred on her pallet, reluctant to face the new morning. Mary Kathleen had cried most of the night. Finally the baby had quieted down, and she had fallen into a deep sleep.

She got up and peeked around the curtain that separated the bed from the rest of the room. Beau was still sleeping soundly. He was lying on his stomach, his golden hair tousled appealingly like a small boy's, face burrowed into the pillow, arms wrapped snugly around it. Tight bunches of corded muscles stood out in his forearms.

He looked young and innocent. Charity wanted to brush the hair off his forehead and kiss him awake. She knotted her hands into fists in an effort to control her wayward fingers that itched to bury themselves in those loose waves.

Since it was still early and she felt lazy this morning, she stretched out on her pallet again. It would be sheer tomfoolery to become physically attracted to Beau; still, she couldn't deny that she found him more fascinating every day. He had recovered from the tea the squaws had given him with no long-lasting effects. She had found the dregs of herbs in her teapot, but she had no idea what they were—a mixture known only to the Kaw.

Beau had described the effect as wanting to sleep, but also everything had been funny. Embarrassed, he'd admitted that he'd giggled, which seemed to bother him more than the attempted kidnapping. The memory of him sleeping in the road while she bartered with Laughing Waters and Little Fawn over him brought a flush to her face. She, Charity Burk, bartering for a man. How low would she go?

The days had passed without incident since that afternoon four weeks ago. The two women had stayed away from the cabin, and Beau was slowly regaining his strength. With proper food and plenty of rest, he had begun to shed his pitiful gauntness, and his body grew strong and sinewy again. She glowed with pride when she remembered the way he looked that day in the stream, half frozen, thin as a reed.

Every day he seemed more thoughtful. He helped with Mary Kathleen as much as his condition allowed. She realized how thankful she was to have him around. Trading her emerald brooch had been a small sacrifice for a large reward.

A smile curved her mouth. She rolled over and hugged her pillow tightly against her, remembering how grateful Beau had been when he'd learned Charity had intervened and saved him a second time.

He'd been too overcome by the tea to know he'd been captured or how Charity had accomplished his release. He couldn't remember anything beyond the first few swallows of the hot liquid Laughing Waters had talked him into drinking.

She thought of how sick he'd been afterward. He'd suffered a splitting headache for three days, but she figured it only served him right. He should have known better than to trust the two squaws, but then, she shouldn't have left him alone with them. It was her fault, too. They wouldn't have given him the tea if she'd been there.

She sighed. She couldn't blame Laughing Waters and Little Fawn for their infatuation with Beau Claxton. He was bathed, clean shaven, and breathtakingly handsome now.

One truly exceptional man.

He was up and about more now. His tall, imposing frame loomed over her small one as they moved within the confines of the cabin. Although she warned herself not to, she had started feeling content and secure again, the way she'd felt when Ferrand had been close by.

At times she caught Beau's blue eyes studying her as if he felt the same sort of contentment—or maybe that was only wishful thinking on her part. Regardless, he was polite and a joy to be around. They'd talk for hours on end, passing Mary Kathleen back and forth between their laps when she became fussy.

It was then that Beau would confide in her how he was looking forward to returning to his family in Missouri. He spoke fondly of his brothers, Cole and Cass, and told her of the stunts they'd pulled together on Willa, the family housekeeper.

He talked about his ma's biscuits and Willa's chicken and dumplings, and how much he loved them both. One evening he asked Charity to help him write a letter to his family, informing them of his injury, yet assuring them he was healing properly. They moved to the table where the light was better, and while Beau talked, Charity penned the letter in her neat, legible hand. The following day, she made the long ride into Cherry Grove and mailed the missive for him, although she had been terrified that his family would come looking for him and take him home. Away from her.

She sighed, recalling how she had felt unusually lonely on her ride to town and back. With Beau safely sleeping behind the dividing curtain, she'd slipped outside and sat for a while, listening to the lonely wind on the prairie, broken occasionally by the howl of a coyote or the gentle *whish* of the tall grass and realized how empty her life would be without him.

Even now, she found herself thinking about it and sinking ever lower into self-pity when she reviewed her own gloomy circumstances. She missed her mother and father unbearably, and she thought it would be sheer heaven to curl up on her old feather bed beside her sisters, Jenny and Sue, and pour her heart out to people who really cared. Then, after a visit with her family, and a good long cry, it would be good to return to her homestead and find a man like Beau waiting for her.

She closed her eyes and fought the yearning stirring inside her. She wished Beau would forget about going back to Missouri. She hadn't mentioned marriage to him again, but it still seemed like a good arrangement to her.

They might not ever love each other the way they'd loved Ferrand and Betsy, but it wouldn't be hard for her to adjust to living with a man like Beau, with his kind ways and gentle nature. In time, she felt sure their mutual respect could bring them a union that would be, if not passionate, at least comfortable.

Her eyes flew open and she wondered why she was thinking such nonsense. The very best she could hope for from Beau Claxton would be an act of mercy in her behalf, not love and undying devotion, with a passel of golden-haired babies thrown in.

Still, she knew that once he was gone, there'd be a large void in her life. Maybe even larger than the one Ferrand had left. He had been gone so long it was sometimes hard to remember how much she had loved him.

The sun went behind a cloud, and the room suddenly turned a dreary gray, as gray and sad as Charity felt this morning. She found herself deliberately dawdling as her mind turned to another weighty problem, one that only served to drag her sagging spirits even lower.

Something had to be done about Ansel. For the past week he'd visited the cabin daily, and on each visit his behavior had been more irrational. Though she hated to admit it, she'd concluded that Letty's death had left Ansel temporarily unstable.

At times he acted as though Charity were Letty. On other occasions he was totally at a loss as to where his wife had gone. He still paid little attention to Mary Kathleen, sometimes behaving as if he resented the child.

His continuing confusion worried Charity, but she didn't know what to do about it. Beau said it was natural; he hadn't known up from down for months after Betsy died. Time. Ansel needed time to come to grips with his situation.

Charity wasn't so sure. Once, she'd thought about asking Ansel to stay with her so she could take care of him until he could cope again, but she knew that would be improper; besides, the house couldn't hold another person. It was full now with her and Beau and the baby.

On top of everything else, Beau's suggestion that she marry Ansel to get the help she needed with her land kept popping into her mind. Apparently that was her only alternative. Once he returned to his old self, she would ask him to marry her. She realized she was trying desperately to persuade herself that it was the only solution left, but the thought left her cold.

Ansel was a reasonably young and vital man, and once he got past the shock of losing his wife, he would be a good provider, but right now he wasn't ready to take a wife, and she wasn't ready to take on a man who didn't seem to know who she was most of the time.

Ferrand surfaced in her mind. She had loved him desperately. The weeks and months after his death had run together into one dark blur, but he was gone and she was left to go on. If her husband had lived, she would never be having these thoughts of another man, wouldn't have needed or wanted anyone else. However, times had changed, and a woman did what she had to in order to survive. She needed a man to help with the work, and the only way she could get one in an acceptable manner was to marry him.

She tried to visualize what it would be like to be Beau Claxton's woman. He would take good care of his wife. Look at the way he mourned for Betsy. If she had to choose between Ansel and Beau, she knew which one she'd pick.

She shouldn't be thinking of Beau this way—surely it was sinful, and disrespectful to her late husband's memory, but her mind seemed bent on tormenting her.

If there had been close neighbors there would surely be talk about a man living here, but Beau was still basically incapable of impropriety, which would be the last thought on his mind. He was a gentleman through and through.

What if he knew what she was thinking? She would be so ashamed. Decent women didn't have thoughts like that, did they? She couldn't help her thoughts, but she didn't have to linger over them.

A brisk rap on the door interrupted her musings. Charity bolted upright and pulled the blanket up around her shoulders.

She heard Beau stirring. "Someone's banging on the door," he mumbled after the second loud knock.

"I can't imagine who's calling this early."

"Better answer it before they wake the baby." She heard him roll to a sitting position.

The rap came again, and Beau called, "You want me to get it?"

Charity sprang to her feet, pulling on a thick wrapper.

She scampered barefoot across the floor, pushing the heavy mass of dark hair over her shoulder. She pulled the door open a crack. Her mouth dropped when she saw Reverend Olson and his wife standing on her doorstep, smiling warmly at her.

"Good morning, my dear. I hope we're not disturbing you." Reverend Olson's kind face reminded Charity of her father, and she was always glad when the reverend and his wife stopped by for a visit.

But not today.

This morning she wanted to shut the door in their faces. She was reluctant to reveal Beau's presence. Once the neighbors found out that he was staying with her, gossip would be inevitable. As far as she knew, only Ansel knew about him, and she preferred to keep it that way. She was aware of the mussed pallet on the floor, of Beau, half-dressed and sitting on the edge of the bed behind his curtain, of Mary Kathleen sleeping in her makeshift crib.

What had seemed so natural now seemed tawdry. She had a man living in her house. A man who had been seriously injured, but would they understand? These were good, caring people, and she couldn't bear to disappoint them. Well, the secret would be out now, and there was nothing she could do except brace herself and brazen it out.

Cherry Grove was a tight community, and its residents were unyieldingly straitlaced. For them, right was right and wrong was wrong, and there was no middle ground even if a man had nearly died.

Deep down she knew her neighbors wouldn't judge her harshly

for nursing an injured stranger, but she knew there would still be some who'd argue that it wasn't proper for a man and woman to live under the same roof without the sanctity of marriage, especially when the woman happened to be a young widow like Charity Burk and the man was a handsome widower.

It wasn't like they were misbehaving. Beau had been a complete gentleman, and she had been careful to keep the curtain in place during the evening hours. Since he no longer needed daily care, she didn't see him lying on the bed. They were living under the same roof, but in different worlds. Would the good reverend and his wife understand the forced arrangement?

"Reverend Olson. . . Mrs. Olson. How nice to see you." Charity swallowed. Her fingers nervously plucked at the collar of her wrapper. "You must forgive me; I'm afraid I've overslept this morning."

"We heard you've been quite busy, dear." Mrs. Olson leaned forward, her blue eyes twinkling. She spoke in a soft, compassionate tone. "Has your unexpected visitor been keeping you awake nights?"

Charity smiled lamely. They knew about Beau. "Yes. . .some. . .but I don't mind."

Reverend Olson looked hopeful. "Well, may we come in to see her?"

"Her?" Charity vacantly stared at him.

"The Latimer babe. We understand you're caring for Ansel's child." Reverend Olson inclined his head. "We were wondering if we might see the little cherub."

When she realized they'd come to see Mary Kathleen, Charity felt limp with relief. "Oh. . .of course! But she's still sleeping—perhaps you could stop by another time?"

Reverend Olson glanced from his wife to Charity with a benevolent expression. "I'm afraid that would be most inconvenient, dear. We plan to make several calls today. But I promise we won't take up much of your time, just a few minutes."

"I'm not dressed."

"We'll wait in the buggy while you get yourself together," Mrs. Olson suggested brightly. The elderly couple would not be easily deterred.

"Yes, well, I'll only be a moment." Charity gave them a hesitant smile; then, closing the door, she sank to the floor in despair.

Now what was she going to do? Reverend Olson and his wife would know she was caring for a man in her house, and then brows would lift. "Who is it?" Beau asked. His voice drifted across the room, breaking into her frantic thoughts.

"It's Reverend Olson and his wife!"

The fire in the stove had died, and Charity felt goose bumps rising on her arms. She hurriedly crossed the room to stoke the embers into a rosy glow.

"What do they want?"

"They want to come in and see Mary Kathleen. I don't know how they found out I have her, but they did."

Beau poked his head around the curtain, unshaven, hair on end. "Should I hide?"

She added more fuel to the fire and turned back to face him. She knew she couldn't complain about the incriminating position she found herself in. It wasn't his fault, and nothing could be done to correct it now. She would just have to tell the truth and pray that Reverend and Mrs. Olson would understand. "Where could you go? We'd better get dressed. They're waiting."

Ten minutes later Charity opened the door and smiled cheerfully at the reverend and his wife, who were waiting patiently in their buggy. "You may come in."

For the occasion Charity had put on her best yellow wool and tied a matching ribbon in her hair.

Reverend Olson helped his wife off the seat, and they hurried inside.

Rebecca Olson was engaged in lively chatter when they entered. Shrugging out of heavy coats, the couple made for the cheery fire, warming their hands. They stamped their booted feet, trying to thaw out. The cold winter day promised snow by evening.

Charity clasped her hands tightly and braced herself. Rebecca stopped in mid-sentence when she caught sight of Beau.

He stepped around the curtain wearing a pair of Ferrand's faded denim overalls and a dark cotton work shirt. To Charity he looked unusually tall and handsome this morning. She suddenly wished he looked fifty years older and six inches shorter, with eyes that were as pale and nondescript as Ansel's.

It would make her explanation much more believable.

"Why. . .hello." Rebecca smiled hesitantly and offered her small, gloved hand to Beau. "You didn't mention you had company, Charity." The reprimand in her soft voice was unmistakable.

"How thoughtless of me," Charity apologized.

"Good morning, ma'am." Beau stepped forward and took Rebecca's hand. "Such a cold day to be out." His voice dripped charm like molasses off hot biscuits.

Rebecca glanced at her husband. "It won't be long before travel will cease until spring."

Charity drew a deep breath, unclasped her hands, and stepped forward.

"Reverend Olson, Rebecca, this is Beau Claxton. He's—he's been my guest for the past few weeks."

"Oh?" Rebecca's smile slowly faded. "Your guest, dear?"

"Beau had the misfortune of meeting up with a wounded wolf in the stream, and as a result, he was gravely injured. I've been looking after him until his injuries heal." Charity tried to sound breezy and carefree, and as if it were the most natural thing in the world for a single woman to care for a stranger in her home.

Rebecca glanced at her husband. "Oh. . ."

"Why, that must have been a terrible experience. It's a miracle you survived, young man." Reverend Olson reached to clasp Beau's hand. "I guess that explains the bandages."

"I'm afraid without Mrs. Burk's excellent care, I wouldn't be here today," Beau admitted.

"Oh dear." Rebecca's eyes anxiously studied the angry welts still visible on Beau's face. "I do hope you're feeling better, Mr. Claxton."

He flashed her a melting smile. "Please. Call me Beau."

The pastor's wife colored; her face turned three shades of rose. "Beau. What a lovely Southern name. Are you from the South?"

"No, ma'am. I'm from Missouri."

"Missouri? I have a sister in Kansas City." Although the elderly couple was trying to be cordial, Charity saw the wary glances Rebecca sent her husband. She knew they were unnerved by Beau's presence and didn't know what to make of the situation.

"Well, my, my, why don't we all sit down and have a cup of coffee?" Charity invited, hoping to smooth over the awkward situation.

"Coffee would be nice," Reverend Olson agreed. "But we can't stay too long, Rebecca. We do have other calls to make, and it looks like weather will be moving in soon."

"Yes, dear. We'll only stay a minute." Rebecca turned back to Beau. "Exactly where in Missouri do you hail from, Mr. Claxton?"

"It's a small town, River Run—not far from Springfield." Beau held a kitchen chair for Rebecca, and she slipped into it gracefully.

"Now, we'll only stay a minute," Rebecca reiterated. Charity began to pour coffee. "Claxton. . .Claxton—you wouldn't happen to be kin to the Claxtons of Savannah, would you?"

"As a matter of fact, I am." Beau smiled. "My father's family is from Savannah."

"They are?" Rebecca glanced at the reverend expectantly. "Did you hear that, Reverend? He's a Savannah Claxton."

Rebecca's minute proceeded to drag into an hour, then two, and before Charity realized it, suppertime was drawing near.

Rebecca had become enamored of Beau. Throughout the afternoon he'd entertained her with exciting war tales about his brother and himself and stories of the Savannah Claxtons. Charity and the reverend shared Mary Kathleen, periodically changing diapers and warming milk.

While Charity prepared the evening meal, Reverend Olson gave up on an early departure and dozed peacefully in the chair before the fire. The morning sunshine had turned to clouds, and outside a cold rain pelted the windowpanes.

During supper the conversation was cordial, but Charity occasionally caught a renewed note of disapproval about Beau's remaining at the Burk cabin while he recovered.

"The reverend and I would be happy for you to stay with us until you're well. Isn't that right, Reverend?" Rebecca prodded.

"Hummph. . .uh. . .well, of course, dear." Reverend Olson cleared his throat and reached for a third biscuit. "Mr. Claxton would be most welcome to share our home."

"I do appreciate your offer, Rebecca," Beau said. "But I'd like to stay here awhile longer. I notice Mrs. Burk has a few fences down, and I thought before I went home, I'd help out a bit to repay her for my keep."

Charity glanced up from her plate in surprise. Their eyes met and held for a moment, and she tried to convey her gratitude.

Why would he do this? Did it mean he actually planned to stay on and help her with the land, or was he only trying to pacify the reverend and Rebecca? Charity felt her pulse trip. She smiled at him, and he smiled back.

"But, Beau, dear, you're not going to be able to mend fences for weeks." Rebecca was clearly appalled that he'd consider remaining at the house.

"I'm doing better every day, ma'am, but I thank you for your concern." Beau's gaze slid easily away from Charity's and returned to the food on his plate. "Another week or two and I should be up and able to work. If this mild weather holds, I'll start on that fence. Winter isn't a good time, but I'll do what I can."

Charity decided a change of subject was in order and promptly mentioned Ansel Latimer, inquiring whether the Olsons had noticed Ansel's odd behavior since Letty's death.

They agreed they had, and Charity discovered Ansel had told the Olsons of Mary Kathleen's whereabouts. She was relieved when they devoted the remainder of the supper conversation to that topic.

It was late when the reverend and his wife finally prepared to take their leave. Charity held an umbrella over their heads and walked them to the buggy, while Beau put Mary Kathleen down for the night.

"He's a perfect gentleman," Rebecca said. "So tragic about his young wife."

"He loved Betsy very much."

Reverend Olson helped his wife into the conveyance, tucked a warm fleece robe over her legs, and then ambled around to check the rigging while the two women continued to chat. The rain had slackened to a cold, fine mist.

Charity wrapped her shawl tighter and smiled. "I'm so glad

you stopped by, Rebecca."

She laughed. "We didn't intend to take up your whole day."

"We didn't mind at all." Charity was surprised how easily she'd begun to include Beau in her statements.

Mrs. Olson glanced toward the front of the buggy. The reverend was busy adjusting the harness. She turned back to Charity. "Dear, I don't know how to say this. . .but I feel that I must."

"Say what's in your heart, Rebecca."

At that moment Reverend Olson walked back to the buggy. "All ready, dear?"

"Well. . ." Rebecca paused. "I was about to remind Charity that while I find Mr. Claxton a perfectly delightful man, there will most assuredly be others in the congregation who'll question the propriety of this—this unusual arrangement. Don't you agree, Papa?"

"Hummph. . .well, yes, dear, as a matter of fact, I've been thinking the same thing," he admitted. He turned to Charity, his faded eyes growing tender with concern. "Now, mind you, I'm not judging, but I'm sure you're aware it isn't proper for two. . .uh. . .single adults to share the same roof, no matter how innocent the arrangement may be." He cleared his throat nervously. "Once the town hears a man is living with you, there will be talk, Charity, and I'm afraid it will be unkind, my dear. Mrs. Olson and I don't want to see that happen."

Charity's chin rose, and she knew she looked stubborn. "Talk doesn't bother me, Reverend. And he isn't living with me. He's staying here until he's strong enough to move on." Surely even the most judgmental couldn't fault an act of kindness.

"I'm aware of that, dear, but we must protect your reputation."

"We're not alone," Charity argued. "I'm taking care of Letty's baby until Ansel returns, and Beau is a sick man. Where is the impropriety?"

Reverend Olson shook his head. "I'm afraid that's beside the point. There will be talk, so I'd like to suggest Mr. Claxton reconsider our offer to stay with us until his recuperation is complete."

Charity lifted her chin a notch higher, determined that gossips wouldn't control her life. "Are you saying you and Rebecca will inform the town about my houseguest?"

"Certainly not!" Rebecca objected, clearly horrified that they'd be accused of such betrayal. "But you know a thing like this will eventually leak out. We're only thinking of you, Charity. We don't want to see your reputation harmed."

Charity's face crumpled like a child's, and her brave facade faded. "I know. . .but it's so unfair. We aren't doing anything immoral," she insisted.

"We know that, but other people won't be so understanding," Reverend Olson predicted. "I want you to promise me you'll talk to Mr. Claxton about moving to our place, soon as possible. I'm sure your secret will be safe for a few more days, but after that. . ."

Charity looked deeply into his eyes and understood he wasn't being self-righteous. He was genuinely concerned for her welfare, and he was right. There would be talk, and it wouldn't be pretty.

"Promise us you'll at least think about it, dear," Rebecca coaxed. "I'll take excellent care of your young man. Soon the snow will be so deep we won't be able to take him home with us."

Charity swiped at the tears starting to roll down her cheeks, wondering when she'd become such a crying ninny. "I'll speak with Beau about your offer," she conceded.

Reverend Olson patted her shoulder then reached into his pocket for a handkerchief. "I think you'll see that it's for the best, dear."

But Charity didn't see it that way. When Beau left, she would be alone.

Just her and Mary Kathleen to face the long winter.

&

Beau watched from the cabin window as Charity chatted with the Olsons. Judging from her solemn face, he had a hunch he knew the subject of their conversation. Him. He hadn't thought of it before, mainly because at first he had been too sick to care, and then because it had seemed so natural, but his staying here would cause talk. About Charity. He couldn't have that. It would be a sorry way to repay her for all her kindness.

The Olsons disappeared into the swirling mist, and Charity walked slowly back to the house. She opened the door and stepped inside, her expression subdued. Beau waited for her to speak, and when she didn't, he figured he'd better.

"The Olsons get away all right?"

She looked startled. "Oh yes, they're gone."

"Nice people, especially Rebecca."

She fingered her apron, her gaze distant as if her mind was a hundred miles away. More likely just down the road—to the community. "They are very nice. Surprising that she knew your relatives."

"Yeah. Guess the world's not as big as it feels."

She gave him a weak smile and started to pick up her pallet. Beau took the bedding from her. "Let me do that. You have other things to take care of."

She stiffened as if he had reprimanded her. "I can do it."

"I know you can, but I want to help." She was one stubborn woman. He studied her flushed face. "Mrs. Reverend giving you a hard time over me?"

She looked up and then glanced away, but not before he saw the gathering tears.

"Hey, don't cry." He ached with the desire to take her in his arms and wipe her tears away.

Mary Kathleen whimpered, and she moved away to see to the baby's needs. Beau watched her, wishing he could do something to make her feel better. He was only too aware of what the talk would be like if the people in town found out about him.

He would have to leave. He knew it as surely as he knew his own name.

Chapter 8

After supper Charity slipped off to catch a breath of fresh air. It had been a worrisome day. The Olsons arriving so early and catching her still in her nightclothes had been bad enough, but Beau's presence had really upset the applecart. Fortunately, Rebecca had liked Beau, but it hadn't been difficult to see what she was thinking. Never had Charity felt so embarrassed, and the thing that upset her the most was that nothing improper had happened between her and Beau, but she knew enough about the way people's minds worked to realize no one would believe that.

Reverend Olson's advice drifted in and out of her thoughts. Moving Beau to the Olsons' residence would be the sensible thing to do. But could she let him go? She felt an inner peace when he was near, one that had been sadly lacking in her life since Ferrand's death. And if she wasn't mistaken, Beau felt that same harmony. If he left now it wouldn't stop the talk. Maybe make it worse. She could just hear people claiming the Olsons had forced her to give him up. Either way, she would be considered a scarlet woman. It wasn't fair.

Should two lonely people—each in need of the other—be denied friendship merely to appease those who had nothing better to do than find fault where there was none? It seemed unjust to Charity that anyone should take this precious gift away from her. She and Beau weren't hurting anybody, so why should they be denied the pleasure of each other's company for the remaining few weeks before he returned home?

An hour later she was still seated on a bale of hay, staring up at the stars. Beau came out of the house and paused to enjoy the night. "Mind if I join you?"

She smiled, scooting over to give him room, grateful to have him—for right now, anyway. She wondered what he thought about the Olsons' visit. He had offered to hide, so he must have realized the impropriety their situation posed. Although where he thought she could find a place to hide a man his size baffled her. A one-room cabin didn't offer much in the way of hiding places. He could have sat behind his curtain while the Olsons were here, but she had her doubts that would have worked, either.

Besides, it would have been dishonest.

He sat down beside her, wincing as he slowly eased his injured leg into place. "Seems like you can see more stars on the prairie than anywhere else."

"Is your leg bothering you today?"

"It stiffens up when I don't move around enough."

"But you're doing much better." Charity wrapped her shawl snugly around her shoulders. "It's so cold."

"I never liked cold weather," he said. "Old Man Winter is seldom friendly."

An involuntary shiver trickled down her spine at the thought of another winter alone.

Winters in Kansas were long and harsh, bringing numbing temperatures and unbelievable snowstorms. Charity knew a Kansas blizzard could be a terrifying spectacle. Without warning, dark, billowing clouds would roll across the sky, unleashing blinding bursts of snow. Wind and snow could sweep across the plains with the force of a cyclone, taking a heavy toll on livestock and people. Communication with the outside world could be cut off for weeks at a time, and travel was impossible. Nothing moved until hundreds of men could dig openings through the drifts. In early fall Charity stored a winter supply of stove fuel and stocked up on canned goods, flour, sugar, and salt. She had moved the livestock closer in so she could care for them in bad weather.

She rubbed her hands down her arms to warm them and turned her thoughts to a more immediate concern. "Is the baby still sleeping?" Mary Kathleen had dozed off in Beau's arms while Charity cleaned up after their evening meal.

"I think the reverend and his wife wore her out." Beau chuckled and added solemnly, "Thank goodness."

Charity laughed at his open candor. "I thought you liked children."

"I do, but I was under the impression they slept once in a while."

"I think most of them do, but Mary Kathleen seems to be a bit confused about when she should be doing her sleeping—day or night. But with all the excitement today, we should be able to get a good night's sleep for a change."

Silence stretched between them. She sensed Beau studying her beneath lowered lashes. "What are we going to do about that situation?" he asked.

"The baby?"

"I don't mean to criticize, but it appears to me that Ansel is a sick man. Doesn't look to me like he's going to be able to take care of a baby for a long time. . .if ever."

Charity sighed. "He's troubled, all right." If anything, he slipped more out of touch with every passing day.

"What are you going to do? Keep the child indefinitely?"

"I promised Letty I'd take care of her. Ansel's a fine man. Given time, he'll accept her death. It was so sudden for him." She only wished she were as confident as she sounded.

"I'm not sure that's wise, Charity. You're getting mighty attached to the baby. Wouldn't it be better if he hired someone to care for Mary Kathleen until he's better?"

Charity turned to him with mock surprise. "I'm getting attached? I've noticed she has you wrapped snugly around her little finger."

Beau's laugh was guilty as sin. "She's a charmer, all right."

"She's more than a charmer, and I wouldn't feel right about anyone else taking care of Letty's child. I love caring for her." He was right, of course. Giving up Mary Kathleen would be like tearing out her heart, but she knew eventually it would come to that. As much as she loved the baby, Ansel had first rights.

"Seems like a lot of work on top of everything else you have to do."

"I don't mind." She really didn't. The baby was a lot of work, but she was so precious. Letty lived on in her daughter. Mary Kathleen's hair, the color of her eyes, even her smile reminded her of the sweet-natured young woman Charity had called friend.

They sat in silence for a while, studying the star-studded sky, sharing a contentment that neither of them questioned.

"You're quiet this evening," Beau finally remarked.

"Am I? I guess I'm just thinking."

"Must be serious," he teased. "Usually you're a real chatterbox."

Charity shrugged. "Nothing profound."

"Your thoughts wouldn't have anything to do with the reverend and his wife, would they?"

Charity glanced up, surprised by his astute perception. "What makes you say that?"

"I noticed they weren't any too happy about me staying here with you."

"I expected their disapproval." Or she would have if she'd thought about it, but expecting and coming up against it weren't exactly the same thing. The Olsons' disapproval would be mild compared to the way others would feel. Beau would leave when he was able, but she would have to live here knowing how the people in town felt about her. She would always be the woman who'd had a man living with her without marriage vows.

Still, if Beau would stay, she would gladly face the gossip for the privilege of having him here. *Lord, does that make me a bad woman?* She had been lonely for so long; she couldn't bear the thought of being alone again.

"It bothers you, doesn't it?"

Charity refused to look at him. "Well, surely Kansas isn't all that different from Missouri when it comes to morality."

"Morality? No, but we've done nothing to be ashamed about."

She finally met his gaze. "I see their point, Beau. I might think the worst if I were in their place and didn't know the true situation."

"Now that they know I'm staying here, Reverend Olson will explain the circumstances. They're God-fearing folk. Any one of them would likely do what you did."

She shook her head. "I'm not worried. I know I'm not doing anything wrong, and Ferrand always said that's all that counts. I sleep with a clear conscience." She wouldn't let idle talk dirty her feelings for Beau.

They sat in silence until he straightened his leg. "I guess I should give serious thought about taking the Olsons up on their offer to move in with them."

Charity closed her eyes and bit her lower lip, forcing herself to answer. "I suppose that would be the proper thing to do."

Beau stood up and lifted his gaze to the sky. A pale moon washed the landscape with light. "You always for doing the proper thing?"

The question surprised her. "Well, most of the time I try to do what's right, but I guess I've gone astray a few times." Her mother had said she was the most stubborn and contrary of her three daughters, but she'd never done anything really bad before. Not evil bad. "I'll wager you usually did what was right."

"Don't tell my ma, but I've slipped up a few times, too. It's best to do what you think is right, but what you think is right and what other people think is right is often a different story."

She glanced up, her breath leaving a frosty vapor. "You think this is one of those times?"

He lifted his shoulders. "Could be."

She sighed and turned her attention back to the night sky. "The situation isn't exactly proper. I suppose we'll be faulted for it whatever we do, so if you want to go I'll understand, but you're welcome to stay."

He fell silent. Then, "I suppose we could just sit tight for a while and see what happens."

Charity felt her heart leap with expectation. It was the closest he'd come to agreeing to stay. "There will be talk, but the Lord sees the true story."

He bent over, his features solemn in the moonlight. "If you don't have any objections, I'd like to stick around for a while longer. I'd leave at first light if I thought it was best for you, but I'd worry about you and the baby if I rode away now. I've been doing some thinking since the reverend left." His voice softened in what she accepted as an attempt to spare her feelings. "I can't marry you, not that you wouldn't make a fine wife, but I guess Bets was sort of it for me. . .you know."

"I wasn't expecting you to offer me your love, Beau." Her voice quivered and she tried to hold it steady. "I know how much you loved your wife."

His tone dropped. "I wouldn't marry any woman without giving her my all. It wouldn't be proper. Marriage is sacred and not to be taken lightly. A man and woman should be committed to one another before they enter into such an arrangement."

"But sometimes it doesn't work out that way," she said softly.

"I know it doesn't, but it should, and just because I can't marry you don't mean that I can't see that you're in a real bind. I'd like to help you out. Since I'm going to be laid up another few months, I could lend you a hand. I know I've never said it in so many words, but I'm beholden to you for saving my life, Charity. I'd like the opportunity to pay you back, if you'll let me."

"It wasn't all me," she reminded him.

"I know Laughing Waters and Little Fawn helped, but you're the one who took me in and sewed me up and sat up nights with me." He laid his hand over hers. His touch was warm, even though the night was icy. "I won't be forgetting what you've done. You're a good woman, and I'd be proud if you'd let me repay your kindness. There's no reason I can't stay till spring. By then I should have your land in good enough shape that you can claim your title. I'd be glad to do that for you, if you'd let me."

At another time in her life Charity might have refused his offer, pointing out that she neither wanted nor needed his sympathy. She didn't want him to stay because he felt beholden to her, but she guessed it was better than nothing. Sometimes you had to settle for what you could get. She'd discovered the hard way that no man—or woman, for that matter—could make it on the prairie alone.

She would've preferred he stay because he wanted her companionship. Nevertheless, she'd accept Beau Claxton on any terms.

Her hand gently closed around his. The touch was like nothing she'd previously known. "If you want to stay, I'll be grateful to have you."

"There's bound to be ugly talk when the town finds out I'm here. Soon as I'm able, I'll be headed to town for wire to string fences. If they don't know about me by then, they'll be finding out."

"Talk doesn't bother me long as I know it's not true."

His hand gently squeezed hers. "I say we see this thing through together. I could stay in the lean-to, if that would help any."

"You'd freeze to death with no heat. And it wouldn't stop gossip because you're here whether you're in the lean-to or sleeping behind a curtain in the house where it's warm. I've never let anyone freeze yet, and I don't plan to start now."

He still held her hand. "I wouldn't do anything to hurt you. I want you to know that. I respect you too much."

She smiled and clung to his hand, unable to speak over the large lump in her throat. He wanted to stay, if he was sure it was all right with her. It was more than all right with her. It was wonderful.

She wouldn't have to face another winter alone.

They started back to the house, and Beau wondered if he was doing the right thing. He knew all too well how vicious gossip could be. People who prided themselves on high standards expected everyone else to live by their rules. He knew how it would look to the people of Cherry Grove, him living out here in the same house with a young widow. For that matter, he knew how Ma and Willa would feel about it. Cole and Cass would understand, but understanding didn't always mean approval.

Usually he would ignore troublemakers, but this was different.

He couldn't stand by and let Charity be judged unfairly. But if he gave in to gossipmongers and moved to the Olsons', he'd have to leave her and Mary Kathleen alone. That wouldn't be right, either. On top of trying to run her homestead without a man's help, she'd been good enough to take him in and nurse him back to health and care for a newborn child that wasn't hers. And now the town would be down on her for what she'd done, when in fact she'd been the Good Samaritan.

What kind of a man could walk off and leave a woman to face the severity of a Kansas winter alone? She didn't have enough buffalo chips to last more than a couple of weeks, and he knew exactly how little food she had on hand. She'd tried to stock enough for winter, but him being here had used up most of her provisions, and keeping the cabin warm while he had been so sick had taken a toll on the stove fuel.

He glanced down at her in the moonlight, noticing the curve of her lips, the contours of her face. Funny, lately when he dreamed of Betsy he had trouble remembering her features. It was Charity's face that haunted the late-night hours. He didn't want it to be that way. No one could ever take Betsy's place in his heart, no one.

Her hand touched his as gentle as a butterfly caress. "Don't worry. I know I'm safe with you here. It means a lot that you'd offer to stay. No matter what people say, God knows we're innocent and that's what really counts."

Beau swallowed hard, surprised at the wave of tenderness that threatened to seize him. "That's right. God knows."

His hand gently squeezed hers, and he struggled against the need to take her in his arms. He was surprised to discover he wanted to, and he might have, if thoughts of Betsy hadn't surfaced, reminding him it wouldn't be loyal to her memory.

All he had left of Betsy were his memories, and he figured if he let those go, Betsy would be gone. Forever.

But if he left Charity here to fight the elements alone, she'd be gone, too. Seemed like God had laid out a pretty tough choice. Regardless, the course was set. He'd stay and face whatever the consequences.

Lately he'd been doing some thinking about God, and his thoughts had shamed him. He knew enough about the Bible to know God hadn't walked away from him. "I will never. . .forsake thee." He knew those words by heart, knew what they meant. He couldn't run far enough to get away from his Creator. Beau Claxton might have shut God out, but that didn't mean God had forgotten Beau Claxton. All the time he had stumbled around in a fog, not knowing or caring where he went, God had watched over him, even directed his steps. Had God brought him to Charity? He was beginning to think so.

Heavy snow fell off and on the next two weeks. As the fine white flakes mounded around the cabin, the predicted trouble arrived, but in a form Beau least expected.

He was feeding Mary Kathleen her first milk of the morning. Charity bustled around the kitchen fixing breakfast.

The smell of fresh coffee, buttermilk biscuits baking in the oven, and bacon sizzling in the cast-iron skillet filled the room.

Fire burned brightly in the stove. The relentless wind whistling across the frozen landscape made little difference to the occupants nestled inside the warm room. Outside, dwarfed by endless sky and sweeping plains, the Burk homestead seemed hardly more than a snow-covered mound on the prairie.

Charity stood on tiptoe and looked out the window at the swirling flakes of pristine white. "I love snow, and I suspect we'll be getting more than our share this year." She rubbed the steam from the glass with her elbow.

"I thought you hated winter." Beau set the baby's milk aside then tipped Mary Kathleen over his shoulder and gently patted her back.

Charity caught the paternal act out of the corner of her eye. Beau performed the task so naturally now that he seemed to enjoy taking care of the baby. Though he said Mary Kathleen was growing like a ragweed, the infant looked tiny draped over his broad shoulder. And he had no room to talk. He was filling out rapidly these days, becoming an impressive man in his own right.

Charity couldn't help but feel a strong surge of pride at the way her small family thrived under her care. She had to remind herself every day that they weren't really her family, only temporary gifts the good Lord had sent to see her through another long winter.

She didn't know when Ansel would come to his senses and show up to claim Mary Kathleen. She didn't like to think about losing the infant, but she'd learned long ago to live for the day and let tomorrow take care of itself. Trust in God one day at a time. Whatever happened, she knew He'd see her through.

"I don't mind snow so much, but I hate the wind and cold."

"Well, if it makes you feel that good, maybe you ought to come out and help me today," Beau teased. "No sense sitting in the house and missing all the fun."

Though Charity had argued that he wasn't strong enough yet to work, Beau had already begun taking over chores. The day before, he'd fed the cow and cleaned out the chicken roost. This morning, he said he wanted to make some much-needed repairs on the lean-to. She worried he'd use up his hard-won strength, but she was learning Beau Claxton didn't take orders. He was definitely his own man—and stubborn to boot.

Charity moved away from the window and returned to the stove to check on the bacon. "I'd be happy to help you out," she said, "but I must insist that you let me do the hard part."

He winked. "If you insist."

Charity knew he was teasing. He wasn't a man to stand by and let a woman do his work, even though his injuries still pained him. But she was certain she could do more than he allowed her to. Yesterday they'd had a discussion over workload. She couldn't wield a heavy sledgehammer to drive the posts into the hard-packed ground, but she could lift the posts from the wagon and have them waiting in place.

Beau wouldn't hear of it. He said she had enough to do taking care of the baby and keeping meals on the table. While he was around, he'd do the heavy work. Charity winced when she recalled another incident when they'd gotten downright snappish with each other.

Beau had been gathering chips, slowly and cautiously, while the pile beside the house had steadily mounted.

Charity was sure that he was overdoing it, so she'd bolted outside four or five times to caution him to slow down.

Each time she'd appeared to give him advice, Beau had promptly, but politely, sent her back into the house. "Go bake bread or something," he'd said. When she'd kept popping out the door to repeat the same warning again and again, he had finally lost patience with her.

"I used to help Ferrand all the time," she complained.

He'd lowered the ax, leaned on the handle in disgust, and fixed his blue eyes on her till the pupils had looked like pinpoints. "Well, I'm not Ferrand. And I'd sure appreciate it if you'd march right back in the house and nail your feet to the floor so I can get my work done."

Nail her feet to the floor! Why, that stubborn pain in the neck! Willing her voice to remain calm, she'd replied in a strained but pleasant tone, "You don't have to remind me you're not Ferrand. He would never have spoken to me in that tone. Besides, I was only thinking of your comfort. You're a fool to work this hard so soon after your accident."

"I feel fine. I want you to quit acting like a mother hen, constantly clucking over me. I'm going to gather fuel until I get enough to last us for a few days, and I don't want to hear that back door flapping every five minutes like a broken shutter in a windstorm. Do I make myself clear?"

Charity took a deep breath and squared her shoulders, her temper blazing hotter than a blacksmith's iron. "I'll see that you're not disturbed again." She tossed her head, marched back into the cabin, and slammed the door loudly enough to send Mary Kathleen into a startled howl.

They hadn't spoken to each other the rest of the day. By the following morning, they'd both concluded they were living too close in their tiny quarters to remain silent indefinitely, so they resumed communication.

Charity snapped out of her reverie and reminded Beau that breakfast was on the table.

He laid Mary Kathleen back in her bed then washed his hands. Charity took the pan of biscuits out of the oven and poured their coffee.

"Smells good," he complimented, and she realized he always had something nice to say about her cooking. He was a delight to cook for, liked anything she set before him. Since he was feeling better, he ate like a harvest hand at every meal.

"Thank you. I hope you're hungry."

He grinned. "I'm always hungry for your cooking."

She smiled back, relishing the compliment.

They sat down to eat, and someone knocked at the door.

Charity glanced up from her plate with a curious frown. "Now, who could that be?"

"I'll get it." He winked at her solemnly and pushed away from the table, sending her pulse thumping.

When Beau opened the door, she saw his expression change from amused to baffled. Charity peered past him to see Ansel standing in the doorway. He wasn't wearing a coat or hat, only dirty overalls and a thin cotton work shirt. His shoulders were covered with a thick dusting of snow. His body shivered uncontrollably, and his teeth chattered so badly he could hardly form words.

"I-I-I want to se-e my ba-b-by."

"My word, man. Where's your coat?" Beau reached out and pulled Ansel inside the shelter. Charity hurried to assist him.

"What's happened to you?" Charity had never seen him looking so disreputable—so unkempt. He was filthy, and his clothes looked as though they hadn't been washed in weeks. He'd lost so much weight his overalls and shirt hung loosely over his skeletal frame. She wrinkled her nose at the rank, offensive odor accompanying him. His unusually long hair was dirty and hung in matted strands around his face. Charity found it hard to believe that this was the same Ansel Latimer she'd known so well. He'd always been so clean, so careful about his appearance. Letty used to laugh about how often he used to change his clothes, and he'd had his hair cut every two weeks on the dot.

"I co-me to se-e my ba-b-y," Ansel repeated, his voice almost belligerent now.

"Of course you can see Mary Kathleen—"

"Who?"

"Mary Kathleen," Charity repeated. "That's what we've been calling her, Ansel. It's the name Letty wanted. I hope you like it."

Ansel seemed to momentarily forget the topic. His gaze

quickly shifted, his eyes roaming insolently over Beau's tall frame. "Who's this man?"

"Why, it's Beau. The man who was injured. Don't you remember?"

"I don't know him." He dismissed Beau abruptly. He glanced around the room.

Charity sent Beau a curious look. If he hadn't been here Ansel's strange behavior would have frightened her.

"Where's my baby?" Ansel's voice rose a notch. "I want to see my baby!"

"Let's get you warmed up first," Beau said. "Come over to the fire, man. We can't have you getting sick."

Charity realized he was worse. Much worse. He was acting crazy, and she was afraid he'd suffered a complete breakdown. "Let's sit down and have a cup of coffee. You must be nearly frozen."

She reached to take his arm, but he jerked away as if her touch burned him. He looked her up and down with the same contemptuous glance he'd given Beau earlier. "You Jezebel," he accused hotly, his voice edged with hate.

Charity stared in stunned disbelief. "What?"

"You're a shameless woman, Charity Burk. . .shameless!" he repeated, his eyes filled with rage.

"Wait a minute." Beau reached over and pulled Charity protectively to his side. "You have no right to speak to her in that tone."

"She ain't nothing but trash!"

"Ansel"—Charity managed to find her voice—"what's wrong with you!" She was shocked by more than his language. What had prompted him to come with such outrageous accusations? They'd been friends for years. Why would he turn against her like this?

He eyed her with disgust. "Don't try to lie to me. I've heard the talk. You're living in sin with this man, and you've got my baby daughter in your vipers' nest," he sneered. "Well, I'm here to deliver her from the hands of Lucifer."

"Oh Ansel." Charity sagged weakly against Beau. "I don't know what you've heard, but it isn't true—"

"Lies! Nothing but lies!" Ansel stepped back, his eyes flaring wildly. "They say this man's been living out here for weeks. Can you deny it?"

"He has been, Ansel, but we're not living together—not the way those people are implying." She'd expected repercussions, but not like this. Ansel knew she'd done all she could to save Letty. She'd taken care of his daughter while he'd not even bothered to come and see if she was all right. He knew about Beau, had expected him to die from the wolf attack. Now he acted like he'd never seen the man lying pale and unconscious right here in this room.

He glared at her, hatred filling his eyes. "Lies! Nothing but dirty, filthy lies, you sister of Satan!" He spat the words as if they'd left a bitter taste in his mouth.

"All right, I think that's about enough, Ansel." Beau stepped forward, his fingers curling into fists. "I want you out of here, or I'll throw you out."

Charity reached to stop him from carrying out his threat. "No, Beau. He's ill—"

"I know he is, but he's not going to talk to you that way," Beau stated, his eyes hard. "Not after all you've done for him."

"I come to get my baby," Ansel said calmly. Suddenly all trace of emotion disappeared. "It's time I be taking her home."

Charity glanced urgently at Beau. "No. . .he mustn't take her."

She knew Beau understood and agreed. He nodded, stalling for time. "You can't take your baby today. The weather's too bad. It would be better if you came back for her after the storm clears."

Ansel's chin jutted out and he turned belligerent again. "I can take my baby any time I want!"

Beau shook his head. "You're a sick man—you need help. Let me take you into town and—"

Ansel started backing toward the doorway, his eyes wild. Charity held her breath when he paused beside Mary Kathleen's bed. He glanced down and saw the sleeping baby, and his face suddenly took on the plaintive look of a small child's. "Ohhh. . .Letty. . .she looks like Letty."

"Ansel. . ." Charity eased forward, hoping to divert his attention so Beau could remove the baby from harm's way. "Let me fix you a cup of coffee, and then you can hold her and see how pretty her eyes are. They're amber—like Letty's."

He looked up. "I can hold her?"

"Of course you may hold her."

He reverted back to normalcy. He straightened his stance and moved with somber grace to sit quietly in a kitchen chair. Charity drew a breath of relief. She poured the coffee and fixed him a plate of food. Poor man; he looked like he hadn't had a decent meal in weeks. He drank the coffee Charity set before him and chatted amicably with Beau about the weather and spring crops.

After a while Beau nodded to Charity and she brought Mary Kathleen, placing the baby in her father's arms. Tears sprang into the father's eyes as he gazed down at his baby daughter. "She does look like my wife." His voice held a reverent awe as he brushed one finger lightly over the baby's cheek. Mary Kathleen laughed and waved her fists.

He looked at Charity, his eyes filled with wonder. "She's real pretty, isn't she?"

"Yes," Charity said softly. "She's a beautiful baby." It broke her heart to think Letty would never see her precious daughter.

He kissed the baby's forehead and smiled at Charity and

Beau. "I know I've been acting real strange, Charity, but I think seeing my baby has helped me understand that Letty's gone," he admitted. "Maybe as soon as I have a few weeks to get my life back in order, I'll be able to take my daughter home and be a proper pa to her." His eyes misted again. "She would've wanted that, wouldn't she?"

"Yes, she would."

"Losing Letty. . .well, I can't tell you what it's done to me."

"I know. You don't have to explain, Ansel." Charity patted his shoulder consolingly. People handled grief in different ways. She hoped Ansel had the worst behind him. Maybe he could start to heal now.

"Do you think I can take the baby outside?" he asked. "The snow's so pretty. I feel like Letty would be there with us, too. I'd like my daughter to experience snowfall with me. That would be all right, wouldn't it?"

Charity was touched by the earnestness in his eyes. What would it hurt to let him take her out for a minute? "It's cold out there. You can only keep her out for a short time."

He nodded. "I wouldn't want her to take a chill. I'll be careful with her, I promise."

Charity hurriedly went about gathering the baby's blankets to comply with his request.

While Ansel cooed and talked to Mary Kathleen, Beau followed her across the room, whispering out of the side of his mouth, "I don't like the way he's acting."

Surprised, she paused to glance up. "Why? He seems like his old self, Beau."

"That's my point. He was crazy as a loon a few minutes ago."

"I've been concerned about him, too, but I think seeing his baby has finally helped him to come to grips with Letty's death."

"What about the way he was talking to you?"

"He must realize he was mistaken. He'll apologize before he leaves; you wait and see. He's acting like the Ansel I've always known. I think with a little time, he'll be back to normal. You heard him. He's even planning on taking the baby home in a few weeks."

Beau remained skeptical. "I guess you know him better than I do. I hope you're not being foolish. I don't want you or the baby getting hurt."

She reached out and touched his arm, deeply moved by his concern. "I can't deny Mary Kathleen's father the right to be with her, and it will do him a world of good."

"I'll abide by whatever you decide," Beau conceded. "I just hope you're not making a mistake."

She squeezed his hand. "Thank you." How could it be a mistake to let Ansel spend time with his daughter? A baby had a way of changing things. Only good could come from this poor man being with his baby girl.

She shook her head at the irony, thinking of Beau's concern. If she was going to be hurt, it wouldn't necessarily be Mary Kathleen who'd break her heart. Come spring, Beau would be leaving. . . . She shook off the thought and hurried to bundle the baby properly for the brief outing.

"I'll only keep her outside a moment," Ansel promised, worriedly tucking in Mary Kathleen's little hand that persistently poked its way out of the blanket.

"A little fresh air won't hurt her, but she shouldn't be out long," Charity cautioned a second time. "The wind's sharp today."

"I'll be careful with her."

Beau opened the door and Ansel stepped outside, still talking to his baby in low, soothing tones.

"I might as well fill the fuel box," Beau offered, reaching for his coat. Charity began to clear the table.

"It is getting low." She knew Beau wanted to keep a close eye on Ansel and Mary Kathleen. If it made him feel easier, she wouldn't object. "Would you mind throwing these potato peels to the chickens?"

Beau crossed the room to take the small bucket out of her hand. Their fingers touched; their eyes met unexpectedly. Charity felt her breath quicken when she looked into his warm blue eyes. For an instant she found herself envying Betsy.

Strange, she thought, *to envy a dead woman.* But Charity realized that she'd gladly trade places with his deceased wife if, for only one second, for one brief second, Beau would look at her with the same love he had so fiercely reserved for Betsy. She knew it could never be, but it didn't keep her from wishing.

"This all you want me to take?" His voice was strained, and Charity thought his eyes looked vaguely troubled.

"Yes. . .that's all."

He nodded. "I'd best see about Ansel." He started to walk away, but she saw him hesitate. He turned and faced her, his face lined with worry. "I suppose gossip about us living together has started. That's what Ansel meant about hearing talk."

"It wouldn't surprise me."

"I don't like folks thinking that."

"We agreed we didn't care," she reminded him.

He acted as if he wanted to say more, but changed his mind. "I'd better check on Ansel."

Charity watched him walk to the door and open it. He adjusted his hat low on his forehead and then smiled at her. The door closed behind him, and she turned back to clearing the table.

Suddenly, the door flew open, and Beau stood in the doorway, his features tight with fury. "That lying, thieving scum is gone."

"What?" Charity's hand flew to her throat.

Beau stepped into the room, removed his hat, and angrily shook off the snow. "He's gone, Charity. There's not a sign of him anywhere."

Her hand covered her mouth. "Oh, dear God. . .the baby! He took the baby?"

Beau nodded curtly. "I'll saddle the horse and go after him, but I don't know. . . . The snow's coming down heavier now."

Charity crossed the room in a daze, trying to make sense of his words. "Beau. . .Mary Kathleen. . ."

"You don't need to remind me, Charity. He's taken her!"

Charity's composure crumbled, and as naturally as if it happened every day, she moved into the haven of his arms. She knew she had taken him by surprise. He held her stiffly at first, until she began to cry. Then his arms folded around her, and he pulled her closely to him.

His arms felt unbelievably good. He smelled of soap and smoke and fresh outdoors. There were still traces of snow on his shoulder, cold and wet against her cheek. She buried her face in the warmth of his neck and cried harder. It was all her fault. She'd been a fool to let Ansel take the child, and now Mary Kathleen would pay the price of her misplaced trust.

"There's no call to start crying," Beau whispered tenderly, smoothing her hair with one large hand. "He couldn't have gotten far. I'll find him and the baby before any harm's done."

"It's my fault," Charity sobbed.

"No, it's mine. I should never have taken my eyes off him."

"I want to go with you."

He grasped her shoulders and held her gently away from him. His blue eyes locked gravely with hers. "You should stay here in case he decides to come back."

"Oh. . .yes. . .he might come to his senses and bring her back." It was a hope to cling to, but she was so frightened. Mary Kathleen out there in this weather? She was so tiny, so helpless. And Ansel. . . *Oh God, be with them, please.*

The blue in Beau's eyes deepened to cobalt. "I'll ride out and see what I can find. Will you be all right?"

"I'll be fine." She dabbed her eyes with the corner of her apron. "Hurry, Beau. It's so cold out there."

Beau smiled reassuringly. "The baby's bundled tight. She'll be fine."

Though Charity tried to muster a weak smile in return, fresh tears rolled from the corners of her eyes.

Beau reached out and caught the two tears with his thumbs, tenderly brushing the dampness away. "I have to go."

Charity nodded, too overcome by emotion to speak.

He looked at her for a moment; then very slowly he pulled her face to his and touched her lips briefly with his own. Just as quickly, he stepped away, almost as if he had done something he shouldn't. "I'll be back soon as I can."

He turned, placed his hat back on his head, and opened the door. "Be careful if Ansel comes back. I don't think he'd hurt you, but you keep the gun close—and don't hesitate to use it if you need to."

Charity nodded, her knees threatening to buckle from his unexpected kiss.

He went out the door, closing it firmly behind him. Her hand came up to reverently touch her mouth, where his taste still lingered. The kiss was only his way of reassuring her that everything would be all right.

She knew that.

But it was the most wonderful kiss she'd ever experienced, and she'd hold it forever within her heart.

The wind-driven snow lashed Beau's face. Heavy white flakes settled on his eyelashes, almost blinding him. He waded through deep snow to the lean-to where the horses had taken shelter from the storm. The wind howled while he saddled the bay stallion with fingers numb and clumsy with cold.

Father, I don't have any idea which way to go. Help me find them before it's too late. Latimer could be anywhere out there. Did he have a horse or was he in a wagon? Surely he wouldn't be on foot. No one could survive a Kansas blizzard without shelter.

Beau swung into the saddle and rode away from the cabin, peering through the heavy curtain of snow, trying to locate tracks. His thoughts turned to Charity, knowing she would be pacing from the window to the door, praying for Ansel and Mary Kathleen and for him.

He thought about the way she had fussed over him the other day while he was gathering buffalo chips. She sure was cute when she got all flustered that way. It had been the first time he'd ever seen her lose her temper, and he'd discovered he rather liked her spunky nature.

The way she'd felt in his arms a moment ago. . .she'd fit just right. She always had that pleasant lemony smell, and her hair had been like silk under his hand. She had felt so small, so sweet it almost took his breath away. Charity Burk was a special woman, and someday she'd make some man real happy. He regretted it couldn't be him.

He turned the horse to face the wind, praying he'd find Latimer and the baby in time.

He had to find them. Charity was depending on him.

Chapter 9

Lamps were burning when Beau returned. Charity had spent the day alternately pacing the floor, praying, and wringing her hands in frustration. When she heard the horse approaching, she rushed outside without bothering to put on her coat.

Snow was still falling heavily, blanketing the ground with deep layers that made it difficult for her to walk. Beau was dismounting when Charity waded through deep drifts to meet him. Her gaze desperately searched his arms for a small bundle. When she saw there wasn't one, tears sprang to her eyes. "You didn't find her?"

"No." Beau quickly led the horse into the lean-to. Charity trailed behind.

"There wasn't a sign of him or the baby?"

He released the cinch and lifted the saddle, glancing at her. "You shouldn't be out here without a coat."

Charity clasped her hands around her shoulders, trying to keep her teeth from chattering. The wind whipped snow around the corners of the lean-to. They had to shout in order to be heard.

"Get back in the house!" Beau ordered.

She refused to leave. "What are we going to do about the baby?"

Beau put the saddle away, slipped the bridle off, and pitched a forkful of hay to the horse. Without a word he drew Charity under the shelter of his arm and propelled her toward the house. Heavy snowflakes mixed with sleet stung her face. Wind buffeted them. Charity stumbled and would have fallen without his supporting arm.

Beau forced open the door, and they struggled inside. Heat wrapped around them like a warm blanket. Charity caught her breath, stunned by the sudden relief from the gale-force winds and bitter cold.

Once inside, he gripped her shoulders and turned her to face him. "I managed to pick up Latimer's tracks about a mile out, but it started snowing heavier and I lost them."

"Oh Beau!"

"He's taken shelter somewhere along the way. He knows the baby can't survive in this storm," he consoled her.

"But he isn't thinking straight."

"He proved he can have lucid moments this morning. He's found shelter, and he and the baby are all right."

Her eyes searched his, and she had a feeling he wasn't as confident as he sounded.

He released her, dusted off his hat, and stomped the snow from his boots. She quietly crossed the room to stoke the fire. He was half frozen and worn to the bone. It would be hard for him to accept defeat.

When she turned around, she noted the way worry and fatigue deeply etched his face, and she longed to go to him to offer comfort. She knew he'd grown as fond of the baby as she; yet she also realized it wasn't her place to hold him.

He moved closer to the fire to warm his hands, and she noticed his stiff movements. The wounds were bothering him again.

"You must be exhausted." Charity helped him remove his

snow-crusted coat. "Sit down by the fire and I'll dish up your supper." She hung his coat on the peg by the door and hurried to the stove. He sat in the split-bottomed rocker warming his hands as she went around filling a dish with stew and pouring hot coffee.

"Supper's ready."

He got up and walked slowly to the table, shambling a little out of weariness. She ached with the desire to place her hands on his shoulders and massage away the soreness of overstressed muscles. Afraid her ministrations wouldn't be welcome, she turned away to hew thick slices of bread from a fresh-baked loaf.

After he'd eaten and she'd cleared the table, they sat before the stove. She let her expression silently beg him for some morsel of solace.

"We wait, Charity."

"For what?"

"We wait until we hear something. . .one way or the other."

Mutely she stared back at him, crushed by the finality in his voice and aware he was no longer pretending that all would be well. He was being brutally frank now. He couldn't know any more than she what the next few hours would bring.

Wait. The hours ahead loomed over her with a foreboding as dark and wild as the storm raging outside her home.

She found comfort in the thought that she would not be alone during the wait. Beau would be with her, and God was there. He'd take care of Mary Kathleen. She had to believe that.

She silently crept into Beau's arms, and they stood before the fire holding each other, trying to absorb each other's grief in the only way they knew how.

The night passed slowly. Charity found rest impossible. She lay awake staring into the darkness, seeing Mary Kathleen's precious face. She had promised Letty she'd take care of her baby. God forgive her, she had broken that promise. Not intentionally, but the result was the same.

Beau had recovered enough to move about now. He'd insisted Charity return to her bed; he'd taken the pallet before the fire. Tonight he tossed about on the makeshift bed, and she knew he was restless and unsettled.

She stirred and called softly to him, "Are you all right, Beau? Do you need anything?"

"I'm fine; don't worry about me."

Thirty minutes later, he got up and stirred the fire. Charity dressed and came out to join him. They rocked and drank coffee. Beau started talking. He reminisced about happier times, carefree boyhood days spent with his brothers. Charity told him about Ferrand, her sisters, and how she longed to see them all again. Ferrand on the other side.

The endless night dragged on, and they talked of many things. The wind howled and buffeted the small dwelling. Occasionally they heard the sound of sleet hitting the windowpane. The fire burned low, filling the room with a rosy warmth. Charity gazed up at Beau, knowing he was talking to ease her burden, trying to help her the only way he knew how, and she was grateful God had sent him to her. She couldn't imagine what this night would have been like without him.

It occurred to her that neither she nor Beau had spoken much of Ferrand or Betsy tonight. The discovery encouraged her. Maybe they were both moving away from their pasts.

"How will he feed the baby?" Charity asked once, returning to the subject uppermost in their minds.

"He'll find a way. It's his child—a man takes care of his own."

A man like Beau Claxton would, she reflected, but Ansel Latimer was a sick man. She remembered his dirty, disheveled appearance, his lack of a coat or hat. He hadn't taken care of himself. Would he know enough to take care of his daughter?

By first light the knock they'd been praying for sounded at the door. Beau gently restrained Charity when she bolted forward. He went to answer it.

Reverend Olson stood on the doorstep. Snow dusted his shoulders, and his kindly features were lined with weariness. "I know you must be sick with worry."

"The child?" Beau asked.

"She's with Mrs. Olson. Ansel brought her by late last night."

Charity joined Beau at the door, and he put his arm around her supportively. "Is she. . .all right?"

"She was cold and hungry, but she'll be fine. Mrs. Olson is spoiling her outrageously right now."

Charity sagged against Beau's side. "I'll get dressed, and we'll go get her—"

"Charity." Reverend Olson's expression changed. "May I step in, dear?"

"I'm so sorry. Of course. You must be half-froze."

The reverend stepped inside. Snow was coming down in large, puffy flakes; the wind was bitter cold. Pale morning light revealed a forbidding landscape buried under a heavy load of ice and snow. Beau closed the door.

"I'll fix you something warm to drink," Charity said.

Reverend Olson nodded, his expression grateful. He held his hands out to the stove, the heat sending steam rising from his damp overcoat. Charity brought mugs filled with hot coffee, and he cradled the cup in his hands, standing in silence for a moment.

While they drank coffee, Reverend Olson told them how Ansel had suddenly appeared on his doorstep the night before, cradling the baby in his arms, talking wildly.

"He was talking about Beau and me, wasn't he?" Charity held his level gaze.

"I'm afraid he is very ill. Somehow he finally comprehended Beau was staying here, and he was convinced the two of you are living in sin."

When Charity started to protest, Reverend Olson stopped her with an uplifted hand. "Surely you must know what the town is saying, dear. We discussed this at great lengths during my last visit, and if you recall, this is precisely what Mrs. Olson and I feared would happen. Apparently you preferred to take the risk. Beau has remained in your care rather than moving to our home for safekeeping."

Charity's eyes dropped, but Beau straightforwardly met the reverend's gaze. "We've committed no sin."

Reverend Olson's expression, kinder now, still held condemnation. "I know, my son, but surely you must see the impropriety of your situation. People are narrow-minded at times, and their tongues will continue to wag as long as you remain here with this young woman."

"Narrow-minded people find fault where there is none, Reverend. Charity needs my help. Soon as I have her land in proper order, I'll be moving on—and not a day sooner."

Beau watched the preacher's eyes grow cold. He knew how his being there must look to outsiders, but they hadn't done anything wrong, and he wasn't going to act like they had. Charity Burk was a lady. Circumstances had brought him into her life, but it hadn't been her choice, and she had committed no sin.

"You're making a grave mistake, young man." Reverend Olson shook his head. "What you're doing will remain to haunt Charity long after you've taken your leave. You must consider that as well."

"Charity and I are in full agreement on what we're doing."

Reverend Olson was right in what he said, but Beau could not walk away from this woman. She needed help. It could have been Bets out here alone. He would have wanted someone to help her, however improper the arrangement appeared.

"Then I must warn you," said Reverend Olson, his tone solemn, "the child cannot be returned to your care."

A low cry of protest escaped Charity. "Oh. . .please, no. . ."

"Ansel has left the child with me, and I cannot, in good faith, return her to this situation."

"Exactly where is Latimer?" Beau demanded. "He has no right to steal the child and give her to you! Charity has been the only mother Mary Kathleen has known. You have no authority to take her away from here."

"I don't know where Ansel is, but he has every right to place the child where he feels she will be properly cared for. He is Mary Kathleen's father."

"He's insane." Beau slapped his hand on his thigh.

"I pray that isn't the case. I prefer to think he's a very troubled man, but regardless, we have a search party looking for him at this moment. He was barely lucid when he left the child last night. He wasn't wearing a coat. The townsfolk are concerned he won't survive the storm unless we find him soon."

"You have no right to keep that child. No one could give her any better care," Beau maintained.

"If Charity were married, there'd be no question," the reverend reiterated. "Or if Ansel sees fit to return the child to her, then I suppose there would be nothing I could say. We'll simply have to find Ansel and try to ascertain what is best for both him and the child at this point."

Charity glanced helplessly at Beau. He set his jaw in a hard line and crossed the room to put on his coat. "I'll be riding back to town with you, Reverend." He was going to find Ansel and bring that baby home if it was the last thing he ever did.

"Oh Beau." Charity followed him to the door. "You can't go out in this again. You were out all day yesterday—"

"I'm going." Beau cut her protest short, and she watched silently as the two men prepared to leave.

"I don't want you worrying. We'll be all right." Beau faced her when they stood in the doorway a few minutes later. She handed him a sack of food she'd hurriedly assembled.

He looked down at her, seeing the fear in her eyes. She was worried about him. And there was something else, something he'd seen only in Betsy's eyes. He swallowed and looked away.

"You be careful." She gave him a warm red woolen scarf she'd been wearing. One she'd knitted and given to Ferrand on his birthday. "Be sure to wear this. The wind is terrible."

Beau smiled and winked at her, hoping his eyes silently conveyed his appreciation for her concern. "Thanks. You take care, too."

He tucked the sack under his arm, pulled his hat low on his forehead, and nodded to the reverend. "I'm ready if you are, sir."

The search parties had split off into small groups. Beau and Reverend Olson met up with two of the men as they rode into the outskirts of Cherry Grove.

All four riders reined their horses to a halt. Lanterns burned brightly in the blowing snow. "Gentlemen, this is Beau Claxton," the reverend introduced them. Their horses pranced restlessly, their breath blowing frosty plumes in the cold night air.

The two men assessed Beau silently, their expressions easily discernible. "You the one living with the Burk woman?" Jim Blanchard finally ventured.

"Mrs. Burk was kind enough to care for me while I was ill," Beau returned evenly. "And I sleep and take my meals there, but

I don't 'live' with her." Though Beau spoke quietly, there was an underlying edge of steel in his tone.

Jim Blanchard shot Troy Mulligan a knowing grin. Beau noted the snide exchange, and he eased forward in his saddle, casually resting his gloved hands on the horn. "I'd be mighty grateful if you gentlemen would be so kind as to pass the word along. I'd not take kindly to anyone who'd say otherwise."

His smooth voice had such an ominous tone it promptly wiped the smirks from both men's faces.

"Gentlemen, we're wasting time," Reverend Olson reminded patiently. "There's a sick man out there somewhere who needs our help."

The men agreed to search in opposite directions and meet back hourly to report any progress. Beau rode north; the reverend, south; Jim Blanchard, west; and Troy Mulligan headed east.

The wind continued to pick up. Icy pellets fell from the leaden skies. Beau rode for over thirty minutes without one encouraging sign to indicate Ansel had gone that direction.

He realized even if there had been tracks, the snow would quickly have covered the trail.

Sleet stung his face, and he paused once to tie the woolen scarf Charity had given him over his mouth. His hat brim sheltered his forehead. The faint smell of lemon lingered in the fabric, and Beau closed his eyes for a moment, drinking in her fragrance. The thought of her waiting and praying back at the cabin gave him the strength to push his horse forward in the ever-deepening drifts. He thought of Ansel out in the storm with no warm clothing to protect him and offered up a prayer for the poor lost soul. He'd been where Latimer was, everything lost and nothing left to hope for, and it was an awful place to be.

It was nearing dawn, and there was still no sign of the man.

When Beau had reported back to the other men, he found that they, too, had been unable to shed any light on Ansel's whereabouts, but they'd all agreed to keep looking.

The storm had increased in intensity and the men were exhausted, but no one was ready to give up. Beau headed back out again, knowing it would take a miracle to find anyone in this blizzard. His face felt numb, and he could no longer feel his hands in the fleece-lined gloves he wore. The drifts were nearly up to his horse's belly. Beau knew he was going to have to turn back soon.

The horse topped a small rise, and Beau reined him to a sudden halt. His eyes scanned the fields below him, and his heart sank.

On the ground, Ansel lay peacefully. Frozen to death.

Beau closed his eyes, despair washing over him. He sat atop his horse on that cold rise, looking at the new father. What an awful, lonely way to die. Why had he neglected to come in from the cold? But he knew the answer better than anyone. Ansel didn't care about living, not without Letty.

Did any man have the right to judge another? Beau slumped wearily over the saddle horn, staring at what once had been a vital, loving man. He searched his soul and found he couldn't condemn Ansel. Only God knew what this man had gone through, and only God had the right to judge. Beau couldn't help but feel Ansel had found a peace most folks would know nothing about.

He knew exactly how deeply Ansel had suffered. Hadn't he felt just as hopeless many, many times after Betsy's death? But through the grace of God and his mother's prayers, some inner strength had kept him going for another hour, another day, another week, always with the hope that the hurt would eventually ease. Like Ansel he'd had trouble accepting the change death had brought. But Latimer had been alone, and Beau had family. It shamed him now that he'd run away from the people who loved him most. It also bothered him that he hadn't talked to Ansel. Maybe it would have helped if the grieving man knew someone else had walked through the same dark valley.

The only thing he could fault Ansel with was that, like himself, he had loved too deeply.

It only took a few minutes to ride to where Ansel lay. Beau gently lifted the lifeless body in his arms and carried him to his horse. He removed a blanket from his bedroll and wrapped it securely around the body, though he wasn't sure why. Maybe because Ansel looked so cold.

Before he secured the body to the back of the horse, he stood gazing down into the man's face, which looked surprisingly serene.

What had been his last thoughts? Beau wondered.

He was now beginning to believe that faith was a journey, not a destination. If only Ansel could have known the difference. The realization jarred Beau to his very core. He knew that if his life was to change, if he was ever to regain hope, he had to trust that though tomorrow would have its share of trouble, no man was asked to carry his burdens alone. That God's grace was sufficient for any need he might have.

Beau reached out and gently touched the cold cheek. "If it helps any, I understand. I'll do my best to see your daughter's cared for."

He wanted to say more, but he didn't know anything to add. Surely there had to be more profound words to speak at a time like this, but he guessed he'd have to leave those words to the wisdom of Reverend Olson.

He climbed onto his horse to take Ansel home.

A grave was never a pretty sight. Ansel couldn't be buried until a spring thaw, so folks had gathered around the Latimers' root cellar to say good-bye. Friends and neighbors had been called upon to bury the dead. In a matter of weeks circumstances had set aside these particular mourners to put to rest another victim of what seemed like a never-ending tragedy for the Latimer family.

Snow lay deep on the ground, and the small group huddled against the cold wind to listen to Reverend Olson talk about the "deeply troubled soul" of Ansel Latimer.

Beau stood beside Charity, solemnly listening to the minister's words. A weak sun slipped in and out of mushroom-shaped clouds, which promised neither rain nor shine. The icy wind whipped the mourners' coats about their legs, making the forced gathering more miserable than it already was.

Reverend Olson's voice sounded far away when he read from Isaiah. "He giveth power to the faint; and to them that have no might he increaseth strength. Even the youths shall faint and be weary, and the young men shall utterly fall: but they that wait upon the Lord shall renew their strength; they shall mount up with wings as eagles; they shall run, and not be weary; and they shall walk, and not faint."

The reverend closed his Bible and wiped his eyes. "Ansel was weary; God gave him rest. Weep not for this good man, but hold tightly to the Word of God, our source of strength."

Our source of strength. Beau had not depended on God enough for that strength. He searched for a meaningful reason why so much heartbreak should come to one family, why so much misfortune should be thrust upon one innocent child. He could find none.

Mary Kathleen was alone now here on earth.

Who would see to her needs, rejoice over her first tooth, send her to school, or walk her down the aisle when she grew into a lovely woman? He realized, with a pang, how proud he'd be to do all those things for her.

Although Reverend Olson hadn't spoken again of the baby's welfare, Beau knew Mary Kathleen wouldn't be returned to Charity. And judging from the sadness on her face, Charity knew it, too.

Beau had watched her going about her work the past two days with a quiet despondency. When he'd attempted to cheer her, she'd politely dismissed his overtures with a wan smile and a soft reprimand: "Don't worry about me."

The cabin was a forlorn place without the baby. He knew Ansel's death bothered Charity, too. In times like this it was easy to wonder if something couldn't have been done or said to prevent the tragedy.

He knew Charity missed the baby. At night Beau had heard her crying into her pillow, and he'd wanted to go behind the curtain to comfort her. Instead, he'd lain staring at the ceiling, feeling her misery as deeply as his own, agonizing because he had no way of easing it.

Then the guilt had set in, keeping him awake long after Charity had dropped into an exhausted sleep. A lot of the blame for her trouble rested on his shoulders. If he had gone to live at the Olsons' the way the reverend had wanted, Mary Kathleen would have been allowed to remain with Charity. His being there had brought this condemnation on her. Deep within his soul he knew a way to spare her this agony.

It would only take a brief marriage ceremony.

A seemingly simple solution, yet by offering to marry her, wouldn't he inadvertently be allowing her to exchange one anguish for another? Granted, the Olsons would be happy to return Mary Kathleen to Charity's care if she was properly wed, but Beau knew it would be unfair of him to marry her. While he certainly liked and respected Charity, he wasn't sure if he could ever love any woman again.

Betsy's death had changed him. He'd loved her with all his heart—but she was gone, and he had been left damaged and broken. The wound in his heart hadn't healed. Maybe it never would. Since both he and Charity had experienced good, loving marriages, would it be right for them to settle for security and companionship and never again know the depth of love they'd each shared with their deceased partners? It seemed to Beau that wouldn't make either one of them happy. There was always the chance Charity would meet someone she could love. Did he have the right to tie her to a loveless marriage? *Father, show me the right thing to do.*

He knew love came in many forms. He loved Wynne, Cole's wife, but not the way he had loved Betsy. If anything ever happened to Cole, Beau knew he would take care of Wynne and provide a good life for her and Cole's child. Maybe he could love Charity the same way he loved his sister-in-law, purely platonically.

Charity had been good to him, as good as any woman he'd ever known. He owed her his life. And since he was relatively sure no other woman could fill Betsy's void, why was he being so stubborn about marrying her?

He couldn't deny there was a strong attraction between them, but he was sure it grew from being so lonely for so long. Charity hadn't forgotten Ferrand any more than he had forgotten Betsy.

If he could save Charity's land by sacrificing a few months out of his life, why shouldn't he? Once the land title was in her hand, and he was assured she could take care of herself, he could always go back to Missouri. She would never try to hold him against his will; he knew that. The day she had asked him to marry her, she had promised to let him leave with no obligation the moment she could claim her land.

Beau realized Reverend Olson had invited the gathering to

pray. They bowed their heads and the minister's voice boomed encouragingly over the frozen countryside. "The Lord is my shepherd; I shall not want. . ." The voices of the mourners blended somberly together as they recited the Twenty-third Psalm.

Beau saw tears seep from Charity's eyes. He reached to clasp her hand and squeeze it reassuringly as his deep voice joined with hers in the moving recitation.

"Yea, though I walk through the valley of the shadow of death, I will fear no evil: for thou art with me. . ."

Beau could see heads begin to lift when Charity absently moved into the shelter of his side. He knew tongues would wag anew, but at the moment, she needed someone to lean on, and he had about made up his mind—like it or not—that he was the only one she could count on.

The top of her head barely reached his shoulder. The small feather on her black hat danced in the wind. She huddled against his coat, seeking shelter from the elements. She glanced up, and their eyes met. Her gaze searched his imploringly, crying out for his quiet strength, and Beau was more than willing to give it to her.

The dreary day was suddenly obliterated when she smiled, and as if they were speaking only to each other, they recited the comforting thought: "Surely goodness and mercy shall follow me all the days of my life: and I will dwell in the house of the Lord for ever."

Beau believed those weren't just words written a long time ago, but a firm promise a man could depend upon. His eyes lovingly brought the message home to her.

Maybe the words would make Ansel Latimer's death easier to bear. He knew she blamed herself for letting him take Mary Kathleen, but there was enough blame to go around. He should have known a man in Ansel's state of mind couldn't be trusted.

The service ended, and the crowd wandered away.

Few chose to stop by the Burk sled to offer words of comfort after the service. Most of the mourners conveniently dispersed to the safety of their carriages for the return trip.

The reverend and Mrs. Olson paused briefly, clasping Charity's hand. Their eyes spoke of deep sympathy because they knew she'd lost another close friend, and their words were kind and reassuring. Beau noticed Charity holding tightly to Rebecca's hands, and he saw the older woman trying to comfort her. He'd also noticed the other women giving them a wide berth. They acted like they were too good to associate with Charity. It hurt him to see the look in her eyes when she experienced the women's behavior.

When the last of the mourners had gone, Beau and Charity sat in the sled staring at the closed cellar door. The Latimer homestead would go untended until better weather.

The sound of the wind rustling through brittle branches was a lonely one. The sun had disappeared behind a cloud again, enveloping the earth in a shroud of gray that seemed fitting for the sad occasion.

"I hate death." Charity's voice sounded small and frightened in the cold air.

"It's as much a part of life as being born."

She turned to Beau, her face childlike now. The wind had whipped her cheeks red, and her moist eyes reminded him of pools of sparkling emeralds. He had never seen her look so pretty—or so lost. Since coming to the Kansas frontier, she'd seen more than her share of death, and he knew she needed to know there was more to life than this terrible, crushing sense of loss. "It hurts, Beau. It hurts." Her voice broke and tears slid down her cheeks.

"I know it does." He reached over gently and cupped her face in one large hand. His eyes held hers. "I wish I could make it easier for you."

"You do, just by being here."

She smiled through her tears, and the sun suddenly broke through the clouds in a splendid array of light, bathing the cellar and the small sleigh in a pool of ethereal warmth.

Or did it only seem that way because that's how Charity made him feel? When Beau glanced up, the clouds were as dark and dreary as they'd been before. He slapped the reins against the horse's rump and turned the sled toward town.

Charity had been aware that Beau had stared at her a very long time. It seemed as if he was struggling to say something but didn't know how.

She had waited patiently but felt disappointment when, after gently brushing her tears from her cheeks with his thumbs, he'd reached to pick up the reins. The horse slowly began to move over the rutted hillside.

Charity turned, staring over her shoulder as the Latimer homestead grew smaller and smaller in the distance.

"I hope he's with Letty," she whispered.

"Yeah, me, too." Beau seemed preoccupied, and after a glance at him, she decided to leave him alone.

A stray flake of snow fell occasionally as the sled wound its way back to Cherry Grove. Charity had mentioned earlier she needed a few supplies and would like to stop by Miller's Mercantile before they made the trip home.

Beau had readily agreed. He needed a new hammer, and he wanted to purchase a quantity of raisins.

"Raisins?" Charity's brows lifted when he mentioned the strange request.

"I'm partial to raisin pie. You know how to make one?"

"Why. . .I've never made one, but I'm sure I could."

"Then I'll get plenty."

She'd make him one for supper. She could make a pie, just had never tried her hand at making a raisin one. But if Beau wanted one, she'd try to comply.

But when the sled rolled into Cherry Grove, Beau drove right past Miller's Mercantile, the Havershams' restaurant, Dog Kelley's Saloon and Gambling House, the Parnell clothing store, the schoolhouse that served as the church on Sunday mornings, and the various other storefronts lining the almost-deserted Main Street.

A plume of white smoke puffed from the chimney of Miller's Mercantile. Charity knew most of the townspeople who were brave enough to venture out on such a cold day would be huddled together around the old woodstove, exchanging tales of Ansel Latimer and, no doubt, the scandalous Charity Burk.

"You just passed the mercantile," Charity reminded him, thinking Beau had been lost in thought and missed his intended destination.

"I know."

The sled came around the corner, and the horse trotted at a brisk pace down Larimore Street. Charity leaned over to assist Beau in correcting the oversight, her breath making white wisps in the cold afternoon air. "Just follow Larimore around, and it will bring you right back to Main."

"I know where I am."

"You do?" His air of confidence assured her that he did, but she didn't understand. As far as she knew, Beau had only been in Cherry Grove one previous time to purchase nails and wire.

"How are you so well acquainted with the town?"

"I'm unusually bright for my age." He winked at her and began to whistle a jaunty little tune, urging the horse to pick up its pace.

Charity sat back and enjoyed the ride, thinking how nice it was to get her mind off of the devastating events of the past few days. Beau seemed to be in an uncommonly good mood all of a sudden, and it made her own spirits lighter. She wasn't in any hurry to face the people gathered at the mercantile, although she knew she'd have to eventually. No one had said anything at the funeral, but their behavior had been cool. That hurt. The name of Burk had always stood for decency and integrity. She hated being the one to bring censure on Ferrand's name.

Beau pulled the horse to a halt in front of Reverend Olson's house a few minutes later, and Charity glanced at him, mystified.

"We're going to visit Mary Kathleen!" She tried to conceal the sudden excitement in her voice. She knew he missed the baby as badly as she did, and she didn't want to put a damper on his cheerful mood.

Beau set the brake and tied the reins to the handle. He got out of the sled and turned to lift her down. She put her hands on his shoulders and felt his strong grip on her waist when he lifted her from the seat. He held her gently for a moment before setting her feet on the ground.

Charity tried to keep up when he opened the gate on the white picket fence and ushered her up the walk. "Beau, I don't think we should drop in unannounced this way. The reverend may still be at the Latimers'."

"A minister shouldn't be surprised by unexpected company," Beau reminded. Before Charity could protest further, he rapped briskly on the parsonage door.

Rebecca answered the summons. Her face broke into a wreath of welcoming smiles when she recognized the visitors standing on her doorstep. "Land sake! Look who's here, Papa!"

"Who?" Reverend Olson poked his balding head around the doorway and broke into a smile when he saw the young couple. "Well, do come in, do come in!" he invited, swinging the door open cordially. "We just got home."

Charity noticed he had a cloth draped over his shoulder, and signs of Mary Kathleen's recent dribbling were in evidence.

"How very nice to see you!" Rebecca exclaimed. She bustled around collecting their coats and scarves. "I didn't expect to see you again so soon."

"Well, I had a few things to pick up at the mercantile," Charity offered lamely, never dreaming herself that she'd be standing in the reverend's parlor, enjoying the delicious smell of a fresh-baked apple pie on this of all days.

"You must stay to dinner," Rebecca insisted.

"I'm afraid we have to be getting back soon," Beau refused politely. "It's starting to snow again."

"It is? Oh dear. I just hate winters, don't you?" Rebecca chattered. "Ansel's service went well, don't you think? So sad. So sad."

Charity nodded, wondering why they were here. She was sure Reverend Olson wouldn't change his mind about letting her have Mary Kathleen.

"You must be here to visit the baby, but I'm afraid she just went down for her nap," Reverend Olson apologized. "She didn't sleep well at all last night. . . ."

"Actually, she hasn't been sleeping well since she got here," Rebecca confessed.

Reverend Olson laughed. "I'm not sure how many more nights I can walk the floor with a screaming baby and still retain a charitable attitude. The good Lord didn't mean for old people to have babies—with the exception of the biblical Sarah, of course."

Charity was about to say they understood and would be happy

to return as soon as they completed their shopping when Beau interrupted. "We'd sure like to see the baby, but that's not what we're here for, Reverend."

Charity's gaze flew up to meet Beau's. "It isn't?"

"It isn't?" Reverend Olson parroted.

"It isn't?" Rebecca echoed.

"No, sir. . .I. . .me and Mrs. Burk want to—to get married."

"You do?"

"We do?"

"You do!" Rebecca clapped her hands together gleefully. "Wait just a minute! I need to straighten my hair."

"Beau!" Charity turned to him, dumbfounded, her heart beating like a trapped sparrow's. She suddenly felt light-headed. He was going to marry her? The least he could have done was tell her.

"Yes. You don't have any objections, do you?" His eyes radiated that stubborn blue she'd come to recognize, and yet they looked a bit sheepish, too.

"No. . .I–I'm just surprised, that's all."

"Well, if we want to get Mary Kathleen back, it seems the only sensible thing to do." Beau took a deep breath and continued. "I figure since we're in town, we might as well get it taken care of."

"You—you don't mind?"

"Wouldn't be doing it if I minded," he said abruptly.

"But, Beau, are you sure you want to do this?" Charity had no idea what had changed his mind, but she didn't want him to do something he would regret in the morning.

"It's the only thing left to do."

"But is it what you want, Beau?" She desperately wished he would say something more reassuring—anything—but did she have a right to question his motives? If he was good enough to help her out, then shouldn't she accept his kindness and not worry?

But "it's the only thing left to do" wasn't the most romantic proposal a woman ever heard.

"It's all right with me if it's what you want."

"I don't have any objections. . .if you don't." She didn't press her luck by asking him if their marriage would be a permanent commitment or only a temporary arrangement. At this point it seemed immaterial.

Beau took a deep breath and straightened his shoulders. "Then let's get on with it, Reverend."

Rebecca breathlessly returned, hair in place, and moments later the ceremony began.

Charity's hands trembled, and her voice could barely be heard when she nervously recited her vows. Beau's hands were steady as a rock, and though he repeated his words woodenly, his voice never wavered.

How vows were exchanged made little difference; for better, for worse, within a scant three minutes, Charity Burk and Beau Claxton had become man and wife.

"Do you have a ring to give your bride as a symbol of your vows?" Reverend Olson asked.

"I'm sorry, sir. I don't."

"No matter. A ring doesn't ensure love." Reverend Olson's kindly gaze met Beau's. "It will be up to you to cultivate love and make it grow, son."

"Thank you, sir."

"You're both good people. I wish you Godspeed." Reverend Olson firmly closed the Bible. "You may kiss the bride—and the baby needs changing."

Chapter 10

Fifteen minutes later, Beau and Charity were standing on the opposite side of the Olsons' front door with Mary Kathleen once again nestled snugly in Charity's arms.

"Did you get the impression Reverend Olson was anxious to hand the baby back to us?" Charity grinned, thinking of the older man's relieved expression when he gave Mary Kathleen to her.

Beau laughed. "Sure looked that way. Never saw anything like the way he hustled around gathering up her stuff."

"He barely gave Rebecca time to say good-bye."

"And he seemed awfully concerned we get an early start home," Beau added.

Charity giggled. "I'll bet he's already curled up in bed sound asleep."

"I wouldn't doubt it."

They stepped off the porch together and walked to the sled. Charity waited while Beau settled the baby comfortably on the seat, making sure she was well protected from the inclement weather. Then he turned to assist her.

He lifted her slight weight easily, his strong arms suspending her momentarily in midair as his eyes met hers. Charity grew a little breathless as she stared back at her handsome husband, and she suddenly found herself wishing the unexpected alliance between them could somehow be a permanent one. She knew she would do everything within her power to make it so. Was it possible she was falling deeply in love with Beau Claxton?

Whatever had caused him to change his mind about marriage, she was grateful. She would have welcomed his presence in her life regardless, but she would be a fool not to recognize the difference wearing his name would make to other people.

"Charity. . .about the ring. . ."

"Yes?"

"I'm sorry I didn't have one to give you."

"It's all right." As if she cared about a ring when she was Mrs. Beau Claxton.

"And. . .I'm sorry I didn't ask you proper. . .to marry me. I. . .well, this wasn't easy for me. . .or you. . . ."

"I understand." She smiled, hoping to assure him that it didn't really matter. Her mind vividly replayed the kiss he'd given her at Reverend Olson's request. It was brief, emotionless, nothing more than a polite ritual, but it had sent every nerve in her body singing.

"I've been giving the problem serious thought." His expression turned solemn, and she realized what he was trying to say was important to him. "I've lain awake more than once considering it, and I think we made the only reasonable choice."

She nodded, too busy wondering what it would feel like to touch his hair to pay much attention to his words. Would it feel soft or coarse and springy? And his mouth. Beautifully shaped, with full, clearly defined lips that looked warm and tender.

Her eyes widened with guilt when she realized that he was aware of the way she was shamelessly regarding him. A slow grin spread across his features, the devilish smile crinkling the corners of his eyes.

For a moment he looked as if he wanted to kiss her—really kiss her this time, and her heart stood still. But the moment passed, and before she knew it, he was quickly walking around the sled and taking his place beside her without further ado.

The stark white frozen countryside looked different, filled with an ethereal beauty she knew had nothing to do with the lowering sky and everything to do with the brief ceremony that had bound them together as husband and wife. Mrs. Beau Claxton. She tried it out in her mind, liking the sound of it. Beau climbed into the sled beside her and turned the horse toward Main Street.

The stop by Miller's Mercantile was kept brief because of the worsening weather. The store was busy, and Beau offered to hold Mary Kathleen while Charity made her purchases. She noticed the sideways glances sent her way by the female population of Cherry Grove. The men seemed a shade too friendly, as if she had lost the right to be respected. She went about choosing her purchases with her head held high, well aware of the spots of color burning her cheeks.

Beau carried the infant around the store, acting very paternal, pointing out various articles to the child, which Mary Kathleen could not possibly understand or appreciate the meaning of. Charity watched when he paused and whispered conspiratorially about a certain rag doll Santa Claus might be persuaded to bring her next year, if she promised to get her outrageous sleeping schedule back in order. His endearing behavior warmed Charity's heart.

When her purchases were completed, the baby exchanged hands so Beau could shop. Charity browsed through the bolts of brightly colored yard goods.

Agnes Troxell, one of the town's busybodies, sidled up close to her. "My, Mr. Claxton's a right nice-looking man, isn't he?"

Charity tried to keep her expression serene as she met the inquisitive brown eyes. "Yes, he's a very handsome man."

"How long is he planning on staying out at your place?" Agnes's nose fairly quivered in her pursuit of juicy gossip she could repeat at the Ladies' Guild.

"Why, where else would a husband stay except with his wife?" Charity asked, pleased to note she sounded genuinely surprised.

Agnes's face fell. "Husband? You're married?" Her expression turned to skepticism. "Who performed the ceremony?" she demanded.

"Why, Reverend Olson, of course." This time Charity allowed herself to sound even more surprised that Agnes would ask.

Several other women had gathered around, listening to the exchange.

Agnes flushed an alarming red. "Well, just when did this wedding take place?"

Charity raised her eyebrows. "Why would you want to know?"

Bethany Dierckson's lips quirked in a barely suppressed smile. Mary Kathleen chose that moment to start fussing. Charity bounced her gently and inclined her head in a half bow. "It's good to see you ladies again, but if you'll excuse me, this youngster needs attention."

She walked away, knowing she had set a limit on the amount of poison Agnes Troxell could spew. Bethany was a good woman. She would do what she could to put a stop to the gossip.

Beau wandered down to the hardware section.

"This is the finest one we have in stock," the proprietor, Edgar Miller, proclaimed. He handed Beau a heavy hammer. "The head is forged iron, and the handle is solid oak."

Beau examined the tool carefully. Assured it would serve his needs well, he agreed to buy it and turned his attention to the vast array of hoes, rakes, spades, ropes, and kegs of nails. When he'd satisfied his curiosity about all the shiny new farm implements, he moved on to examine the food staples behind the counter on long rows of shelves.

There were large containers of soda crackers, coffee, tea—black and Japanese—starch in bulk, bottles of catsup, cayenne, soda, and cream of tartar, often used in place of baking powder.

The floor of the mercantile was lined with barrels. There were two grades of flour—white and middlings, as well as coarse meal and buckwheat flour. Large barrels of Missouri apples, sacks of potatoes, turnips, pumpkins, and longneck squashes were in plentiful supply. There was more: salt pork in a crock under a big stone to keep the meat down in the brine; vinegar; salt; molasses; and three grades of sugar: fine white—twenty pounds for a dollar—light brown, and very dark.

The counters were brimming with baskets of eggs—three dozen for a quarter—and big jars of golden butter, selling for twelve and a half to fifteen cents a pound. There was cheese all the way from New York, maple syrup, and dried peaches and apples.

"Do you have any raisins?" Beau asked.

"Raisins?" Edgar scratched his head thoughtfully. "Afraid not. . .but I could probably get some from over in Hays."

"How long would it take to get them here?"

"Depends. If the weather cooperates, they should be here in a couple of weeks or so. They'll be right costly, though."

"I'll take four pounds."

"Four?"

Beau nodded. "Four should do it."

While Edgar wrote the order, Beau looked at the row of watches and rings displayed in a glass case beneath the counter. His attention was immediately drawn to an exquisite emerald brooch that lay nestled on a bed of royal blue velvet. Something about the brooch reminded Beau of Charity. The stones were elegant and the design intriguing. The delicate piece of jewelry seemed out of place among the large watches and gaudy baubles surrounding it.

"May I see the brooch, please?"

Edgar glanced up and smiled. "Lovely piece, isn't it?" He moved over to unlock the case and gently lifted the box containing the brooch, placing it on the counter for Beau's inspection.

"Just got it in a couple of days ago," Edgar volunteered.

"It's beautiful." Beau lifted the pin from the velvet box. The green stones caught the light, and it suddenly occurred to him why the piece of jewelry reminded him of Charity. The stones were the exact shade of her eyes.

"Yeah, a couple of Indian squaws come waltzing in here day before yesterday and offered the brooch in trade for three bottles of whiskey and a handful of peppermint sticks."

"You don't say." Beau turned the piece over and examined the craftsmanship closely. It was worth more than three bottles of whiskey and a handful of peppermint sticks.

"I'll make you a good deal," Edgar offered.

"How much?"

The price Edgar set was completely out of line, especially in view of the fact he'd just revealed what he'd given for the brooch. However, Beau knew the man would have no trouble finding someone who'd pay the exorbitant price.

"Thanks, but I'm afraid that's a little too steep." He regretfully placed the brooch back in the box. He'd gotten married today, and he didn't have anything to give his new bride. The brooch would have made a nice gift.

Edgar slid the box back into the case and Beau started to walk off. He suddenly turned and went back. "How much did you say those raisins would cost?"

Edgar repeated the price. The brooch would cost four times what the raisins would, but by not buying the raisins, he'd have the money to buy the brooch. He wanted Charity to have it.

"Then cancel the raisins, and I'll take the brooch," Beau said, grinning. He hadn't had a raisin pie in over a year; he guessed he could do without one a little longer.

Edgar smiled. "A gift for your lady?"

"Yes. I married Charity Burk about an hour ago. I think she'll enjoy the brooch more than I'd enjoy the raisins."

Beau's grin widened when he saw Edgar's jaw drop.

Charity was quiet on the way home. It was getting dark, and they still had several miles to go before they reached the cabin. The baby was sleeping and seemed unaffected by the night air. Beau urged the horse's steps to a faster trot.

"You cold?" he asked.

"A little." The weather was uncomfortable, but Charity didn't mind. She was still bathed in a warm glow from the unexpected turn of events. She barely noticed the discomfort. The baby was back in her arms and she'd just married Beau.

She didn't see how she could complain about a little thing like bad weather. God had certainly blessed her this day.

"I'd hoped to make it back before dark," Beau apologized. "Guess I spent too much time browsing in the mercantile."

"I don't mind. I'm fine."

"You think the baby's cold?"

"She doesn't appear to be." Charity reached down and adjusted the heavy blanket surrounding Mary Kathleen like a cocoon.

They'd ridden in silence for a few minutes when Charity remembered. "Were you able to get the raisins?" She'd gladly bake him all the pies he wanted.

"No. . .Mr. Miller would've had to order them."

"Oh. How long would it have been before they'd arrived?"

"He said about a month."

Snow began to fall again. The horse briskly trotted down the road, pulling the sled containing the newly formed family.

Charity let her thoughts wander as the last vestige of twilight faded. The world around her became a fairyland of white. Snow sifted down in earnest now.

She longed to snuggle closer to her husband's large frame, but she wouldn't. He would surely think her forward, and just because they were married, she couldn't take such wifely liberties. It was still to be determined to what extent he intended to participate in the marriage.

Her gaze drifted shyly to him, and she found him immersed in his own thoughts. His hands deftly handled the reins while he drove the sled. She thought how nice it was to have a man perform that task for her. She'd never liked driving the prairie alone at night. It would be too easy to miss the road and get lost.

Would he expect a marriage bed? The thought jumped unexpectedly into her mind, startling her. It was shameful to be thinking such thoughts, but the prospect sent goose bumps skittering up and down her spine.

Would she object? The answer came more easily than the question: not at all. She was prepared to be his wife in every aspect. Even if he planned to leave her in the spring, it would not change her feelings. She would seek his comfort, tend his needs, and share his life for as long as he chose to remain with her.

And when the time came for him to leave, she would see him off with a smile and good wishes. She'd made herself that promise, and she intended to keep it.

Charity shifted on the seat, adjusting the blanket more tightly around her. The darker it became, the colder it was.

"You might be warmer if we moved closer together." Beau's suggestion was spoken so casually that Charity wasn't sure if it was an invitation or request. "Slide the baby onto your lap. She'll probably be warmer there anyway."

"Oh. . .well, yes. Thank you." Charity carefully repositioned the infant and then edged closer to him until she felt her hip make contact with his solid thigh.

She was so aware of him, not only aware of his masculinity, but close enough now to note his distinct scent: a combination of soap, leather, wool, and the elements.

"Better?" Beau glanced at her and smiled.

"Yes, thank you."

They were closer than they'd ever been, and Charity felt her limbs getting weak.

Christmas had come and gone with little fuss but much warmth. Since she'd lost Ferrand, Charity had considered Christmas just another lonely day on the prairie. But with Beau here, the day had been as special as when she was a small child. He had shot a turkey, and she had made stuffing and baked a pumpkin pie.

Before they ate, he had reached for her hand. "I think I'd like to say grace—if you don't mind."

She nodded, bowing her head and closing her eyes. Mind? She was elated that his trust and hope in the Lord was gradually coming around.

"Lord," he began, "I want to give thanks to You today. For my life, for this woman who cared for me when I couldn't care for myself. Thank You for Mary Kathleen and what this little girl has brought into our lives—peace, joy, living proof that life goes on. When I look at this innocent baby I am reminded of Your love—a love that goes far beyond our understanding. Today we celebrate the gift of Your love: You gave Your Son, Jesus, for our sins. I couldn't have done the same, Lord. And I'm beholden to You. Amen."

"Amen." Charity blinked the wetness out of her eyes and passed the bowl of sweet potatoes.

She was brought back to the present when Beau finally broke the strained silence. "Seems like we should be saying something a little more meaningful, doesn't it?"

"Meaningful?"

"I mean, it is our wedding day. . . ."

"Seems we should have something to say, all right." Charity fondly recalled the day she and Ferrand had married. Birds had been singing, and the grass had been a rich, lush green carpet for her to tread upon. The church had overflowed with well-wishers, and there had been baskets of flowers and a large wedding cake.

"Was the weather nice the day you married Betsy?"

Until now Charity had been able to view and talk about Betsy in a charitable light. But now, the casual mention of her name sent streaks of jealousy shooting through her when she thought about the intimacy Beau and his first wife must have shared on their wedding night.

"Yes, it was a warm fall day. The leaves on the trees were gold and yellow and brown. . . ." His eyes took on a faraway look, and Charity wished she hadn't brought up the subject.

"What was the date?" It shouldn't matter; yet, for some reason, she had to know.

"Second of October. What about you and Ferrand?"

"June second."

Silently each pondered the coincidence; it was the second of January—their wedding day.

"I—I was quite surprised when you asked Reverend Olson to marry us," Charity confessed. "But very thankful."

"The gossip was bothering you, wasn't it?"

"A little," she admitted. "But I would've seen it through." It hadn't been easy facing the accusing stares. The few times she'd ridden into town for supplies had been disconcerting, but having Beau remain with her had been worth it.

"No need for either one of us to be the source of malicious gossip. Talk should quiet down now."

"I hope you don't mind, but I—I told several women at the mercantile we were married now."

"I don't mind. I mentioned it to Mr. Miller myself."

Charity grinned. "You did? Well, thank you."

"You should've seen Edgar Miller's jaw hit the floor."

"He's the biggest gossip of all."

"That's why I made sure he was the first to know about the marriage. His tongue will have a chance to cool down now."

Charity sighed. "I surely hope so."

"By spring I should have the land in good shape," Beau predicted. He urged the horse across Fire Creek and headed north.

"With the two of us working it shouldn't take long," Charity agreed.

She wanted to ask if he still planned to leave then, but selfishness stopped her. She wanted nothing to interfere with the happiness she was feeling.

"Charity. . .about our marriage. . ." Beau paused, apparently hesitant to broach the subject.

Charity felt the conversation was about to take a more personal turn. "Yes?"

"I know you must be wondering if I expect to claim my. . ." Beau's voice trailed off. She was sure if she could see his features clearly, he would be blushing!

Her lofty spirits plummeted. She braced herself; next he would tell her that he had no intention of claiming his husbandly rights because he didn't want to make love to anyone but Betsy.

Beau started again. "I. . .well, I think we would. . .of course, we both need to. . .well, we should talk about. . .but then it's not going to be exactly the same. . ."

He appeared to be having a hard time making his point.

"Are you trying to say you don't plan to be my husband. . .not really?" Charity offered gently, hoping to help ease his dilemma.

Beau's gaze flew to meet hers. "No. . .I wasn't trying to say that."

"You weren't?" Charity's pulse jumped with his rather adamant denial.

"No. . .I didn't mean that at all. I meant it might be sort of. . . embarrassing at first. Well, you know. It might take us a while to get used to. . .get to know each other. . . ."

"You mean, you think we should give it time?" Charity agreed.

"Yes, that might be wise," he said.

She settled deeper into the blanket. A few moments later she scooted closer, pressing herself tightly against his side.

Beau was aware of her movements. He shifted his leg so it was resting more fully against hers. "I was thinking how nice it will be to get home," he remarked. The horse trotted along in the falling snow.

"It will be nice. The fire will feel exceptionally good this evening." She slipped her hand into his.

His hand tightened perceptibly on hers. He had no idea what was happening to him. He found himself thinking of Charity in a new way, as if the marriage vows had freed him from the chains of memory binding him to Betsy.

Well, why not? he argued, trying to still the faint twinge of conscience pulling at him. Betsy was gone. And he was still a young man, and the woman beside him now was his wife.

But you haven't given one single thought to whether you'll be staying with this woman come spring, his conscience reminded. *You went off half-cocked and jumped into marriage without giving the future much thought.*

"I hope the baby decides to sleep tonight," Charity said softly.

"It won't hurt her to cry a little. I think we're spoiling her."

"No," she agreed. "It won't hurt to let her fret for a spell."

Charity's head had somehow drifted to his shoulder, and she turned and pressed her face into the warmth of his neck. He guessed she was feeling some of the same emotion that choked him.

"How much farther?" she whispered.

"Another mile."

He glanced down and caught his breath when he saw their mouths were only inches apart. "Don't go to sleep on me," he urged.

She looked up at him, her heart in her eyes. "Now you're being silly."

Charity, her heart overflowing with love, watched Beau carry the baby into the cabin. She loved him. Maybe not in the exact way she'd loved Ferrand, but it was very, very close. She gathered up the blanket and prepared to jump down from the sled when she saw him come to an abrupt halt. He glanced back over his shoulder and called to her, "Did you leave a lamp burning?"

Charity glanced toward the cabin window and frowned when she saw the warm, golden ray of light spilling out across the freshly fallen snow. "No."

He returned to the sled to grab his gun and hand the baby back to Charity before he turned toward the house again.

"You stay here until I see what's going on."

"Beau, wait. It may be dangerous!" Charity scrambled off the seat. Beau strode back and kicked open the door, gun drawn and positioned.

The young man sitting at the table looked momentarily startled at the hasty entrance. Quickly recovering, he invited in a dry voice, "Well, hello. Do come in."

Charity quickly stepped behind her husband, her eyes widening when she saw the splendid, dark-haired man sitting at the kitchen table.

His boots were off, and his stocking feet were propped casually on the table. He had achingly familiar turquoise blue eyes and shamelessly long, thick black eyelashes. His hair was outrageously curly, and he looked as ornery as sin.

The man grinned, flashing a set of brilliant white teeth at her. "About time you and big brother were showing up."

Chapter 11

Beau shot an irritable scowl at his younger brother. "You always did have a way of being in the wrong place at the wrong time."

Cass Claxton flashed a roguish grin. "I've ridden for two weeks, through rain and snow and dark of night, just to see how my big brother is getting along, and he acts like I was some varmint come crawling out of the woods."

Cass was being melodramatic. The boy couldn't help it; it was in his nature. Still, it didn't make Beau any happier. How had he gotten here so soon?

"How'd you find me?" Beau pulled Charity into the room and closed the door. "Don't mind him," he said, nodding toward his younger brother before he crossed the room to lay Mary Kathleen down in her bed near the hearth. "It's my brother, Cass. He's harmless."

Charity smiled uncertainly. Her frozen fingers worked to untie the strings of her bonnet.

Cass grinned and pushed back from the table to get to his feet. A cocky, devil-may-care attitude stood out all over him, and Beau wanted to tell him to behave. "Well, hello, ma'am. You must be the lovely Widow Burk." He politely tipped his hat.

Charity grinned, not at all sure how to take his cavalier attitude. She glanced at Beau for guidance.

"She used to be Mrs. Burk," Beau said easily while busily removing the baby's warm bunting. "How'd you get here?" He hadn't seen an extra horse in the yard.

"I brought a sled from town. It's out back. I wasn't sure where to stable the horses." With undisguised curiosity Cass watched Beau settle the baby.

"How did you find me?" Beau turned his full attention to the guest.

"Your letter was pretty clear about where you were. When I reached Cherry Grove, I asked around. An old man gave me directions to the Burk cabin. When it started getting dark and you failed to show up, I began to wonder if I had the wrong place."

"We had business to tend to. Why'd you bring a sled?"

"You know Ma and Willa," Cass complained. "I had to bring half the root cellar, extra blankets, and medicine in case you weren't being properly looked after." Cass glanced at Charity and his grin widened. "All that worrying for nothing. Looks to me like you're being taken care of real well."

Beau frowned. He didn't like his brother's tone of voice, or the disrespectful innuendo. "Mrs. Burk has been good enough to take care of me while I was ill. I owe her a great deal, including my gratitude and respect."

Cass shook his head. "That's what I meant. We all appreciate what she's done for you."

So Cass had brought provisions. It was like his mother to think of everything. Beau gave Mary Kathleen a fatherly pat and walked over and warmly clasped his brother's hand. "Good to see you, Cass."

Charity looked from brother to brother, and Beau could see

she felt left out. He could understand that. Cass might be spouting off, but one could look at him and see not only love but a deep respect shining in his eyes. The Claxton boys were knit tightly with one another with an intangible bond that would be hard for an outsider to penetrate. Loyalty ran deep and strong among the brothers, and he thanked God for it.

Cass Claxton clasped Beau's hand tightly, his face turning somber. "You're looking a whole lot better than I'd expected."

Beau shrugged. "It was close, but, thank God, I'm on the mend."

"We've all been worried about you, Ma in particular. You've been gone a long time." There was an unspoken reproach in the statement.

Beau remembered Cass was the one who couldn't understand his need to leave. Now he shrugged, realizing there was no way to explain to his brother the unrelenting darkness that had invaded his heart when Betsy died. The need to get away from all that was familiar. "I'm sorry I haven't written sooner," he said. "I should have done better."

Cass nodded. "We understood, but we couldn't help wondering if you were all right."

"The family all okay?" Beau asked.

Cass grinned. "Doing fine."

"Ma?"

"Strong as an ox."

"Cole?"

"Healthy as a horse."

"Wynne?"

"Pretty as a picture."

"Did your teachers ever mention anything about enlarging your vocabulary?" Beau asked.

"Nope."

Beau good-naturedly clapped his brother's shoulder. "Come here. I have someone I want you to meet."

The two men turned their attention to Charity, who was standing by the fire looking out of place. She smiled, and Beau walked over and placed his arm around her waist. "Cass, this is my wife, Charity."

For a moment Cass was stunned by Beau's unexpected announcement, and his face showed it. But to his credit he managed to regain his composure quickly. "Your. . .wife! Well, how about that." He brushed his hand down the side of his tight-fitting denims and graciously extended it. "Welcome to the family, ma'am. You're sure going to be a lovely addition."

"Thank you, Cass. I'm so happy to meet you. Beau has spoken of you often."

"He exaggerates," Cass objected. "Once you get to know me, you'll find out I'm fairly decent."

Charity laughed. "I can assure you, it has all been very complimentary."

"Don't tell him that," Beau protested. "I won't be able to live with him." He watched in amazement as his younger brother poured on the charm. How did he do it? Cass and Cole both could be as sweet and as slick as warm honey. He'd never had the gift himself. He could be smooth enough with an older woman like Rebecca, but with one closer to his own age he wasn't so smooth. Maybe because he'd never practiced the art. Betsy had won his heart when they were both young, and he'd never looked at another woman.

"So, you've remarried." Cass's gaze drifted nonchalantly over to Mary Kathleen's crib. "Been. . .married long?"

Charity spoke up quickly. "Oh no! Uh. . .the baby. . .she's not Beau's."

Beau looked at her with a stunned expression. "She isn't?" He turned to Cass. "Now is that anything for a bride to tell her husband?" he said in feigned disgust.

"Beau!" Charity looked horrified.

Beau sent her a roguish grin. He watched her face flush a bright scarlet. His arm tightened affectionately around her. "The baby's parents are dead, and Charity and I have been taking care of Mary Kathleen," he explained. "We're hoping we'll be given permanent custody of the child, once things settle down."

Cass had a strange expression on his face, like he wasn't sure that would be a good idea. Beau figured he was remembering the day his baby died with Betsy, but if that was what he had on his mind, he hid it well. Cass peered down at the sleeping Mary Kathleen. "You don't say? Been taking care of a new baby, huh? She's real cute."

"We think so," Beau said proudly.

While Cass filled them in on recent happenings, Charity cut thick slices of pie and made a pot of fresh coffee.

"Wait until you taste her pie," Beau bragged. He was proud of her cooking. She hurried around to wait on them, so pretty and flustered at having unexpected company. Charity Burk. . .Claxton was a woman any man would be proud to have carry his name.

Cass leaned back in his chair. "Makes good pies, huh?"

"Best I've ever eaten."

"Better than Ma's?"

"Almost as good."

The lamp had burned low when it was finally decided that they had more than one night to visit.

"I hope I'm not putting you out by staying a few days," Cass apologized.

"Not at all!" Charity said. "I'm thrilled to finally meet a part of Beau's family."

"Well"—Cass began to yank off his boots—"just tell me where to roll up. I'm so tired I could sleep on a thorn and not know it."

Beau watched his new wife, realizing that in all the excitement it hadn't occurred to either of them that their privacy was going to be affected by Cass's unexpected arrival.

"Well, I suppose you'll be sleeping. . ." Charity grappled awkwardly with the problem of where to put him.

"Outside," Beau interjected.

Cass's face fell. "In this kind of weather?"

Before Beau could answer, Cass glanced down and saw the neatly made pallet by the fire. A relieved smile replaced his earlier frown. "You always did like to pull my leg. I suppose I'll take the pallet. It's been a long day."

Charity smiled lamely. "Yes. . .well. . .good night."

Cass paused. "You're sure I'm not putting you out?"

"No," Beau muttered.

Charity smiled. "Don't be silly."

Beau loved his brother; of course he did, but he sure had a bad habit of turning up at the worst time.

Charity turned away. Her bed seemed to suddenly dominate the tiny room. She edged timidly toward the mattress while Beau banked the fire for the night.

Cass settled himself on the pallet.

Charity proceeded to pull the curtain across the room. Once she was assured of a modicum of privacy, she began to undress while listening to Beau bid his brother a good night. A few moments later, he parted the curtain and stepped into the small cubicle.

The intimate area suddenly looked stiflingly small.

"I'll get up with the baby for her night feeding," Beau offered. He sat down on a chair and began unbuttoning his shirt. "That way you won't have to. . .dress."

"Thank you." She mouthed the words, vividly aware of Cass sleeping in the same room. "It's so late; I'm surprised she hasn't awakened before now."

"I guess she's real tired."

Charity fumbled for her gown hanging on a small hook and glanced self-consciously at Beau. "Would you mind. . .?"

Beau turned his head and she quickly readied herself for bed.

"All right. . .I'm through."

She busied herself turning back the blanket.

Beau remained in the chair.

She lay stiff with apprehension, awaiting the moment he, too, would be under the blankets. She had no idea where her earlier boldness had fled, but it had completely deserted her now.

Beau leaned over and blew out the lamp, throwing the room into total darkness.

Charity lay perfectly still, thinking how much she'd always hated darkness. Fears tended to be amplified, doubts reborn, and small problems inflated to overwhelming obstacles when there was no light.

Many nights she'd slept with a lamp burning so she wouldn't have to face the emptiness. Now that she was married again, would that horrible loneliness finally be over? she wondered.

"Aren't you coming to bed?" she whispered.

"No. Best I sleep in the chair."

Frustration swept through her. She supposed he was right. She could still hear the wind howling outside, the tick of the clock, the baby making soft sucking sounds in her sleep, Cass's soft breathing as he dropped deeper and deeper into untroubled sleep. With Beau beside her, it was as if her life had been miraculously sorted out and put back into order.

For a moment he sat quietly, lost in his own thoughts.

She wondered if he was thinking of Betsy. It would be only natural, of course. She didn't expect him to forget his first wife, but she wanted him to think of her tonight. Ferrand's face floated through her mind, and she sighed. Betsy and Ferrand were part of their past. Tonight was the beginning of their future. A future together, she prayed. It would be easier if she thought Beau loved her, but she knew he had only married her because he considered it the right thing to do.

He reached over and took her hand. His presence was comforting in the darkness. She remembered the sinewy muscles, the tuft of springy hair above the opening at the throat of his long johns. His familiar scent surrounded her, and she clung tightly to his hand.

"I'm sorry about tonight," he whispered.

His voice sent a flood of sensations through her like warm honey, all breathtaking, all mysterious, all inexplicably exciting.

"I understand. I guess the only thing that's really important is that you're here. . .that we're together," she returned softly.

It occurred to her that neither she nor Beau had mentioned to Cass that this was their wedding night.

Not that she supposed it would have made any difference. He was here, and they couldn't turn a man out in the teeth of a Kansas blizzard. He'd die out there. She could sense Beau's frustration, but Cass was here and they'd have to make the best of it.

He'd come in answer to the letter she'd mailed last month. She had a sudden fierce wish she'd thrown the envelope away, not mailed it, but of course she couldn't have done that. She had to do what was right, and keeping news of Beau from his family would have been terribly wrong.

She caught her breath when a horrible thought occurred to her. What if Cass had come to take Beau home with him?

Could she give him up now? *Please, God, let me have this winter. If I have to give him up in the spring, I will, but let him be mine for a while.*

Cass was as strikingly handsome as Beau. If Cole, the older brother, was any more handsome, she didn't think her heart could stand it.

Not that she was expecting to ever meet Cole or Wynne or any of the Claxton clan. Eventually Beau would leave, and she wasn't going to tell herself anything different. Today meant only that he loved Mary Kathleen enough to give her a mother.

Beau had been silent, but now he whispered, "I'm glad to see my brother, but his timing's a little off."

She laughed softly, feeling more at ease. "We couldn't turn him out."

"We can't? It sure is tempting."

She snuggled deeper into the sheets, savoring the moment. This wasn't the wedding night she had anticipated, but maybe it was best this way. Perhaps Beau had been right in the first place. They needed to take it slow, get used to thinking of themselves as husband and wife. Having him here was enough. For the first time in a long time she would fall asleep with someone holding her hand. For a while at least, she could feel loved again.

Beau sat quietly, wondering how he'd sleep in the straight-back chair. It would be a long night. This wasn't the way he had pictured their wedding night. Sitting here with Charity so close was pure torture. He thought of the way they used to talk into the night, Charity in the bed and him on the floor, sleeping on the pallet where Cass was now snoring. He'd never felt this passion then, this desire to hold her. Never wanted to kiss her.

What had made the difference? A few words spoken before a preacher? Evidently the marriage ceremony had resurrected feelings he'd wanted to forget. He breathed in lemon scent. Her scent. She always smelled good.

"What are you thinking?" he whispered.

"I was thanking God for sending you my way," she whispered back.

He felt humbled. She was thankful for him? He'd ruined her reputation and subjected her to a marriage with little hope of surviving. For all she knew, he'd be gone in a few months, and she was thankful? He sighed.

Lord, I don't deserve this woman. I don't deserve much of anything the way I've acted this past year, but it seemed like I couldn't help myself.

He had a feeling God knew what he'd gone through and understood. God always understood. Beau felt humbled. He'd always been so sure of what he wanted and knew how to go about getting it. Then he'd lost hope. Maybe he had to reach the place where God was all he had, to realize God was all he needed. Beginning tonight, he intended to trust more and appreciate his blessings while he had them.

Like Job in the Old Testament, Beau had lost all he valued in one day. But God had given him new blessings, *"good measure, pressed down, and shaken together, and running over."*

"The LORD gave, and the LORD hath taken away; blessed be the name of the LORD."

He smiled into the darkness. *I don't deserve a second chance, Lord, but I'm glad You don't give me what I deserve. I'll try not to let You down again.*

Charity stirred and he pulled a blanket closer to her chin, feeling protective. He had a family now—Charity and Mary Kathleen. They couldn't take the place of Betsy and the unborn child he'd lost, but they could make their own place in his heart. He bent to kiss his wife good night.

"He'll only stay a few days," Beau promised when their mouths parted.

Charity nodded and returned the kiss.

"Just a few days," he whispered.

It was indeed a strange wedding night, but as the fire began to die down, Beau accepted the circumstances. Wasn't like he hadn't encountered a change in plans before.

Chapter 12

Two weeks later, Cass was still there. When Beau inadvertently mentioned the large amount of work he had to accomplish by spring, Cass decided to stay for a while and lend a hand. He insisted it was the only proper thing to do.

He couldn't stay much longer, though, because the few storms they'd had would soon give way to howling blizzards, making travel impossible until spring.

When Cass had been there for three days helping Beau, Charity was amazed at the amount of work the two of them had completed despite the bad weather. They came in at the end of the day, laughing and talking. Charity had supper on the table; Cass stood in front of the stove basking in the brothers' friendship.

She was used to Cass's striking good looks now. He was handsome, but he didn't make her pulse race the way Beau did.

Beau washed his hands and reached for the towel. "I guess we're going to lose our favorite guest."

Charity glanced up from setting the table. "What do you mean?"

Beau grinned. "Cass has decided he'd better start home before we get snowed in."

Charity's heart hit the bottom of her stomach. Would Beau decide to go with him? If he wanted to go with Cass she wouldn't be able to hold him. She turned her back to the men, fumbling with the oven door. What would she do if he left? She could not face losing this man.

"That's right," Cass said. "I've helped Beau about all I can until spring. I need to be heading home."

Charity set a pan of steaming corn bread on the table. "We'll miss you." She was proud that her voice sounded so steady. "Supper's ready."

Grinning, Cass took a couple of steps before his left foot caught on the pallet where he slept at night. "Whoa!" he exclaimed, fighting to retain his balance.

Charity watched, horrified, as he fell, hitting the floor with the grace of a fallen oak tree.

Beau crossed the room in four steps. "You all right?"

Cass sat up, looking dazed and holding his foot. His face contorted in pain. "My ankle—I think it's broke."

Charity dropped beside the fallen man, her hands deft and sure as she probed the injured ankle. "Beau, help me. We've got to get his boot off before that foot swells so much we have to cut it off."

Beau took the boot in his large, capable hands, moving it gently back and forth while Cass sucked in his breath. "That hurts."

"I know it hurts," Beau said. "But Charity's right. You want me to take it off this way or cut it off after it swells?"

"Take it off," Cass muttered between clenched teeth. He kept quiet until the boot was removed to reveal an ankle already swelling and turning blue. Charity moved the appendage experimentally back and forth. "It's not broken," she said. "Just badly sprained, but you'll have to stay off it a few days."

Beau glanced at Charity.

She looked back.

"Well, little brother, looks like we're going to have the pleasure of your company a little longer. You can't ride with that foot."

Cass shook his head. "I guess you're right. I just hope we don't get another blizzard before I'm able to leave."

Charity felt almost relieved that Cass had to stay. She'd be happy to keep him here until spring if it meant Beau would stay, too. She'd seen the bond between the two brothers, and she knew if anyone could convince her new husband to leave, it would be Cass.

Beau had only married her to save the land and to provide a home for Mary Kathleen, and she appreciated it, but now that he was her husband for real, she wanted more.

Given time, she'd find a way to keep him here. God willing.

Nine more days passed. Beau and Cass were sitting at the table finishing breakfast, and Charity was getting the wash ready to hang out to freeze dry on the line.

She'd fixed a solid meal—cured ham and eggs with biscuits and gravy. Cass had eaten with enthusiasm, but Beau had been quiet. He hadn't talked much, and when she inadvertently touched him while serving, he had flinched away. She knew his brother's extended visit was getting on his nerves. It would have been different if they had any privacy, but in a room this size, there was no way to be alone. Beau's even disposition was beginning to suffer.

Even Cass was beginning to notice his brother's unusually sour behavior. Beau had snapped at him twice over something so trivial it had made both his and Charity's brows lift in astonishment.

"Would you mind watching the baby while I hang the wash?"

Charity asked as soon as the last breakfast dish was washed and put away.

Beau was sitting in front of the fire, pulling his boots on.

"How long will that take?" he asked sharply.

Charity glanced up. "Not long. Why?"

"I can't get anything done if I have to stay in the house and babysit," he barked.

Charity sighed. Indeed he was in a very foul mood these days.

"I'll watch Mary Kathleen," Cass offered.

"You can't watch Mary Kathleen and drive nails at the same time!" Beau snapped.

Cass looked at Charity and shrugged good-naturedly. "I can't watch Mary Kathleen and drive nails at the same time. Sorry." He held his forefinger up as an afterthought occurred to him. "But I would, if I could." Charity detected a mischievous twinkle in his eye now as he tried to smooth over Beau's uncharacteristic bad humor.

"I'm capable of watching Mary Kathleen," Beau grumbled. "I merely asked how long it'd be before I could start on my work." The tone of his voice left no doubt that his work was far more important than hers, but she let the thinly veiled implication slide.

"Fifteen minutes at the most," Charity bargained.

"Make it ten."

"I'll pin as fast as I can." She shot him an impatient look, picked up the basket of wet clothes, and sailed out the door, letting it bang shut behind her.

Still seething, she marched to the clothesline, flung the basket on the ground, and began to haphazardly pin diapers and washcloths in a long, disorderly row. She knew what was causing Beau's ill temper, and she could sympathize, but she was getting tired of his sour disposition. The past two weeks hadn't exactly been a bed of roses for her, either.

Her conscience bothered her; Cass still being here was her fault. His sprained ankle would have healed if it hadn't been for the poultices she carefully applied twice a day. She'd been careful not to choose anything that would hurt him—just a various mix of herbs plus a good handful of stinging nettle—with the results that, although Cass could walk better, his ankle was still red and swollen and he couldn't wear his boot.

The deception shamed her, and she knew only too well what Ferrand would have thought about her behavior.

For that matter, she didn't want Beau to know.

He wouldn't understand, and she wouldn't want to tell him the truth, but she had to keep Cass here. Beau would go with him when he left. Her new husband didn't love her the way she loved him. He was a one-woman man, and that woman was Betsy.

Submerged deep within her self-pity, she forgot to keep an eye out for danger.

A nut-brown hand suddenly snaked out and clasped her arm, and she nearly swallowed the clothespin she'd just wedged between her teeth. She jumped and squealed.

A tall, muscular brave was standing next to her. Where had he come from? She hadn't heard a thing.

"Mhhhhhhh?" Her wide eyes peered helplessly up at his imposing height. She prayed Beau was watching from the window, but she knew that was unlikely.

The brave eyed her impassively. "You White Sister?" His voice was deep and gruff. She was so terrified that if he'd asked her if she was Mrs. Wa-kun-dah, she'd have agreed.

Wordlessly she nodded.

The brave's eyes narrowed. "Why White Sister have stick in mouth?"

"Mhhh. . ." Charity hurriedly reached up and removed the clothespin. "I–I'm hanging wash."

"Hanging wash?" His black eyes looked confused. "How White Sister hang wash? Red Eagle wash in water and water cannot be hung up with funny-looking sticks."

Charity hoped he didn't expect an answer. Her heart was pounding, and her knees had turned to pulp. He wasn't Kaw; she was sure of it. Cheyenne, maybe? Handsome, with high cheekbones; a proud, aristocratic nose; and long black hair that whipped freely about in the blustery wind. He wore buckskins, moccasins, and a massive buffalo robe draped over his broad shoulders to ward off the cold morning air.

"Did. . .can I do something for you?" she asked, wondering if he'd come here to harm her. Maybe he'd been hunting and when he noticed her hanging the wash he'd grown curious. She prayed that was the case.

"No can find Laughing Waters."

"Oh?" Why would a man who looked like this be hunting Laughing Waters? She could understand why Laughing Waters would be hunting him. The way the two sisters had latched on to Beau, she was sure they wouldn't let someone like this man get away.

"Laughing Waters tell Red Eagle, 'White Sister make good medicine.'"

"Oh. . .Laughing Waters said that, did she?" Charity felt a quiver of apprehension. She made terrible medicine. Beau would have died if Laughing Waters and Little Fawn hadn't stepped in.

The brave crossed his arms and stared. "Squaw heap big sick. White Sister make good medicine."

Charity decided he must be trying to tell her that his wife was sick and Laughing Waters was not available to tend her.

"I'm not very good. . . . Laughing Waters and Little Fawn are much better at this sort of thing," Charity hedged.

"No can find cuckoo sisters," he announced flatly.

"Well, I. . ." Charity searched for a reasonable excuse to deny his request but failed to think of one. "What's wrong with your. . .squaw?"

He rubbed his stomach. "Bad hurt."

"Oh. Well, come with me, then." She had no idea what the problem could be, but she figured a good dose of castor oil couldn't harm and might cure his under-the-weather squaw.

Charity traipsed into the cabin with the brave following close behind. Beau and Cass caught sight of the pair, and their mouths dropped open.

Beau scrambled for his gun. Cass sprang to his feet, every muscle tensed and ready for combat. Charity ignored them.

Without a word of explanation, she hurried to the cabinet and extracted a large bottle then poured a small portion of the contents into a fruit jar. Screwing the lid on tightly, she handed the jar to the Indian. "Make squaw drink."

The brave held the jar up to closely examine the thick, gummy substance. He scowled. "Make squaw drink?" He shook his head. "This not look like something to drink."

"I know. It looks awful, but it will help."

The brave, evidently taking her at her word, nodded. He cast a sour look in Beau and Cass's direction, his gaze flicking over them in a contemptuous manner, as if they weren't worth worrying about; then he turned back to Charity. "Red Eagle thanks White Sister."

If the castor oil didn't do the trick, Charity sincerely hoped that, at least in this particular instance, his gratitude would be short-lived.

Red Eagle turned and marched with a royal dignity to the door and made a quick exit, the jar of castor oil held carefully in the crook of his arm.

"Just who was that?" Beau demanded as the door closed behind him.

Charity shrugged. "I have no idea. I was hanging the wash and he approached and said his squaw was sick and needed medicine."

Beau looked incredulous. "You mean, out of the clear blue sky, he walked up and asked you for medicine?"

"Yes, he did, but that isn't unusual," she pointed out. "The Indians around here are rather straightforward when it comes to something they need."

"You've never met him before today?" Beau challenged.

"If you mean is he a friend of mine, no, he isn't." She didn't appreciate the insulting insinuation in his voice. What right did he have to act like he doubted her word?

"But he was quite a striking man, don't you think?" she added, with a flirtatious glance in his direction.

She was pushing her luck, and she knew it.

Beau stared coolly back at her. "I hope you mentioned you were under a man's protection now—just so he doesn't get the idea of coming around when I'm not here," he countered tersely.

Charity saw Cass grinning at Beau's splendid performance of a jealous husband, which didn't make her feel any better. Undoubtedly that's all it was—an act.

Her chin lifted with unmistakable defiance. "I don't believe we got around to that subject."

Their eyes locked in a silent duel.

The silence stretched uncomfortably. Charity decided to wait Beau out. Let him speak first. But he was so stubborn he'd sit there until violets bloomed in the spring before he'd give in.

"Well, well." Cass awkwardly reached for his coat. "Guess we best be getting to those chores, Beau. We're burning daylight."

"I'm right behind you." Beau swiped his coat from the peg and opened the front door. He glared at Charity. "You're through hanging wash?"

"It certainly looks that way!"

The door snapped shut.

Charity watched from the window as the two men left. Cass favored his bad ankle, and she felt a sudden renewed stab of remorse for what she was doing.

God, I know it's wrong, and I'm asking You to forgive me.

She knew He wouldn't, though, because even at that moment she had a pan of herbs simmering on the stove, ready to apply a new poultice.

The next morning, bright and early, a sharp rap sounded at the door.

Both Charity and Beau went to answer it.

"I'll get it."

"I'll get it," Beau corrected.

"I'm perfectly capable of answering my own door."

Their gazes locked obstinately.

Beau gave in first, and Charity opened the door.

The handsome brave who'd caused all the trouble the day before stood before them, his face wreathed with an ecstatic grin.

"White Sister makes strong medicine." He held up three fingers. "Many papooses!"

Chapter 13

The bell hanging over the door to Miller's Mercantile tinkled melodiously when Beau and Cass stepped inside. Cass wore a boot on one foot and a moccasin on the other. Seemed like those herb poultices of Charity's weren't helping much. The foot was still swollen. The store was empty, except for Edgar, who was busy putting turnips in a large barrel.

"Morning, Mr. Claxton." The storekeeper wiped his hands on his apron and stepped behind the counter. "What can I get for you today?"

"I need nails, wire, and a few more fence posts," Beau said.

"Sure thing. Just got a new load of posts in yesterday. Who's that you got there with you?"

Beau introduced Cass to the friendly proprietor.

Edgar cordially reached out and shook Cass's hand. "Thought you two must be brothers. There's a strong family resemblance. Where you from, Mr. Claxton?"

"Missouri."

"Missouri, huh? Never been there. Always wanted to go; just never got the opportunity."

Beau told Edgar the amounts he needed, and Edgar wrote it

all down on a large, thick pad.

"Got those raisins in," Edgar mentioned.

Beau glanced at the large glass jar of raisins sitting on the shelf. He could buy the raisins, and Charity could make a pie. . .or he could save the money and apply it toward a new plow this spring. He quickly tossed the temptation aside. Charity needed a plow more than he needed raisins. "Thanks, but I'll be passing up the raisins today, Edgar."

"Just thought I'd mention it."

"Appreciate it."

While Beau and Cass browsed, Edgar went about filling the order.

The door opened again, and a small, rather harried-looking man entered the store, accompanied by a girl who appeared to be his daughter.

She was a beauty with an exquisite figure and lovely amethyst-colored eyes. Her golden blond hair, scooped up into a mass of ringlets, trickled down the back of her head beneath the brim of the latest Paris fashion.

She had a wide-eyed, innocent-looking appearance, but her full lips formed a petulant pout as if she'd just finished sucking a lemon.

Beau noticed Cass glancing up and taking note of the new arrivals before he promptly returned his attention to the shirts he was examining.

The bell tinkled again, and Reverend Olson entered the mercantile. Catching a glimpse of Beau, he immediately came over and struck up a conversation.

"How's Mary Kathleen?"

"Growing like a weed."

"And your new bride?"

"She's just fine."

The reverend chuckled. "I hope the baby is allowing the newly-weds some privacy by sleeping longer periods of time."

Beau flashed a tolerant grin. "She's not bothering us."

And Mary Kathleen wasn't. It was his own baby brother, who was right now eyeing the blond beauty that'd just come in, trying to pretend all he had on his mind was buying a new shirt.

"Well, I haven't been able to locate any of Ansel's or Letty's kin. I've sent letters, but as yet, I haven't received an answer," Reverend Olson admitted. "Now, the Farrises have offered to look after the baby, if you and Charity want, but with nine in the family and another one on the way. . ."

"Mary Kathleen's doing fine with us," Beau dismissed abruptly. "Charity would be lost without her."

Reverend Olson gazed kindly back at Beau. "And what about you?"

Cass approached the two before Beau could answer. "I don't believe you've met my brother, Reverend. Cass, I'd like you to meet Reverend Olson."

The two men shook hands. The reverend's smile was as pleasant as always. "Will you be staying in Kansas long, Cass?"

Funny. That was the question uppermost in Beau's mind, too.

"I will not have that filthy, disgusting piece of slime on my back!"

The men pivoted at the sound of a woman's shrill voice raised in anger.

"Now, Susanne, dear. . ." A small, harried-looking man ducked hurriedly as a bolt of material came sailing over his head and landed with a thud at the feet of the three men, who stood watching the developing ruckus with growing curiosity.

"I am sick and tired of having to look like a—a common peasant all the time!" With one fell swoop, the young woman angrily cleared the table of calico, cotton, and muslin. The mercantile suddenly looked as if it had been hit by a cyclone.

Edgar made a sound between a gasp and a moan at the sight of his valuable bolts of fabric scattered on the floor.

Beau smothered a grin. Turn that little spitfire loose and she'd trash the mercantile in nothing flat! What she needed was a good spanking, but her daddy didn't look capable of administering it.

The girl turned tail and flounced over to rifle through the display of ribbons and fine laces. Beau noticed Cass staring after her. He'd better be careful. That one would be hard to handle.

Cass, Reverend Olson, and Beau haltingly resumed their conversation as the girl's father gathered up the bolts of material, mumbling something softly under his breath about having only suggested the material might look nice on her—nothing to get all that upset about.

"As soon as the swelling in my ankle goes down and the weather holds, I'm planning on heading back to Missouri," Cass said, answering the reverend's interrupted inquiry.

"Well, I'm sure Beau has appreciated having another set of hands to help with the work." Reverend Olson cautiously eyed Susanne, who, having moved to the rack of cooking utensils, was plainly trying to eavesdrop on the men's conversation.

"Susanne McCord is a high-spirited girl," he whispered. "Extremely spirited."

"Acts like a spoiled brat," Cass observed curtly, looking shocked by such an unladylike display of temper. "The woman has the manners of a goat."

Susanne heard his remark, and her perfectly arched brows lifted with disdain. When Cass shot her an impervious look that not only matched hers but topped it, she quickly moved on.

Beau grinned. His little brother wasn't used to getting high-toned looks from a woman. All the females back home had practically stood in line to talk to him. Could be the boy was a trifle spoiled.

"Oh dear. Well, remember, I didn't say that," Reverend Olson insisted nervously. "The McCords are new in town. Leviticus is a retired circuit judge. He and his daughter came from back East, and it seems the girl hasn't quite made the adjustment her father had hoped she would."

The men drifted apart, trying to remain detached in the wake of a wildcat loose in their midst. Beau thought nostalgically of his own even-tempered wife waiting for him back at the cabin and thanked the good Lord he hadn't been rescued by an ill-tempered harridan like Susanne McCord.

His thoughts soured. Charity had been distracted lately. He had a feeling she was regretting jumping into this hasty marriage. A woman like Charity didn't give her heart lightly. He knew she still loved Ferrand. How did you compete with a dead man?

A few minutes later, Cass was forced to duck again when he heard Susanne scream and a bottle of perfume sailed over his head to smash noisily against the west wall.

His head shot up, and his hands moved defiantly to his hips. Beau watched with interest, figuring Cass was planning on teaching Miss McCord some manners. He hoped his brother was up to the task. The girl ignored the men, diverting her full attention to bullying poor Edgar Miller.

"Why don't you have something as simple as a spool of red thread? You have every other color," she accused. "Why don't you have red?"

"I did have red," Edgar said, eager to console her, "but Ethel Bluewaters came in yesterday and bought the last—"

"Incompetent fool! Sheer incompetence!" Her eyes narrowed threateningly. "It's a lucky thing you have the only mercantile in town, Mr. Miller, or I would certainly take my business elsewhere!"

Edgar had a scrunched-up expression, and Beau figured he prayed daily that such colossal good fortune would befall him. "Miss McCord, I have a new shipment of thread coming in next week, and I'm sure there will be plenty of red—"

Edgar's apology was interrupted when she bombarded him with a barrage of spools. "I wouldn't buy your stupid thread even if you had it!"

He cringed and ducked, throwing his arms over his head protectively. The spools continued to bounce off the counter. . .and off his balding skull.

"Susanne, dear! You must stop this!" Leviticus sucked in his breath and drew up his slight five-foot-two frame to boldly confront his daughter. "Mr. Miller can't help it if Ethel Bluewaters bought his last spool of red thread!"

"The service here is wretched!"

Edgar looked like he was holding on to his temper by the grace of God.

Reverend Olson clucked. "Dear me. What an exhibition."

Cass shook his head. "Why would Edgar put up with that kind of treatment?"

Beau grinned. "I figure prudence is the only thing keeping him silent. The man values his life."

"Now, dear"—Leviticus balled his fists up tight—"now, dear, we just can't have this! You'll just have to go back home until you can get yourself under control."

Cass leaned against the doorway, arms folded. "Would you look at that? She's managed to tree two grown men without firing a single shot."

"Amazing," Beau agreed. "But you have to consider the men. Neither Leviticus nor Edgar are a match for her."

"That's perfectly all right with me." Turning her nose up haughtily, Susanne lifted the hem of her skirt and swept past her father with the regal air of a queen holding court.

She paused momentarily when she came face-to-face with Cass, who by now had stepped over to deliberately challenge her path through the door.

"Get out of my way, cowboy." She spat the words out contemptuously, her eyes flashing with renewed anger.

Cass grinned insolently and his dark eyes glittered. He reached up and pushed his hat back on his head. "And if I don't?"

Beau, watching, figured this would be a battle of the wills. No way would Cass allow any woman to push him around.

After a tense pause Susanne hauled off and hit Cass squarely between the eyes with her purse. The blow was unexpected and explosive. Cass staggered, groping blindly for support. Beau tried to grab him before he fell, but missed. Susanne slammed out of the mercantile, rattling windowpanes and sending jars dancing merrily across the shelves.

Cass slid to the floor. Beau looked down at his brother. "I don't suppose you've ever heard 'Hell hath no fury like a woman scorned'?"

Cass shook his head.

"Well," Beau sighed, offering him a hand, "you have now."

Charity opened the front door and scanned the flawless expanse of blue sky. It was an extraordinarily beautiful day.

She wished now she'd ridden into town with the two brothers when they'd asked her this morning. Instead, she'd stayed behind to do her weekly baking. By late morning she'd finished six loaves of bread, and three sweet-potato pies were cooling on the windowsill.

The pies reminded her of Beau's penchant for raisins, and the idea suddenly came to her. By now Mr. Miller should have received the shipment from Hays.

First thing tomorrow morning she'd bundle up Mary Kathleen and make the hour's ride into Cherry Grove. Beau would be overjoyed when he came home to find his favorite pies bubbling in the oven.

"You feeling any better?" Beau noticed Cass wasn't quite as pale as he'd been earlier, though he still complained of a throbbing headache.

"That woman's meaner than a two-headed snake," Cass grumbled.

"You shouldn't have provoked her," Beau reminded him. "You need to leave a woman like Susanne McCord alone."

"You don't have to worry about that. I hope I never meet up with that spitfire again."

They rode on for a few moments in silence, enjoying the unseasonably warm afternoon. "You know, you've been as testy as an old cow missing her calf," Cass accused, reminding Beau of his own display of bad temper of late.

"I know," Beau said simply.

"Well?"

"Well what?"

"Well, what's gotten into you? You never used to be so short-fused. I don't know how Charity puts up with you."

Beau shrugged.

"Exactly how long have you two been married, anyway?"

"How long have you been here?"

Cass looked confused. "What's that got to do with anything?"

"Because we'd just gotten married the afternoon you arrived," Beau said curtly.

Cass's jaw dropped. "Are you—you've got to be pulling my leg."

Beau shook his head.

"You mean to tell me. . .you and she. . .?" Cass sputtered.

Beau nodded. He watched Cass put two and two together.

"Well, well." Cass mulled over this surprising bit of news. "It's beginning to dawn on me what your problem might be. No wonder you've been on edge. Why didn't you say something?"

"I don't know. Maybe I wasn't exactly sure if I would be doing the right thing if we consummated our vows," Beau confessed.

"Now, what's that supposed to mean? She's your wife, isn't she?"

"Yes, but the marriage isn't what you think."

As the two men rode along through the bright sunshine, Beau filled Cass in on the past year of his life. At times his voice filled with emotion as he relayed how miserable he'd been until that fateful day the wolf attacked him in the stream.

He spoke of how Charity, along with two Indian squaws, had worked to save his life. "I'm real grateful to all three of them. I guess it was touch and go for a while. I don't remember much about it. Most of the time I was out of my mind."

"We never knew you were hurt so bad," Cass said.

"I wasn't in any shape to write letters," Beau admitted. "Charity insisted I send word home and even wrote the letter for me."

Cass looked at him. "Seems like Charity has done a lot for you."

"She saved my life, with a little help from Laughing Waters and Little Fawn." Beau thought about the two Indian women's determination to marry him, but decided not to mention that. If he knew his brother, Cass would rib him about it, and you could count on him to spread the news to Cole as soon as he got home. They'd never let him hear the last of it.

"What happened to her husband?" Cass asked.

"He was killed in the war." Not every family had been as fortunate as the Claxtons. All three brothers had gone off to fight, and they'd all come back home in reasonably good spirits.

He told Cass about Mary Kathleen and about Ansel's untimely death. "You know, Cass, I felt just about that hopeless myself for a long time. I figure it's pure luck that I'm still alive."

Cass frowned. "I think Ma's prayers had more to do with it than luck. You know she wouldn't want to hear you talking like that. Neither would Betsy, for that matter."

Beau sighed. "You're right. God's been good to me, and I haven't thanked Him enough. I'm realizing it more every day."

"Are you going to stay here in Kansas, or are you bringing Charity back home to Missouri?"

"I figure I'll stay here. Charity needs a lot of work done before she can claim her land. I should have it in good shape by spring."

"Charity seems like a good woman," Cass ventured.

"She is; one of the best," Beau agreed.

"There's something that bothers me," Cass said. "You've said you were sorry for her. You're grateful she saved your neck. You told me all the reasons you married her, but you've never once said you love her, and you've never said you intend to make this marriage permanent. Are you saying you plan to leave once Charity has the title to her land?"

Beau fixed his gaze on the winding road. A muscle twitched in his jaw. "I'm saying I'm not sure what I'm going to do."

"Well, look here, Beau. If you're not going to stay with her, do you think it's fair to. . .to. . .well. . .act married?"

"I don't know."

"Do you love her?"

Did he love her? It had been such a long time since Beau had felt love, he wasn't sure he would even recognize the feeling again. But yes, he thought he did.

"I don't know. . . . I still think of Bets."

"She's gone, Beau," Cass reminded him gently. "We all loved Betsy, but you have to go on. She'd want it that way."

"I know. It's been real hard for me, Cass."

"I think Betsy would approve of Charity," Cass said. "I don't think your conscience ought to bother you there. She seems like a fine woman. And she's beautiful. You have noticed that, haven't you?"

"Of course I have," Beau admitted. "Living together all winter. . . well, it would be impossible not to."

Yes, Charity was beautiful. He knew other men found her desirable. Even his baby brother had sent a few glances her way.

That was another thing that bothered him, the way Charity didn't seem in a hurry for Cass to move on. The way she fussed over him sometimes, putting poultices on his ankle, set Beau's teeth on edge. He wasn't a jealous man; still, Cass was the best-looking one of the Claxton men. He couldn't help wondering if Charity hadn't noticed.

Cass interrupted his thoughts. "But you're not sure you love her enough to make a lifetime commitment?"

Beau laughed mirthlessly. "Who knows how long a lifetime is going to be?"

"Well"—Cass sighed—"you'll have to decide what to do about Charity, but I'll make it a little harder on you." He flashed his brother a grin. "The weather's real nice, and it looks like there's going to be a full moon tonight. I'll saddle up and ride out to do a little. . .uh, fishing." He winked knowingly. "Been meaning to do that, anyway."

Beau shook his head, but he couldn't deny the thrill of expectation that shot through him at the thought of being alone with his wife. "Leaving me and Charity all alone," he concluded dryly.

"You'll still have the baby—unless Mary Kathleen wants to go hunting with me."

"I doubt she will. She's out of bullets."

Cass grinned and spurred his horse into a faster gait. "Well, what are you waiting for, big brother?" His grin widened. "We're burning daylight."

Chapter 14

Charity turned from feeding the chickens when the horses galloped into the yard. Beau threw the reins to Cass and announced that he was in need of a hot bath. She looked surprised by his strange request, especially since he seldom took a bath in the middle of the week, but she quickly set about filling kettles and putting them on the stove to heat.

After supper Beau dragged in the old washtub, laid out a bar of soap and a fresh towel, and drew the privacy blanket.

He then proceeded to bathe, shave, comb, and brush. By six o'clock he was clean as a whistle, though he wasn't sure what he was hoping to accomplish with the improvement. Throughout his preparations he'd weighed the dangers of embarking upon the course lurking in the back of his mind. Was it wise to wholly enter this marriage?

They were married in God's sight. But Beau needed to be committed in his heart. Irreversibly faithful.

Neither he nor Charity had false expectations concerning their arrangement. He'd been honest with her; he knew she needed his help to gain the title to her land. He was willing to do that. It would be impossible for him to remain under her roof as long as they were both single. Marriage was the only answer to their immediate problems. Yes, they desired each other. The past month had proven that, but would desire be enough to get them through a lifetime, if he chose to remain here come spring?

Bets had died over a year ago. Sixteen months. It seemed like a lifetime. Would it make a mockery of his vows to Betsy to bring another woman into his heart this soon?

He wrestled back and forth with the weighty questions until he grew short-tempered again.

"I thought you were going hunting!" he snapped. Cass was sitting in the rocker playing with Mary Kathleen when Beau's accusation ricocheted across the room.

Charity glanced up from the sampler she was working on and frowned. "My goodness, Beau, why would he be going hunting tonight?"

"How should I know? He said he was going." Beau sent a pointed look in Cass's direction. With typical Kansas unpredictability the weather had warmed, melting the snow. The temperate weather wouldn't last, but hunting was possible.

Charity frowned. "How can he hunt in the dark?"

"He's coon hunting," Beau said. "Best time to hunt coons is after dark."

Cass sprang to his feet and carried Mary Kathleen back to her crib. After nuzzling her fat cheeks affectionately, he kissed the baby good night then reached for his coat.

"Don't look for me to be back till late," he warned. "I may even do a little fishing while I'm out."

"Don't rush on our account," Beau grumbled.

Charity's expression suggested that she found Cass's odd behavior as puzzling as Beau's. "Fishing? Tonight?"

"Thought I'd take advantage of the mild weather. Won't be many more days like this one," Cass predicted. He eased the brim of his hat back on his forehead. "You two have a nice evening."

"Beau?" Charity laid her needle aside, clearly concerned.

Her husband shrugged. "A man's got a right to go fishing if he wants."

When Cass opened the door, he came face-to-face with Susanne McCord.

He drew back in defense. "What are you doing here?"

"Mr. Claxton?"

"Yes."

"Mr. Cass Claxton?"

He frowned. "That's right."

Susanne glanced from Beau to Cass, clearly confused. "Oh. . .I didn't realize you were Cass," she murmured.

Cass's expression was about as friendly as a head cold.

Susanne took a deep breath and primly drew up her shoulders. "It really doesn't matter. I'm here on a purely business matter. I wonder if I might have a word with you, Mr. Claxton."

"What do you want with me?"

"Our conversation will be brief," she assured him.

Charity approached the doorway, pulling a wrap closer. "Won't you come in, Miss. . ." She smiled and looked to Cass to provide the guest's name.

The set of his steel jaw indicated he wasn't going to hand out any information.

"Why, yes, thank you. I will come in." Susanne quickly stepped into the cabin before Cass could argue. She nodded pleasantly at Beau when her skirts brushed past him.

Beau closed the door and wondered why the spitfire wanted to talk to Cass. Had she come to apologize for her outrageous behavior this morning? The idea seemed unlikely; the woman didn't look to be the type that would admit she was sorry for anything.

"May I get you something warm to drink, Miss. . .?" Charity

glanced helplessly to Cass again. "A cup of tea or coffee to help ward off the chill?"

"Miss McCord won't be staying long enough to socialize," Cass said.

Charity looked shocked by Cass's rude behavior. Her eyes switched to Beau, and he grinned and shook his head. Cass and Susanne reminded him of a couple of hound pups, snapping and snarling for no reason.

Charity wasn't aware of Miss McCord's earlier behavior; he'd have to inform her. Cass hadn't been in any mood to talk when they got home, especially about how he had been bested by a woman who didn't reach to his shoulder.

Susanne returned Cass's fixed gaze, her nose lifting a notch higher. "Why, thank you, Miss...?"

"Mrs.," Charity supplied. "Mrs. Claxton."

Susanne's eyes reverted coolly back to Cass. "I was about to say, I don't care for anything to drink, Mrs. Claxton. I'm here to speak with Cass."

"Then Beau and I will take a short walk and let you two talk in private."

Cass objected. "No need to do that. Whatever Miss McCord has on her mind won't require privacy."

"I would like to speak to Mr. Claxton alone," Susanne reiterated stiffly.

Charity checked on the baby then smiled encouragingly at Susanne and reached for her shawl. "Take all the time you need. My husband and I will enjoy the outing."

"Thank you ever so much." Susanne moved closer to the stove. Shortly afterward, Beau and Charity closed the door behind them.

"Who is she?" Charity asked when she and Beau stepped off the porch and began their walk.

"Susanne McCord. She and her father were in Miller's Mercantile this morning where she made quite an entrance."

The recollection of Cass's unfortunate encounter with the highly temperamental Miss McCord brought a grin to Beau's face.

"She seems like a lovely young thing."

Beau wrapped his arm around his wife's waist and drew her close to his side. "You think so? Well, let me tell you what that 'lovely young thing' did to my little brother."

When the door closed, Cass squared off to meet his adversary. "What do you want, Miss McCord?" There was no time for mundane pleasantries; he did not like this woman. His gaze impersonally skimmed her petite frame elegantly sheathed in an outfit he figured had set poor Leviticus McCord back a pretty penny.

Susanne cleared her throat. "I understand you're from Missouri?"

"That's right."

"And you plan to return there soon?"

"I might."

"You're not being the least bit cooperative. But it really doesn't matter." She smiled, flashing dimples. Cass figured that was the way she dazzled the young men in Cherry Grove. Unfortunately, he'd been around awhile; he was tough to dazzle.

She fluttered her eyelashes. "When you leave, I want you to take me with you."

He shifted his weight to one foot, staring at her as if he hadn't heard her correctly. "You want what?"

"I want you to take me to Missouri," she repeated.

Cass laughed. He pulled off his coat and draped it over a chair back.

Susanne tapped her foot. "I'm prepared to offer you five hundred dollars provided that you'll safely escort me to my aunt's home in Saint Louis."

Cass knelt in front of the stove, poker in hand. "Where would you get that kind of money?"

"That's none of your business," Susanne informed him. "But I assure you, I have it. It's imperative that I leave this gopher hole they call a town and leave it immediately!"

"Imperative to whom?"

"Imperative to my sanity," she snapped. "I cannot stand the thought of living in Cherry Grove, Kansas, another moment."

She eased forward, her eyes mirroring desperation. She reached out to clutch the sleeve of his coat. "You must help me. You are the only sane person in this backwater town who is smart enough to leave." She spat out the observation as if the words left a bad taste in her mouth. "When I overheard Reverend Olson telling Edgar Miller that you were planning to return to Missouri, I knew this was my chance to escape."

Cass coolly eyed the hand clutching his sleeve. Susanne released the fabric. Her expression went from arrogant to pleading.

"Mr. Claxton. If you would be so kind to see me safely back to Saint Louis, I will pay you handsomely. Once I'm there, Daddy will understand how unhappy I've been in this—this rat's nest, and he'll let me stay. Oh! There will be parties and balls and lovely gowns when I'm under Aunt Merriweather's supervision." She gaily whirled around the hearth, caught up in her flight of fantasy. "Daddy will be overjoyed to let me stay in Saint Louis once he knows that I will never come back to Kansas. Never." She paused, her face flushed prettily from the heat. "Well?" She tipped her head flirtatiously. "Will you do it?"

Cass's expression was calm and aloof. "I'd rather be horsewhipped."

Susanne's brows shot up. "You mean you won't?"

"Not on your life, sweetheart."

"And if I increase my offer to six hundred dollars?"

Cass shook his head. "You don't have six hundred dollars."

Her eyes darted away momentarily, but seconds later they switched back to meet his with defiance. "I do have the money and more, and I'll pay whatever you ask if you'll take me with you."

Cass sighed. "Miss McCord, not only will I not take you to Missouri for six hundred dollars, but you could sweeten the deal with a herd of longhorns, a ranch in Texas, and a chest of gold, and I still wouldn't take you to a dog fight."

Her eyes dripped ice. "You're despicable."

He shrugged. "So are you."

"Why won't you take me?" she demanded.

He smiled. "Because I don't like you, Miss McCord."

She cocked her chin rebelliously. "I didn't ask you to like me. I don't like you, either, but I see no reason why personal feelings should interfere with a business arrangement. If it would help, I'll promise not to even speak to you during the journey."

Cass walked over to stare thoughtfully out the window. "Does your daddy know you're running around asking strangers to take you to Missouri?"

"What do you think?"

"What would he do if he found out?"

"He'd be upset, naturally. But he isn't going to find out—unless you tell him, and I doubt you will. Apparently, you're not the sort to involve yourself in other people's business."

"I'm not going to tell him." Cass turned and walked back to the fire. "Nor am I going to take you to Saint Louis."

She shot him a scathing look. "Exactly why don't you like me? Until this morning, we didn't know the other existed, so how can you not like me?"

"I know you about as well as I plan to know you." The scene

in the mercantile said about all he needed to form an opinion of Susanne McCord.

"Why?" she persisted.

"I don't like little girls with nasty tempers."

She sighed. "You're upset about what happened this morning. Well, it was your own fault. You should never have blocked my way."

"You're lucky you're still standing," he reminded her. "What kind of woman goes around hitting a man for no reason?"

Her face colored, which surprised Cass. He hadn't figured she had a repentant bone in her body. "Then you refuse to take me?"

"That's about the size of it."

"For any price?"

"For any price."

"You won't change your mind?"

"No, ma'am."

"Then I suppose I've said all I came to say."

Cass tipped his head politely. "It's been a real pleasure, ma'am."

Susanne walked to the front door, pausing with her hand on the latch. "If you should change your mind—"

"Do you have a hearing problem?"

She yanked the door open. "I'd appreciate it if you'd take a look at my mare before I return to town."

"What's the matter with her?"

"She developed a slight limp just before we got here."

Cass grumbled something uncomplimentary under his breath, but he followed her out to the sled.

"She's thrown a shoe," he said a few minutes later.

"What does that mean?"

"It means the horse will need a new shoe before you can leave."

She sighed, drawing her collar tighter. "Can you fix it?"

He straightened. "Lady—"

"I'll pay you for your services, sir!"

There wasn't enough money in the world—Cass took a deep breath. "I'll see what I can find."

Smiling, Susanne slumped lower onto the seat.

Thirty minutes later Cass had the horse reshod and ready to travel.

"Which direction is Cherry Grove?"

Cass glanced up from a final check of the hoof. "What?"

"Do you have a hearing problem? What direction is Cherry Grove?"

The muscle in his jaw tightened. "You don't know?"

She shook her head. "It was still daylight when I came. My father only moved me to this horrible area three months ago. This is the first time I've ventured out on my own."

"And you chose to come two hours before dark? To the west," he said curtly and turned back to the horse. "Okay," he said a minute later. "You shouldn't have any trouble."

He glanced up to confront two large violet pools swimming in tears.

"Now what's wrong?"

"I'm afraid. I don't think I can find my way back to town." She sniffed.

"Just follow the road, lady."

"I—I have a terrible sense of direction," she confessed. "And this is the first time I've ever traveled. . .alone."

"You'll make it fine," Cass said. His chin set in a stubborn line. "Light your lantern, and give the horse her head. She'll find the way."

Susanne's hands trembled when she reluctantly accepted the reins he offered.

"What if she doesn't? What if I become lost—and it snows again? I could perish—then my father would hold you responsible for my death." Her small teeth worried her lower lip. "Knowing Father, he would sue for lack of responsibility—"

Cass glanced down the darkened road then back to her. "Stop the 'poor me' act, Miss McCord. I'm not buying it. You'll be all right. You have a gun, don't you?"

She shook her head. "I never thought of bringing a gun. Besides, I wouldn't know how to use one." Her sniffling grew more pronounced. "Suddenly I have this most wretched headache, and I'm beginning to feel faint." She sounded ready to collapse on the spot.

Cass shook his head. She actually thought he was buying this performance?

She sniffed and blew her nose daintily into a lace handkerchief. "I do hope I don't just faint dead away and have to remain here—with you—in that small cabin for. . .well, who knows when I might be able to travel?"

Resigned, Cass helped her out of the sled and they walked toward the house. He was whipped. She'd have to stay the night. But not a moment longer. Her little tricks wouldn't work on him.

"Will Mr. and Mrs. Claxton mind having an unexpected houseguest?" she asked.

"They won't mind," Cass lied.

Charity looked up in surprise when they entered the room. She and Beau had gotten back from the walk. "You haven't left yet?"

Cass strode to the fire. "Miss McCord's horse threw a shoe."

"Oh. . .I'm sorry."

"But you fixed it," Beau prompted.

Cass met his brother's eyes. "I fixed it, but now it's dark, and she's afraid she can't find her way back to Cherry Grove."

"Can't you drive her back?"

"She's developed a wretched headache, and she feels faint."

The brothers exchanged a series of trapped looks.

"You do?" Charity immediately moved to welcome her guest. "May I do something for you?"

"Maybe. . .if I could just rest a spell," Susanne said softly. She glanced at Cass and smiled.

Beau looked on helplessly when Charity moved Susanne to the bed. "You just lie down in here. I'll bring you a cup of tea—nothing like a cup of hot tea to chase away a headache."

"You're ever so kind."

"Can't you do something?" Beau hissed when the two women disappeared behind the privacy curtain.

"What do you expect me to do? Let her wander around on the road in the dark? That woman doesn't know up from down."

Beau's lips thinned. "I suppose the hunting trip is off."

"Would it accomplish anything now? I'll stay by the fire, thank you."

"Well, it's going to be another long, miserable night," Beau predicted.

Cass glanced at the drawn curtain, where female voices could be heard. "Tell me about it."

Chapter 15

The women carried on the brunt of the conversation over breakfast. Beau and Cass ate steadily, commenting only out of necessity. The moment the last egg was eaten and plates were removed and washed, Susanne announced that she was leaving.

Cass refused to look up from his plate. "Tell Leviticus that he has my prayers."

"I will indeed, sir." She flounced away from the table, addressing her remarks to Charity. "I so appreciate you letting me spend the night. If I ever do get to Saint Louis"—she paused to give Cass an aggrieved look—"you must come for a long visit."

"Oh—I don't think I'll ever get to Saint Louis," Charity admitted, "but thank you for the invitation. Perhaps we can correspond occasionally?"

Beau thought his wife's smile seemed a trifle strained. A little of Susanne McCord went a long way.

Cass hitched the McCord sleigh, and without further ado Miss McCord set off for Cherry Grove—concocting, Beau suspected, a lofty explanation for a father who was sick with worry. Leviticus would have no way of knowing that his daughter had spent the night at the Burk homestead. For all he knew, the willful Miss McCord was off in a ditch somewhere.

Beau and Cass left shortly after to spend the morning repairing fences on the north section. The morning had dawned sunny and bright and promised a mild day for late January, though snow lay deep on the ground.

Before he rode out, Beau managed a rare moment alone with his wife. Drawing her into his arms, he kissed her soundly.

"My, my," Charity murmured, breathless when he finally relinquished his embrace. "What's this all about?"

Beau rested his cheek on the top of her head, nuzzling her hair. "I'm thinking how lucky I was that day at the stream."

"Lucky!"

"Sure. You found me. What if someone like Susanne had come along first?"

"Are you suggesting Susanne McCord isn't your ideal companion?" She grinned, closing her eyes when his lips lightly traveled the base of her throat.

"The good Lord must have been put out with Leviticus the day that woman was born." He stole another kiss, interrupted by Cass, who'd returned to the house to search for his forgotten gloves.

With a regretful sigh, Beau released her. "I wish Ferrand had built you a bigger house."

"He would have if he'd known I'd need one so badly," she bantered back.

Beau winked and kissed her forehead then reached around her for his coat. "See you at dinnertime." Looked like the weather would hold awhile longer. It had been days since the last snow; maybe spring would come early this year. "I won't be back until dark."

"Mary Kathleen and I will be waiting for you."

When the horses rode out, Charity quickly finished her chores and dressed Mary Kathleen warmly. If she hurried, she could make the trip into Cherry Grove to purchase raisins and be back before Beau discovered she'd gone.

Sun was streaming brightly among a scattering of fleecy clouds. It would be a perfect day for a short winter outing.

She put on a lightweight jacket, which she wouldn't need but wanted to take along just in case. Kansas weather could be fickle—just like a man's affection.

She led the harnessed horse from the lean-to then went back to the cabin and carried Mary Kathleen to the waiting sled.

"Easy now, Jack." She spoke to the horse while she settled the infant on the board seat then climbed up and took hold of the reins. Suddenly she thought to take the shovel along in case she might need it. She retrieved the shovel, tossed it in the back of the wagon, and climbed onto the seat again. After checking to make sure Mary Kathleen was warm enough, she gathered up the reins and set off for the hour's ride to Cherry Grove.

Charity lifted her face to the sun, drinking in the marvelous treat. She couldn't remember when she had felt this good. She hummed the hauntingly sweet melody "Aura Lee" to the baby as the horse trotted briskly down the snow-packed road.

The sled runners skimmed effortlessly through Fire Creek and picked up speed when Charity urged the horse into a fast trot. If she didn't dawdle at the mercantile, she'd have plenty of time to share a cup of tea with the Olsons before starting back. Beau wouldn't be home until dark. By then she'd have the raisins tucked away and dinner on the table. He would never suspect she'd made a trip to town.

A small, puffy cloud passed over the sun, but Charity didn't worry about it. What was a cloud on a lovely warm day like this? Besides, she was having too much fun thinking about her husband's sheer joy when she brought those two hot pies out of the oven. Though a small, insignificant token, the celebrating of their marriage would not go unnoticed.

Charity glanced up when an unexpected chill crept into the air. A second cloud now skimmed the sun. Even as she watched, the cloud was joined by two more, then three. The sky had been perfectly clear a few minutes ago. Now it was clouding up, and the wind had a sharp bite.

She decided she'd better stop long enough to readjust Mary Kathleen's blankets and put on her light jacket. It only took a minute to perform the simple tasks, and she was ready to move on.

A Kansas blizzard could move in faster than a jackrabbit outrunning a prairie fire. After careful study of the darkening clouds, she concluded they were nothing to be overly concerned about. But just in case. . .instead of sharing a cup of tea with Rebecca and Reverend Olson, she would buy the raisins and start home immediately. She clucked her tongue, and Jack's big hooves clopped noisily back onto the road.

Thirty minutes later, the first minuscule flakes started to drift lazily down, melting as soon as they touched the ground.

Charity still wasn't concerned about the abrupt change in weather. It would be about as far to turn back as it was to go on, and the snow appeared to be nothing more than flurries. But it was getting noticeably colder, so she set the horse to a brisker gait. Mary Kathleen, cuddled in her warm cocoon, stared with big eyes at the snow drifting down like tiny feathers to dot the wagon seat. Charity reached over to brush the accumulation off the infant's blanket.

"It's getting cold, isn't it, darling? We'll sit in front of Edgar's fire and toast our toes when we get there."

Snow continued to fall in the same gentle manner. The pristine beauty had always fascinated Charity. She watched the pea-sized flakes float peacefully from the heavy, leaden sky, marveling at yet another one of God's wondrous creations. She hoped this was the last snow of the season, but she knew that was wishful thinking. They still had February and March to contend with—months when they got their biggest snowfalls. The wind suddenly shifted directions, and the snow fell in earnest now. Periodic wind gusts whipped the wagon about on the road. Charity gripped the reins tighter and urged Jack to greater speed.

The wind steadily picked up strength, swirling snow back into her face, taking her breath away with its growing ferocity. It was increasingly evident that once she reached Cherry Grove, she'd be forced to wait out the blizzard. Beau would be worried—she hadn't left a note saying where she was going.

She was a mile from the town when panic set in. By now, Mary Kathleen was cold and crying, and Jack was becoming increasingly spooked by the storm's freakish nature.

Drifts built beside the road so quickly that Charity found herself losing her sense of direction. If it weren't for the aid of familiar landmarks, she knew she'd soon be hopelessly lost.

She reached a hand over to soothe Mary Kathleen's frightened screams, finally admitting to herself that the trip had been a mistake. At the first sign of trouble she should have turned around and gone back home.

From all indications this was going to be a full-blown blizzard, and she and the baby would never survive the storm if she didn't find shelter—and soon.

Above all she must keep her head. She'd reach appropriate shelter and wait for Beau to find her.

But Beau has no idea where you are, her mind shouted. Stinging sleet lashed her face. She had been so intent on keeping the trip to town a surprise she hadn't thought of possible danger and the need to leave a note.

She stopped Jack in the middle of the road and gazed helplessly at the chilly alabaster prison in which she found herself. She realized with sinking despair that Beau wouldn't know where to begin looking for her.

Not the vaguest idea.

The blizzard hit full force as Beau and Cass finished setting the fourth fence post.

"Looks like it's going to be a bad one!" Cass shouted above the rising wind.

"Let's head in!"

The two men quickly gathered their supplies, loaded up, and kicked their horses into a full gallop.

Snow swirled around the riders. Once the two men stopped and tied bandannas around their noses to ward off the stinging air. By the time they reached the cabin, the horses were having difficulty navigating the deepening drifts.

"I've never seen a storm move in so quickly," Cass remarked. They rubbed down the horses and secured the lean-to. "I wonder if that snippy little twit made it home before the storm hit."

"Susanne?"

"Do you know another snippy little twit?"

"She started early enough to outrun the storm. I've heard of freakish blizzards, but this is the first one I've ever dealt with." Beau glanced over and noticed Jack's stall was empty. "Where's Jack?"

"I don't know. Maybe Charity turned him out to pasture before the storm."

The men bent into the wind and slowly made their way to the house. Beau shoved the door open and was surprised when Charity wasn't there to greet him.

The brothers stepped inside. Beau paused when he saw the room was empty. The fire burned low in the chilly room. There was no sign of Charity or the baby.

"Charity's not here. Where is she?"

"I don't know. Maybe she's out trying to help the stock?"

"She wouldn't have taken the baby with her." Beau jerked the door open and scanned the swirling mass of white. Encountering nothing but endless drifts of mounting snow, he felt the knot in his stomach tighten. Where was she?

He stepped out of the house and made his way back to the lean-to, oblivious now to the howling storm. There wasn't a sign of the stock, except for the two oxen, Myrtle and Nell, contentedly munching hay in their stalls.

He strode behind the lean-to, and his heart sank when he discovered the sled missing.

He quickly threw a saddle across the mare. Cass entered the lean-to and automatically started saddling his animal.

"She's probably fine, Beau. She may be caught at one of the neighbors'—"

"Charity wouldn't be out on a day like this," Beau said shortly. "If she'd planned to visit anyone she would have said something about it this morning. Or left a note."

The men remounted. Cass handed Beau one of the two wool scarves he'd brought along. He tied one around his neck and pulled it up to cover his mouth. "Where do we start?"

Beau shook his head. The full implication of Charity's unexplained absence closed in on him. "I don't know."

"I say we try the neighbors first and then head toward Cherry Grove," Cass suggested.

"Cherry Grove? She wouldn't be going to town."

"You don't know that."

"And you do?"

"No," Cass admitted, "but I figure that's where I'd be going if I had a husband and a small baby and I'd been cooped up in the house for a spell."

"In the middle of a blizzard?" The horses shied nervously when a violent gust of wind threatened to collapse the drafty lean-to.

"The weather was like a spring day three hours ago."

Beau wasn't going to waste time arguing. Cass's reasoning might seem insane, but it was bound to be better than his own right now. He pulled up into the saddle. Charity and Mary Kathleen were out there somewhere. "Let's get moving."

"We'd better stay together," Cass warned.

Beau was well aware how crazy it was to ride off in a storm. They could be risking their lives, but Charity's and Mary Kathleen's lives were at risk. He felt sick to his stomach when he thought about losing them.

"Let's go." Beau viewed the worsening storm. A fresh feeling of despair threatened to engulf him. "Where are you, Charity?" he whispered. "Where are you. . .sweetheart?"

Charity's feet and hands were numb. She'd searched for over thirty minutes, but she had found nothing in the form of shelter. During the process, she'd managed to run the sled off the road and into a steep ditch. One runner had sunk into a deep drift, and the rear end was tilting grotesquely to one side. She crawled to the back of the sled and laid Mary Kathleen on the floor then lay down beside her. Huddled in the warmth of the baby's blankets, she began to pray.

Dear God, help us. That's all her mind could repeat. *God, help us.*

The day wore on. Snow continued to fall in wet, heavy sheets. Charity managed to stop the baby's periodic crying by letting her nurse from the cloth she'd brought along. Ice had formed in the milk, and Mary Kathleen angrily spit the liquid out of her mouth, but Charity forced her to drink enough to momentarily pacify her. She wondered what would happen when the milk was gone. She'd only brought one jar.

Mary Kathleen eventually cried herself out. She now seemed fascinated by the snow. Charity knew the child was getting colder, and she had no idea how much longer an infant could survive in the falling temperatures.

By afternoon both she and the baby had started to doze.

Charity lay next to Mary Kathleen, vacantly watching the snow slowly begin to bury the sled. She tried to make herself stir, recalling how Ferrand had once told her about a man who'd frozen to death. The man succumbed to the temptation to sleep; a deadly mistake, he had warned her.

Charity forced her eyes open, but her lashes were becoming frozen. Soon they drifted shut on her snow-covered cheek.

Beau. . .don't let me die. . . . Don't let me die.

Beau and Cass searched the back roads, methodically wading their animals through deepening drifts, checking nearby homesteads. Beau's worry amplified with each negative shake of head. Not one person knew of Charity's whereabouts.

They stopped at Bill Cleveland's only to find he hadn't seen her, either. No one had, Beau thought in despair. *Charity, where are you?*

Bill followed them out to the horses. "I've been abed for a couple of days. Just got up the first time about an hour ago." He coughed a deep, rasping noise that threatened to tear through his chest wall. "Let me get old Duke saddled and I'll go with you."

Beau shook his head. "You wouldn't last an hour out here, Bill. Go back to the fire."

"But I want to help," Bill argued. "The widow Burk's been such a good neighbor to me. Brought food when I was flat on my back last fall."

"You can pray." Cass held out his hand, and Bill reached to take it. "We'll find her."

Bill nodded. "I'll be praying. Never doubt it."

Beau had been brought up to believe in the power of prayer, though he'd gotten out of the practice. That was about the only thing they had going for them right now.

Next stop was Jacob Peterson's dugout. Beau banged on the door. Jacob stuck his head out and blinked snow out of his eyes. "What's all the commotion?"

Beau quickly dispensed with the introductions. "I've been helping Mrs. Burk around her place."

"I know who you are." Peterson motioned for the two men to come inside.

Beau entered the dugout with Cass following behind. Both men stomped their boots, knocking off the wet snow.

"Charity's missing. She didn't happen to stop by here today, did she?" Beau asked.

Jacob turned thoughtful. "Missing, you say? In this weather? That's bad."

"Yes, sir." Beau knew how bad. If they didn't find her soon,

Charity would die out here. The baby, too.

Jacob stooped to add another piece of wood to the fire. "Haven't seen her. You check with the Joneses? They live 'bout a mile on down the road."

Beau shook his head. "Not yet. She didn't leave a note; that's unusual. It started out to be a nice day, so I suspect she decided to go for a visit."

Dear God, let that be true. Right now, let her be holing up somewhere drinking hot tea and eating cookies in a safe haven—though where that would be Beau didn't know.

Folks were talking; they wouldn't take kindly to Charity and the baby showing up on their doorstep.

"Kansas weather's as fickle as love," Jacob said. He took a couple of cups from the board shelf fastened to the wall and filled them with hot coffee. "Get this inside you. Maybe it will warm you up a little, anyway. I'll saddle my mule and help you look."

"You can't do that," Beau protested. The man was eighty if he was a day. He wouldn't last thirty minutes in this weather.

Jacob paused in the act of reaching for his coat. "Son, I ain't got many more years left. If I die trying to save a woman and a baby, then so be it."

"You wouldn't get past the lane, and I'd have to bring you back. Sorry, but you'd just slow us down."

Jacob's expression turned old and defeated. "I know you're right, but I can't hardly stand by and do nothing."

Cass spoke up. "You'd be more help if you'll join Bill Cleveland."

"How's that?"

"He's praying right now."

"I can do that," Jacob said. "I'll sure be bending the good Lord's ears tonight." He paused. "Lot of talk going around—some real unkind toward your lady. But I never believed a word of it. If I'd been in Mrs. Burk's shoes I'd likely have done the same thing. You boys take care. I'll be on my knees before you're out the door."

Seconds later, Beau and Cass rode off, wool scarves thrashing in the wind.

"We have to split up!" Beau had to shout to make himself heard above the shrieking storm. "Charity and the baby are out there somewhere. I know it, Cass. We'll have a better chance of finding them if we ride in different directions. It's risky to separate, but we're running out of time."

"Agreed!" Cass shouted. "I'll veer east; you take the road to town!"

Beau reached across his saddle horn and clasped his brother's hand. "Be careful."

"You do the same." Their eyes silently conveyed both men's fear.

"If we don't find them before nightfall, go back to the house. I'll meet you there."

Cass nodded.

It made Beau ill to consider the possibility, but he knew if they didn't find Charity and the baby by dark, they would have to wait until morning. By then, it would be too late.

"Don't worry. We'll find them," Cass said.

With a brief nod Beau acknowledged the hope, then reined his horse away and disappeared into swirling snow.

Cass reined in the opposite direction.

Charity woke with a sudden start. She was in some sort of cave. A white one. And she was warmer.

Outside she could hear the wind screeching, but the sound was muted, softer somehow. Less terrifying.

She cautiously flexed her fingers, trying to determine if they were frozen. To her relief, they moved. Though bright red and stiff, she could wiggle the appendages, but the effort was painful.

Her gaze circled the cubicle; she and the baby were completely buried beneath snow.

Buried alive.

She bit back a scream when panic seized her. She had to get out. Their body heat had melted enough space to shift positions. The sled bed provided some protection. A dim light filtered in from overhead.

She clawed at the drifts, trying to dig her way out, but gave up after a few futile attempts. She sank back down beside the baby. It was hopeless. She didn't have the strength to break through the packed layers of snow. Her gaze searched Mary Kathleen's face. The baby's eyes were closed. She lay deathly still. Charity's heart caught in her throat. Was she still breathing? She touched the round baby cheek and found it warm to the touch. Mary Kathleen's breath was feather soft against her hand. Charity sighed in relief. She was sleeping.

Thank You, God. Don't let her die, please.

Somehow she had to keep the baby warm until help came.

Tears pooled in her eyes. She felt a tremendous sadness overtake her, and she laid her head beside the baby and lovingly patted the helpless infant. Help? Who could find them now with the snow piled high above them? No one could see them.

No one would find them until spring thaw.

Charity knew she couldn't survive the elements for long, and she would die. She lay across the foot of the blanket, warming Mary Kathleen with her body heat, peacefully awaiting the moment her life would slip away. She'd heard of small children's lives being saved by parents sacrificing themselves to keep their little ones safe. She was prepared to do that for the precious baby

Letty had left in her care.

Oh Letty, I'm sorry. I should have taken better care of your daughter.

She thought of Beau and how much she loved him. Loved him. She loved him! As much as or more than she'd loved Ferrand. How she wished now that she'd told him how much she cared. She'd started to, many times, but she'd always stopped herself because she was afraid he'd think she wanted him to make a similar declaration. She'd convinced herself he didn't want to hear her foolish prattle, and if he ever said those words she wanted it to be because he meant them, not because he felt obligated to speak. Betsy still lived so deeply in his heart that no other woman would ever be able to exorcise her ghost.

Oh Beau. . .Beau. . .I love you. . . .

Would Ferrand be there to meet her when she passed from this life into the next? And Letty? Would she be waiting to hold her precious daughter? She heard herself chuckling, her voice sounding hollow against the walls of snow. Would she even remember what her first husband looked like? The Bible seemed to indicate that she would, and yet there would be no marriages in heaven.

Would Beau be saddened by her death? Had he made it back before the storm hit? If she survived, would she ever be able to win his love? Her mind turned from tormenting her to playing tricks on her. Strange tricks.

She saw Beau coming to her. She could see the way the corners of his eyes crinkled endearingly, and a sigh escaped her. She eagerly reached out to touch him.

He caught her hand and brought it to his mouth. His eyes, his beautiful blue eyes, probed deeply into hers. They were in a room. . .alone. . .a lovely, quiet room with candles burning low in crystal holders and flowers, lots of beautiful flowers filling the room with their perfumed fragrance.

Her breathing turned shallow. His mouth caressed hers.

Charity could feel her sleep deepening. Her strength slowly ebbed as the illusion wove its way in and out of her mind. In the rare moments when she was lucid, she realized she was hallucinating. . .but oh, such lovely agony.

If she had a pencil and paper she would leave Beau a note. A simple message: "I love you. Forgive me for never telling you so."

She should have told him.

Sometime during the fantasy it occurred to Charity that even if Beau was looking for her, he wouldn't be able to find the sled. Snow completely covered it now.

Feeling as if she were suspended from somewhere far above the sled and looking down, she saw herself struggle out of her petticoat. She watched, spellbound. She saw herself sit up and begin to feel around in the sled for something to slide the dark muslin onto. She'd made the garment from some of Ferrand's old shirts.

Her hand found the shovel she'd brought along, and with stiff fingers she tied the piece of fabric around the handle and hoisted the shovel into an upright position.

In the smooth, unbroken surface of snow, a long makeshift flag began to flap at half-mast.

She lay back, watching the fabric whip in the icy wind. Curling around Mary Kathleen, she closed her eyes. Pictures in her mind faded. She gave herself over to the question that haunted her.

Would she recognize Ferrand? He had blue eyes. . . no, green. . . .

Darkness was closing in.

Beau's horse plowed laboriously through deepening drifts, moving noticeably slower. He knew the animal was close to dropping from exhaustion, and yet he couldn't make himself turn back. He'd die with Charity—but he wasn't turning back until he found her.

He was running out of time, and he blamed himself for listening to Cass. He should be searching south or west, not north. Charity had no reason to go to town. She had supplies to last the winter. Why had he let Cass talk him into riding to Cherry Grove when he knew better?

He pushed on, pausing frequently to cup his hands around his mouth and shout, "Char–i–ty!"

"Char–i–ty!"

Time after time, the wind blocked his effort and flung the words mercilessly back in his face. He nudged his horse forward, his shoulders hunched against the howling gale.

The horse squealed. She stumbled and suddenly went down, her heavy weight dropping into the folds of the wet snow. Beau exclaimed under his breath and waited until the horse struggled to regain her footing.

This was insane. He was going to kill both the horse and himself if he didn't turn around soon; yet he couldn't turn back. *Charity. Mary Kathleen.*

He suddenly realized he was in love with Charity and that child.

He set his jaw. He wasn't going back until he found them. If the storm took his life, so be it. God had already taken a wife and child; this time he was going to fight with everything he had to keep these two.

He steeled himself against the bitter wind and rode on. His gloves had frozen to the reins, but he was past feeling the cold. He was aware of nothing except the pitch and sway of his horse as she labored through building drifts. He ignored the growing ache in his heart.

Hope was starting to dim when he spotted the flag.

The horse slowed. He squinted through the blowing snow at the piece of dark fabric flapping crazily in the wind.

Inching forward in the saddle, he peered through the swirling flakes and then clucked to his horse, and the mare eased forward. Holding the lantern high above his head, he followed the mellow beams across the snow-crusted earth. He inched closer. The flag—the signal—was a woman's petticoat.

Sliding off the horse, he began to run. Deep drifts impeded his progress, but he ran on. When he reached the flag, he dropped down on his knees and began furrowing through the packed snow.

"Charity! Charity? Are you in there?" He ripped off his gloves with his teeth and dug faster.

His fists frantically busted drifts, tears blinding him. Gut-wrenching fear turned to searing white-hot anger and frustration. She had to be in there. She had to be!

"Charity! Are you in there? Answer me!" Snow flew in a furious white cloud.

Howling wind hammered him. He bowed his head, turning his back on the gale, and continued to dig, his hands frantically clawing at the packed snow. She was there, beneath the heavy drift. He could sense her presence.

God, help me. Let me be in time.

Snow had not only drifted in dense ridges, the wind had twisted it until it was almost impossible to tunnel through.

When his hand hit the side of the sled, his motion ceased. For a moment he sat back on his heels, breathing heavily. Large red stains dotted the snow. His hands were raw and bleeding.

Then he heard her.

A weak voice snatched away by the wind, but recognizable, and the sweetest sound this side of heaven. "Here—I'm here, Beau."

His sobs turned to hysterical laughter, and he dug faster, unaware of the cuts on his hands, scooping the snow up in large armfuls and flinging it wildly into the wind. He shouted her name. "Charity!"

"Chariiittty!"

He saw her hand first and then caught a glimpse of her sleeve. Alternately laughing and crying, he uncovered her and the baby and caught them both up tightly to his chest.

"Oh God. . .oh God. . .thank You. . . . Thank You. . . ."

He held the baby in one arm and covered Charity's face with kisses, clasping her close against his chest then releasing her long enough to claim her mouth again and again.

"I didn't think I was going to find you." He cupped her face with one hand, meeting her eyes in the weak lantern rays. "Are you hurt? Are you all right?"

"I'm. . .co-co-ld, B-B-B-ea-u."

"Oh sweetheart, I'll take you home where it's warm," he promised.

"Th-th-the ba-b-by?"

Beau gently uncovered the thick layers of blankets to encounter a tiny pug nose, which suddenly wrinkled in disgust at being awakened so abruptly. Mary Kathleen let out a wail that threatened to permanently impair his hearing.

The familiar bellow was music to Beau's ears. His face broke into a radiant smile. "She's fine!"

He pulled Charity and Mary Kathleen back to his chest and

squeezed his eyes shut in pure joy as he held his family tightly in the shelter of his arms.

"Both my girls are fine, Lord." His voice broke before he finished in a ragged whisper. "This time I'm not going to be forgetting Your mercy."

Chapter 16

Beau shifted Charity, who still held tightly to Mary Kathleen, to one arm and knocked on the Olsons' front door. They'd made it this far. God had been good. Snowdrifts nearly blocked the road now, but once he got Jack unhooked from the sled, he'd put Charity and Mary Kathleen on his horse, and they'd managed to come through the storm with their lives intact.

Reverend Olson opened the door, shock registering on his features. "Beau? Come in!" He quickly summoned Rebecca, and they welcomed the half-frozen family in from the storm's fury.

Beau explained what had happened, but before he had finished, Rebecca was helping Charity and the baby into the bedroom. Reverend Olson was already pulling on his coat to go for the doctor.

He returned within the hour after rooting Dr. Paulson from a deep sleep. The good doctor had then made the cold trek to the parsonage to examine the weary travelers.

An hour later the doctor entered the parlor and set his worn leather bag down on the piecrust table. A fire blazed high in the hearth, and the smell of fresh coffee permeated the air. "I think they're both mighty lucky," he told a haggard-looking Beau. "Another hour out there in this storm and it could have been too late."

Exhausted, Beau could barely keep his eyes open. The fresh

cuts on his hands were pure agony, but he hung on the doctor's words. "They'll be all right?"

The doctor smiled. "Mother and child are doing fine. With proper care, they should regain full strength."

Beau slumped with relief, realizing he had been holding his breath. "Thank you. . . . Thank you, Doctor."

"Don't thank me, young man; only God could have pulled this one off. I'm glad I could help. That's a right nice family you have there, but I'm guessing you already know that."

Beau knew his eyes were brimming with tears, and he didn't care.

Rebecca came in from settling the infant. "Happen to have an extra piece of chocolate cake, Harlow. Couldn't interest you in it, could I?"

"You know I'd risk any kind of weather for a piece of your chocolate cake, Rebecca. Thank you; I'd love some."

"How about you, Beau—won't you join us?"

"No, thank you, Mrs. Olson. I'd like to talk to my wife, if I could."

Dr. Paulson followed Rebecca to the kitchen. Beau walked to the window and lifted the thin curtain. The storm still raged, but he felt an inner peace that he hadn't known in a very long time.

Thank You, God, for giving them back to me. I'm going to take good care of them from now on. I've learned my lesson; I should have studied Your Word more when I lost Bets, not less. I should have held on to hope instead of bitterness.

"Who comforteth us in all our tribulation, that we may be able to comfort them which are in any trouble, by the comfort wherewith we ourselves are comforted of God. For as the sufferings of Christ abound in us, so our consolation also aboundeth by Christ."

How many times had Beau heard Ma recite 2 Corinthians 1?

Enough for the verse to have stuck with him. The wisdom had gotten lost in his grief. It was going to be up to him to regain his trust, but he could do it. God had given him another chance for love.

He swallowed hard against the lump in his throat. He felt like the prodigal had come home.

"You say your brother's still out there?" Reverend Olson inquired.

"I hope that he's found shelter by now. I've been praying that when it got dark, he returned to the cabin." Cass was a reasonable man; he'd have given up the search at dark, as agreed.

Reverend Olson cleared his throat. "By the way, Beau, I've heard from Ansel's and Letty's families."

Beau turned slowly from the window. "And?"

"It turns out that Ansel's father passed away a few months back. Phedra Latimer is finding it hard to cope with her husband's death. I'm afraid she'll be unable to take care of Mary Kathleen at this time."

"And Letty's kinfolks?"

Reverend Olson sighed. "Letty's parents would love to take the child, but poor health makes it impossible. They regretted to inform me that they are not able to care for a youngster." He shrugged apologetically. "Children are for the young and healthy, Beau."

Beau turned back to the window, deeply troubled. "Put Mary Kathleen with strangers?"

"They wouldn't be strangers. They'd be Letty's kin. Of course, Mary Kathleen would have to grow to love them. And then there'd be the problem of sending the child back East, but these decisions don't have to be decided tonight. You're sure I can't have Rebecca fix you a bite to eat?"

"No, thank you. I'd like to see my wife."

"Then you run along. Rebecca and I will look after the baby. Mary Kathleen's sleeping soundly. The doctor says she shouldn't have any lasting effects from her adventure." A tender light entered the reverend's faded gray eyes. "You know, Beau, it was the Lord's hand that allowed that sled to be buried in the snow. It surrounded your wife and the child and conserved their body heat. It saved their lives."

Beau's eyes met the reverend's. "I know where the credit belongs, sir."

"Just wanted to make sure you did." Reverend Olson smiled. "See you in church when weather permits?"

"Yes, sir, you will."

"Now, I believe you have a wife you want to see."

Beau smiled. "Yes, sir."

"Then why are you hanging around here talking to an old codger like me? Go to her, young man!"

Charity's room was dark when he stepped inside. She stirred and opened her eyes as he cautiously approached the bed.

"Hi."

"Hi. I thought you might be asleep."

She sighed. "Just getting warm."

The bed creaked when he sat down on the side of the mattress.

"Baby all right?" she asked.

"She's sleeping. Reverend Olson said he and Rebecca would look after her tonight. You need your rest. Are you warm enough?"

She nodded. "Finally."

"Good."

Charity reached out and gently took hold of his hand. "Lie down beside me."

Beau shook his head. "I—I don't want to disturb you. The doctor says you need your rest." He couldn't see her face in the dark, but the plea in her voice drew him like a moth to a flame.

"Please. I need you beside me."

He carefully eased to his side and lay down beside her. Then he wrapped his arms around her small body and drew her close.

She sighed, burying her face in the warmth of his chest. "I love you, Beau."

"I love you, too, Charity."

His mouth searched and found hers, and he kissed her with a passion that words could not convey. The will to fight was gone. The war that had been raging inside for over a year was over.

"Tomorrow we go home." Beau sat on the side of Charity's bed, an air of excitement in his voice.

"I know, and I can hardly wait."

She had weathered the close call amazingly well, and this afternoon the doctor had pronounced her fit enough to travel. Beau leaned over to steal a kiss, his eyes sparkling like a small boy's. "Cass was afraid you wouldn't make it home before he left, so he brought you and Mary Kathleen a present by this afternoon."

"He did? A present for me! Where is it?"

"Not so fast." Beau held up his hand. "I'd like to give you my present before you open his."

Her eyes widened with excitement. "Why?"

"Because mine's better than his."

"Beau!" She laughed. "How do you know?"

He shrugged. "I asked him what he got you, he told me, and so I know mine's the best."

"You're terrible."

"Yeah, I know that, too." He grinned and stretched out beside her, waving a small, wrapped box before her eyes.

She started to reach for the box, and he playfully drew it back. "Not so fast."

"I thought you wanted me to open it."

"I do, but I want you to beg for it first."

"Beg for it?" Charity laughed. "It's that nice?"

"I think so."

She rolled over to face him and traced a lazy finger across his cheek and over the outline of his lips. "Please, please, please, please, please. How's that?"

"So-so."

Her eyes softened to liquid pools. "Oh Beau. I love you. I don't need presents; God has given me everything I ever wanted."

Catching her hand, he held it tightly. "When I thought I'd lost you and Mary Kathleen I knew—well, again I thought I didn't have anything left to live for." His voice cracked with raw emotion, and he remembered what it had been like looking for her, the gripping fear that had ridden through the night with him. He saw the tears in her eyes.

Her lips quivered. "I love you so very much. That's all I could think of while I waited for you to find me and the baby—and how I so desperately wished that I had told you of my love, long before now."

Beau toyed absently with a strand of her hair, intrigued by its softness. "You know, I'm kind of glad it happened this way."

"What way?"

"This way. God showed me how easily I could lose love again. I'd been a blind, stubborn, bitter fool until two days ago." He squeezed her hand tightly. "I'm sorry. I should have told you how I felt sooner, but I still had Bets in my heart."

It was a hard thing for a bride to hear, but she had to know.

"And now?"

"Now I've let her go. Though I suppose she'll be with me from time to time, I realized that God had given me a second chance at love." He paused, still trying to sort through his new feelings.

Charity smiled. "I don't resent your feelings for Betsy. Betsy and Ferrand were our first loves, and they'll always hold a special place in our hearts. But we're older now. We share a different kind of love. I'm content with that."

"I love you, Charity. Deeply and forever. Maybe not in the same boyish way that I loved Bets, but what I feel for you in some ways is bigger and more—well, downright scary, to be honest."

She grinned. "And that frightens you?"

He pulled her ear closer, whispering, "It should scare the dickens out of you. Now, what about Ferrand?"

"I will forever hold him in my heart." Her hand reached out to gently caress her husband's face. "He was my first love; you are my last."

He reached for the small box. "This is your wedding gift."

She took the box and slowly slipped off the ribbon. "I'm afraid I have nothing to give you. I was going into town to buy raisins to make you a pie when the storm came up."

"You almost got yourself killed over raisins?" She was doing that for him? The realization only made him love her more.

"I wanted to do something special for a wedding gift. You saved my life. . .and I had nothing to offer you."

He shook his head. "You've given me back my life. That's enough."

Smiling, she removed the paper and opened the box. Her eyes widened, and she gently fingered the emerald brooch. "Oh Beau."

"I hope you like it. I got it at the mercantile the day we got married, and I've been waiting for the right time to give it to you. A couple of squaws traded it for food and blankets." He reached out and gently stemmed the moisture suddenly streaming down her cheeks. "The color of the stones reminded me of your eyes."

Charity cradled the brooch in her hands, Ferrand's grandmother's brooch, and then pressed it to her heart. Laughing Waters and Little Fawn must have tired of the trinket and traded it off. She wouldn't dream of telling Beau that long ago another man had given her the same gift; Beau's gift meant just as much. She would cherish the token as deeply as she'd treasured Ferrand's gift.

"My beloved husband, have I told you how very much I love you?"

"Yes, Mrs. Claxton, but I'd have no objections to hearing it again." He smiled. "For the rest of my life."

&

"I still say you should wait till all the snow's melted." Charity frowned when she passed the sack of ham sandwiches up to Cass. "It's February. There could be another storm any day!"

Cass glanced at Beau and shook his head. "Your woman frets too much."

Beau grinned. "I love her anyway."

"I've hung around over a week waiting for you to get home, and now you don't want me to leave." Cass grinned and then softened his banter. "My ankle's fine now—strangest thing—the swelling's gone down, and I need to be getting home before another blizzard hits. You two don't want me underfoot all winter now, do you?"

"No," Beau said.

Charity shrugged. She couldn't put those poultices on him forever.

"That's what I thought." Cass climbed into the sleigh and tapped his hat back on his head. "I'll be seeing you again one of these days. Ma'll have me dragging another sledload of pickles and preserves out to you, thinking you all will be starving to death."

Charity pulled the blanket up closer around Mary Kathleen to shield her from the sharp wind. "You're welcome any time. And thank you again for the lovely handkerchief. I'll wear it close to my heart."

Beau leaned over and kissed his wife. "I'm going to ride out a ways with Cass. I'll be back."

She smiled. "Take your time. We'll be waiting."

He swung into the saddle. "Let's go, little brother. We're burning daylight."

The sled and rider moved out of the yard down the snowy pathway. For several miles the two brothers rode in compatible silence. Then as they crested a small rise, they reined their horses to a stop. Beau swung out of his saddle and stood beside the sleigh.

"Well, looks like I'll be going it alone from here on."

"Yeah. I'd best be getting back to Charity and the baby. Tell Ma I won't be coming home this spring."

Cass grinned and reached for the reins. "Didn't figure you would be."

"Yeah." Beau stared contentedly at the snow-covered plains. "Sorta feels like I am home."

"You got yourself a fine woman," Cass admitted. "You going to adopt Mary Kathleen?"

"Figuring on it. Then planning on having a couple more sisters, and maybe two or three brothers to look after the girls."

Cass chuckled. "That's good. Ma likes being a grandmother."

"Yeah, can't wait till she sees my baby." Beau met his brother's gaze evenly. "Mary Kathleen's about the cutest little thing you've ever seen, isn't she?"

"She's cute, all right."

Beau's grin widened. "I think so, too. One of these days you'll settle down and have one almost as cute," he predicted.

Cass hooted merrily. "Don't count on it. No woman's going to rope and hog-tie me until I'm good and ready."

Beau shook his head skeptically. "Don't be too sure. A thing like that can slip up on a man before he knows it."

"Not on me, it won't." Cass released the brake. "Best be moving on. I'm burning daylight."

"You take care. Tell Cole and Wynne we'll write. Maybe they can make the trip out to see us someday."

"Sure thing. You behave yourself, big brother."

"You do the same, little brother."

Cass shot him an arrogant grin. "Not a chance."

Beau threw his head back and laughed, his merriment rumbling deep in his chest.

Cocky kid, he thought affectionately. *Someday some woman will come along and tie his tail in a bowknot.*

He took a deep breath and held it, tipping his face up to drink in the cold sunshine. It felt good to be alive. Real good.

A Note from the Author

Dear reader,

I hope you have enjoyed Beau's story. It's an adventure telling the stories of the lives and loves of these Wild West Brides for you. I pray the struggles they endure and the lessons they learn will cheer you. The men have their troubles—and their fears—but I hope I've shown them taking comfort in the knowledge that they're never without help in their faith walk. And neither are we.

If you identify with Beau and his loss of hope, don't feel alone. There are seasons in all of our lives when we struggle to keep the faith—even this author. When you need a good dose of God's Word during difficult times, here are some of my favorite scripture passages: John 14:27, John 14:1, Hebrews 10:35–36, and Galatians 6:9.

God bless you! And keep the hope—joy comes in the morning.

THE MAVERICK

BOOK 3

Prologue

Kansas frontier, 1868

The wind had a sharp bite to it, but overhead the sun shone brightly on the eastern rim. Cass Claxton guessed a man couldn't ask for much more in the first week of February. The sled zipped along the icy road, and a smile formed at the corners of his mouth. He set the brim of his hat lower on his forehead, and his cobalt-blue eyes surveyed the endless expanse of Kansas sky.

The visit with his brother Beau and Beau's wife, Charity, had been good, but he was eager to get home before another storm hit. Winters in Missouri were contrary, but he didn't think they could hold a candle to Kansas blizzards. Beau had nearly lost his wife and baby daughter last week when a whiteout had taken them by surprise and almost cost them their lives. The good Lord had smiled on Beau that day. He'd lost one wife to a rattlesnake bite; Cass didn't think his brother could stand another tragedy.

No doubt about it—the newly formed Claxton family was blessed. Cass remembered the solemn way Reverend Olson had reminded the family that it had been nothing short of a miracle that Charity and Mary Kathleen had survived after being buried in snow for five hours by that sudden storm.

His smile returned when he thought about how happy his

brother was now. And it was high time. It had taken a long time for Beau to get over the death of his first wife, Betsy, but thanks to the good Lord and a sweet little Kansas widow by the name of Charity, it now looked like he'd make it just fine.

The way Beau had loved his first wife and now Charity sometimes puzzled Cass. As far as women were concerned, Cass could take them or leave them. And he'd done just that, more times than he cared to admit.

There was no way a woman was going to hog-tie and brand him. He'd never met a woman he'd want to be around much longer than a week—with maybe the exception of Wynne Elliot. Now there was a woman.

The image of her crimson hair and dancing sea-green eyes came back to haunt him. He probably should have married her when he'd had the chance, but there was no use crying over spilled milk. Cole, his eldest brother, had married Wynne, and Cass had to admit he'd never seen a happier couple.

Of course, Beau's wife, Charity, wasn't all that bad, either. She'd make Beau a fine woman—no arguing that point—but marrying was the last thing on Cass's mind. He wasn't anywhere close to settling down and raising a family. He had a peck of wild oats to sow before any woman dragged him to the altar—if one ever did.

He gave a sharp whistle and set the horse into a fast trot. The runners ate up the frozen ground. He began whistling under his breath. Directly ahead he spotted four riders approaching. The horses were coming fast, their hooves thundering over the packed snow. Cass wondered where they were headed in such a hurry.

The riders drew closer, and Cass frowned, noting that one of the arrivals was that infuriating Susanne McCord.

The woman had been nothing but a thorn in his side since the day he'd watched her throw a temper tantrum in Miller's

Mercantile. He'd hoped last week's blizzard had gotten her, and then checked his uncharitable thoughts. He'd like to make it out of Kansas without running into her again, but it looked like his luck had soured.

He decided to politely tip his hat and ride on by and was about to do just that when the foursome reined up in his path. Caught by surprise, Cass hauled back on the reins, bringing the sled to a sudden stop.

Leviticus McCord; his daughter, Susanne; Reverend Olson; and a large man wearing a tin star sat stiffly in their saddles, staring back at Cass.

Cass touched the brim of his hat. "Reverend."

"Mr. Claxton."

The horses danced about, breathing frosty plumes into the brisk morning air.

"What brings you out this way so early in the day?" Cass asked. Silently seething, he ignored the young woman on the dapple-gray mare. His blood still boiled whenever he thought of how Susanne McCord had hauled off and hit him between the eyes. Then the silly twit had had the gall to look him up a few days later, at his brother's house, and offer him the exorbitant fee of five—even six—hundred dollars to take her back to her aunt in Saint Louis.

He'd flatly refused, and none too nicely. He wouldn't take Susanne McCord to a catfight, let alone back to Missouri, and he'd wasted no time in telling her so.

It had been dark by the time she had accepted his no. She had started to cry. She'd pleaded that she felt too faint and frightened to find her way back to town. Cass had had no recourse but to let her stay the night under Beau's roof, but he'd sent her packing at first light.

Now here she was again, looking down at him with that

superior smirk that made him so mad he couldn't see straight.

"We're looking for you!" Leviticus interrupted before the pastor could speak.

"Me?" Cass's grin slowly faded. Why would Leviticus McCord be looking for him?

The sheriff motioned for Cass to comply. "Mr. Claxton, would you mind climbin' down off that sled?"

"It depends. . . ." Cass glanced back to Revered Olson expectantly. "What's going on?"

The reverend apologetically met Cass's gaze. "I believe you've met. . .uh. . .hummruph. . .uh. . .Miss McCord?"

Cass spared a glance in Susanne's direction. "I've met her."

Susanne nodded from beneath the veil of an ostrich-plumed hat, her violet eyes mocking him.

"Met her? Met her!" Turning scarlet, Leviticus shouted louder, "I should hope he's met her?"

Cass's eyes snapped to the irate father. "I've met her."

"Cass. . .uh. . .this is most difficult, son," Reverend Olson began in an uneasy tone. "Would you mind to step down for a moment?"

Susanne appeared to be sniffing loudly into a lace hankie. Her sobs shook the mass of waist-length blond ringlets, and the silken strands of hair shone like spun gold in the morning light.

Cass wrapped the reins around the brake and in a lithe motion landed on the ground. Something was wrong. He could feel it. "What's the problem?"

The men dismounted and stared at Cass for a moment. Then Leviticus exploded, "What's the problem?"

Cass realized where Susanne had inherited her volatile nature. The five-foot-two retired circuit judge was now hopping around in the road with his fists balled into tight knots.

"What's the problem?" Leviticus repeated, pausing long enough to draw an indignant breath before shaking his finger under Cass's nose. "I'll tell you what the problem is, you. . .you young whippersnapper! You sullied my daughter, and you're going to be held accountable!" He stomped his left foot, nearly dislodging his felt bowler.

Cass shifted his stance to eye the judge sourly. "I've what?"

"Sullied my daughter!" Leviticus shrieked. "Disgraced, soiled, tarnished!"

Cass's gaze narrowed. "I know what the word means, sir."

"I should hope so!"

"Now, now, gentlemen, let's all calm down," Reverend Olson advised. "I'm sure we can settle this matter without hollering to raise the dead."

Cass met the pastor's eyes. "What is he talking about?"

The reverend looked to Susanne then to Cass. "Well, it seems that you and. . .you and Miss McCord spent a night together recently. Am I correct?" Cass could see that the reverend sincerely hoped that he wasn't. The preacher was a friend of Beau and Charity's, and Cass didn't like to see him so uncomfortable.

"Spent the night with her?" Cass shot a reproachful eye toward the woman in question. "No, sir, I did not spend the night with her—not like she's insinuating."

"Oh yes, you did!" Susanne accused. She sniffed loudly.

Cass shifted his weight a second time, and his eyes sternly pinpointed her. "I did not." He knew as well as anyone that her accusation meant war. A man didn't trifle with a woman in these parts unless he married her.

Susanne heaved a tolerant sigh and dabbed at her streaming eyes. "I told you he would take this attitude, gentlemen."

"Now hold on a minute." Cass turned back to Reverend Olson.

"I don't know what she's told you, but nothing happened that night—"

"So, you did spend the night with my daughter!" Leviticus accused.

"I didn't spend the night with her. My brother and his wife were present—"

"She was gone all night!" Leviticus bellowed. "How do you explain that?"

"She was there because she felt too 'faint' to make the trip back to town. I was there. . .but so were my brother, Beau, and his wife. If you won't take my word for it, you can ask them. . . ." Cass's voice trailed off when he began to realize that the more he tried to explain, the more he appeared to incriminate himself.

Leviticus glanced pointedly at the sheriff, and Cass could see the wheels in his mind turning. The entire town of Cherry Grove knew that Beau Claxton had stayed with the widow Burk months before he'd married her. Cass broke a sweat, though it was a cold day.

"Papa"—Susanne turned watery eyes on Leviticus—"it would be a waste of time to ride all the way to the Claxton place; I'm feeling delicate this morning. The wind's so cold." She shivered. "You know perfectly well that Beau Claxton would say anything needed to protect his no-good brother." Her voice trailed to a whine. "Can't we settle this matter quickly?" She lifted one hand to her brow as if faint.

Cass shot her a scathing look. "Susanne, this is not funny." The seriousness of the situation was beginning to sink in, and he was getting uneasy. And mad. Just plain mad at the woman. "Nothing happened the night you stayed at Beau and Charity's, and you know it. I should have sent you packing, and I would have if you hadn't lied to me when you said you were feeling faint."

He shifted his attention to Leviticus. "Sir, your daughter approached me that night and offered me five hundred dollars to take her to Saint Louis—even upped the offer to six hundred."

Leviticus's face turned varying shades of scarlet.

"I said no." Cass didn't mind telling on the silly twit. Now Leviticus would see how thoroughly rotten a daughter he had.

The distraught father leveled his gaze on his daughter. "Did you do that, Susanne? Did you offer this man six hundred dollars to take you to Saint Louis?"

Susanne gasped, batting long black eyelashes. "Gracious no, Papa! Where would I get that kind of money?"

Leviticus turned to Cass. "Where would she get that kind of money?" Cass figured that Leviticus knew his daughter's penchant for lying, but he felt obliged to ask.

"I don't know!" Cass snapped. "She offered me money; she didn't say where she was going to get it."

"Mr. Claxton." Leviticus stretched to his full height. His diminutive stature wasn't all that intimidating, but it struck the proper respect in Cass. "Susanne doesn't have six hundred dollars. Great day, man! I barely have six hundred dollars! That's a fortune!"

"I understand, sir." He did understand. Six hundred dollars was a lot of money, and the little schemer had been lying about that, too! "But that's what she offered me—six hundred. . . ." Cass felt a sinking sensation when he began to realize that he was in deep trouble this time.

Leviticus straightened, tugging his velvet waistcoat into place. "If my daughter says she didn't offer you the money, then I must assume she's telling the truth."

"But she's lying!"

Leviticus shot his daughter an exasperated look but continued. "Whether she offered the money or not, she says you took advantage of her that evening, and I can't take the risk. You have to make an honest woman of her. Restore her integrity."

"Now, hold on—"

"No, you wait a minute," Leviticus said, his eyes narrowing. "You're about to take a wife, son."

The conversation had slipped beyond the point of reason. Cass whirled and was about to climb back into the sled when he felt the barrel of a shotgun tapping his right shoulder. He slowly turned to meet the sheriff's cold, assessing eyes.

"You want to take a few minutes to reconsider your hasty decision, son?"

Cass froze. The clear implications in the man's tone made him rethink a quick escape.

"Son"—Reverend Olson reassuringly laid a hand on Cass's shoulder—"you best think this thing through."

"But, Reverend." Cass stared back helplessly. "I haven't been near Susanne McCord. . . . She hit me. . .and it left a knot the size of a goose egg." The reverend had to know the extent of what he was dealing with!

Reverend Olson nodded. "In Cherry Grove, we tend to take the woman's word in matters of this delicate nature. I'd suggest you marry the girl, and then try to resolve the matter in a more satisfactory manner." His eyes indicated the overwrought father.

Marry Susanne McCord? Cass would rather throw a rope over the nearest tree and hang her!

Leviticus helped his daughter off the mare. She rested her slender hand on his arm. "You do believe me, don't you, Papa? I wouldn't story about an awful thing like this. I warned Mr. Claxton he'd surely be facin' my papa's wrath. That's what I said. . .but I do declare he wouldn't listen. . . ." She broke off tearfully and buried her face in a lace handkerchief.

Leviticus wrapped a protective arm around her trembling shoulders. "I believe you, daughter." His chin firmed. "Sheriff," he prompted in a righteous tone.

The sheriff stepped up, and Cass looked at Reverend Olson pleadingly. "Are you actually going to let them do this to me?"

The clergyman sighed and opened his Bible. "Do you, Cass Claxton, take Susanne McCord to be your lawfully wedded wife?"

"No, I do not!"

Reverend Olson turned patiently to the bride. "Do you, Susanne McCord, take Cass Claxton to be your lawfully wedded husband?"

She sniffed, daintily blew her nose. "I suppose I'll just have to, under these dreadful circumstances." Her lovely amethyst eyes peered at Leviticus woefully. "Don't you agree, Papa?"

Her father patted her hand. "You just relax, darlin'. Papa will see to it that your virtue is protected."

"Virtue—that's rich!" Cass exploded. "She doesn't know the meaning of the word!"

"Oh Papa. He's just so dreadful. Do I really have to marry him?" Susanne peeked at Cass from behind her handkerchief.

"Lady, all you have to do is tell the truth—if you have it in you," Cass said through gritted teeth. He'd never raised a hand against a woman, but given half a chance, he'd gladly strangle Susanne McCord at that instant and worry about forgiveness later.

Reverend Olson droned on, apparently hoping to dispense with the unpleasant matter as quickly as possible. "Do you promise to love, cherish, and obey, till death do you part?"

"Welllll. . .I. . .I suppose I can. . .if I must. . . ." Susanne glanced at Cass. "I do."

Reverend Olson turned back to Cass. "Do you promise to

comfort, honor, and keep her, in sickness and in health—"

"I wouldn't pull a mad dog off her!"

"—forsaking all others, till death do you part?"

Cass took a deep breath and closed his mouth. Nothing short of a miracle was going to stop this atrocity. Didn't the woman have one ounce of respect for marriage—for God's Word? A man and a woman didn't marry lightly.

The sheriff lifted the barrel of the gun a notch higher. "Say you're gonna forsake all others till death do you part, boy, or I'll blow a hole through your chest."

"I will not."

The sheriff pressed the shotgun firmly against Cass's rib cage. Cass sent a frantic look at Reverend Olson.

Reverend Olson sighed. "You'd better say you'll take her for your wife, son. The marriage won't be legal otherwise."

The gun nudged him again. "Wanna live to see thirty, boy?"

Cass thought about it: death—or life with Susanne McCord. Still he didn't answer. He felt the gun press tighter in his side.

"All right! I do!"

Reverend Olson snapped the Bible shut. "I now pronounce you man and wife." He lifted his brows hopefully. "I don't suppose you'd like to kiss the bride?"

Cass stared stoically ahead. "I don't want to kiss the bride."

The reverend sighed. "I didn't think so."

Five minutes later, Leviticus stored the last of Susanne's baggage in the back of the sled.

"Take care of my daughter." Leviticus reached up to shake his new son-in-law's hand. Cass sullenly ignored the offer.

Leviticus laid a small pouch filled with several gold pieces on the seat beside Cass. "She's a good girl," Leviticus told him in a hushed whisper. "Just a mite determined at times."

Cass thought that had to be the understatement of the year.

Reverend Olson, the sheriff, and Leviticus remounted. With a nod, they prepared to leave.

"You be sure and write your papa the moment you reach Saint Louis," Leviticus reminded.

"I promise. You take care now! I love you!" Susanne McCord Claxton blew kisses.

The small party turned their horses and trotted off in the direction of Cherry Grove.

Cass whistled sharply, and the sled lurched ahead. "You are not going to get away with this," he warned.

Smiling, she slipped her arm through his. "I believe I just did, dear husband."

"Don't call me that."

"Why? I'll grant you permission to call me your wife. . .but only until we reach Saint Louis." She laughed merrily.

"I'll be calling you a lot of things before we reach Saint Louis," he promised.

"Tsk, tsk, such a sore loser! You should have accepted my gracious offer when I first offered it," Susanne pointed out, primly adjusting her skirts. "You'd have been much better off—six hundred dollars richer and still single."

"You don't have six hundred dollars!"

"But you don't know that for certain," she pointed out.

"Your own pa said you didn't."

"My own pa doesn't necessarily know everything," she reasoned. "You'll discover, Mr. Claxton, it's so much simpler to let me have my way."

"And you'll discover your conniving ways are going to be dumped on your aunt's porch so fast it'll make your head spin," Cass snapped. "I'll take you to Saint Louis, but once we're there this absurdity is over. This so-called marriage will be annulled. Immediately."

Susanne twisted in the seat and waved her handkerchief at Leviticus, who by now was a speck in the distance. "Bye-bye, Papa. I'll write real soon!" She turned back to the conversation. "And you'll find that all I wanted in the first place was to go to Saint Louis." She heaved a sigh of contentment. "I'll be only too happy to have the marriage annulled, darling, the moment I reach my aunt Estelle's. However," she said, pausing to smile at him, "it was truly a touching ceremony—wouldn't you agree?"

Rotten. Cass had no doubt about it. The girl was just plain core rotten.

Chapter 1

Six years later
St. Louis, Missouri

Thunder cracked then rolled along the quiet residential street. A young woman hurried on her way, her hand placed strategically on top of her head to prevent the gusty wind from carrying off her plucky straw hat.

Susanne McCord didn't mind the inclement weather, but she did wish the rain could have held off for another thirty minutes. Fat drops peppered down on the cobblestoned streets, scenting the air with the smell of summer rain.

She smiled, thinking of the changes the past six years had brought. She'd arrived at her aunt Estelle Merriweather's a spoiled, flighty, temperamental young woman yearning for fun and parties. Instead she had found a dedicated woman struggling to maintain a small orphanage in her home. Now her aunt was gone, and Susanne was in charge of the children.

Her shoes skipped gingerly over the gathering puddles, her eyes scanning the numbers printed on the towering houses. The three-story frame dwellings nearly took her breath with their lovely stained-glass windows and hand-carved doorways.

When lightning flashed as bright as a noonday sun, she peered at the address scrawled on a scrap of paper that was fast becoming soggy in her hand.

Her feet flew purposefully up the walk as the heavens opened to deliver a torrential downpour. Pausing to catch her breath, Susanne stood for a moment under the shelter of the porch eaves, watching the rain pelt down. She noticed the old lamplighter, already soaked to the skin, hastily making his way down the street.

She called out, inviting him to take cover with her. He turned and scurried up the walk, his head bent low against the driving rain.

"Terrible, isn't it?" Susanne commented as the white-haired gentleman removed his top hat and shook the rain off.

" 'Tis for certain, little lass." He grinned, and his wizened face broke into a wreath of wrinkles. He set his lantern down and extended a friendly hand. "Thaddeus McDougal here."

Susanne returned his greeting. "Susanne McCord. It looks like we're in for a good one." Susanne had never acknowledged her married name, nor did she ever plan to. Since their journey from Kansas to Saint Louis, she had not seen Cass Claxton again. They had parted on bad terms, with Susanne declaring she would see him again when hades froze over.

Thaddeus sighed. "Aye, it does at that, lass."

"Well, we can always use the rain."

" 'Tis true, 'tis true." Thaddeus glanced about the massive porch, mild curiosity on his face. "Wasn't aware the old house had finally been sold."

"Oh, I don't think it has." Susanne noticed that the house was not in the best of repair. The porch sagged, the paint was peeling, and several shutters flapped haphazardly in the blowing rain. It didn't matter, though—it looked beautiful to her. "I'm here to see about acquiring its use."

"Eh? Well. . ." Thaddeus's pale gaze roamed over the peeling porch ceiling. "Old Josiah would be upset if he could see his house now. Used to brim with love and laughter, it did." His eyes grew misty with remembrance. "Josiah never had children of his own, you know, but he took in every stray he could find. Fine man, he was. The world lost a bit of sunshine when Josiah Thorton was laid to rest."

"I never knew him," Susanne admitted.

"Fine man." Thaddeus sighed again. "Well now, little lass, why be you tryin' to acquire such a big old barn of a house?"

"I'm looking for a place big enough to be a home for nine children."

"Nine children!" Thaddeus took a step back, eyes wide. "Beg pardon, miss, but you don't look old enough to have nine wee bairns."

Susanne smiled at his obvious bewilderment. "I'm overseer of a small orphanage. The bank has been forced to sell the home we're presently living in, and someone mentioned that this house was empty. I've looked unsuccessfully for weeks for somewhere to move the children, so when I heard about the house, I hurried right over." Her forehead creased with a frown. "I'm sorry to hear the owner's passed on."

Losing Aunt Estelle's house had been a blow, but running an orphanage was not a profitable business venture, and Estelle had been forced to mortgage her home for operating expenses.

Now Susanne was desperate to find somewhere to shelter the children.

"Aye, Josiah died about a year ago."

"Then his family will be disposing of the property?"

Thaddeus frowned. "Josiah didn't have any family—leastways, not that I know about. Rumor has it that he had a business associate, though. Could be he can tell you what's to be done with the house."

"And how might I contact this business associate?" Susanne hoped that wouldn't prove to be another time-consuming delay. The orphanage had to be out of its present location by the end of the month.

"Well. . ." Thaddeus stepped over to the legal notice nailed to the porch railing and peered through his wire-rimmed spectacles. "It says here that anyone wanting information about this property should contact a Mr. Daniel Odolp, attorney-at-law."

Susanne took a small pad from her purse and prepared to scribble down the address. "Does Mr. Odolp reside here in Saint Louis?"

"Aye, his office is close by." Thaddeus read the address aloud for her.

"Oh, that's not far."

"Only a wee jaunt."

"I wonder if Mr. Odolp would still be in his office."

Thaddeus reached into his waistcoat and took out a large pocket watch. He flipped open the case and held the face of the watch toward the receding light. "Depends on how late he works. It's nigh on six o'clock."

Six o'clock. Susanne doubted Mr.Odolp would be working this late, but since she'd be passing by his office anyway, it wouldn't hurt to check. "Thank you, Thaddeus." Susanne replaced the pencil and pad in her purse and reassessed the inclement weather. It wasn't raining hard—just a nice, steady drizzle. "I'll go by and see if Mr. Odolp is still in his office," she decided.

"But it's still raining."

Susanne shrugged and gave Thaddeus a bright smile. "I won't melt."

"Well now, you just might. You're an unusually pretty piece of fluff with that flaxen hair and those violet-colored eyes. If you had wings you'd look like an angel," he finished wistfully.

"A half-drowned angel, surely, but I appreciate the lovely compliment. It's been nice talking with you, Thaddeus." Susanne reached down and quickly removed her shoes and stockings then her hat. It was senseless to ruin them. Her toes peeked out from under the hem of her skirt.

Thaddeus grinned. "A barefoot angel. Nice visiting with you, lass." He picked up his lantern. "I must be about my work. It'll be full dark soon."

Susanne watched the old lamplighter step off the porch. A chance meeting, and now they would go their separate ways. One set out to light folks' pathways; the other to find a home for nine waifs and strays.

Aunt Estelle had been a devoted, God-fearing woman who had taken seriously the commandment to give a cup of cold water in Jesus' name. No child had been turned away from her door. When Susanne had worried about unpaid bills, her aunt had quoted her favorite scripture: *"Be kindly affectioned one to another with brotherly love; in honour preferring one another; not slothful in business; fervent in spirit; serving the Lord; rejoicing in hope; patient in tribulation; continuing instant in prayer; distributing to the necessity of saints; given to hospitality. Romans 12:10–13."*

Estelle Merriweather had lived those words. She had been patient when times were hard, diligent in prayer, rejoicing in hope, and believing that God would provide.

Susanne dodged another puddle. Well, she had been as patient as possible, which she acknowledged wasn't saying all that much, and the good Lord knew she spent a prodigious amount of time on her knees. But she felt the hope in her own heart was a feeble candle flame compared to the blazing torch of steadfast confidence that had filled her aunt's every waking moment.

Still, she had learned to trust in God's tender care. She sighed. Hope. It was all she had to cling to.

"Lord, I'm hoping You will help me get that house."

Saint Louis, Missouri, had been the gateway to the West for adventurers, explorers, traders, missionaries, soldiers, and settlers of the trans-Mississippi. Founded in 1764 by Pierre Laclede Liguest, a French trader, it began as a settlement for the development of the fur trade. One hundred and ten years later the area had turned into a thriving waterfront town where cotton, lead, pelts, gold from California, and silver from New Mexico poured through shipping lanes along the busy Mississippi levee. It was said that Saint Louis was admired for her hospitality, good manners, high society, virtue, and the sagacity of her women.

One such woman hurried through the night, intent upon her mission. Susanne could hardly believe her good fortune when she rounded the corner leading to the landing and saw the faint lantern glow spilling from a window of a second-story office.

Prominently displayed in bold black print across the window was DANIEL R. ODOLP, ATTORNEY-AT-LAW.

She covered the short distance to the building and climbed the steep stairs leading to the second floor. A few minutes later she tapped softly on Mr. Odolp's door.

"Yes?" boomed a deep voice that brought nervous flutters to Susanne's stomach. The man sounded like a giant.

"Mr. Odolp?"

"Yes!"

"I. . .I wonder if I might speak with you?"

Susanne heard a shuffling then the sound of chair legs being scraped across a wooden floor. Heavy footsteps approached the doorway.

She swallowed, her throat gone dry. With only a small tallow candle splitting the shadows of the dark, narrow, forbidding hallway, she suddenly wished she'd decided to wait until morning to make her visit. Just as she was turning to leave, the door was abruptly flung open.

"Yes?"

The man standing in the doorway was indeed a giant, at least six feet five. Bushy dark brows nested over his beady black eyes. His face was pockmarked, and his jowls hung heavily on his neck. Sweat beaded profusely on his ruddy forehead.

Susanne thought he was the most unattractive and intimidating man she'd ever encountered.

"Mr. Odolp?" she asked meekly.

"I am Mr. Odolp!" he barked. "Good grief, woman, are you deaf?"

Susanne drew herself up stiffly, perturbed by his appalling lack of gentility. "No, sir, but I shall be if you continue to speak to me in that tone."

"You called my name," he boomed, "and I answered. You implied you wanted to speak to me, and when I opened the door, you asked again if I was Mr. Odolp. Naturally, one would assume you have a hearing problem."

Susanne jumped as he bellowed again.

"Yes, I am Mr. Odolp!"

"Well, you needn't keep shouting." She lifted her skirts and brushed past him.

He closed the door and stalked back to his desk, his eyes grimly surveying her bare feet. "Where are your shoes and stockings, young lady?"

Susanne glanced down and blushed. Her shoes were still in her hand, along with her hat and stockings. She must look as strange to him as he did to her. "I'm sorry. . .it was raining."

"What brings you to my door at this hour?" the attorney demanded, curtly dismissing her stammering explanations. He sat down and reached for a wooden box filled with cigars, selected one, bit off the end, and spat the fragment into the wastebasket. His chair creaked and moaned with the burden of his weight.

Susanne flinched at his lack of manners, but her demeanor remained calm. "I understand that you're handling Josiah Thorton's estate?"

"I am." The lawyer held a burning match to the cigar and puffed, blowing billowing wisps of smoke into the air.

The humidity in the room was stifling. Susanne fanned smoke away from her face. "I was wondering if Josiah's house is going to be sold."

"Which one?"

"Does he have more than one?"

Mr. Odolp turned his face upward and hooted uproariously. "Does he have more than one? You're not serious!"

"I'm afraid I didn't know Mr. Thorton personally."

"I'm afraid you didn't, either." Mr. Odolp fanned out the match, propped his feet on top of his desk, and took a long draw on his cigar. "Exactly which house did you have in mind, honey?"

Susanne felt her hackles rise at his growing insolence. "The one on Elm Street. And my name is Miss McCord, sir."

"Well, what do you want to know, Miss McCord?"

"Some details about the house. For instance, who will be disposing of the property?"

"The house was jointly owned."

"By whom?"

"Josiah and his business partner." Mr. Odolp brought his feet back to the floor and stood up. He lumbered to the files and rummaged for a few minutes before extracting a thick folder. "Since Josiah had no immediate family, we're waiting to see if anyone steps up to claim his estate." Mr. Odolp grinned as though he knew his next remark would certainly shock her. "Josiah's partner wants to be sure there aren't any illegitimate Thortons waiting in the wings."

Susanne was taken aback by his speculation and annoyed at his continuing impudence in a lady's presence. "And if there aren't?"

"Then the Thorton estate reverts to Josiah's partner." Mr. Odolp sighed, and Susanne detected a note of envy. "A sizable fortune, I might add. The partner will then decide what he wants to do with the property."

"Exactly how long will it be before a decision is made?"

"Six months or longer."

Susanne walked to the window and looked down on the rain-slicked streets. She pursed her lips thoughtfully. The house was exactly what she was looking for. Undoubtedly there were others available in town, but none so well suited to her purpose.

She'd hoped to stay in the house longer, but six months would be sufficient. If she could persuade Josiah's partner to lease the house to her for six months, it would alleviate her immediate problem. At least she and the children would have a roof over their heads until she could make other arrangements. "Would it be possible for me to speak with Mr. Thorton's business associate?"

"I see no need to bother him. What is it you want?"

Susanne turned from the window, meeting his beady eyes. "I would prefer to speak to the partner in private, Mr. Odolp."

"And he would prefer you to speak to me."

"Then let me phrase it differently." Susanne let a hint of

coolness creep into her manner. "I insist on speaking to Josiah Thorton's business partner."

"You can't."

Susanne arched one brow. "Does the name Silas Woodson ring a bell with you, Mr. Odolp?"

"The governor?"

"Yes, the governor of Missouri." Susanne tapped her finger on her cheek thoughtfully. "You see, Uncle Silas would be quite distressed to learn of this conversation—"

Daniel Odolp's eyes widened. "Now, now, let's not jump to conclusions. I'll help you if I can." She could almost see him thinking that if the governor was the chit's uncle, he'd better be a bit more cordial. His manner changed abruptly. "I don't like to have my clients bothered. . .but in this particular case I'm sure I can bend my rules a bit."

He reached hastily for a pen and paper. "Now, I'll just jot down the name and address of Josiah's partner. There's no need to tell him where you got this information, of course—"

"None at all."

Daniel slapped the piece of paper into her hand. "How is your uncle these days?"

"Oh, very busy."

"I can imagine."

Susanne nodded. "He and my dear mama are brother and sister, you know."

"No, I didn't know."

"Well, I must be off, Mr. Odolp." She folded the paper carefully and slipped it into her bag. "Thank you for your cooperation."

Daniel rose and extended his hand, his manner noticeably more pleasant. "Always happy to oblige, Miss McCord. Must you be leaving so soon?"

Susanne smiled. "I do wish I had time to stay and chat."

"Stop by anytime. Always happy to visit."

"I will."

Susanne clutched her shoes, stockings, and hat as she walked to the door. She'd pulled it off! Aunt Estelle would have disapproved of her tactics, but under the circumstances even she would tolerate this one tiny deception. "Good evening, Mr. Odolp."

"Good evenin', ma'am. You say hello to the governor for me."

"I will. He'll be ever so pleased to hear from you." Once safely outside, Susanne hurried down the steep stairway and out onto the street, still grinning from her victory. She did have one qualm—mainly that God might not approve of her methods. "Lord, I'm sorry if I sort of edged outside of the bonds of truth, but You know I just have to have that house. There is no other answer."

Pausing to catch her breath under the streetlight, she reached into her purse and carefully unfolded the paper the attorney had given her. Her eyes widened, and she felt a hot flush creep up her neck when she read the name printed in bold black letters.

Cass Claxton.

Cass Claxton! She had to force back a rush of hysteria. Great day in the morning! Cass was Josiah Thorton's business partner?

Late-afternoon sun spilled across the Aubusson carpets in the elegant room. Golden rays bathed the fine furniture and the tasteful art hanging on pewter-colored walls. Dark mahogany bookcases contained the finest array of world literature. Cass Claxton was a wealthy man in earthly ways, but when it came to keeping a woman happy he was poor as a widow's mite.

"It is getting late," the young woman observed.

"So it is." He shuffled through a stack of papers, finding that his heart wasn't in the upcoming social event. Shadows had lengthened and turned to a rosy hue when Laure Revuneau eased from the window and approached the desk.

"*Mon chéri*, you will make us late for the party," she reproached. "Can this work not wait until morning?"

Cass lazily grinned at her, stemming her hopes of serious reprimand. "Laure, my love, I can think of a hundred things I'd rather do with you than attend another one of your Saturday soirees."

She sighed. "Chéri, I do not understand you at times. They are not merely soirees. My father is the French consul. I have many responsibilities, not the least being to uphold Papa's image."

He reached out and caressed the curve of her cheek. Drawing her into his arms, he kissed her. Kissing always silenced a woman's complaints.

"Mon *pauvre* chéri," she whispered when their lips finally parted. She sympathetically traced the tip of her finger around the outline of his lips. "Do you truly hate my parties so?"

"With a passion. So why do you insist that I attend?"

"Because, it. . .it is something a man of your importance should do."

Cass threw back his head and laughed heartily at her simplistic reasoning.

Laure affected a pout. "Do not laugh at me, mon chéri. Someday we will be called upon to host many parties in our own home," she reminded.

He tensed at her thinly veiled reference to marriage—her hints were coming up with unnerving regularity these days. "I'm sure your social responsibilities must be burdensome, but may I say you handle it with elegance and charm that other women can only envy."

"Oh, *merci*, chéri. I have wondered if you'd noticed." She moved gracefully across the room to adjust a vase of fresh flowers.

Cass sat down behind the desk, his eyes going back to the documents in hand. "Would it honestly upset you if I failed to attend the party tonight?"

Laure looked distressed but not surprised by his inquiry. He'd never enjoyed social functions, so it couldn't have been a surprise to her. He watched as she carefully rearranged a large white magnolia. "You have pressing business?"

The sun's sinking rays formed a halo around her hair, making it appear as rich as black velvet. Watching her domestic efforts, Cass smiled. She was lovely, rich, and God-fearing. And he wasn't in love with her.

There had been many women in his life, and none could match Laure Revuneau's beauty. But marriage—his marriage—was the last thing on his mind.

"Business could wait," he admitted, returning to the subject. "I'm just not in the mood to socialize."

She tilted her head coquettishly. "You are not in the mood for my company?"

"My dear, you are lovely to look at, but I'm not in the mood for a party."

Laure finished the busywork, then turned and faced him. "I wish you would change your mind. Many of your business associates will be there."

"I thought it was some sort of charity function," Cass murmured absently.

"*Vraiment*, truly, but the guest list is quite impressive. I've invited everyone having the tiniest bit of social prominence—"

"And money," he speculated.

She laughed softly. "*Oui*, most assuredly those who have *richesse*?"

Cass knew her angle. He was arguably considered to be the

most eligible yet the most unobtainable bachelor in town—and the young Frenchwoman was not unaware that he was a highly successful entrepreneur with valuable connections to the wealthiest people.

Cass had contacts that Laure drew upon regularly. Because of his various holdings in shipping, cotton, lead, and even silver from Mexico, he could be a real asset for a man in her father's position.

Laure's candid admission of where her values lay annoyed Cass. The last thing he wanted was to mingle in a smoke-filled room with the idle rich. "Why don't I make a donation to whatever it is you're supporting and let it go at that?"

Laure arched a supercilious brow, her smile tantalizing. "I don't want to press you for more than you can afford. I realize you have your own charities."

He frowned at her. "I don't know what you are talking about."

She smiled. "I met Reverend Dawson yesterday. He told me how grateful their church is for the new steeple you provided them."

Cass shrugged. "They needed a steeple. I had the money. Nothing to make a fuss over."

"And the new organ for the Methodist church? The wagonload of meat and vegetables for the Sheltered Souls Mission? Ah. I know your secrets."

"Not all of them, surely." He smiled at her. "That doesn't mean I have to attend every charity benefit in town."

Laure turned, and Cass noticed that her lower lip curled with displeasure. "Please, mon chéri. . .you must come. . .for me?"

Cass hated it when she—or any woman, for that matter—tried to pressure him. "Laure, I don't want to argue about this."

"But Papa will wonder where you are. . .and so will my friends!" She crossed the room and knelt beside the desk, grasping his hand.

"Please! It will be the last party I will ask you to attend this week." She stared up at him, eyes wide with expectation.

"This week?" Cass shook his head with amusement. It was Friday.

"Say you will come, chéri." Laure lightly kissed the palm of his hand.

"Laure. . ."

"S'il te plaît?"

He sighed, realizing she was going to be stubborn about it. "All right, but I won't promise to stay the evening."

"Merci *beaucoup*, mon chéri!" Joyfully she wrapped her arms around his neck and kissed him breathlessly. "You will not regret it, chéri. . . . I promise."

He wasn't optimistic, but it was difficult to refuse her when she looked at him with those wide turquoise eyes.

"I will instruct Sar to prepare your bath." Laure rose and leaned over to kiss him fiercely. "Try to arrive before dinner. It will please Papa."

Blowing one final kiss, she hurried from the room, leaving a faint trace of her expensive French perfume in the air. When the study door closed behind her, Cass rested his head against the chair back. He didn't plan to hurry. He even toyed with the idea of going back on his promise to attend the party, but after mulling over the consequences such a reversal would bring, he concluded it wouldn't be worth all the tears and fury.

Afterward he would stop by the club for a visit. An hour or two of complete solitude. It had been a lucky day when his old friend, Josiah Thorton, had asked young, callow Cass Claxton to come to Saint Louis and be his business partner. Cass had worked hard and been instrumental in expanding their investments, and he'd prospered beyond anything he'd ever dreamed.

He leaned back in his chair, thinking that sometimes he longed for the old days on the farm with his brothers, Beau and Cole, and his mother, Lilly. In his drive for wealth, he'd neglected important things like family and nieces and nephews—and friends. It had been months since he'd corresponded with Trey McAllister, a man who had become like a brother in the days following the war. There were times when he felt the price for worldly pursuits had been too high. Cole and Beau were happily married, but love had escaped him. While he lived in an imposing house, its emptiness often mocked him.

Cass thought with dread of the evening ahead, but having convinced himself that his concession was the only way to keep peace, he got up from the desk and went in search of the waiting bath.

Shadows lengthened as the carriage carrying Susanne drew to a halt in front of an impressive rose-red brick home. The railing of the house's charming cupola matched the one that ran the length of its wide veranda. To the left, a beautiful rose garden captured her attention. She had debated whether to postpone her business until morning, but then decided that since she was in the vicinity, she would approach Cass on her way to the charity function she was about to attend. She swallowed. Meet the lion in his den, so to speak.

Lion? Stubborn mule was more like it.

Susanne sat for a moment staring at the lovely old two-story home, wondering when her estranged husband had become so prosperous. But then again maybe he'd always had money. She realized she knew nothing about Cass Claxton other than the bits of information she'd been able to extract when he'd escorted her to Saint Louis six years ago.

Six years. Was it possible that the days and months had passed so swiftly? She felt the familiar guilt, remembering the way she'd tricked Cass so mercilessly. She was deeply ashamed of what she'd done when she remembered the selfish lengths she'd gone to to get her way, but at the time she'd been desperate. She had been certain that she couldn't have stood another moment in Cherry Grove, Kansas, and since Papa wouldn't hear of letting her travel to Saint Louis alone, she'd thought her only alternative was to use Mr. Claxton as a pawn.

She winced when she recalled the pall of black silence that had hung between them during the endless journey. Justifiably, he'd been furious and had spoken only when absolutely necessary—to bark a warning or issue her a brusque ultimatum. Then, on her aunt Estelle's front lawn, he had dumped her—and that was the most charitable way Susanne could describe it—and tossed her the small pouch of money Leviticus McCord had given him following their shotgun ceremony.

He had issued one final, tight-lipped decree: "Have this outrage annulled!" A nagging twinge reminded Susanne that she had never gotten around to it. Not that she had taken her vows seriously—far from it—but she had never filed for the annulment. She'd assumed there was no hurry. Cass had returned to his home in River Run, and she'd felt certain that she'd never see him again.

A real marriage, a binding one, to Susanne's way of thinking, began with a snow-white wedding gown, a church, flowers, and a host of well-wishers, not with an embarrassed minister, a sheriff carrying a loaded shotgun, and a bewildered groom—a stranger—pleading for mercy in the middle of a dusty road. But she supposed she should have kept her promise and followed through on the annulment. Well, she was certain of one thing: Cass Claxton had not pined away for her. Most likely, he'd filed for the annulment the moment he'd gotten home.

Stepping lightly from the carriage, she instructed the driver to wait, then turned and proceeded up the flagstone walk.

A lovely dark-haired beauty about her age was coming out the front door. As Susanne approached, the woman greeted her softly, "*Bon soir, madame.*"

Susanne returned her smile. "Good evening. Is Mr. Claxton in?"

"Oui." The dark-haired woman's eyes ran lightly over Susanne.

"Thank you. . . . Merci."

The young woman distractedly responded, "*Pas de quoi. . . .*"

Susanne stood before the brass door knocker, fashioned in the shape of a lion's head, trying to bolster her courage. She peered closer at the fierce image, thinking the symbol apropos for Claxton. She knew that what she was about to do would not be pleasant. Cass would not be pleased to see her again, and she couldn't blame him. But the needs of nine homeless children were far more important to her than a bruised ego.

She turned slightly to watch the striking young Frenchwoman step into the waiting hansom cab sitting at the side entrance. Who was she? Susanne mused. *A maid?* She seriously doubted it, considering the woman's appearance and the cut of her stylish gown and cloak. *One of Cass's lady friends?* Apparently her dear "husband" was managing to amuse himself in his wife's absence.

The philistine brute!

She drew a resigned breath and reached for the brass knocker. Cass Claxton didn't scare her. Whether he was pleased to see her or not, they had business to discuss.

And please, dear Lord, let him be civil. I know what I've done to him is awful, but I'm willing to make amends if You will open the door for me. Thank You, Father.

"Excuse me, sir, there's a young lady in the drawing room who wishes to see you." Sar's towering frame dominated the doorway to Cass's bedroom.

The black butler's height of six feet seven inches could be disconcerting for all who were not acquainted with the man's genteel ways and impeccable manners. His hands were as large as ham hocks, his heavy features far from attractive. But anyone who knew Claxton's manservant could and would attest to his kindness and gentle heart.

For the past three years Sar had run Cass's household with a tenacious spirit and a firm hand. Cass commonly referred to Sar as his right arm, and no other man had so rightfully earned Cass's trust and respect.

"What young lady?" Cass kept his attention centered on the stubborn cravat he was trying to tie.

"She says her name is McCord, sir."

"McCord?" Cass sighed and irritably jerked the cravat loose. The name failed to register with him. "Can you do something with this thing?"

Sar stepped forward, and within a moment the task was effortlessly completed.

"I don't know how you do that," Cass reflected absently. "Would you hand me my jacket?"

"About the young lady, sir?" The servant retrieved the double-breasted topcoat and held it as Cass slipped it on.

Reaching for a hairbrush, Cass tried again to control the springy mass of dark hair still damp from his bath. "Tell the lady I'm indisposed. She'll have to make an appointment to see me on Monday."

"Are you feeling ill, sir?"

"I feel fine."

"The lady was quite insistent about speaking to you this evening."

Cass laid the brush down on the dressing table. "It's late; my business for the day has been concluded. If the lady wants to see me, she'll have to come back Monday."

"I'll convey your message, sir."

"Oh, and have the carriage brought around." Cass reached for the black top hat lying at the foot of the bed. "I'm ready to leave."

"Yes, sir." Sar bowed politely. "Will you and your lady want a bite to eat when you return, sir?"

"No. Miss Revuneau won't be returning with me. I plan to stop by the club later." Cass glanced up and flashed Sar an insightful wink. "You and Sarah Rose can take that evening walk early, can't you?"

A smile brushed across the man's face. "Yes, sir, I'm sure we can."

Susanne looked up as the butler approached. "I'm sorry, madam. Mr. Claxton is not receiving guests at this time."

"Oh?" Susanne's brow lifted with surprise. "Did you tell Mr. Claxton that Susanne McCord wishes to speak to him?"

"Yes, madam, I informed Mr. Claxton of your wishes."

"And he refused to see me?"

"Mr. Claxton requests that you make an appointment to see him Monday morning."

"Oh, he does, does he." Susanne shot a reproachful glance up the stairway. Did she dare try to sidestep this giant and force her way into Cass's bedroom? He had every reason not to see her, granted, but she'd come this far. If she left now she'd never find the nerve to come back.

She measured the manservant with a critical eye. He was twice—three times—her size. There was no way she'd be able to make it up the stairs without his stopping her.

"Then I suppose I have no other choice but to comply to Mr.

Claxton's request." She nodded coolly. "Good evening."

Sar opened the door. "Good evening, Miss McCord."

Susanne was leaving by way of the front entrance when Cass left from the side entrance of the house. He paused momentarily to enjoy the early evening air. The temperature was beginning to cool; a bank of dark clouds hung in the west, hinting of rain before sunrise. Suddenly his attention was drawn to a young woman just entering a carriage at the front entrance. A flash of homespun cotton and the door to the carriage closed. Moments later the carriage disappeared in the gathering twilight.

McCord. Cass frowned as the name Sar had mentioned earlier popped unexpectedly into his mind.

McCord? Susanne McCord?

He quickly shook away the alarming thought. It couldn't be the same woman. God wouldn't do that to him.

Seconds later he stepped into his carriage, and the conveyance pulled away.

Chapter 2

The French consul's elegant mansion blazed with light when Susanne emerged from her carriage a short time later. She glanced down at her homespun dress, her best, but perfectly improper for the event. Money was scarce as hen's teeth at the orphanage, and food was needed more than fine dresses. The French consul had invited her tonight with the charitable intention of introducing her to men and women who would be only too happy to contribute to the small orphanage once they learned of the pressing need. Susanne was prepared to make the plea.

Yet she was in a foul mood. Her "husband's" lack of cordiality hadn't surprised her, nor had his insolence. See him Monday, indeed! She didn't have the time or tolerance to play silly games with him. She needed to face him, face his wrath, clear the air, and move on. He would never take pity on her, but he had seemed the type who loved children. Once on the road to Saint Louis they'd run across an entire family without shoes. He had promptly taken them to the mercantile and purchased each member a pair of the finest leather money could buy. Then he bought the children a large bundle of peppermint sticks. At the time Susanne had thought he was addled and rude, but later she realized he must be a man who believed and followed the Lord's command: "Love thy neighbour as thyself."

Gathering her skirt in her hand, she started up a walk lined with towering hickory and walnut trees. Blooming roses heavily perfumed the air, and the occasional streaks of lightning in the west suggested more rain.

Susanne dolefully recalled how Slade Morgan had asked to escort her to the gala this evening. When she'd explained to him that she wanted to make a brief stop before the party, Slade had consented to meet her later. As it turned out, her stop had been so brief that he could have accompanied her easily. She nodded to a young couple who strolled past arm in arm, and hurried up the walk.

She found herself wishing again that tonight's festivities were being held solely to benefit Maison des Petites Fleurs, or House of Little Flowers. But the small group of homeless waifs had been Aunt Estelle Merriweather's personal crusade, so the hodgepodge flock rarely received outsiders' attention. The nine children were regarded as less than ideal youngsters—street urchins who had stolen for survival, eaten their meals from garbage cans, and fought tooth and nail for the right to exist in a sometimes cold and callous world.

The memory of dear, colorful Aunt Estelle brought the first smile of the evening to Susanne's lips.

Estelle had had a heart as wide as the ocean. Susanne fondly recalled how her aunt, without a word of recrimination, had welcomed the frightfully overindulged daughter of her baby brother into her home six years ago.

Over the years Aunt Estelle managed to channel Susanne' s zest and eagerness for life in more sweet-natured directions. She taught her niece the rewards of asking politely instead of rudely demanding. She had shown Susanne the wisdom and power of a twinkling eye and a gracious smile. And she had encouraged her to live her faith, not pretend it.

When Susanne put it all into play she had reformed practically overnight. Now God meant something to her other than words in the Bible. Their daily walks together were more precious than gold to her; she had given her life completely to serving and pleasing Him. She stopped stamping her foot and petulantly tossing her head of golden curls. No longer headstrong, she had become a lady. Estelle had watched a lovely young woman rise from the shell of the original Susanne McCord, like a beautiful butterfly emerging from its ugly cocoon.

Estelle had shown the same zeal and enthusiasm with the nine orphans. She saw them not as thieves and misfits but as needy children crying out for love. Society's lack of compassion toward these children had haunted Susanne's aunt. So one cold, snowy morning she had gone out into the streets, gathering the town's homeless young ones to her ample bosom, telling them something miraculous, something they had never, ever heard before. They were loved.

Aunt Estelle had confided that the dark eyes that had stared back at her with open skepticism had seemed forbidding. However, one by one, their small, dirty hands had clutched the material of her skirt, and like the Pied Piper, she'd led them down the streets of Saint Louis, past the shops and doorways of the town's most respectable and prominent citizens and into the first real home they had ever known.

She had found an elderly couple to attend to the children while she personally handled their religious training and the financial burden. She had taken in washing and sewing and extra baking in order to stretch the budget. It had been a rigorous undertaking, born of love, but she declared it had been worth her every sacrifice to ensure the boys and girls a decent childhood.

When Estelle had passed away a year ago, the awesome responsibility of keeping the small group intact had fallen to Susanne. At times, keeping the wolves from the orphanage door had seemed nearly impossible. Estelle had not been a rich woman, and she had left too little money to keep the orphanage operating.

Leviticus McCord had sent what money he could spare, but it was not enough. Estelle's house was heavily mortgaged in order to pay the orphanage bills. Finally the bank had been forced to sell it in order to settle her estate.

Susanne had been able to keep food on the table by first depleting the small inheritance her mother had left her, then by working as a seamstress. But now that they'd lost the very roof over their heads, she wasn't sure how much longer she could manage to hold on. *Hope.* The word Aunt Estelle had charted her life by seemed like a dim star, barely seen and vanishing when looked at directly. If Susanne couldn't talk Cass into letting her have the Josiah Thorton house she had no idea how they could carry on. She couldn't turn the children back onto the streets. Not after they had experienced a real home and been part of a family. She couldn't bear to think of that happening. No, she had to have that house. It was the only answer.

Harlon and Corliss McQuire, the elderly couple who helped look after the children, refused wages, insisting that they needed very little except room and board. Susanne knew the two of them had grown to love the children as their own, but she felt guilty about their working for nothing.

One fund-raiser like tonight's, and the children would be secure for a whole year, she thought wistfully, wishing again they didn't have to share the largess. However, she would settle for the lease to Cass Claxton's rose-bricked house. She stepped onto the large veranda.

Slade Morgan waited in the shadows of the portico. Susanne approached, and he stepped forward and bowed graciously to kiss her hand. "How lovely you look this evening, my dear." Slade was an encourager to her cause; they'd met one day in the park, and he was the force behind the French consul's efforts to obtain financial support for the kids.

Susanne broke into a smile. The charming, debonair riverboat gambler's easygoing manner and silver tongue managed to capture the attention—as well as the hearts—of most women. She prayed for his soul daily.

His effect on Susanne was no less energizing.

She curtsied demurely. "Sir, you're ever so kind."

Slade gazed back at her, fondness registering in his eyes. "Kindness has nothing to do with it. You are, without exception, the most beautiful woman here tonight."

"May I take that to mean you have already examined the other ladies in attendance?" she bantered, knowing full well that he had. A romantic relationship between them would never come to pass, but she thoroughly liked the man. He had been a solid friend these last few months. Many times he'd left baskets of meat and cheese and fresh fruit on the orphanage doorstep, fiercely denying that he'd been the benevolent soul responsible for the blessing. But Susanne knew where the bounty came from.

He feigned astonishment. "Are there other women present?"

Grinning, she looped her arm through Slade's, and he led her through open french doors into a large ballroom, where elegantly dressed men and women whirled around the floor to the strains of violins and harps.

The ballroom looked splendidly opulent. French-cut glass

chandeliers flickered brightly overhead, their gaslight fixtures illuminating the rich red tapestries draped artfully at the great long windows. There were massive bouquets of summer flowers atop carved stone pedestals and priceless paintings on every wall, The marble floor was magnificent, having been polished until it reflected the pastel images of the ladies' gowns like a shimmering rainbow.

Susanne found herself thinking that she could care for her nine homeless children for the rest of their lives with a mere fraction of the money represented in this room.

"It's marvelous," she whispered under her breath.

"Stuffed shirts," Slade confided. "But rich ones."

Didier Revuneau spotted Slade and Susanne when they entered the ballroom. Taking his daughter's arm, he gently moved her through the crowd to greet the late arrivals.

"*Bienvenue*, my good friend, bienvenue!" The French consul reached out to grasp Slade's hand in greeting.

"Good evening, Consul."

"You have met my lovely daughter, Laure?"

"We've met." Susanne noticed that Slade's eye grazed the lady with lazy proficiency. He bowed. "Good evening, Miss Revuneau."

Laure graciously acknowledged the greeting, her wide turquoise eyes openly admiring the handsome gambler. "Monsieur Morgan."

"Ah, such a lovely young flower you bring with you tonight." Didier's eyes were warm as he bowed and lifted Susanne's hand to his mouth, lightly kissing the tips of her fingers.

Susanne curtsied. "It is an honor to meet you, sir."

"Ah, but the honor is all mine, ma *chérie*."

"And who is this, Monsieur Morgan?" Laure's voice was soft but crisp as she demurely slipped her arm through Slade's with such a familiar ease that it made Susanne wonder exactly how well they knew each other.

It was rare for a man of Slade's reputation to be invited to such a prestigious gathering, but then Susanne knew that her friend was widely accepted in the community despite his questionable occupation.

Slade glanced affectionately down at Susanne. "Miss Revuneau and Consul, may I present Miss Susanne McCord."

"Ah." The host nodded. "From the orphanage, yes?"

"Yes. Thank you most kindly for your invitation."

Laure inclined her head demurely. "I believe Mademoiselle McCord and I share a mutual acquaintance."

"Yes, I believe we do." Susanne had the distinct impression that the consul's daughter might be better acquainted with Cass than she.

"Monsieur Claxton," said Laure.

"Monsieur Claxton," Susanne confirmed. So here was the reason—and a decidedly lovely one—her husband had been indisposed earlier.

"Did you see Cass?" Laure asked.

"No," Susanne admitted, waiting to observe Laure's reaction.

"Oh." Laure's full lower lip formed into a pretty pout. "I am sorry."

"So was I."

"You are good friends with Monsieur Claxton?"

"I was there on a business matter."

Laure's expression was noticeably more guarded, but the tone of her voice remained pleasant. "Perhaps you will be granted another chance. Cass promised to come to the party. He should arrive very soon."

Susanne felt her pulse take an expectant leap. "Oh?"

"Yes. . ." Laure's attention was momentarily diverted by Susanne's rather plain attire. The dress was simple, but Susanne knew it was also becoming to her. "I was admiring your lovely dress earlier. Is it not the one shown in the recent issue of *La Modiste Parisienne*?"

"Oh my, no. I could never afford to purchase such a gown. I'm afraid I only copied it," Susanne admitted.

"You made this dress?" Laure's brows lifted.

"Yes. I'm delighted you like it."

"It is exquisite," Laure complimented and then returned her attention to Slade. "You must promise me a dance later."

Slade inclined his head politely. "Of course; I would be honored."

"Enjoy the evening," Didier said. Susanne detected a merry twinkle in his dark eyes. "And your lovely lady."

"Thank you." Slade glanced at Susanne. "I'm sure I'll enjoy both."

The consul and his daughter merged into the crowd, leaving Susanne and Slade free to mingle.

"She is lovely, isn't she?" Susanne's gaze still lingered on the consul's daughter.

"Laure?" Slade chuckled. "Indeed, she is quite a woman." He eased her toward the refreshment table, where he poured two cups of cold punch.

"Slade. . ." Susanne was annoyed to discover that she was actually curious about Cass's relationship with the French beauty, though she hadn't the vaguest idea why. She had never considered Cass appealing—and they mixed like oil and water.

"Yes?"

"I was wondering about Miss Revuneau's friendship with Mr. Claxton."

Slade's eyes met hers with a look of amusement. "Friendship?"

"I was on my way to speak to Mr. Claxton earlier, and when I was coming up his walk I saw Miss Revuneau leaving."

Ordinarily, Susanne would have felt ill at ease prying like this, but she knew Slade wouldn't think her boorish—friendship had freed them to discuss their thoughts.

Slade's left brow lifted inquisitively. "Why would you be going to see Cass Claxton?"

Color flooded her cheeks. "I told you; I needed to discuss a business matter with him."

"And Laure was leaving?"

"Yes."

Slade's smile, brimming with male perception, confirmed the obvious. "I would guess they'd spent the afternoon together."

"Oh. . .they are seeing each other?" Susanne deliberately kept her inquiry casual. It really was none of her business. The moment Cass discovered that she was here sparks would fly. *Oh Father, I don't want to be at sword's point with the man—grant me the temperament to handle our situation with gentleness and grace.* How many times had she prayed the simple prayer? God was not hard of hearing, and His memory was perfect, so why did she continually ask the same thing?

Thank You for answering my prayer, Father.

Now. That was that. She wasn't going to think about it anymore, but simply proceed as though she and Cass were able to talk sensibly and reason like adults. All she needed was the use of a house he owned—and only for a mere six months. Surely the good Lord would not have to work a miracle in this instance.

"I believe you could say that." Slade smiled.

It was Susanne's brow that lifted this time. "Seriously?"

"If Laure has her way. Cass has been a difficult man to get to the altar, but Laure is a determined young lady." Slade leaned closer and lowered his voice. "I've heard she's planning a Christmas wedding."

Susanne glanced at the dark-haired belle, whirling around the floor with one of her many admirers. "Oh really? How interesting." "*How very interesting*," she added under her breath. *So he had the marriage annulled and failed to notify me. The cad.*

Around ten, Slade suggested he go in search of more punch. Heat suffused the crowded room. Susanne agreed and drifted toward the veranda for a breath of fresh air while she waited.

She strolled along the railing, listening to the peaceful voices of nature blending in muted harmony. A full moon shone overhead; the earlier rain had vanished.

She allowed her thoughts to drift, feeling relaxed and more optimistic about the children. Somehow things always had a way of working out. If worse came to worst, she could always take the children to her father in Cherry Grove. Leviticus had mentioned in his last letter that he would be willing to provide a home for the orphans in Kansas, but Susanne feared Harlon and Corliss were too old to make the long trip, and she didn't have the heart to leave the couple behind. The children were family to her, and so was the elderly couple. It would be best for all concerned if she was able to keep her flock in Saint Louis, where Harlon and Corliss could remain a part of their lives.

She knew what Aunt Estelle would say. "Ask the Lord. He will direct your paths." She purely hoped He wasn't directing her path toward Cherry Grove, Kansas. Surely God could see it would be better for them to remain here in Saint Louis.

Straight ahead, Susanne saw a man step onto the veranda and pause to admire the evening. Light spilled from the ballroom, and she recognized Cass Claxton's familiar stance.

Proud.

Confident.

Her heart thumped in her chest. *Coward*, she silently chastened. He's just a mortal man. And a bullheaded one at that.

She paused, staring at her husband, taking in the head of curly dark hair and powerfully broad shoulders. The years had added an attractive, virile maturity to him. In fact, he now possessed devilishly good looks. He had been heavier when she'd last seen him, almost stocky from what she remembered, and now he looked leaner, older, and wiser.

More inflexible.

Unapproachable.

Dressed in black, with a gray-and-white-striped silk waistcoat, his polished boots showing not a speck of dust, Cass looked every bit the successful young entrepreneur he was reported to be. He carried his top hat in one hand while the other curled around a malacca cane—a rich brown walking stick made from the stem of a palm tree. How had the rough ex-soldier she had known been transformed into this picture-perfect dandy?

She stood quietly in the shadows, not ten feet from him, afraid to breathe. How would he react when he saw her? She was afraid she knew. He would be none too happy.

As though sensing that he was being watched, he straightened and turned.

And their eyes met.

Even the cicadas and tree frogs seemed to be holding their breath with strained anticipation as Cass and Susanne stood, staring at each other.

His eyes, even more of a vibrant cobalt blue than she remembered, narrowed as they coolly assessed her. Her cheeks warmed beneath his masculine appraisal.

Susanne stood immobilized, holding her breath, preparing

for the explosion. Would he detonate with pent-up anger? Or would he turn and walk away without a word? She prayed that he wouldn't walk away. She didn't want to cause a scene, but for the children's sake she would if necessary.

His gaze centered on her, Cass calmly fingered his cravat. In a voice as relaxed as if they had last seen each other only yesterday, he murmured, "As I live and breathe, if it isn't Miss McCord. Hades must have frozen over."

Susanne McCord! Somehow her presence wasn't a total surprise. Trouble was likely to show up anywhere, even at a private party.

"I heard you were here," she said, her tone calm.

Cass felt surprisingly in control of this sudden turn of events. He was proud that he had sounded so casual. He intended to be every inch the suave, sophisticated gentleman, but wasn't sure he could pull it off.

Their gazes remained fixed—reminding him of wild animals caught in a snare.

She was prettier than he'd remembered. Her once too-slim body had rounded gently to form appealing curves. Only her eyes were familiar, a defiant deep violet lined with long, sooty lashes. She wore her hair differently—more refined and sophisticated than six years earlier—but he'd wager she was still the devious little schemer.

"Looks like the rain has passed us by," he remarked, hoping to keep the unexpected encounter as impersonal and brief as possible. He hadn't seen Susanne McCord or thought about her in years, but her appearance suddenly brought back the black day six years ago when, at the wrong end of a shotgun barrel, he'd been forced to marry the devious twit. Cass did not hold the memory dear. He couldn't imagine what Susanne McCord was doing here at Laure's party, but he didn't intend to stick around long enough to find out.

"It does appear that way." She edged toward him.

He debated whether she intended to block his way to the ballroom, and he hoped she would think otherwise.

Taking a second step closer, she said, "I'm glad you're here. I'd like to talk—"

He interrupted. "Make an appointment." Turning, he started back to the ballroom.

Boldly, she stepped forward, throwing her slight weight in his path. Once again their eyes locked.

Cass casually sidestepped, and she dogged his movement. He hadn't forgotten the misery she had dealt him when he'd angered her by deliberately blocking her path in Miller's Mercantile six years ago. Out of the blue, she'd ruthlessly brought him to his knees with one swift, retaliatory blow of her purse to his head.

Facing her, he said calmly, "You are blocking my way."

"I know—excuse me, but I do need to talk to you, and there's no sense in me making an appointment when I can say what I have to say and be done with it." A pleasant smile remained intact on her rosy lips, but he thought it seemed a trifle more forced.

"We have nothing to talk about—and don't try hitting me again."

Her cheeks flamed, and she had the decency to look repentant. "I wasn't going to strike you!"

The sharp exchange between the couple started to draw attention.

Cass glanced uneasily at the growing cluster of curious onlookers. "What do you want?"

"I want to talk to you."

"I'm busy."

"You are not!"

Seizing her by the wrist, he pulled her back onto the veranda.

"Let go! You're hurting me!" She wrestled to free his hold as he sent a weak smile in the direction of the bewildered guests watching beyond the glass door.

Moments later he backed her against a baluster in a secluded corner of the porch. Their eyes locked in a glacial stare.

"What are you doing here, Susanne?" His face was inches from hers now, his voice ominously low.

"Let go of my arm," she demanded.

"Not until you tell me why you are here."

Dipping her head, she sank her teeth into the back of his hand then twisted loose of his grip so swiftly he could do nothing but let go.

Sucking in his breath, he stared at the row of small, even teeth marks on the back of his hand. "You little spitfire," he hissed.

Her eyes met his. "You weasel! Is this any way to treat a woman you married?" She used both hands to straighten her gown.

Cass glanced over his shoulder, alarmed that her remark might be overheard and misunderstood. "What do you want, Susanne?"

She lifted her chin regally, snapped her fan open, and moved deeper into the shadows. "Why, dear, dear Cass, whatever makes you think I want something?" she inquired.

"Why, dear, dear Susanne," he mocked in a tone far from sweet, "because you always do."

"Perhaps if you had consented to see me when I came by your house earlier, you'd know what I want," she reminded him.

"I had no idea it was you."

"And if you had known?"

His eyes narrowed. "I would have set the dogs loose."

He noticed that his response didn't surprise her, but that only confirmed that she hadn't changed over the years. She was going to be as easy to reason with as a grizzly bear with a thorn in its paw.

"You should have made an effort to see who it was before you sent me away," she accused.

By now the curious guests had starting filing back into the ballroom. Cass made a mental note to extend apologies for the unseemly display. "I was busy."

"Yes. I met her on the way in."

He flashed what he knew to be a lazy, arrogant grin guaranteed to ruffle her feathers. "Then you understand why I didn't want to be disturbed."

She refused to take his bait. "Tsk, tsk. The woman must be desperate for male companionship." She dropped her voice, and he knew what she was about to add would cook her goose, but poor Susanne was powerless to let her opportunity pass. She didn't prove him wrong. "Once a weasel always a weasel."

She had to know that once she'd bitten the whey out of him she'd ruined any chance of civility now. Whatever she wanted, she'd just sealed her chances of ever getting it from him.

Cass fought the urge to strangle her. He knew it was useless to try and outwit her in a war of insults—he'd tried that six years earlier and had lost hands-down. All he could do was stand his ground.

She watched warily as he ran a hand through his hair. "What are you still doing in Saint Louis, Susanne?"

"I live here, remember?"

"I remember." But he'd tried to forget. He assumed she had married and by now was in the process of tormenting her husband to death. "I thought you'd moved on by now."

"Ah, then you've thought of me over the years," she said.

A wicked smile curved the corners of his mouth. "Not even once." That wasn't true; he'd thought she would be civil enough to send him a copy of the annulment, but she hadn't. Other than that, he hadn't thought of her.

She sighed. "A pity. And here I thought you were pining away for me all this time."

Cass chuckled mirthlessly. "What a dreamer."

"I would think the more proper question is, what are *you* doing here in Saint Louis? I thought you'd be in River Run."

Cass casually set a booted foot onto the rail next to her and stared into the darkness for a long time.

"It's none of your business," he finally said, "but if you must know, I returned to River Run for a few months before an old friend wrote and asked me to join him in a business partnership here in Saint Louis. So I came back."

"Josiah Thorton," she murmured absently.

His eyes snapped back to meet hers. "How did you know Josiah Thorton?"

"I didn't. I just know that he was your business partner. . .and that he died, leaving you heir to his estate."

Cass didn't fancy her knowing anything about his business. "Where did you hear that?"

"Never mind where, I just did. Actually, it's Josiah's house that I came to see you about earlier."

"Josiah's house?" Cass studied her guardedly. "What about it?"

"I want you to rent the house to me."

"Rent the house to you?" Cass found the request odd, even for Susanne McCord. "I wouldn't rent my horse's leavings to you."

"Nor would I accept them," she snapped.

"Then what makes you think I would rent Josiah Thorton's house to you?"

"I know you won't rent me the house, but I'm hoping—and praying—that when you hear that I have nine children who desperately need that house, you'll be willing to at least listen to what I have to say."

For a moment silence filled the air as Cass slowly digested her words. *Nine kids?* Suddenly he threw his head back and laughed uproariously. His jollity continued to grow, and by the puzzled look on her face he could see that she was frantically reviewing her remark to see what was so amusing that it could send him into fits of mirth.

"What's so funny?" she challenged.

Cass pointed at her, his eyes filling with tears. "You. . .and nine children!" He slapped his hand on his thigh and broke into another boisterous round of laughter.

She watched with a jaundiced eye. "What's so funny about the children and me?"

As quickly as his gaiety had erupted, it came to a sudden halt. His studied her dispassionately. "I can't imagine any man living with you long enough to father nine children. Did you marry a simpleton?"

She smiled. "Yes. But that's beside the point. The children don't have fathers."

His jaw dropped.

"Not that," she accused. "They aren't my children. Technically."

"I didn't think so!" He burst into laughter again.

"If you can pull yourself together, I'll tell you why I have them," she said curtly.

"Oh yes." He wiped tears from his eyes. "I'm all ears."

"The children are orphans. My aunt Estelle took them into her home to raise, and after she died I assumed responsibility for their care."

He'd believe that when it was announced that, through an unforeseen technicality, the South had won the war! "Of course you did! Grasping, conniving, spoiled Susanne McCord giving unselfishly of herself to nine homeless children. Sounds exactly like you, my lovely."

"You don't believe me."

"I couldn't hope to live long enough to believe you, Susanne."

"Then I suppose it would do no good to plead with you to lease Josiah Thorton's house to me?"

"None whatsoever." Cass was not a heartless man, and he regretted that innocent children would suffer from his refusal—if she was telling the truth—but the truth was foreign to this woman. He wouldn't help Susanne McCord cross the street, let alone rent Josiah Thorton's house to her. She was out of his life, and he intended to keep it that way.

"Mr. Claxton"—Susanne's eyes locked stubbornly with his—"I know you and I haven't exactly been friends." She stoically ignored the choking sound he made in his throat and continued. "But I fail to see how you could let our personal differences stand in the way of providing a home for nine helpless children. I beg you to reconsider. I understand you have accumulated wealth beyond what most people can imagine, and you surely have no need for such a large house. Please reconsider; I'm desperate."

"Come now, Miss McCord, if what you claim is true, and you've turned into an unselfish saint, which I don't believe for a minute, then why are you making it sound as if I'm the one responsible for the children's misfortune?"

"You have the house," she said simply.

He lifted his brows wryly. "There are no other houses in Saint Louis with twenty-four rooms?"

"I'm sure there are, but none so ideal and none that I can afford. I'm afraid I can only offer a pittance to repay you for your kindness and generosity." She nearly choked on the praise. "But the children and I will paint and clean and weed the gardens for a portion of our keep."

"What makes you think you could afford what I would ask?"

"I'm not sure that I can, for we have very little money. But when I saw the house, I knew it was exactly what the children needed, even though it's old and run-down and needs a mountain of repair. Why, no one would think about purchasing it in the condition it's in now. Of course, I had no idea you owned it—"

"I don't. It belongs to Josiah Thorton."

"But he's dead, and you're the heir to his estate and the one most likely to inherit it, along with the rest of Mr. Thorton's vast holdings."

Cass's eyes narrowed. "And who told you that?"

"I can't say who told me, but wouldn't it be to your advantage to have people living in Josiah's house, people who would maintain the dwelling until the estate is settled?"

"And what happens once the estate is settled? Suppose I have a potential buyer interested in purchasing Josiah's house. Would the kindhearted, generous 'weasel' then throw you and your nine little orphans out of the maintained dwelling?"

"Well...I'm not sure what would happen in that case." Susanne had learned long ago to take life one day at a time. "It's possible—if I can't find another house at that time—I might be forced to take the children to my father in Cherry Grove, but I don't want to do that right now. With winter approaching, the long journey would be extremely difficult for the elderly couple who helps me run the home," she confessed.

"I hate to hear that, Miss McCord, because I can't help you." Cass straightened to face her. "It looks like you're going to have to trick someone else into helping you out of your mess this time."

She felt her temper rising. "You can't help me—or you won't help me?"

He grinned. "Both. I can't because Josiah's house is not mine to do with as I please—his estate won't be settled for months yet. And I won't because. . ." His eyes skimmed her insolently. "Well, I think we both know why I won't, don't we? Oh, by the way, I never received those annulment papers. Where are they?"

"You are heartless," she spat out. "Cold, uncaring. Selfish!"

"Weasel," he mocked. He touched his index finger to her chin in silent warning. "Watch it, sweetheart—your halo is wobbling."

She was going to explode. He'd really done it this time. Squaring her shoulders, she called out to his retreating form, "We don't have to have twenty-four rooms, you know. We can make do with far less!"

"Forget it."

"Don't you have any house you could rent to me and the children?"

"Not even one. Good evening, Miss McCord." He threw his head back and laughed merrily.

Susanne stamped her foot. Good evening, indeed!

The man was an intolerable muttonhead who was going to pay for his high-handedness.

And pay dearly.

Chapter 3

Susanne had reached the end of the line. Her options, slim at best, had run out. "I'm sorry," she told the children that night, "but we have no other choice. We must start for Kansas at first light Monday morning."

Susanne McCord did not quit, not when a matter touched her heart, and the children's plight tore at her compassion. She'd broached the lion's den and confronted the insufferable Cass Claxton twice, begging him to reconsider. On both occasions he had turned a deaf ear and told her in his most holier-than-thou tone that it would take an act of divine intervention for him to rent her a glass of water, to say nothing of Josiah Thorton's house.

She'd left enraged each time to scour the town for other prospects, praying for that divine intervention he was so smugly sure she'd never find.

And she hadn't found it.

Lord, are You listening? I really believed You'd help me get that house.

She'd been so sure keeping the children in Saint Louis was the best thing for everyone concerned. It wasn't as if her determination to coerce Cass Claxton into letting her have that house was a selfish desire or even a spur-of-the-moment decision. She'd prayed about it long and often. For some reason God hadn't seen fit to answer her prayers. How could she hold on to hope when her way seemed blocked every direction she turned?

She sat at the orphanage's round dinner table, hands folded, trying to gauge the reactions on the bright young faces. The children—Aaron, sixteen; Payne, fourteen; Jesse, nine; Doog, eight; Margaret Ann, six; the twins, Lucy and Bryon, five; Joseph, four; and Phebia, three—digested the news with solemn gazes.

The children knew of her diligent search to find a home large and inexpensive enough to house them. She also knew the worry lines on her forehead tonight told them that the miracle they had hoped for had failed to materialize. In three short days they had to vacate Aunt Estelle's house. The bank would take possession of their home and pass it on to the new owner. The children would be on the street again. That must not happen. They had learned to trust and to enjoy a fairly stable life. She could not and would not let them return to the sort of desperate existence they had once endured. There was nothing left now but to notify her father and arrange transportation to Cherry Grove. The challenge was overwhelming, even for a woman of her fortitude.

"Are we gonna ride in a wagon?" Jesse picked up an ear of corn and gnawed on a row of tender kernels. The late garden was producing nicely. Susanne would pick the last of the produce and take it with them.

"We have enough money to buy a wagon and a team."

Funds from her personal savings were meager but sufficient. "We cannot hope to find a wagon that will be large enough for all of us to sleep in, but we'll ask the Lord to keep the weather mild so that we can sleep on pallets beneath the wagon at night. Corliss and Harlon will sleep inside."

Susanne tried to read Corliss's reaction to the news as the matronly woman went about quietly dishing potatoes onto the youngest child's plate.

Phebia was the baby of the household, a gurgling, brown-eyed, chubby-faced tot who had been left on the Merriweather doorstep two years ago by a mother who could no longer care for her. Estelle had been eager to welcome a ninth stray into the fold, and the other children had joined in to help with Phebia's upbringing.

"I know it's not the ideal time to embark on a journey," Susanne admitted quietly, "but if all goes well, we should reach Cherry Grove in six to seven weeks."

She knew the journey would be long and arduous, but it was only the end of August, and she figured that with God's help, they would reach their destination before the first heavy snow. She was relieved to see both Corliss and her husband nodding as she spoke, supportive as usual of any request she made of them.

"How are we going?" Harlon asked.

"Well, the most sensible way to go would be to take a boat up the Missouri River to Westport then buy a wagon and supplies to transport us on to Cherry Grove, but because of our lack of funds, we won't be able to do it that way. We'll travel by wagon, keeping to the main route crossing the state."

The old man nodded. "I'll see to getting the wagon and a team first thing in the morning."

"Thank you, Harlon. Wes Epperson, at the livery barn, said he might have one he'd sell cheaply." Susanne absently reached to cover Doog's fork in a mute reprimand when he prepared to launch a pea at an unsuspecting Bryon. "I think you'll like Cherry Grove," she told the children—although she herself had never been happy there.

When her mother died, Susanne had longed to return to the parties and gaiety of Saint Louis; she'd begged Leviticus to let her go back to Aunt Estelle's, where she'd spent much of her younger years. Leviticus had ignored his daughter's pleading and instead insisted she move with him to Cherry Grove to begin a new life. The decision had forced Susanne to take her own action.

Cass Claxton was elected to take her back to Saint Louis.

The marriage ploy had worked like a charm, though Susanne realized now that using such underhanded tactics had been reprehensible. She thought about her last encounter with Cass and knew deep down that he was absolutely right to resent her. She was no longer the irresponsible, willful girl she had once been, but she had to admit her earlier selfishness still disturbed her deeply. God had forgiven her, but she was slower about forgiving herself. Cass would never forgive her.

Now, when she most desperately needed Cass's help—or more accurately, when she needed the house he controlled—she knew she could never convince him that she had changed.

She sighed, and her father's words came back to haunt her: *"You've made your bed; now you must lie in it."*

"Will them Indians git us?" blond, gray-eyed Jesse asked. He wrapped a string bean around his forefinger.

Susanne smiled. "You've been listening to the big kids in the neighborhood again. They are just trying to scare you. There are no hostile Indians left between here and Cherry Grove, and I'm sure the good Lord will see us through."

Aaron, the oldest of the boys, said quietly, "Ma'am, what about the border ruffians?"

A shudder rippled down Susanne' s spine. The threat from marauding gangs of ex-soldiers, both Union and Confederate, was still very real along the Missouri-Kansas border. "Like I said, the Lord is our shield. We'll be very careful to stay out of danger."

"It will be all right," Margaret Ann chimed in.

Susanne had always contended—out of Margaret's hearing

range—that Margaret was a thirty-year-old trapped in a six-year-old's body.

"What may I do to help, Miss McCord?" Margaret inquired sweetly.

"I'll make a list tonight of duties that will be assigned to each of us. I'll have it completed by breakfast tomorrow morning." Susanne sipped her coffee, trying to read the children's faces again. She was relieved to see that they seemed to take the turn of events in stride. Over the years, under Aunt Estelle's tutelage, they had become exemplary kids.

Margaret and Payne stood up and began to clear away the dishes, while Corliss wiped Phebia's hands and face and lifted her out of the wooden high chair. She handed the child her favorite doll, Marybelle, and then swatted her lovingly on the bottom.

"Jesse, it's gettin' late. Time for Phebia and Marybelle to be off to bed."

"Yes, ma'am." Jesse pushed back from the table and led Phebia, who immediately popped her thumb into her mouth, out of the room.

"The wood box is gettin' low." Aaron reached into his pocket and slipped his cap onto his head. "I'll be filling it, Miss McCord, before I turn in."

"Thank you, Aaron," Susanne replied absently. She reached for the small slate and piece of chalk.

The remainder of the children dispersed from the table in an orderly manner. Harlon disappeared into the kitchen and returned with the coffeepot, lifting his bushy white brows expectantly at Susanne.

"I've had plenty, thank you."

Corliss bustled off to the kitchen to supervise the cleaning. Harlon sat back down at the table. The clock on the mantel chimed six times while he methodically scraped the bowl of his pipe. Susanne scribbled on the slate, deeply absorbed in making a list of supplies she would need to purchase for the long journey. Money was tight, but she had been known to stretch a dollar until it cried for mercy. Thanks to Cass, she would now have to stretch it until it dropped dead of overuse.

She knew very little about wagons and teams and the proper food to carry on such a long trip, but she had spent hours that morning at the general store, talking to an outfitter. Clifford Magers had explained to her that when she went to select a wagon, she must make sure that it was strong, light, and constructed out of well-seasoned timber—especially the wheels, since they would be traveling through a region that was exceedingly dry this time of year. He warned Susanne that unless the woodwork was thoroughly seasoned, constant repairs would be inevitable.

She'd have to travel light, he insisted, no matter how strong the urge to take along furniture, potted plants, iron stoves, and grandfather clocks. He emphasized that should she succumb to temptation, the heavy items would only have to be discarded by the wayside later, in order to conserve the animals' strength for their long journey.

In selecting her team, Clifford advised mules rather than oxen because they traveled faster and seemed to endure the summer heat better. But when she'd gone to the livery later that day, she discovered that mules were priced higher than oxen.

Wes Epperson told her he thought she'd be smarter to buy oxen over mules, assuring her that oxen stayed in better condition and were able to make the journey in the same amount of time. He contended that oxen would be less likely to stampede.

Susanne would have preferred mules, but with her limited funds, she supposed oxen would have to be her choice.

She glanced up, aware that Harlon had been watching her for

the past few minutes. She smiled encouragingly. "Is there something you'd like to suggest, Harlon?"

"Yes, ma'am."

Susanne laid the chalk aside and folded her hands over the slate. "I'm listening."

"Have you given any thought to the dangers a young woman and nine children will be facing once we're out on the trail?" he began quietly.

She sighed, sensing that all along Harlon had harbored misgivings about her decision. "I know there will be dangers, and I'm not happy about having to go, but taking the children to my father is our only hope of keeping them together."

"With all due respect, Miss McCord, I think we need a man—a good, strong man who knows the wilderness—to lead us on such a long journey."

Susanne sighed. "I've thought about that, Harlon, but I have no such man, and it isn't as if we're traveling to some faraway place like California or Oregon," she argued. "I'll have you to help me. You're a man."

"I'm an old man," Harlon reminded gently. "I can't do anything but hunt for game and haul freshwater to the camp each night. You need a young man, a man strong enough to protect you, wield a bullwhip, and drive a team of oxen."

Susanne realized he was right, but what choice did she have? She didn't know such a man, and her scarcity of funds prevented her from hiring anyone.

"Maybe we can hire a bullwhacker to drive the team," Harlon mused.

"I don't know a bullwhacker, and even if I did, I wouldn't allow such a bully to travel with us."

Everyone knew a bullwhacker was the biggest show-off on a

wagon train. His casual brutality to animals was deplorable, and he usually kept the women and children in constant fear. "Besides, I can use a bullwhip myself," she said. A former suitor had taught her how to handle a bullwhip almost as well as a man. She'd become accurate enough to swat a fly off the rump of an ox before the ox even knew a fly was there.

"Well, 'course, it's your decision," Harlon conceded. "I just wanted to make sure you'd thought about what we're gonna be up against."

"I have, Harlon, and I agree with everything you're saying, but I'm afraid we have no other choice. We will have to make the trip alone." She reached over and squeezed his hand encouragingly. "Aaron and Payne are developing into strong young men, and they will be able to drive the oxen. And though they haven't had much experience with a rifle, I'm sure they will learn quickly. The girls will pitch in to do all they can. You'll see; we'll be fine." *Easy to say*, she reflected. She knew only too well the dangers involved, but she would have to take the risk.

Harlon drew thoughtfully on his pipe as she tried to convince him it would be a memorable journey. She knew what he was thinking—that it would be memorable, all right! Susanne knew Harlon had traveled with a wagon train back in the fifties, and he could still tell about the torrential rains, blazing sun, freezing winds, and the dust—miles and miles of swirling dust—that got into the eyes and clothes and food, tormenting the weary travelers until they thought they would lose their minds. She'd heard him talk about the flies and the sickness. . . . Well, it would be different this time. It had to be.

Since God hadn't helped her get the Thorton house, dare she hope He would guard them on this trip? *I'm sorry*, she mentally apologized. *It's not that I don't believe, because I do. I'm just not sure what You want me to do.* It hardly seemed possible that God would want her to set off this time of the year with nine children and an elderly couple traveling all the way to Kansas by themselves. Even she could see the enormous potential for disaster.

"You'll see; we'll make it just fine," she said again before turning her attention back to her list.

"Well, I hope so," Harlon muttered.

A few minutes later he pushed away from the table and slowly got to his feet. "It sure would make it easier if you had a husband to take us all to Cherry Grove," he said almost wistfully.

Susanne glanced up from the slate. "Yes, it certainly would make it easier."

"Well, don't be frettin' none over what I've said." Harlon sighed as he stretched lazily. He shuffled over to wind the clock. "Me and Corliss will do everything we can to help get those young'uns to their new home. The good Lord will see us through. He always has."

"He always has." She nodded. "I've been praying about it, Harlon, and I don't think we have a thing to be concerned about." She was doing her best to keep up a good front, although truth be told, she was scared half to death thinking about everything that could go wrong.

Harlon nodded and announced he was going to turn in.

Susanne distractedly bid him good night.

The lamp had burned low when she finally blew out the flame. She closed her eyes and clasped her hands around her waist, trying to ease the stiffness in the small of her back. Harlon's earlier comment drifted back to her: *"It sure would make it easier if you had a husband."*

Reaching for the candle, she rose to make her way to the darkened stairway, thinking about his observation.

Suddenly her hand paused on the railing.

"It sure would make it easier if you had a husband." Harlon's words echoed through her mind again, taunting, offering an almost prophetic challenge. *"Someone who could take us to Cherry Grove."*

Her feet absently claimed a second stair then hesitated again. It would make it considerably easier if she had a strong young husband to help out. He could safely escort them, and they could all stop worrying. She stood in the darkness, scowling thoughtfully.

Well, maybe she had a husband—a good, strong, reasonably young husband who was more than capable of escorting them on such a journey. And why shouldn't he? Wasn't he partly to blame for her having to make the journey since he'd refused to rent her Josiah's house?

Susanne, there's no way on this earth that you could ever talk Cass Claxton into escorting you to your own lynching. . .well, maybe he would agree to take me to that, she amended grudgingly. But he would most assuredly refuse to take her, two seventy-year-olds in failing health, and nine homeless children to Cherry Grove, Kansas.

She took another step and then paused. No, he would never do it. . .unless. . .

Unless. . .

She smiled and then moved with purpose as she hurried up the steep stairway, confident that if she put her mind to it, she could find a way he would.

Maybe it was time to show that smart-alecky Cass Claxton that Susanne McCord still had the upper hand when she wanted it.

Monday morning dawned with a slow, steady rain dripping from the eaves of the Claxton estate. In the distance occasional thunder rumbled, but all in all, the gray, cool morning was ideal for working. However Cass found he had to struggle to keep his mind on the papers spread out before him.

He sat at his desk trying to concentrate while Laure sat watching him.

"Oh, mon chéri, why must you always work? Could we not go for a ride in the countryside?"

"It's raining, Laure. Don't you have mission work you should attend to?"

"Oh—I am not in the mood for mission work. Can we not have a picnic in the gazebo? It would be so lovely, even though it is raining. Come—don't be such an old workhorse."

Moments later he found himself gazing into her turquoise-blue eyes and admonishing her in what he hoped was his sternest voice. "What am I going to do with you?"

"Ah, but I am shameless when it comes to you, mon chéri." She smiled and lightly traced the outline of his lips with her forefinger. "Please? A simple picnic."

A sudden rap on the study door interrupted them.

Laure groaned when Cass shoved back and went to answer the summons. "Tell Sar we do not want to be bothered," she said.

Cass grinned and opened the door. "Don't be so eager, love. There is time for both business and pleasure."

She frowned when a more persistent knock sounded.

He found Sar waiting with an envelope in his hand.

"Yes?"

"I'm sorry to bother you, sir, but a telegraph message just arrived. I thought you would want to see it immediately."

"Oh?" Cass took the envelope. "Thank you, Sar." He closed the door and crossed the room, opening the missive to peruse it.

"What is it, mon chéri?"

A frown creased his forehead. His eyes quickly scanned the puzzling message.

NEED HELP STOP COME AS QUICKLY AS POSSIBLE STOP BEAU

"Is it bad news?" Laure moved to stand by his side, her eyes searching the message over his shoulder.

"I'm not sure. It's from Beau."

"Your brother?"

"My brother in Cherry Grove. He must be in some sort of trouble." Cass absently pitched the piece of paper onto the desk and strode briskly toward the doorway.

"Where are you going?" Laure demanded.

"To Kansas." He flung the door open and shouted for Sar.

"Kansas!" Laure wailed. "But you cannot! You will be gone for weeks! And there is a party Friday night."

"You'll have to attend without me."

"But this is most terrible!" Laure ran out of the study, trying to keep up with his rapidly retreating form. "When will you be back? How long will you be gone?"

"Don't know, and I'm not sure," he murmured distractedly. "I'll let you know." Bounding up the stairs two at a time, he shouted, "Sar! Pack a bag! I'm leaving in five minutes."

"But, mon chéri!" Laure paused and slapped her hand against the railing angrily when Cass continued his ascent. "Cherry Grove, Kansas?"

Rain fell in heavy sheets. When Susanne received the wire answering her inquiry, she smiled grimly and destroyed the paper.

Father, forgive me. But I know no other way. I realize I have already broken another promise—to make amends to Cass and then to leave him alone—but there's no other way to get the children to Kansas. If You will see us safely to Cherry Grove, I will step out of Cass's life forever. And this is one promise I will keep.

She sent one more wire to her father then hurried back to the orphanage to gather the flock, who had been in preparation the past two days for the journey. The small entourage left Saint Louis around eight in the morning. Jesse, Doog, and Margaret Ann walked behind the wagon and were soon struggling to keep up. Aaron and Payne sat on the narrow wagon seat, manhandling the reins. The newly purchased covered wagon rolled cumbersomely over the soggy ground. The children were forced to step lively as the wheels on the large prairie schooner sluiced through deepening ruts. It wasn't a fit day for man or beast to be about, but Susanne prayed the weather would clear by early afternoon.

"Keep moving, children. The rain will surely let up soon!" Susanne glanced anxiously over her shoulder when Aaron urged the oxen up a steep incline. The creak of harness and leather filled the air as the massive animals labored to pull their heavy load.

Harlon rode ahead on a mule he'd purchased, hat pulled low on his forehead in an effort to shield his face from the rain. Corliss rode in the wagon and tried to entertain the younger children. Now and again she popped her head out to keep an eye on the ones walking.

Because the weather was warm, the children had been instructed to tie their shoes together and hang them over their shoulders to prevent them from wearing out the leather on the long journey. Susanne couldn't afford to buy new shoes this winter, so not one complaint was heard.

Phebia rode next to Payne on the wagon seat, hugging her doll, Marybelle, to her chest to protect it from the pelting rain.

"Me want to go hooooome." She had begun sobbing almost the moment they'd left the city limits. "Me getting all wet!"

Susanne momentarily climbed into the wagon and tried to explain that they couldn't go home—they had no home—but to Phebia's three-year-old mind, the explanation was useless. The child had already wearied of the journey.

The oxen topped a rise in the early afternoon, and Aaron halted the wagon to allow sufficient time for the smaller children to catch up. Susanne rested against the back of the wagon bed, studying the rain-soaked horizon and trying to shake the depression that had been with her since waking that morning. Overhead the sky threatened more rain.

They'd been traveling for more than four hours, and she was certain they had covered only a few miles. No matter how hard she tried to convince herself that she could do it, the long trip loomed bleak ahead of her. *When the rain lets up, we'll be able to move faster,* she reasoned. Gray clouds hung low, shrouding the earth with a pewter mist. Suddenly the sky opened up and poured.

Harlon galloped up beside the wagon and had to shout to be heard above the torrential downpour. "I be thinkin' it might be a good time to stop for dinner!"

"I think you're right!" Susanne called back, thankful for any reprieve.

"There's a grove of sycamores 'bout a quarter mile on up the road. Looks like as good a place as any to make camp."

"I'll follow you!" Susanne was taking her turn driving the team, and she fought to keep the animals moving as lightning streaked wildly across the sky, followed by earth-rattling thunder. Phebia screamed. Marybelle's straw-colored hair wilted in the rain.

"Phebia, darling, Marybelle will be fine." Susanne chanced a quick pat on Phebia' s knee before she was forced to turn her attention back to the team.

Her sympathy only served to remind Phebia of how thoroughly miserable she was, and she bawled even more loudly.

Susanne herself was close to crying a few minutes later when she heard the back wagon wheel lurch then slip deeper and deeper into a quagmire.

Corliss poked her head through the canvas opening. "What's going on?"

"The wheel—I think it's stuck!"

Susanne stood in the midst of the cloudburst, hands on her hips, surveying the wheel that was hopelessly mired to the hub. Phebia screamed harder. There wasn't a thread of dry clothing left on any of them, and if Susanne could have gotten her hands on Cass Claxton at that moment, she—well, her behavior wouldn't be Christlike.

Cass traveled fast and light. His horse covered the ground in smooth, even strides despite the worsening weather. Within fifteen minutes of the time he'd received Beau's message, he was on his way. His mind raced with the possibilities that might await him when he reached Cherry Grove. Beau was ill? Something had happened to his wife, Charity? Surely it wasn't their little girl, Mary Kathleen. . . . She had been a healthy, rosy-cheeked infant when Cass had last seen her, but that had been more than six years ago. Had something happened to her—or maybe to the twins, Jase and Jenny?

He flanked the stallion harder; worry lines creased his face. Perhaps something had happened to Ma. . .or Willa, the family housekeeper. . .or his older brother and his wife, Cole and Wynne.

Forgive me, Lord. . . . I should have kept in closer touch with the family. He'd become a loner; he knew it. But when a man was single it was hard to stay in touch with people. Particularly when a good portion of his time had been taken up with making money and taking care of his business. He'd been a fool to put personal wealth ahead of family ties. How long had it been since he'd seen most of them? Four, maybe five years.

The horse topped a rise, and he abruptly reined the stallion to a halt. The animal was already winded, and Cass realized he was pushing too hard. Running the horse to death was not only cruel and senseless, but would cost him more delay. He rested against the pommel of the saddle, allowing the horse to catch its breath and cool down. His eyes skimmed the valley below, focusing on a covered wagon in the near distance, contortedly leaning to the left side. Several figures milled about in apparent confusion while a couple of young lads tried to unhitch a cow and a goat that were tied behind the wagon. A large chicken crate remained fastened to the side of the wagon, its occupants flapping their wings and cackling loudly in the confusion.

Pioneer family in trouble, Cass concluded. He sat watching what appeared to be an elderly man and woman, along with a younger woman, struggling to free the wheel from a muddy confinement. He could see now that there were children—a whole slew of them—adjacent to the mud hole that imprisoned the spoke wheel.

After studying the situation for a few minutes, Cass decided the wheel was going to be impossible to free the way they were going about it. He shifted uneasily in the saddle, grappling with his conscience. His first instinct was to swing around the wagon and be on his way. It wasn't his problem. If he stopped to help, he could be delayed for an hour or longer, and he could hardly afford the wasted time. However, he could plainly see that at the rate they were going, the family would be stuck until the sun came out and the road dried.

And some of those kids sounded real unhappy. The desperate wail of a small child sobbing her heart out drifted on the wind.

He yanked his hat lower, hoping to overcome his conscience. He'd never claimed to be a Good Samaritan. . .but he was a decent sort, and he knew he couldn't just ride by and ignore the situation, much as he'd like to.

Ma would wring him dry if she ever heard that he'd ignored a soul in trouble.

Sighing, he picked up the reins, wishing at times that he'd been raised a heathen. It would have made his choice easier. He clucked to his horse, figuring he might as well ride down there and get it over with so he could be on his way.

As he approached the wagon, he quickly recognized Susanne McCord, and he felt his expression go from open to incredulous. No. It wasn't possible. Not her.

Rain spilled in rivulets off the brim of his hat. He sat on his horse and stared down at her. It was uncanny how this woman turned up to haunt him! He didn't know why the good Lord continued to throw her in his path, but here she was, her wagon bogged down in a muddy slough, while nine children stood helplessly beside the road, looking to him as if he had just come off a mountain with stone tablets in his arms.

"What are you doing here?"

"I think I could ask the same." Susanne turned to look back at the wheel. She stood ankle-deep in mud. "How fortunate we are that you've come along."

Cass coldly met her look. "I fail to see anything fortunate about it." He wouldn't put it past the wench to have set him up again, but she couldn't have known that he would be traveling this particular road at this particular hour.

She brushed a strand of damp hair out of her eyes, apparently ignoring his brusque tone. "You can see we are in a good deal of trouble. Would you be so kind as to lend a hand?"

"Ha!"

She blushed, casting an apprehensive glance toward the older couple, who were so engrossed with the problem at hand that they didn't appear to have heard the exchange. "There's no need for sarcasm," she reproached. "We are in need of a good strong back, and yours should do nicely."

Cass was about to tell her what she could do with that idea when he turned sharply at the sound of the elderly man groaning with misery. The fellow strained against the large pole he was manipulating in a vain effort to pry the wheel loose.

"Harlon, your heart!" his wife called.

Cass glanced back at Susanne, struggling with his conscience.

The littlest girl burst into renewed tears, setting up a wail that would raise the dead. "Me sooo wet and hungrrry!"

She held a doll; its flaxen hair trailed through the mud as the child dragged it by the feet when she made a beeline toward Susanne. The little girl buried her face in Susanne's rain-soaked skirt and howled.

"Please, Cass. We need your help. There are other people involved here, not just me," Susanne pleaded. Several of the other children tried to comfort the sobbing toddler.

Swinging out of the saddle, Cass shot Susanne a pointed look that he hoped clearly said *Just so you understand, I'm only doing this for them.* He motioned for the two oldest boys to step up.

Over the next few hours differences were set aside and the group worked as a team to free the trapped wheel.

Harlon wanted to help but couldn't, so he and Corliss were

put in charge of feeding the younger children their noonday meal.

Susanne proved to be more of a hindrance than a help. Cass gruffly ordered her to step aside when he and the boys heaved and tugged on the stubborn wheel. In an open effort to appease him, she would obediently step away, but moments later she would be back in the thick of the action, working alongside the men.

At one point he found her arms locked tightly around his midsection when the oxen, Aaron, Payne, Doog, Cass, and she formed a human chain of brute strength.

Midafternoon, exhausted and knowing that the animals needed rest, Cass called a halt to work. Wearily the entourage sank down to the saturated ground to eat the fatback and cold biscuits Corliss pressed into their hands. Since the downpour refused to let up, anything more substantial was impossible to fix.

The children milled around, making the best of the situation, but Cass and Susanne chose to eat their food in a withdrawn and uncommunicative silence.

Handing Cass a third biscuit, Susanne finally decided to make an attempt at civility. "I'm sorry there's no hot coffee."

Cass accepted the peace offering, but she could see that his mind was still on freeing the wheel. "I've lost a good four hours," he muttered.

"Oh?" Susanne bit into her second biscuit. "Are you going somewhere important?"

Cass turned to give her a baleful stare. Rain spilled from the brim of his hat in torrents. "Now, why would you think of that? Isn't this the sort of weather any man in his right mind would go out riding in for the pleasure of it?"

She shrugged.

"Obviously, I'm going somewhere."

She took a bite of bread. "What a coincidence that we should happen to run into each other this way."

"Yeah, what a coincidence," he returned dryly.

"It was a stroke of good luck for us, but I'm sure we'll be able to free the wheel soon and then be on our separate ways."

She lifted her brow inquiringly. "Where was it you said you were going?"

He swallowed the last of his biscuit and stood up. "I didn't say."

"Oh." It was apparent that he didn't care to elaborate, and Susanne didn't push the issue.

He shoved off to address the wheel.

Struggling to her feet, Susanne smiled brightly. "I'll be there in a minute!"

It was late afternoon before they managed to free the wheel. The old wagon lurched forward, and Harlon, Corliss, and the children shouted with glee. Payne and Aaron stood back with big grins spread across their youthful faces. Only the whites of their eyes and teeth showed through the thick layers of muck caked on their noses and faces.

Doog suddenly bent, scooped up a handful of mud, and flung it at Jesse. The day's tensions eased as quickly as they had come, and soon the ensuing mud war caught everyone in its spontaneity.

Susanne glanced warily at Cass, who looked no better than she, and abruptly they joined in the fun.

Susanne thought the mud balls Cass hurled at her had entirely too much velocity to them, but she stood her ground and returned fire in a wholehearted attempt to go him one better.

The participants were a pitiful sight to behold when a truce was finally called. Even Corliss and Harlon were covered with mud, having been innocently caught in the cross fire.

"You look funnnny." Phebia pointed at Susanne, who gagged and spit out a clump of mud.

"Land sakes, I never saw such goings-on!" Corliss complained. She rounded up the smaller kids, shooing them to the back of the wagon where a bar of lye soap and the water barrel awaited.

Cass followed the crowd, and Susanne made belated introductions. She didn't go into detail about her and Cass's prior history, saying only that they'd met before.

Once he was presentable, Cass walked away from the boisterous group and headed for his horse.

Chapter 4

Susanne glanced up from scrubbing mud out of Lucy's hair and saw that Cass was leaving. "Margaret, come help Lucy, sweetie," she murmured under her breath. "There's something I need to do."

Cass frowned when she strode purposefully toward him. He reined the stallion in the opposite direction, but she was faster than his intent. Her hand snaked out and grabbed the bridle, impeding his departure.

"I want to talk to you," she stated flatly.

"Sorry. I've already wasted a whole day."

"I seriously doubt you'll consider what I have to say a waste of your time," she promised.

"Anything you have to say I'd consider a waste of my time, Miss McCord." He cut the reins to the left, and she was forced to step aside.

"Make that Mrs. Claxton," she corrected. "Mrs. Cass Claxton," she repeated a little louder when he showed no signs of staying.

The words—fighting words—stopped his departure cold. He reined up.

She saw his back muscles tighten, almost as if he knew what

was coming next. Without turning around, he spoke in a voice so ominous that it should have made her think twice about what she was about to do.

"Mrs. Cass Claxton—now, what's that supposed to mean?"

"If you'll stop being in such an all-fired hurry to get away from me, I'll tell you what that means."

Cass turned his horse and walked the animal back to where she stood. He sat staring at her for a moment; then he slowly dismounted. His blue eyes fixed on hers with a soundless warning. "All right, what are you up to this time?"

"I need your help, Cass. Badly. That's what I've been trying to tell you." She swallowed and dropped her gaze.

The disgusted sound that came from the back of his throat was not encouraging. "Don't you ever let up?"

She took a step, her voice now brimming with underlying urgency. "I will let up; I promise. If you'll help me this one last time I will never bother you again."

He bent forward, tipping his hat politely. "Can't do it, lady. Sorry. I got troubles of my own."

So. He was going to hold to his stubborn, mulish pride. All right. She didn't want to match his heartless tactics, but he left no other choice. She lifted her eyes to meet his. "You have more trouble than you think."

"What did you mean by that 'Mrs. Cass Claxton' remark?" he repeated, and she took small comfort in the fear that now started to creep into his self-satisfied expression. He could bluff all he wanted; she knew the truth—ugly as it might be.

His expression dropped from forced tolerance to looking tempted to draw his gun on her, so she decided to divert the blow. She preferred not to antagonize him, but she knew that was impossible. Her mere existence annoyed him. "You're on your way to Cherry Grove, aren't you?"

For one imperceptible instant she thought she saw his mouth slacken with disbelief. "No."

"You're not telling the truth."

"Okay. Suppose I am on my way there?" This time he swung out of the saddle, apparently ready to stand his ground.

"I need you to take the children and me to Cherry Grove with you," Susanne said before she lost her nerve.

"Over my dead body."

She smothered the urge to strike out. Instead, she kept her tone pleasant. "Mr. Claxton, if I could have arranged that I would have long ago. I think, for your benefit—and for that of your French lady friend—you'd best consider what I have to say."

Cass shifted his weight impatiently. "Laure? What does Laure have to do with me taking you, two elderly people, and nine children to Cherry Grove, Kansas?"

"Listen, and listen well, Mr. Claxton. If you escort us there, then I in return will hand you signed annulment papers dissolving our marriage."

"I should have a copy somewhere, shouldn't I?"

She smiled. "I don't think so; I never applied. Did you?"

"Me? I thought you'd file—" He stiffened. "I told you to take care of it."

"You told me a lot of things, sir."

His eyes narrowed. "Are you telling me that our 'marriage' is still—?" The news apparently rendered him temporarily scrambling for a scathing denial.

"I believe you heard me correctly."

Coherent thoughts appeared to fail him. "Just what makes you so cocksure I'm even going to Kansas?"

She quickly focused on her hands. "I'm. . .not sure you are. . . .

I just assume you might be, since I know you have kin there. You said no sane man would be pleasure riding in weather like this."

"Look, Susanne." She felt mildly relieved that he was at least using her name now. "I am not taking you or anyone else to Cherry Grove. I'm going to travel hard and fast, and I can't be dragging twelve other people along with me."

"We'll keep up," she promised. "Just help us drive the team, and make sure we're not attacked by marauders or wolves or the like."

"Now, how am I supposed to do that?"

"You can," she said, firmly believing that even though he was a miserable excuse for a human being, his knowledge of the land was invaluable. "The boys and Harlon will keep us in fresh meat and water, and I promise we won't ask anything of you if it isn't necessary."

"Just that I get twelve people to Cherry Grove without incident."

Susanne didn't like to think of it that way, but that was the general drift. "Yes."

He grinned. "Well, now. How about this? The day you hand me the signed annulment papers will be the day we'll discuss my getting you to Cherry Grove with your pretty little head intact."

"I can't t give you the papers this moment because I don't have them!" *Oh, dear Lord! I'm slipping. Grant me patience. Grace. Strike me deaf so I can't hear his taunts.*

Cass turned back to mount the horse. "Then consider the subject closed."

She reached out and grabbed the bridle. Their gazes locked in silent duel. "Just to Cherry Grove, then you're free of me. Forever."

His eyes darkened. "And if I don't agree to your blackmail?"

She shrugged. "I'm in no hurry to remarry. Are you?" The silent message rang out like a bell. She could hold out on the annulment, never sign the papers even if he filed, contest the annulment in court, do a hundred thousand things to make his life miserable. She wouldn't, of course, but at the moment the unspoken threat was the only remaining weapon in her arsenal.

She waited for his reaction. When it finally came, it was nothing close to what she had expected.

He simply stared at her, a muscle working tightly in his left jaw.

"Cass?" She edged forward, extending her hand to him, aware that the matter distressed him. "I promise, I will give you the annulment. . . . Please don't think I enjoy using underhanded tactics. . . . But you must see that my situation is impossible without your help—"

"Susanne, I wish I could believe you."

She deserved that. Reestablishing trust wouldn't be easy, and she had treated him abominably.

"I will do better, Cass. I won't even come around you. The children are my only concern."

"We've been married for six years?"

She nodded hesitantly. "Yes—on paper only. But that needn't upset you. If you're on your way to Cherry Grove, then what can it hurt if we ride along? I think we could make it fine on our own, but Harlon needs an experienced man to see us through the wilds." She bit her tongue, wanting to add "and I can think of no other man with your vast experience," but she knew he would construe the remark to mean women—which is how it was meant to be taken. So she refrained. "I promise you, the very day we reach Cherry Grove I will file for the annulment. There won't be any trouble in having the mock marriage set aside."

Guilt that she would take God's solemn ceremony so lightly flooded her, but she had asked for and received forgiveness. She swallowed. "After that, why, you'll never see me again."

His eyes shifted to the covered wagon swarming with children then on to Corliss and Harlon, who were sitting in the wagon looking as though they were about to draw their last breath. She waited, wondering if he was a man strong enough to put pride aside in lieu of common sense.

"If I say no, you will lie and say the vows had been consummated. Your father, Judge Leviticus McCord, will make doubly sure that the marriage was duly recorded in order to protect his daughter's sterling reputation."

"I've changed, Cass. I wouldn't do that. But I would fight to prevent the annulment long as I could." He couldn't know that she was telling the truth; she had a bad history of falsehoods and willful nature. But she meant every word.

He laughed. But not from humor. She recognized ugly disbelief, and she knew she had earned his lack of respect.

"Will you help us?" She waited for the answer, not sure what she would do if he refused her. There were no more tricks in her arsenal.

Cass shook his head wordlessly. Then, shooting her a look that could have sent a strong man to his knees, he mounted the stallion.

"Aren't you going to say anything?" she asked.

He calmly turned the horse toward the wagon. "The moment we get there, Susanne. I want those signed papers in my hand the same day."

Relief flooded her. She nodded. "You have my word."

He snorted.

Thank You, God. I know I don't deserve this grace after the underhanded way I've made him help. But this promise I will fulfill. One day after arriving in Cherry Grove, barring any technicalities, Cass will have his freedom.

She didn't have the slightest idea why the thought should make her so sad.

"You think them border ruffians will attack us and steal our wagon?"

Cass slowly cracked an eye open and stared into a pair of solemn gray ones. "I thought you were supposed to be fetching wood."

"I was." Jesse gestured toward a small pile of limbs and twigs lying at Cass's feet. "Now what about them outlaws?"

"What about 'em?" A fly buzzed in a lazy circle above Cass's head as he lowered the brim of his hat to shade his eyes from the glare of the midday sun. The past two weeks had been gruesome. Rain. Heat. Kids. Everywhere he looked a kid came into view. Susanne kept her promise to stay away from him, and the old folks went to bed so early he barely knew they were around. For a while the kids had steered clear of him. Phebia still wouldn't have anything to do with him, and Aaron and Payne had walked around him like a coiled rattler. Jesse had been the first to open up, and the others had followed.

"They gonna kill us?" Jesse asked.

"I don't imagine so."

"How do you know?"

Cass glanced at Susanne, who was standing in the stream doing wash. "Because they're never around when you need them."

Susanne overheard the remark. She wrung out a shirt and laid it across a flat rock to dry. Sunday was a day of rest—if washing, cooking, and standing guard over the camp while the men went hunting was considered rest.

The night before, they had been blessed to find a grove of tall pines adjacent to a clear-running stream to make camp. After morning chores were finished they gathered for Bible study. Harlon, who enjoyed leading, had a tendency to name his lessons. He announced his chosen scripture, Romans 12. "Today we're going to be studying 'How to Behave Like a Christian.'"

Susanne stiffened at the first verse, aware that Cass was watching her as Harlon's voice boomed out, adding emphasis she felt was entirely uncalled for. "Let love be without dissimulation."

The words fell upon her heart like stones as he continued. "Be kindly affectioned one to another with brotherly love."

She had lied to force Cass into marrying her and then tricked him into accompanying them on this dangerous journey, taking him away from his comfortable home and his business. She certainly hadn't been kind to Cass. Hadn't been acting like a very good Christian, either. *I'll do better,* she vowed silently. After all, she should live her beliefs before the children.

Harlon wound up his scripture reading. "Rejoicing in hope; patient in tribulation; continuing instant in prayer; distributing to the necessity of saints; given to hospitality."

Susanne sighed. Why was it so difficult to do what was right and so easy to do wrong? And rejoicing in hope? Her troubles were too overwhelming, too enduring, to leave much room for rejoicing.

Cass shot her a sardonic glance from beneath the brim of his hat, and every bit of her remorse vanished. Susanne glanced at the children gathered around them and hardened her heart. She would make it up to him after he delivered her charges to Cherry Grove. They were her first priority. Cass was a grown man. He could take care of himself. The children couldn't.

After Bible study, they gathered around the fire, where Corliss had a kettle of stew simmering. Susanne helped dip up the fragrant mix of meat and vegetables simmered in home-canned tomatoes.

"Mr. Cass?" Margaret Ann stared up at him, her eyes inquiring. "What's dissimulation?"

Cass hesitated; then a note of malice crept into his voice. "Why don't you ask Miss McCord?"

Susanne felt the heat rise in her cheeks. "I assume you caught the part about distributing to the needs of the saints and being given to hospitality? It seems you've been a trifle slack in those areas." After all, if he'd agreed to let her have the house he owned they wouldn't be traveling overland to Kansas.

Cass quirked an eyebrow. "Ah, but I've never considered you a saint."

Susanne opened her mouth to give the unspeakable cad a lesson when Corliss intervened. "Will the two of you please remember this is the Lord's Day? I'll not have any childish squabbling; you hear me?"

"Yes, ma'am," Cass muttered, looking disconcerted.

Susanne pressed her lips together, suppressing the words threatening to spill out. The title of Harlon's Bible study shamed her. "How to Behave Like a Christian." She sighed. *I'm sorry, Lord. Forgive me again.*

Why did she let Cass upset her like this? She picked up the ladle and started dishing out seconds. The mischievous gleam in Cass Claxton's eyes didn't do anything to improve her disposition.

After lunch, the children wandered off to fish and swim, openly enjoying their reprieve from the long days. Actually they'd made good time, considering the obstacles a group of their size confronted daily. She and Cass had avoided each other. The kids knew something was wrong, but not one had mentioned the strange conduct.

Corliss and Harlon noticed the animosity between Cass and her, but they were polite enough to ignore it. Susanne knew Harlon was too relieved to hear that Cass had agreed to travel with them to ever question why.

She had wondered how the children and Cass would get along. Sometimes she still worried that he might lose his temper with them, but she thought he'd shown a surprising amount of forbearance for their constant chatter and endless curiosity.

Aaron and Payne were clearly in awe of this man who seemed to know everything. The two boys were never far from Cass's vicinity, even though they rarely tried to get his attention.

Phebia was the only one who still kept herself at bay. Cass had made several attempts to win her trust, but the three-year-old remained skeptical when it came to the tall, dark-haired stranger who had come so suddenly into their lives.

All in all, the days were beginning to settle into a routine, and Susanne was thankful. She began to think her worries were groundless, that the trip might pass without incident. And Cass would be out of her life forever.

She pretended to be absorbed in her work while she listened to the conversation taking place a few feet from her.

"Bryon, leave my gun alone."

Bryon's inquisitive fingers persistently crept over to explore the shiny Colt revolver Cass wore strapped to his right leg. The weapon was an enduring source of interest to the boys, who were familiar only with the old-fashioned muzzle-loading rifle Harlon kept in the wagon for protection.

Moments later Susanne heard Cass warn Bryon again; the child's curious fingers had started to creep toward the pistol a second time. Even Doog and Jesse were eyeing the weapon with a determined look in their eyes.

"Can't you see Mr. Cass is trying to sleep?" Payne admonished the smaller boys. He leaned against the trunk of a tree whittling a new whistle—for Joseph, Susanne guessed. "Why don't you go find something to do?"

"Don't want to," Bryon said.

"Then let's take a nap," Aaron threatened.

"Don't want to!"

Four-year-old Joseph walked up and straddled Cass's chest. "Don't want to, either!" he joined in.

Cass sighed and sat up, lifting Joseph from his chest.

Corliss looked up from her mending and sharply admonished, "You children, git! Let Mr. Cass rest!"

"It's all right, Corliss. I promised Harlon I'd help fix the broken harness," Cass said.

"Now that you're awake, will you show us your gun?" Bryon persisted.

Susanne had to turn her head to keep from laughing out loud.

Even Margaret and Lucy looked up when they saw that Cass was going to oblige. Dropping the articles of clothing they'd been scrubbing, they scampered quickly from the stream when the shiny gun came out of its holster.

Cass squatted down on his haunches, and the children gathered around him. Only Phebia, clutching her doll, chose to stand to one side and watch instead of participate.

His strong baritone gentled. "A gun can either save your life or take it. You have to learn to respect whatever kind of weapon you decide to carry. This particular pistol is what they call a percussion revolver." He checked the empty chamber before he handed it butt-first to Aaron.

The young man's hands trembled with excitement when he took the gun and examined it closely.

"The thing about a percussion revolver is its firepower," Cass continued. "Like a breech-loading weapon, a revolver can be loaded and fired rapidly. You can put six shots in the cylinder of a percussion firearm and fire it in a matter of seconds. That's quite an improvement over the time it takes to fill a muzzle loader with powder and ball and cap it."

Doog, Jesse, and Bryon pressed closer, eager for a turn to hold the gun.

Aaron reluctantly passed the pistol to Payne for his inspection.

"Mr. Cass," Margaret Ann said primly, "a gun is necessary, but isn't it also dangerous in the hands of an inexperienced shooter?"

Cass flashed a crooked grin at her. "Very good, Margaret. Like anything else, you have to take the bad with the good. There's a possibility of the revolver discharging several chambers at once. The flashback of hot powder and gases from the gap of the barrel and cylinder could seriously injure a man—or woman."

Lucy flinched and moved closer to Cass, draping her arm protectively around his neck. "Throw it away," she insisted. "Me don't want you hurt! I wuv you!"

Susanne wasn't surprised to hear Lucy's flourishing declaration of love. Clearly she'd been enamored of Cass from the moment he'd joined them. Cass had that effect on women.

"I don't want you hurt. I love you." Susanne automatically corrected the child's English and wrung out a muslin petticoat.

At the sound of her voice all heads shot up. Chatter ceased.

Susanne glanced up, startled to see that they were staring at her. Her cheeks grew hot when she noticed Cass's eyes fixed on her. He met her flustered gaze, and he grinned. She realized the cad was amused by her innocent blunder! They'd mistaken her statement for a declaration, not a simple correction.

Even Corliss had misunderstood. She sat gaping at Susanne, needle and thread suspended in midair.

"Land sakes! You all know what I meant." Susanne dropped her head sheepishly and focused her full attention on the collar of Harlon's flannel shirt. How one man got so dirty was beyond her!

The children's eyes turned back to the pistol, but Susanne's unsettled feeling lingered. She noticed that though Cass continued to talk to the children, his eyes repeatedly strayed back to her. And the man was still grinning!

She ignored the sudden butterfly swarm in the pit of her stomach, grimly conceding that, try as she may, she was finding it increasingly hard to ignore the fact that he was an exceptionally appealing man.

Susanne wasn't aware of just how serious her attraction had grown until she stepped out of the wagon a couple of mornings later and saw Cass stripped to the waist, shaving.

She stood frozen in the shadow of the canvas, staring at him as he lifted his chin, eyed himself in the small mirror tacked to the tree, and drew the straight-edged razor across his cheekbone.

The sight of his bare chest covered with a mat of curly dark brown hair made her look away in guilt. Other than her father's, Susanne had never seen a man's chest—and most assuredly Leviticus McCord's chest looked nothing like the solid ridge of muscle she now found herself staring at again.

She shook away the disturbing image, ashamed of herself. She should be about her work, not ogling a man, but her eyes refused to budge from the tightly corded muscles that rippled along his arms when he leaned closer to the mirror, carefully shaving his upper lip and then around the long, dark sideburns.

Laure Revuneau popped unexpectedly into her mind, and she felt a stirring that was very close to jealousy. How often had Cass embraced the lovely Frenchwoman?

Susanne was startled to find that the question intrigued and annoyed her; she deliberately set her feet in motion.

It didn't matter how many women had been in her husband's life. He'd made it clear to Susanne that she would never be one of them, no matter how badly she was beginning to wish that she'd started out on a better footing with him.

She rounded the corner of the wagon, pretending not to notice his presence as she filled the coffeepot and swung it over the fire.

Corliss appeared, and they exchanged morning greetings. The older woman flapped the skirt of her apron and made clucking sounds as she gathered the six white laying hens and one rooster that she released from the chicken coop each night. The chickens seemed to sense when it was time to move on. They flew into the portable coop without a backward glance.

Giving both women a perfunctory look, Cass said good morning, while Phebia came around the corner, dragging Marybelle by her heels.

"Poor Marybelle's going to have a knot on her head," Cass observed when Phebia came to a stop beside him. She stood silently staring up at him.

He set the razor aside, reached for a towel, and wiped the stray remnants of shaving cream off his face. "Something I can do for you this morning, Miss Phebia?"

Susanne was amazed at the way he handled the child's continuing reticence, allowing her ample time to warm to him. He would make a wonderful father, she realized and was astonished at her observation. A few short weeks ago she wouldn't have wished Cass Claxton on her worst enemy, let alone an innocent child.

Phebia remained silent, but a few moments later Susanne saw her tug at Cass's trouser leg.

He glanced down, and the little girl cautiously handed the rag doll to him. After a brief examination, Cass noted out loud that Marybelle was missing an eye. He reached for his shirt, slipped it on, and acknowledged soberly, "This looks serious."

Motioning for Susanne, who had been listening to the exchange while she'd dropped slices of bacon into a large iron skillet, he ordered briskly, "Nurse McCord. Prepare for surgery."

Playing along with his theatrical manner, Susanne dramatically passed the fork to Corliss and went to the wagon to fetch her sewing box.

Moments later Marybelle lay on a large, flat rock, her one remaining eye staring sightlessly up at the mock medical team.

Nurse McCord located a new eye (that almost matched the old button), and the doctor set to work. Phebia watched with rounded eyes when Cass's surprising nimble fingers drew thread in and out of Marybelle's tender cotton face. "This should only take a few minutes," he told the anxious mother.

Operation completed, the patient rested comfortably—with one green and one blue eye.

"How did you do that?" Susanne whispered. "My father couldn't sew a button on his shirt."

He grinned. "Sewn up so many cattle, horses, and dogs it comes second nature."

Before Susanne could pronounce the patient fit, Phebia scooped the doll into her arms and squeezed her tightly.

Cass reached for his hat and adjusted it on his head, grinning at the elfin three-year-old. "You know, Phebia, if you carry Marybelle in your arms instead of letting her face drag on the ground, she'll be likely to keep her eyes longer."

Nodding, the child started to skip happily away when she suddenly paused and turned around. Slowly she walked back to Cass. Crooking one finger, she motioned for him to lean down.

Phebia is going to kiss him! Susanne observed. The child had come so far from the day they found her on the orphanage doorstep.

Cass obligingly crouched to her level, and the child's brown eyes somberly met his blue ones.

Suddenly Phebia's forefinger and thumb darted out, clamped

onto his nose like a vise, and twisted.

"Phebia!" Susanne dropped her sewing basket and bolted to break the child's grip. Wrestling the child's steely hold, she demanded that she stop.

Cass wobbled back and forth, trying to retain his balance.

Finally Phebia gave his nose one final jerk then calmly released it, stuck her thumb in her mouth, and skipped away to join the other kids.

Cass fell backward onto the ground and lay there for a moment.

"Oh Cass!" Susanne knelt beside him, brushing dirt off his shirt. "Did she hurt you?"

"Yes!" He rubbed his nose, which was now a glaring red. "I've fought with men twice my size and come out in better shape." He stared up at a laughing Susanne. "What's so funny? The kid nearly took my nose off!"

"I think that's Phebia's way of accepting you," she offered. She covered her mouth, suppressing a giggle.

"Accepting me!" His fingers examined his smarting nose for broken cartilage. "I'll have to blow my nose out of my ear from now on. She's maimed me for life."

Susanne gave him a helping hand, which he grasped, and she pulled him to his feet, determined to ignore the way her heart jumped when their hands touched.

"You know something?" he asked, slapping dust from his pants with his hat.

Susanne worked hard to maintain a sober face. His nose was fairly glowing. "What?" Had his eyes always been that blue? They were beautifully expressive—even when angry.

"The kid reminds me of you."

The likeness hit her the wrong way. Had she been expecting a compliment? From him? That was as likely as snow in August. She whirled and marched back to the fire. She wasn't about to pursue the remark, because no matter what she did, he managed to find fault with her. She'd gone out of her way to be nice to him lately, but he hadn't bothered to say one kind word to her.

"Don't walk away from me while I'm talking."

"When you say something worth hearing, I'll listen," she tossed over her shoulder.

But she felt sure it wasn't imminent.

Chapter 5

Trouble, Cass decided, was his middle name. And he'd been right to hold off on marriage and having kids. God had not equipped him to be a family man. The next morning, he reluctantly agreed to keep an eye on Phebia while Susanne, Corliss, and the other children went off to pick the last of the wild berries.

While he shaved, Phebia played with Marybelle around his feet. He had to sidestep twice before he could convince her that she should go feed Marybelle a late breakfast and get out of his way.

To his relief, the child bought the idea and raced to get a biscuit from the supply box. She sat on a nearby rock, taking intermittent bites and then squashing crumbs into Marybelle's unyielding mouth while Cass finished shaving in peace.

He was wiping soap from his face when he heard Phebia let out a scream that raised the hairs on the back of his neck.

He whirled. "What's wrong?"

"Caw-doo. Me want caw-doo!"

Cass stared back at her blankly. "Caw-doo?"

She nodded succinctly.

"Caw-doo, caw-doo," Cass murmured. He glanced around the

camp, wondering what in the Sam Hill caw-doo meant.

"Caw-doo!" Phebia demanded, her tone turning more belligerent.

"Caw-doo. . ." Cass was getting frantic. A thought came to him, and his heart nearly stopped. Kneeling beside the rock where Phebia perched, he whispered hesitantly, "Did you do something in your britches?"

Cass hoped to high heaven that wasn't the case. He'd never had to deal with anything like that before, and he wasn't sure he could.

Her eyes narrowed, and her face puffed with indignation. She shook her head and cried out, "Caw-doo!"

"Okay. Caw-doo." Relieved, Cass started grabbing anything in sight, trying to figure out what she wanted.

He held up her bonnet.

She shook her head. No.

He held up the remainder of the biscuit she'd been eating.

"No!"

A bar of soap.

"No!"

A towel.

"No! Caw-doo."

"Why don't you sit there and suck your thumb until Susanne gets back?" he offered, knowing that he shouldn't be encouraging her to continue a habit they'd all been trying to help her break, but he was stumped.

Phebia stood up and stamped her foot, clearly outraged by his stupidity. "Caw-doo!"

Cass felt sweat starting to trickle down his back.

After several more futile attempts, he sat down on the rock beside her, admitting defeat. "Phebia, I'm sorry, but I don't know what you want."

He glanced up, relieved to see Aaron rounding a corner carrying a bucket mounded with berries.

"Hi."

"Aaron, you got any idea what caw-doo means?" Cass asked.

"Water."

Cass looked up, startled. "Water?"

"That's what she calls water." Aaron grinned at Phebia. "You want a drink of water, squirt?"

Phebia eagerly nodded. "Me want caw-doo!"

Cass watched while Aaron led her to the water bucket and reached for the dipper.

Caw-doo, Cass thought irritably. Imagine that. He could have sworn it would be something you'd step in, not drink.

Five men rode into camp late that afternoon. Cass and Aaron were off hunting to replenish the dwindling meat supply. Harlon had stretched out in the shade of the wagon, taking a much-needed rest, and Corliss sat on an overturned bucket mending Doog's shirt. Susanne looked up as the four rode into the small clearing, and she knew in an instant this could be trouble. They were a ragtag bunch—none too clean, and unshaven. Three wore overalls with the sleeves of their red long johns serving as shirts. Battered felt hats crowned their heads, and each one packed a sidearm and had a rifle in the saddle boot.

The way they eyed her left Susanne feeling uneasy. She was used to more respect, even from Cass. However, she knew better than to show a sign of weakness. Her chin lifted, and she waited for the men to state their business.

"Ma'am." The biggest one tipped his hat. His undersized, shrewd eyes, almost eclipsed by the broad expanse of his hat, squinted back at her.

Susanne nodded and gripped the wooden spoon she'd been using to stir a batch of corn bread. Who were these ruffians, and what did they want? She spared a glance at the encroaching tree line, wishing Cass would return. From the corner of her eye she saw Harlon sitting up and slowly edging closer to his rifle.

"Bull Hanson here," the big man said. "We've been traveling quite a spell. Don't guess you'd be able to spare a hot meal?"

Susanne swallowed. She did not want these men spending any time in the camp, but she could hardly say no. The unwritten code of the trail required that she offer them hospitality. She had a feeling nothing she could say would make any difference anyway.

Aware too much time was passing with no answers from her, she hastened to reply. "Of course. Supper will be ready in an hour or so, which will give you time to take care of your horses."

A second man, the lower half of his thin face covered with ragged stubble, edged his horse forward. His gaze skimmed the camp. "You all traveling alone?"

Susanne shifted her grip on the spoon. "My husband and oldest son are hunting. They should be back any moment."

"That so?" The thin man grinned. His eyes raked her. "Now why would he go off and leave a pretty little thing like you all alone?"

I'm not alone." Susanne indicated Harlon and Corliss and the children.

"Seems like something's missing," the man said. "Like maybe that husband of yours is just a story you tell people?"

"That's not true." Susanne heard the catch in her voice. *Oh Cass, come back. Hurry.*

A shot sounded, followed by a second one, and the big man, Bull Hanson, lifted his head to listen.

Relief swept Susanne. "That's him now. He'll be back to camp soon, likely bringing fresh meat for supper."

The third man, cleaner than the others, young but with an air of competence about him, gathered up the reins, turning his horse. "Reckon we'd best ride on, Bull."

The big man appeared to consider the thought before shaking his head. "No. That stew smells powerful good. I believe we'll stay."

He dismounted and the others followed suit, tying their horses to saplings and gathering around the fire. Susanne went about her work, aware of five pairs of male eyes following her every move.

Corliss gathered the children into the shelter of the wagon; Harlon stayed close to his rifle. Every passing moment seemed like an hour.

Cass, where are you? I need you.

But even if he came back, he'd be outnumbered, and walking in unaware of the scruffy company. There must be some way she could warn him, but her mind refused to cooperate.

Cass approached camp carrying the young doe Aaron had shot. He'd fired simultaneously, but his bullet missed. The kid had taken a lucky shot and dropped the deer. His first, judging from the big grin he wore like a badge. A break in the trees allowed Cass a full view of camp. He stopped, eyeing the five men seated around the fire, their attention centered on Susanne. He motioned for Aaron to wait.

The boy's eyes grew wide when he saw the visitors. His voice dropped to a stage whisper. "What are you going to do?"

"I don't know." Cass lowered the deer to the ground, looking over the situation. After a minute, he motioned to Aaron. "You come in from the south. I'll work my way around and approach from the north. Don't move a muscle until you hear me whistle."

Aaron nodded and Cass moved away, walking quietly. When he was in position, he whistled, low but clear. He noticed the way the men tensed, covertly looking around the campsite. Probably outlaws. Copycat scum spawned by admiration for the James boys and the Younger clan.

Once even Cass had admired Frank and Jesse James, believing them to be victims fighting for their rights. Over the years his view had changed when he came to realize the truth. Frank and Jesse might have started out with noble intentions, but they had turned into renegades, outlaws who would rather steal than work.

He eyed the five who stood around the fire. Dirty, spiritually corrupt men, preying on the weak. The Jameses and Youngers had a touch of class. This bunch wasn't in their league. Probably a good thing he and Aaron hadn't been in camp when they'd arrived. At least this way they had an element of surprise in their favor.

Cass stepped from the concealing brush and advanced toward the campfire. Five pairs of eyes watched him, the men's expressions calculating. Susanne looked relieved, and Harlon relaxed perceivably. Cass looked past the men, nodding as Aaron strode from the thicket, rifle held in a casual yet thoroughly businesslike manner.

The big man made a small gesture and the others settled back, their expressions becoming less watchful. Cass strode into camp, moving easily, rifle at the ready. "Afternoon."

The leader stepped forward and extended his hand. "Hanson's my name. Bull Hanson. Your missus invited us to stay for supper." He glanced at Aaron. "Fine-looking son you got there."

Cass shifted his attention to Susanne, noting the flush staining her cheeks, but her eyes met his readily enough. He guessed she'd run a bluff. This was one time he appreciated her spunk.

"Sure thing." He shook Hanson's hand. First man he'd met who was as tall and imposing as Sar. "Glad to have company. Payne, you and Jesse help Aaron carry the deer in and we'll get it dressed."

He passed Susanne on his way to the wagon and dropped his hand on her shoulder in a possessive manner, eyeing Bull Hanson as he did so. The faces of the outlaws remained neutral, revealing nothing. Cass had a bad feeling about the company. Had this band managed to stumble in on them, or had they been trailing a lone wagon, waiting until Susanne and the children were left with only Harlon to defend them? Starting tomorrow he was teaching the three older boys to use a gun.

The boys carried the deer into camp, and Cass strung it up from the branch of a white oak tree, preparing to remove the skin. One of the strangers, the cleanest one, came over to watch. His brown hair was in need of a haircut, but his hazel eyes were steady and nonthreatening. Nothing was said for a few minutes, and then the stranger took out a knife and stepped in closer. Cass tensed, waiting for what would come next.

The man grinned. "Slim Watkins here. Just trying to help."

"Help's always welcome." Cass slit the skin down the inside of one leg. "You from these parts?"

"I'm from a lot of places," Slim said. "Some of them I can even go back to."

Cass smiled. "We're just passing through ourselves."

"A word of advice," Slim said. He stepped closer. "You see that scrawny dude eyeing your wife? Watch out for him. He'd as soon shoot you in the back as look at you."

"Can't see why he'd do that." Cass's stomach tightened at the thought. He'd noticed the thin man with the wolfish grin, but figured Bull could keep his men in line.

"Oh, Joe Killen doesn't need a reason. He just plain likes to hurt people. See one like that once in a while."

"Seen some in the war," Cass admitted. "Never cared for the type."

"Me neither. You fought in the war? Which side?"

"The South."

"I'm a Johnny Reb myself," Slim said.

Cass knew the war could bind men together in a way that had nothing to do with where a man came from or what kind of work he did. He knew Beau and Cole felt the same way. The men they had fought with were like family.

"I don't think you'll have a problem with this bunch." Slim helped pull the hide loose from the carcass. "But if Joe or Bull starts something I'll weigh in on your side. Just wanted you to know."

"Why would you do that?"

"I draw the line at some things." His eyes wandered back to the fire site.

"Then why would you ride with scum?" Cass deftly slit open the deer, removing the organs and placing them into a bucket Slim held.

"I'm thinking seriously of parting ways. My mama didn't bring me up to run with the likes of Bull and Joe."

"A man needs to stay close to his raising," Cass agreed. "I got a good mama myself. Been too long since I've seen her." Before he went back to Saint Louis he planned to drop by River Run—eat some of Willa's chicken and dumplings.

"Yeah." Slim watched as Cass sliced the fresh meat, getting it ready for the fire. "Think I'll be riding back to the Missouri Boot Heel before much longer. There's not much future in outlawing."

"Never much wanted to die with my boots on," Cass agreed. "I'll take a feather bed and my family anytime."

Slim hefted the pan of fresh meat. "I'll take this to your wife."

"Any chance of you all riding out after supper?" Cass asked.

"Can't say what Bull might do." Slim turned and walked back to the campfire. Cass watched him go, wondering if the young stranger was being truthful or if he was trying to pull a fast one. Get them relaxed and off guard so Bull could move in and catch them by surprise. That wasn't going to happen.

He finished dressing out the meat and carried it to the fire, where Corliss and Harlon would take care of it. Susanne already had thick steaks sizzling over the flames. The scent of cooking meat blended with the smell of simmering stew and a skillet of baked corn bread. No wonder the band of outlaws chose to stay for supper.

One by one the men got up from supper, stretching. Slim carried his dishes to a fallen log where Corliss bent over a pan of soapy water, doing cleanup. "That sure was a fine meal, ma'am. Believe it was one of the finest I've eaten in a spell."

Susanne heard his remark and decided if all the men were like him she wouldn't mind having them around so much. She didn't like the way the skinny one, Joe, looked at her. Several times she'd seen him watching Cass with a calculating gleam in his eyes, as if wondering if he could take him. She wouldn't put it past the outlaw to shoot a man in the back if he thought he could get away with it. That's why she had slipped into the wagon and gotten her own derringer—the one that she had inherited from Aunt Estelle. Her aunt had been a woman of many talents, one of which was the ability to use a pistol—and the determination to use it if necessary. Susanne hoped she had the same resolve.

Lord, I wouldn't shoot a man unless it was absolutely necessary; You know that. But if these men made one move toward hurting a member of her party it would become necessary in a hurry.

The men looked as though they were settled in for the night, something Cass didn't want. He moved over to stand beside the rifle he'd left leaning against the wagon, one hand lingering close to the butt of the pistol hanging at his waist. "So you got far to ride tonight?"

Bull Hanson looked up, suddenly alert. His eyes took in Cass's vigilant stance, Harlon standing at the end of the wagon bed, rifle close by. Aaron leaned against a tree to the right of them, weapon dangling from the crook of his arm. Bull's teeth clamped on his lower lip for a minute as he apparently weighed his options.

"Thought we might spend the night here. Heard there was a group of renegades working this area. You folks might be in the need of a little protection."

"Oh, I think we can handle ourselves just fine," Cass told him. "Wouldn't want to delay your ride."

Slim rose to stand a little to the left. "We might ought to ride on, Bull. Got a ways to go."

Bull looked at him, considering. "You buying in to this?"

"No. Just think it might be the smart thing to do. Looks like these folks can take care of themselves."

The outlaw's eyes narrowed. "Maybe. Like you say, Cass here and old Harlon look pretty capable." He slowly got to his feet. "Time to saddle up, boys."

"Now, let's not be in any hurry," Joe said. "Seems like this here's a good place to spend the night. Lots of services, if you get what I mean."

Cass was quite certain that he understood what the man had in mind, and if he dared put a hand on Susanne, he was going to need an army of doctors to put him back together again.

Bull turned slowly and faced Joe. The man took a step backward. "I said, let's ride. Unless you got a different idea?"

"No, let's ride." Joe backed toward his horse. Cass let his hand rest on his pistol. He planned to make it clear the men had outstayed their welcome. The outlaws mounted up and slowly rode out, the silence so deep the only sound was the creaking of saddle leather. At the edge of the clearing Slim twisted in the saddle and lifted his hand in farewell. Cass nodded an acknowledgment. He hoped the young man followed through on his intentions and left the gang.

Cass motioned for Harlon and Aaron to stay on alert. He wouldn't put it past the outlaws to circle around and come back. It looked like he was going to stand guard tonight.

Susanne helped Corliss get the children ready for bed.

Phebia resisted all efforts, claiming she needed to stay awake to take care of Marybelle. "Her's afraid of the dark. And those ole men might come back."

"Then you need to take her to bed with you and cover up her head so she won't be afraid. And Cass won't let 'those ole men' hurt you, darling."

The child's indignation rose. "Her can't breathe with her head covered up."

"I see. Well, really, I do believe Marybelle will be just fine if you hold her tight and tell her a bedtime story."

"Me don't know any stories. You tell her story."

"Not tonight. I still have work to do. I'll be in plain sight if you need anything."

Phebia sighed and held the doll up against Susanne's face. "Kiss Marmarbelle good night."

Susanne obediently kissed the doll and then dropped a second kiss on the little girl's forehead. "Sleep tight. Don't worry; God will keep you and Marybelle safe."

Phebia nodded. "God and my Cass."

Susanne smiled. "Mr. Cass will watch over you, too." They

bowed their heads and Phebia made her petition to God.

The child then turned on her side, arm curved over Marybelle, and stuck her thumb in her mouth. Would they never break her of that habit? Apparently not. Phebia had a mind of her own.

Susanne finished cleaning up the campsite and leaned back against the wagon bed. Harlon and Corliss must be asleep, judging from the duet of snores coming from behind the canvas covering. A loud snuffling hoot from Harlon, and a lighter fluttering gasp from his wife.

She thought about the older couple, how they looked after each other on the trail. More than once she had caught them holding hands, and Harlon often looked at Corliss as if she were still the most beautiful woman in the world. Sometimes she envied the couple the love they shared.

A silvery moon rose overhead, throwing patches of light over the clearing, turning shadows into black pools of darkness.

Susanne felt restless. The band of renegades had frightened her more than she liked to admit. If they had been traveling without Cass it could have been very different. She was so thankful he had agreed to stay with them, and to do him justice, he was keeping his part of the bargain. The children adored him. Harlon deferred to him on every decision, and Corliss flat-out catered to him, but unfortunately, he made it clear he had no time for Susanne McCord.

She wandered across the clearing, drifting closer to the deep shadows beneath a large oak tree. A hushed whisper reached her ears. "If you're going to walk around out here, at least have enough sense to stay in the shadow."

She stopped, pulse racing. "Cass?"

"You're lucky it's me. What would you do if Bull Hanson or Joe Killen was waiting out here?"

"I thought you were asleep." She edged into the tree line, trying to spot him.

"I would be if I could be sure we weren't going to have unexpected company."

"You think they might come back?"

"It's a possibility or I wouldn't be out here. Do I know they will return? No, but I'm not taking the risk."

Pausing, her eyes adjusted and she located him. "You'd protect me?" She felt joy rising like a bubble in her chest. He cared enough to protect her?

"I'd have to. Otherwise I'd have to take care of these kids by myself."

She tried to determine if there was a smile in his voice and decided probably not. Cass Claxton didn't do any smiling when she was around. "I see. You don't care what happens to me."

"I didn't say that. I wouldn't turn a dog over to those men."

He was comparing her to a dog? How charming. And infuriating. She moved close enough she could smell the smoke from the campfire on his clothing. *Let's see what Mr. Claxton is made of.*

"You care nothing at all for me?" She breathed the words into the night, for his ears alone. She didn't believe him; somewhere deep in his heart he had to care a little.

"Is there a reason why I should?"

His words had a rough edge that she didn't think came from anger. Being unable to see him heightened her senses. Hearing his words without seeing his face gave a different impression, and she had a feeling Cass Claxton wasn't as immune to her as he tried to pretend.

"Why shouldn't you? We're traveling together, and for the first time we have the opportunity to get acquainted. Why not relax and enjoy each other's company?"

"I'm not sure I want to get acquainted, but exactly what do you have in mind?"

"Why, nothing in particular." She faltered. "But technically, we are married—"

"Only technically."

"Only technically," she grudgingly agreed. "But we should at least pretend to get along. For the children's sake."

"I'm not good at pretending. And I don't want you for a friend. Every time I get close to you I end up with more trouble."

"You surely can't blame me because those men rode into camp. What do you think I could have done to stop them?"

"There was nothing you could do, but if they come back it will be because of you."

She hesitated, stunned by what he was saying. Why hadn't she thought of that before? Those men wouldn't come back to harm the children or kill Cass and Harlon. If they came back, it would be for her. The thought made her sick to her stomach. She reached out to touch him, needing the comfort of his presence. The feel of his arm beneath her hand, the muscular strength of him, sent a tingle of awareness through her.

He tensed, and she moved away. "I'm sorry. I didn't intend to disturb you."

"I'm not disturbed."

Susanne felt a new element inserting itself into their presence. Something she hadn't wanted or welcomed. When had she stopped thinking of Cass as someone she could use and begun seeing him as an attractive man she would like to know better? How could she have fallen prey to this man? The moment that he could free himself of her he would be gone, and she would never see him again. The last thing she needed was a lifetime of unrequited love.

She turned to go and stumbled over a root, pitching forward.

Arms closed around her. She leaned against his chest, struggling against the sensations racing through her mind. This was Cass Claxton. She hated him. She loved him. She was. . .confused.

His face was only a few inches from hers. She could feel his breath against her hair. Slowly, sweetly, he turned her and their lips met. She closed her eyes, drifting. Her arms reached up to encircle his neck as a wild sweetness surged through her until she was floating in a rising tide of joy.

He released her, gently but firmly removing her arms from around his neck. "I think you'd best turn in for the night."

Susanne drew away, stung by his rejection. For a moment she stared at him; then shame sent her reeling. What had happened to her? Had she thrown pride out the window where this man was concerned?

"Yes, of course," she murmured. She stepped back, moving away from him until she left the shelter of the shadows, edging out into the clear, cold light of the moon. Her fingers brushed her lips, marveling at his taste.

"Good night, Mr. Claxton." Her voice trembled.

"Miss McCord."

She walked away, torn between shame and exhilaration. Had she really behaved in such a wanton manner? After a moment she decided that she had. Oh dear. She was so frightened at her feelings.

Terrified that she would lose her heart to this man and never regain it.

Chapter 6

Cass had spent a restless time standing guard. He still wasn't sure they'd seen the last of the outlaws—especially the one called Bull—but he could be wrong. He had a feeling the man could be as mean as sin when he took a notion, and he had no real desire to tangle with him.

Susanne, still clearly peeved about last night's chance encounter, avoided him. Watching her, he could tell her anger simmered barely beneath the surface as she went about breaking camp.

He was going to ignore her. He had slept only a couple of hours, and his disposition wasn't the best this morning. He had too much on his mind to worry about an ill-tempered woman. Beau's telegram still concerned him; how much trouble was his brother in, and what kind of trouble? At the back of his mind he wrestled with the blooming attraction he felt for Susanne and the way she'd felt in his arms. Memories of the kiss they'd shared plagued him. The woman meant trouble with a capital *T*. He had to steer clear of her or risk getting more deeply involved.

He wouldn't be caught up in another situation with this aggravating female, no matter how much she egged him on. If he wanted that annulment—and he surely did—Susanne McCord was off-limits.

When Susanne sailed around the corner carrying a pan of dirty dishwater, Cass was crouched beside the wagon checking the left front axle.

The sight of him set her off again. Arrogant, self-centered cad. The way he'd kissed her, taken advantage of her innocence. She preferred not to remember the way her knees had gone weak as a newborn kitten and her pulse had fluttered like a trapped butterfly. She had been caught off guard. She would never intentionally let a man like Cass Claxton kiss her.

Determined to avoid another scene with him, she whirled and started off in the opposite direction, but suddenly her footsteps slowed. Cass was preoccupied with the wheel, apparently unaware that she was even in the vicinity. So like him. Pursing her lips, she struggled against the overpowering urge to fling the greasy water at him.

You've changed, Susanne. You don't behave like a hooligan anymore.

Still, it would serve him right for treating her the way he had last night—though she knew if she followed her impulse, it would be tantamount to waving a red flag at a salivating bull.

But he deserved every nasty, revolting, repulsive, obnoxious ounce of water in this pan.

Before she fully realized it, she had tiptoed closer to the wagon. When she was within firing range, she straightened and reared back to take aim. Cass stood up and turned to face her as the water flew out of the pan, headed straight in his direction.

His features went momentarily blank before what she was doing registered. His eyes widened with incredulity, and he dodged to one side in a vain attempt to avoid the onslaught, but his defense came too late. The dishwater hit its target squarely on the bull's-eye, leaving soggy bits of bacon rinds dangling limply from the front of his drenched shirt.

Jerking herself upright, Susanne could see that he was livid. She braced herself for the eruption that wasn't long in coming.

"You. . .you. . .what did you do that for?" he bellowed.

She looked at him with round-eyed innocence. "Oh my, I'm so sorry. I didn't see you."

He wiped greasy water from his eyes. "Don't try to pull that. You didn't see me? Like thunder you didn't! You always throw dishwater on the axle?"

A chunk of garbage dangled from his shoulder. He angrily flicked it aside.

She smiled smugly. "This morning I did." She shrugged, ignoring the blistering looks he sent her way. "Guess we'd better be getting a move on."

Susanne turned, aware that he was peevishly fanning the front of his shirt, mumbling things under his breath she was sure a lady wasn't supposed to hear.

"Sure has started off to be a fine day so far," she observed.

Cass was still eyeing her when she sauntered away, swinging the empty dishpan in her right hand.

Midmorning the wind kicked up. Aaron drove the team while Corliss rode on the seat next to him. Susanne walked behind with the children.

Harlon wasn't feeling well this morning—summer complaint, he thought—so about an hour ago he'd climbed into the back of the wagon to catch a short nap.

Susanne kept falling behind to oversee Lucy, Bryon, Joseph, Phebia, and Margaret Ann when they paused to gather armloads of wildflowers that grew along the roadway.

They'd forded a small creek a while back, the water shallow enough that the children waded across, splashing and laughing. Susanne watched their fun, thinking how life on the trail had changed them. Days spent in the sun had given the children a tanned, healthy look, so different from the city pallor. Eyes alert, cheeks rosy, full of energy, they followed the wagon, running as much as they walked, shouting out each new discovery from birds' nests to the pretty pebbles Phebia stuffed in her dress pockets.

Margaret Ann walked beside Susanne, leading Lucy by the hand. "Are we getting close to Kansas?"

"I'm afraid it's still a long way yet. Are you tired of living on the trail?"

"Oh no."

Susanne smiled at the dignified tone of voice. If women ever got the vote, as some claimed they eventually would, Margaret could very well be the first woman president, and she'd do just fine.

Now the child looked up with a serene expression. "I wish we could go on forever like this. It's so enjoyable."

"Enjoyable in what way?"

Margaret Ann shrugged. "You know what it was like back in Saint Louis, worried about money all the time. We don't need money on the trail."

Ah, the innocence of children. Yes, they were surviving, mostly because of the fresh meat the men brought in, but they were running short of other staples. They would have to restock once they reached Westport. Susanne prayed daily that their meager supply of money would be sufficient. Aunt Estelle's voice echoed in her mind. *"The night is always darkest before dawn. Hope in the Lord."*

Well, there must be one spectacular, blazing dawn headed this way, because to her mind the night was about as dark as it could get. *Hope in the Lord.* Easy to say, difficult to do when everything was going wrong. She shook her head, wondering what it would be like to have such an unwavering faith as her aunt had lived by, so that no matter what happened, you could rejoice in hope.

Susanne sighed. It must be something that came with spiritual maturity; apparently she was still growing.

"Miss McCord?"

"Yes, Margaret Ann?"

"I feel closer to God on the trail than I do in church. Is that a sin?"

"No, dear. I feel the same way. Churches are built by men, but nature is God's creation."

"Then why do we go to church?"

"Because it is a commandment—we are not to forsake the gathering together to worship—and because we want to praise and worship the Lord."

"I see. So it is all right to worship God in church and outside, too."

Susanne hugged Margaret Ann. She was such an adorable child. "It's always right to worship God, darling, wherever we may be."

Margaret Ann sighed, relief evident on her features. "I'm glad to get that settled. Now I need to check on Phebia. She tends to be unruly sometimes."

"She does at that." Susanne watched as Margaret Ann scampered away to check on the younger girl. How could anyone have abandoned a special child like Margaret Ann? But then all the children were special. She loved every one of them as though they were her very own. A soft sigh escaped her. Would she ever have children of her own? Would she ever find a man that she could fall deeply and hopelessly in love with? Enough to marry—truly marry and spend the rest of her life loving?

Susanne kept a wary eye on Cass. From the smoldering glances he sent in her direction she supposed he was still angry. Why did she do her best to torment him? No wonder he despised her so. Her conscience nagged her. *God, I'm such a contrary soul. Can't You give me a few redeeming qualities?*

She thought of Cass's outraged expression and gave a muffled laugh. All right. Maybe she was past help. God was no doubt ready to wash His hands of her. Cass certainly was. She needed to be nicer to him. No more taunting or teasing. She would be as dignified as Margaret Ann.

A tall order; one Susanne doubted she could deliver.

Cass rode a good distance to the rear, keeping a close eye on the group. He'd seen nothing to indicate that renegades were still in the area, but that didn't mean they weren't there. Although the Civil War had been over for several years, the violence spawned by the conflict had never gone away. Frank and Jesse James, the Youngers, and others had inspired a number of gangs who would rather prey on the helpless than work for a living. But for now, the small group was making steady progress. Threat of trouble seemed remote for the time being. He took a moment to count his blessings. Health. Life—many a man had lost his during the war. Family.

Father, I have nothing to complain about—just praise for Your grace. I thank You for safekeeping and returning me home to my family. Lord, I guess what I'm trying to say is that I thank You for everything.

He caught a glimpse of Susanne and thought about the way she could rankle him without trying. *Well, almost everything,* he amended.

The wind continued to pick up, and he found his attention drawn more to Susanne's skirt than to anything else. The heavy gusts would snatch up the flimsy cotton and toss it as high as her head, providing Cass with a glimpse of white pantalets.

What was wrong with the woman? Didn't she have any sense of modesty? They were traveling through strange territory, and not everyone they met could be trusted. The surrounding tree-covered hills and hollows could hide a dozen renegade groups bent on causing trouble. He couldn't be expected to fight them all.

Keeping Susanne under control was harder than herding coyotes. Get her out of one mess and she fell into one even worse.

He nudged his horse's flanks and quickly rode up beside her. "Are you aware your pantalets are showing?"

Susanne glanced up startled. "What?"

"Every time the wind blows, your pantalets show."

She drew back defensively. "I beg your pardon! What business is it of yours?"

"None at all, I'm just the fool who'll have to rescue you if some stranger decides he likes what he sees. If you can't think of your own safety, you might at least think of the others."

He could feel the heat of her anger when she glared up at him. "I've told you several times I can take care of myself."

"Sure you can. Ever heard of sewing buckshot in your hem to keep your skirt from flying over your head?"

Her chin lifted with a stubborn set. "I have not heard of sewing buckshot in my skirt to keep it from flying over my head," she mimicked.

"Woman, you're driving me over the edge."

"It wouldn't be a very long journey, now, would it?"

All right now. He'd had enough. Cass leaned down and scooped her up, hauling her into the saddle in front of him. Almost immediately he recognized his mistake.

"What do you think you're doing? Put me down this instant!" she demanded. The children stopped walking and stood watching the skirmish in wide-eyed fascination.

She twisted to confront him. Their faces were inches apart when she took a deep, self-righteous breath and said in a disgusted rebuke, "You should be ashamed of yourself!"

He grinned, aware that she knew he'd been angry when she had doused him with dishwater. Payback time had arrived. "That will be the day!"

"You. . .you heathen!" She struggled to free herself, and he gripped her tightly to keep from dropping her. Now that he had her, what was he going to do with her? An idea occurred to him, and he liked it. It was time he taught this contrary woman a lesson.

"You might as well pipe down," he warned. "If you don't have the good sense to keep yourself covered, then I suppose I'll be forced to see that you do."

"What do you mean, covered?! I was covered! I can't help it if your heathenish thoughts—"

Cass cut her off. "Payne, you see to Jesse and Doog. They're wandering too far ahead." He hit his horse on the flank and it trotted off, with Susanne loudly protesting.

"This is an outrage, and I demand that you set me down this instant! What do you think you're doing?"

"You think you can do such a good job of taking care of yourself; I'm going to give you the chance to try."

She stiffened in his arms, looking suddenly afraid. He squelched a stir of compassion. Somehow he had to make her understand the seriousness of their situation. Hadn't the woman learned anything in the past six years?

"What are you talking about?"

He noted with satisfaction that although she made an obvious effort to sound in control, her voice had a slight tremor.

"I thought I'd set you down out here on your lonesome and let you walk back."

Her eyes narrowed to viperous slits. "You wouldn't dare."

"Oh, wouldn't I? Maybe you'll get lucky and not be forced to fight off big Bull Hanson. I'm betting he could pull you into the saddle even easier than I did."

Her eyes widened at the implication of his words. "Cass. You're just teasing; aren't you?"

"Why should I tease about something like this? Besides, you have it coming after that trick with the dishwater."

He was surprised to see a shamed expression cross her face. She took a deep breath and looked past him, avoiding eye contact. "I'm sorry I wasn't more observant. There's no excuse for my behavior, and I apologize."

"The fact that I'm about to set you afoot doesn't have anything to do with your heartfelt apology, does it?"

"No, it doesn't." She pressed her lips tightly together and sighed. "I'll try to be nice to you from now on."

"Susanne, you don't know the first thing about being nice." Deciding they'd come far enough to teach her a lesson, he turned the horse and rode back to camp.

But as he expected, her show of repentance didn't last long. "You conceited, disrespectful worm! You don't have the slightest idea what I'm like."

Cass put spurs to the horse. "I know all I want to know."

"I've said I was sorry for that, and if you were any kind of gentleman you would accept my apology."

"I'll accept your so-called apology the day you hand me the annulment papers."

"You'll get your papers as soon as you deliver us safely to Cherry Grove." After a few moments of silence she said, "There isn't anything I like about you."

He grinned, knowing he was about to infuriate her further.

"You didn't complain when I kissed you."

He heard her soft intake of breath and chuckled. Her hand shot out to smack his leg, but he quickly thwarted the move and halted the horse beside the wagon.

"Put me down!" she gritted through clenched teeth.

"Well, anything you say, darling."

He released her, and she sailed off the horse, hitting the ground with a solid thud.

"Cass Claxton!" she wailed.

Cass sat on the horse, grinning, waiting to see what she would do.

All of the unexpected commotion caused Corliss to stick her head out of the back of the wagon. "Everything all right back here?"

"Everything's fine, Corliss. Miss McCord insisted on walking." Cass tipped his hat at Susanne. "Don't tire yourself, darlin'."

Corliss looked blank for a moment then shrugged and dropped the curtain back in place, as if to say whatever was going on, she didn't want any part of it.

Lucy grasped on to Margaret Ann's hand, looking as if she might burst into tears at any moment. Susanne calmly picked herself up out of the dirt and stalked toward the wagon.

Cass watched her walk away, thinking he might have been a little rough on her. He didn't know what it was, but something about Susanne McCord brought out the worst in him. Lilly Claxton had not raised him to treat a woman with anything less than respect.

But then Ma hadn't met Susanne.

Late that afternoon the wagon topped a rise, and they spotted a small caravan traveling about a mile ahead. Susanne counted the wagons out loud: "One, two, three, four, five."

"And fifteen to twenty head of cattle," Cass observed.

"You think they'll let us join them?" Susanne asked. Cass's

warnings were beginning to sink in, and she'd feel a lot safer with reinforcements.

He took off his hat. "I'll ride ahead and see if they'd mind if we hook up with them."

"Seems like the smart thing to do," Harlon agreed. "We'll wait here until we get a proper invite."

Thirty minutes later Cass returned bearing the good news: they were welcome to join the wagon train.

That night, six wagons camped in a pasture after getting permission from the owner. They formed the customary pear-shaped corral, the pole of each wagon pointing outward, and the hub of the fore wheel of the next wagon set close to the hind wheel of the wagon just ahead of it. The exact placement of the wagons formed an enclosure large enough to pen the animals belonging to the train. It also provided a defensive arrangement that made an attack unlikely. The chances were slim that a group this large would run into trouble in Missouri or eastern Kansas, but the danger was greater in Oklahoma, where the rest of the train was headed.

The women quickly formed a comfortable relationship. When the children had been safely tucked in that night, they sat around the fire, stitching handiwork and exchanging small talk. The men enjoyed their pipes and cigars while they discussed the weather and whether they were likely to encounter hostile Indians farther west.

The ladies openly expressed concern about savages when they crossed into Oklahoma, though most agreed the threat was small. With the casual friendliness of the trail they accepted Susanne into their midst, showing interest in her new quilt pattern. Their companionship was bittersweet because Susanne knew the friendships she made here would be short-term. They would be leaving the wagon train when it reached Westport. She and her family would travel on to Kansas, while the others would journey south into Oklahoma.

She glanced up from the quilt she was piecing when she heard Cass excuse himself, saying that he was going to turn in early.

Ernest Parker's teenage daughter, Ernestine, sprang to her feet to say good night. It was evident from the look in the young beauty's eyes that she'd developed a full-blown case of puppy love for the blue-eyed, curly-headed stranger, who promptly rewarded her with a smile guaranteed to melt any woman's heart.

Susanne watched Cass get to his feet to say good night with mixed feelings. The events of that afternoon still lingered with her. He'd been hateful today, but in her heart she knew she had deserved it. What had gotten into her? From the moment they'd met she'd gone out of her way to provoke him. Even worse, although she didn't understand her emotions, a part of her wanted them to be friends—even more than friends. She had to admit no other man had ever touched her life in quite the same way, making her feel so aware, so vibrantly alive. . .so in need of. . .something. *Love?* she wondered.

She'd had to remind herself twice this evening that she would be three times a fool if she were to let herself fall in love with Cass Claxton. He was a rogue and a rascal who'd treated her as badly as she'd treated him.

When they reached Cherry Grove and she handed him the annulment papers, that would be the last thing he'd ever want from her. She was confident that she would never see him again. She knew that he had every reason to want her out of his life, but the realization didn't make her growing feelings for him any easier to accept.

Why do I do the things I do? she silently agonized. *Why couldn't I have been the perfect lady, one who would have captured his heart instead of his ire? A soft-spoken Christian lady.*

Now it was too late to hope he would ever see her as anything but the headstrong, stubborn girl he thought her to be. In her heart she couldn't blame him for despising her. By an act of defiance and deceit, she still shared his name, but it would be a woman like Laure Revuneau who would eventually win his heart.

Dear God, how do I make amends? Perhaps he could forgive if given the chance. You forgave me—even died on a cross for me.

But Cass was not God. He came close in the children's eyes, but still he was not their Maker.

It shamed her to know that Ernestine Parker's lovesick gaze was not the only one that followed Cass's tall form when he strode toward the wagon. Susanne was ready to admit, at least to herself, that she was falling in love with the very man she'd so foolishly forced to marry her.

And there was nothing she could do to hold it back.

The following morning Lucius Waterman's voice rang out a warning: "Steep hill comin' up!" His words echoed down the line.

Susanne eased the team to a halt when Cass rode up beside their wagon.

"Better let Aaron take the reins. Looks like there could be trouble," he said.

Susanne lifted her hand to shade her eyes from the hot sun and squinted up at him. "Can he handle the team?" Aaron was wiry and slight of build, although he insisted he was as strong as two grown men put together.

"He can handle it." Cass assessed the hill. "It's a bad one, though—steep, with little room for error."

"What will you do?"

A frown creased his forehead, and she knew he was trying to

determine the safest angle of descent. As far as she could see, there didn't seem to be one. Having the wagon fall and break beyond repair while being windlassed down the steep grade wasn't something she cared to think about.

Susanne climbed down from the wagon, and Cass dismounted and stood beside her. He removed his hat and ran his sleeve over his forehead. "Get the children together and keep them at a safe distance," he said quietly. "Tell Harlon and Corliss they'll have to walk down the hill. I don't want anyone near this wagon except Aaron and me."

Susanne's eyes lifted to meet his. "It's bad, isn't it?"

"Just do as I say," he repeated softly. He adjusted his hat back on his head.

"Then I'll drive."

"Do as I say, Susanne. Aaron and I will take care of the wagon. You and the children stay back."

Knowing it was useless to argue, Susanne went in search of the children while Cass drew Aaron aside. She could see the two talking, and her heart filled with pride. It was almost as if he were her husband, teaching their son one of life's lessons. Then a terrible sense of dread filled her. If either one of them should be seriously injured, she didn't think she could bear it.

The train sprang into activity. Women called out to children, and men started unloading some of the heavier pieces off the wagons and setting them beside the road.

When two of the women realized they were parting with family heirlooms, they started weeping and begging their husbands for compassion. Stern-faced, the men kept about their work, though one kept apologizing and assuring his wife that he was only doing what had to be done.

Since Susanne and Corliss had brought nothing but the bare

necessities, the McCord wagon was ordered to the head of the line.

"Payne, you and Jesse scout around for the biggest log you can find," Cass called as he knelt to check the left front axle. The axle was low on lubricant. "Doog, tell Susanne I need the bottom side of a bacon slab."

"Yessir!" Doog scampered off, and Harlon hurried over to help. By the time Doog returned with the requested bacon rind, Harlon and Cass had taken off the white oak wheel. Cass took the bacon fat and carefully wrapped it around the axle hub. Moments later the wheel slipped back into place.

"Think that'll work?" Harlon asked.

"It should."

"Mr. Claxton?" Ernestine Parker stood at Cass's heels, her eyes wide with worry. "You do be careful, you hear?"

Cass winked, and a flush stained the girl's cheeks. "I plan to do that, Ernestine."

Payne and Jesse returned, dragging the biggest log they could handle.

Reaching for the ax, Cass told Payne to grab the long hemp rope lashed to the back of the wagon and follow him. They tied the log to the back of the wagon to act as a brake. Cass eyed it, doubts forming in his mind. He surely hoped this worked. If it didn't, he and Aaron were in for a rough ride.

When he was confident that everything was in order, Cass swung into the wagon beside Aaron. He removed his hat and wiped his forehead on his shirtsleeve. "Well, I can think of things I'd rather be doing."

Aaron swallowed, his Adam's apple bobbing. "Yes, sir. Me, too."

Cass turned to face him, a slow grin forming. He'd developed a real affection for the boy. "I suppose you know how to stay on a woman's better side?"

Aaron frowned before a sheepish grin formed on his youthful features. "Well. . .uh. . .there are a couple of things I've been meaning to have you clear up for me."

Cass chuckled. "Son, there's a couple of things I still don't know."

Aaron's grin widened. "Yessir!"

"You've noticed that pretty little Ernestine Parker, haven't you?"

Aaron's Adam's apple bobbed again, and he flushed a deeper red. "Yessir. . .a little."

"A little, huh?"

"Yessir. . .a little."

Cass grinned, deciding the boy was relaxed enough to start. "You about ready to get this wagon down the hill?"

"Yessir!" There was a slight tremble in the youth's voice, but Cass saw that his hands were steady when he picked up the reins.

"Then let's get this over with so the women can stop their fidgeting."

"Yessir."

"I want you to take it real easy. Keep the reins good and tight, and ease the animals down real slow. The tree will act as a drag, but it's up to you to see that the animals don't get away."

"I can do that, sir."

Cass clasped one of Aaron's thin shoulders confidently. "I'm counting on you."

He swung down from the wagon and turned to give a sharp whistle, signaling that they were ready to take the first wagon down. The other members of the train stopped what they were doing and came to watch.

"I'll need a couple of volunteers," Cass called out. He pulled on a pair of leather gloves.

Matt Johnson and Lewis Brown stepped up. Young men with

strong, sturdy backs.

Glancing around to see where Susanne and the children were, Cass found them standing off to the side, looking worried. Susanne tried to smile when her eyes sought Aaron. Cass realized the boy was young to have so much responsibility thrust upon his shoulders, but kids grew up fast on the trail.

Sweat stained the back of Aaron's shirt. He gripped the reins so tightly that his knuckles turned white.

Cass took his place at the back of the wagon. "Okay, son, let's—"

"Cass!" Susanne shouted.

Cass glanced up. "What?"

"Please. . .be careful!"

He nodded curtly, surprised that, for a change, she wasn't cheering him on to trip downhill and be trampled by a herd of longhorn.

"Let 'em roll!" he shouted.

The wheels on the wagon began to turn. Cass, Matt, and Lewis latched onto a rope that trailed behind the tree, letting their weight act as an additional drag.

The crowd of onlookers collectively watched when the wagon began to laboriously descend, easing down the incline. The hill wasn't long, just steep.

Aaron gripped the reins, fixing his eyes straight ahead. Sweat poured down the sides of his dust-streaked face. Cass could hear him urging the animals in low, soothing tones to take it easy.

The harness creaked and the brakes protested. The team strained to move the now contrary wagon. Overhead, clouds blocked the sun as a threat of rain sprang up.

Cass watched the sky, praying that a thunderstorm wouldn't break out before they'd gotten all of the wagons safely down the hill. *God, we could use help here.* He dug his heels in, trying to keep his feet under him when the wagon threatened to careen down the steep slope.

Susanne held her breath, trying to ignore the tight band of fear suddenly gripping her middle. Her heart was in her throat, her eyes riveted on Cass. She could see the muscles in his arms bunching tightly when he strained against the rope. The wagon dragged him and the others like rag dolls down the hillside.

She wished she could take his place, that she was the one in danger, not him. It wasn't fair that he could be injured—or perhaps killed—trying to help her.

The wagon picked up speed, rolling faster. Men's anxious shouts echoed through the countryside. Aaron threw all of his weight against the reins, trying to force the animals to slow down. A fierce gust of wind nearly took the canvas off the wagon when the first clap of thunder sounded.

Susanne closed her eyes and prayed in a frenzied litany. "Don't let them be hurt, don't let them be hurt, don't let them be hurt."

Minutes seemed like hours; the heat closed in around her. She felt light-headed and faint, and the children's excited voices seemed to come to her from far away.

Suddenly a whoop went up, and she felt her knees buckle with fear.

"They made it!"

Her eyes flew open. Tears of relief streamed down her cheeks when she saw that the wagon was safely at the bottom of the hill. She could see Cass—his clothes filthy now, but blessedly safe and sound—calmly untying the rope in preparation for the next wagon.

A flurry of clamoring feet swept her along in their wake as the children rushed down the hill to meet him.

Margaret Ann and Lucy descended on Cass like a whirlwind,

throwing their arms around his waist, nearly dragging him to the ground in their exuberance.

Aaron hopped from the wagon, his face flushed with victory and his wide grin assuring the others that he was going to be hard to live with for a while.

Ernestine, who'd been headed for Cass, stopped and blushed prettily when Aaron turned his smile in her direction. He winked—a gesture he'd picked up from watching Cass—and the teenage girl's face turned a deep crimson.

"Bet that was fun, huh?" Doog prodded Cass, his eyes conveying his deep longing to be old enough to do such an exciting thing.

"Never had so much fun," Cass teased. He tried to control the girls, who bounced around his feet like grasshoppers.

Margaret Ann demanded a hug, then Lucy, then Phebia, and of course, Marybelle. Cass knelt down to oblige the ladies, though he pretended to be wary of Phebia. Susanne grinned. The little imp still had an unnerving way of latching on to his nose when he least expected it.

Susanne arrived when Cass finished the hugs and stood up. Giving a cry of relief, she threw herself into his arms. "Oh. . . I thought you were going to be killed."

His arm tightened around her as naturally as if he'd held her a hundred times before. "Me? I'm invincible—haven't I mentioned that?"

She grasped the back of his head and hugged him with all her might.

Susanne hadn't realized what she was going to do. She hadn't planned to show the depth of her feelings, but now she realized she was glad she'd done it. And she would die if he cast her aside in front of the children.

After a long moment, he gently set her aside, his eyes filled with amusement. A grin started at the corners of his mouth when he surely recognized the alarm growing in her eyes. "Why, Miss McCord," he challenged softly, "I didn't know you cared."

"I. . .I didn't know, either," she confessed.

His amusement disappeared, and the blue of his eyes darkened when he contemplated the meaning of her admission. "Well, well, what do you know about that."

She held her breath when he looked at her. It was as if he were seeing her for the first time.

Their gazes continued to silently assess each other. She prayed that he would be kind, that he wouldn't openly reject her. *Please, God, don't let him reject me this time. Not this time.*

He glanced down at the children and winked; then, gathering Susanne in his arms, he hugged her warmly. "Thank you, Miss McCord. Sure do appreciate your concern."

For a moment she was caught by surprise, but then she enjoyed the unexpected kindness. His arms felt exactly as she thought they would: superbly masculine, exciting—wonderful.

She sighed and stood on tiptoe, her arms encircling his neck more tightly. "Thank you," she whispered into his ear.

If it hadn't been for the children, she would have shamelessly stayed in his arms forever. But the sound of embarrassed giggles broke the spell.

Cass eased out of the embrace as quickly as it had begun. "Storm's about to break. I've got the other wagons to see to," he said gruffly.

A new, headier thrill shot through Susanne when she realized that he was as shaken by the embrace as she was. "Yes, of course," she murmured.

He turned to the children, who were still chortling. "If you children don't have anything better to do than stand around giggling at the old folks, I'll find something to occupy your time," he warned.

Squealing, they scampered in all directions.

Susanne watched Cass walk back up the hill, her heart overflowing with love.

The storm's already broken, Mr. Claxton, she thought with a grin. *You just don't know it yet.*

Chapter 7

The wagons stopped at the brink of a swift-moving creek Monday morning. Matt Johnson rode his big bay out into the stream, trying to gauge the depth. "I think it's all right," he yelled back to the ones waiting on the bank. "Hold upstream and aim for that gravel bar. Should be a good place to pull out."

Cass watched as the other wagons eased into the water one by one. The force of the water and the loose gravel in the streambed caused the Waterman wagon to shift sideways, but Lucius Waterman cracked his bullwhip and the oxen changed course, struggling to the bank.

Aaron sat on the wagon seat, holding the reins. Cass rode up beside him. "You ready for this?"

The young man nodded. "I'm ready."

"All right. You see where that wagon went wrong? Aim about six feet upstream from where Lucius crossed and I think you'll be fine." Susanne, Corliss, and the children rode inside the wagon. This stream was too deep and too fast to wade across.

Aaron nodded, and when his turn came he drove out into the water as steady and sure as if he'd been doing it all his life. Cass smiled. He was right proud of the boy. He'd do to ride the river with. As a matter of fact, every one of these kids was first-rate. A man would be proud to claim any of them as his own.

After the wagon was safely across, Harlon rode the sorrel out of the water, sitting easy. *A good man,* Cass thought. The elderly gentleman had done what he could to pull his weight on this trip. Made a real hand.

Cass caught his breath when the horse slipped and went down, taking Harlon with him. Before Cass could reach the struggling horse and man, the animal rolled onto its side and Harlon disappeared under the water. Corliss screamed and jumped from the back of the wagon to race to the edge of the bank, wringing her hands.

When Cass approached, the horse struggled to its feet and surged toward the shore. Payne jumped to catch the bridle, bringing the animal under control. Swinging out of the saddle, Cass fought to keep his balance against the strong flow. The reins slipped out of his hands, and his animal took advantage of its freedom to head for shore.

Harlon surfaced and tried to regain his footing, slipped, and went under again. Cass lunged, catching hold of his shirt. He hauled upward, bringing the older man's head above the water.

Payne waded toward them, slipped on a rock, and fell with a mighty splash. Immediately he was back on his feet, plowing toward them. Between them they got Harlon upright, but he floundered, a deadweight. Cass grabbed him under one arm and motioned for Payne to do the same. Struggling, one slow step after the other, they managed to drag the older man to shore.

They laid him on the rocky shingle, and Corliss pushed them aside to kneel beside her husband, "Oh Harlon. You're hurt," she gasped.

Harlon coughed, spitting up water. "Think my leg's broke, and

I nigh drowned. Guess Cass and the boy saved my life."

Cass coughed, spit water on the ground, and then said, "I think Payne saved us both. I wasn't having much luck getting you on your feet."

He knelt and examined the older man's leg. "It's broke all right. I can set it, but it's going to hurt."

"Hurts now," Harlon said. "Might as well go ahead and get it over with."

"Aaron, you and Payne get me Susanne's quilting frame. It will do as splints."

"My quilting frame?"

He looked up to find Susanne standing beside him. "You got a problem with that?"

"No. Of course not. I suppose you'll need something to bind it to his leg? I'll rip up an old petticoat."

When the items arrived, Cass took the frame from Aaron and carefully measured the wood. "Cut it right here. Okay?" He indicated the length.

"Sure." The two boys went to work and shortly handed Cass the narrow, sturdy pieces of pine.

"All right now, Harlon, we're going to pull that leg back in place and splint it. Bear with us." He pulled, with Aaron holding the older man by the shoulders. The leg gradually eased into position, and Cass quickly bound the splints in place. Harlon hadn't made a sound, but he had gripped Corliss's work-worn hand so tightly that she had winced. With Cass on one side and Aaron and Susanne on the other, they carried the injured man to the wagon and made him comfortable.

Cass patted Harlon' s shoulder. "I'll be back to check on you later. You need anything, have Corliss call and we'll come running." He glanced at Corliss. "Do we have any whiskey on hand?"

She shook her head. "Nary a drop."

Sweat dripped off Harlon's forehead. "Sure glad you were here, Cass. I owe you one for this."

"You don't owe me a thing. You're going to have some real pain."

"It can't get much worse," Harlon said with an attempt at a smile. Cass walked over to take the reins of his horse from Doog.

"Is Harlon going to be all right?" the boy asked, his youthful features pale.

"He should be fine. These things happen. He'll mend." Cass prayed that he was right and not misleading the boy. Harlon was aging, and his bones would take time to heal.

Doog grinned and scampered off to join the others.

Cass took his position at the rear of the train, thinking of Harlon. It was a common trail accident. Apart from his concern for the old fellow's recovery, he realized that the accident meant there would be one less hand to help with the work.

It could take months—or longer—before Harlon would be on his feet again, but he was lucky to have come out of it with his life.

They had been on the trail for five weeks, and Cherry Grove was a little more than a hundred miles away. Cass was confident that he could get by; Aaron and Payne were old enough to accept extra responsibilities.

The October mornings had a nip to them now. He knew it wouldn't be long before Indian summer gave way to howling winter winds. They should reach their destination long before that, so he wasn't concerned.

After supper that evening he walked to the back of the wagon to visit Harlon, who lay on a mattress looking peaked, with his foot propped up on a pillow. Cass could see the older man was suffering. "Can I do anything for you? If you need it, just name it." He wasn't a man to drink, but he knew whiskey's medicinal purposes, and if Harlon needed something he'd try to oblige.

"Thanks, son, but I can't think of a thing I need."

Cass perched atop a bundle in the wagon and leaned back against the frame.

"I'm much obliged to you for settin' the leg," Harlon said. "I told Corliss I don't know what we'd have done if you hadn't been here to help us."

"You don't need to thank me. I was glad to help."

"You've been a real godsend to Susanne—well, to all of us. I hope you know that."

Cass appreciated the praise but found he was uncomfortable with it. "Susanne's a strong woman. She'd have made it with or without my help."

Harlon's eyes twinkled. "She's not as strong as you might think, boy."

Cass fell silent; he guessed Harlon could sense he would prefer to drop the subject because he glanced resentfully at the splinted leg. "I could just kick myself for breakin' this gol-burned thing! I'm as helpless as a turtle on its back," he complained.

Cass smiled. "You'll heal."

"Well, I shore hope so. I don't want to be no trouble to anyone." He reached for his pipe and smoked in silence for a while. Someone in the train strummed a guitar, the sound adding to the peace of the evening.

"Gettin' colder," Harlon observed.

"Yes—change is in the air."

Susanne's and Margaret Ann's voices approached the wagon.

"Margaret Ann," Susanne was saying, "before you go to bed I want you to run over and ask how old Mrs. Medsker is this evening."

"Yes, ma'am," Margaret Ann replied and skipped off to do as she was told. Cass heard her return within minutes. "Mrs. Medsker said she didn't think it was any of your doin's how old she is," Margaret repeated.

Cass grinned when he heard Susanne's sharp intake of breath before she skirted Margaret off to Winoka Medsker's wagon to explain the misunderstanding.

"How come a nice-looking chap like you never took a wife?" Harlon asked. "Seems to me that a man your age ought to have his own children's mistakes to chuckle about."

Cass shifted uncomfortably at the question. "The right woman's never come along."

"Maybe you haven't looked in the right place," Harlon said, and Cass wondered if he was thinking about Susanne.

"Harlon, I'd like to talk to you about something."

"Certainly."

"I guess I'm asking your advice."

"All right."

"Bull Hanson and his men have been following us for days. They dropped out of sight for a while, but they're back now."

Harlon glanced up, a frown on his brow. "Is that right?"

"What do you think he wants?"

Harlon drew on his pipe thoughtfully. "Hard to say."

"I've been wondering whether I should let it pass or pay a visit to Mr. Hanson one of these evenings."

"I don't know, son. The man 'pears as ornery as a caged skunk to me."

"I don't want him scaring the women."

"No, we couldn't put up with that."

"What do you think I should do?"

"Well, I think I'd wait him out. If he shows any sign of trouble, you can deal with him then. There's no use raisin' a stink if he's merely travelin' the trail with us."

"I guess you're right." Still, Cass didn't like the close quarters; it made him edgy.

"Keep a close eye on him."

"I plan to."

Harlon drew on his pipe again, sending a plume of smoke rolling out of the wagon. "You don't suppose the women have noticed him?"

"I don't think so. Susanne would have mentioned it if she had."

As much as Susanne irritated him, Cass didn't want her subjected to a man like Bull Hanson.

Harlon sighed. "Well, maybe we're just borrowin' trouble."

Cass's gaze followed Susanne when she and Margaret Ann emerged from the Medskers' wagon. He didn't know why he found the outlaw's presence so disturbing, but he did.

"Yeah, maybe we are."

But even Aaron mentioned Bull Hanson's continuing presence a few days later. His young features were stoic as he watched Cass saddle up. "Have you noticed Hanson and his thugs have been following us for days now?"

"I've noticed."

"What do you think he wants?"

Cass shrugged.

"You think he has his eye on Miss McCord?"

Jerking the cinch tighter, Cass frowned. "I think if he's fond of wildcats he's on the right trail." He swung in the saddle and adjusted his hat low on his forehead.

"You're not worried about him?"

"Not in the least."

Aaron grinned. "I guess you know how to handle the likes of

Bull Hanson. He's awfully big, though."

"A man's size doesn't mean that much." Cass winked. "It's his will that counts."

Aaron nodded. "Mind if I ride behind your saddle this morning?"

"You're not driving the wagon?"

"No, sir. Miss McCord said she was going to."

"Climb aboard."

The horse trotted through camp; Cass spotted Susanne rolling up the night's bedding and storing it in gutta-percha sacks.

Their gazes met, and he tipped his hat mockingly.

She stuck her tongue out at him.

"Miss McCord's a right fine-looking woman, isn't she?" Aaron remarked when Cass spurred the horse into a gallop.

"I suppose she'd do in a pinch," Cass allowed. If a man was desperate, which he was not.

Early that afternoon the train of wagons stopped to water the stock in a wide brook. Indian summer had turned hot as a smoking pistol. The cool, clear water felt heavenly, and the weary travelers splashed the liquid on suntanned arms and faces. The children's delighted squeals could be heard for more than an hour as they laughed and played in the bubbling water. When they were loading to leave, a new wagon rolled in.

"Oh brother!" Susanne muttered irritably when she saw that the old buckboard was decked with an outrageously gaudy yellow-fringed awning.

A wagonload of fallen angels.

Protective mothers hurriedly gathered the children and herded them into the wagons in an effort to shield their young eyes from the unsavory sight. Husbands followed suit, but not without one or two curious glances at the new arrivals.

However, the less-than-cordial welcome didn't dampen the

spirits of the scantily dressed women. The women piled out of their buckboard and headed straight for the water.

Within minutes they were cooling in the stream, oblivious to the resentful looks fired in their direction. There wasn't actually a beauty in the lot, but that didn't seem to discourage the men's rapt attention.

Susanne kept a close eye on Cass. He and Aaron sat on the horse with their eyes glued to the spectacle going on before them.

Even Payne's and Jesse's eyes were rounder than usual. They peered around the corner of the wagon, gawking. Corliss hollered for them to git, and their heads quickly disappeared.

A buxom redhead focused on Cass. She gave a come-hither smile, displaying her dazzling white teeth and full cherry-red lips. "Hello there, handsome. Nice camping place you got here." She reached into the pocket of her dress and pulled out two thin cigars. She lit one and offered the other to Cass. His mouth curved into a lazy smile, and he leaned down and took it from her. He put it, unlit, between his teeth.

It was clear to Susanne that the redhead had snagged his undivided attention.

"Afternoon, ma'am. Mighty warm today."

"Yes, it is," she agreed in a sultry Texas drawl.

"You ladies traveling far?"

"Far 'nuff." She lowered her lids demurely. "Where y'all goin'?"

"Kansas."

"Sure 'nuff? Why, I have a dear old grandma who lives in Wichita."

"That so?"

"Sure 'nuff. Are you by any chance going to Wichita?"

Cass shook his. "No, ma'am, afraid not."

"Well, that's too bad. . . . Listen, sugar, we'll be stopping not far down the road tonight. Maybe you'd like to drop by, so I could give you a letter to mail to my dear, sweet grandma once you reach Kansas."

Susanne had heard enough. She reached for the bullwhip under the wagon seat, stood up, whirled it around her head a couple of times, and let it fly.

Cass heard the deafening crack of the whip about the same time his cigar splintered into oblivion.

Stunned, he lifted his blank gaze to encounter Susanne's snapping eyes. Bits of tobacco fragments swirled in the air.

"It's time we were on our way," she snapped.

The butt of his cigar dropped from his lips and rolled down the front of his shirt before it dawned on him what had happened. His face turned crimson, and for the first time in his life he was speechless. Had she swung that whip? By grab, she had. Swung that bullwhip at him! Cut the cigar in half. No woman had ever treated Cass Claxton in such a manner. And he wasn't in a mood to take it now.

He clenched his jaw, feeling the veins standing out in his temple. *Lord, why did You make this woman so blamed ornery?* Rile her and no man was safe in her vicinity! He swung off his horse, intent on teaching her a lesson. Before he could move, Margaret Ann blocked his path.

"Mr. Cass. Think what you're doing."

He peered down at her. "What?"

"I believe you might mean bodily harm to Miss McCord. Is that right?"

"You better believe it."

"Do you think force ever solves anything?"

He drew a deep breath. Wasn't it too bad Miss Have-My-Own-Way-Or-Bust McCord didn't have one-tenth the common sense of this child? The world would be a far better place.

"Well?" Margaret Ann's direct gaze brought him to his senses.

"Probably not." But it sure would help him to let off a load of steam. He heaved a sigh and reluctantly climbed back on his horse, feeling he had been taken to the woodshed by this moppet. Fine thing when kids started taking their elders down a notch.

Susanne wielded the whip a second time, and the wagon lurched forward. The other drivers followed suit, and the train started moving.

Once they were out on the trail she glanced back to see if Cass and Aaron were following. She was relieved to see that they were, although they were trailing at a distance.

"Guess I showed that Jezebel that she best not mess with my husband and expect to get away with it," she muttered tightly under her breath. She swung the whip again and sent it blazing over the oxen's heads. Oh, her temper had gotten the better of her; she'd gone too far this time. Cass would be mad as a hornet and yell at her or worse for embarrassing him in front of the whole wagon train, but he'd deserved it.

A grin escaped her when she recalled the horrified look on his face when he'd realized what she'd done. *But he 'sure 'nuff' had it coming, Lord.*

Camp was quieter than usual that night. Since Mort Harrison had the first watch, he was preparing to take up his post. Meanwhile, Buck Brewster sat beneath a tree, playing his violin—a sweet, lilting refrain that floated pleasantly through the wagons.

Cass lay on his bedroll, looking up at the stars. It was a clear night, and the heavens were ablaze with God's handiwork.

Aaron and Payne had rolled up beside him, and he sensed that the two boys had something on their minds. He could wait until they were ready to say whatever it was that was bothering them.

"You got a pa?" Aaron asked.

"My pa died a short while after I was born," Cass said. "My mother raised me with the help of an older brother."

"I think mine's dead, too," Payne admitted. "I can't be sure, though. Been on my own for as long as I can remember."

"Sure would be nice to have a pa to talk to—or maybe a ma," Aaron mused.

"Mothers are nice," Cass admitted, remembering his own mother and how long it had been since he'd last seen her.

A few minutes passed before Aaron finally broached the subject Cass figured was uppermost in his mind.

"Cass...those women we saw today..." He sat up and his voice trailed off.

Cass squelched the urge to laugh. These boys were on the verge of manhood. They didn't have a pa to confide in, so he guessed he'd been chosen to answer their questions. "What about them?"

"Well"—Aaron cleared his throat—"they weren't nice women, were they?"

"Probably not."

Aaron was quiet for a moment, and Payne sat up. "A man's not supposed to have nothing to do with that kind of woman...is he?"

"I guess it depends on the man. Some men take their pleasure where they find it, but a steady, God-fearing man would prefer to find a good woman and settle down and raise a family."

"The Good Book says that kind of behavior is evil," Payne reminded.

Cass nodded and added quietly, "The Good Book also says 'Judge not, that ye be not judged.'"

"Have you ever been. . .acquainted with one of those women?" Aaron asked.

Cass sat up and stared at the stars, wishing the conversation were a little easier to handle. "Rule number one: a gentleman never kisses and tells."

"Even if he's been kissing with one of them women?"

Cass eyed Payne dryly and considered the question. "Especially if he's been kissing one of those women. How do you know so much about 'those women'?"

Payne flushed. "Well. . .I saw this book one time. . . ." He stopped, and a sheepish grin formed.

Cass nodded. Youngsters were curious, but he needed to explain the difference in women. "There's nothing that can compare with a decent, God-fearing woman. Like the Bible says, a good woman is worth more than rubies."

"Rubies?" Payne asked. "They're worth a lot of money, aren't they?"

Aaron sounded puzzled. "What's it mean, she's worth more than rubies? You can't put a dollar amount on a person."

"No, you can't," Cass agreed. "It means that having a woman who loves the Lord and tries to do right standing beside you is a blessing straight out of heaven."

"Well, maybe, but—" Payne began.

But Cass interrupted. "You can trust a woman like that with your life. She'll be there when you need her, work with you, pray with you, and raise your children to be God-fearing adults."

Cass thought of the way Susanne had tricked him into marriage and felt his ire rising. He tamped down on his anger. Right now he had to make the boys see the difference between a sober, decent, God-loving woman and the other kind.

"I have a mother who loves God and raised her boys to do

the same. I've wandered off the straight and narrow a few times, but my mother's teaching always brought me back. That's the way it is with the right kind of woman. No matter how much you're tempted to do wrong, you'll never want to disappoint the woman who loves you and believes in you."

"Well, I suppose the kind of woman you're talking about is all right," Payne said. "But it seems to me the other kind is more exciting."

"That's where you're wrong," Cass said. "The kind of woman you'll want to tie up with will smell like wildflowers after a rain; she'll have skin as soft as cotton; and her hair will feel like French silk when you run your fingers through it. She'll be gentle by nature, and she'll have a way of making a man feel eager to come home at night."

"What about the other ones?" Payne asked. "I already know what I'm supposed to want."

"Well, the Bible says the wrong woman will lead a man to destruction. You have to realize there are some 'bad' females. Some are misguided, and some do what they have to do to survive. I treat all women with respect, and I'd suggest you do the same. When you meet up with a woman, you treat her like a lady, no matter what other people think of her. If a man trifles with a woman, then walks away, he's nothing but a piece of trash."

The three lay back to stare at the stars. Silence surrounded them.

"What kind of woman do you think Miss McCord is?" Payne asked.

"Payne, she's a good woman!" Aaron gasped. "Isn't that so, Cass?"

"I would imagine."

"Don't you know?"

Cass realized he didn't know anything about Susanne, other than she was like a burr under his saddle most of the time. *What sort of woman is she?* he wondered. Beautiful, yes, he couldn't deny that. Over the last six years, she'd turned into a lovely woman, charming when she wanted to be, and a blessed saint when it came to dealing with children.

"I think I'll just try out a few of the other kind before I look for a nice woman," Payne decided. "Seems like that'd be the practical thing to do."

Cass winced. "What part of this conversation were you not listening to?"

He made a mental note to take Payne aside for a more detailed discussion of the subject. It appeared that the boy had missed a point somewhere.

"Well, how are you gonna know who's what?" Payne asked, clearly confused. "Miss McCord—she's real pretty and I think she's nice, but how am I going to know unless I try out a lot of women?"

"Gentlemen"—Cass rolled to his feet, thinking he'd ride back along the trail and see if Bull and his men were camped anywhere in the general vicinity—"it's getting late."

Aaron looked up and winked. "But Miss McCord's pretty hard to overlook, ain't she?"

Cass chose to ignore the question. "Go to sleep. I think I'll take a ride."

"I've been thinking. . ." Aaron said. "There ain't no woman gonna hog-tie and brand me; not if I can help it!"

Yeah, Cass thought, *you've got a lot to learn about women, son.* He'd once felt the same way until he met up with an angry father and a shotgun-toting sheriff. And he'd been paying for it ever since.

Cass paused to speak to a young woman who sat in a large

rocking chair just outside one of the wagons. She was trying to soothe her fretful infant, who'd been ill for days.

"How's the baby tonight?" he asked.

"I think she feels a mite hotter than she did earlier." Mardean Gibson's wan smile gave mute testimony to the strain she was under.

Cass touched the baby's forehead, and his brow furrowed with concern. "Do you need another bucket of cool water?"

"No, thank you. Boyd said he'd fetch me one when he got up." Boyd and Mardean had been taking turns sitting up nights with the infant. Cass felt sorry for the young couple. Still teenagers, they were barely more than children themselves.

"I'll hold your baby if you'd like to rest a spell," he offered.

Mardean gazed tenderly at the sleeping child on her lap. "I'm beholden to you, Mr. Claxton, but I want to stay with her," she said softly.

Giving Mardean's shoulder a friendly squeeze, Cass smiled. "If you need anything, you let me know."

Her face brightened momentarily. "Thank you. I surely do appreciate your kindness."

Susanne had just pulled the pins from her hair and was about to give it a thorough brushing when she saw Cass come walking back through camp. She was surprised to see that he was still awake.

The fires had burned low, and Buck Brewster was slipping his fiddle into its case, preparing to retire for the night.

Susanne watched the exchange with Mardean, and a feeling of envy engulfed her.

What she would give to have Cass speak to her with such compassion, such concern, such caring. . . . Her thoughts wavered.

She watched him walk to where his horse was grazing.

Now, where did he think he was going at this hour? He picked up his saddle and slung it over his shoulder. Suddenly she was sure she could guess. He had to be going to visit those women.

He's going to see that redhead, she thought. And the two of them were not going to spend their time composing a letter to dear old Grandma in Wichita!

Scalding tears sprang to her eyes, and she swiped them away angrily. She tried to tell herself that she didn't care. But she did care, desperately.

Somewhere a legal document had been recorded verifying the hasty marriage. She wouldn't even try to fool herself into believing that a mere piece of paper could prevent him from seeing other women, but not in her presence. She would not allow him to disgrace her by running off in the middle of the night to cavort with one of those women of easy virtue.

She walked toward the wagon, conceding that her logic might be flawed. After all, no one on the train knew that she and Cass were married, so he could hardly disgrace her in their eyes.

But she knew they were married. And the thought of his spending time with another woman when he'd avoided her—his own wife—like the plague set her blood boiling.

How dare he even contemplate such a thing? No decent, godly man would dream of visiting one of those. . .those. . .women. Didn't he know the Good Book frowned on such behavior?

She paused, hands clenched into fists, and did some serious thinking. The Bible warned against being unequally yoked with an unbeliever. She struggled to remember whether Cass had ever talked about his spiritual beliefs. Was he a Christian? If so, didn't he know what he was thinking of doing was wrong? Better for her to punish him than to let him set his feet on the road to destruction and risk God's wrath. Why, she would be doing him a favor by stopping him.

Then it hit her. Sometime during the past weeks, she had unconsciously begun to think of Cass as her property—her man. Now she asked herself if a woman didn't have a right to protect what was hers, even though what was hers had never wanted to become hers in the first place. She frowned. That sounded complicated, but she knew exactly what she meant.

She reached the wagon, and her hand fumbled under the seat for the bullwhip while she kept her eyes trained on Cass. He was acting as if he were simply about the business of saddling his horse for an innocent moonlight ride. Well, she was about to change his destination.

Cass had one foot in the stirrup when he momentarily paused. Cocking his head to one side, he thought he could detect the sound of a whip oscillating in midair.

The meaning of the ominous whir suddenly sank in, and he braced himself for what he knew was coming.

The soft *wisp, wisp, wisp* grew louder.

"Susanne, you'd better think twice," he warned, glancing over his shoulder.

She stood behind him in her nightgown, covered by an enveloping wrap, whirling the whip above her head. "Where are you going?"

"That's none of your business."

"Oh yes, it is."

Wisp, wisp, wisp, wisp.

"Susanne—"

"You're not going to that woman." A menacing *crack* split the air, and Cass clamped his eyes shut and gripped the pommel tightly as he felt the back of his shirt split in half. He sucked in his breath, waiting to feel his blood gush, but he gradually realized that she hadn't touched his flesh—a fact, he decided, that had most likely saved her life!

"Don't push me, Cass. I can draw blood," she warned in a tight voice.

"What's this all about?" he demanded, stunned to realize that for once his voice sounded thready instead of cocksure.

"You are not going to that woman."

"What woman?"

"That woman!"

"What woman? I wasn't going to meet a woman—I was going for a ride!"

He didn't know why he was bothering to inform her of where he was or was not going. She didn't own him. He started to turn around and tell her so when the whip cracked again.

This time it sliced through his sleeve and separated the fabric cleanly from his shoulder.

"Don't lie to me! You were going to see that woman!"

Cass had had enough. He whirled and lunged at her, catching her around the waist. She jerked back, and he reached for the whip. Susanne fought like an enraged cat, clawing and scratching. She punched him in the chest with her free hand while the other held the whip out of reach. It was an unequal contest, and his strength easily overpowered hers. They fell to the ground, and he landed on top of her, hearing the breath go out of her with a *whoosh*.

"Get off me, you big oaf!" she gasped.

He sat up and, with a strength born of pure rage, snapped the whip in two and threw it as far as he could send it.

"I have another one!" she said. She didn't make any effort to sit up, and he guessed he'd knocked the wind out of her.

He glared at her. "Miss McCord," he said in a voice so ominous that even he felt the hair rise on his arms. He wouldn't strike her, would he? "You are sorely getting on my nerves, woman."

"You were going to that. . .that woman," she accused. For some strange reason she sounded as if she was about cry.

"I was not—and what if I was? You have no right to be telling me what I can do! I'm doing what I said I'd do. I said I would get you, the children, Harlon, and Corliss to Cherry Grove safely, and I'm trying my level best to do that. Now, woman, you've browbeaten me, badgered me, bullwhipped me, and bad-mouthed me about all I'm going to stand for. You're going to stop. Do you understand?"

"I am your wife!"

His jaw dropped. He couldn't believe she'd said that. "My wife?"

"Your wife. . .I am, you know—no matter how hard you try to deny it!"

"I don't want you to be my wife! I've told you that a hundred times."

"But that doesn't change the fact that we are husband and wife," she argued. "And the Good Book says a man and woman should cleave together."

"Hold on. What's cleave mean?"

"I don't know—it's beside the point. They're to stay together—and you're not even trying to obey the Word."

"Let me get this straight. You're suggesting that just because of some idiotic, meaningless ceremony that took place in the middle of a road six years ago, I should actually consider myself married to you?"

"Well. . .yes." Their eyes were still locked. "I. . .I wouldn't object—truth is, I'd be honored."

"Me and you?" he repeated, feeling as if she had just asked him to step before a firing squad.

"Don't sound so shocked. We could be. . .married."

Cass slumped, resting his face in his hands. For a moment he thought he was going to break down and cry like a baby. Then he started to see the humor in this situation. His body heaved with barely suppressed hilarity.

Susanne stiffened, her eyes blazing with fury. "What is so funny?"

"You!"

She struggled to sit up. "I fail to see how my offering to be your wife should be so hilarious."

His hand snaked out, grasping her shoulder. "Now, wait a minute." Slowly he eased her back to the ground. "I didn't say I wouldn't accept your offer."

"You would?" She didn't sound so sure of herself.

He managed to keep a straight face, knowing that to consider her offer seriously would bring more trouble than it was worth. This woman was a spitfire, a wildcat, and the biggest obstacle he'd ever tried to overcome. She was a beautiful albatross who also happened to be his wife, albeit in name only. And he had a vested interest in making sure it remained in name only.

She took a deep breath. "So now what?"

The moonlight turned her hair to silver. A faint fragrance of woodsmoke from the campfire tinged the air. Cass found himself remembering how soft her lips had been, the way she had fit in his arms the day they lowered the wagons down the hill. Susanne McCord. . .Claxton. For a minute he was tempted, and then common sense intervened. She might be pretty, but he still had half a mind.

"You can go where you like; I'm going for a walk. Without you."

She clenched her fists. "You're rejecting me again?"

"That's right. You're nothing but trouble, and if I ever get free of you, I'm going to be mighty particular the next time around."

"You. . .you. . ." she spluttered.

"And you want to know what makes me the maddest?" He could feel the slow burn of anger rekindle. "The fact that you think I'd have anything to do with one of those women. I might not be perfect in the eyes of God, but I do make an effort."

She stared up at him, mouth open. "But I thought. . ."

"Thought what?"

"Laure. . .Miss Revuneau. . ."

"Laure Revuneau is a decent woman, active in her church and involved in mission work. What gives you the right to insult her?"

"Well. . .I. . ."

"At least she's never tricked a man into marrying her, or taken a bullwhip to one."

"Well—you don't know that!"

"Good night, Miss McCord. Sleep well." He turned and walked off, wondering where she kept the other whip. Finding it and destroying it would be his next move.

Chapter 8

The following morning when Susanne rounded the wagon, she found Mardean sitting in the rocker, cradling her infant to her bosom.

Tears rolled silently down the girl's cheeks when Susanne knelt beside her. She reached out to smooth a stray lock that had fallen across the young mother's forehead. The girl looked exhausted. "Mardean. . .is the baby worse this morning?"

Mardean lifted her red-rimmed eyes, and Susanne saw in them the depth of human misery: Mardean's child was gone. She rocked back and forth, quietly holding her infant's lifeless form.

Sometime during the night, her baby had passed away.

Susanne didn't know how things could get much worse. Why did the world have to be so complicated?

A bright sun shone overhead, birds chirped, and the squirrels chattered noisily in the trees. It didn't seem a proper day for a burial.

The small group stood around the shallow grave as Lucius Waterman spoke the words of interment. His voice was solemn when he opened his worn Bible and read from Matthew 19:14: "But Jesus said, Suffer little children, and forbid them not, to come unto me: for of such is the kingdom of heaven."

Lucius glanced at the bereaved young couple. "Nothing can replace the loss of this sweet infant, or ease the pain you are feeling right now. This suffering is too new, too fresh to easily endure. But I want you to know that the loss of this baby wasn't a punishment for your sins. God didn't take your baby to cause you grief.

"There'll be other babies, and you'll love them and care for them, but you'll never forget this one, your firstborn. Now, I want you to hear me out. When it seems you miss her so much you can't go on, you close your eyes and picture this sweet child healthy and happy, running through fields of flowers, the wind fresh and cool against her face, the sound of laughter and music filling the air.

"Then I want you to remember your child isn't lost to you. She's there, in heaven, waiting, and someday you'll meet her in a joyful reunion in the presence of Almighty God."

Susanne stood between Cass and her own brood, wondering how she would cope with such loss. Was her own faith strong enough to see her through the tragic ordeal? She felt it was; but then why did she despair when it came to Cass? She'd asked the Lord to intervene, to help her make amends. Now she, like Mardean, must trust that He loved His children and heard their cries.

The children that stood quietly beside her were not her own, yet she loved them all as dearly as if she'd carried them in her womb. Her heart went out to the young grieving father, Boyd. He stood tall with his arm around Mardean, who openly sobbed. Susanne could see that he was trying to be brave, even as his own grief streamed from the corners of his eyes.

Lucius spoke words of comfort and encouragement as Boyd and Mardean, along with their friends, listened in silence.

Susanne could feel a kindness in all of them, a deep understanding. The grim reaper often lurked on the trail; not a soul here was unaware of the dangers that could befall them.

Lucius closed the Bible and took stock of the small group. "Let us pray." Lifting his gaze upward, he began in a reassuring voice, "Father, we know not why You have called Sari Gibson home today, nor do we question Your will. Grant her parents the strength they will need to see them through their loss. Lend us the strength to give comfort and sustain Boyd and Mardean through the dark days ahead. God, we pray that You grant mercy to us all. Amen."

Four men stepped forward. Susanne could hear the scraping of the shovels. She knew each thrust of dirt would lay bare Mardean's heart.

The service broke up; others broke camp, allowing the grieving parents the last remaining moments with their child.

Susanne could see the young couple standing next to the mound of fresh dirt, holding tightly to each other.

She wondered if she would ever experience the kind of love Boyd felt for Mardean. If a tragedy befell her, to whom could she go for comfort? *I know I could go to You, Father, but I desperately need someone human to hold me. Lord, I feel so alone.*

Her eyes searched for Cass. She found him busy hitching the team to the Gibsons' wagon, and she suddenly needed the assurance that he was nearby.

Gathering the last of their supplies, she stowed them in their wagon then ambled over to where he was working.

Perched on the tongue of the wagon, she watched him adjust a piece of harness. He didn't seem to notice her, but she was strongly aware of the way the sun glinted on his hair, the way his appearance had changed from the rather dandified city man to a tanned, rugged man of the saddle.

Phebia ran up, crying. She'd smashed her thumb—the sucking one. With solemn eyes, she silently extended her injury to Cass.

"I don't think it's serious, but I'll bandage it," he reassured her.

Minutes later Phebia skipped happily away, dragging Marybelle by the hair, her injured thumb encased in a huge snow-white bandage.

"Maybe now she'll stop sucking the thing," Cass remarked when he turned his attention back to the harness.

"She seems to rely on you more and more in all her crises."

Cass shrugged. "She's a good kid."

Susanne sighed and clasped her hands in her lap. "Real sad about the Gibson baby, isn't it?"

He glanced her way, but he kept working. "It is."

"I'll never get used to the thought of death." Her eyes misted when they wandered back to Boyd and Mardean. "I know we shouldn't question God's will, but you wonder why He would want to take a baby."

"God didn't promise there'd be no pain here on earth. Losing a child is one of the hardest things a man or woman has to accept."

She looked at him. "You sound as if you've had firsthand experience."

"A few years back my brother lost both his wife and the child she was carrying." Cass jerked the leather straps together. "The loss almost killed him."

"I'm sorry."

"Meant to be. After a year or so he married a little gal named Charity, and from what I hear, he couldn't be happier. God has a way of turning loss into victory if we allow Him."

"Would that be Beau?" she asked softly, trying to ignore his words. She'd never gotten accustomed to losing. In fact, she had devoted a large part of her life to making sure she didn't lose. She didn't even like to think about loss. She'd met Beau Claxton years ago when she'd gone to the Burks' cabin to ask Cass to take her back to Saint Louis. That night with the others sleeping soundly, she had hatched a plot to force Cass to marry her and take her with him when he left. An act she now realized hadn't worked out exactly the way she had planned.

"It was Beau," Cass acknowledged.

"Do you have other family?"

"An older brother, Cole. And my mother. They live in Missouri. And Trey McAllister. He fought with my brothers in the war and since has become almost like family."

"No sisters?"

"No sisters."

She was pleased to discover that they could carry on a normal conversation without fussing. It felt good for a change. Maybe they were making progress, she thought wistfully, realizing that it would probably last only long enough for her to finish her next statement.

"Cass?"

He glanced up. "Yes."

"There's something you need to know."

"All right." He didn't seem overly curious, and she realized nothing she could say would surprise him. She guessed he'd learned to expect the worst from her.

"I sent you the telegram from Beau."

Cass never looked up. "Doesn't surprise me," he said quietly. "Knowing you, I've sort of suspected it. Seemed like you were too certain of my destination for our meeting to be purely coincidence. I'm just relieved to learn that Beau isn't in trouble. That did worry me considerable."

She blinked, stunned by his benign acceptance. "You're not angry?"

He looked at her this time, long and hard. "Would it do any good if I were?"

"No." She lowered her gaze to study her hands. "I know it was an awful thing to do."

"You seldom do anything that's nice where I'm concerned."

She looked away again. "I know."

"Exactly why do you do these things, Susanne?" he asked. "What drives you to be so ornery?"

"I don't know. . . . I suppose because nobody ever cared enough to stop me."

"Your folks never taught you the wisdom of asking for favors instead of bullying your way through life?"

"They tried; certainly Aunt Estelle taught me right from wrong. But after Mama died, Daddy was so wrapped up in his grief that he went off into his own little world. Seemed to me the only way I could get his attention was to throw fits, make demands, and act perfectly outrageous. When I found out that he wasn't going to come out of his shell long enough to do anything about it, then I suppose I just got worse." Maybe that was when she had started making sure no one ever ignored her again. Now, looking back, she could see her behavior must have appeared to be childish and out of control to others.

She lifted her gaze, aware her eyes were bright with unshed tears. "What my father didn't realize was that I was hurting, too. When I lost Mama, I didn't know where to turn or what to do. It isn't right to make a fourteen-year-old face death all alone. I needed him, Cass, but he wasn't there. Then he up and moved us to Cherry Grove to begin a new life. I didn't know anyone at all. I was sure that my world had come to an end."

"Did you ever let your father know you felt this way?"

"No." She sighed. "He wouldn't have understood. He's a good

man, but he hasn't the faintest idea of how to deal with a child."

"So you were lonely and miserable, and you decided to trick me into marrying you and taking you back to Saint Louis."

"I see now how terrible that was, but at the time I thought it was my only hope. I was sure that if I could just return to my aunt, then everything in my life would be all right again." She sighed, glad to have her weighty confession finally out in the open. "I always felt loved and wanted by Aunt Estelle. I guess she had a way of making everyone feel that way."

Cass stopped what he was doing and stepped over to tilt her chin up to meet his gaze. "Susanne, I'm going to tell you something, so listen to me. You don't bully people into loving you. You earn people's love by being honest and decent, by being a woman of your word. That gets their attention every time."

"Maybe it isn't attention I want," she whispered. "Maybe I want to be loved the way Boyd loves Mardean."

"I know of nine children who think you've hung the moon."

"I know. . .but sometimes I despair that no man will ever love me," she added softly.

"That's foolish."

She smiled, feeling tears sting her eyes. "Maybe I want to be loved by a man like you."

Their eyes met, and she wasn't sure of what she read in his gaze. . .pity. . .sympathy. . .maybe something entirely new. Could it be a grudging realization that she wasn't as bad as he'd thought she was?

"Then I suggest you give a man like me a reason to love you," he said simply.

They studied each other, his expression void of emotion. She was unprepared for the surge of affection he triggered in her. Could he see how deeply she loved him? She wasn't sure she wanted that.

Right now she was too confused in her thinking about Cass Claxton. One minute she wanted him so badly she wanted to cry and the next she was plotting ways to get even.

"Mr. Cass! Mr. Cass!"

They looked up to see Jesse dashing headlong in their direction.

Cass frowned. "What is it, Jess?"

"Doog. . ." Jesse was panting so hard he could barely get his breath. "Doog. . .fell. . .over a cliff."

"A cliff?" Startled, Susanne sprang up from the tongue of the wagon. "Where? When?"

"Just now. Down by the river. Hurry."

Cass paused long enough to grab a rope; then the three raced through camp, shouting for extra hands to help with the rescue.

Corliss poked her head out of the canvas flap of their wagon. "What's going on now?"

"Doog. . .he's fallen over a cliff!" Susanne shouted.

"Land o' mighty!" The flap fell back into place. "I'll be there soon as I find my shoes."

The growing assembly fought their way through dense briars and thickets, tearing off the prickly vines that angrily snatched at their clothing. A stitch formed in Susanne's side, but she ran on, her shorter legs barely able to keep up with Cass's long strides.

They ran for what seemed like a long time before Jesse skidded to a halt. He pointed to a patch of brush. "There," he panted. "Just behind those bushes."

Motioning to the others to stay put, Cass moved to peer past the heavy thicket. The abrupt drop-off on the other side shocked him. Moving farther, he stood on the edge of a near-vertical drop of fifty feet that ended on the rocks of a dry riverbed.

"Doog! Where are you?"

"Down here," came the weak, frightened reply.

Cass leaned even farther over the edge and spotted Doog about halfway to the bottom. He had one arm wrapped around a small cedar tree that jutted from the side of the cliff. Cass saw immediately that the tree was all that was keeping Doog from the perpendicular drop below him.

"Are you all right?"

"My arm hurts."

"Is he all right?" Susanne crowded closer.

"I think so," Cass yelled over his shoulder. "Stay back."

Cass glanced up to see Ernest Parker and Boyd Gibson already tying a loop on the end of a rope. He was stunned to see Boyd, but here he was, temporarily putting grief aside to help another.

Mardean stood behind Susanne, placing a gentle hand on her shoulder. She had just buried her own child, but she was here, lending silent support.

"Doog, I'm going to lower a rope. I want you to grab it and tie it around your waist," Cass ordered.

"I can't. . . . My arm's all funny looking, and it hurts real bad!"

"Is it broken?"

"I don't know. Maybe."

Cass pushed to his feet, his eyes gauging the firmness of the soil at the cliff's edge. He didn't want to dislodge rocks that would harm Doog. He turned back to Susanne. "I'm going down there."

"Oh Cass. Be careful."

They quickly tied a loop into a second rope and dropped it around Cass's waist. Ernest, Lucius, Boyd, Matt Johnson, and Lewis Brown took hold of the opposite end. Laurence Medley, Mardean's father, stood by to help oversee the operation.

"We're ready anytime you are."

Cass realized he might be putting his life in their hands. He removed his hat and handed it to Susanne. "Here, make yourself useful and hold this for me."

"Please"—Susanne's eyes locked helplessly with his—"please. . .I'm so worried."

He grinned. "You worry too much."

Her lower lip trembled, and his smile faded. "I'll be all right. . .okay?"

She nodded wordlessly.

In a completely uncharacteristic gesture—at least toward her—he reached out and tugged her nose playfully then turned to face the four waiting men. "Gentlemen, I hope you have strong grips."

Moments later the men carefully lowered Cass over the cliff.

Susanne couldn't bear to watch. She turned and buried her face against Martha Waterman's shoulder.

The cliff was almost vertical and was composed of loose shale rock that made climbing up impossible. Cass moved as carefully as he could, but dirt and rocks still rained down on Doog.

"You still all right, Doog?"

"Yessir."

"Any particular reason you picked today to walk off a cliff?" Cass asked, trying to keep the boy's mind off his problem.

He was about ten feet above Doog when the rope went slack for an instant and then tightened again. A fine sweat broke across his forehead. He paused, braced his feet against the wall, and tightened his grip. "Everything all right up there?" he yelled.

"Sorry. We've got you now."

Doog's voice trembled. "I was just chasin' a rabbit, and I was runnin' real hard. . . ."

Cass eased down another few feet until he was level with the boy. "We're going to get you back up on top."

"Good."

"You scared?"

"A little. . . What about you?"

"A little. Your arm hurting you?"

"Yessir. Is Miss McCord up there?"

"Yes, she is."

"I'll bet she's scart, huh?"

"She looked a mite peaked. Hold on while I figure out how to get you tied into this rope."

"Okay. Mr. Cass?"

"Yeah?"

"Better hurry. Them snakes are making me kinda nervous," Doog admitted.

"Snakes?" Cass paused, his heart sinking.

Doog nodded his head toward the cliff on the other side from Cass. "There's two big old rattlers lyin' on a ledge just over there a few feet. One's just kinda lyin' there lookin' at me."

Oh Lord—say it isn't so. Cass wasn't afraid of snakes, but he didn't necessarily cherish the thought of having a tea party with two of them while dangling at the end of a rope.

He could see them when he leaned away from the cliff face and looked past Doog. Sure enough, they were big ones, lying there sunning themselves.

"Listen, Doog. Stay perfectly still. Don't move a muscle." Cass deliberately kept his tone neutral, hoping to keep the boy from knowing what they were up against.

"My arm hurts."

For a moment Cass had forgotten about the child's injured arm. "All right. . .let me think for a minute." He could feel sweat trickling down his back; his eyes focused on the snakes. This was not going to be his day—he could feel it.

"Cass, are you all right?" Susanne's anxious voice came to him from far up the cliff.

"We're doing fine!" he called back.

One of the snakes opened its mouth and moved from a full coil into an S shape. Cass's skin crawled.

"Just fine," Cass repeated softly, hoping to believe it. *God? You watching? Fine doesn't exactly cover it, but I guess You know that.*

"Are rattlers likely to attack?" Doog asked when he noticed Cass's reaction to them.

"Not usually, son."

"But sometimes?"

Cass kept his tone impartial. The last thing he needed was for Doog to spook and try to scramble away from the reptiles. "Doog, how much does your arm hurt? If I put this loop around your waist it will slide up into your armpits when they start to pull you up. Can you stand that?"

Doog kept glancing back at the snakes. "I'm not sure. Can they pull both of us up at once?"

Cass did some quick mental calculations. The boy was light; maybe sixty pounds. He was uneasy about the strength of the men and the rope if they had to go up together.

"Susanne!"

"Yes!"

"Tell Lucius we may have to come up on the same rope. Ask him if he thinks they can handle us both."

Seconds later her voice echoed, "They say they can if they have to."

Doog looked at the snakes again and gave a start. "Mr. Cass, they're moving. I think they're coming this way."

"Don't move. Just don't move."

Still dangling from the rope, Cass slowly tried to edge past the boy and get between him and the snakes. His movement seemed to awaken the one who had looked to be asleep the whole time.

"Bad idea," he said to himself.

Doog looked down as if he thought he might try to escape by letting go of the tree.

"Don't look down," Cass cautioned softly. "We can't go down. We've got to go up."

The boy obediently lifted his eyes. "I'm scart," he whispered. "Real scart, Mr. Cass."

"I know. You're going to have to climb over to this side of the tree and get on my back. They can pull us both up at the same time."

Cass looked closely at the boy's face, trying to gauge his ability to do what was being asked of him.

Doog swallowed. "I'll try." He shifted his feet, trying to find a solid spot that would support his weight for the move.

Out of the corner of his eye, Cass saw one of the snakes was moving their way. He didn't seem angry and he wasn't rattling, but he was on the move.

I've got to buy us some time. Disregarding his earlier "don't move" strategy, Cass scrambled to the other side of Doog. Bracing his left foot against the cliff face, he placed his right boot squarely in the snake's path. Then he waited.

Sure enough, the snake crawled onto the toe of his boot. When it was about one-third of the way across the boot Cass kicked out and the snake sailed through the air to the rocks below.

"Now, Doog, before the other one wakes up, get up here and hang on to my back, just like a piggyback ride." With an urgency born of fear, the boy did as he was told.

Holding on to the rope with his left hand, Cass reached his right hand around his back under Doog's seat to help support the boy's weight.

"Now pull!" he yelled. "Pull for all you're worth."

Immediately he felt the tug of the rope as those on top went to work. Doog was making a small whimpering sound, not unlike a scared puppy. He was trying hard not to cry, and Cass had a quick thought of admiration for the lad's courage.

Cass felt sweat stream down the sides of his face. Doog's good arm threatened to choke him. Then the pulling stopped.

What's going on up there? he thought. That's exactly what he would have yelled if he could have gotten any sound by Doog's arm.

Then he heard some confused yelling, and the pulling started again.

"Hold on, Cass," Susanne yelled. "Hold on."

Slowly they were pulled upward. Cass tried to get some toeholds in the cliff face and help the men above, but the loose shale kept flipping away. Someone yelled, "Quit all that flopping around down there. You're making it harder!"

So he held on tighter than ever and hoped they would reach the top before he blacked out from lack of oxygen.

Doog kept repeating, "Please, God, don't let us fall. Please, God, don't let us fall." Cass found his prayers in unison with the boy's.

After what seemed like hours, they were high enough that strong hands reached out and took Doog from Cass's back. Cass scrambled up another foot or so and lay with his upper body on the ground and his feet still dangling over the precipice.

After a few minutes of rest he stood up. Doog was on his knees a few feet away, trying to catch his breath and compose himself. Susanne was kneeling in front of him, trying to assess the seriousness of the injury to his arm.

Cass walked over to the boy and whispered in his ear, "I don't see any need to let Miss McCord and the others know about our little friends down there. It would only upset them. Women are real funny about snakes, you know, so why don't we just keep this between us men?"

Doog nodded without raising his head. "From now on I'm gonna be real funny about 'em, too."

When Susanne looked up and saw him, Cass thought she might stand up and give him a big hug. Instead she kept worrying over Doog.

Corliss ran her hands over the boy's upper body and diagnosed his injuries: a sprained shoulder and a bruised arm. She prescribed a sling and a period of rest. Doog, who was openly distressed by all the fuss that the womenfolk were making, tried to wriggle from her grasp and edge toward the other boys.

Ernestine Parker fawned over Cass, patting his arm. "I declare, you're so brave, Mr. Claxton. I could never have gone down into that terrible old creekbed."

He smiled down at her. She was a pretty girl—would make some lucky boy a good wife in a few years. "It wasn't all that bad." He thought of the snakes and suppressed a shudder. No, it had been bad. Real bad.

"Are you all right?" Susanne asked. She laid her hand on his sleeve.

"I'm fine. Nothing to get upset over." Cass and Doog exchanged a conspiratorial glance, and both grinned.

Susanne's eyes took note of Cass's sweat-stained clothing, and she shook her head. "I'll bet it was terrible down there."

He shrugged.

Phebia marched over and immediately demanded that he remove the bandage from her thumb. Since it had only been for show anyway, he complied.

"Good!" She popped the thumb back into her mouth.

"Folks, we best be gettin' on the trail," Lucius warned. "We've lost nigh onto four hours today."

The group wandered off toward their camp, talking among themselves about all the strange happenings the morning had brought.

The children clustered around Cass and Susanne when they started walking. Cass casually placed his arm around Susanne's waist; Corliss fell into step, carrying Phebia and Marybelle.

Doog was loudly extolling his adventure to the other boys, omitting the part about the snakes, though Cass could tell it pained him to leave it out. Without that part, it sounded as if he'd simply fallen off a little hill and Cass had come down to fetch him.

Cass smiled down at Susanne as they walked along, enjoying the lovely fall day, thinking that they looked like a real family as the twelve of them sauntered down the road together.

A real family.

What was he thinking?

Chapter 9

Sunday morning, members of the wagon train gathered for an early morning service. Pre-service talk among the men centered on hunting and the weather.

Lucius stood before the group holding his Bible. "Our text today is taken from the thirty-first chapter of Psalms. 'Be of good courage, and he shall strengthen your heart, all ye that hope in the Lord.'"

Lucius looked out over the small congregation. "Be of good courage. Let those words take root in your heart. Life is hard; bad things happen to good people. Sometimes we don't know where to turn next, but our God is a merciful God who longs to bless His people if we give Him a chance.

"Don't let trouble bow you down and cause you to take your eyes off the goal. Be of good courage, and God will give you strength—His strength—for everyone who hopes in the Lord."

As Susanne listened to the familiar words, it seemed Lucius spoke directly to her. She felt she gained a message from God—and Aunt Estelle—to have hope in the Lord. Sad that she often lost sight of that hope. *Father, help me to remember that whatever happens, You are there. Give me Your courage and strength, Lord, because I sure don't have any of my own.*

Susanne had seen firsthand how God had blessed her aunt

and the work she had done at the orphanage. He hadn't stopped loving the children because they had left Saint Louis. He would take them safely to Cherry Grove. She had to trust.

Jay Lassiter strummed his guitar, while Buck joined in with his fiddle. Voices rose in singing "Amazing Grace." Susanne added her soprano. She could hear Corliss's rich alto, and surprisingly, Cass contributed a fine baritone.

After services the members scattered to their midday meal. Corliss had outdone herself with fricasseed squirrels and a rich hickory-nut pie. Susanne knew she would miss the bounty of the Missouri countryside when they left the hills behind to enter Kansas. The prairie had its blessings, too, but she had come to know and love the Ozarks.

After dinner, Cass took the older boys with him, saying that he would enjoy the company. Susanne and Corliss and the younger children carried the dirty clothes to a small stream, taking advantage of the layover to catch up on laundry. Wash days never occurred on Sunday back in Saint Louis, but life on the trail was different. Here one did what one could when one could. It was also the only time they could catch up on the week's gossip without the men being around to scowl at them. They chattered like magpies as they went about their work sudsing and wringing out garments.

Susanne helped Corliss with most of the laundry, but shortly before two she announced that she and Phebia were returning to camp to begin the baking.

Corliss absently waved her off, never missing a lick in telling her story about how Jesse had put a frog in Bryon's bedroll two nights ago, describing the howl the five-year-old had sent up.

After feeding Phebia a biscuit and a cup of milk, Susanne put her down for a nap. Almost everyone had drifted out of camp by the time she turned her attention to bread making. She had just dumped several cups of flour into a large wooden bowl when she heard footsteps approaching. She glanced up and was startled to see Joe Killen, one of the renegades who had stopped at their camp a few weeks earlier.

The man stood looking at her, a grin spreading across his dirty features. He tipped his hat politely. "Afternoon, ma'am."

Susanne stepped back when his foul smell assaulted her.

"Mr. Killen. . . What are you doing here?"

His eyes traveled over her, and her skin crawled. "I thought you might be sparin' me a cup of coffee, ma'am."

"Well. . .I suppose I can." She didn't like the idea of this man around while Cass was gone, but she didn't want to be rude. She moved to the large pot hanging above the fire, poured coffee into a tin cup, and handed it to him.

His fingers brushed hers when he took the cup. "Thank you, ma'am. I'm right beholden to you."

Susanne nodded and quickly stepped away. She was dismayed to see him amble over and settle himself comfortably upon a rock a few feet away from where she'd planned to work.

Deciding she could do little about it, she concentrated on mixing the dough.

"Right purty weather we're havin'." He took a sip from the cup.

She nodded, fixing her eyes on her work.

"Sure was sorry 'bout the old man a-breakin' his leg. At his age it'll take a spell to heal."

Reaching for the salt, Susanne felt lightning in the pit of her stomach. How would he know Harlon had broken his leg—unless, of course, he'd been following them?

"Where is the rest of your party, Mr. Killen?"

"Jest call me Joe, honey."

She let a warning light enter her eyes when she turned and

evenly met his gaze. "My name is Mrs. Claxton."

"I know what your name is." His insolent gaze skimmed her.

"Then use it when you speak to me."

Joe grinned. "I like a woman with spunk. Makes the game worthwhile."

She didn't answer, and he added, "Bull and the other fellers are camped down the road a ways."

"I'm surprised. It was my understanding that you had business elsewhere. I would think you could travel much faster than we can."

"Oh, we ain't in no hurry," Joe said. "Just kinda like to take our time and enjoy the scenery—you know what I mean?"

Susanne knew.

"Where's your man today, Mrs. Claxton?" His tone remained friendly, but Cass's earlier warning about the outlaws made Susanne leery. She wondered how far away he was.

"Are you referring to Mr. Claxton?" she returned coolly.

"Yeah, Mr. Claxton. Where he be off to on such a fine day?"

"He's hunting nearby."

"That so?" Killen peered at her over the rim of his cup, and he took another swallow. "You know, if I had me a fine-lookin' woman sech as you, I'd be sending them young bucks off to do my huntin'."

The implication in his voice hung heavily between them.

Susanne continued her work, determined to ignore him. Surely he would move on.

"I suppose the old man is around?"

"Harlon's. . .resting in the wagon." Susanne didn't want him to think that she was alone, without protection, so she quickly added, "He's here in case there's any trouble."

Killen glanced toward the wagon some thirty feet away. "Is that a fact? 'Course, there ain't much an old feller with a broken leg can do, now, is there?"

"Not much," Harlon's voice agreed. The barrel of his gun slid out the back of the wagon and leveled at the center of the outlaw's chest. "But ol' Myrt here can sure get her point across!"

The tin cup clattered to the ground. Killen sprang to his feet, jumping back when the hot coffee seared the material of his shirt. "Here now, I was just makin' conversation. T'ain't no call to be gettin' all riled up!"

"You git on out of here, Joe Killen. We don't take to the likes of you comin' around botherin' our womenfolk." Harlon kept the gun trained on his target.

By now Jesse, Doog, and Joseph had returned to camp. They stood watching the tense exchange with wide-eyed curiosity.

The outlaw sent an uncertain look in Susanne's direction.

"He means what he says, Mr. Killen. You'd best be moving on."

A look of sheer hatred flared unchecked in the renegade's eyes. "All right, but you'll be regrettin' this, missy," he yielded in a voice so tight that Susanne barely caught the message. He whirled and stalked off.

The boys raced to Susanne, their eyes aglow with excitement. "What'd he want, Miss McCord?" Doog asked.

Susanne drew the boy close, distractedly giving him an assuring squeeze. "Nothing, Doog. . .just a cup of coffee."

But Susanne knew what he had wanted, and the realization sent a cold chill down her spine. The man was evil, and so was his ugly pack waiting just beyond the shadows.

She turned to the wagon and said, "God bless you, Harlon. God bless you!"

The men had a good hunting day. Even Laurence Medley killed a small doe. That night there was fresh venison steak for all.

After supper Cass took Aaron and Payne down to the river to wash. The three whooped and yelled as they plunged headlong into the icy water. The shock nearly snatched their breath away. They waded to the bank to lather themselves with the bar of soap Susanne had supplied.

Jesse and Doog sat nearby, skipping rocks on the water.

"Don't see any sense in washing again," Doog complained. "We just bathed last night, so we got a whole week to go before we need to put ourselves through that again."

The sun was sitting behind a row of towering sycamore, casting a mellow glow on the red and gold leaves shimmering with vivid splashes of color. The air already had a sharp bite to it, and being wet didn't help matters. Cass washed faster.

"How many rabbits did ya kill today, Payne?" Doog wanted to know.

"'Bout six, I guess."

"How 'bout you, Mr. Cass?"

"Twelve rabbits and four squirrels."

"Man!" Doog exclaimed. "I'll be glad when I get old enough to go hunting. Fact is, I'll be glad when I get old enough to do anything."

"What did you boys find to do to keep out of trouble?" Cass asked.

"Nothin'. We just sat down here and threw rocks in the river while we listened to them women cacklin' like a bunch of ole settin' hens." The boys giggled.

"Hear anything interesting?"

The two looked at each other sourly. "Not a thing."

Socially acceptable again, the men waded out of the water, shivering. They toweled off and put on clean clothes.

"That outlaw came to camp today," Doog announced.

Cass's hands suddenly paused in buttoning his shirt. "Bull Hanson?"

"Nah, that other one, Joe Killen. Boy, he is nasty dirty!" Jesse made a disgusted face.

"What'd he want?"

"Miss McCord said he just wanted a cup of coffee," Jesse relayed.

"But Harlon had to turn the gun on him," Doog said.

Cass finished dressing and sat down to pull on his boots, digesting the news. He hadn't talked to Harlon tonight. The older man was asleep during supper. Since his leg was keeping him up nights, Corliss hadn't wanted to disturb him.

"Why did Harlon turn the gun on him?" Cass asked.

Doog was about to skip another rock when he let his arm slip back to his side. "Don't know. . .'cept I think maybe he wasn't bein' real mannerly to Miss McCord."

Cass stood up, suddenly hot with anger.

Aaron reached to restrain Cass with his right arm. "Best check with Harlon afore you get all riled. Doog's stories aren't too reliable at times."

"They are so!" Doog turned to Jesse. "Didn't that ole outlaw come to camp today?"

Jesse lifted his eyes to Cass. "He did, Mr. Cass. Honest."

"Aaron, look after things here," Cass said. "I have business to tend to."

"I'm coming with you." Aaron stepped forward, meeting Cass's eyes.

"I appreciate your offer, but I can take care of this matter myself."

"I know you can, but there be four of them. I figure that's two apiece."

Cass grinned. "You think you can handle two?"

Aaron drew his unimpressive stature to its full height. "Yessir."

"Then I guess you and I better go teach a low-down piece of nothing a few manners."

"Can I go, too?" Payne was on his feet in a flash.

"I need you here," Cass said as the five walked back to camp. "With Harlon down, I have to leave a man here to help the women."

"Oh. . .all right," Payne said. "But I'd rather go with you."

"Staying here is important. Someone has to look after the women, and, like I said, it needs to be a man."

Payne's chest puffed with pride. "I can handle it."

"Gentlemen, I think we'd better keep this under our hats," Cass advised as they drew closer to the site. "The women will get all fussy if they know where we're going."

The boys nodded, conveying the silent pledge to keep the mission quiet.

"Man, I don't like girls!" Doog complained. "They're always taking the fun out of everything."

Cass sympathetically clamped his hand on the boy's shoulder. "Try to hold that thought, son."

Susanne glanced up when her men walked into the clearing. She felt such warmth when she thought of how the boys idolized Cass. It was apparent that Aaron respected and loved him deeply, and she wondered what the boy would do once they reached Cherry Grove and Cass left.

She watched Cass and Aaron break away and pause to talk with Harlon for a moment. Seconds later, the two emerged from the wagon, matching strides on their way to saddle the horses.

Realizing they were about to leave again, Susanne abandoned the dishwashing to run to catch up with them.

"Cass!"

He paused and turned at the sound of her voice.

"Where are you going?"

"Aaron and I have a little business to conduct," he said easily, his tone too quiet to suit her.

She frowned. "Business—tonight?"

"We won't be gone long."

She looked doubtfully from Cass to Aaron. "You be careful. . . ."

Cass nodded. "We plan to."

She turned and started away then paused, reaching out to clasp his arm.

Cass looked at Aaron and grinned. He pulled Susanne close for a reassuring hug. "You're worrying again."

"I can't help it. It seems to me you're storying about where you're going." She had an uneasy feeling that Cass was keeping something from her.

He drew back innocently. "Me? Story to you?"

"Don't you look so innocent, Cass Claxton!" She brought her hands to her hips. "You'd story to me in a minute." She turned to Aaron. "Is he storying to me?"

Aaron shrugged and gave her a sheepish grin.

Chuckling, Cass drew her back into his arms. He gave her another hug before he turned her in the direction of camp. "Go wash your dishes, woman."

Susanne still had a niggling feeling in the pit of her stomach that something wasn't right as she watched him walk away.

Exactly what it was she wasn't sure, but she had a feeling it wouldn't take her long to find out.

The moon was high when Cass and Aaron returned to camp. Susanne thought she'd never seen two more disreputable-looking characters in all her days.

Their clothes were filthy, their shirts torn at the shoulders, and both were sporting the biggest, blackest shiners she had ever seen.

They got off their horses and turned to face her, their expressions guilty. She saw that each had a pumpkin tucked under his arm.

"You've been fighting!" she accused, drawing her wrapper closer against the night chill. She'd lain awake for hours, listening for their return.

"Fighting?" Cass shot a knowing glance at Aaron, and they both grinned. "We have not. We've been picking pumpkins." He gallantly extended his bounty to her.

"I hope you didn't steal these."

"Nope, we sort of—well, they were lying around and we took them," Cass said.

Corliss's head emerged from the back of the wagon. Seeing Aaron's sorry condition, she squired him off to patch him up. That left Cass in Susanne's care.

"I have never seen such goings-on!" Susanne usually borrowed one of Corliss's standard sayings when she didn't know what else to say. Quietly she set the pumpkin aside and stepped over to help Cass at the improvised washstand.

He good-naturedly shrugged her away, insisting that he didn't need any help.

Susanne decided that whatever he'd been doing, it had left him in a good mood. He was buoyant and elated, completely unconcerned that she'd been up most of the night, worrying herself half to death.

After pouring water into the enamel basin, she reached for a bar of soap.

"If you've been out all this time consorting with that woman. . . ," she began, remembering the redhead who'd been itching to get her hands on Cass. If that woman continued to fool with her husband. . . She couldn't finish the thought. "I can't believe you'd subject Aaron to such—"

"Redhead, redhead! Is that all you can think about?" Cass complained. "Do you honestly think I'd let a woman do this to me?" The flying cloth garbled his words.

Susanne wrung out the cloth and started scrubbing his face much as she would have scrubbed Phebia's. "I don't know what to think of you! And I didn't say anything about a redhead—you did!"

"Ouch! That hurts!"

"You'd better not have taken Aaron out to teach him things he shouldn't know!"

"Aaron is sixteen years old. What he doesn't know he should be learning." She heard his swift intake of breath when the soap found an open wound. "Will you stop it? I can wash my own face!"

"What have you been doing, Cass?"

"I told you; I had business to take care of."

"And you involved Aaron in your rowdy shenanigans?"

"He's a great kid." Cass's voice held nothing but respect for Aaron, the boy that no one had wanted.

Susanne didn't know what the two had been up to, and it didn't seem likely she was going to find out. But there was no way on earth she believed they'd been out picking pumpkins.

"You should be ashamed of yourself!"

Cass sighed. "You're not going to let up on me, are you? All right, I'm ashamed of myself."

"You are not!"

"I know it, but I figure you're not going to pipe down until I say that I am."

Irritated, Susanne dabbed white salve on his cuts, silently admitting that she'd been more scared than angry. From all appearances they had been fighting. She felt a smile threatening when she wondered how their opponents must look. "It's a wonder you weren't shot."

"Not a chance. I'm smarter than that."

She helped him out of the soiled shirt, handed him the washcloth, and went to get a clean shirt from his pack. By the time she returned he looked more presentable. She handed him the clean garment and walked to the dying fire to pour a cup of coffee.

Frost had settled on the ground; a bright harvest moon hung overhead. The midnight hour gleamed as bright as day. Susanne turned and finally smiled, noting the relief on his face when he accepted the silent truce. She handed him the tin cup. "Drink this. It'll help to warm you."

He slipped into his coat, his gaze locking with hers. "Thanks. Why not stay and share a cup with me?"

She was surprised by the invitation. It was the first time he'd asked her to join him—for any reason—and she fought the urge to read more into his unexpected request than simple gratitude.

"Thank you. I would enjoy a walk." She busied herself pouring a second cup of coffee as he walked over to pick up his bedroll. Moments later they left camp so that they wouldn't disturb the sleeping children.

Side by side, they walked until they came to a grassy knoll, where Cass paused.

Susanne helped unfold the blanket. "Nights are getting cooler," she remarked. They sat down and settled their coffee cups on the ground.

"Another month and the snow will be flying. Would you like my coat?"

"I'm warm enough, thank you."

They sat for a moment in compatible silence, sipping the coffee.

Susanne spoke first. "Killen paid a visit to camp this afternoon."

"That right? What'd he want?"

She frowned, thinking about the vile man and his crude remarks. "He asked for a cup of coffee, but I think he was up to no good. Harlon had to ask him to leave."

"Oh?"

"Aren't you a little surprised he's still around?"

"No."

"You don't think he intends to cause trouble?" She thought about mentioning the insinuations Killen had leveled at her, but she knew if she did it would only add to Cass's troubles, so she left out details about the visit. She was confident that Harlon had properly discouraged the man from coming around again.

Cass sipped his coffee. "I'm not worried about Joe Killen, and there's no need for you to be, either."

"Well"—Susanne was confident that Cass could handle whatever trouble the Killen man could cause—"I'd sure be happier to know that he was a hundred miles on down the road."

They shared the silence again.

When Susanne thought of something to say, she had to cover her mouth to stifle her giggles.

Cass drew his brows into an affronted frown. "What's so funny?"

"You. . .you look like you tangled with a wildcat!" *And lost,* she added silently.

A muscle quivered in his jaw, and she could tell that he was trying to restrain his amusement. "You think it's funny, huh?"

Her eyes gleamed with merriment. "Yes. . .I never knew a jack-o'-lantern could be so ferocious!"

He shrugged, gazing up at the moon. "Go ahead and laugh."

Had she upset him? She didn't think so. "Thank you, I believe I will!"

Susanne broke into a renewed round of mirth, and by the time she was near tears, Cass had decided to join her. He knew that he looked a sight, but it had been worth it. He and Aaron had taught Joe Killen a lesson tonight that the man would never forget.

He wasn't about to tell her where he'd been because if she found out that he'd gone to take care of the man who'd insulted her, she'd assume he'd done it as a favor to her—which he hadn't. Anyway, he didn't think he had. He was pretty sure he'd wanted the outlaw out of his own hair. He'd been relieved to see that Slim Watkins had left the group some time back. He'd liked the man. A thought struck him. How had Aaron known there were only four men in the outlaw camp? He grinned in the darkness. The kid had been spying on them. The boy had grit.

"You remind me of the time Jimmy Lonigan pushed me into a mud hole," Susanne teased. "I declare, I was a mess. My face was caked with mud, my dress was ruined, and the lovely yellow ribbon Mother had tied in my hair that morning looked like a soggy noodle. I was mortified. I pitched a temper tantrum of such magnitude that my teacher was forced to send one of the younger boys rushing out the door to get my mother to come take me home." She laughed merrily. "I refused to go back to school for two weeks, and I'm sure the teacher thought that was too soon."

Cass could imagine her fit; he'd witnessed a few. "What made Jimmy Lonigan want to push you into a mud hole?"

Susanne looked down at him, managing to keep her features deceptively composed. "Why, I just can't imagine! I was such an angel!"

They broke into laughter, and Cass thought it was a nice change from being at each other's throat.

"I remember being embarrassed in front of the whole school once." Cass gazed across the moonlit meadow as the corners of his mouth lifted with amusement. "My brother Beau had brought a frog to school and stuck it in Elsbeth Wilson's lunch pail. Elsbeth was a real pain. Her folks were rich, so she had more than the rest of us, but she was miserable. She always looked like she'd been eating persimmons. When she opened up her pail, that bullfrog jumped out onto her desk and swelled up with a loud *barrroopt*! You could have heard Elsbeth screaming for miles."

"What did the teacher do?"

"Because I'd laughed the hardest, the teacher thought I'd put the frog in her lunch pail, so she made me sit in the front of the room all afternoon, holding that frog on my lap, apologizing to Elsbeth every few minutes for being 'unsociable and crude.'"

Susanne giggled. "And your brother didn't say a word in your defense?"

"Are you serious? Beau sprang out of his seat, pointed a self-righteous finger in my direction, and hollered that I shouldn't have been so mean and that he was gonna tell Ma on me when we got home!"

They shared another good laugh. When their merriment died off, Cass swiveled to look at her. "I'll bet you were one of those prissy little girls in frilly dresses, with your hair in big blond curls that hung down to your waist."

She nodded. "Mother insisted on neatness. But Butch Michaels was forever dipping a curl in his inkwell."

"He was probably sweet on you and wanted to get your attention."

"Oh, he got my attention, all right! I gave him a black eye every Monday morning. It got to where he'd run when he saw me coming out the door."

Cass grinned.

"I was pretty terrible most of the time."

"You haven't improved a whole lot since."

Susanne glanced up, and he winked at her.

"Oh, you. . . How would you know what I'm like?" she accused. "You've never taken the time to get to know the real me. You're always blustering around, shouting at me, acting as if I'm about to give you a black eye every Monday morning."

"Butch Michaels has my sympathy," he said dourly. "I've experienced a couple of your black eyes."

Susanne knew that he was speaking figuratively, of course. "I'll admit that in the past I gave you reason to feel that way about me, but I wish I could convince you that I've changed, Cass. . .even if I do backslide a bit occasionally."

"A bit? I'd say your lapses are more like rockslides."

"Nevertheless, I am better."

Than what? he wondered. "If that's what you think."

"It's what I know. I'm really not a bad person."

He shrugged. "Who am I to argue? You were the perfect lady the day we met," he conceded dryly. "You recall the incident? I happened to get in your way when we were in Miller's Mercantile—"

"You didn't just happen to step into my way," she corrected. "You deliberately blocked my path."

"But you do recall the incident? You had just bounced fifteen or twenty spools of thread off Edgar Miller's bald head because he didn't have a certain color you wanted."

Susanne blushed. "That was a long time ago."

"The memory is vivid."

"I said I was sorry."

"Since then you've tricked me into marrying you at the point of a shotgun, tricked me into taking you to Cherry Grove, deliberately thrown dishwater on me, and with the aid of a bullwhip, shamed me in front of a whole lot of women. That same night, you turned the whip on me again, nearly peeling the hide off my back because you'd gotten it into your head that I was riding off to meet a redhead—"

"That whip never touched your back!"

His eyes narrowed. "A fact, I might add, that saved your life."

She grinned when he continued.

"In the time I've known you, you've browbeaten me, cussed me, spat on me, threatened and coerced me more times than I can count on both hands—now, tell me again how you've turned into such a nice person! I'm having a real hard time believing that."

She knew he was right. She had treated him wretchedly. A heartfelt sigh escaped her. "I wish we could start over."

He fell silent, and she wondered if she had made him angry again. But a moment later he said quite calmly, "Well, I guess there's no law that says we can't."

Her eyes drew to his face, and his steady gaze assured her that she hadn't heard wrong. "Do you mean it?"

"I mean it. I don't enjoy this bickering any more than you do, and for the sake of everyone else, I think we should try to get along with each other. I can't say I'm ever going to forget what you've done, Susanne, because I'm not sure I ever could. I'm the kind of man who likes to control my own destiny—and I sure plan on having the only say about who I marry. No woman's ever gonna hog-tie and brand me. But I'll concede that people can change, if they want to."

Susanne's heart tripped and thudded at his words. "Thank you," she said softly. "Does that mean you do believe I've changed?"

"That means I'm going to work on it a little harder."

"Thank you. . .because I'm beginning to care for you quite deeply."

"Well, just don't let it get out of hand," he warned.

"What would you say if I told you that I wasn't trying to mislead you the other night? That I really wanted to be your wife?" She knew the question was wanton, shameful, but it popped out anyway.

He slowly lifted the brim of his hat to look at her.

"I do, you know," she said.

He lowered his hat again. "I thought we'd been all through this."

"I understand." She fixed her eyes on the moon, staring hard, determined not to cry. "I don't want to push you into anything. It's just that I get so lonely."

He brushed a stray lock away from her forehead. "I guess I can understand that. You're trying to be everything to everyone. You must feel completely worn down sometimes."

"It's not the children or Corliss and Harlon," she said fiercely. "I love them like they were my own."

"Then what is it?" he asked, and she could have wept at the gentleness in his voice.

"It's just that sometimes I wonder if I'll ever find someone to love me. I want what every woman wants—a home, love, family."

"You have the family," he pointed out.

"In some ways, but you know what I mean."

"I know. I guess most everyone wants the same things. Both of my brothers are married with good wives and children, but somehow settling down never interested me. I might be missing something, but a hunch isn't enough to base a marriage on, Susanne. When a man and woman agree to join their lives together before God, it's serious business."

"Very serious," she whispered. "I used you, Cass. All I could think of was getting away from Cherry Grove. I never thought about what I was doing to you."

Susanne couldn't bear to look at him. All those years when she hadn't seen him, she hadn't given a thought to what her deception had done to him. What if he had married during that time? His marriage would have been a mockery because of her.

"I promise you, Cass; I'll never use you again." And she meant it. Never again would she manipulate him. Never again would she impose her selfishness on him. From this moment on, she would love him as deeply and as wholly as she knew how, even if he never loved her in return.

Cass was strongly aware of the woman at his side. She was desirable; something about her touched him in a way a woman never had. He knew she had changed, and that she would make some man a good wife. He'd never taken to the idea of settling down, being burdened with responsibilities. Life was too sweet, too exciting to swap his carefree existence for the staid, never-ending sameness of married life. It might be all right for Cole and Beau. But not for him.

"I don't think you have to worry. Someday a man will come along and he'll fall head over applecart in love. You're going to have all the things you want. Be patient. Somewhere God has the right person for you."

"But not you."

Did he imagine it, or did he hear a tinge of sorrow? "Not me. I'm selfish, Susanne. Maybe we're too much alike—willing to go to any lengths to win."

"Spoiled? Self-centered? Determined to have our own way?" she ventured.

He shrugged.

"But we've changed, Cass. Neither of us is like that anymore. We've grown up."

"Maybe, but not grown up enough. I've got a hunch we can either one be mighty headstrong when we want to be. Like you with the dishwater."

"And you dropping me off the horse."

He laughed. "I'm sorry about that."

"You are not," she accused. "You enjoyed every minute of it."

"Yeah—I did," he agreed, sobering.

She shifted to look at him again. "If we can't be man and wife, can we be friends?"

"I think we could manage that." He held out his hand and felt hers—warm and fragile—accept the offer. "Friends."

For a disturbing moment he found himself wondering what it would be like to take Susanne as his wife. After all, she had changed. Or he had.

He quickly discarded the notion. That kind of thinking would surely lead to trouble.

Friends. Susanne tried the word out for size and found it had a nice sound, but it wasn't close to what she wanted. Somehow, in spite of her best intentions, she had fallen in love with Cass Claxton. She had never wanted to feel this sweet longing for his presence, never chosen to have her heart leap at the sound of his voice, never asked for this total misery when she thought of the prospect of never seeing him again once they reached Cherry Grove. She had his answer, though. He preferred the single life to marriage. Especially when it came to being married to her.

He stood up and reached down to pull her to her feet. She stood beside him, feeling small and helpless. . .and lonely. She didn't want another man; she wanted Cass—wanted him with all her heart.

They walked back to camp in silence. Susanne left him to spread out his bedroll with the boys while she went back to her pallet where the girls were sleeping.

Phebia muttered in her sleep, and Margaret Ann rolled over to administer a soothing pat. "There, there, everything's all right."

The child calmed, and Margaret Ann rolled over on her side to look at Susanne. "Miss McCord?"

"Yes, Margaret Ann?"

"Where have you been?"

Susanne swallowed her surprise. She was being questioned by a child? And a child who was at the moment staring at her as if expecting an answer. She decided to tell the truth. "I've been talking to Mr. Cass."

"I see."

For a wild instant, Susanne thought perhaps she did. Then reason prevailed. Margaret Ann was extremely intelligent, but even she had no idea of the relationship between her and Cass.

"Is he going to stay in Cherry Grove with us?"

"No, he isn't."

"I see." Margaret Ann seemed to mull this over. She was silent for the space of five seconds, and Susanne dared to hope the subject was closed. She should have known better.

"Can't you ask him to marry you?"

"I couldn't do that." Mostly because she was already married to him and he couldn't wait to get rid of her, but she couldn't tell Margaret that. She couldn't tell anyone. Her pride would never survive the humiliation.

"I see."

If she says that one more time, Susanne thought, *I will scream.* The child had a decisive, thoughtful way of thinking and speaking that made her offhand remarks sound as though she were the mother and Susanne were the child.

"Why not?"

"Women don't usually do the asking."

"I see. Well, that seems like a very silly rule if you ask me."

Susanne figured she could share a few thoughts on the risks of asking—or rather forcing—a man to marry you, but she had no desire to dispel the child's dreams.

Thankfully Margaret Ann closed her eyes and ceased talking. Susanne lay back on her bedroll, staring up at the stars. Usually when she saw the night sky she felt overwhelmed by the majesty and glory of God's handiwork. Looking up at the heavens made her feel small and insignificant in comparison. Tonight she barely noticed. All her thoughts were centered on her husband. Why couldn't she have him? After all, they were married. Why should she allow him to just walk away? There had to be a way to hold him.

Please, God, let there be a way. . . .

Cass looked up from inspecting the lead ox's foot to see Margaret Ann approaching. For once she wasn't leading Lucy around, and her expression said she was dead serious about something. Cass felt a prickle of alarm. When this kid got something on her mind, she was hard to shake.

"Good morning, Mr. Cass."

"Morning, Margaret Ann. Sleep well?"

"Very nicely, thank you, but I do believe Miss McCord had a restless night."

"Oh?" He wasn't going to touch the topic.

"I believe she was with you until rather late."

"We took a walk—talked a little." He didn't like being on the defensive. What right did this child have to question him?

"I see."

How could anyone her age pack so much meaning into two words?

"Are you staying with us once we reach Cherry Grove?"

Clay lowered the animal's foot and straightened to face her. "No, I'm not. I'll be returning to my home in Saint Louis. I have business to take care of there."

"We need you." Her eyes were faintly accusing.

"You'll get along fine. Miss McCord will be there and Harlon and Corliss."

"But they're not you."

Cass drew a deep breath. If he didn't answer, maybe she'd go away. He had enough sense to know it wasn't going to be that easy.

She fixed him with a stern gaze that cut right through excuses. "If I asked you to marry Miss McCord, would you?"

He eyed her stoically. "Did she put you up to this?"

"I haven't spoken to her this morning, but it does seem a sensible solution."

"Well, it isn't."

"Why not, pray tell?"

"People marry because they love each other."

"Miss McCord is very lovable."

He shook his head. "Look, Margaret Ann. It doesn't work that way. Miss McCord has her life, and I have mine."

Margaret Ann sighed. "Adult reasoning is so lame at times." She turned to leave, and he breathed a sigh of relief, feeling the way he'd felt when he'd been seven and accidentally thrown a rock through the parlor window, breaking the glass and shattering Ma's double-globed lamp with the hand-painted pink roses on it. Margaret Ann's tone of voice reminded him of his mother's when she pointed out how irresponsible it was to throw rocks at glass. Except staying married to Susanne wasn't irresponsible; it was insane.

So why did Margaret's solution make perfect sense?

Chapter 10

By the end of the week, the wagons rolled into Westport, Missouri, where Susanne, Harlon, Corliss, the children, and Cass prepared to say good-bye to their new friends before continuing west to Kansas.

Westport was the first major city the travelers had come across since leaving Saint Louis. Even though it wasn't large, the town took the cake in confusion, the trademark of the embarking point for the West.

Three trails left from here: the Oregon, the California, and the Santa Fe. A strange mixture of people thronged the streets, and for the first time they saw Indians. Wild-looking men, bronzed, with long black hair and piercing black eyes.

Phebia had taken one look at the men and declared, "Me don't like Kansas."

"We're not in Kansas yet," Susanne said. The Kansas border was a short way out of town.

"Me don't like it anyway." Phebia poked out her lower lip in a familiar pout.

They stocked up on supplies at Boone's Trading Post, and Cass treated them to a meal at Yocum's Tavern, a place where many of the travelers ended up for one reason or another. At Susanne's request they attended church, choosing Union Church, founded by a Methodist missionary. The Presbyterians, the Christian Reformers, and the Baptists had met here, too, until they could find suitable locations for their own houses of worship. The brick exterior was handsome and imposing.

Inside they settled on the wooden pews, breathing in the fragrance of beeswax and freshly laundered curtains. Susanne listened to the rustling of ladies' skirts, the soaring notes of the organ, and felt comforted. There was something special about coming together to worship God, whether the worshippers gathered in a stately building or around a campfire. She remembered Jesus' promise: "Where two or three are gathered together in my name, there am I in the midst of them."

It was a morning to enjoy. The children were quiet and well behaved, the music lively and spirited, the sermon inspiring. For a moment Susanne could pretend they were like the other families attending. Anyone looking at them would think they were a husband and wife with a sturdy, growing family.

They shook hands with the minister on the way out and wandered down the street to have Sunday dinner at the Harris Hotel. Corliss and Harlon had elected to stay with the wagon, so as soon as they finished eating they walked back to join them. Susanne felt it had been a glorious morning. The last time they would worship in church until they reached Cherry Grove.

Cass had business acquaintances in Westport, and a prominent man-about-town, Mr. Adrian Holland, came out to the train to meet him. Susanne sat in the shade of the wagon mending Jesse's trousers, which had been torn so many times they appeared to be held together with patches. Cass noticed Holland watching her.

After greetings were exchanged, Cass broached the subject

he'd been thinking of since getting into town and hearing the talk. "I hear there's money to be made in Santa Fe shipping."

"Possibly," Holland agreed. "That's if gangs don't attack the train, robbers don't ambush you, wagons don't fall apart, animals don't go lame or die on you, and you don't lose everything trying to ford a river."

Cass grinned. "You're saying there's a risk?"

"A big risk," Holland agreed. "But worth it. You'd need a good wagon master, one you can trust."

"You know one?" Cass asked.

Holland nodded. "Know three, actually. The best is a shyster, and you have to watch him. He knows the country, though, and he's never lost a wagon yet."

"So why is he out of work?"

"Because he also likes to fight. Got in a squabble and broke up Yocum's Tavern. Now he's in jail until he can pay for damages, which he can't since he gambled and drank up his last paycheck."

Cass noted the information. When he came back this way he'd check into the situation. He was always looking for new ways to expand. Santa Fe trading would be a new direction for him. After he completed his business and Holland had left, Cass got up to check on the livestock and met Susanne's disapproving expression.

"Now what?" he asked. She had a way of looking at him with Margaret's discerning eyes.

"Surely you're not going to do business with that dreadful man."

"Holland?" Cass shrugged. "He's a pillar of society, deacon in the church."

"Not him. The one in jail."

"Oh, him." He shrugged again. "The man's a good wagon master. Why not get him out of jail and put him to work? He'd be grateful, and I'd have a good man to get my wagons through. Everyone's happy."

"I suppose so. Making money means a lot to you, doesn't it?"

"Why wouldn't it?"

"I don't know. Why does it? You tell me."

"Well, think of all it can do." He paused, sensing the trap.

"Yes, big houses, fancy clothes, and fancier friends."

He winced at the scorn in her tone. "There's nothing wrong with having a few luxuries."

"I suppose not. And if you're feeling guilty, you can always hold a benefit where everyone who is anyone can eat and dance and gossip and listen while some poor wretch espousing a good cause begs for money."

He heard the bitterness in her voice and knew the source. "Did you get much from the Revuneau benefit?"

"Five hundred dollars. I'm financing the trip with it. But what I really needed—a home for the children—wasn't even considered. And you know why? Because children like these were considered a nuisance. Until Aunt Estelle took them in they ate out of garbage, stole for food, and slept in doorways. They couldn't be ignored, and your friends wanted them to go away."

He cringed. The rebuke in her voice even sounded like Margaret. He had three houses he could have let her have, and he'd laughed and walked away. Not because he cared about the properties one way or another, but because he hated Susanne McCord. He looked at her now, with her head bent over a boy's ragged britches, hands roughened from hard work. Her hair was drawn back in a roll on the back of her neck, her face tanned brown by the autumn sun. She didn't have Laure Revuneau's exotic flare, but she was lovely, with a grace and sense of dignity that earned his admiration and respect.

Corliss joined them, and Cass walked away, alone with his thoughts. He'd come to know the nine orphans. Might as well admit it—he loved them. Even Phebia, who had an unerring attraction to his nose. It was a wonder the appendage hadn't lengthened by several inches, the way she tweaked it.

He thought of Susanne's compassion for the underdog, and he knew a footloose bachelor interested in money and the power it brought could never be what she needed. Not only could he not be a part of her life, she would be desperately unhappy in his world.

If he claimed her for his wife, she'd have to give up the children, and he knew she would never agree to that. But there was one thing he could do. He would personally underwrite the needs of the orphanage. As long as he had a dollar, Susanne and her brood would never want for food or shelter. Cass expected a warm, sweet burst of satisfaction over the decision. After all, it was the sort of tribute that should warm the cockles of God's heart. But if the Almighty was pleased with his decision, there wasn't any sign of it. In fact, Cass was left with the disturbed impression that his heavenly Father had a few unresolved issues with him yet. He also had a feeling Ma wouldn't be all that happy with him, either.

The members of the wagon train gathered for one final evening together. Tomorrow they would be on the trail again—Cass and Susanne and their brood headed for Cherry Grove and the rest on their way to Oklahoma. Susanne knew she would miss Mardean, Winoka Medsker, Lucius Waterman, and Buck Brewster's sweet fiddle music. The group had formed close bonds, and several of the people had become like family to her.

But everyone seemed determined to substitute happy faces for tearful good-byes. After supper, the women brought out the pies and cakes while Buck tuned up his fiddle for dancing.

The camp took on a festive air as the weary travelers set their troubles aside and, as Corliss put it, "just let their hair down for a spell."

By mid-evening Susanne was breathless and rosy cheeked from the strenuous activity. The men had kept the women dancing nearly every jig. Susanne whirled through reels, square dances, and waltzes. Ernest Parker called the squares while Buck and his fiddle skipped through one tune after another. Although she had danced with every man in the group, some more than once, Cass remained on the sidelines. She figured he had forgotten her or was deliberately ignoring her.

She saw Aaron stealing a kiss from Ernestine and made a mental note to talk to him. *Well, maybe not. Better have Cass do it.* Aaron might take the lecture better from another man. *Another man?* The word caught her attention, but she realized it was correct. Aaron had changed from a shy, awkward boy to a competent young man. The trip had been good for him.

Finally Cass stood in front of her, and she knew she'd been waiting for this moment all night. "Miss McCord, may I say you look right fetchin' tonight," he complimented.

"Oh, I do thank you, kind sir," she returned, matching his airy tone. "Your silver tongue just makes me feel ever so giddy, but I was beginning to fear that you were never going to come over and 'fetch' me."

"Been waiting for me, huh?" He threw his head back and laughed. Sobering, he winked and extended his left arm. "Let's take a walk."

Something had changed in their relationship since the night they'd talked. He seemed more at ease with her, less prone to being provoked, more willing to cooperate. "I thought I was going to have to whip Ernestine Parker and take you away from her," she said, accepting his arm.

He winced. "I thought I was going to have to ask you to."

"I believe Aaron's got his eye on her."

Matt Johnson stepped over to claim Susanne. Cass motioned the man away. "Later, Matt."

Smiling, Susanne nestled closer to his side, and they stepped into the deepening shadows.

"Sorry I didn't have time to eat with you and the children," he apologized. The darkness wrapped silky arms around them.

"We missed you, but I'm sure Laurence appreciated help with the broken axle."

"Lucy still cranky?"

Susanne nodded, mechanically carrying on the conversation, but her thoughts wandered.

"Maybe she's just tired of traveling."

"Maybe, but it won't be long now before we're home."

She cuddled against him, happy to be there as long as it would last. Someday he would leave, but tonight he belonged to her.

Her old nature surfaced, nearly choking her. Why should she be forced to give him up? She wouldn't! There had to be a way to convince him to stay with her. He was her legal husband, after all.

Her legal husband. That was the problem. As long as their marriage was in name only, Cass would not feel obligated to stay with her. It was really a fairly easy problem to solve. . .but did she dare? It would be far worse than anything she'd done to him so far. Evil. God would turn away in disgust.

"Cass?"

"Hmmm?"

"Do you ever think about me as a woman?"

He appeared to be weighing his answer, and she wondered if

she had overstepped her bounds. Finally he said, "If I were to be completely honest, Miss McCord, it would only make your head swell."

She savored a flood of satisfaction. She drew back to gaze into his eyes. "Then you do."

"I never said that."

"But you do." She felt her stomach tie in knots as he gazed back at her.

"All right," he confessed. "I do."

She reached out to trail her fingers tenderly down the side of his face. He moved back as though her touch unnerved him.

"Then don't leave me," she urged in a broken whisper, suddenly wishing she had more control over her emotions. She had been struggling so long to find herself, to know the real Susanne McCord, but it had taken this man to show her that she could be the woman she'd always longed to be. She didn't know how she could bear losing him.

"Susanne, it's settled. I'm not ready to settle down to one woman. . . . I may never be."

"Not even Laure Revuneau?" Susanne knew she was out of line, but she had to know what he felt for Laure.

"Laure?"

"I believe she is hoping for a Christmas wedding, with you."

She felt him tense. "She's free to hope all she wants."

Her pulse leaped expectantly. "Then you aren't planning to marry Laure?"

He sighed. "My only plans are to return to Saint Louis and attend to my business, which has been sorely neglected of late."

Her eyes met his unashamedly. "I'm going to say something you're not going to like."

"Then don't say it."

"I'm in love with you, Cass—deeply in love."

His face changed and became hard. "Susanne. . .don't do this—"

"I am, Cass. I'm sorry, but I am." She stopped and caught his face in both hands. "I love you, and I will never, ever give up hope that someday, no matter what I've done in the past, you will return my love."

"Susanne," he warned, pulling her hands away and drawing her face to his chest, "you're making me nervous."

He was weakening; she could sense it. And wasn't that her plan?

"You always have been a mite skittish," she acknowledged, "but you can't stop me from loving you. You're the best thing that has ever happened to me."

"No, Susanne. It'll do no good for either one of us to think that way. I can't return your love. We bring out the worst in each other."

She wondered who he was trying to convince: her or himself.

She thought of all the times she had rejected other men—easily, cruelly, and without much thought for their feelings. She guessed the good Lord had had His fill of her nonsense and had sent Cass Claxton for her penance.

But if He had, she would gladly accept her punishment and pray that the Lord would see fit to extend it.

&

Later that night, when everyone was safely tucked in bed, Cass took his bedroll and went in search of a place to sleep. He had watched Susanne move about camp, preparing for bed, and he admitted that he was drawn to her, no matter how hard he fought against the attraction. Her earlier pleading had nearly broken his resolve. No woman had ever had this strange effect on him, but he wasn't cad enough to claim her as his wife then ride away and leave her.

He spread the blanket on the ground and walked to the creek to wash up. When he returned five minutes later, Susanne—his wife—was lying on the blanket.

He stared down at her, shifting on one foot impatiently. He didn't have the strength to go through this again.

"Hello." Her smile was beguiling and meant nothing but trouble. "Lovely night, isn't it?"

"What are you doing here?"

She shrugged. "Why are you always so cranky?"

He could feel defeat settling in like a noose. "I guess a man wouldn't need to be overly smart to see what you're up to."

"I am your wife."

She was right. They'd said their vows before God. She was his—as surely as if they'd repeated the words in church. But still. . . consummating their marriage would only lead to trouble. He just knew it.

Cass thought if he ignored the invitation she might go away. He lay down and turned his back on her. He felt her settle beside him, smelled the lilac fragrance of her hair. He rolled over to face her, and that was a mistake. Now there was no turning back. Her lips, satin soft, met his as the moon slid behind a cloud, and as surely as Adam succumbed to Eve, he surrendered to the serpent.

The wagon train left the next morning amid fervent handshakes, hugs, and tears. People got real close traveling together. Most would never see each other again. Cass had unexpectedly walked up on a tender scene: Ernestine Parker weeping in Aaron's arms. He backed away, regretting his intrusion on the young folks' final moments together, but not before hearing Ernestine promise to write.

The sun was a red ball on the horizon, and lacy rose-colored clouds floated overhead. Late October had a bite to it. The children wore light jackets and shoes, which they would remove when the sun climbed higher. Susanne pulled her worn sweater tighter around her. She hated what she'd done last night. What she had perpetrated had been deceitful and inexcusable. Once again she had tricked the man she loved. She couldn't say her morning prayers for fear God would strike her dead. Now they were truly man and wife, but would it make any difference to Cass? She feared it wouldn't.

Jesse strode alongside. "I like it being us again, don't you?"

"It's nice," Susanne agreed. "But I'll miss some of the people in the wagon train."

He considered this. "Do you think Cass will stay in Kansas with us?"

"No," she bit out. He would not change his plans—especially now.

"He might if I ask him," Jesse said. "He likes me."

"He won't stay—and I forbid you to ask him, Jesse. I mean it. Don't ask him."

"Yes, ma'am." Jesse eyed her curiously. Bryon wandered off the trail, and he pointed at him. "Guess I'd better help Doog. He can't keep an eye on Bryon and Joseph, too."

Susanne watched the ensuing tug-of-war between Bryon and Jesse. The younger boy determined to go his own way and the older just as determined to keep him with the wagon. They were good boys. She didn't see how Cass could ride away from them and never look back.

Corliss raised the back flap of the wagon and looked out. "Bryon! You quit giving Jesse trouble. You hear me?"

Phebia ran up to Susanne. "Me so tired."

"All right, I'll give you a lift." She squatted so Phebia could climb onto her back, clasping the child's legs in front of her. Thin arms circled her neck, and she felt a curly head resting against her shoulders. "Would you rather ride in the wagon?"

"No. Want to be with you."

Susanne's heart swelled with love. If God never gave her anything more, He had given her these children, and she was grateful. The travelers forded a small creek bordered by wild plum, which in early summer would have been loaded with fruit. Now the branches only bore leaves, which were drying and falling to litter the ground. They would reach Kansas too late to lay up food for winter. She remembered only too well the blizzards that could sweep across the plains. They would need so many things, and her supply of cash was pitifully low.

The prairie was flatter than Susanne remembered and covered with tall grass, taller than the youngest children. Phebia, Bryon, Joseph, and the twins needed to stay with the wagon. If they wandered out in that waving sea of grain they could be lost, unable to find their way back.

She sighed. Seemed like she just traded one set of worries for another.

Late morning, Cass rode up beside Susanne and Phebia. "Do you like Kansas any better this time around?"

"I'll make do," Susanne answered, unable to look at him. She felt so ashamed of her trickery. "I'm not the same person who left here."

"Really?"

She sensed that he had started to make a cutting remark about the way she'd changed, but didn't. Somehow the contrived wedding ceremony didn't matter that much anymore. It seemed so long ago and involved two different people.

"Is your father expecting you?"

Susanne hitched Phebia up higher on her back. "I wired him we were on our way, but he has no way to send a reply. He's willing to take us in, though."

He pointed to a strange little animal sitting up on its hind legs staring at them. The twins made a dash in that direction, and immediately there was a shrill whistle, which seemed to come from a dozen different places. The little animal disappeared.

"Prairie dog," Cass said. "A colony of them."

"Dogs cute," Phebia said. "Get me one, Mr. Cass."

I'm not fast enough to catch a prairie dog," Cass said. "Besides, you don't want one. They're wild animals."

"I do so want one." Phebia stuck out her lower lip in a familiar pout.

"When we get to Cherry Grove I'll find you a puppy. That will be better, won't it?"

Phebia cocked her head to one side, considering. "That will be better. Let me down, Miss McCord." Once on the ground she ran toward the wagon, good spirits restored.

Cass grinned at Susanne. "She's a charmer."

Susanne didn't smile. "What are you going to tell her when you leave?"

Color rose to his cheeks. "I'll stay if you want me to, Susanne."

She remembered their agreement. Pretty words, softly murmured words, but no misconceptions. "What do you want, Cass?"

He shook his head. "I'm not ready for marriage and responsibilities—I know I'm a little late, but you want the truth."

Yes, she wanted the truth. "I'll keep my part of the bargain," she promised. "However, it's possible you're making a mistake."

He fixed his gaze straight ahead. "I'll stay. You say the word."

She finally lifted her eyes. "We need to be going. We're holding up the group."

His eyes sought hers. “Do you want me to stay?”

“Not until and unless you choose to make a life with me.”

“Susanne—”

She turned and walked off before she could change her mind.

They had been on the trail to Cherry Grove for a week. One of the oxen had pulled up lame and delayed them. The day started out warm for October. The air was heavy, muggy. A dark line of clouds outlined the western horizon, and a scorching wind whipped the grass in undulating waves. Cass felt the hair rise on his arms, a sure sign of electricity in the air. From all indications this was going to be a raging Kansas thunderstorm.

He rode up beside the wagon, calling to Harlon, “Think it’s going to rain?”

“Like pouring water on a rock. Better find a place to weather the storm.”

“Storm?” Susanne looked up, shading her eyes with her right hand. “The sky is clear—not a cloud to be seen.”

“Look over there.” Cass pointed west, and she looked where he indicated. Clouds foamed toward them. A sullen rumble of thunder reached her ears. A forked tongue of lightning licked the sky.

“Put Phebia and the twins in the wagon. The rest of you keep up. I don’t want to lose you.”

Susanne didn’t argue; she followed his instructions. After putting the younger ones in the wagon, she scooped up Lucy and carried her. “Margaret Ann, you and Doog and Jesse get behind the wagon and keep up, you hear?”

“Yes, Miss McCord.” Margaret Ann’s voice was as serene as if she’d just been offered a cup of tea.

Jesse and Doog looked apprehensive, but they fell in step.

Cass heard Corliss soothing the younger children. Clouds roiled like a boiling pot.

Aaron, following Cass's directions, drove the wagon into the shelter of a low limestone bluff, barely higher than the top of the wagon. They quickly unhitched the team and hobbled them under the lip of the bluff. Livestock taken care of, Cass ordered Susanne and the children to get inside the wagon.

"What about you?" she shouted above the rising wind.

"I'll stay with the animals!"

Aaron and Payne stubbornly refused to seek shelter. "We'll help."

Cass frowned. "It's going to rain like dumping water out of a boot." Huge drops splattered the ground, emphasizing the warning. "It's going to be a bad one."

"If you can take it, we can," Aaron replied.

A solemn-faced Payne grabbed the lead rope and pulled the oxen closer to the bluff. The storm struck with a blast of thunder that set the animals fighting the restraining ropes. A blaze of lightning blinded Cass. He pulled his hat lower and hunched his shoulders against the driving rain.

&

Susanne had her arms around Lucy and Margaret Ann. Phebia huddled on her lap. Corliss held the twins, and Doog and Jesse crouched close to Harlon. Each thrust of wind rocked the wagon until it seemed it would surely tip over. The canvas covering cracked and popped, and Susanne wouldn't have been surprised to see it tear apart, leaving them exposed to the storm's fury.

Thunder boomed like an explosion. Susanne's ears rang from the force.

Margaret Ann raised a tearstained face. "I really do not like

Kansas, Miss McCord."

"Me want to go home," Phebia wailed.

Lucy shivered against Susanne. "Are we going to die?"

"Oh no, darling. God will take care of us. Don't worry; the storm will pass."

"I do think God could do something about the noise." Margaret Ann jumped when another roar split the sky. "I believe I'll mention it to Him as soon as it's quieter."

Susanne stifled a hysterical laugh, imagining Margaret Ann facing God and saying, "I see." Having experienced her own interrogation, she knew exactly how He might feel.

The storm eventually blew past. Susanne climbed out of the wagon to face Cass and the boys. Payne looked shaken, a little pale, but he wore an air of quiet pride. They hadn't lost an animal, although Cass's horse had broken the rope. Aaron had caught it before it could bolt.

"Are you all right?"

"We're fine," Cass said. "I couldn't have held them by myself. The boys saved the day."

They made camp, building a fire to dry out their supplies. Corliss and Susanne fixed an evening meal, and they all retired early. Afterward she lay in her bedroll, staring up at a sky full of stars. The storm had passed; the night calmed.

But a storm still raged in her heart.

Chapter 11

A small party of buffalo hunters—one hunter, two skinners, and a cook—rode in late one afternoon. Their red wool shirts were dirty, their corduroy breeches stained, and the high Western boots they wore hadn't seen a coat of polish in years.

Corliss and Susanne, happy to welcome company, cordially invited the men to stay for supper. The hunters accepted their gracious offer and went about settling their stock for the night.

When Cass, Aaron, and Payne rode in from hunting, Susanne took one look at Cass and knew he was in a howling temper. He glared in her direction, looking like a Kansas thundercloud.

"Susanne, I want a word with you!" he ordered. He swung off his horse and handed the reins to Aaron, barely acknowledging the visitors' presence as he strode through camp.

Susanne rolled her eyes. Wiping her hands on her apron, she whispered to Corliss, "The king has bellowed."

Cass had been friendlier lately—not what you might call pleasant, but not inclined to snap like a chained dog every time she got close. There had been no chance for intimate talks or romantic moments, and she was relieved. Guilt hung heavy in her mind.

Evidently something had riled him now, though she had no idea what. She'd been careful not to cross him, but if Cass Claxton thought he could bully her he had another think coming. He might be her husband. . .yet he wasn't. So God's command about obedience to the husband didn't apply.

Cass's rules.

Corliss chuckled, and Susanne knew she was concerned and yet amused by Susanne's and Cass's open hostility to each other. Susanne had passed the wagon and heard Corliss and Harlon discussing the strange alliance one night when they thought everyone was asleep. Although they had no idea what was causing the couple to behave with such animosity toward each other, they both seemed to feel that Susanne was attracted to Cass Claxton and that Cass was attracted to Susanne. However, they had agreed they were both so mulish that they'd go to their graves before either of them would admit it.

Susanne had burned at the thought. Well, she guessed it was true that eavesdroppers never heard anything good about themselves.

Now Corliss placed her hands on her hips and frowned, a sure indication that she was getting ready to impart wisdom whether Susanne wanted to hear it or not. "You know, girl, Harlon's beginning to fret about the growing standoff between the two of you. He took an instant liking to that young man. Cass is doing a fine job. You might think about that."

"I do think about it, and I'm more than willing to be friends. I'm not the one causing trouble." Susanne knew Harlon hoped she might make a match with Cass. If the older man only knew the true situation he would be even more befuddled. She was confused; and she'd been the bride at that so-called wedding.

"Harlon thinks he's taking a shine to you. Why else is he

busting himself to help us?"

"Harlon couldn't be more mistaken. Mr. Claxton wouldn't be helping us it weren't for the children. He's a softy where they're concerned."

Corliss lifted both brows. "Maybe so, but I've seen that look in a man's eyes before. He's got something on his mind, and it ain't driving us to Cherry Grove, Kansas. I know a man with a hankering for a woman when I see one."

"If he's 'hankering' for anyone, it's for the woman he left behind." Laure's lovely smiling face rose up to haunt Susanne. The young Frenchwoman had a captivating beauty she couldn't hope to compete against. Satin and lace did something for a woman that homespun never could.

She could see why Laure was interested in Cass, but there was a problem. Cass, even though he wasn't happy with the situation, was married, and he would be until he delivered his charges safely to Cherry Grove. If Susanne couldn't talk him into staying—convince him that she was the love of his life—then she would release him from what he considered a hateful alliance.

Cass bawled again, and Susanne took a deep breath, wishing she had the freedom to tell him what she really thought of his bossiness.

"Better go see what he wants," Corliss encouraged. "Margaret Ann and I will take care of the biscuits."

"It better be important," Susanne muttered under her breath. She handed the spoon to Margaret. She was at no man's beck and call, particularly Cass Claxton's.

Ignoring the watchful eyes of their visitors, she strode through the camp in the direction of his voice.

She found Cass preparing to wash for supper. He'd stripped his shirt off, causing her a stab of momentary distress. Why a bare chest should fascinate her so she wasn't sure. She just knew that it did.

"Don't you ever keep your clothes on?" she snapped.

He glanced up. "Who yanked your chain?"

"No one yanked my chain. . . . I'm worried that the girls will see you this way."

He lifted an inquisitive brow. "Is that the reason for your concern, or does it fluster you to see me without a shirt, Miss McCord?"

"The name is Mrs. Claxton," she reminded in a carefully controlled tone, "and no, it doesn't 'fluster' me to see you without your shirt. I'm from Missouri. I've seen mules without saddles before."

For a moment she thought she saw a hint of a smile twist the corners of his mouth, but then he turned away and started pouring water into the enamel washbasin. "I see you're in another one of your aggravating moods."

"Did you want me?" she said curtly. He had no right to ride into camp and bellow out for her as though she were his handmaiden and then act like he thought she was "flustered" by seeing him without a shirt. Granted, she had trouble looking away. . .and he knew full well they were more than friends.

"Afraid not, but it looks like I have you anyway." He reached for the bar of soap.

Susanne watched the tight play of muscles in his forearms when he worked up a thick lather. "I don't have time for games. What do you want?"

"I see we have company."

"There's nothing wrong with your eyesight."

He leaned over and scrubbed his face and neck. "Do you know who those men are and what they do?"

Susanne wasn't sure if it was disapproval or mere curiosity she heard. Was this why he had called her away from her chores? Her eyes traveled the width of his broad shoulders and paused. "No. . .I mean, I assume they're probably family men who'll appreciate a hot meal and a bit of pleasant conversation."

Cass rinsed off his face and neck and reached for the towel. He rubbed the cloth over his face, eyeing her dispassionately. "Well, you assume wrong."

Tiny water droplets interspersed throughout the cloud of hair splayed across his chest. His dark curls clustered in damp ringlets, and her fingers itched to brush them back off his forehead. Exposure to the wind and sun had bronzed his complexion, making him—if possible—even more appealing.

Susanne caught her shameless reflections and averted her gaze. "Then who are they?"

Without taking his eyes off her, Cass reached for a clean shirt and slipped it on. "Buffalo hunters."

Her eyes lifted to meet his. The explanation was meaningless. "So?"

He finished buttoning the shirt and, with his eyes still firmly fixed to hers, casually tucked in the loose ends. She glanced away, uncomfortable in the face of his casual indifference. He treated her with the same offhanded manner he exhibited toward the children or Corliss. Not disrespectful, but as if he didn't think of her as a woman, or as if the other night had never happened. She felt a sudden urge to make him look at her the way she was sure he looked at Laure Revuneau.

"So," he mimicked, "by inviting those particular men to supper, we're now likely to attract the attention of every Indian within a fifty-mile radius."

She wasn't sure if it was the word *Indian* or her own wayward thoughts that caused her heart to suddenly hammer in her throat. Susanne knew only too well what a thoroughly aggravating creature Cass could be, but he was smart and experienced, and she knew she had better take him at his word.

She felt color flooding her cheeks. "I'm. . .sorry. . . . I didn't know."

It occurred to her that he might be deliberately amusing himself. He knew what she was thinking, and he loved to aggravate her, yet nothing in his manner indicated deliberate agitation. On the contrary, if Susanne hadn't known better, she would have sworn that he was looking at her with the same undeniable interest that she felt toward him.

For an electrifying moment, blue eyes seared deeply into violet ones, and Susanne was aware of nothing more than his overpowering presence and the uneven cadence of her breathing.

Then, as if they simultaneously realized what was happening, their gazes split. Cass reached for his hat, and Susanne eased to a safer distance on the far side of the makeshift washstand.

The incident left her puzzled and shaken. She found it hard to concentrate. Cass picked up the conversation in a tone that made her wonder if the events of the past few minutes or the time they had spent together had touched him. How could something so life-altering to her have meant so little to him?

"We'll have to hope there isn't a scouting party on the hunters' tails."

Susanne was confused. "Why would Indians follow them?"

"Because they hate them. Unlike the Indian, who kills the buffalo for his own survival, the white man kills for business and pleasure." He picked up his gun belt and buckled it around his waist. "The Indians depend on the buffalo to supply medicine, cooking utensils, blankets, garments, boats, ropes, and even their tents. They use the sinews to make bowstrings and thread for sewing. After the tribe has enjoyed the fresh meat of the kill, the women cut the rest of the meat into strips and hang it on racks to dry in the hot sun."

"To make jerky?" She knew that but had forgotten.

"Later they pound it into powder and make pemmican, which will keep for years. There's still plenty of buffalo roaming the plains, but every buffalo killed is a threat to the Indians' existence. The white man's irresponsible slaughter continues to drive the herds farther afield, and I've heard some predict that the time isn't far off when the vast herds roaming the land will be only a memory."

"That seems impossible," Susanne mused. "I've heard my father tell stories of seeing thousands of buffalo moving across the plains."

"That's true, but it will change if the white man continues to kill buffalo for personal gain. How many will be left in ten, twenty years? Trust me; the Indian will do everything in his power to kill the men who threaten his survival."

"So if the Indians discover that we befriended the hunters, then our lives may be in danger?"

He absently dusted his hat against the side of his legs. "No 'may be' about it. Our lives are in danger."

"Oh Cass. . .I'm sorry. Corliss and I were just trying to be neighborly when we invited the hunters to stay for supper."

"Susanne, I want you to listen to me." His tone was firmer than she'd ever heard it. "There's something else you need to know. By their appearance, I figure these men have been on the trail for a while. My guess is they've been on a hunt somewhere in Kansas, Colorado, or Oklahoma, and they're on their way home. Now, I want you to heed what I'm about to say: a beautiful woman will be hard for them to ignore." His eyes locked with hers. "I want you to go out of your way to avoid any personal contact with these men. Serve supper, then disappear and let Corliss and the girls clean up. These men have no morals; you've never been around this sort."

"All right." Her pulse fluttered. Did he really think she was beautiful? She'd been around men all her life and was used to being admired and appreciated. But if Cass Claxton ever had a good thought regarding her, she had yet to notice it.

"With a little luck, the hunters will move on in the morning, and nothing will come of your misplaced hospitality."

"What about the Indians?"

"You let me worry about the Indians. You do what I say and leave immediately after the meal. I don't want to have to save you if one of those men gets out of line."

"You think they'd be disrespectful?"

"I think that would be the least of your worries. I hope you're smart enough to see the wisdom of my advice."

She knew he was waiting for her chin to lift with her usual rebellious pride. Just for that, she'd show him. "You sound as if you honestly care what happens to me."

"Me care about you?" He threw his head back and laughed.

Susanne gritted her teeth in an attempt to control her temper.

"Honey, if I were looking for female company, I'd find me a sweet-talking woman."

"Like Laure Revuneau?"

His sly grin spoke louder than words. "Now, there's a fine woman. Soft-spoken. Godly. Slow to anger, holds her tongue—a real lady."

"Are you going to marry the 'lady'?" She was glad to see the question momentarily stilled him. "You didn't answer my question."

He tipped his head subserviently. "How could I marry anyone, my lovely, when it seems I am already encumbered by a previous commitment?"

"My dear Mr. Claxton. You don't have to worry about me," she snapped. "I do not plan to 'encumber' you, so rest easy."

"I'm not worried. Even if a man took a wild fancy to you and dragged you away, you wouldn't be gone long. Once he'd spent a few hours with your spunk he'd be bringing you back so fast it'd make your head swim."

"Is that so?" She could feel herself slipping, but he was downright exasperating. Squaring her shoulders, she took a deep breath and volleyed back. "You don't believe God has a say in who you'll marry?"

"Well, sure. . .when I ask Him."

"You polecat. I've never had a problem attracting suitors."

He grinned, but he didn't rise to the bait. "Tell me"—his gaze moved over her dispassionately—"is there anything in particular that I'm supposed to find impressive?"

Her eyes narrowed with warning.

"Oh. . .I'm supposed to notice how pretty you are. . .or no, wait. It's your hair, isn't it? Lovely. Never a hair out of place."

Her hand shot up to smooth the messy locks.

"I suppose you could catch a man without resorting to a shotgun," he allowed.

She squelched a rising rush of anger. "I don't reckon I'd need a shotgun," she said. "The man I'd marry would be smarter than that."

"Touché."

Susanne knew that Aunt Estelle was rolling over in her grave right now, but she was determined to get his goat. He was the only man who had persistently ignored her. Men had been known to fawn over her, shower her with extravagant compliments to snare her attention. They had begged for her hand in marriage, but she had blithely broken their hearts. She had never met a man who matched her in spirit, with maybe the exception of this lout, and he wouldn't even concede that she was a woman!

"I've never been interested in you, and I don't see why you would expect me to be interested now, so what are we arguing about?" he asked, his voice only mildly polite.

Their gazes met in a defiant deadlock. "Can't you at least admit that I frustrate you?" Surely she had some effect on him! He couldn't be that apathetic.

"Nope. Unless you count right now. You're in my way and delaying my supper."

Determined to beat him at his game, she edged closer. "Most men would be interested in their wives. But, then, maybe you're not like most men."

He picked up the wash pan and slung the water against a handy tree trunk.

"I am not married," he calmly stated.

"Hogwash."

"And I'm not like most men. The men I know would have wrung your pretty little neck long ago. Considering the circumstances, I've shown remarkable restraint."

"Restraint!" she choked out. "Why. . .you. . ."

"Precisely." He grinned. "I feel the same way about you, dear 'wife.'"

"I've apologized for my behavior, and you haven't. Don't you know what the Bible says about forgiveness?"

"I certainly do, but no sooner do I forgive you for one thing than you do something else downright unfriendly. Forgiving you is a full-time job. I do not have the patience of Job."

Susanne pulled the tattered remains of her dignity around her like a cloak. The man was marking time until he could safely dump her and the children in Cherry Grove.

She must quell her hope. *Dear God, I'm through. Through trying to make him care. Hope is only a word now; a meaningless word. You are not going to honor my hope.* Cass was lost to her. She had to accept that.

But defeat hurt so much.

Cass wondered why he liked to antagonize her so much. With her cheeks flushed and those violet eyes snapping sparks, she was about the cutest thing he'd seen in a long time. Pity she was such a spitfire—and even more regretful they'd started out on the wrong footing. Susanne McCord was a force to be reckoned with, and he reckoned he didn't know what to do about her.

Susanne Claxton, he corrected. She had tricked him into giving her the name, and he admitted it had a certain ring to it. He brought his thoughts sharply into line. What was he thinking? This woman had deceived and manipulated him every time he got near her, and now he was in deeper than ever. It was too late for an annulment; now a divorce would have to take place. Not exactly something the Lord would approve of. What would Ma say? And Beau and Cole?

His life would decidedly be less of a challenge without Susanne around. Still—he liked to aggravate her.

"A buffalo hunter might want you," he said.

Her hand came up to strike him, and he caught it, holding fast. She tried to pull away, and he blocked the effort. Caught off balance, she fell against him, and his arms caught her.

He looked down, meeting her startled expression. Violet eyes gazed up at him; her parted lips were soft, sweet, and he felt a surprised flicker of—what? Interest? Attraction?

Love.

God, please, no. Not that.

He felt her go limp against him, and the sudden realization

that she was not immune to him pleased—and worried—him. He shifted her closer, surprised to discover that she was tiny. She felt exquisite and delicate in his arms. Things he had barely noticed before.

He lowered his head until his lips brushed hers, light as the silken seeds of the milkweed plant growing alongside the trail. The touch of her mouth against his sent a longing racing through his veins. He kissed her again, slow, sweet. So this was the feeling. The one he'd heard described so often. The one he'd never believed possible.

Susanne stiffened, pulling away. "What do you think you're doing?"

He drew a deep breath. He tried to brazen it out by guilelessly staring back at her. "Why. . .isn't this what you want? I'm only trying to keep my wife happy."

"You're disgusting." She spat out the words. "You act as if you despise me one minute then the next you try to take advantage of me."

Cass's mouth dropped. "Take advantage of you? You've been chasing me for weeks."

"I never."

"You know you did. I can't turn around without stumbling over you."

Her face turned so red he thought she would explode. "You brute! You called me over to warn me about the hunters."

His gaze lightly caressed her mouth. "Now who's being cranky?" He tweaked her cheek.

She jerked free. "Miserable skunk!"

He flashed an exasperating grin. "I thought I was a weasel."

"Skunk is only one name for your miserable species!"

She whirled and stumbled over Margaret Ann, who had

silently approached the warring couple.

"What is it, Margaret Ann?" she demanded, her voice shaky.

"Corliss said to tell you supper's ready."

Shooting Cass a dismissing glance, Susanne picked up her skirt and marched off, leaving Cass not as unscathed by the encounter as he would have hoped. His eyes followed her as she walked back to camp. He could still taste her kiss, and he had a feeling that sleep wasn't going to come easily tonight.

"You comin', Mr. Cass?"

"I'll be along in a minute, Margaret Ann," he said absently. Shaken, he reminded himself that Susanne McCord was not a woman for him to get involved with. She had bested him in every confrontation they'd ever had. A Claxton was supposed to have enough sense to know when to cut his losses. With Susanne, he'd never been ahead. She'd outthought him, outmaneuvered him, and just plain outfought him every time.

He tried to sort out his confused feelings and turned up empty-handed.

Actually most men would find his wife desirable. Too desirable.

After supper the children gathered around the hunters' wagon. They looked over the .45 Sharps rifles, along with Winchesters, Remingtons, and Springfield Trapdoor models. The boys were full of questions.

Payne picked up one of the more than fifty Green River and Wilson skinning knives lying in the bed of the skinners' wagon and reverently turned it over in his hands. The wagon had too many bull, calf, and cow hides to count.

"You say you've been in Colorado?" Harlon hobbled over to sit next to the fire. Cass figured the old cook would soon have their visitors reciting the tall, adventurous buffalo tales that were designed to make the children's eyes round with wonder.

"Yep, up near the border." Hoyt Willis stretched his long legs out before him and propped his head back on the seat of his saddle.

Cass thought the buffalo hunter had his stomach full of home-cooked grub, and judging from the foul odor it was the first time he'd taken off his boots all week. Cass assumed the hunters had observed the Indians' custom of hunting buffalo in September when the cows were fat.

"We'll go back once we've had time to visit our families and collect our money for the hides."

"You independent, or working for someone?" Not that Cass really cared. He was making conversation, keeping an eye on the man.

"Independent."

"Got a wife?" Harlon asked.

"A wife and ten young'uns just waitin' for their pa to come home."

Cass judged the hunter to be close to forty. The man stank like a polecat. His shirt was saturated with animal blood and dried pieces of flesh where he'd wiped the skinning knife, his beard matted to his face. Cass hoped Hoyt would be considerate enough to take a bath and change his clothes before he saw his family again. Although judging from the man's rough exterior, he didn't hold out much hope.

Cass got up from his seat at the fireside and moved back into the shadows, far enough away not to be noticed, but close enough to observe. Hoyt Willis, like Joe Killen, was the one to keep an eye on. Killen, by all signs, had moved on and was no longer a threat. But Willis was a new one. Cass had seen the disappointment on the buffalo hunter's face when Susanne had obediently disappeared after supper.

The night sounds closed around the camp and the men relaxed. Wood popped, sending showers of sparks flying.

"Where did the woman go?" Hoyt casually asked Harlon.

"Corliss? Why, I imagine she's getting ready for bed."

"Not your wife. The other one."

"Susanne?"

"Yeah, Susanne."

Harlon filled his pipe, lighting it with a coal from the fire. "I'm not rightly sure. Why?"

"No reason." Hoyt tipped his hat over his eyes. "She and the Claxton man hitched?"

Harlon chuckled. "Nope."

"He seems right protective of her."

"Yes, that's his job."

A slow smile curved the corners of Hoyt's mouth. "She's not married, huh?" The hat brim hid his eyes.

"Nope, she's not married."

Hoyt rolled to his side and settled his head more comfortably against the rolled blanket. "Right nice-looking woman," he commented.

"That she is. Imagine Cass thinks so, too."

"Yessir." Hoyt's mouth curved into a satisfied smile. He settled deeper under the blanket. "Right nice—you say Claxton has no claim on her?"

"No claim, but he wouldn't take nicely to a man showing any disrespect."

Cass stood in the shadows, fighting the urge to call the man out and teach him some manners. Problem was Hoyt had friends, and all Cass had was Harlon. Not real good odds. Just the same, if this unwashed, coarse-smelling specimen of humanity laid a hand on Susanne he would personally break his arm. She was a Claxton—even if no one knew it and she had come by the name dishonestly.

Claxtons took care of Claxtons.

Chapter 12

The Maison des Petites Fleurs Orphanage arrived in Cherry Grove a little before noon on Wednesday. Skies were overcast, and a bone-chilling wind blew from the north. October had finally gotten down to business.

The wagon rolled down Main Street, and Susanne took in the familiar sight of Miller's Mercantile. She breathed her first sigh of relief since she'd left Saint Louis. The journey was finally over. The Lord—and Cass Claxton—had seen them safely through.

She pulled the team to a halt.

Corliss lifted the flap, a big grin dominating her rawboned features when her eyes took in the row of storefronts. "Well, bless my soul, am I ever glad to see this!"

Susanne sighed, her own smile rather happy. "We've made it, Corliss. We've finally made it."

"Amen, and praise the Lord!"

Edgar Miller was sweeping off his porch. He squinted, apparently trying to make out the new arrivals. Susanne saw his balding head bobbing up and down with curiosity. She lifted her hand to give him a friendly wave. "Hello, Mr. Miller!"

Eyes widening, Edgar nearly dropped his broom when he

recognized her. He suddenly turned tail and shot back inside the mercantile, slamming the door firmly behind him.

Cass rode up beside the wagon and stopped. Resting his hand on the saddle horn, he grinned at Susanne.

"Better raise a white flag, Miss McCord. I believe the troops are getting nervous."

Meeting his laughing eyes with an impervious look of her own, Susanne firmly gathered the reins in her hands. "Very funny, Mr. Claxton."

Cass was still chuckling when she clucked her tongue and set the wagon into motion.

Nothing had changed in Cherry Grove. The sleepy little town wasn't much, but she knew there were a lot of good, God-fearing people living here, people who would see to the children's physical and spiritual welfare. She saw that the Havershams still had their restaurant, and it looked like Doug Kelly still ran his saloon and gambling house. She wondered if the saloon still served as a church on Sunday mornings. The town wasn't nearly as bad as she'd thought it was six years ago. It was a nice place, actually, one she was sure that she and the children would grow to love.

Once they were settled, the children would come to know and respect Leviticus, and she and Cass could—

An unsettling realization overshadowed her resurrected hope. In days now Cass would ride out. He had become so much a part of all their lives that it was hard to imagine how she and the children were going to manage without him. Susanne didn't want to imagine a day without him, let alone the rest of her life, but she admitted that she had no power to prevent him from leaving. She'd used every trick—God forgive her—in her arsenal, and she had lost the war.

The wagon turned the corner, and Reverend Olson's house came into view. Susanne could see Rebecca standing on a chair, cleaning windows. The parson's wife glanced up, seemingly startled when she recognized Susanne driving the wagon. She quickly recovered and began tapping on the panes of shiny glass, making staccato sounds. Smiling, Susanne waved at her.

The door to the parsonage flew open, and Olson hurried out, struggling into his jacket.

Susanne was anxious to see her father. Though they'd corresponded regularly, she hadn't seen him in six long years. She wondered how much he'd changed. He'd always had a penchant for gooseberry pie and lemon cake, and she giggled when she pictured her wiry little father having developed a round belly and rosy cheeks. She couldn't wait until the children met him. Susanne knew they would adore him, and Harlon and Corliss would welcome the hours of companionship Leviticus would provide.

Although he didn't always know how to relate to children, he was generous to a fault. At Christmastime, he would see to it that the orphanage had the biggest, brightest, most beautiful tree in town. There would be apples, nuts, and oranges to fill each stocking, and the house would be bursting with the mouthwatering smells of succulent roast duckling, tasty mince pies, delectable spice cakes, and—

Her thoughts wavered when Leviticus's house suddenly came into view. She sawed back on the reins, halting the team. For a moment she sat, dumbfounded, staring at the scene before her.

Susanne heard Corliss's sharp intake of breath, then her awestruck prayer: "Dear God in heaven. Have mercy on us all."

The chimney, silhouetted against the gray sky, was the only thing left of Leviticus McCord's house. The rest had burned to the ground.

Cass rode up beside the wagon, grave-faced.

Susanne stared up at him, too shocked to speak.

He climbed off the horse and onto the wagon seat, drawing her into his arms.

"Cass. . ."

"Shhhh. It will be all right, Susanne."

The reverend appeared momentarily taken aback when he saw Cass Claxton holding Susanne McCord in his arms. "Oh Miss McCord. . .I'm so sorry I wasn't able to warn you."

Lifting her face from the haven of Cass's chest, Susanne stared back at the reverend, still unable to comprehend what was happening. "Warn me?"

"Yes. . .your father. . .he's. . ."

His words slowly began to penetrate her numbed senses, and her face suddenly crumpled. "Papa?"

Reverend Olson glanced at Cass. "You'd better bring her to the house. We can talk there."

"Come on, sweetheart." Cass lifted her gently off the wagon seat and drew her protectively against his side. "Corliss, you'll see to the children?"

"Of course."

"Aaron, drive the team and follow us back to the reverend's house."

"Yessir."

Cass remounted his horse then reached down and pulled Susanne up behind him.

She wrapped her arms around his waist and held on tightly, terrified to let him go. Papa was gone. She had no one now. "Cass. . .Papa. . .?"

Nodding solemnly at the children who stood staring up at him with open curiosity, Cass reined the horse around and walked the animal back to the parsonage.

Rebecca was waiting with a pot of hot tea and a heart filled with compassion. The reverend suggested that he and Susanne step into his study.

Alarmed, she glanced to Cass for assurance.

He nodded. "You want me to come with you?" he asked.

She shook her head dazedly. "No. . .I'll be all right." She followed the pastor into his study, and the click of the door closing was like a blow to her heart.

Rebecca reached out and pressed a reassuring hand on Cass's shoulder. "Come sit beside the fire. You must be weary." Cass belatedly removed his hat. "Thank you, ma'am." When they were seated, Rebecca reached to pour the tea, but Cass suddenly jumped to his feet, his tormented eyes focused on the study door. The sound of Susanne's anguished cries broke his heart.

"Please, Mr. Claxton," Rebecca urged softly. "This is very difficult. . . . Later she will need you more."

Cass slowly sank down, stunned by the unexpected event. His blue eyes pleaded with Rebecca, trying to make sense of it all. "How. . .when. . .?"

"Two weeks ago, in the middle of the night. No one is sure how the fire started. By the time it was discovered, it was well out of hand."

"And Susanne's father? He wasn't able to escape?"

Rebecca shook her head. "They found Leviticus still in his bed."

Cass woodenly accepted the cup of tea she offered.

"We knew that Susanne and the children were on their way here. That's all Leviticus talked about once he'd gotten the news she was coming. We've felt so helpless knowing we could do nothing to prepare her for the tragedy that awaited her."

Rebecca blotted her eyes. "My, how Leviticus looked forward

to seeing his only child again, and the children she was bringing to fill the emptiness in his life." Overcome by emotion, Rebecca tried to stem the flow of tears rolling from her eyes. "He had such fine plans, such high hopes. He would sit for hours and tell anyone who would listen how they were all going to be so happy. . .and now. . .now what will happen to them? Leviticus and the home they were coming to are gone. Everything is gone."

Cass's gaze went back to the study door. Rebecca's words drove deeply into his heart.

The children were homeless. Again.

Later that afternoon Susanne asked Cass if he would take her to visit her father's grave. He said he would, and they left right after supper. Rebecca had insisted that they stay the night at the parsonage, saying that they'd all put their heads together in the morning and come up with a solution.

At the sight of the fresh mound of dirt, Susanne caught her breath and turned away, realizing that she'd been praying all afternoon that it wasn't true. But it was. Her father was dead without ever knowing the transformation that had taken place in his daughter. She had wanted to surprise him, to let him actually see how she had changed.

Cass silently drew her back into his embrace and held her tightly. Her anguish overflowed, and her tears came again.

"He never really knew me," she whispered brokenly. "And I never really knew him."

She was forlorn that Leviticus would never know how much she'd loved him, how much she'd appreciated the love and devoted care he'd given to her. And she had never once thought to say thank you.

Was it possible for a child to fully realize how deeply and unselfishly a mother and father gave their love, never asking, but freely sacrificing whatever was required to see their child happily and safely to adulthood? What other relationship on this earth could boast of such love, such unending commitment that asked nothing in return? How strange, she thought, that children failed to understand such love until they had young ones of their own.

She recalled how one day she had selfishly demanded that her papa walk through snow up to his hips to buy a silly little bauble she'd decided she had to have. He'd worked all day hauling water to the cattle and walked home, but at her insistence he'd trudged to the mercantile in a blizzard to do her bidding.

Hours later he'd returned, cold and exhausted, bearing a red peppermint stick and the shiny spinning top she'd wanted. She'd jumped up and down with joy in their warm, cozy parlor while Leviticus had shed his sodden clothing and Mama had wrapped a warm blanket around his shoulders. Susanne could still hear the way Leviticus's teeth had chattered. He'd stuck his feet into a basin of hot water to thaw out.

Mama had raced around the kitchen, fixing tea and liberally lacing it with brandy to keep him from catching his death, while Susanne had watched the colorful top twirl 'round and 'round in the middle of the floor, unconcerned about her father's near-frozen state.

She recalled thinking she was the luckiest girl in the world to have such a fine papa who would buy her such extravagant things. Now she knew how fine Leviticus had really been, not because he could afford to buy his daughter a spinning top but because he'd loved her enough to walk three miles in the snow to purchase a silly toy that meant nothing to him but everything to a five-year-old child.

"*Leviticus McCord,*" Susanne could still hear her mother scolding, "*you're spoilin' that child somethin' terrible!*" But Leviticus had only laughed and candidly admitted that it was true, but he didn't care. Then he had taken Susanne onto his lap, opened the family Bible, and as her chubby fingers had worried the top 'round and 'round in her hands, he'd begun to read her favorite story to her, the one about Mary and Joseph and the little babe born in a manger.

The tears came faster now, and Susanne desperately wished she were that child again. After her mother's death the relationship between father and daughter had changed. Each had been wrapped in their own individual grief, and they had grown apart rather than closer. She was aware that a good part of the blame lay with her. She had hoped they would have a chance to get to know each other as adults, but that dream had now been denied her.

Drawing her gently away from the graveside, Cass supported her slight weight back to the reverend's buggy. He lifted her up onto the seat, and their eyes met and held.

"Tell your papa good-bye, Susanne."

Drawing her shoulders up determinedly, Susanne turned, and with tears streaming down her cheeks, she said loud and clear, "Good-bye. . .and thank you, Papa!"

She glanced back to Cass, and a radiant smile suddenly broke through her tears. "Do you think he heard me?"

Cass smiled. "I think he heard you."

Darkness closed around them. Cass picked up the reins, and the horse began moving away, leaving only Leviticus—and the good Lord—to know for certain.

"My stars! Look what the dogs have dragged up!" Beau Claxton stood gazing at his brother, shocked to find him standing in the doorway of his cabin.

The two brothers slapped each other on the back, laughing and whooping like two young boys. Charity, Beau's wife, moved away from the stove, smiling. Cass swept her up and swung her into the air.

"Cass Claxton, put me down!"

"Great day, girl, you're fat as one of Ma's old sows!"

"Beau!" Charity wailed. "Tell your brother that I'm not fat; I happen to be carryin' your babies!"

Retrieving his wife's squirming body in midair, Beau lowered Charity to her feet, kissing her soundly on the way down.

"Another set of twins?" Cass teased, his eyes pivoting to the three children looking up at him with wide-eyed innocence. "Great day in the morning!"

Beau looked at Charity and winked. "Just obeying the commandment to go forth and replenish the earth."

"He didn't mean all by yourself, brother," Cass admonished with a grin. "What's for supper? I can only stay for a short while."

"You'll stay the night!" Charity protested. "We haven't seen you in years!"

"Sure." He reached out and ruffled the oldest child's head of red hair. "I have to get acquainted with my nieces and nephew, don't I?"

"You'd sure better!" Wrapping his arm around Cass's shoulder, Beau walked him over to the fire. "What are you doing here? Children! Come over here and meet Uncle Cass." Beau motioned for the children to come to him. "You remember Mary Kathleen? She was just a baby last time you saw her, and these are the twins, Jason and Jenny."

Cass grinned and shook each child's hand solemnly. "Nice-looking family, Beau."

"Thank you." Beau beamed with fatherly pride. "It is, isn't it?"

While the men caught up on the news, Charity fixed supper. After they'd eaten the thick slices of cured ham, hot corn bread, and steaming bowls of brown beans, Charity hugged each man and then discreetly excused herself, saying she wanted to put the children to bed early.

When she'd disappeared to the loft, Cass sat staring pensively into the fire. Beau got up to wind the clock.

"I see you've built on to the cabin."

Beau grinned. "Had to—the young'uns started coming and we ran out of room. Put the loft on last year. So, what brings you back in our direction?" Beau asked as he finished with the clock and added a few more chips to the stove.

"It's a long story, but at the moment I'm trying to find a home for nine children."

Beau's hand paused in midair, and he grinned. "Nine, huh? Your women all catch up with you at one time?"

"No, my women didn't all catch up with me at one time," Cass mimicked.

"Whoa!" Beau's brow lifted curiously. "We're a little touchy, aren't we?"

Cass supposed that he was, but he was tired and he had to get the children settled somewhere. Phebia had cried for two days, wanting the home she'd been promised. "I'm in one big mess, Beau."

"You're serious, aren't you?"

"Dead serious."

Beau sat down to give his full attention. "All right, I'm listening."

Cass took a deep breath and then began to tell of his recent journey from Saint Louis—of the orphanage, the children, and the fire. He was candid about everything except Susanne McCord and her forcing him to marry her six years ago. That was too humiliating to admit, even to Beau.

"Why would you agree to escort a pack of orphans to Cherry Grove?" Beau wondered aloud.

"I did it as a favor."

"For the older couple you mentioned—Harlon and Corliss?"

"No, it wasn't for them. I agreed because the woman who runs the orphanage was in a bind."

"Really." Beau stared into the fire thoughtfully. "What's her name, and how good-looking is she?"

"That didn't have anything to do with it."

"I'll bet!"

"Seriously, Beau, it didn't. I ran into their wagon outside of town on my way to—on a trip I was taking." He wasn't going to mention Susanne or the problem yet. "They hadn't gotten two miles out of town, and already they were stuck in a mud hole. When I stopped to help, the woman made me see how desperate they were for a man to help them make the trip to Cherry Grove. I couldn't just ride off and leave them stranded, now, could I?"

"Since when?"

"Come on, Beau, you know me better than that."

Beau chuckled. "A year ago it wouldn't have surprised me one bit to hear you'd left twelve people stranded along the road. Maybe there's hope for you yet. So you agreed to bring nine children, two seventy-year-olds, and the woman back to Cherry Grove. You know, I really have to wonder about that."

Cass sat up straighter, his face animated. "You wait until you meet these kids—you're going to love them! There's Aaron—he's sixteen—and Payne—he's fourteen. I've been teaching them all about hunting! Then there's Jesse, Doog, Bryon, Margaret Ann. . . Wait until you meet Margaret Ann—you won't believe this child. She thinks she's thirty years old—and you will, too, once you talk to her—but she s only six. Then there's Lucy and Phebia. Phebia is three and still sucks her thumb, although we've all been trying hard to break her of it. And then there's Joseph, who's as cute—"

"Whoa! Wait a minute! Are you sure these aren't your kids?"

"Of course they're not my kids, but lately I've been thinking it wouldn't be so bad having a couple of my own," Cass admitted.

Beau grinned. "Ma would insist you marry first."

Cass sighed. "I'm aware of that."

"So, you were bringing the kids and the old people and the woman from Saint Louis, and when you got here, you found that the house that was meant to be the new orphanage had burned down?"

"That's right. And I've looked everywhere for the past two days to find a house large enough to serve as an orphanage, but there isn't anything." He had debated about taking them all back to Saint Louis and giving them Josiah's house, but with the first snows approaching, he realized that Harlon and Corliss would be in no shape to make the return trip.

Beau seemed pensive as he thought about the problem. "I can think of only one fire that's happened around here lately, and that was Judge McCord's house over in Cherry Grove—you remember him? He had a daughter named. . .what was it?. . .Susanne? You had that run-in with her at Miller's Mercantile."

Cass looked away. "Seems like I do recall something like that."

"You recall meeting her?" Beau hooted. "Why, she knocked you upside the head with her purse. Left a knot the size of a goose egg, didn't she?"

"I said I remember Susanne McCord," Cass interrupted tersely.

How could he forget her? She was on his mind day and night; now she and her nine kids were in his heart.

"I just asked. You all right? I don't believe I've ever seen you so edgy."

"Look, I might as well tell you because there's no way I'm going to be able to keep it from you. Susanne McCord runs the orphanage. I said I would help her get the children to Cherry Grove safely."

Beau cocked his head, eyebrows raised.

"It's the truth."

"How many guns did she have pointed at you?"

"None! Actually one, but not that day."

"All right, all right, you don't have to take my head off!"

"I need your help, Beau. Stop messing around and get down to business. I'm running out of time."

"How can I help? I don't have a house big enough for three kids—soon to be five—let alone nine!"

"Then you're going to help me build one."

"You and me? Build a house that big?"

Cass nodded. "And however many men I can hire to help us. Susanne needs a home for those kids, Beau, and I'm not going back to Saint Louis until I know they have one."

"Well, well, how about that?" Beau said softly. "What's your main concern here—the kids or Susanne?"

Cass refused to look up. "Just be in Cherry Grove first light tomorrow morning."

&

Susanne walked down the street from the parsonage to the ruins of her father's house. Evidently the fire had roared through the old frame structure, giving Leviticus very little chance of escaping. She wondered how it had started, then realized it didn't matter. Papa was gone.

Aunt Estelle's words came back to her. "*You have to keep moving and hope in the Lord.*"

Hope. Susanne realized she had no hope left. She was bone-dry. Nothing had gone the way she planned.

My plans.

The words echoed in her mind. Perhaps that had been the trouble. She had made the plans and then expected God to bless them, running ahead of what God had in store for her. Her mind traveled back over a long list of transgressions. When had she ever truly hoped in the Lord? Sitting in church, it was easy to hope. Going about her life, faith came easy. Her hope had been centered firmly in her belief in Susanne McCord's ability to have her own way.

She regretted misleading her father about Cass. He had gone to his grave believing the lie she had told. Not only had she hurt Cass, she had deceived the one person who had trusted her.

That wasn't all she had done, either. She'd manipulated Cass into bringing them to Cherry Grove, and she had taunted and teased him and manipulated him into consummating their marriage vows. Well, her chickens had surely come home to roost. What was she going to do now?

She thought of the Bible study Reverend Olson had conducted in his home last night. They had gathered around the big kitchen table, eager to learn. The text was on Abraham and how he'd run ahead of the Lord. Growing tired of waiting for God to provide the promised heir, he had taken matters into his own hands, creating a problem for everyone concerned.

She thought back to all the times she had promised to place her hope in the Lord. She'd even asked God to grant her the courage to hope in Him, but every time she had turned away to follow her own plans. Running ahead of God, so sure she knew what was best, had handed her a problem for which she had no solution. Tears ran down her cheeks as she realized she had never really trusted Him. A part of her had always held back, wanting to be in control.

She, Susanne Claxton—she would use the name privately—had taken matters into her own hands and made a royal mess. She stared at the blackened chimney pointing an accusing finger at the sky, knowing she had reached the end of her rope.

"I'm sorry, so sorry," she whispered. "Forgive me." The words caught in her throat.

"Lord, maybe I had to arrive at the place where You are all I have to realize You are all I need. But I'm ready now to submit to Your will. Show me what You want me to do, and, Lord, I promise, no matter how much it hurts, I'll give Cass his freedom. I never should have deprived him of it to start with."

She took a deep breath. "Take charge of my life. Show me what You want me to do. I promise from now on I'll wait for Your leading."

She thought of what she had admitted and realized something else needed to be said. "I was wrong to put my wishes ahead of Your plans for me and for the children. I was so sure I had to have a certain house, so sure I had to come to Cherry Grove, so sure Cass had to bring us. I've done a lot of damage to a lot of people. It's too late to ask forgiveness from some of them. But I beg You to forgive me. And. . ."

She sighed. There was one more thing. And it would hurt more than anything she'd ever done before.

"And, Lord, I will never again do or say anything to bind Cass to me against his will."

Chapter 13

With Beau, Aaron, Payne, and the twenty additional men that Cass was able to hire, the house was under a roof in three and a half weeks. It took a crew of five men to build the fireplaces alone. The orphanage could move in, though the house wouldn't be completed for months.

And what a glorious house it was. Fifteen rooms, seven fireplaces, five spacious bathrooms complete with claw-footed tubs, and the most modern, up-to-date kitchen conveniences Edgar Miller could have shipped from Hays, depending on weather. The house had running water piped straight to the bathrooms and kitchen, sparking the envy of every housewife in Cherry Grove.

Cass wouldn't let Susanne see the house until it was almost completed. But her excitement and anticipation surpassed even the children's, so late one Saturday afternoon Cass borrowed the reverend's buggy and drove her out to the building site.

Situated on thirty-five acres of prime land, the house was built in a grove of towering oak trees that would encourage cool breezes in the summer and provide a sturdy shelter against winter winds.

The horse's hooves clopped up the winding drive as Susanne's hands came up to cover her mouth, on the verge of squealing when she saw the magnificent sight spread before her.

Cass grinned, watching her turn speechless in wide-eyed wonder. "I wanted it to be larger—and it will be eventually. The carpenters require several months to complete the interior. When we need additions, they'll build on for us, but since you're so crowded at the reverend's I told them to just get you into the house. I figured Rebecca and the reverend need a little peace and quiet."

Having thirteen unexpected guests for nearly a month couldn't be pleasant, Cass had reasoned, especially since four of the children were either ill with chicken pox or coming down with it.

"Oh Cass, I've never seen anything like it!" Susanne's eyes lit with joy. "It must have cost a fortune!"

He reined the horse to a stop in front of the house, and they sat for a few moments, admiring the carpenters' craftsmanship. The dwelling was superb, both in quality and construction. Two stories of wood and stone supported tall columns and sweeping verandas.

"The men will finish up the stonework by late tomorrow. The remainder of the furniture will be here Monday, and we should be able to get you moved in on Tuesday morning," Cass said as he set the brake and stepped out of the buggy. "You won't have all the conveniences for a while, but you'll be comfortable."

"Oh, it's lovely. . .simply lovely. . . ."

He turned to lift her down but instead held her suspended in the air for a moment, his dancing eyes teasingly meeting hers. "Is that all you can say—that it's lovely?"

She smiled down at him. "How about, thank you, Sir Galahad, because you surely must be the noblest knight in all the land."

Cass shook his head, indicating that she needed to do better.

She shook her head inquiringly. "No?"

"No."

"Then perhaps a kiss from the fair maiden?"

"Perhaps you know one?"

"Sir—" she dropped her gaze demurely—"I was one, until Sir Galahad rode into my life." Her mouth dipped to brush his lightly. Cass could feel the thunder of his heartbeat.

"I should apologize, fair maiden. I don't know what came over me," Cass said. "Can you forgive me?"

"The fair maiden not only forgives you, sir, but pledges her undying love," Susanne whispered.

He drew back, the teasing light in his eyes gone. Once he had her and the children comfortably settled, he would be gone, taking with him only a memory of days that meant more to him than he liked to admit. "I believe you were interested in seeing the house?"

"Oh yes. . .I can hardly wait."

Tucking her against his side, he led her up the steps leading to the circular veranda.

"Cass, has Reverend Olson said anything to you about why we're together?"

"I've noticed that he and Rebecca have exchanged a few inquisitive looks." Cass chuckled at the kindly minister's confusion. Though the reverend had presided over their hasty vows six years ago, neither Cass nor Susanne had given him reason to think their marriage would last.

"I should sit him down and explain what's happened," he conceded.

"I think you should." Susanne looked up at him and grinned. "Then come and tell me, because I still can't understand it."

"Someone will have to explain it to me first." Cass had lain awake nights, wondering how he'd suddenly found his life so entwined with Susanne's. They shared an easy camaraderie now, one that he knew he was going to miss.

They opened one of the two large doors and stepped into the

front parlor. Long, elegant windows lined the room, bringing light in from the east. A stone fireplace to lend warmth in the winter centered on the west wall.

Susanne's hands flew up to cover her mouth again when she saw the mammoth room. "Oh my. . ."

"Come Christmas Eve, I want Aaron and Payne to cut the biggest, nicest tree they can find," Cass told her. "When they bring it home, I want you to make it a night the children will never forget. They can string popcorn and berries and make chains from colored paper. I'll send some of those tiny candles they can put on the branches, but you'll have to watch and be sure that they don't burn themselves. And be sure to make Phebia take a nap that day, so she won't be so cranky that she can't enjoy it. And have Jesse and Doog hold Joseph up to the tree, so he can get his share of the fun, and—"

Susanne laughed. "Cass Claxton, I never dreamed you were so sentimental!"

He grinned sheepishly. "Christmas is a special time for family. I want this year to be the best the children have ever had."

They strolled to the kitchen, holding hands. Susanne was taken aback when she saw the long work counters, two cookstoves, three sinks, and a colossal icebox to cool milk, butter, meat, and vegetables.

"I've never seen such luxury," she murmured, her eyes taking in the rows and rows of copper-plated pots and pans hanging over the cookstoves.

Cass took her arm and led her to the window, pointing to a large structure still under construction behind the house. "That's going to be the washhouse. I wanted it to be away from the main quarters so that you and Corliss won't be bothered."

"Bothered?"

"I've arranged for three women to come in four times a week to do the wash."

Susanne turned, flabbergasted. "For how long?"

"From now on."

"But Cass, I can't afford to pay three women to do our wash!"

"I know you can't, but I can. There'll also be a couple of men who'll do the yard work, two who'll keep you in wood, a tutor for the children, a man who'll supply fresh meat year-round. Three local farmers will keep you in fresh vegetables, milk, eggs, and the fruit in season. Sadie Withers and Wanda Mitchell will be coming in daily to do the cooking so that you and Corliss won't have anything to do but look after the children. I've arranged for you to have unlimited credit at Miller's Mercantile, so you can buy staples and the children's clothing and shoes. Use it. I've spoken with the doctor in town, and he's been instructed to forward any bills pertaining to the orphanage to my offices in Saint Louis, including those incurred by Harlon and Corliss and yourself. Every month, you'll get a sizable check for incidentals you might need."

He paused and lifted an inquiring brow. "What have I overlooked?"

She looked at him in awe. "Your sanity! I can't accept such generosity."

He drew back, affecting a mock bow. "It isn't for you; it's for the kids." And for her, but she wouldn't take it unless he stretched the truth.

"Cass. . .I don't know what to say. Your kindness is overwhelming, but—"

He took her arm again and guided her to the next room. Their footsteps echoed across the gleaming pine floor. "No buts. You should know by now you're not going to win an argument with me."

Like he had ever had an argument with her he hadn't lost.

The dining room was large and airy with space enough to seat fifty guests. "The children will need the extra room for the friends they'll be bringing home over the years," Cass explained.

An adjoining room with back-to-back fireplaces looked out over a meadow, providing the children with restful surroundings to do their schoolwork. Next to it was a medium-sized study, where Susanne would transact business pertaining to the orphanage. The room had a smaller, more intimate feel, with a cozy fireplace tucked into one corner and four large windows across the south wall.

To the left, a separate wing housed Susanne's and Corliss and Harlon's bedrooms.

Cass suggested that they view Susanne's quarters after they'd taken a tour of the upstairs. Leading her up the long, winding staircase, Cass then led her down the hallway, where they peeked into each of the children's bedrooms. Every room was large, bright, and cheerful. Susanne could visualize the astonished looks on the children's faces when they saw their new home.

Susanne thought her heart would burst from happiness. There was only one thing to mar her joy: the knowledge that Cass would not be there to share it with them.

"Now. The best part," he said.

"There couldn't be more."

"Ah, but there is."

They went back down the stairway, arm in arm. At the bottom Cass turned her in the direction of the wing he had left for last. "I thought you might enjoy having the bedroom on the left, though you're free to choose any one you want."

He paused before a closed door and gave her a wink that threatened to stop her heart. "This is the only fully completed room, and for some reason, I am partial to this one." He reached out, turned the handle, and the door swung open.

Susanne was unprepared for the sight she found. The four-poster bed, the armoire, the chiffonier, and the dressing table were made of the finest, richest walnut. The draperies, the bedspread, the pillows, the fabric on the settee in the adjoining sitting room, the chaise lounges, and the numerous chairs scattered about were sewn in delicate shades of lavender and blue. Lush baskets of ferns hung in the corner windows where fading rays of sunlight shone through the windowpanes. Outside the window was a large pond where a couple of waterfowl paddled through the peaceful water. Susanne's eyes took in the small dressing room, a closet the size of a room, and the private bath with gold-plated handles and faucets.

The room was so beautiful that tears welled in her eyes. "Oh Cass, it's wonderful. I don't believe it."

Cass leaned against the doorway, watching her. "The lavender reminds me of your eyes; the blue warns me how much I'm going to miss you and the children," he said softly.

Not daring to look at him, she kept her eyes fixed on the waterbirds and said in a broken voice, "You're leaving, aren't you?"

"First light, Wednesday morning," he verified softly.

She wouldn't hold him; he'd stay because he loved her or not at all. She was through manipulating.

"Susanne. . .if you want—"

"I won't stop you. . . . I only wish you wouldn't go."

"There are times I wish I didn't have to go. But I do."

Swallowing the lump crowding the back of her throat, Susanne turned, smiling. She had made God a promise; she would honor it. "We'll miss you."

Placing her hands on either side of his face, she closed her eyes.

He pulled her to him, his lips skimming hers. Suddenly he drew back when salty wetness slid down her cheeks. "Don't cry," he probed gently.

"I'm sorry. I'm doing exactly what I promised I wouldn't do."

"Getting weepy on me?"

"Yes."

Stemming the flow of tears with his thumbs, he reminded softly, "I haven't gone yet."

Her heart was in her eyes. "You've brought me here to say good-bye, haven't you?"

He sighed, tenderly drawing her head back down to his chest. "It's not easy for me, Susanne."

She understood; it wasn't easy for him to walk away. He had deep feelings for the children—she knew that, but the knowledge didn't make it any easier for her.

For a long moment they said nothing; then he gently tipped her face up to his and kissed her. Her breath fluttered unevenly through her lips to his, "I never knew it could hurt so badly."

"What?"

"Loving you."

"Please, don't make this any harder," he whispered raggedly.

Tears ran unabashedly down her cheeks. "I'm afraid I'll never see you again."

His breath was warm and sweet against her mouth. "I'll never be very far away if you or one of the children needs me."

"Oh Cass, how will I ever let you go?"

"You have to, Susanne. Don't try to force me to stay."

No, she wouldn't do that. She'd learned the hard way you couldn't hold anyone if they didn't want to stay. She wouldn't stand in the way of his leaving, but it would break her heart to let him go. Particularly now when she held the one weapon that would bring Cass Claxton to his knees. And she'd promised God she wouldn't use it.

Cass had hoped the house would ease Susanne's pain over their parting. He realized now that while it might help, nothing would make it easier for her. Or for him. How had they come to this point? Sometimes he wanted to stay, but he wasn't sure if he could love only one woman after so many years of running from them. He knew what he felt for her must come powerfully close to lasting.

They wandered out on the veranda, sitting down in the cane-bottomed rockers provided there. Cass watched her out of the corner of his eye, half-expecting her to beg him to stay. He hoped she wouldn't; it was hard to deny her anything. He'd enjoyed building the house, taking pleasure in imagining her and the children enjoying the luxury and comfort they'd never known. He'd pictured Phebia running through the house, Jesse and Doog sliding down the banisters, Margaret Ann's common-sensical remarks.

Most of all he'd pictured Susanne moving through the rooms, going about her work, resting on the spacious veranda. Now he realized he'd pictured himself there, too.

She rested her hand on his arm. "I do appreciate all you've done for us. Life will be so much easier now."

"It's not enough, is it?" He hadn't meant to ask the question. The words had popped out.

"It has to be."

"It will be all right; you'll see."

"No, it won't. Being back here where it all started makes me realize how badly I behaved. God must be punishing me for what I did to you."

He was silent for a moment, searching for words. "In that case,

He must be punishing me, too. My part in this hasn't been all that admirable, either."

She smiled. "I wonder what it would have been like if we'd started differently. Would you have found me desirable?"

He chuckled. "Well, I sure do at this moment." The smile faded. "You are lovely, dedicated, and wise—far wiser than I."

Unshed tears sparkled in her eyes.

For the hundredth time Cass wondered if he was doing the right thing. Could he leave her—ride away and not think of her and the children day and night?

She reached out, touching his face. "I'm afraid you'll forget me."

"Forget you?" He clasped her hands and held on tightly. "I make you this promise, Susanne. Until I draw my last breath, I will never forget you."

He couldn't forget. It would be better for them both if he could.

Chapter 14

Winter's first snow sifted down in fine, powdery flakes when Bryon, Joseph, Lucy, and Phebia huddled around Susanne's skirt, their eyes openly indicting Cass for desertion. He stoically saddled his horse, dismissing the silent pleas. Even Margaret Ann had shed some of her sophistication when the cold fact that he was leaving became evident.

A cold wind whipped the tails of the heavy sheepskin jackets that Cass had recently purchased for the boys. Jesse, Doog, Payne, and Aaron stood by, watching his departure in stony silence.

Delaying as long as prudent, Cass summoned enough nerve to turn and face his accusers. The forlorn faces he found waiting weren't encouraging.

He cleared the goose-egg lump in his throat and adjusted his hat, settling it lower on his forehead, carefully avoiding any particular gaze. "Well, guess that about does it."

Corliss offered him the sack of food she and Susanne had prepared earlier. "Just some chicken and biscuits—won't last long, but it'll be more appetizing than jerky."

"Much obliged, Corliss. I appreciate it." Cass tucked the food away in one of the saddlebags. "I talked to Harlon earlier, but tell him I said good-bye again."

"Shore will. . . . You take care now, you hear?"

His eyes softened. "I will, Corliss."

"How long will it take you to ride to Saint Louis?" Susanne asked, finally stepping forward.

Cass was forced to meet her gaze, though he didn't want to. They had said their good-byes last night, and it hadn't been easy. "Ten, twelve days. . .depends on the weather."

"You could sell your horse in Westport and take a boat the rest of the way," she said. "It'd be faster."

"I don't mind. I need the time."

A faint smile touched her lips, and he knew she was trying to make it easier for him. "You take care of yourself. Snow's going to be deep."

He gazed down at her. Was he doing the right thing? He came up with the same unyielding answer: he didn't know.

"You'll write?" she whispered.

"Yes. . .you do the same."

"Of course."

Turning to face the children, he looked at the faces he had grown to love, fighting the building emotion that was pressing heavily against his chest. "You kids mind your elders."

There was a combined mumbling of "yes, sirs" before Phebia buried her face in Susanne's skirt and began to sob.

Reaching out, Cass lifted her into his arms and forced her to look at him. "You're a big girl now, Phebia. Big girls don't cry."

Tears of misery rolled silently out of the child's eyes. There were many things the three-year-old couldn't comprehend, but he knew Phebia sensed that he would no longer be there to patch her hurts and make them better. "They do when their daddy leaves," the little girl whispered.

"You want to pinch my nose?" Emotion clouded his speech.

Phebia shook her head no.

"Will you give me a kiss before I go?"

She nodded. Cass removed the thumb from her mouth, and she leaned over and pecked him on the mouth.

He winked at her. "Not bad. With a little practice, you'll be breaking some man's heart before we know it."

Margaret stepped forward shyly to offer him a kiss. She was joined a few moments later by Lucy. How he loved these kids, he thought. He held tightly to the three small bodies.

Phebia suddenly backed away and extended Marybelle to him. Cass grinned and obediently gave the chosen one a kiss. But Phebia emphatically shook her head. "Marmarbelle go with Papa," she said firmly, extending the doll to him again.

Cass lifted his brows. "You want me to take Marybelle?"

Her face broke into a radiant smile. "You Marmarbelle's papa!"

He nearly broke down. "You sure you don't want Marybelle to stay here and live with you?"

She shook her head again.

"All right. I'll be a good papa to Marybelle." He carefully tied the doll onto his saddle horn.

Openly shaken now, he turned and knelt down to hug Joseph then Bryon. Rising to his feet again, he shook hands with Doog and Jesse. "You boys behave yourselves."

"Yessir."

"Yessir."

Cass could feel his eyes mist. He reached out and clasped Payne's hand—a man's hand now. "I'm counting on you to keep the smaller ones under control."

"I will, sir."

"You see that you do."

And then it was time for Aaron.

Aaron's eyes remained stoically fixed straight ahead as Cass, too overcome by his deep feelings for this young man, simply reached out to squeeze his thin shoulder. Then he turned and walked blindly to his horse.

"Cass."

His foot paused in the stirrup at the sound of Susanne's voice.

"Yes?" he answered without turning around.

She was suddenly by his side, her hand gently on his arm, silently willing him to turn and look at her.

But he refused. Keeping his head down, he said in a voice gruff with emotion, "Susanne. . .let's get this over with."

Wordlessly she pressed an envelope into his hand.

Recognizing the significance of the long legal envelope, a blanket of pain suddenly settled over him. The divorce papers.

"These are the papers I promised you. All they need is your signature," she said softly. "I signed them last night."

He swung up onto the saddle, tucking the envelope inside his jacket. "See that you write."

Her eyes confirmed her love, told him that she would always love him. "You do the same."

He kicked the horse. The children stood huddled against the driving wind, watching him ride out of their lives as simply and as suddenly as he had ridden in.

"Mon çhéri, I do not know what has gotten into you!" Laure Revuneau paced the floor of Cass's study, wringing her hands with frustration. "I did not hear from you the entire time you were gone. And now that you're back, you've been ignoring me for weeks."

Cass sat at his desk, staring out the window. Heavy snow was falling in sheets. But it was no heavier than the sense of depression that had plagued him since he'd left Cherry Grove ten weeks earlier.

Laure crossed the room to stand before him. "You have not been to see me since you returned. Have I done something to offend you, mon chéri?"

He pushed back from his desk, hoping to avoid the question in her eyes. He didn't know why, but Laure wasn't the woman for him. He had started to compare each one he encountered with Susanne, and it annoyed him. "You haven't done anything wrong, Laure. I've been distracted lately." He walked to the fire and picked up the poker.

She followed him. "You are not so terribly busy now, *n'est-ce pas*?"

He studied the fire, realizing that the time had long passed to be honest with her. He had told her nothing of Cherry Grove or Susanne McCord, and he didn't plan to. But he also realized that he had no plans to continue their relationship. "I'm sorry, Laure." He knelt to stir the fire. "I'm leaving for Atlanta within the hour."

He knew she was stung by his rejection; her expression showed her displeasure. "You're leaving again?"

"My business has suffered in my absence. I will be traveling often in the next few months."

"But. . .what about us?"

Cass straightened, turned to face her. "I think you would be happier if you sought more reliable companionship."

She lifted her head proudly. Laure Revuneau had more

dignity than he thought. She inclined her head. "If that's what you want."

"Laure. . ." He heard the familiar note of despondency creeping back into his voice. "I don't know what I want."

A tap sounded at the door as Laure gathered her ermine cloak and prepared to leave. "Perhaps you will reconsider when you return from Atlanta."

"I won't reconsider."

Laure opened the door to find Sar waiting. She turned back to Cass and smiled, her eyes issuing a challenge. "I do not give up easily."

Cass smiled wanly. "Take care, Laure."

Her eyes softened with perception. "Whoever she is, I hope she deserves you."

Sar stepped back to allow Laure room to exit. When she was gone, he walked into the room and Cass turned back to the fire.

"Another letter has been delivered, sir."

Cass glanced up expectantly.

"Again it's postmarked Cherry Gro—" Sar didn't get to finish before the letter was snatched from his hand.

Cass tore into envelope eagerly.

"Will there be anything else, sir?"

Cass wasn't listening. He strode to his desk, his eyes hungrily roving over the piece of paper.

"Very good, sir." Sar closed the door behind him.

Seating himself at the desk, Cass's eyes focused on Susanne's neat penmanship:

Dearest Cass,

I hope this letter finds you happy and well. The

Christmas tree fit in the window as beautifully as you predicted it would. Aaron and Payne took the smaller boys, and they scouted the woods on Christmas Eve, looking for the perfect cedar.

That evening we placed the lovely candles on the tree, and the children strung popcorn and made chains from the colored paper you sent them. When they were finished, the tree was truly a magnificent sight.

Aaron and I took turns holding Phebia and Joseph, so he could place the star of Bethlehem on top. Joseph was so proud. Later we gathered around the tree and I read the story about the angel appearing to the Virgin Mary, telling her she had been chosen to be the mother of the Christ Child, and how Joseph and Mary had made the long trip to Bethlehem only to find no room at the inn.

For days afterward, our Joseph was quite adamant that he had a wife named Mary and that they had journeyed to Bethlehem on a donkey, where they'd developed a case of bad sniffles because they'd had to sleep in a stable.

Corliss and I finally got the children to bed and asleep by midnight, only to be up again before five. The older boys were ecstatic over their new rifles, and the girls simply adore their dollhouses. Of course, Bryon and Joseph thought their bicycles topped everything. Where in the world did you find such silly contraptions?

Well, I must close and get to bed. Tomorrow Doog and Jesse are in a spelling bee at school. Can you imagine that?

We think of you every day, and your name is mentioned quite frequently in Margaret Ann's prayers.

Respectfully yours,
Susanne McCord

The first buds of spring were bursting open on the oaks when Doog came running up the drive, waving a letter in his hand.

"It's here!"

Susanne dropped her sewing, and children flew out every door. Making her way carefully down the steps, she prayed that it was news from Cass. "Is it from him?"

"Yes!" Doog answered.

When the letter was in her hand, Susanne closed her eyes and held it close to her heart for a moment, imagining that she could smell his familiar scent. Of course she couldn't, and at the children's indignant insistence, she ripped into the letter and began to read aloud:

Dearest Susanne, Harlon, Corliss, Aaron, Payne, Doog, Jesse, Bryon, Joseph, Margaret Ann, Lucy, and Phebia,

Please do not take in any more children until I can acquire a longer pencil.

Susanne paused to glance up sheepishly. "He's silly, isn't he?"

"Read us more," Joseph demanded.

"All right." She went on:

I have been traveling many weeks now, and I am very weary. At times I think I will sell everything I have and retire, but after a good night's rest, I change my mind again. Hope you children are minding well and keeping up with your homework.

Take care of yourselves.

Love,

Cass

Margaret Ann frowned. "Is that all?"

Susanne sighed. Cass couldn't be accused of being long-winded. "That's all."

Dearest Cass,

Is it ever hot! If we owed someone a hot day, we could have paid him back a hundred times lately. The temperature has soared dreadfully for days, and the children are getting cranky. Aaron and Payne have taken the smaller ones to the pond to swim every afternoon, though I had to scold Joseph again today. He chases my pretty swans until they are exhausted.

Harlon is up and about. Feeling right, he says to tell you. Corliss says she's feeling tuckered out because of all the heat. Phebia has just about stopped sucking her thumb, though she does have an occasional relapse.

I received the signed divorce papers. Thank you.

I trust you are well. I had a spell last week of not feeling so well, but I am much better now.

We thought of you the other night at supper; we were enjoying that stew you like so much.

Take care.

Respectfully,

Susanne McCord

P.S. I almost forgot, Bryon and Lucy wanted me to tell you that they've each lost another front tooth. You should see them when they grin! They insisted that I enclose their teeth—hope you don't mind.

The oaks were bursting with color as Doog came running breathlessly up the drive again.

Susanne ran out of the washhouse. "Is it here?"

"It's here!"

She flew across the yard, her heart thumping erratically. "Give it to me."

Not waiting for the other children this time, she tore into the letter, her eyes eagerly devouring his words:

Dear Ones,

Since I'm in California, I decided to visit the ocean today. I sat for a long time looking out across the water, thinking of you. I was reminded of what a great distance separates us. Sometimes I worry that you don't have everything you need, and that makes me worry even more. If you should ever want for anything, you have only to ask. Don't worry about money. I have all we could ever need and more. I used to think money could make a man happy, But I'm beginning to realize that there are more important things in life.

Take good care of yourselves—I miss all of you in a way I find hard to put on paper.

Love,

Cass

P.S. Susanne, be sure that the kids have big pumpkins for Halloween. I mean it. I'm getting tired of you being so frugal.

Dear Cass,

The children had the biggest pumpkins in town; I hope you're happy. Do you realize you are spoiling these children shamelessly? Take care.

Respectfully,

Susanne McCord

Dear Susanne,

I'll spoil the children if I want to. I miss you all.

Cass

"The old-timers are predicting at least nine inches by morning," Sar remarked. He set a tray filled with sandwiches and a pot of tea on the study table.

Cass answered absently. He sat staring into the fire, his fingers folded above the bridge of his nose, staring unseeingly at the glowing embers. Susanne was on his mind constantly lately. Her memory tortured him at night, and today he'd passed a woman on the street who'd reminded him of her. The response had been painful.

What was he going to do about Susanne McCord? About the children?

He got up and walked to the window to pace restlessly. It had been close to a year since he'd seen them. Eleven months. How much the children must have grown! Why didn't he go to them? How much longer was he going to feed his senseless pride that no longer required feeding? he wondered.

Regardless of what Susanne had done to him in the past, he could no longer deny that he was in love with her. She had changed. He had seen her change from a spoiled brat to a compassionate, loving woman. So what was he waiting for? Why did he keep torturing himself like this? The reasons he'd given for leaving her didn't seem to make sense anymore. He didn't want to be a footloose bachelor, and he'd trade all the money in the world to feel Phebia tugging on his nose again.

Suddenly he stopped pacing. He wasn't going to wait any longer. He was going to go after her.

His eyes caught sight of a buggy pulling up in front of the house, and he groaned.

Company—the last thing he needed or wanted. He was about to tell Sar that he wouldn't see anyone when he noticed a boy stepping down from the carriage.

Cass leaned closer to the window, his face wreathing with happiness when he recognized the visitor.

"Aaron!" He bolted from the sill.

Sar glanced up from pouring the tea. "I beg your pardon, sir?"

"Sar, it's Aaron!" he exclaimed. He briskly walked across the room and out the door.

"Aaron?" Sar lifted his brow curiously.

Aaron was coming up the walk when Cass flung the door open. The boy broke into a grin as Cass rushed out to engulf him in a warm embrace.

Clapping him heartily on the back, Cass exclaimed, "Aaron, what are you doing here, son?"

"Come to pay you a visit."

Cass held the boy away from him to get a good look. He'd grown at least two inches! "It's good to see you—"

His smile suddenly froze. "Is everything all right at the orphanage? Has anything happened to Susanne or one of the children?"

"No, sir, they're all doin' fine," Aaron insisted with a good-natured grin.

"Are you sure?"

"I'm positive."

Cass began moving the boy toward the house, keeping his arm firmly around him as if he might somehow slip away. "How did you get here?"

"By boat."

"Boat? From Westport?"

"Yessir. I have a part-time job working at Miller's Mercantile, and I used some of the money I've earned to buy a ticket."

"You didn't need to do that. I would have sent you the money to come for a visit."

"I couldn't do that, sir. Miss McCord says I need to be man enough to stand on my own two feet."

"Well, she's right, of course—are you hungry?"

"Yessir."

They walked inside the house, and Cass shouted for Sar to bring more food.

"It's cold out there—and snowing." Cass drew Aaron closer to the warmth of the fire.

"Yeah, but Missouri's not as cold as Kansas."

"Take off your coat and warm yourself. How did you find me?"

"I asked around. You weren't hard to find."

Sar returned with a large tray laden with food. Cass began to fire a million questions at Aaron about the other children.

When he'd answered all of them to Cass's satisfaction, Aaron tore into the slice of steaming apple pie that Sar had set before him.

Cass lit a cheroot and settled behind the desk. "Well, how have you been?"

"Real good. You remember Ernestine Parker?"

"Sure. I remember Ernestine Parker."

Aaron grinned. "Well, me and her might be marrying up next spring."

"Is that so?"

"We've been writing back and forth, and I'm thinking real strong about asking for her hand."

Cass shook his head. It was hard to realize that the boy was old enough to think about such things.

"How old are you now?"

"Seventeen. Ernestine is younger, but I plan on taking real good care of her."

Cass smiled. "Ernestine's a fine choice, Aaron. I'm sure she'll make you an excellent wife."

"Thank you, sir. I hope she feels the same."

"Where do you plan to live?"

"In Cherry Grove. I think Miss McCord can use my help raising those kids. Corliss and Harlon are getting older, and the kids are a handful at times."

Cass nodded, glancing out the window, fondly recalling how there was rarely a moment's peace when the children were around. "How are Corliss and Harlon?"

"Holding up."

"And Susanne?" Cass turned and leaned forward in his chair. "How is she?"

"She's fine, sir. Had you a fine son a few months back."

"Oh yeah? Well, that's good—" Cass started to lean back when he suddenly froze, his face draining of color. He sat up straighter. "Had me a what?"

Aaron's tone changed from friendly to critical in the blink of an eye. "I said, she had you a fine son, sir."

Cass couldn't find his voice.

Moving the slice of half-eaten pie aside, Aaron stood up and drew a deep breath. "Sir, I want you to know I've thought a lot about what I'm about to say—and I know you might not be real happy to hear it, but I've come a long way to say it, so don't try to stop me."

Cass glanced up, in shock at the news that he had fathered a son.

"I don't mean any disrespect, sir, but you've got this coming."

"All right." Cass stood up to meet Aaron's stringent gaze. "Say what you've come to say."

"You're a no-good, sorry piece of trash. . .sir." Aaron doubled his fist and struck out.

Cass lifted a hand to his smarting cheek, astounded by the boy's actions. His eyes narrowed. "I've whipped men for less than this."

Aaron braced himself, looking fully prepared to fight. "Then you'd better get to whipping, sir, because it's the truth." The boy's face reddened with anger.

"The truth!"

"Yessir, the truth."

"You want to tell me why you think it's the truth?"

"Because of what you did to Miss McCord."

"What do you think I've done to her?"

"Sir, I may not know a whole lot, but I think it's plain to everyone what you did to her."

Cass had the grace to blush. "What's all this nonsense about me being a worthless piece of trash?"

"You are one, sir, sure as I live and breathe." Aaron kept his eyes solidly fixed to the snow falling outside the window. "You told me you'd been taught that if a man trifles with a woman and then walks away, he's nothing but a piece of trash."

"And you think that's what I've done?"

Aaron's gaze focused on Cass accusingly. "I know it is."

Cass leaned back in his chair, trying to grasp what had happened. He was quiet for a long moment, trying to muddle through the boy's accusations. "Does Susanne know you're here?"

"No, sir! And she'd skin me alive if she knew. She thinks I've gone to visit Ernestine, but I had to do this for Sammy."

Cass looked up. "Sammy?"

"Samuel Cass Claxton. I believe Miss McCord figured you might want your son named after you and your pa, seeing as how he's dead and all."

Samuel Cass Claxton, Cass thought. *I have a son.* Susanne had had the perfect way to trap him again, and she hadn't. She must have known or at least suspected that she was carrying his child when he'd left her. She'd let him ride away that day, divorce papers in hand, and never said a word.

"Aaron"—Cass's voice broke with emotion—"believe me, I didn't know. . . . She never told me. . . . I never dreamed. . ."

"You mean, she really didn't tell you?" Aaron asked.

"No. . .she never said a word. I wouldn't have left if I had known. . . ." Cass's eyes turned pleading. "You have to believe me, Aaron. I didn't know."

Aaron laid his hand on Cass's shoulder. "Well, then, I think it's time you met your son." He smiled, and Cass saw that the smile was no longer that of a child but of a man.

"I think so, too. You think Susanne will forgive me?"

"Shoot, yes. She's always been downright silly about you."

A proud grin spread across the new papa's face. "When's the next boat leave?"

Reaching into his back pocket, Aaron drew out two tickets. "Tomorrow morning—and I'd be much obliged if you would pay me back for your fare, because I'll need the money for my wedding"—Aaron flashed him an embarrassed grin—"sir."

Chapter 15

Fire popped in the grate; the orphanage had settled down for the night. Susanne cuddled her son in her arms, one hand supporting the head of dark curly hair. She gazed into an achingly familiar pair of blue eyes and sang softly: "Hush, little baby, don't you cry; I'm gonna sing you a lullabye. . . ."

It had been a long, hot summer and fall. She recalled the day she'd finally drawn Corliss, Harlon, and the children aside to explain her expanding waistline. The older boys had taken the news grim-faced.

"I'm carrying Cass's child." She had stilled the horrified looks with a hasty, "We're married—been married for over six years." Then she'd gone on to explain the hopelessly entangled mess she'd made of her life—and Cass's. "I'm so ashamed. I have led that poor man a merry chase."

Harlon cleared his throat and then spoke up. "Does Cass know about the child?"

"Certainly not—and he isn't to know. Ever."

"But, Susanne—you can't deny a man his son or daughter. It isn't right."

She'd thought about that, but the child wasn't his child. It was her child. Cass wanted nothing to do with marriage or responsibility. He'd said so time and again.

"If I were to tell him, Harlon, he would be back in an instant. But it wouldn't be because he loved me or the baby. It would be because he felt an obligation to us." She had looked up, her eyes brimming with tears. "I want him back on his own accord. I want him to love me, Harlon. Truly love me when—if—he ever returns."

Corliss had shaken her head, deep lines etching her forehead. "Don't seem right, child."

It wasn't right, but it was the only solution to the problem. She had been selfish and out of the will of God. Disobedience sometimes demanded a high price.

Susanne glanced up when she heard the sound of the door opening behind her, and her heart leaped to her throat when she saw who was standing in the doorway.

Cass leaned against the frame, his gaze fixed on her. "Forgot to mention something, didn't you, Miss McCord?"

She managed to still her pulse long enough to return his gaze. "No, Mr. Claxton, not that I can think of."

His eyes motioned to the child. "No?"

"No."

"Where did you get the baby?"

Susanne smiled. "Oh. . .he just sort of came. . .late one rainy afternoon."

"Really."

Susanne realized that, somehow, Sammy's father had found out about him. "Who told you?" she asked softly.

"Does it matter?" Cass crossed the room and came to kneel beside her chair. His presence suddenly filled the awful emptiness in her heart, and she murmured a silent prayer, thanking God for sending him back, if only for a visit.

He gazed down on his son, his eyes wet with emotion. "He's a handsome boy."

She drew the blankets aside to allow him a closer look. "We do good work, don't we, Mr. Claxton?"

"We sure do." Cass reached out and lightly touched a finger to his son's chin. "Hi, Sam."

The child puckered up, threatening to break into tears.

Mother and father laughed, momentarily easing the tension.

"How old is he?"

"Four months."

"No kidding! He's big for his age, isn't he?"

"Of course." She avoided meeting his eyes, struggling to keep her emotions in check. The past year had been an emotional seesaw. "Samuel Cass Claxton is going to be exactly like his father. A fine, strong man."

Cass leaned closer, and she felt faint when she detected his familiar smell. She longed to throw herself into his arms and let him kiss away the loneliness of the past year, but she knew she wouldn't. Not this time.

His gaze returned to the infant. The shock of dark hair and arresting blue eyes. "He favors me. Ma will be pleased."

Susanne sighed. He didn't have to remind her of how much the baby looked like him. Sammy was a daily reminder of the man she loved. "Yes, he does, and he has your streak of orneriness, too."

"Mine?" Cass grinned, that affable, crooked grin that tore at her heartstrings. "I'd say he gets that from his ma."

"Oh, now, now," she cooed when the child began to sob harder. "Is this any way to act in front of your papa?"

Cass suddenly caught her hand, turning her to face him. "Why,

Susanne? Why didn't you tell me about our son? How long did you plan to keep this from me?"

Susanne swallowed the constricting knot in her throat. "I don't know—I wasn't sure how you would feel about him, Cass. I know you aren't ready to settle down, and a baby calls for permanence in one's life."

"Feel about him? He's my son."

Susanne drew a long breath. "Yes, but he's my son, too, Cass. How does that make you feel?"

"Maybe that makes him even more special," he admitted in a shaky voice.

"Maybe?" She wasn't sure what he was trying to say. Was he here to claim his son? If he was, he'd have to claim her, too. She wanted Cass Claxton, and this time she was willing to fight for him. "I didn't tell you about our child because I didn't want you to think I was trying to trick you again."

"I wouldn't have thought that—"

"Yes, you would have. You know you would have."

"Well, I don't think that now," he said gently.

"Cass, I love you so deeply it's a physical ache at times," she confessed. "I pray every night that someday you'll return my love, but I'm tired of using tricks and deceit to hold you. I'm afraid if you want your son, you have to take me, too."

"I'd be grateful to have the both of you."

His ready acceptance failed to register. "And you'll have to want me and agree that our lives will be empty and meaningless without each other," she warned. "I'll settle for nothing less."

His gaze traveled adoringly over her then on to his son. "You'll have nothing less. I'm sorry it's taken me so long to realize how I feel, but I had to be sure—for both our sakes. I love you, Susanne Claxton—love you so much—and I'm miserable without you."

"Well, as I say, if you ever want—" She paused, his words finally sinking in. Her eyes widened. "You love me?"

He nodded, slowly drawing her mouth up to meet his. The kiss was long and filled with urgency and longing.

"Oh Cass, why did you leave?" she whispered against the sweetness of his mouth.

"I had to. It's taken me almost a year to realize what's important in my life, but not a day has gone by that I didn't know that I loved you. I said many things to you, Susanne—spiteful things, words spoken in bitterness and anger. I ask you to forgive me—allow me to make amends for my bad behavior."

"But you signed the divorce papers."

"Because I wanted the old marriage over and done with. I want us to start again. I want God and our love to be the ruling forces this time, not manipulation. I'm deeply in love with you, Susanne." His hand reached out to touch her face and her eyes reverently. "Can you forgive me?"

"Oh Cass, if you only knew how long I have waited to hear you say those words."

His smile was as intimate as a kiss. "Get used to it you're going to be hearing it a lot for the next fifty years."

When their lips parted many long minutes later, she prompted softly, "Does this mean you're home to stay?"

"It does."

"What about your business—?"

He laid a silencing finger across her lips. "I've consolidated most of my holdings, and the remainder of my business can be handled from here in Cherry Grove. I'm closing the house in Saint Louis, and I've arranged to have Sar brought here to help with the children—if you have no objections."

She gazed back at him, her heart overflowing with joy. "Of

course I have no objections, but. . .are you sure it's me you want, or is it because of your son—and the children—that you've changed your mind?" She had to know for sure.

"I want you, my love, and my son. . .and my nine other children."

"Oh Cass. . .are you sure? The children will be overjoyed. They love you as much as I do. . . ." She paused and smiled, drowning in the familiar blue of his eyes. "Well, nearly as much."

"Woman, I've never been surer of anything in my whole life—and don't start arguing with me." His lips pressed and then gently covered her mouth.

"Then each and every one of us is yours," she said a moment later. "You don't mind being hog-tied and branded?"

"Not by you."

He reached out to pull her and the baby onto his lap.

"Hey, Sam, me and your ma are getting married—not in the middle of a road at the point of a shotgun, but she and I and our ten children are going to plan the biggest, rowdiest wedding this town has ever seen!" Cass told his son. "I want the whole world to know she's mine, and she's going to stay mine for the rest of her life!" He paused and grinned engagingly at his son. "What do you think about that, Samuel Claxton?"

Sammy Claxton burped.

Cass and Susanne laughed and indulged in another long kiss. Afterward, Susanne whispered, "That means your son thinks your idea sounds simply grand."

He frowned. "No. . . Susanne, a man doesn't use words like 'simply grand'!"

She nodded and revised. "Well, partner, your son thinks that sounds mighty fittin'."

He kissed her. "Better, but we'll work on it."

Three weeks later, Cass stood at the upstairs window, looking down on the activity, shaking his head with amazement. The orphanage was decked out in its very finest. Greenery and colored ribbons adorned each room, while the smell of cedar filled every nook and cranny. The weather had held; the day was crisp and cold. The men he'd fought with—become good friends with over the years—had come. Trey McAllister and others too numerous to name.

The parlor was filled with tables stacked high with gaily wrapped presents awaiting the bride and groom's attention.

A magnificent eight-tiered wedding cake kept Corliss busy trying to keep the children's fingers out of the icing.

There had been a solid stream of buggies arriving for the past hour, with people alighting from the carriages in their Sunday best to witness the exchange of vows between Miss Susanne McCord and Mr. Cass Claxton.

A knock sounded and the door opened.

"Hello."

Cass turned, a smile surfacing on his face as Susanne swept into the room as bright as a ray of summer sunshine on this snow-covered winter afternoon. "It's about time you got here. Come here, woman."

She went willingly to him, and his arms encircled her, one hand at the small of her back. His kissed her. "Ready to marry me?"

"More than ready, darling."

"Then let's do it—the right way this time. With God's blessing."

There was a lot of backslapping and hugging when the Claxton family reunited.

Cass drew his mother, Lilly, into his arms and held her tightly. He hadn't seen her for more than five years.

"Now, where are all my grandbabies?" Lilly turned to Cole's children, engulfing them in big grandmotherly hugs.

"Ma, you better ease up," Cass warned. "You still have my ten to go."

Lilly threw her hands up in despair. "I always said you'd be the one to turn my hair gray!"

Willa, the family housekeeper who'd been like a mother to the Claxton boys, was here, beaming with pride. She swept Cass into her arms and gave him a big kiss.

Wynne was standing by and, by the look in her eyes, eager to talk to the lothario who had jilted her at the altar many years ago. "I can't wait to meet the woman who's finally snagged you," she teased, going into Cass's open arms.

"Wynne, sweetheart, look at it this way: If I hadn't left you standing at that altar, and you hadn't traipsed all over the country looking for me, why, where would my brother be today? In the arms of another woman—"

Wynne Claxton poked him soundly in the ribs. "All right, all right. How many times do I need to say thank you?"

Cass laughed and knelt down to greet his nieces and nephews. "Jeremy, look how you've grown—and your sisters, Tessie and Sarah!" He stood up again, shaking his head with disbelief. "They make you realize you're getting old, don't they?"

Cole was suddenly forced to sidestep when Doog, Jesse, Bryon, Joseph, and Lucy hurtled down the staircase. "Did school just let out?"

Cass threw his head back and hooted. "No, those are just more of mine!"

Beau and Charity arrived with their five children, and the hugs and kisses started all over.

"You're expecting again!" Wynne exclaimed.

Charity nodded, her eyes sparkling with happiness. "Beau says it's boys again."

"It better be; I need more help with the work," Beau teased, giving his wife an adoring squeeze.

Events blurred. Handshakes and greetings were exchanged. Cass grew more nervous. He anxiously checked the time, dragging his timepiece in and out of his pocket.

When he was sure he couldn't wait another moment, the music suddenly sounded the wedding march. He straightened his tie, took a deep breath, and stepped into place next to Aaron and Payne beneath the wide arch of greenery in the parlor.

Phebia, dressed in a miniature replica of the bride's gown, had confiscated Marybelle, and she now carried the doll down the stairway. She entered the parlor scattering dried petals along the pathway, sneaking an occasional suck on her thumb.

Margaret Ann and Lucy followed, dressed in long lavender-blue gowns and wearing circlets of dried flowers around their hair.

Jesse, Doog, Bryon, and Joseph were next, looking spit-shined and polished in their Sunday best. Corliss followed, carrying Sam, who didn't appear to care much for all the commotion. The latter didn't have an official role in the wedding, but it had been agreed by all that the ceremony should be a family affair.

And then the moment Cass had been waiting for arrived.

Susanne descended the stairway, a vision of loveliness in an ivory bridal gown.

Cass's eyes locked with hers as she walked slowly toward him, supported by Harlon's steady arm. They smiled at each other, and Cass savored the heady moment. Reverend Olson officiated over the nuptial ceremony, and this time he didn't have to prompt the groom to accept his vows or kiss his bride. In fact, the assembled guests had reason to wonder if the groom was ever going to stop kissing her.

Susanne finally broke the embrace and covered her face with embarrassment amid the sound of hoots and applause.

Corliss cut the wedding cake. Guests crowded around when the groom lifted his glass, his eyes overflowing with love, and made the first toast to his bride. "Darling Susanne—love of my life. Here's to our first happy year of marriage." He winked then leaned closer and whispered in his bride's ear, "One out of seven's not bad, huh?"

She laughed and kissed him soundly.

"Well, little brother." Cole cornered Cass when they caught a rare moment alone. "Looks like all these years I've worried about you have been for nothing."

Cass's eyes fixed on his new bride, who was busy trying to excuse herself in order to slip away. "She's something, isn't she?"

Cass had finally told his family about his earlier marriage to Susanne and how he'd grown to love the orphans as much as he loved his own son. He'd had to. Lilly had swooned when he told her he had ten children.

Beau drifted over to join his brothers. "I guess Susanne will do in a pinch, but have you two really looked at Charity? Now, gentlemen, there's a woman!"

Cole hooted. "Brothers, no disrespect intended, but Wynne's got your women beat, hands-down."

Beau and Cass both turned to give him a dour look.

The three brothers exchanged identical devilish winks.

"Yeah," Cole said softly, "it looks like the Claxton boys have done just fine."

Samuel Claxton Senior would have been right proud of his sons.

A Note from the Author

Dear Reader,

Well, we've come to the end of the third story in the Wild West Brides series, and I hope when you close this book, you'll feel your hope has been renewed. Just as Susanne struggled with her old nature, we struggle with ours. Day by day we must renew our hope in the Lord Jesus Christ and wait for His perfect plan for our lives. His time is not our time, but in due time, joy will come in the morning!

In your daily devotions, take time to read the following scripture passages on hope: Psalm 9:18, Psalm 119:114, Psalm 103:5, Jeremiah 17:7, Proverbs 13:12, and Lamentations 3:24. Then stand back and watch God work in your life.

About the Author

Lori Copeland, Christian novelist, lives in the beautiful Ozarks with her husband and family. After writing in the secular romance market for fifteen years, Lori now spends her time penning books that edify readers and glorify God. In 2000, Lori was inducted into the Springfield, Missouri, Writers Hall of Fame.